THE THRESHING FLOOR
JEREMIAH'S WARNING TO AMERICA

COLIN BRISCOE

WESTBOW
P R E S S®
A DIVISION OF THOMAS NELSON
& ZONDERVAN

WestBow Press books may be ordered through booksellers or by contacting:

WestBow Press
A Division of Thomas Nelson & Zondervan
1663 Liberty Drive
Bloomington, IN 47403
www.westbowpress.com
1 (866) 928-1240

Scriptures taken from the Holy Bible, New International Version®, NIV®. Copyright © 1973, 1978, 1984, 2011 by Biblica, Inc.™ Used by permission of Zondervan. All rights reserved worldwide. www.zondervan.com The "NIV" and "New International Version" are trademarks registered in the United States Patent and Trademark Office by Biblica, Inc.™

ISBN: 978-1-5127-6224-2 (sc)
ISBN: 978-1-5127-6225-9 (hc)
ISBN: 978-1-5127-6223-5 (e)

Library of Congress Control Number: 2016917772

Print information available on the last page.

WestBow Press rev. date: 11/7/2016

Dedicated to American Family Radio

*"He who gathers crops in the summer is a
wise son,
but he who sleeps during harvest is
a disgraceful son."*

-Proverbs 10:5 NIV

*"His winnowing fork is in his hands,
and he will clear his threshing floor,
gathering his wheat into the barn
and burning up the chaff with
unquenchable fire."*

-Matthew 3:12 NIV

*"The harvest is plentiful but the
workers are few. Ask the Lord of the
harvest, therefore, to send out workers
into his harvest field."*

-Matthew 9:37-38 NIV

I

OBLIVION

"But the way of the wicked is deep darkness.
They do not know what makes them stumble."

-Proverbs 4:19

1

HARM'S WAY

Before the bottom dropped out, the forecast had been favorable. What had begun as a promising day with a brilliant sunrise under a canopy of blue skies in God's country had all of a sudden dissipated. Any memory of a serene beginning had now been enveloped by the ominous clouds looming on the horizon. Even so, it could never be said that it had happened completely by surprise, for there were those who had forecasted its inevitability.

The inclement weather had set in as the wind blew and beat against Simon's vehicle. While the very vessel in which he traveled teetered to and fro down the highway, any safety that its insulated interior had offered deteriorated into a mere illusion.

Still, Simon pressed on without fear not because he had considered the peril of his circumstances but only because he hadn't. Besides, he had a date with destiny, and like most young men, could not be bothered by diametrically opposed pressure systems.

Annoyed by the sudden turn of events, he bemoaned his current predicament, longing for the comfort and ease that the first part of his journey had afforded him. When he had set out on his trip earlier in the day, the conditions demanded little of his idle mind. With heavy eyes and a fist full of Texaco coffee, he had bounded down the road with the chauffeur of the subconscious listlessly weaving thirty-five hundred pounds of Detroit steel in and out of car seat infested minivans and Nodoz aided freighters, while a matinee of inner-theater played trailers from ESPN Classic and Cinemax movies.

When Simon, after many hours of driving, crossed over Twain's mighty Mississippi into the Land of Lincoln, he saw a few of the steamboats down below the rusty Erector Set bridge in the shadow of the Arch. Not surprisingly, any comparisons to Huck Finn on the superhighway of his day were completely lost on him. It was a fact that would have deeply saddened his English professors at TCU who could pull a myriad of deep and fascinating analogies out of a life insurance manual.

Instead, no such deep thoughts entered Simon's mind. It was otherwise occupied as he contemplated the St. Louis Cardinal's pitching rotation while quivering the vinyl of his seat with a rank fart. By all accounts, he had been oblivious and comfortable like most red-blooded Americans. Full of nervous energy, his fingers tapped on the armrest of the door, void of purpose or requisition.

It was then that the springs of the great deep burst forth and the floodgates of the heavens were opened. A cascade of water poured over the windshield warping reality into a smeared mosaic of colors. To Simon it was like looking at the world through the bottom of a shot glass, a thought that immediately caused him to gag on the vile taste still lingering in the back of his throat. It was an unsavory byproduct of the previous night's graduation party. As he struggled to keep his breakfast down, Simon was reminded of the shooting pain that pierced his still incompletely developed pre-frontal lobe.

Break lights flashed before him as the rain came pouring down. Simon slouched in his seat and let out a deep sigh. He looked at a small white cross on the side of the road without really seeing it, before glancing down at his watch that read 1:01 p.m. Thoughtlessly, he mouthed the words of an old Genesis song on the radio, ..."And I've been waiting for this moment all of my life, O'..," as he shook out the watch and then held it against his ear. Nothing. It had died. So it goes. He then picked up his cell phone in the seat next to him only to find that it was actually 1:27 p.m., while he continued mouthing the lyrics..."and I was there and I saw what you did, saw it with my own two eyes..."

Until now the traffic had not been too bad. When the weather was good, autonomous drivers had motored down the interstate virtually impervious to one another's existence.

But now, a prophetic sign foretold of roadwork ahead. That large, orange sign was followed shortly thereafter by another one that promised there would be no exits for the next thirty miles. A third diamond-shaped sign warned of reduced speeds and increased fines.

Simon reluctantly pumped the brakes and glanced down at the speedometer. After driving over a slight bluff, he saw through the swiping of his windshield wipers a long serpentine line of red break lights. He muttered several expletives under his breath and looked down at his dead watch before once again reaching for his cell phone.

Predictably, a fourth sign appeared, indicating that the right hand lane was going to merge with the left within the next half-mile. Simon began to merge before impulsively seizing an opportunity to get ahead. Shrewdly, he yanked on the wheel and punched the gas. The old car first lagged and then lunged into the soon-to-be terminal lane. Racing past the now stagnant line of cars towards an orange and white barricade looming in his path, Simon wrung the steering wheel as if it were an old, wet rag. The tightening line of drivers blurred in his periphery as he surveyed a place to jump back in. Much to his dismay, his fellow travelers insolently hugged the bumper before them leaving Simon no clear opening in the long line of cars.

He was quickly running out of road, when he spotted a small opening between a minivan and an oil tanker. With little room for error, he quickly darted back over into the open lane and slammed on the brakes. Glancing upward, Simon grimaced at the sight of a Peterbilt logo filling his rearview mirror. The screeching of tires and the gush of air released from the truck's brakes engulfed him, then nothing. His heart raced from an elixir of exhilaration and fear.

Finally, Simon exhaled in relief. A horn blasted in protest. "Yeah, yeah, whatever," Simon said aloud, as he gave a condescending wave.

Regardless of origin or destination, make or model, every vehicle eventually conformed to a singular, narrow path. Each time the petrol procession ground to a complete halt, Simon's chances of achieving his ultimate destination before nightfall dwindled precipitously. And when two police cars and an ambulance screeched by him, he resigned himself to the fact that barring a miracle he would not. With that realization, he let out a moan, turned down the radio, and reached for his phone. Swiping away the empty McDonalds's bags from the seat next to him, he picked it up and dialed the number of his godfather in New Jersey. The ring reverberated in his ear several times before the all too familiar voicemail picked up.

"Hello, this is Joseph Hightower with Biotech Therapeutics. I am either away from my desk or out of the office. If you will leave a brief message, I will return your call at my earliest convenience. Thank you."

Simon punched the number one on his cell and said, "Uncle Joe, it's Simon. I hope all's well. Look, I hate to bother you again, but I just ran into a little bit of road construction, and I wanted to check on, you know, uh, the status of the interviews...and if, um, anything new had materialized with the FDA since the last time we talked. When you get a chance, I'd appreciate it if you could give me a call. Thanks."

His shoulders and back writhed with tension, and frustration coursed through his veins. Simon tossed the phone back down on the seat and ran his hand through his hair. Just as he glanced back down at the phone, the time changed from 6:05 to 6:06 p.m. Turning the radio back up, he thoughtlessly mouthed the words of the song, "...Oh, I just gotta know if you're really there, and you really care, Fa fa fa-Fool'in..." Then he leaned way over to the opposite side of the seat and felt for the road map. Doing his best to avoid an accident, he perused the map with the mind's eye still on the road. Guesstimating his current location, Simon tried to calculate how far he might get before pulling into a hotel for the night and what affect that might have on his overall ETA to the East Coast. While surveying the map, his eyes repeatedly jumped up the page to the central portion of the state. As his eyes began to gravitate to one particular location, he felt for the first time the tugging at his heart that a sort of homecoming would be expected to induce.

Just as his heart skipped a beat, the Peterbilt honked. He looked first in the rearview mirror and then in front of him. The line of cars had crept forward some distance, but the sizable gap was evidently more than the already irritated truck driver behind him could bear. With a contemptuous look on his face, he set the map down beside him and picked up the slack.

"All right, all right," Simon growled.

For some time the interstate two-step continued. With each minute that passed, Simon's agitation grew proportionate to his added drive time. Anxiously, he would slide a little outside of the line of cars trying to get a look at whatever it was that held them up. He tried periodically to distract his mind by searching up and down the dial before tuning in to a sports talk radio show that broke through the static and white noise with perfect clarity. Simon feebly tried to focus on the host preaching about the inalienable right of touchdown celebrations and showmanship. But it was of no use. Every few minutes he would habitually look down at his dead watch and then pick up his cell phone to check the time. Without being able to actually see whatever it was that was causing the traffic jam, he directed all of his anger towards humanity as a whole and lamented the misfortune that had befallen him.

"Why does this always happen to me?" he asked rhetorically as he crept past a car on the side of the road with its hazard lights on and hood up, never even once thinking of stopping to help or provide assistance. Just as Simon was about to finally blow a gasket, he pulled around a slow curve only to see the warning lights of the ambulances, fire trucks, and police cars that marked the site of the accident.

"Finally!" he yelled out in exasperation as he sat up and shifted in his seat.

Just then, the weather took a sudden turn for the worse. The turbulent wind grabbed at the car and lifted it while an intense rain pounded the hood. Above the din, he could hear the swishing of the wipers against the inundated glass. As he approached the crash site, he dutifully slowed down in an attempt to get a glimpse of something, anything. Simon strained to see through the kaleidoscope of rain on his driver's side window. To his dismay, all he could make out were state troopers dashing about holding onto the tops of their cellophane covered hats while the storm whipped about their bright orange rain slickers. Simon's eyes rapidly darted about in an effort to penetrate the sheet of rain and the cover of smoke emitted from the safety flares that outlined the crash site. But no such luck, they revealed nothing sensational.

When Simon looked back, the minivan in front of him had already pulled away by nearly a hundred feet.

"Yes!" he exclaimed as he sat up in his seat and applied the gas.

The powerful V-6 roared and water rushed through the wheel well as he surged past a convoy of lumbering freighters, obstructing Simon's view of the next set of construction signs. Despite the portentous weather, Simon, hijacked by his own road rage, threw caution to the wind. Basking in his newfound liberation, he fumbled for his CD case with one hand while the other captained the old Impala.

Just as the rusted out Chevy reached seventy-five miles per hour, the wind ripped and howled through the decaying seals around the windows. Hail crinkled like tinfoil and then rattled like a tight snare drum. A flash of lightening was immediately followed by a sizzling, peel of thunder that resounded in his chest. Simon heedlessly pressed on, defiantly smashing his foot into the pedal, and white-knuckling the steering wheel. Through squinted eyes and pursed lips, he peered into the abyss trying desperately to discern the way. A split second after the cautionary hum of the tires reverberated through him, a pool of standing water grabbed at the car and yanked it toward the guardrail. In a flash, a streak of lightening revealed the danger that lay in his path.

"God…!" he called out, while cursing profanely between gritted teeth as sparks flew. The sound of metal on metal screeched like a legion of demons.

Impulsively, Simon jerked the wheel hard to the left, severely overcompensating. The steel leviathan launched from the guardrail into the far left lane towards an unsuspecting SUV. Catching a glimpse of the blurred object in his periphery, Simon grimaced and contorted his body while pulling down on the wheel hard to the right. In so doing, the almost certain collision was narrowly averted, but now he was out of control as the car wildly fishtailed down the road. Simon dug his shoulders into his ears, locked his arms straight out, and deliberately wrenched the wheel back and forth in a desperate attempt to regain control of the car. Suddenly, a black and yellow striped concrete barricade appeared in his path. His heart sank and his blood ran cold. Everything went into slow motion, and he turned his head and dug his chin into his shoulder.

"God, oh, God," he muttered, as he grimaced and braced himself for the impact.

In another heartbeat, the tires inexplicably gripped the pavement, and the car shot back into the middle of the road. When he opened his eyes, the sparkling twinkle of a chrome fish rapidly swam towards him. Simon punched the brakes and the sparkling fish darted away into the curtain of rain. Then the two tail lights, a license plate, and the rest of the back of the vehicle came into focus.

Simon let out a gush of air and sank back in his seat. For the first time he noticed his heart pounding in his chest and sweat on the palms of his clammy hands. He first glanced in his rearview mirror. Then he looked into each of his side mirrors in utter disbelief that he had survived unscathed. Every fiber of his being was stiff and tingled with great fear and trembling. When the realization that he had somehow been spared finally sank in, he was overwhelmed by a deep sense of gratitude and relief.

"Thank you, thank you," he uttered to no one in particular while the white noise of the radio became audible to him again. With great jubilation, he quickly reached for the phone to tell someone, anyone, about how his life had been spared.

* * *

Simon had driven for maybe a half of an hour basking in his implausible stay of execution. The sequence of events, so vivid and clear, played over and over in his mind. He tried unsuccessfully to call several people in an effort to share his miraculous story of deliverance from the clutches of death. While he enthusiastically dialed in hopes of regaining a cell tower, he failed to notice the subtle changes to the landscape around him. With the sunlight beginning to break through the clouds, the rubbery squeal of the windshield wipers rubbing on dry glass brought him back to reality. When he reached with his still trembling hand to turn them off, he noticed a billboard through a row of trees lining the interstate. It read, "Next Stop, Neoga's Adult Time Superstore."

"Neoga?" he said aloud as a look of confusion swept over his face. Quickly, he fumbled again for the map that had fallen to the floorboard. But before he could reach it, a green interstate sign confirmed his suspicions. It read, "Neoga 6, Mattoon 18, Champaign 36, Chicago 216."

Sitting in a nearly empty parking lot under a sign that read "Adult Time", Simon retraced his course on the map with his index finger. Evidently, his near death experience took place on the outskirts of Effingham, IL. When he lost control of the car, he had inadvertently swerved onto I-57 north instead of continuing on I-70 east. Then, subconsciously, Simon continued with his finger north a few more miles to an isolated spot on the map.

"There it is," Simon almost whispered contemplatively, "Bethel." It was the town where he had spent the first ten years of his life before his dad left and his mother took Simon to live with his aunt in that forsaken town in West Texas. He knew all along that his trip would bring him back to the general vicinity, but at the time he couldn't justify going out of his way just to see it. After all, he hadn't kept up with anyone from the good ole days, and he had a schedule to keep. But now, due to a twist of fate, he was no more than a stone's throw away. His eyes lifted off the map, He looked out over a bean field in the direction of the small, Midwestern town.

Just then his voice mail rang.

"Sure, now I get coverage!" he said sarcastically, only to see that he had missed some calls. It was Joe. Picking it up to listen to the message, he noticed the absurdly flat terrain that defined Central Illinois. Short stalks of corn lined in perfect rows flapped and fluttered in the breeze, stretching all of the way to the horizon. Countryside roads outlined the large rectangles that formed a giant inextricably woven quilt of green, yellow, and black, dotted with farmhouses, barns, and silos. Simon was caught off guard by a warm feeling of familiarity that suddenly swept over him.

Then the message started, "Simon, sorry I missed you. How was graduation? I really wished that I could have been there. I hope the trip is going all right. Be safe. Don't kill yourself getting out here. It looks as though you have plenty of time. The FDA notified us today that we will not hear back from them until early next week, and interviews won't begin until after that. In the meantime, give me a call if you need anything and let me know when you expect to arrive in Jersey, we'll get the spare bedroom ready."

"Ahh!" Simon let slip a vulgar slur while his face revealed a pained expression. He pressed the end button, dropped the phone onto the seat beside him, and tapped the steering wheel, as if he were hammering out his thoughts on a PC. He lowered his chin into his bicep and raised his left eyebrow furtively.

"It's ridiculous," he thought. "There's no point in going that far out of my way. What would I stand to gain? After all, it had been over ten years. That's it!..." He sat up decisively, putting the car in gear. "...I can't think of a single solitary reason to go back there," he concluded as the rusty, old gas-guzzler rolled forward, crunching the gravel under its tires.

In an instant, he was back on the highway heading north towards Bethel. His pulse raced as he considered the years that he spent there as well as those that had passed since.

The miles went by quickly. Then the interstate lifted off of the plains, and the car ascended an overpass. Simon looked expectantly to his right. Off in the distance, rising up out of the cornfields and bean fields, he could see the silhouette two grain elevators and a water tower. Their bases were shrouded in a small, dense cluster of trees and houses. At that moment, the sun ducked under the blanket of clouds in the West and began its downward descent, casting a glaze of gold over the entire valley. The brilliance of it all went largely unnoticed by Simon whose gaze shifted back and forth between the past and all that lie ahead. The nostalgia of an otherwise happy childhood collided with the pain of abandonment. Apprehension and giddiness swirled about with great turbulence deep inside of him. His stomach tightened and his heart ached as he veered from the interstate onto the off ramp and made the turn onto the narrow slab of road connecting the final expanse between himself and home.

Before Simon knew it, he was standing under a streetlight beside his car at the end of a main street that could be found in any small town throughout the Heartland. The afterglow of twilight cast a soft orange hue onto the narrow corridor of withered brick buildings. Everything and nothing seemed to have changed. Somehow each and every feature looked miniature in comparison to the visual rendering of his mind's eye. What stood before him clearly regaled a more prosperous time in the town's history and belied Simon's memory of its Mayberry-like perfection. Ten or so different establishments lined each side of the main drag ranging in a variety of sizes, color, and ornamentation that somehow were now knitted together in a perfect harmony of decay. It was neat and clean and even cliché and, in a strange way, even better than he remembered it.

The glass of the storefronts bore the names of the establishments to which they now housed. To the best of Simon's recollection only a few remained while most of them had been boarded up or closed down. The Post Office anchored the northeastern corner of the street to his left followed by a hardware store that used to be an insurance agency, a real estate office, and the National Bank. Looming over the bank in the backdrop was the iconic water tower. Inscribed on the side of its tank read, "Bethel" in bold letters with the epigram written below, "Center of the Universe." The prodigious grain elevators stood proudly next to it, completing the boondocks skyline. His eyes lingered for a moment at the summit, and he paused to contemplate its rustic grandeur. While he gazed upward, something inside him lovingly nudged the deep recesses of his memory. And even though he was not able to put his finger on it, there was an unmistakable absence. He squinted his eyes and audibly let out a "huh," paused for a brief moment, and then looked again at the panorama in its entirety.

Simon grinned knowingly then closed his eyes for a moment to bask in the comfortable feeling that now flooded his consciousness. When he opened them again they were a bit glossy and reflected the glow of a lone red blinking light that governed the town's busiest intersection. Below the light, just to the right and opposite the bank, sat the Bethel Tavern. Above its doors a neon sign glowed and hummed while moths frolicked and fluttered in the soft breeze of what had become a pleasant spring evening. Then his eyes fell upon the old Harold Trophy and Engraving shop, which sat wedged between the tavern and the public library. A shudder involuntary swept over Simon's whole body as he considered the possibility. "Miss Harold?" he muttered. "Could that old bat possibly still be kick'n after all of these years? No way. She was saggy and crusty a decade ago when she doubled as principal at the elementary school and as the town constable."

Seeing no signs of life, his eyes continued to follow the virtual tour of the downtown resting his eyes for a moment on the library and then the grocery store. It was then that it occurred to him how an inordinate number of cars and pick up trucks lined the street for a Sunday night in a bedroom community. And yet, there were still no signs of life. Just then, in the eerie stillness, something out of the corner of his eye caught his attention. Simon quickly turned towards the direction of the ancient school to see what it was. He furrowed his brow and peered intently into the darkened alley that separated the grocery store and the schoolyard. Nothing.

He turned to the right and scanned the façade of Bethel Elementary School. The old school had defiantly stood the test of time as proclaimed by the etchings in the corner stone that read "1905". A modestly elegant building in its day, it now bore the black eye of a broken window covered in plywood, and Simon had to wonder if it hadn't been condemned altogether.

Still, he was mesmerized by the wealth of memories that inundated his consciousness at the sight of his old stomping grounds. Each memory that swam to the forefront of his mind was more wonderful than the last. Many of them were familiar due to the number of times they had been replayed, while others gushed forth from the most remote compartments of his subconscious and exploded in new richness and clarity. Looking through the backstop to the playground with its swing sets, monkey bars, and swinging gate, a wave of emotion swept over him, and he recalled the innocence of his childhood.

There it was again.

"Okay, that time I know I saw something," he said aloud.

The movement flashed out of the corner of his eye, but this time it was more vivid. His eyes intently fixated on the cellar doors of the school. Dusk had already set in and the doors remained in the shadows cast from a florescent light that illuminated the entryway. His mind examined the still frame of what he thought he saw, because it looked like a *hand* furtively pulling the cellar door shut from within. The thought was immediately challenged by reason. He cocked his head and scowled in consternation searching for the last vestiges of plausible explanations before concluding that his mind must have been playing tricks on him.

"But it was a hand. Wasn't it?" A part of him objected, "That's ridiculous."

"Wow, wait a minute…," Simon said aloud, only now remembering something long forgotten. Just as he took a step towards the school, the door to the tavern flung open at the end of street. Unnatural, yellow light spilled onto the sidewalk while the audible din of laughter and music reverberated off the brick buildings. Simon stopped and turned in the direction of the tavern as his heart skipped a beat. A dark figure stood in its entrance holding the door slightly ajar. It lingered for a time in the entryway, gesticulated wildly to those inside, and then allowed the door to close behind him. Simon glanced towards the school, thought better of it, and walked in the direction of the tavern. After all, it stood to reason that the owners of all of those cars and trucks lining the streets must be congregated inside, and at the moment, that was a comforting thought.

As Simon walked past the trophy shop, he slowed down to get a quick peak inside. A part of him wanted to see if the old principal could still be lurking somewhere in her shop tinkering on baseball trophies or printing band ribbons. It was a thought that immediately reduced him to an apprehensive, awkward school boy, and he had the same pit in his stomach that he used to have at the mere threat of being sent to her office. "Oh man, the paddle," he thought. His eyes scanned the dimly lit shop but met only the dusty trophies and plaques that adorned its walls.

The dark figure that had just exited the bar came towards him, paused, reached into his pocket, and struck a match to light a cigarette. As Simon approached, the man cupped his hands to protect the flame against the mild breeze and brought his face down to meet it. The brief flash of light shone about him, but it only seemed to accentuate the shadows of deep lines emitting from the corners of his eyes and mark the deep crevices of his forehead.

"Hey, how's it going?" Simon asked perfunctorily as he passed by.

The man looked at Simon out of the corner of his beady eyes while he took a deep drag on the cigarette. He nodded in response and grinned through his goatee as he exhaled. Then he stood upright and shook out the match. Simon did not allow his eyes to meet those of the stranger. Instead, he pressed on towards the tavern. After he passed, the man looking on brought the Marlboro down to his chin and scratched it with his thumb. With a smirk, he returned the cigarette to his mouth, put his hands in his pockets, and strode off into the darkness.

When Simon reached the tavern, he opened the door and stepped inside. The booming surround sound and hallow gazes met him in unison. He paused awkwardly for an eternal moment in the entryway, still holding the door wide open behind him. To his amazement, the place was nearly empty. Three sets of eyes glared questioningly at him as though he were alien to them. After measuring him up, their eyes returned to the flat screen behind the bar. When they did so, Simon took the opportunity to look around the room. He was astounded by what he saw. This was no longer the same seedy tavern he had remembered.

Bewildered, Simon looked behind him out through the glass door at all of the cars and trucks lining the streets and then turned again towards the nearly empty tavern. He let the door close behind him and sheepishly made his way towards the bar. Neither of the two patrons acknowledged his presence. A fervently passionate bartender commanded their attention while preaching about the virtues of drafting 27 year-olds and third year pitchers to his fantasy league baseball team.

Simon was thankful for the mild diversion that again gave him occasion to get a better look at each of them. The bartender, a man of some stature, stood with his back to Simon, leaning against the bar with one hand while motioning ardently with the other. His captive audience consisted of one young man wearing a suit with his tie loosened, his shirt sleeves rolled up, and his jacket hanging over the back of a bar stool. The other one sported a Yankees cap with a flat lid pulled down over his eyes. He wore earrings and a silver chain with a large Chicago Bears emblem that dangled between the buttons on his overalls. His hardened expression ran counter to his soft, boyish features.

The two young men clutched their beer bottles like joysticks and looked over a myriad of disheveled papers set out before them. The guy in the suit slumped over the bar, while the other one sat tall on the edge of his seat. Their attention was primarily transfixed on the ESPN Sunday Night Baseball game displayed on a forty-two inch LCD that sat behind the bar. From time to time, they glanced at the bartender and nodded arbitrarily in agreement while Jon Miller's voice boomed the play-by-play.

As Simon reached for a seat at the bar, he casually scanned their features hoping to recognize at least one them.

Suddenly, the bartender lifted the remote control, turned it towards the TV, and muted it with an exasperated expression.

"You two idiots haven't heard a single word that I've said," he said, scolding the two young men sitting before him. A big, hulking mountain of a man with a towel draped over his shoulder, he leaned on both of his massive arms, looking down at some kind of rulebook while reading its contents aloud. When he was finished reading, he continued with his rant.

The two guys who appeared to be in their late teens or early twenties looked past him to the muted television screen.

"Come on' G'," the guy in the Yankees cap said. "Turn id' back up!"

"I'll turn it up when I'm ready to turn it up," the large bartender replied. "I'm not done reading the rules. You guys need to know this stuff! Just because I'm the commissioner of the Fantasy League doesn't mean that I'm the only one who needs to know this..."

While the conversation continued, Simon looked around and was dumbfounded by the changes that had been made since he had last seen the place. As a child he and his family would come here, along with the rest of the town, on "Catfish Night" in a mostly Catholic community. At that time, it was a dingy little dive with a low false ceiling that made secondary smoke a readily renewable resource. It was a dark, depressing place that probably broke any number of health code violations. Outside of Friday nights, it was little more than a watering hole for the seedy, underbelly of the community. That included his father who was a regular fixture.

But now, it had been completely refurbished. The whole place had been gutted and renovated. Someone had invested a small fortune in the striking transformation. The false ceiling had been removed, revealing a magnificent, ornate tin ceiling. Fans hung throughout the room, swirling lazily with soft lights housed in green glass. Tiny diamond shaped windows were replaced by six large panes of glass that started at booth level and went all the way to the ceiling, while neon signs hummed softly illuminating the window frames and beckoning seductively to would be patrons.

Simon's eyes surveyed the rest of the room. A requisite pool table, jukebox, pinball machine, and dartboard resided in the very back of the room. Just to the right stood a makeshift salad bar. Beyond that, there was more seating as the room continued around the corner just out of sight. The walls of the establishment were adorned with pictures of local sports teams, memorabilia, trophies, and plaques. He leaned in close to get a better look at a few of them.

In all, it was like some sort of sports shrine replete with shiny gold trimmings, shimmering oak, sleek leather seats, and a myriad of flat screen TV's, all simultaneously flashing Hi-Def images of Sunday Night Baseball. Then once again Jon Miller's voice boomed from the surround sound.

"Thank you!" the two patrons echoed in unison.

Simon sat down and waited for the bartender to make his way over. It was then that the most heavenly aroma wafted from the kitchen. His salivary glands kicked into gear, and he was overwhelmed by an insatiable craving. Still, the bartender paid him no heed. Instead, he kept his back towards Simon while imploring his friends to pull the trigger on some trades that he was trying desperately to orchestrate.

Finally, he turned towards Simon and put up his index finger, indicating that he would be over in a minute. When he turned around, Simon caught a glimpse of the boy's face trapped in a man's body. It was Little Richey Land, one of his closest friends!

"No Way!" Simon thought in disbelief, as the hairs stood up on the back of his neck. "What are the odds?" Then he thought for a moment. "In a town of a thousand people? Pretty good, I guess," he mused. "It could be him. Right? Maybe not, though, after all Little Richey was...well...little." Simon had to find out for sure.

"Hey, uh, buddy," Simon called out to the hulking bartender.

The guy glanced over his shoulder at Simon with incredulity then turned back. The other two guys at the bar also turned to look at Simon with a perplexed expression on their faces.

"Who's that dude, Rich?" he could hear one of them say.

"Don't know him," Rich answered. "You guys recognize him?"

"It is *him*, no doubt about it!" Simon thought excitedly. Richey Land was a runt, the smallest of all his friends. They did everything together as kids. They ran around town, got into trouble, swam in the creek, explored abandoned houses. But above all, they played baseball. Richey absolutely loved everything about the game. Like most runts, other kids constantly picked on him in the classroom and on the field. As a result, he had a fierce temper and a short fuse, and he constantly felt like he had to prove himself. Nonetheless, he was a great kid at heart and had been a loyal friend.

"Hey, uh, Richey," Simon blurted out.

The bartender jerked his head around. "Hang on a minute, guy," he answered without thinking. The other two patrons sat up this time, looked at each other inquisitively, and then turned back towards Simon.

Rich turned and slowly walked over to Simon.

"Wow, he's huge, 6-4 or 6-5, maybe 250 pounds," Simon thought. "But there could be no doubt about it now. It was definitely him."

Simon was about to speak when Rich interrupted.

"Listen, little man," he said, "I don't like anybody calling me 'Richey'. All right?"

"Little man?" Simon, who was above average height, thought. He nodded affirmatively and decided to take advantage of his autonomy and have a little fun with his old friend.

"Now, you want a draft or a bottle?" Rich asked dully as he tossed a coaster on the bar in front of Simon.

He nearly gagged at the mention of beer due to his exploits the night before. "Just a Coke, thanks," Simon replied.

"Rum and Coke?" Rich asked moving to pick up a glass.

"No, just a Coke," Simon answered.

"A Coca-Cola?" Rich said with disapproval, reaching to a fridge behind the bar.

"Yeah, thanks. Hey, by the way, what's with all of the cars parked out front?" Simon asked while Rich popped the tab and plopped the can of Coke in front of the annoying stranger. "I thought there'd be a bunch of..."

His old friend dragged a newspaper over in front of Simon and pointed his beefy finger at the front page headline. "They're all across the street," he replied, lifting his chin towards the window.

Simon looked over his shoulder in the direction Rich was pointing. It was the Town Hall. By the time he looked back, Rich had already made his way to the other end of the bar and was talking in a hushed voice to the other two guys who kept shooting glances over at Simon.

Spinning the paper around, Simon read the headline, "School Referendum on the Ropes." Beneath it the sub-heading read, *Town Hall meeting on school referendum to be held Sunday, May 15th."*

"Well, that explains that," Simon thought. The first paragraph of the article stated that the school board was proposing a referendum to build a new grade school. The proposal involved tearing down Bethel Elementary School, consolidating with the next town over, and building a new school on a neutral site.

The article struck a cord with Simon, although he didn't know why exactly. Something about tearing down his old school felt like erasing a part his past. While he was reading, Rich and the other guys had gone back to watching the game. Jon Miller announced excitedly, "There's a hit deep in the gap..."

"Yeah, Boy! See what I'm say'n'?" the guy in the Yankees hat yelled out, clapping his hands.

"I don't believe it!" the other one in the suit replied, followed by a deluge of vulgarity.

"I told you, Rob," Rich said smugly, while punching something into his Blackberry. "I know you love the Cubs, but you can't draft their entire team. That's just stupid."

"Das right, what wuz u' thinkin'?"

"Stop with all that ghetto talk, Rocky!" Rob said angrily, while he loosened his tie a little more.

"Wha'? Dats just who I am," Rocky replied, thumping his own chest. "Dats jus' me."

"You don't even know who you are," Rob said jeeringly. "I'll help you out here because obviously you're a little confused. You're a white, farm boy from Podunk, nowhere, U.S.A. who still lives with his mommy and daddy in the basement."

Rocky countered with a volley of his own obscenities and one pronounced gesture.

"All right, cool it you two," Rich said with his chin down, scrolling through stats on his Blackberry.

"I know," Rob said. "It's just another one of his stupid phases. But, this one is really annoying. You can't even understand him half of the time."

"A faze?" Rocky objected.

"Yeah, a phase," Rob countered. "Like when we were little and you wanted to be Zack what's-his-face from 'Saved by the Bell', or your Michael Jordan phase, or Garth Brooks, or..."

"...random Harley guy phase," Rich chimed in without even looking up from his phone.

"Oh, that stupid bandana!" Rob mocked.

"Shut up!" Rocky responded. "Both of you can..." he finished with a flurry of expletives.

"Okay, okay," Rich said, shaking his head in disgust. "Back to reality here. Look, you've got plenty of hitting. What you need is pitching. You and Will need to make a trade. Neither of you have made a single trade all season. I'm calling him and getting his butt down here."

"Will?" Simon thought. "Unbelievable, Will Thornchuk, another one of his best friends that he used to run with in Bethel.

"'His ole' lady' ain't gonna like dat," Rocky interjected.

"What? I don't care what she thinks," Rich snapped back. "Did I tell him to get her pregnant?" Rich asked indignantly. "Is it my fault, he went and knocked her up? He needs to establish who wears the pants early on," he added while dialing the number and lifting the phone to his ear. "What's one beer gonna hurt, he's... Hello? Oh great, it's you. Yeah. No. No!... Just put him on the phone. Just put him on the pho...." He held the phone out for them all to hear, shaking his head. Then he waited. "Yeah, yeah, yeah. Hey, get your butt down here. I don't want any of your lame excuses. Just get down here." Then he hung up.

The intoxicating aroma once again made its way out of the kitchen. Simon's stomach growled in response. "Hey, Richey, uh, I mean, 'Big man'," he said mockingly," do you have anything to eat?"

Rich again slowly made his way over. This time he looked none too pleased.

"Something smells really good..," Simon started to say as Rich dragged over a bowl of stale pretzels and placed them under Simon's nose. Several fell out onto the bar. Rich raised his eyebrows and returned to the other end of the bar.

"He hasn't changed a bit," Simon thought. "Same fiery temper."

"No, I meant, what's that smell coming from the kitchen?" Simon asked with a smile.

"Italian beef, the Sunday night special," Rich answered tiring of the pesky questions from the mysterious guest.

"Oh yeah, I'm starving. I'd love to have some of..."

"Yeah, well, too bad, we're all out," Rich said, pointing again at the pretzels. "Knock yourself out."

"Oh, okay, so that's how it's gonna be," Simon thought to himself. "...Yeah, no," he said aloud. "These are great. Thanks. These should be fine," Simon said sarcastically, lifting one up to show them, before tossing it into his mouth.

Looking around the room at the pictures of old baseball teams, he suddenly had a terribly wonderful idea.

"Richey..."

By now, Rich had lost his patience. "Where do you get off calling me, 'Richey'? Do you think you know me or somethin'? Cause I sure don't know you," he said, punctuating his statement with a couple of derogatory remarks.

"Yeah, you know what, I think I do know you," Simon said with a wry smile. "I played baseball against you back in the day."

Rich furrowed his brow trying to search his memory. "When? Who'd you play for? Ivesdale? Sadorus?" Rich asked trying hard to figure it out. "Oh, it was Sidney, right?

"You're the little kid who couldn't throw a strike to save his life," Simon continued.

Rich's face turned crimson.

Anticipating trouble, Rob and Rocky slid off of their seats and made their way towards Simon.

"Bro', I wouldn't do dat," Rocky said with a look of concern.

Rich threw his towel down on the bar. "You do look familiar. You're one of those Bement jerks, aren't you?" Rich asked as he moved deliberately over towards him.

"What'd we used to call you?" Simon continued to say. "Man, you would get so mad. Short Bread. No. That wasn't it. Short Stuff...No...

"Don't say id," Rocky stammered.

"Short Bus!" Simon said, snapping his fingers. "I knew it. You're 'Short Bus'!"

Rich thrust his big hand across the bar and grabbed Simon by the shirt, lifting him off of his seat. Two other stools fell and hit the ground, making a noise like a revolver going off.

"You little punk...!" Rich snarled, pulling back his fist.

"*Enough!*" an old gravely voice yelled out from around the corner behind a video poker machine.

Everyone stopped, including Rich who was still holding Simon in the air. Each of them bore a look of confusion. But no one was more stunned than Simon.

"Put him down!" a short, old woman snarled, while she dawned a sweater and limped towards the front door.

Obediently, Rich slowly set Simon back down.

As the old lady limped her way over to them, she said, "Don't nothin' ever change? Do I need to take you two to the office or something?"

Simon and Rich slowly shook their heads in disbelief.

"Heaven's to Betsy, Rich," she continued. "Don't you recognize your own best friend?"

"Miss Harold?" Simon uttered under his breath in disbelief.

"Been a long time, welcome back," Thelma Harold said, limping towards the door and opening it. Then she looked at Rob and Rocky. "Well, don't just stand there. Pick up those chairs."

The two boys scrambled to pick up the chairs and slide them back up under the bar. Rich looked deeply into Simon's face still dazed and confused.

As Thelma was going out the door, Will made his way into the tavern.

"Hey, well if it isn't Simon Freeman," Will said with a smile. "What is up, man?"

Still pumped full of adrenaline, the massive bartender leaned forward and looked closely into his old friend's face. A wide grin swept across Rich's face, "Simon Freeman? Holy…"

2

AMONG THE SIMPLE

By the time Rich finished his bear hug, Simon was almost gasping for air.

"I can't believe it, man!" Rich said grinning from ear to ear. "Oh man!"

"I had you going!" Simon said laughing, as he bent over trying to regain his breath.

"You had me all right," Rich replied. "Another second and you would have had all of me."

"What?" Will asked confused. "What's happened?"

"You wouldn't believe it," Rob said. "I thought Rich was going to kill this guy. Who is he anyway? Who are you?"

"Who dat?" Rocky asked with an incredulous expression. "Only da' best centerfielder in the history of Bethel!"

"You have to forgive Rocky," Rich said. "I've told him so much about you, he probably thinks he knows you."

"Na!" Rocky said. "I remember watch'n him play when I wuz a kid."

"You don't remember jack," Rob scoffed. "We're the same age, and I don't remember him."

"He wuz only three years older," Rocky replied. "Sides, I was raised ad' the ballpark."

"Well, it's good to see you," Will said enthusiastically. "Simon Freeman. Wow. Crazy. What brings you back to town?"

"I'm driving to New Jersey for a job interview, and I kind of accidentally got a little sidetracked because a storm...," Simon started to answer.

"You mean the tornado down near Murphysboro?" Rob asked. "Did you see it?"

"Saw it?" Simon replied. "I think I was *in* it."

"What?" Rich asked. "You'd come all the way from Texas and not look us up?"

"Well, I didn't know you'd still be here," Simon said a little embarrassed by the insinuation.

"Where else would we be?" Rich asked.

Simon burst out with a boisterous laugh before realizing that no one else even cracked a smile.

"Well, sit down, man," Rich said adding a few colorful words. "I can't believe it. Man, I'm glad to see you. You want anything?" he asked making his way around the bar. "I'm going to get you a beer."

"Actually I…" Simon started to say.

"Yeah, round of beers!" Will said enthusiastically.

"Oh, look whose ready to party now, 'Mr. I'm-whipped-cause-I'm-getting'-married-next-week'," Rich said sarcastically. "Simon, you still want some of that Sunday night special?"

"I thought you were all out," Simon said as he sat down at the bar.

"That's when I thought you were a stranger," Rich answered. He slid a pitcher of cold beer and six frosty mugs onto the counter. "But, you're not, you're one of us, man," he said as he made his way through the kitchen doors.

Simon could feel the warmth of his welcome, and Rich's words, as corny as it sounded, struck a cord deep inside of him.

Rocky grabbed Simon by the shoulders and steered him to where he and Rob had been sitting. Rocky yelled, "Da' pro'gul son is back in da' house, know what I'm say'n'?" Then he pulled out a stool for Simon and guided him to his seat. "Man, Freeman, I member watch'n you play. You was one baller. Fast. Man, you was fast. Did ya go on and play anywhere?"

"Yeah, a little in college," Simon answered awkwardly. "But, no more ball for me now. That dream died long ago."

"So, what's been going on?" Will asked pulling up a chair beside him.

The group of guys battered Simon with a deluge of questions while Rich worked furiously behind the scenes, slapping down frothing, frozen mugs for each of them. In no time at all, he re-emerged with heaping plates of steamy beef and homemade bread on plates garnished with hot peppers and mustard. "Here you go," Rich said, setting the plate before Simon.

"So what's the job you are interviewing for?" Will asked.

"It's actually a pharmaceutical sales job," Simon answered, before he could take his first bite.

"Really?" Will asked. "Nice. That's a good gig. Big money, a car, great benefits… the works, am I right?"

"Not to mention the chicks," Rob added, enviously. "Have you seen those girls come into Dr. Al-Banna's clinic. Man, they're all unbelievable. And from what I hear, they work like ten to two, right? It's a like a dream job."

"I don't know about any of that," Simon replied with a smile. "But, it's a really great opportunity- the chance of a lifetime."

Before they could dig in and finally appease their appetites, they raised their glasses for a toast. "To the return of one of Bethel's very own," Rich said proudly. They each took a swig, slammed their mugs on the bar, and dug into the feast that had been set before them.

Simon paused momentarily nearly bursting with gratitude over the fortuitous series of events that brought him back here. Lifting his fork, he leaned down over the top of the bountiful provisions set before him and deeply inhaled with his eyes closed. When he opened them again, he looked up at the game on the big screen and caught a glimpse of his own countenance in the mirror behind the bar. He smiled at his reflection sitting amongst old friends. He couldn't have imagined a better homecoming.

"Watcha waiting for, man?" Rich asked. "It's been simmering in the crock-pot all day. It'll melt in your mouth. I promise. Suddenly, Rich let out an expletive as he rushed around the bar towards the front door of the tavern.

"What's the matter?" Will asked, wiping mustard from the corner of his mouth.

"That Town Hall meeting on the referendum just got out, and those guys are heading this way," Rich cursed. "I don't want anybody else in here right now!"

By the time Rich made it to the door, the first two men from the meeting had opened it and were about to walk in. Rich grabbed one of them by the arm with his left hand, forcing him out the door, while his right hand pushed it shut.

The men profanely chided, "What in the world are you doing, Rich?"

"No, no, no. Sorry, private party fellas," Rich answered dully. "The bar's closed."

"You gotta' be kidding me," another man complained from the other side of the glass door. "It's not even ten! You don't close down till midnight."

The men banged on the door and protested adamantly, but it was quite obvious that Rich was not changing his mind. Three more guys approached as Rich slammed the dead bolt shut. All five of the dismayed, would-be patrons yelled at Rich through the glass.

"Come on, Rich...Open the door!" the men yelled from the outside looking in.

They gnashed their teeth and protested profanely, but Rich paid no heed. Instead, he threw his towel over his shoulder and sauntered back to the bar.

"You're gonna do that to me, really?" one called out.

"I don't know you," Rich yelled back with a smirk. "Sorry boys. Special guests only, and you're not on the list." Seeing the futility of it all, the men finally gave up, left the front door, and made their way out into the darkness.

Unmoved by the calamity outside, Rich called to Simon. "Hey, I got somethin' to show ya."

Rich excitedly walked over to the wall behind the pool table, perusing the pictures and memorabilia with his index finger. "Aha," he said as he pulled down one of the pictures from the wall. "There it is."

Simon looked on with curiosity while Rich returned to his spot behind the bar.

"Recognize this?" Rich asked. He was half-giddy as he handed it over to Simon.

Simon wiped his hands on his napkin before reaching for the picture. At first, Simon didn't recognize the photo, and then it all came back to him. It was a photograph of their Little Okaw Valley Traveling League Championship team.

"That was a great team," Rich said proudly tapping the glass of the picture.

"Where you at, Freeman?" Rocky asked with a mouth full of Italian beef while looking over Simon's shoulder.

Simon scanned the photo with an air of nostalgia that oscillated back and forth between extreme joy and bitter pain. It was taken the last summer that he spent in Bethel. In that photo, he had no idea that his father had already decided to leave. Shortly after it had been taken, his mother told him that they would be leaving Bethel and moving to his aunt's house in Texas. That had been twelve years ago.

"He's fourth from the right," Rich chimed in. "He's helping me, Shane, and Will hold up the trophy."

"Where is Shane, anyway?" Simon asked.

"Iraq," Will replied.

"You were the reason we won that game, Simon," Rich said.

"Oh, yeah, right," Simon replied with sarcasm, handing the plaque back to Rich. "You guys probably never won another game without me."

"No, I'm serious!" Rich countered.

"No, really, we didn't win much of anything after that," Will said flatly.

"You mean you guys were actually good at one time?" Rob said sarcastically.

"Let me tell you…no…for real, don't laugh. This is what really happened…" Rich started telling Simon all about the lean years of sports in Bethel since his departure.

From that moment, it was all over. Each of the young men regaled their tales of conquering ball diamonds, frozen gridirons, and hardwood courts like only young men can, with the brevity of a Southern Baptist preacher and the veracity of a used-car salesman. Each partially listened to the other's stories, but only to the extent that it reminded them of something else that they had done or seen or heard. And then they waited, not for the sake of being polite, but for an opening. As the night dragged on, the degree to which the listeners remained engaged was inversely proportional to the amount of time it took for the other to tell the story. By the time it was finished, no one was actively listening anymore. In a time honored tradition of man-speak, no one looked directly into anybody else's eyes. No one gave an affirming grin or an understanding nod. Other times, someone would cut off somebody else to tell their own story, and if better, was justified in doing so. Either way, it didn't matter for they were young. It was the law of jungle, and they had been practicing it for years. There was no pressure, no expectations, and best of all, there were no hurt feelings.

When the mental paper clippings ran dry and the accuracy of the tales came into question, the topic of conversation made its natural transition to a different field of competition- women. Of course, on that subject, they were most familiar with teenage girls who acted like the former but looked like the latter. Naturally, credibility became less and less of a commodity as the tap continued to flow, while explicitness and inventiveness became held in greater and greater regard. With no one to corroborate their accounts, sketchy details and unlikely scenarios were challenged with great discord by their mouths but secretly believed in their hearts because they wanted them so badly to be true. Completely enthralled, each one sat forward on the edge of his stool hanging on to every word as the stories escalated epically. With each new story and each refill, they started to rebuild the deep bonds of friendship.

Then Rob told a story about a friend in the Navy visiting the Philippines.

It's a rare that a story elicits utter silence from a group of 20-year-olds, but like a verbal cold shower, silence was indeed rendered. After the awkward moment had passed, somebody yelled out, "Let's play some pool." And the party raged on until Rich noticed the clock on the wall.

"Man!" Rich said, cursing. "Almost missed it."

"What?" Simon asked.

"It's midnight," Rich slurred as he moved back behind the counter and over to the cash register.

Simon, who was inadvertently trying to play pool with a warped stick, looked back at Rich, bewildered. The room started to spin, and he realized he was more than just a little buzzed. "Yeah, that happens every night from what I understand," he said.

Rich popped open the register, busted out a roll of quarters, and headed for the juke box.

"Na, homie," Rocky answered. "It's tradition. He be puttin' on the Frankie, baby."

"Huh? He do what, to who?" Simon asked.

"Frank Sinatra," Rich replied as he loaded the machine with quarters. "We play Sinatra on the juke box every night at midnight."

"You're here every night?" Simon asked in wonder.

Shortly after punching in GEN3-6, "My Way" rocked the house.

Unsolicited, Rocky, Rob, Will, and Rich broke into some sort of deranged karaoke kinda thing that would have scattered alley cats. What they lacked in pitch and harmony they more than made up in volume and zeal. Will gestured for Simon to come join them. As the last sour notes drowned out ole' blue eyes, they all bellowed at the top of their lungs, "*I did it my way…!*"

The rest of the details of the evening are sketchy at best. By all accounts, the first round of shots began shortly after Franky finished crooning his classic mantra. It was followed soon thereafter with much caterwauling, mostly singing to much less classic hair band tunes of the eighties. While Simon performed what could technically be termed an a cappella rendition of "Welcome to the Jungle", Rich pulled the foot long beer bong off of the wall. He began filling it at the tap while everyone joined in singing.

Sometime around one in the morning t was reasoned that the beer bong had become too cumbersome and inefficient. It was proposed that by cutting out the middle man one could place his head directly beneath the tap and receive an equally substantial amount of beer with only a fraction of the hassle.

Around a quarter of two, there came a knock at the front door emanating from the butt of a County Sheriff's flashlight. To everyone's delight, the public servant just so happened to have played football against Rich in high school. The fortuitous encounter thereby elicited a second round of glory day stories, as well as leniency from any number of laws that had been violated. Being ever so gracious, the on-duty patrolman decided to resume his duties around 3:00 a.m., but not before making each of them solemnly swear that they would not under any circumstances get behind the wheel of a car. They each vehemently swore that they would refrain from any such temptation. Reassured by their sincerity, he put on his hat and proceeded towards the exit. The boys patted him on the back and thanked him for his being "a really good dude" before seeing him out the door.

However, it wasn't long after that that Rob astutely observed that there was no one present representing the female persuasion and suggested that the party take to the road in an effort to seek the more soft and supple company of the opposite sex. All agreed with the practicality of his recommendation. As they staggered towards the door, Simon reminded them of the promise that they had made to their friend in law enforcement. The group agreed that that was a little problematic. Several of them lamented the fact that none of them had even considered this particular scenario at the time. Otherwise, they in no uncertain terms would have agreed to such an egregious oath as the one that the officer had obviously coerced.

It was Rob who pointed out that they had actually only agreed to not get behind the wheel of a *car*. Then everyone turned and looked at Rocky. Once that ethical hurdle was cleared, the greater concern now came from Simon who wondered openly how their enterprise to find female companionship might prove difficult that late on a Sunday night in a town of less than a thousand. Rob acknowledged that it normally would be a valid concern, but assured Simon that he had a solution.

After Rich locked up, they all climbed into Rocky's dad's Limited Edition Chevy Silverado. Had Rocky been in control of his faculties, he would have never agreed to it. However, given his current condition, Rob was able to persuade Rocky to let him drive his dad's brand new truck. Just as Rob put the vehicle into gear, he noticed that Thelma's light was still on in the trophy shop.

"Oh, man, awesome," Rob said with an mischievous grin. He hit the gas, and the truck lunged backwards into the middle of Main Street.

"What are you doing?" Rich asked rather annoyed. "Come on, don't be stupid."

"Oh no," Will said knowingly while looking back at Thelma's store.

The big diesel snorted like a great Rhino just before charging.

"What's going on?" Simon asked with a confused look on his face.

"Don't you remember, Simon?" Rob asked as he put the truck into neutral. "Thelma is the town constable."

"Don't do it…!" Rocky started to say.

But it was too late. Rob punched the gas and slammed it into drive. The roar of the powerful motor and the screeching of the tires echoed off of the buildings lining the tiny thoroughfare. Frenzied, the boys grabbed a hold of whatever they could find. The tires finally gripped the pavement, and the metal behemoth shot off down the narrow corridor leaving a trail of rubber and dense smoke before Rob slammed on the brakes.

Thelma poked her head out the door. Then she went back inside, set down a trophy, threw off her magnifying lens, grabbed her keys, and hobbled to her car. Rob waited patiently down the street looking into the rearview mirror while Will begged him to drive off. Thelma didn't move as fast as she used to. It took a couple of minutes before she got the keys into the ignition, placed her flashing blue light on top of the Buick, and buckled her seatbelt. Meanwhile, Rob casually sifted through Rocky's CD collection before finding a band he could identify with. Soon, AC/DC blasted the sound system. After what seemed like an eternity, Thelma carefully backed into the street, put the car in gear, and hit the makeshift siren. At that, Rob lurched forward and put the hammer down. The chase was on.

* * *

A sliver of light piercing through a tiny gap in the white curtains fell upon Simon's eyelids. The intense laser of light finally seared through Simon's previously impenetrable unconscious state. Up to that moment, the curtains had shrouded him in a blanket of darkness. He was dead to the world. Being unconscious, he had been unable to rouse himself to a state of consciousness. While content in his unconsciousness, he neither knew of, nor longed for, anything more. Simon had fallen into a deep sleep that necessitated an extraordinary external force to intercede and awaken him.

Ultimately, it was the light that pried through an ever so slight aperture from a tear in the curtain and systematically moved across the room as the sun rose in the East that brought him back to life. First, only one eye flickered and fluttered. Then the other. The concentration of the light was harsh and unwelcome at first. He grimaced and blinked turning his head and used his hand to shield its brilliance. But it wasn't long before he basked in its warmth and welcomed its brilliance.

Simon looked around the room not knowing where he was or how he had gotten there. Turning his head to the left and then to the right, he realized that he was laying on an old, worn out couch. He pulled his feet around and sat up. When he did, the familiar pangs of a hangover once again shot through his cerebral cortex with unapologetic recourse for the ill treatment he had subjected it to the night before. Now he was paying the price. The room spun and he tasted his cottonmouth tongue and sandpaper lips. He smacked them purposely, trying to wet them, but the effort was futile. Every fiber of his being yearned for a drink of cold water. Looking once again around the room, he noticed for the first time its filthy condition. There were crushed beer cans, empty Skoal containers, and nasty spit cups laying on the coffee table along with ransacked bags of chips and pretzels. Simon surmised that he must have crashed at one of the guys' houses based on the meager décor and the abhorrent condition of the room.

All of a sudden, his stomach ached and rolled. Sticking his chin down into his chest, he fought hard to hold back from vomiting while eking out a belch. Even though the situation was tenuous, he was somehow able to keep everything down. That was before he saw a half-eaten hot dog sitting in a spit cup on the floor, and that was it. Scrambling off of the couch, he grabbed his mouth and frantically looked for the most plausible location of a bathroom or trash can. Intuitively, he sprinted down a hallway. Grabbing what he supposed was the bathroom door, the urge to purge became more than he could fend off. As he frantically opened the door, Simon projectile vomited all over a bed of large shoes and cleats on the floor of a darkened closet.

Having rid himself of at least a portion of the toxins that had most recently been introduced to his system, Simon stumbled his way to the actual bathroom. A note had been taped to the mirror for him to read. When he pulled off the piece of paper, he noticed for the first time a pale specter squinting back at him. His hair was disheveled and a substantial amount of stubble adorned his chin. At the corner of his mouth was a small unidentifiable piece of food and what was unmistakably some remnants of chaw.

"That explains that," he muttered. It was when he went to wipe the disgusting residue away that he noticed letters written in permanent ink on the back of his knuckles. He quickly turned them around and read "Love" on his left hand and "Hate" on his right.

"Real nice, guys," he said with a scowl and proceeded to scrub at them under some hot water. When he looked up in the mirror a second time, he recognized two other small markings in the shape of tear drops just below his left eye.

"Oh, come on, guys!" he muttered.

Reaching with his left arm this time to wipe it clean, revealed other markings just beneath his left sleeve. Flashing his shoulder towards the mirror and lifting up his sleeve, he looked down and the read the words written in the middle of a broken heart, "Momma Didn't Love Me." He turned and lifted the other shirtsleeve, exposing a barbwire tat.

"Real funny," he murmured with a slight smirk on his face. He looked back again at the splotches of sharpie "teardrops" falling from his left eye.

Simon grabbed a dirty bar of soap. His hands burned as he scrubbed furiously at the markings. But, it was to no avail. In fact, the effort only proved to worsen the condition by creating a large, dark blotch of stain that he would not be rid of for some time. Shaking his head in mild disgust, he picked up the note and read.

"We were trying to 'convict' you to stay a while...ha, ha. If you can't run with the big dogs, stay on the porch. And if you ever want to see your car keys alive again, come down to the baseball field.
-Short Bus

PS- "You know what they say about payback. Pass out next time and it won't be nearly as pretty."

Simon laughed in bemusement realizing that his friend had repaid him in full. They were even, at least until someone discovered the closet full of shoes. He crumpled up the piece of paper and threw it into the trash. Simon glanced at his cell phone, but it was dead. He noticed a clock hanging on the living room wall. Much to his amazement it was well past noon. Suddenly, it occurred to him that he was having trouble recollecting the events from the previous evening after they had left the Bethel Tavern. In an effort to jog his memory and start the recovery process, he decided to jump in the shower. When he reached down to turn the water on, his palm burned again. Surprised, he turned his hand over and looked in bewilderment at the fresh blisters. Then he flipped over his other hand revealing several more fresh blisters.

Looking past his hands, Simon made another discovery. His clothes were filthy. On closer examination, both his shirt and jeans were covered in mud and dark red splotches. He pulled his shirt up to his nose and smelled it, but it held no distinct scent. Alarmed, he immediately checked his arms and legs for any cuts or open wounds. Luckily, there were none. A sense of relief was quickly replaced by disquieting trepidation.

"Man, what did we *do* last night?...

3

COMING HOME TO ROOST

In the heat of the early afternoon sun, Mara slowly bent down to pull up a most unwelcome weed that had sprung up in her beloved garden. She could in no uncertain terms tolerate such an insidious intrusion into her personal sanctuary. As she reached for the base of the insolent, overgrown weed, she felt a sharp prick in the back of her hand. Responsively, she yanked it back and shook it. When she did so, Mara was startled at first to see a little, green gardener snake, flopping wildly from the back of her hand. But after the initial shock, she calmly held out her shriveled hand and observed the serpent through her horn-rimmed glasses.

"You're a feisty one," she scoffed in a gravelly voice, as she watched it dangle and twist in the air.

She pinched its head between her thumb and forefinger. Prying it off of her, Mara grabbed the snake by the tail and held her arm out straight from her body. She limped over to the edge of the garden where a crabapple tree stood and set the snake in its branches.

"Back where you belong," she grumbled.

Just then, she caught the glimpse of an object flying through the air and crashing into her precious garden.

"What on earth?" she muttered angrily. She had no sooner gotten the words out of her mouth when she realized what it was. By the time she had started for the rubber ball, a little boy came scrambling across the street to the edge of Mara's picket fence. She wiped her hands off on the apron that hung over her old-fashioned summer dress, hobbled over to the red rubber ball, and picked it up.

"Ma...Ma'am," a nervous little 6-year-old boy called out while waving to her. "Ma'am can I have my ball?"

But Mara paid no attention to him as she made her way towards the house and reached for the handle of the screen door. The boy looked on hopelessly. Then a voice called from the porch next door.

"Mother Rash," Hannah Grace said. "What do you think you're doing?"

"I'm teaching this boy a lesson," Mara called back undaunted as she pulled open the screen door.

"Mother!" Hannah Grace said while setting her pitcher of water down and walking over to the gate that connected the two yards. Feeling sorry for the little boy, she said to Mara, "You are most certainly not. I am quite sure that he did not purposely kick his ball into your yard." Hannah Grace grabbed the ball out of her mother-in-law's hands.

"Now why'd you go and do that?" Mara protested.

"Don't be an old, crotchety woman," Hannah Grace answered. "He just wants his ball back."

"Kids today don't need to be coddled, they need to learn the meaning of respect," Mara answered sharply. "Did you see what that ball did to my roses? He needs to learn now that there are consequences to his actions."

The boy watched Mara with great apprehension. To him, she looked and acted like the witches straight off of Disney Channel.

Hannah Grace made her way over to him. She smiled sweetly and offered him the ball. "There you go," she said.

The little boy quickly snatched the ball out of her hands and ran. A pretty, young teacher shepherded him back across the street to the playground of the school before waving back to Hannah Grace who returned her gesture.

Mara looked on in disgust, "Hmmph. I spose he'll just do it again tomorra'."

"Why do you have to act like that?" Hannah Grace chided. "Sometimes you're as mean as a rattlesnake. Those kids are scared to death of you! Did you know that?"

"Good!" she snapped. "At least they don't cut through my yard, destroying my garden on their way to school."

"Oh, Mother Rash, what am I going to do…," Hannah Grace began to say before looking at her watch. "Oh Mother, look what time it is, I don't have time to sit here arguing with you. We promised the pastor that we would be down at the church in twenty minutes. Are you going to be ready?"

"Don't you worry about me," Mara answered sharply.

Meanwhile, the little boy had made his way deftly across the street holding the prized red rubber ball with both hands. Still a little shaken by the encounter, he was nonetheless proud that he was able to get the ball from Old Lady Rash's yard…and she didn't turn him into a toad or anything like they said. Usually, once a ball goes into her yard, it is never seen again. He was lucky this time. Weaving his way through the multitudes on the playground, in-and-out of jump ropes, four square, and hopscotch, he moved past the swing sets, under the monkey bars, and back onto the kickball field.

"Hurry up!" an impatient red-haired, freckle faced 11-year-old boy yelled at him.

The little boy picked up the pace, worried that he might be in for it otherwise. Jackson was already mad about Ralph kicking another grand slam over the road. The teacher had made them kick from the opposite direction today after Ralph broke out a window last Friday. That too was a game winning home run, making it three in a row. And Jackson hated to lose.

"What took ya so long?" Jackson asked angrily as he ripped the ball out of the first grader's hands. Then he pulled it way back in his right hand and acted like he was going to chuck the ball at the boy with all of his might. The little boy covered his head and ducked in fear. Jackson laughed contemptuously.

"Come on, Jackson. Give him a break," Ralph yelled out to him from behind the incinerator that they were using as a backstop. His team was still clamoring and high fiving over the latest towering home run. The little boy standing next to Jackson looked at the fair-haired fourth grader full of gratitude.

"Ha! What a loser," Jackson replied, sneering at the little boy. Slowly, he walked back to the pitcher's mound and added calculatingly, "Do-over."

"*What?*" Ralph exclaimed. "What are you talking about? Do what over?"

A riotous clamor arose from Ralph's team.

"It was foul, so Do-over!" Jackson snapped back.

"Are you kidding, me?" Ralph objected, as he started for the mound. "The ball sailed straight over Roger's head in right!" Just as Ralph made his way across the third base line, Jackson pulled out his old ace in the hole.

"And another thing, I don't want any of these little boys to play with us anymore," Jackson said shrewdly. He bounced the ball forcefully and then caught with two hands. He hated to lose and took no shame in winning at any and all costs, a quality that had been carefully nurtured by his father, Lexus.

"If it was foul, why didn't you say anything right after I kicked it?" Ralph challenged. His team crowded around him in support. "Everybody *saw* it."

Jackson paused for effect because he was also partial to grandstanding. "I didn't have to say nothin' cause it was obvious that it was foul," Jackson answered, beaming with arrogance. "So, do-over."

"*No!*" the boys yelled out again in earnest.

"Do-over!" Jackson yelled at the top of his lungs.

"You're a liar and a cheat Jackson Helrigle!" a little chubby boy with glasses chided above the noise of his teammates. "I'm going to tell Miss Passimons!"

"Shut up, '*Porker*!'" Jackson yelled back as he dropped the ball and started for the chubby boy.

"My name is Parker!" the chubby boy replied as he started for the teacher.

But Ralph stuck out his tan, sinewy arm and stopped him.

Jackson walked over and stood nose to nose with Ralph. They were cousins only in the sense that their mothers were sisters. Jackson stuck out his pale arm and poked a finger into Ralph's chest. Being about the same height and age, they stared with daggers into one another's eyes.

"Either it's a do-over or we can start the whole game over without the little ones," Jackson continued. He knew that Ralph was a push over. "They're just in the way."

Ralph slapped away Jackson's finger from his chest. "As long as the teams are even, what's it matter?" he objected.

The younger boys stood by watching with great angst at the prospect of being excluded from the game that they loved to play each and every day.

"Teacher said they've got to play," the chubby boy raged at Jackson, lifting his chin and peering through his thick glasses.

Jackson reached over and shoved him hard to the ground. Parker hit the ground with a dull thud into the soft, saturated ground. All of the other boys, even the youngest of them, cackled with laughter.

"Miss Passimons? Ha. Go tell her. She ain't gonna do nothin' about it," Jackson said. The boys glanced back over their shoulders to the teacher standing at the far end of the playground wearing her bug-eyed sunglasses and spinning her whistle in large, concentric circles. Even Parker knew that taking their case to her would only be a humiliating waste of time. She was on the verge of retirement and had long since opted for her own serenity over exacting justice. Jackson sauntered back over to red rubber ball and picked it up. He now stood holding it and all of the cards.

"All right," Ralph said. Everyone looked at him in surprise. "It's a do-over, but only if the little boys still get to play."

Jackson looked over his shoulder and spit on the ground beside him and then looked at all of the boys on the game field. "Okay. Everyone can play, accept him!" Jackson answered, pointing his bony finger at the chubby boy.

Ralph glanced over to Parker without saying a word and shrugged. The boy looked back at him knowingly. With his shoulders slumped over, he slowly made his way over to a shade tree by the field and plopped down. He sat Indian style leaning on his hands with tears rolling down his cheeks.

"Okay. Still eight to five, we're winning, and Ralph's up," Jackson said with a wry grin on his face.

The little boys scattered to their previous positions and the game played on in accordance within the laws of the schoolyard.

Just over Parker's shoulders in the distance, two of the third grade girls stood whispering in hushed tones and giggling with their hands cupped over their mouths. They glanced around to see if anyone had been looking before they scurried around the corner of the school building that was off limits. Once on the other side, the two girls, prettily dressed climbed up onto the cellar doors of the school basement and got settled in to share in the juicy gossip about their favorite subject.

"What did he *say*? What did he *say*?" one of the girls asked with great anticipation.

Just then, a little boy popped up out of nowhere and stood looking scornfully at the two little girls. The girls shrieked grabbing on to one another before realizing whom it was.

"Simon Adamson!" one of the pretty little girls said. "You nearly scared us to death. What on earth are you doing? Get out of here!"

But the pale, dirty-faced little boy's expression did not change. "You're not supposed to be here," he said in a low voice through his gritted teeth.

"You're not either," the girls countered without budging.

"This is my spot!" he said again scowling with his chin down in his chest.

"Nu-uh, we were here first," one of the girls replied.

"*Get out of here!*" he yelled. His shoulders were heaving up and down, and he seethed with anger.

By now, the girls were more than a little annoyed with him but decided to try a different tact.

"Simon, just give us a second. Go over there and let us talk," one of them offered diplomatically. "Then we will go away and you can come back over."

"No! Get outta' here or else," he threatened, holding his arms straight down with clenched fists. "This is my spot."

"You can't *make* us leave," the other girl who was twice his size objected.

"Don't you know what I am?" he said showing his teeth and hissing as he moved toward the girls. "I'm warning you."

They couldn't help it. Both of the pretty little girls burst out in laughter. Then one of the girls looked at him doubtfully and said, "I'd like to see you try."

Around the corner, Miss Passimons was about to blow the whistle to end the recess before two shrill screams echoed off of the brick building over the schoolyard.

A little girl jumped out around the corner, cupped her hands, and yelled hysterically to the teacher.

"*Miss Passimons! Miss Passimons!*" a hysterical voice screamed.

* * *

The pastor looked up from his desk out the Venetian blinds of his office, biting his lip while waiting for the perfect word to come to him. From his vantage point, he could see the playground of the school across the street from his parish. He was seeing, yet not noticing the chaos that was unfolding before him. Resolute, he sat forward, raised his fingers over the keyboard, pecked a few lines, and then relaxed again in uncertainty. After some deliberation, he looked up again out the window and finally noticed the children excitedly running around the corner of the grade school building. Intuitively, he surmised that it must be a fight for there had been many of them over the years around that very corner even when he himself was a student there.

When he looked down again at the screen before him, he frowned and shook his head in disgust at what he had just written. As he deleted the entire paragraph, the teacher herded a small child around the corner. Holding each other close, they walked to the entrance of the school with a throng of students in tow. By the time the pastor looked back up, the teacher had already guided the student into the building and out of his sight while leaving the masses at the front door.

With a sigh, he sat back in his chair and looked over the top of his bifocals to re-read the first part of his weekly sermon. He took a sip of his green tea and set it back down as he licked his lips. Mouthing the words out loud, he squinted hard and mustered up the courage to go at it again. He sat tall in his chair, flexed his fingers, and began pounding on the keys with an air of determination. After some time, he took a deep breath and exhaled out of his nose in mild frustration. It was then that he glanced down at the icon at the bottom of his computer screen. The pastor winced in disgust as if he just caught a whiff of something putrid. Involuntarily, he shook his head in an effort to vanquish the uninvited thought. But the trick only temporarily thwarted the temptation. In the end, it was to no avail. His eyes gravitated once again to the icon. That old familiar elixir beckoned to him as it had so many times in the past. With a jittery hand, he slowly reached for the mouse and obediently moved it and clicked. The soft blue light flickered and fluttered in the reflection of his bifocals before his sad eyes.

After he was through, the good pastor pushed away from the desk in self-loathing. Resting his elbow on the arm of an old, swivel chair, he leaned his head against his fist and looked out the corners of his eyes through a second window on the opposite side of the room. There he noticed two young girls not more than thirteen or fourteen years old walking down the street. Carrying their backpacks slung over their shoulders, they bounced and be-bopped around one another like two wild butterflies. At second glance, it became evident that they were furiously texting on their cell phones. Periodically, one would stumble into the other only to be pushed back in playful retaliation. Every now and again, they doubled over, laughing uncontrollably. Periodically, they would flip their backpacks over their shoulder again, pull their long, shimmering hair back out of their eyes and continue on their way. Like watching a silent film, the pastor could only speculate at what they were saying or giggling about. But true to that medium, it was all the more lovely to not know. Their expressions of pure joy and youthful innocence transcended mere words. Still leaning on his fist, he surrendered an envious half-smile.

"The one on the left has to be Sharon," the pastor thought.

He couldn't recall the other girl's name though he had seen her around town many times before. As he watched, it became quite obvious that the two of them were very close friends. The girls strode their way slowly down the tree-lined road out of sight.

"Ah, to be so young and carefree," he said aloud. Then he sat up, rubbed his face with both hands, and began to delete his entire sermon.

* * *

What the pastor didn't know was that the young girls were actually texting each other as they made their way home from school. It was a couple of miles, but when they walked together it was all too short of a distance which explained the snail's pace.

Looking down at her phone, Sharon opened her mouth in melodramatic surprise. "Un-uh," she grunted as she slapped Shannon on the shoulder. "I can't believe you said that. Oh yeah? Well,..."

In rebuttal, she pecked away at her phone, but before she finished one of her "fave" songs came on.

"Oh wait, oh wait," Sharon shouted. She stopped, put her hands out, and looked down at the ground intently as if for a lost contact. "Yes, it is! Here, here..." she said, as she reached for one of her earpieces, pulled it out, and offered it to her longtime BFF.

"Ahh!" Shannon screamed through a wide smile after she had finally inserted the earpiece. They both screamed together in unison. "Ahh!" With their heads close together, they started dancing and singing to some new female artist's first hit single. "It's a love story baby just say, 'yes'..." the girls wailed.

The brake lights flashed from a passing car that quickly came to a screeching halt up the road.

"Who was *that?*" Mike shouted to his best friend Sean over the stereo blasting "Sensual Seduction." As he sat up and peered into his rearview mirror, he reached over to turn down the volume.

"I dunno," Sean answered. He pulled his ball cap off of his moppish, brown hair and leaned out the window to get a better look.

By now the girls had taken notice of the car, but played it off masterfully as though they hadn't. Sharon reached for her phone and sent a message to Shannon.

"Whoisthat???"

"OMG! that's mike jones' car! don't know who's with him. hope its sean king!!!"

"Oh, I know who that is," Sean said looking back down the street at the two girls. "That's who I was telling you about, dude. That's Shannon Payne!"

"Dude, you were right, man. She's definitely hot," Mike said. "She's only gonna be a freshman?"

It had been obvious to everyone including both Shannon and Sharon that Shannon had been developing at a much faster rate than her best friend. In fact, it had been a bit of a running joke between the two of them because they had always been the exact same size and shape since they met in second grade. Now, Sharon wore bras because of pure practicality while Shannon wore them out of necessity. Sharon and Shannon's hipless figures had made them virtually invisible to the older boys until recently. Now, Shannon's hourglass shape filled out her miniskirt to the point that she had inadvertently flagged down two soon-to-be seniors. Still, regardless of any differences, they would always be the best of friends. It said so in their eighth Grade yearbooks.

"Dude, back up, back up," Sean urged Mike.

Mike threw the Escort into neutral, before slamming it into reverse. Miraculously, the transmission responded one more time as the front tires squealed out a dark patch of rubber on the asphalt. The car wildly swerved back and forth as it backed down the road toward the expectant girls.

"I can't believe it!" Shannon squealed in excitement, grabbing Sharon's arm. "They're coming back."

Sharon smiled and asked nervously, "What do we do? What do we do?"

"Let me do the talking," Shannon whispered excitedly.

The car grounded to an abrupt halt next to them.

"Hey," Sean coolly uttered as he leaned out the door on his folded arms. His tan, muscular arms flexed involuntarily in the late afternoon sun.

"Hey," Shannon responded casually while tucking her long hair behind her ear. She glanced back at Sharon and shot her a quick smile before looking back again at Sean with a placid expression. "You, uh, want something?" she asked. Sharon rolled her eyes in disbelief, and then catching herself, looked around as if bored.

"Aren't you Shannon Payne?" Sean asked.

"Uh, Sean King, you know exactly who I am," she responded with a smirk walking over to the car. "We've know each other forever."

"Well, uh, yeah, kinda, but..." Sean stammered. "Who's your friend?"

"Sean, don't be stupid. You know Sharon too. Ga' what's gotten into you?"

"Hi," Sharon said with an awkward wave while holding onto her backpack with both hands and swiveling slowly back and forth.

"Oh yeah, hey," Sean said disinterested.

Shannon walked over to the car and leaned through the window, forcing Sean to move back in his seat.

"Whose car is this?" she asked coyly. She turned her head towards Sean whose face was mere inches from her own.

"Oh, hey," Sean answered, his heart racing. "This is Mike Jones. He just moved here this spring."

"Oh, Hey, Mike," Shannon said, acting if she had never even noticed him before.

"What's up?" Mike said, while giving a wave with his hand that rested on the steering wheel. "What are you guys up to?" he asked.

"Nothin', we're just heading home," Shannon answered, looking around the interior of the car.

"You want a ride?" Mike asked hastily. "We can give you a ride, if you'd like."

Sean gave him a look of disgust, like his dad used to give him as a kid when he scared the fish away by tripping over the tackle box on the floor of the boat.

"Or whatever," Mike added in an effort to salvage the situation.

"Oh, I don't know," Shannon responded coolly. She looked back at Sharon on the sidewalk and mouthed. *"Yes!"*

Sharon raised her eyebrows worrying about what her older brother would say. Well, actually, she knew what he would say. He would kill her, and then he would tell their mother to ground her for an eternity.

"I guess so," Shannon said.

"Cool," Sean answered. He opened the door, jumped out of the car, and held the seat back for the girls to crawl inside. Shannon took a step towards the car and motioned to Sharon who hesitated at first. Bugging her eyes out and tilting her head, Shannon mouthed the words to her friend, "Come on!"

Sharon looked down the road towards home and then back towards the car, before crawling into the back seat.

Shannon followed her, accidentally bumping into Sean as she passed by. "Oh, sorry," she whispered.

Once the girls were inside, Sean jumped back in the car, slammed the door, and pounded out a rat-i-tat-tat with his hands on the dashboard that elicited a cloud of dust.

Looking back into his rearview mirror, Mike's eyes locked with Sharon's for a brief moment.

"You guys listen to Snoop Dogg?" Mike shouted as he cranked up the volume. The girls nodded with contrived enthusiasm at the set of dreamy blue eyes looking back at them in the rearview mirror. But, when the eyes again turned to the road, the two girls looked at one another and simultaneously feigned hurling. Huddled close together in the back seat, the bass shook them to their core, and they smiled with great anticipation at the prospect of their own "Love Story."

Mike unwisely looked back again at the girls in rearview mirror when he hit the gas pedal. As a tried and less than true method of teenage boy flirtation, the car spit out some loose rocks and leaped forward. Without warning, another car suddenly appeared coming from the opposite direction. Mike jerked the steering wheel, as did the driver of the other car, narrowly averting a head-on collision.

* * *

Without slowing, the teenagers sped off. The other car pulled off to the side of the road in front of one of the older, more neglected, Victorian homes that lined the quiet street. A young man in his early twenties jumped out of the old, rusted out beater, hurried around to the back of the car, and opened the trunk. After rummaging around for a few minutes, he re-emerged with two armfuls of groceries cradled tightly by his spindly arms. He made his way up the cracked sidewalk, pausing only to lift his bony knee in an effort to gather the bags that were slipping away. Once he collected himself, he ascended the rickety old steps onto the porch and hit the screen door several times with his sharp elbow.

The scrawny, young man whistled joyfully as he waited for someone to answer. After a time, a pretty, young woman with black hair and blond highlights came to the door. The young man dipped his head and smiled warmly. Unceremoniously, the girl opened the screen door and leaned against it, holding it open as the scrawny young man entered the rundown house. The girl hesitated in the doorway for a brief moment as she pulled her long, untamed hair back into a pony tail. When she raised her arms, it pulled her shirt up high enough above her cutoffs to reveal a belly button ring and a tiny tattoo just above her hip. Then she made her way back into the house.

Simon looked on unwittingly as the screen door slammed behind the girl. He was otherwise preoccupied listening to a voice mail that he missed from earlier in the morning as he walked down the street. By the time his uncle's message had ended, he found himself standing at the corner of a white picket fence that lined an immaculate, manicured yard. His hand holding the cell phone dropped to his side. Simon could not believe what he saw. The rickety house that he grew up in had been completely gutted and refurbished. To his utter amazement, the exterior had been painted with a surprisingly tasteful shade of pink while the shutters and a wrap-around porch were contrasted in white. He looked to the ragged house on the left and then back to the withered one on the right in order to get his bearings. There was no doubt about it. That was home or at least it used to be.

He peered a little closer and squinted his eyes a bit, as if he were trying to find the gloomy, slate flecked paint and the droopy porch with loose shingles hidden under the now picturesque exterior. For a fleeting moment, he could see the drafty old house beneath its recent facelift. The image quickly faded and was enveloped by the beautiful, eclectic home that now stood before him. Incredibly intricate neoclassical details outlined the entire home from the eaves to the wrap-around porch. Decorative window frames held ornamental, paned glass, reminiscent of the turn of the century while an American flag hung from one of the columns on the porch like it was 1941. The only flicker of similarity between what he remembered from his past and what lay before him now was the general framework of the house and the great oak in the front yard, faithfully holding a tire swing. Otherwise, there was no comparison. Someone spent a great deal of time and resources transforming a John Steinbeck novel into a Norman Rockwell painting.

Simon was at a loss for words as he gazed upon the lawn that was dotted with toys before the front door of the house was thrust open by a small child, bursting out onto the porch chasing after a golden retriever. The boy looked to be about 5 or 6 years old with dark hair and dark complexion. After him came another boy who appeared older than the first, followed by a little girl. By the time the first little boy reached the gate, a woman came out the front door calling out to them as she reached back to shut the single-glass paned door.

"No, no, no…don't let the dog out," she called to them in a thick accent. She was also of dark complexion with dark hair that flowed out from under a distinctive looking scarf. "Children. Put the dog back inside. Back you go now. Yes, that's it put him back inside. Okay. Now go, get in the car."

Simon thought the inflection of her speech may have been Middle Eastern or Indian, but he couldn't be certain. He watched covertly as the shiny new Land Rover backed out of the driveway, paused in the street, and rushed off in the opposite direction. Absentmindedly, he closed his cell phone that was incessantly beeping and tucked it back into his pocket. For another minute, he gazed upon the house. The whole experience was so surreal. Finally, his eyebrows lifted above his glassy eyes, and he gave out only a slightly audible, "Wow." He turned, put his hands into his jeans pockets, and headed for the ballpark.

* * *

By the time he wandered through town, past the grain elevators, and over the railroad tracks, he had completely lost his train of thought. Simon lifted his head skyward towards the top of the concrete elevators. Something deep inside was still lovingly nudging him, demanding to be dealt with. Just as he was about to identify it, the narrow street lined with maple trees opened up before him, and he stepped out into the bright sunshine. To shade his eyes from the bright light, he cupped his hand and placed them above his furrowed brow. It was then that he realized he was standing on the corner of the old Bethel ballpark. For a moment, Simon was once again at a loss for words. Suddenly, it was as if he was once again that same little boy standing on that very same corner, staring at that very same ball diamond, and dreaming of playing in the Majors. Such a powerful infusion of whimsical innocence overwhelmed him that he had to actually make a conscience effort to remind himself that the final chapter to that dream deferred had already been written. And there would be no going back or second chances to do it all over again.

In a flash, his mind retraced the steps that led to the dream's demise, and a hollow, empty feeling mourned in its wake. Regret and dejection wrestled with his pride, taking it almost all of the way to the mat. Within a fraction of a second, he was systematically reliving all his shortcomings and failures while his ego did damage control by offering up a myriad of excuses. Taking solace in a series of snippets from his carefully guarded mental highlight reel, Simon resuscitated some sense of self-confidence. After all, before the injury, he *was* pretty good.

It wasn't long before he was able to appreciate all of the wonderful memories of playing the game. A slight grin spread across his face until it broke into a full fledged smile.

Then he noticed the dramatic changes that had been made to the ballpark itself in the time that he had been away. Rich had told him about the improvements that the president of the bank, Lexus Helrigle, had made to the field. The red, rickety snow-drift fencing that had previously lined the field and the warped light posts that presided over it had since been removed and replaced with a shiny new chain link fence and towering metal poles. Concrete replaced the dirt floors of the sunken dug outs. Even more impressive, batting cages and bull-pens had been erected down either foul pole while a home run fence displayed the sponsors that were responsible for funding the dramatic transformation. Even the rusty, metal Pepsi-Cola scoreboard had been replaced with the most modern digital technology.

Just to the right of the field, a concession stand had been constructed complete with indoor restrooms. A shiver involuntarily ran up and down Simon's spine at the thought of the glorified, cinder-blocked porte-potty that used to reside just outside the foul pole in right field. It was every player's nightmare to have an "emergency" at the Bethel ballpark. What was passed off as a restroom, was in all actuality little more than a forsaken bunker with a plank that had two holes cut out of it, exposing a most ungodly smell. Indelibly implanted in his brain, the foul odor stirred once again his nostrils. He chuckled and shook his head perfunctorily to erase the unpleasant memory.

From somewhere behind the newly constructed concession stand, Rich came barreling around the corner, driving a Mule that carried a full load of sand. As Rich made its way through a side gate onto the game field, Simon noticed for the first time the carefully manicured playing surface that would have rivaled TCU's home field.

"Wow, that's unbelievable!" he uttered.

Rich slowed down and carefully made his way across right field to second base where two young men were standing. One was leaning against a rake, while the other sat on second base with his head down staring at a phone that he clutched with both hands. Simon walked over to just behind home plate and leaned against the base of the flag pole. As he looked up at the stars and stripes residing over the park, he noticed for the first time several signs that had been attached to the top of the backstop that proudly displayed the Bethel Dixie Youth Baseball League's recent champions. All four segments of the fence that soared above home plate were covered representing titles of various age groups and divisions. Simon read down the list of Dairy League Championships, "2001, 2002, 2003, 2005, 2006." It was impressive to say the least. Who would have thought that somehow tiny Bethel would have become some sort of little league baseball dynasty.

Rich cut the Mule off, reached for the shovel, and then noticed Simon for the first time. He whistled to get Simon's attention and motioned for him to join him out on the field. As Simon made his way out of the dugout and stepped onto the clay, that same old magical feeling swept over him. He took in a deep breath as he looked around at the major overhaul that had been made to the rugged sandlot of his memory.

"Hey, look, here comes death-warmed-over," Rich mocked, noting the pale complexion of his old friend as a result of the previous evening's festivities. Simon shook his head in disgrace and then playfully hopped over the third base line like Turk Wendell as he made his way over to the guys. As he approached them, it became apparent that they were trying to add sand to the infield around second base to absorb some of the water that had fallen in the torrential downpour the day before.

Rich started shoveling the sand onto the field while the other two guys appeared to be in some kind of debate. One of them was flailing his arms excitedly while the other shook his head in opposition. By the time Simon had reached them, Rich had had enough of their antics.

"Would you two shut up already," he chided. "I'd like you to meet someone. This is Simon Freeman. Simon this is Joey Campbell and George Lukas."

They appeared to be in their late teens or early twenties. The one leaning on the rake reached out his hand towards Simon.

"Hey, nice to meet cha'," George said. "Wow, looks like they got you with the Sharpie."

"It's pretty noticeable, huh?" Simon asked as he absentmindedly tried to wipe away the dark smudge from his cheek.

The other one who had been holding his Blackberry while gesticulating wildly skipped all pleasantries.

"Hey man, you can settle something for us," Joey said. "Do you think…"

"Oh, Joey, shut up, man, he doesn't care," George objected. "No one wants to hear about any of that. Where are your manners? You just met the guy."

"I'm just saying," Joey retorted. "He's perfect. He's a completely objective third party. Neither of us know him. He's completely unaware of…"

"I apologize for the rudeness of my friend here," George said, butting-in a second time.

"See there you go again," Joey said as he pulled on the bill of his crimson ball cap, adorned with a bright, white H'.

"Ignore those two," Rich chimed in as he scooped another shovel full of sand and spread it carefully onto the clay. "They're always like this."

"Okay. Fine. Joey wants to know if, in your opinion, it is a waste of time to argue over something that has no definitive answer," George said.

"See, stupid, like I said!" Rich mocked as he scooped another shovel full of sand from the Gator.

"No, no…I want to know if he thinks it is *worthwhile* to discuss an issue that does not have a definitive answer," Joey responded. "It's all in the way you phrased the question. See. You already tainted his opinion by bringing the words 'waste of time' into his sub-consciousness." Then he kicked some excess sand onto George's Birkenstocks.

"I don't know," Simon answered with a perplexed expression on his face. "I've never really given it much thought to be honest."

"Nor should you," Rich grunted.

"That's just it," Joey replied. "He doesn't have to consciously think about it because it comes naturally, right? People just do it. They consider and discuss things that can't be proven, because it uncovers a common consciousness of absolute truth."

"What?" George said with a pained expression. "No, that just proves that you're a moron who learned a bunch of fancy words your freshman year of college.

He doesn't ever think about it because it is just nonsense. He's an educated...
where'd you go to school?" he asked turning towards Simon.

"I just graduated from Texas Christian," Simon answered, looking inquisitively
at Rich who just shook his head while scooping out another shovel full of sand.

"TCU, the Horned Frogs, right?" George said. "Cool. Joey just finished his first
year at the University of Illinois where he unlocked the mysteries of the universe."
And then he turned back to Joey. "See. Another normal person who never thinks
about any of this junk."

"He's not even told you what we're talking about," Joey said to Simon. "George's
taken the whole thing out of context and already unduly influenced you. Let me
break it down into simpler terms. If you discuss something, even though it has no
definitive answer, you learn more about the subject while discovering more about
yourself. And if you are conscious of it, then you can unlock trends and common
beliefs. Those beliefs become your *truth*."

With a furtive sigh, Rich took the unused rake from Joey's hands and went to
work, smoothing out the sand.

"For example, here's what I said before you walked up, 'If I had drafted Manny
Ramirez with my second pick in the draft, I would be leading the fantasy league
right now."

"And I said, 'That's stupid,' George countered. "Why even waste one milli-
second discussing that. It's a mute point. There's nothing to gain by discussing it
because we don't know what *would* have happened. It can't be proven. It would be
like saying 'who is the greatest athlete ever? Michael Phelps or Michael Jordan?'"

"Jordan," the other three young men answered in unison.

"But that's just it!" Joey blurted out. "By exploring something that cannot be
proven, he uncovered an unconscious truth that is common to us all. Last night I
was reading a book by Thomas Mann and he..."

"Look, shut up already," Rich said before Joey had a chance to finish. "I really
don't care. When he first left for college he was reading Sports Illustrated. Now,
'Yoda' here stays up half the night reading about native American folklore on
Wikipedia," Rich said to Simon sarcastically.

He turned to Joey and George. "We've got work to do," Rich said. "Somebody's
got to get this field ready. The teams are going to start showing up. If it isn't ready,
Lexus is going to be ticked. I have to get another pile of sand. Do something useful
and rake. Finish smoothing this out till I get back."

Joey frowned as Rich forced a rake into his hand.

Simon was thankful for the opportunity to change the subject. "So, there's a
game today?" he asked.

"No. Just a couple of preseason scrimmages," Rich answered, climbing back
onto the Mule. "But the first one starts at 4:30, so the teams will be here soon to
warm up."

"Got another rake?" Simon asked.

"You really want to rake some sand?" Rich asked. "I thought you needed to hit the road."

"Na'," Simon answered looking around at the field. "I just got a message from my uncle saying that it looks like it will be another week now before they start interviewing. So, I've got a little time."

"So, you can hang around here for a couple more days!" Rich replied enthusiastically, yelling over the noise of the motor. "Hey, you can go to Will's bachelor party Friday night."

"Really, I gotta...," Simon started to object.

Before he could answer, Rich revved up the engine and headed back towards the sand pile.

"What are you interviewing for?" George asked.

"A pharmaceutical sales position," Simon answered as he grabbed a rake off of the ground and began smoothing out the sand.

"Ah, no, man, you're kidding," Joey said with a look of disgust.

"No way," George added. "Even McCain hates those guys."

"Oh, really?" Simon replied, doing a poor job of pretending that he knew or cared who 'McCain' was.

"Haven't you been following the election?" Joey asked almost exasperated.

"No," Simon replied while carefully smoothing out a pile of sand.

"So, how are you going to know who to vote for?" Joey pressed.

Simon laughed out loud. He stopped raking and looked up at them before realizing that they were serious.

"I don't know," Simon said, returning to his work. "I probably won't. I'm not into politics..."

Both Joey and George, appalled by his response, took a step closer before they both started in on him.

"You're kidding!" they exclaimed in unison.

"I can't believe that," Joey continued. "What were they teaching you down there? Man, if you're not a part of the solution, you're a part of the problem. It's time for a New World Order, a changing of the guard. And Obama is the guy who can do it. The Millennials are going to change the world.

"Last week, George and I hitchhiked to Des Moines to go to a rally, and Obama was hammering a message of 'Hope and Change'. No more politics as usual. You should have seen the crowds! It was like he was a rock star."

"Oh, yeah? That's cool I guess," Simon said completely disinterested, reaching out again with his rake and pulling it back in.

"Yeah, dude, he's the next Abe Lincoln!" George added. "I'm telling you."

"But pharmaceuticals, I'd really reconsider that one if I were you," Joey said. "There's so much more out there to do than be a slave to the status quo of corporate America and Wall Street. There's a couple of cool websites you can go to..."

Thankfully for Simon, Rich pulled up on the mule with another pile of sand.

Simon lifted his head momentarily before flipping the rake over in order to finish smoothing out the area that he had been working.

"Awesome," Rich shouted over the motor. "Good work fellas. Now, hurry-up. Let's take care of the area behind third base. Lexus just got here."

All four of them looked over to see a black Cadillac Escalade pull up, followed by a yellow Hummer. A fair haired boy jumped out of the Cadillac carrying a Nike baseball bag. The driver of the chromed-out SUV, who appeared to be one of the coaches, climbed out of the driver's side, placed his Oakley's on his head, and surveyed the field. By that time, the driver of the Hummer had also emerged. He walked around the back of the vehicle and opened the rear gate. A red-headed boy climbed out holding his glove in one hand and a Mizzuno bag in the other.

"Great, it's Lexus all right," Rich murmured. "Man, we've got to get this done, he's gonna have my butt. Come on. Let's get going. They're going to want to start on time."

"So, they're the guys you were telling me about?" Simon asked.

Rich jumped out of the four wheeler and started quickly unloading the sand. "Yep," he replied. "Besides being the president and vice president of The First National Bank of Bethel, they are the biggest donors of the booster club."

"Awe, man, Rich," Joey said, looking down at his watch. "I hate to do this to you man, but remember, we've gotta catch a train. So..."

"Nice," Rich retorted. "You guys are gonna take off *now?*"

"Sorry, man," George answered apologetically. "We're going down to Shiloh where the tornado hit."

"Are you're going down there to help or something?" Simon asked, somewhat impressed.

"Yep, life's all about the experience, man," Joey replied, haughtily.

Then the two young men headed off towards one of the dugouts. "Yeah, we're going to check it out for ourselves" George added. "See ya."

"Nice meeting you Simon," Joey yelled back with a wave. "I'd think twice about that pharma gig if I were you. Bad karma, man. Bad karma."

"Are they for real?" Simon asked Rich. "I mean, that's pretty cool that you guys are helping with the tornado cleanup."

"Uh, yeah right, not exactly," Rich scoffed. "Those guys are a couple losers. Leaving me high-and-dry again. They can go 'experience' somebody else working for a change." Then he looked around at everything that had to be done in the next 15 minutes. "Hey, man. I can't pay you anything, but if you chalk the lines, I'll get your dinner and all the beer you can drink tonight at the tavern."

"It's a deal," Simon replied with a smile. He wrinkled his brow quizzically and asked, "Hey, does Amtrak stop somewhere near here?"

"What? No way!" Rich answered, swearing profusely while he raked out the sand at third base. "Those two idiots are jumping the next freight train heading to Decatur."

4

FEET THAT NEVER STAY AT HOME

Prepping the field took a whole lot more work than Simon had anticipated, but somehow the two of them were able to mold the infield into a playable surface. By the time they had finished chalking the batter's box, it was a thing of beauty. Rich picked up the line of string from left field and began to roll it up as both of them surveyed the fruit of the labor with great satisfaction.

While they had been working, Simon didn't even have time to take note of the number of players and coaches that were now warming up for the scrimmage. The teams were broken up into various stations all through the outfield. One coach, who appeared to be in charge, would call out "Rotate" as he twirled his finger in the air. Within seconds, each of the players would gather their equipment into their bags and hustle to the next station. While Simon was taking it all in, Rich walked toward him at home plate, rolling up the remaining string.

"It's a little different from when you and I played, huh?" Rich said with a laugh after noticing Simon's expression.

"That's an understatement," Simon replied. "It's so well orchestrated. It reminds me of my first practice at TCU."

Suddenly, a bellowing horn like that of an 18-wheeler swept over the diamond. It was followed by a deep thumping sub-woofer that pounded in their chests. The source of the commotion came from behind left field. Some sort of 3-wheeler on steroids carrying a clothesline came barreling down a country road towards town. As the contraption came more clearly into view, Simon could tell that it was a farm implement. It had a huge tank on the back with long arms and hoses tucked behind. On the side of the tank was the word "Monsanto."

When the vehicle had almost bounded down the road past the ball field, Simon noticed the Mercedes-Benz symbol that had been welded to the front hood. Then he saw Rocky hanging out the window waving his Yankees cap. The deep thumping bass loosened its grip on Simon's chest as the crazy contraption continued barreling down the road.

"What on earth was that?" Simon asked with a laugh.

"That? That was Rocky Land driving a fertilizer sprayer," Rich answered in a disdainful tone.

"Mercedes?" Simon asked.

"What?" Rich answered. "No. Rocky wrenched that emblem off of some old heap and welded it on himself. And that noise was that rap clap-trap from his forty-two inch Bose sub-woofer that he installed in the back. His daddy got him that cush job. He's basically set for life.

"Wow," Simon replied. "Good for him."

"Now, what were you say'n before Vanilla Ice distracted me?"

"Nothing," Simon answered. "I was just saying how impressed I am at the level of coaching and the skill of the players."

"Oh yeah, can you imagine how good we could have been if we had ever been coached? I mean *really* coached," Rich said almost bitterly.

"Yeah," Simon agreed. "I think all we did was take turns hitting and catching fly balls. Remember that? Sometimes we'd stand in the field for what seemed like hours, bored out of our skull waiting for some doofus to hit a stinkin' pitch."

"That ain't the way it is anymore," Rich said. "We've invested a ton of time, effort, and money into our program and it's paid off. If the kids buy into it, then they can be a part of something very special. But, they gotta make that commitment."

"Yeah, I saw all of those championships," Simon replied, pointing to the back-stop.

"Awesome, isn't it?" Rich said. "Helrigle, Livingood, and myself have poured our heart and soul into this program. And now Bethel is like the Mecca of Dixie Youth baseball in Central Illinois. Kids come from all over to play in our program."

"What are the ages?" Simon asked.

"Ten and under. After that they go on to travel ball. The plan is to keep growing the program as these kids get older."

"And how many teams do you have?"

"Four in Bethel. But, there are twelve other teams overall in the entire county."

"Who all coaches the Bethel teams?" Simon asked.

"Me, Lexus, and Wilson coach the three most competitive teams," Rich answered. "Each year for the past six years, one of our teams has won the Dairy League Championship. The fourth team is coached by a guy named Jeremy Warner. He's a youth pastor at the new church just outside of town. He stepped in when Shane was deployed to Iraq.

"But, he has no clue what he's doing," Rich said. "We couldn't find anybody else. I don't even know if he ever even played. Last fall, he picked up all of the rejects, and you just have to scratch your head. We've tried to help him, but he won't invest the time that it takes to put together a great team. So, naturally, they get mercy-ruled just about every game.

"You'll see them in the second game. My team scrimmages Jeremy's after the Angles and the Rays play. We have been looking for another coach because it's really a disservice to the kids. They don't play year round. They're never hitting in the cages. I don't think any of them have a hitting coach. In the end, they're the ones who suffer. Plus, there have been rumors..."

Suddenly, a voice boomed from right field. "Rich, can we take infield now or what?" Lexus yelled before spitting out some sunflower seeds.

"Yes, sir!" Rich called back before turning again towards Simon. "Never mind, I'll tell you all about it later. Hey, how would you like to make a few bucks umpiring?"

"I don't know," Simon said in a cautious tone. "I've never umped behind the plate before."

"Don't worry about it," Rich replied. "I'll do it in the first scrimmage, and you can do it in the second. It's easy money. The second game won't matter anyway. It's going to be a blowout. You don't even need to know all of the rules. Just act like you know what you're doing and nobody will say a word, I promise. Besides, it's fifty bucks to work behind the plate"

Simon raised his eyebrows and said, " I could always use fifty bucks! Easy money, huh?"

* * *

The first scrimmage was a well played game. Simon was a little nervous umpiring on the base paths, but he felt great just to be on the field again. It wasn't playing, but it was the next best thing. Besides, it didn't take him long to get settled in. Rich helped him with where to stand and what to look for. Not surprisingly, the hulking bartender was in complete control behind the plate. More than once, Lexus went off about a call, but each time Rich was able to recite the rule that supported his decision.

"Wow, is that guy serious?" Simon said to himself under his breath. "It's a scrimmage. Take it easy."

Simon realized very quickly that the coaches, players, and parents took it very seriously. Both pitchers were so good that the innings went by quickly. The Devil Rays' pitcher, a red-headed kid named Jackson was even throwing some nasty curve balls.

Luckily for Simon, there were no real close plays or difficult calls for him to make in the field because he often found himself watching the game like a fan. Several kids made diving catches of fly balls and backhanded stabs at a couple of grounders. In the end, the Rays and their red-headed fireballer, whom Simon assumed was Lexus' son, won the day.

As the first scrimmage was finishing up, players from the two teams playing in the night-cap began to arrive and warm up on the other side of the home run fence. After the Devil Rays and the Angels had shaken hands in the traditional fashion, Rich carried a fungo bat out to home plate to hit some grounders to his infielders. He picked up a catcher's mitt near the dugout and tossed it to Simon.

"Can you catch for me?" Rich asked with a grin.

As Simon slipped the glove over his fingers, that old feeling, like a narcotic, hijacked his brain. He punched the mitt several times before putting it up to his face and deeply breathing in the leather.

"All right, goin' to first!" Rich called out. But before he tossed the ball into the air, he paused and turned to Simon. "Take a look, Simon," Rich said, pointing at a figure jogging towards them. "Here comes Warner now."

When Simon looked up, he recognized the young youth pastor immediately. "That's him?" Simon asked. "I saw that guy earlier today, taking groceries into the Cler's old house."

Rich paused for a moment with the fungo bat draped over his shoulder as he squinted his eyes and gazed at Jeremy. "Huh. Interesting." Then he drilled a grounder to the third baseman, "Goin' to first!"

"Hey, I'm sorry I'm running a little late," Jeremy called out to Rich as he clutched the fence with one hand while the other one held an old pea-green, army satchel draped over his shoulder.

Rich barely acknowledged him with a wave of the hand. "You got twenty minutes to get warmed-up," he told the youth pastor.

Simon intermittently kept an eye on Jeremy as he met his team in right field. He high fived his players and rubbed some of the heads of those who swarmed around him jumping up and down. His team was a stark contrast to the other three teams. Besides being highly disorganized, their overall skill level seemed to be extremely low. More than that, there was a visible difference between the players' builds. Rich's kids looked like athletes. They already had that V- shaped build. What's more, they moved like athletes, while Jeremy's players were shaped more like U's and I's and moved more like Weeble Wobbles and praying mantises.

Still, the biggest difference between the two teams was their maturity level. Besides being undersized, members of Jeremy's Padres were much more likely to play in the dirt, or get distracted by a bird flying over, while a scorching line drive narrowly missed taking their heads off. Mostly, they looked like a bunch of misfits and numbskulls.

When Simon looked over at the bleachers on the Padre's side, there were two mothers sitting on opposite ends, clapping quietly and offering a few words of encouragement. On the other side of the field, the Yankees had a sea of families sitting in lawn chairs lining the entire fence. Even for a scrimmage, they were rather raucous and intense from the opening pitch.

The glaring differences between the two squads paralleled that of the two coaches. Rich, a mountain of a man, was full of fire and intensity while Jeremy, diminutive in stature, sat on the bench with his legs crossed laughing and cutting up with his players. Simon could see what Rich meant by his assessment of Jeremy's coaching ability. It wasn't long before the score had gotten out of hand and the mercy rule was enforced. Simon couldn't help but feel a little sorry for the Padres and their fearless leader.

However, the kids on the team seemed to be getting over the loss very quickly. In fact, most of them didn't seem to give it a second thought. Instead, they smiled and made tiny dust storms by dragging their feet through the infield as they shook hands with the proud, domineering Yankees. Jeremy seemed almost apologetic as he went to shake hands with Rich. It was one of those David and Goliath snapshots.

As Jeremy shuffled his way back over to his team, he was almost immediately swallowed-up by the players. Simon heard him ask rhetorically, "Who wants a piece of gum?" And they all screamed with delight. Meanwhile, the Yankees were being berated for their lack of focus and consistency at the plate. Rich debriefed them on the finer elements of their game that needed attention if they were to win the ultimate prize. Rich's demeanor and tone set a definite level of expectation for the team that was clearly understood by everyone including the parents who stood nearby listening intently.

When it was over and everyone had gone home, Rich locked-up the last of the equipment, jumped in the Mule, and roared back to home plate where Simon picked up a bat and took a couple of swings. When he did, the fresh blister on his hand rubbed unkindly against the handle of the bat.

"Huh," he muttered, looking down at the wound while trying to recall how it got there.

"Smooth," Rich said. "You always had a smooth swing."

"Yeah, right," Simon replied. "It does bring back a lot memories., though"

Rich leaned on the steering wheel and glanced over his shoulder towards the playing field.

"Is their anything like the feeling of being out their, playin'?" Rich asked.

"No," Simon answered. "I guess not."

"Too bad you're not sticking around for a while," Rich lamented. "We sure could use your bat on my slow-pitch softball team."

"Probably not," Simon said. "But thanks." After a short pause Simon blurted out, "But, hey, these kids are awesome. I cannot believe how good they are. We were never that good. I don't think I hit like that Livingood kid until I was in high school."

"Yeah, he's the real deal," Rich responded. "But, we were terrible tonight. A lot of those hits would have been outs against a good team. We've got to be more disciplined at the plate. Otherwise, Helrigle and Livingood will take us to the woodshed."

"What?" Simon said. "You've got to be kidding me. You've got some studs out there too."

"Sure, we have potential," Rich quickly added. "We're still probably a player or two away from having a really competitive team. But, hey, I owe you a beer. Come on. Jump in. Let's go."

"Twist my arm," Simon said with a smile on his face as he hopped into the Mule. "But you're crazy if you don't think your team is awesome."

"Oh man, we are so far from where we need to be," Rich replied as he sped off towards the tavern. "I told them, 'yes', we persevered and won the title last year. But last year was last year. We can't be satisfied. Each individual needs to ask himself, 'How can I get better?' Ya know? 'What is my role on the team?' 'What can I do to help us reach the ultimate goal?'...it's all a process...we're in constant pursuit of perfection..."

With great passion, Rich preached on and on about the virtues of winning and losing while Simon listened with the excitement of a child listening to his favorite bedtime story.

* * *

When Simon and Rich entered the tavern, the first person they saw was Rob who was sitting alone at the bar. He was wearing his suit with his jacket once again draped over the back of the chair. His tie was undone, and his sleeves were rolled up. With a cigarette dangling in his left hand, he hovered over a mostly empty beer mug like a lioness protecting her cub. He had been pouring over the latest fantasy baseball magazines for quite some time as evidenced by the empty beer bottles making a semi-circle around him.

"Well, if it isn't Robin Ateitup?" Rich said, jeeringly. "Rip anybody off today with that Whole Life garbage?"

"Ha, ha," Rob scoffed. "You guys been playin' in the dirt with a bunch of 10-year-old's?"

"At least we can say we did *something* today," Rich answered defensively. "How's business here at the bar? Looks like you're kill'n it again today, as usual." Then he turned to Simon. "Rob, here, is a death hustler."

"I sell life insurance," Rob replied. "Is that a crime?"

"At least, it looks like you're trying to do something about that sorry fantasy league team of yours," Rich mocked before noticing a bunch of dirty glasses that had been piled up from earlier in the day. "Ah, would you look at this?" Rich snarled. He turned and called towards the kitchen. "Brad, what's up?" Why are all these dirty glasses sittin' out here?" He slid around the bar, turned on the water, and poured dish washing liquid into the sink.

"Looks like you have a little mascara running down your cheek, Tex," Rob said to Simon with a cruel laugh. "Is that the latest fashion statement in Dallas?"

"Yeah, real nice," Simon answered wiping his hand compulsively over his face. "So, you're the one responsible for this, huh? What goes around, comes around."

"I must admit, I had some help," Rob replied.

While the sink filled, Rich slid a frothy, frozen mug of beer over to Simon. Then he grabbed one of the publications that Rob had been sifting through.

"All of the reading in the world's not gonna help your woeful team," Rich said. "See if you can help him out there, Simon."

"At least I haven't devoted my entire life to virtual reality," Rob said as he wadded up his napkin and threw it at Rich.

"Rich knows his fantasy baseball, huh?" Simon asked.

"Let's put it this way, he's seven games up six weeks into the season," Rob answered.

"What did I tell you before the draft?" Rich asked grabbing a broom and beginning to sweep up.

"Come prepared," Rob reluctantly replied.

"And..."

"Don't drink and draft," Rob muttered as he rolled his eyes.

"Yes, thank you." Rich answered.

At that moment, the door of the bar swung open, and Rocky entered wearing Carhartts, gold chains, and a flat billed Sacramento Kings ball cap.

"Hey, did dat refer'ndum pass last night?" Rocky asked as soon as he walked in. "Cause' I'm gonna be *teed off* if it did. Know what I'm sayin'?"

"No, nobody knows what you're saying," Rob said scornfully.

Before Rocky could answer, he saw Simon sitting at the bar next to Rob. He leaned sideways and brought his fist up to his mouth. "Whoa, look who still ere', my boy, Simon. Thought you'd be gone by now." Rocky clutched hands with Simon and gave him a half hug before sitting down on the bar stool next to him.

"Yup, still here," Simon replied. "You, uh, got a big interest in politics these days, Rocky?"

"Wha'?" Rocky asked with a perplexed look on his face.

"Weren't you asking about the referendum?" Simon asked.

"Yeah, yeah, my ole man said if we gotta pay more taxes he's gonna take it out of my 'lowance," Rocky replied.

Rob chided him, followed by a vulgar comment. "What's the matter? You afraid your little entitlement program's gonna be shut down?" Rob asked.

"Rocky's dad owns a ton of acres of land," Rich said to Simon as he scrubbed the dirty glasses.

"Wouldn't want that well to run dry, would you Rocky?" Rob chided.

Rocky smacked Rob on the back of the head. "At least, *I* ain't out rippin' off old people. I got a real job."

"At least I'm not out sucking in fertilizer and weed killer all day," Rob answered. "Say, you might want to take a look at your own life insurance plans, Rocky Carcinoma."

"Speaking of which, I saw your ride today, Rocky," Simon said, tactfully changing the subject.

"Sweet, ain't it?" Rocky said, beaming. "Did all dat myself."

"No, Rocky, to answer your question, they didn't pass the referendum," Rich said, jumping into the conversation. "All they could agree on was to kick the can down the road. They've scheduled another couple of town hall meetings later this summer."

"Coo'," Rocky said, relieved.

"I don't get it," Simon said. "Why does the new school have to be paid for by a property tax?"

"You're back in Central Illinois," Rich said as he dried the glasses and hung them up. "We don't have any oil, just land. So, the only way to raise money for new schools is to raise taxes on the few people who own it. Have you seen the rest of town? Most of the jobs have dried up and gone outta the country. Ain't nobody got any extra money laying around here."

"'Cept Jack," Rocky said, chiming in. "And Helrigle and Livingood and…"

"…and your dad," Rob interrupted.

"Okay, so you named about one percent of the population," Rich said, flipping around one of the magazines.

"Hey, hands off!" Rob said, pulling it out of his gigantic hands. "I gotta figure out who I want to put in the lineup tonight before I go to my next appointment with that old bag, Mrs. Silverson."

"Can I see the rosters?" Simon asked enthusiastically. "Maybe I can help you put together a lineup for tonight."

"You know, Simon, now that Shane is stationed in Fallujah, we have an opening for another team in our fantasy league," Rich said, as though he were making some kind of tantalizing offer.

The four guys sat at the bar reading through the latest stats in the soft glow of the flat screen TVs as Baseball Tonight boomed through the establishment. The voices of Karl Ravech and Peter Gammons were soon drowned out as more and more patrons began to fill the tavern for the Monday night special.

"Man, I'm callin' Will and getting his rear end over here," Rich said after he dropped two plates of brats and onion rings in front of Simon and Rocky. "This might be the last night that we can all hang out before Freeman heads off to Jersey and forgets all about us again."

"Where is Will?" Simon asked.

"Probably still over at the bank closin' it down cause Helrigle and Livingood were both at the ball field today…ah, and there it is," Rich said, looking down at his cell. "What excuse do you think he is going to give this time? Ah, he just texted that he has to study for a stat class. That wuss!"

Rich poured a pitcher of beer and slid it over to the guys along with a couple more frosty mugs. The ice slid slowly down the side as he hammered away again at his cell, shaking his head in disgust.

After much cajoling and a month's worth of texts, Will finally caved like he always did and made his way through the crowd at the entrance of the bar to where they sat.

"Thornchuk!" Rocky yelled.

"Hey, look who's here!" they all yelled at once over the crowd noise, high fiving one another as their buzz began to kick in. Will got some indication of how long they had been sitting at the bar when Rocky jumped up and gave a series of heavyweight body blows to his midriff before giving him a big hug.

"Easy, champ. Easy," Will said, patting Rocky on the back before he climbed back onto his stool.

It wasn't long before Will caught up with them. Rich saw to that. If this was the last night that he would hang out with his old buddy Simon, Rich was determined to make sure that it would be one that his old friend wouldn't soon forget. While the drafts flowed, the guys bantered back and forth over everything from fantasy league lineups to the all-time greats in sports history.

Simon was having such a great time that he wasn't aware that the dark of night had set in or that the majority of the dinner crowd had since dispersed and gone home for the evening. Rob had long since missed his 8 o'clock appointment with Mrs. Silverson.

"She's half senile anyway," Rob reasoned. "I'll just tell her that she was mistaken and that we had scheduled it for Thursday night. I better not read about the old bag in obits tomorrow, or I'll be upset. Besides, it's easier to sell after the prune-people go to Wednesday night service anyway."

"What? Why?" Will asked.

"Because," Rob replied, after forcing a deep, disgusting belch. "Church makes the 'blue-hairs' think of heaven, and heaven makes them think of death, and death makes them think of life insurance. It's a beautiful thing! Right, Simon?"

But Simon had been far too wrapped up in a much more important argument with Rich, "Best all time running backs in the MFL, huh?" Simon sputtered.

"MFL?" Rich asked with a chuckle. "That'a boy. Have another drink. And you can't say 'Walter Payton.' Everybody around here says, 'Walter Payton," Rich said almost exhausted by the tiring argument.

"Because he is," Will, Rob, and Rocky responded in unison.

"All right, I'll say Emmitt Smith," Simon said smugly.

"What? Emmitt Smith. *Please*! Cut him off!" they all jeered and taunted.

"And I'll tell you why Emmitt Smith is the best running back ever…," Simon started to say before suddenly having an undeniable urge to hit the restroom. "…after I get back from the can."

That only elicited more jeers and trash talking from the guys, "You don't even know. You have no argument. You can't think of anything to say. My grandma could have run behind that offensive line."

"One of you better be ready to defend your boy, Payton!" Simon taunted, sliding off of the stool. "Cause I'm going to be comin' hard with it. Get your arguments ready. I'm gonna categorically lay it all out for yall…when I get back." Simon didn't realize just how much he had been drinking until his foot hit the floor, and he bumped into the empty barstool next to him. When he reached the bathroom door, he held it open for a moment and called back to the guys one more time. "Be ready…No. 22…best of all time!"

"All right already, just go," they shouted, throwing napkins and straws and coasters in his general direction. Will and Rob were already hammering away on their phones trying to find as many Walter Payton stats as possible for firepower before Simon even got his pants unzipped.

The tavern had completely cleared out, leaving just his friends at the bar. As Simon entered the restroom and saddled up to the urinal, he read a short blurb underneath a picture of the latest local high school baseball phenom. It was taken from the Ford County Chronicle and posted for his reading pleasure on the wall above the urinal while he relieved himself. As it so happened, he had time to read the entire article. By the time he finished, he thought of what might have happened had he and his mom stayed in Bethel.

As he shook the water off of his hands into the sink, he also shook off that regretful thought and resumed his mental checklist of systematic apologetics to defend Emmitt Smith. He may not know anything about politics, but he knew a whole lot about America's Team. With a smirk on his face, he grabbed a paper towel out of the dispenser. "Okay, I've got it!" he said to himself. He couldn't dry his hands off fast enough to get back out to the boys who were waiting for him.

He grabbed the handle, pulled back, and readied himself for the debate while forgetting to check his zipper.

"Okay, who thinks they're ready to take me on?" Simon profanely yelled out after bursting through the door. When he looked up, the entire group turned towards him in silence. Only they were not alone. Standing in the middle of the pack was the most beautiful girl he had ever seen. She was wearing an incredible blouse that accentuated a figure tightly packed into the shortest of miniskirts. And then he noticed her angelic face.

After an awkward moment of silence, the crafty young lady looked from one side to the other. She put a hand on one hip and answered him in a voice that dripped of honey, "I'll take you on!"

She lowered her chin and lifted her eyes towards him with a most seductive smile. After seeing the dumb look on Simon's face as he stood there speechless with his pants undone, the guys fell-out laughing.

"I can't stay long," she said coyly.

Simon slowly limped towards the group with his head hung low while the guys fell all over themselves, insisting that the young lady stay for a drink or two. When she graciously accepted their offer, each of them competed to pull up a chair closest to the mystery girl with the striking figure. Finally, it was Rob who successfully guided her onto the barstool beside him, while the others jockeyed shamelessly for position.

Rich remained behind the bar through the entire melodrama. He poured her her usual while the half-inebriated young bucks levied a bevy of lines and questions in an effort to either grab or hold her attention. Will looked down at his cell phone to see the long list of texts that his fiancée had sent to him before turning his phone off completely.

Embarrassed, Simon was left on the very fringes of the herd. Rather than being completely forgotten, he slid around to the side of the bar where he could at least get a glimpse of the young lady. Rich glanced over at Simon and caught him staring at the stunning brunette. The young lady leaned toward Rich as he handed her the drink. Her dark curls fell softly from her shoulder exposing more of her shimmery neck. Simon couldn't help but let his eyes fall to a gold cross dangling in front of that wondrous, soft cleft.

"You're so good to me, thanks baby," the girl said as she gave Rich a kiss on the cheek. The others looked on jealously.

Rich offered up a halfhearted smirk and said, "Hey, there's someone that I want you to meet." Then he made his way to the side of the bar where Simon sat. "This is Simon Freeman. He was my best friend growing up." Rich said proudly, putting his grizzly bear arm around Simon's shoulder.

She finished sipping her first drink out of the tiny straw and looked up through mesmerizing, green eyes.

"Mmm," she said swallowing her drink. "Sorry. Nice to meet you, I'm Jez," she said with a beautiful smile that almost made him feel unworthy to hold her gaze. "If you're a friend of Rich's, you're a friend of mine."

She leaned over the bar towards him, reaching out her hand to shake his. When she did so, her chest pressed against the bar, exposing an hour glass figure. Much to the dismay of the other guys, she held it for a fraction of a second longer than necessary.

"Nice to meet you," Simon said sheepishly before ducking his head. He was intimidated by gorgeous young women and unsure of what, if anything, he would ever have to offer a girl like that. After all, he didn't have a job, or money, or a nice car...at least not yet.

Simon nodded without anything clever or interesting to say, and in a flash his window of opportunity was gone. The pack overwhelmed her again. It was always that way for girls like Jez. And it had always been that way for shy guys like Simon. Because he was a handsome guy, his shyness was often misconstrued as arrogance and indifference.

Simon could only look on as she laughed wildly at the guys' lame jokes and outrageous come on lines, flipping her hair back over her glossy, tan shoulder. Then she would lean in close to them, sometimes even putting her hand on their arm or on their knee as she spoke. Rocky, sitting on the far side of her, tried the hardest to dominate her attention. But, he wasn't having much luck.

"Poor guy, doesn't even know that she's completely out of our league," Simon thought. After only a relatively short period of time, the young college grad had already resigned himself to defeat and self-loathing.

While Rocky went on and on about his boring job, Rich casually strode over to where Simon sat.

"Now she did it," Rich said. "Never let Rocky talk about his job."

"Why?" Simon asked, conceding a smile.

Rich whispered out the side of his mouth to Simon, "Rocky thinks that just because it's what he does all day that it's interesting. She will be lucky to get out of that chair for the next hour. He takes no hints and leaves no breaks or pauses for his victim to make a subtle escape."

"Nice," Simon replied. "Well, at least he's trying. You got to give him credit for that."

"Hey, why don't you go bail her out?" Rich suggested as though he just thought of it.

"What?" Simon snapped. "Nah. She's not into me. Besides, I don't know what I'd even say."

Rocky sat forward with a twinkle in his eye, as he began to recount the everyday happenings of his work, spraying the fields with pesticides and fertilizer. Before long, Jez didn't even bother to look interested. Instead, she stared at her drink, stirred it several times, and took another long sip. Still Rocky did not seem to notice. Or, if he did notice, he did not seem to care. He just kept on talking at her.

Rich took the opportunity to saddle up next to Simon, "So, what do you think of her? She's hot, right?"

The question might as well have been rhetorical. There was no sense in stating the obvious. What else was obvious to Simon was that he had no chance and imparted the fact to Rich.

"What?" Rich said. "You're playin' it perfect, man. She can't stand it when guys don't give her the time of day. Besides, I think she kind of likes you." When he finished the last sentence, Rich stood up, raised his eyebrows, and slung his towel over his shoulder. Then he went back to his perch behind the bar.

"Come on, no way," Simon thought. But oddly enough, Rich might have been on to something. His resignation to anticipated rejection actually came across as confident indifference to Jez, which in turn made him seem like a challenge to her. It wasn't often that she got the opportunity to be the hunter.

As Rocky jabbered on about pork belly prices and heads of cattle, Simon would periodically glance over to Jez only to find her looking back at him.

Could he be imagining it or was it merely an alcohol induced narcissism?

"Now that was not my imagination!" Simon thought. "She definitely looked over at me that time and even raised one eyebrow. Na'. I've got to be imagining it."

Then nothing. A few more minutes and still nothing. It was almost as if she were toying with him. With a furrowed brow, he took another drink.

Meanwhile, Will, Rob, and Rich had already moved on. It didn't take much for them to get their fill of Rocky's incessant clamoring. Instead, they talked about how to hold a circle-change while Simon did his best to feign interest in the conversation. But, he couldn't take his eyes off Jez. Suddenly, she threw Simon a little change-up of her own.

She leaned tightly against the bar, further accentuating her figure. Simon sat up in his seat, took a deep breath, and watched intently out of the corner of his eye. Completely enthralled, he was caught off guard and without reaction when she caught him staring. Before he could play it off, she surrendered a wry grin while making no effort to inhibit his view.

Simon was stunned by the implications of her reaction. His mind raced as the possible inference of their exchange, including what course of action to take, if in fact what just happened was what he thought just happened.

"This could be the most memorable night of my life!" he thought with great anticipation.

5

STEPPING INTO THE NOOSE

From out of nowhere, Jez lashed out at Rocky for not picking up on her obvious signals.

"Rocky, can't you take a hint?" she asked, before finishing off another drink. "I get one night a week off, and I'm not going to waste it sitting here listening to your stupid farm report!"

The other guys were momentarily taken aback before bursting into laughter. Rob nearly fell off of his stool, while Will doubled over. Rocky was clearly hurt by her brutal honesty. He slowly slid off his bar stool and shlepped off to the other side of the bar while the guys unmercifully rubbed it in.

"Oh, come on, Rocky!" Jez said, completely irritated. "Don't be like that!"

"Come on, Rock," Rob exhorted as he took another drag on his cigarette.

"Yeah, forget about it!" Will said now feeling a little bad about the whole thing. "Come back over, have another beer. You're still my best man."

Just then, Rich remembered what he had told Simon. "Hey, Will," he blurted out. "I forgot to tell you. Simon's coming to your bachelor party Friday night."

"Oh, okay," Will replied.

Rich turned back to Simon and said, "You said that the interviews were delayed, right? So, actually you could make the reception too."

Will looked a little caught off guard by Rich's presumptuous request. Simon could feel the tension between them.

"Nah, don't worry about it," Simon said to Will.

"Wouldn't that be awesome, Will?" Rich asked. "Come on."

"Yeah, that's a great idea!" Rob said in agreement.

"Well, yeah, I guess that would be..." Will answered.

"Listen, I don't want to impose..." Simon started to say.

"Cool, it's settled," Rich replied, clapping his meaty hands together.

"I'd have to ask Rachel, she's the one putting together the..." Will began to say, before Rich shot him a look.

"Of course, I'm sure she'd say yes," Rich said, challenging him. "What does she care? He's you're friend. It's your wedding too, right? Or is she going to be making all of your decisions for you from now on?"

Seeing the awkward exchange, Simon made an attempt to bail Will out, "That's cool man, I've really got to be heading to Jersey anyway." When he finished his sentence, he noticed Jez staring at him intently with a pouty expression.

"Nonsense," Rich chided. "You said yourself that you could use the cash."

"I did?" Simon asked, amazed. "When did I...?"

"I can put you up for a couple more days at my place, until my mom gets back from Florida," Rich said. "The East Coast is expensive man. You'd be better off hangin' here with us and saving up some money. Will...?"

"Yeah, Simon, I'd love to have you there, really," Will said, obediently.

Simon was certain that he couldn't impose on Rich or put Will out, until Jez chimed in with a cunning smile. "Yeah, Simon. Hang out with us in Bethel for a while."

That got Simon's attention. There was no escaping that entreaty. As he looked across the bar at her intoxicating smile, that was all the affirmation that he needed.

"Well, I mean, I don't want to get you in trouble with Rachel," Simon said to Will.

"Nah, man" Will answered, with a smattering of profanity. "Sometimes it's better to ask for forgiveness than permission. You can be my personal guest at the wedding."

"Reception," Rich said correcting him.

"Reception, wedding, whatever," Will said just before he took a big swig from his bottle of beer.

Simon looked around at his friends. With an air of appreciation, he tossed one more glance at Jez who waited expectantly for his reaction.

"Well, if Will doesn't care, then, sure, I'd love to go," Simon said.

Will then took it a step further, "If money's an issue, I could even get you a part time job, and you could stay as long as you needed to."

Rob, who had been listening with mild interest to the entire conversation, spoke up. "Ya know, Simon," he began, taking a freshly lit cigarette out of his mouth, "if you needed a place to stay, I've got a friend who owns an apartment that's vacant right now. I could talk to him. I bet he'd be willing to make a deal with you."

"Nah...," Simon said. "I'm just staying until Saturday. Let's not get crazy here. That's it."

"What job could *you* get him?" Rich asked Will with skepticism.

"At the elementary school," Will answered. "It's just a summer gig, cleaning up the school, and getting it ready for next year."

"O' man," Rocky sputtered, coming out of his funk. "Da' schoo'? Oh man, no thank you!"

"Like a janitor or something?" Simon asked Will. "My mom would love that. Get a college degree and go to work for minimum wage as a custodial engineer."

"Actually, it's not minimum wage," Will said. "It's actually pretty good money. I had a cousin do it a couple of summers ago. At that time, it was payin' about ten dollars per hour, I think. Anyway, he said it was cush. Nobody watched over him. He'd get there when he wanted, work when he wanted, leave when he wanted. Take naps. Whatever. He said it was the easiest money he ever made."

"I don't care!" Rocky said emphatically. "You couldn't pay me enough to work there."

"What?" Rich asked in disbelief. "Why not? I barely make more than ten bucks an hour here, and I gotta sit here and serve a bunch of bums like you losers."

"'Cause that place is haunted, bro!" Rocky adamantly replied.

Rich and Simon laughed out loud, but Rocky was dead serious.

"Oh, come on!" Rich whaled with a broad smile.

"Yeah, right," Simon echoed.

"No," Rob said with a very serious expression. "I believe it."

"Me, too," Will said, nodding in agreement. "Freaky."

"You guys are a bunch wusses," Rich said with an incredulous look. "I'm embarrassed for you. What do you think, Jez?"

She cussed and said, "That place has always creeped *me* out."

"Strait!" Rocky exclaimed, as he swallowed his pride and rejoined the group.

"Actually, I thought it was condemned when I pulled into town yesterday," Simon said.

"That was because Ralph Livingood kicked a rubber ball forty yards and broke a second story window," Rich said as though he was impressed. "Kid's a stud. The school *should* be condemned, not because it's full of ghosts, because it's filled with asbestos. And if it weren't for some of these greedy farmers around here, we could build a new one."

"Woe, woe, woe!" Rocky protested.

"All of a sudden, you've got an interest in public education?" Will asked Rich sarcastically.

"Not exactly, but if they built a new school, I bet Helrigle and Livingood could get them to tack on a pretty sweet ballpark. We need more practice fields."

"I thought as much," Will said smugly. "It all goes back to baseball."

"The place is old, and I definitely did not care for going down to that freaky basement when I was a kid," Simon said. "Not to mention, Principal Harold used to scare the daylights out of me." Remembering himself, he glanced around the corner to make sure she wasn't hiding behind the poker machine again. "But haunted? That's funny. What makes you think that it's actually haunted?"

Will, Rocky, and Rob all started in at the same time.

"Oh, man. There was this one time..."

"'Caus'. We wuz…"

"You should have been there…it was crazy."

Simon smiled at Rich in disbelief at their friends' ridiculous reactions, but Rich appeared to be less than amused.

"Shut up, I'm tellin' it," Rob said above the din, putting his arms out straight to his sides and gesturing for the others to be quiet. "When we were in fourth grade, we climbed up the fire escape…"

"You mean the one that's like an enclosed metal slide going up to the chorus room?" Simon asked interrupting.

"Yeah, that one," Rob continued. "It was me and Will. We climbed up to eat our candy bars and drink our sodas that we had gotten at the grocery store…"

"We used to do that," Simon said.

"…And we heard some footsteps, so we peered through a tiny crack in the door," Rob said gravely. After pausing for effect he said, "And there was *no one* there."

Jez objected with a vulgar slur as an expression of shock swept over her beautiful face.

"Shut up!" Rich said. "That's so stupid. You guys are morons."

"Man, I was there," Will said. "All I'm sayin' is we heard the steps and no one was there."

"That's it?" Simon asked laughing.

"Nah. Dat ain't it," Rocky sputtered, completely engrossed in the topic. "Tell'm G'. Tell'm 'bout Band Night. Forgetting himself, he added, "You are not going to believe this. Listen. Listen."

"What happened?" Jez asked enthralled. She too was getting drawn in to the story.

"Oh no, *this* again?" Rich said. He was beginning to let his aggravation and impatience show.

Simon chuckled at his old friend. He was thoroughly enjoying watching the three guys telling their stories. They were completely into it. However, Rich was obviously disgusted with the whole thing, and Jez… Jez was just enjoyable to look at.

"I'm telling you, it happened," Rob said. "It was Band Night. And me, Will, and Rocky…"

"We were like in 5th grade," Rocky added.

"Can I continue, what in the world?" Rob said to Rocky with a look of disgust.

"Yeah, yeah, go ahead," Rocky said, flipping his hand at Rob to proceed with the story. Then he leaned in closer with his eyes wide open.

"Like I was saying," Rob continued. "We were in 5th grade, and we were at band night."

"You know band night, where they tell the parents how great it is for their kids to be in band, and then they try to get them to sign up and buy an instrument," Will said.

"Yeah, so we snuck out of the gym where they were talking to the parents, and we went down to Ms. Lotman's old room. We were just messing around. And the chairs were all up on the desks, you know, for the janitor to sweep. And in the far corner of the room one of the chairs fell down and scared the daylights out of us. I'm telling you, none of us were around that chair. But we didn't really think much about it until we put the chair up, and then another one falls at the other end of the room. That freaked us out a little, but when we put that one up, another one fell..."

"Man, I've never ran so fast in my life!" Rocky said, forgetting his newly acquired dialect.

"Oh, what are you talkin' about?" Will asked. "I climbed over both of you getting out of that room."

"Come on," Rich said. "I'm sure you guys were running around the room and knocking them loose or something."

"Ya know Ms. Lotman died in that room, didn't you?" Rocky asked.

"So! It doesn't mean she haunts the room," Rich said, laughing. "Right, Simon?"

But Simon was caught a little off guard. While Rob was telling the story, Simon suddenly remembered an incident that happened years ago while he was in Ms. Lotman's room. After he had gotten in trouble for not doing his homework, he had to miss recess and serve a detention by himself.

In an instant, his blood ran cold when he suddenly remembered the hand that he thought he saw pulling the cellar door shut just last night. He almost mentioned it but thought better of it.

"What? Oh, yeah, that's pretty weird all right," Simon answered with a slightly forced chuckle.

He wasn't about to say anything in front of Rich. The rationale, sober part of him knew that it was all just a bunch of harmless stories. Still, he wasn't exactly flippant about it either.

"You know, I had a terrible dream the day after Ms. Lotman died," Jez started to say. "In the dream, I was walking down the hallway towards Ms. Lotman room. It was dark, and the red Exit sign was the only thing glowing in the hall. And I was frightened. And as I got closer to the room, Ms. Lotman stuck her head out around her door. At first, she was so peaceful looking. She was so nice, you know. It kinda relaxed me. Then her face turned dark and sinister, and she smiled this wicked smile. Then from behind the door she flashed a long knife at me."

By this time, Will, Rob, and Rocky were quiet and sullen. Even Rich, because he could see the fear in Jez's eyes as she relived the dream, became somber.

"Then what?" Rocky anxiously asked.

"Then I woke up crying, calling for my grandma," she said. "It was terrible. It was something in her face, you know? I'll never forget that dream as long as I live."

"That's pretty creepy," Will said. "But you know that Ms. Lotman is not who's haunting the school."

"No?" Simon asked. "Then who? Wait a minute. I do remember something about all this. There was some crazy story about a teacher who supposedly killed all of his students, right? We used to play some game on the playground...what was it?"

"Don't tell me you've forgotten about the legend of Jessie Joseph and Adam Potter," Rich said with a sarcastic tone as he rolled his eyes. "Yep, that old wive's tale."

"I never actually thought any of that was true," Simon said. "At least, I always told myself that it wasn't true. I just thought that it was some dumb story that the older kids told the younger ones to freak them out."

"No, it's all true," Rocky answered, nodding his head in dramatic affirmation.

"How'd the story go again?" Simon asked. "Something about drowning them during a field trip or something?"

"Yeah, that's it, kinda," Rob said. "This is how it *really* happened."

"This is where it gets good," Will said to no one in particular.

"Are you crying, Rocky?" Rich asked. "Don't tell me you're actually crying!"

"Nah, my eyes always water when I hear scary stuff," Rocky answered plainly.

"Then why are you cryin' now?" Rich asked sardonically as he dumped out Rob's ash tray.

"Go on with what you were saying, Rob," Jez said as she smacked Rich's arm.

"Well, it goes back seventy-two years now," Rob began. Without realizing it, everyone except Rich leaned in a little closer. They were so quiet that the ceiling fans could be heard swirling above them. "There was this teacher at Bethel Grade School named Jessie Joseph. This was back when there were maybe 400 people total living in Bethel. It was a real tight knit community. Everybody knew everybody. Well, in those days, the classes were so small that each teacher taught two grades in the same classroom. Jessie happened to teach the youngest kids."

"So, first and second grade were in the same room," Will added.

"Right," Rob went on. "See, people didn't realize it but ole' Jessie was some kind of real sicko. Every day he would take the students up to the chorus room next to the stage in the gym, where no one could see them, and he would have the students do the most heinous stuff you can think of."

"Like what, to who?" Jez asked with a disgusted look.

"Like the worst kind of stuff you can think of," Rob answered.

"*What* kinda stuff?" Jez asked again.

"My grandma wouldn't say...," Rob replied. "...She used to say that what he did to them was 'unspeakable.' But anyway, so he's doing this for like months and months until the kids start acting funny at home. Then the parents start asking questions. One of them takes their kid to the doctor to ask about bruises, and the next thing you know the whole town is in an uproar."

"How old was this 'Jessie' guy at the time?" Simon asked.

"Probably like 21 or 22 years-old," Rob said. "So anyhow, Jessie gets wind of it and decides that he can't let the kids tell everybody what he's been doing to them.

By now, it's like spring, and he gets the idea to take the kids on a little 'impromptu' picnic trip. But what he really intends to do is, because it's spring, right, and the creeks and rivers were all flooded, he's going to drown the kids and say that it was a bad accident and set it up to look like that. Only, he can't just drive the bus off a bridge into the creek, right?"

"Which creek?" Jez asked.

"The Embarras River," Rob said. "The one just outside of town here."

"Out by Potter's farm?" she asked again. "The one by the old rundown farmhouse up on the hill?"

"Stop interrupting this fascinating story," Rich said sarcastically to her.

"I just wanted to know where," she said sheepishly.

"Why didn't he just drive the bus into the creek with the kids in it, and be done with it?" Simon asked suspiciously.

"Well, he could I guess, but he was probably afraid that some of them might make it out, and he couldn't take that risk. I guess he decided that he did not want to take any chances. So, he sets up the kids on a little scavenger hunt or something, and he starts picking them off, one by one, taking them over to a secluded spot and drowning them in the river. And he's just laying them all out in a row on the bank, so that he can put them back into the bus and then drive it off a bridge or something into the water."

"No way!"

"How horrible."

"I know," Rob agreed. "After a while, everything is going according to plan. He is down to the last two kids. He's got one of them, holding him under water. And he looks up and somehow one of the boys had crossed the creek and was watching him from the opposite shore. When the boy realizes what is happening, he takes off running. Jessie knows that he's probably in big trouble, cause how's he gonna catch up with this kid? He decides to get rid of the eleven bodies that he already has on the bank lying in the tall weeds before going after the boy who got away. So, he tosses them into the raging creek and drives the bus off the bridge into the water."

"Why did he do that?" Simon asked quizzically. "That doesn't make any sense. Surely, he'd go after the boy that got away."

"Nobody knows why," Rob said.

"Maybe, he had to get rid of the evidence though, first," Will proposed. "I mean, the kid was on the other bank, by the time Jessie got around to the other side who knows which direction the kid might have taken, not to mention who might stumble upon them out there. They weren't far from Potter's farmhouse. Besides, the guy's a psycho right?"

"I bet he figured he'd just stick with the plan and make up some story about the kid who got away," Rob said. "Then it would be his word, a trusted, law-abiding citizen, versus that of a 6 or 7-year-old kid. Who knows? Anyway. He couldn't find the kid, so he went back to town with soaking wet clothes, tellin' his story and hoping that he could get to Adam Potter before anybody else did. He looked and looked for this kid. They even made a coffin for his body, thinkin' they'd eventually find his body in the creek with the rest of them. After the funerals were over, three days or so later, they find Little Adam Potter hiding in the bottom of the well of his dad's farm, crying. Once he told them what had happened, old Jessie was done for."

"So, what happened to Jessie Joseph?" Jez asked.

"Oh, this is the scary part, this is cool," Rocky said, rubbing his hands on his thighs in anticipation.

"He was hanged in the public square…without any trial or *anything*," Rob said. "The only public execution ever in Bethel. But before they dropped Jessie from the scaffold he cursed the town, swearing that he would get his revenge from the grave."

"Sounds like a Scooby-Doo episode," Rich said mockingly.

"Yeah, except that's actually how it happened," Will said.

"Oh, come on, it's just a bunch of coincidences," Rich argued.

When Rich said coincidence, Simon shot an inquisitive glance over to him.

"What's coincidences? Like what?" Jez asked.

"I can't believe you don't know this," Rob said, annoyed.

"Well, I only lived here a year with my grandma," she answered, defensively.

"Oh yeah," he said. "Well, from the time Jessie cursed the town till this day, a series of tragedies have occurred in Bethel. Ever since the day he died, some teenager or some kid has been killed every six years for the past seventy-two years. It's like a pattern or something. And *this* is the sixth year since the last one."

"You mean died," Rich said. "They died. People die, like in accidents and what not."

"Six years ago there was a suicide," Rocky said, ignoring Rich. "Dude jumped off of the grain elevator. And that same year a kid named Michael Newdow died in a car crash. The skid marks show that he swerved to miss hitting something, but they never found out what. Probably Jessie, huh? Six years prior to that …"

"And there was that guy back in the eighties, what was his name? Timmy or Jimmy," Will added. "Remember him. They found his remains on the side of the road. He died execution style. You're telling me that was an accident?"

"Jimmy Barnes," Rich said, dryly. "That was a drug deal gone bad. Everybody knows that. That one doesn't count. It wasn't some ghost of Jessie Joseph. He ticked off a drug dealer. Besides, he wasn't even from Bethel."

"So, you have thought about it!" Will said with a big smile on his face.

"What? Now why would I waste my time sitting around thinking about something so stupid," Rich answered as he picked up a Fantasy Baseball magazine.

"Well, what about the 6-year-old who suffocated and died in the closet of the first grade classroom?" Rocky challenged.

"What, there's no oxygen in a *closet?*…" Rich snapped back while rolling his eyes and shaking his head.

"So, you don't believe any of it?" Jez asked.

"Yeah, right," Rich said while flipping through the pages of the magazine. "Tragedies happen in every town. Like every six years Jessie Joseph returns from the grave to exact his revenge on Bethel until when. What is it?..."

"Until someone comes to end the curse..."

"...the curse, yeah right," Rich said along with Rob at the end in an effort to make fun of him.

"Who's the 'Someone'?" Jez asked.

Suddenly, out of nowhere, a strange feeling swept over Simon as though a freshly unearthed time capsule that revealed a distant memory of what some crazy old lady once said to him in church when he was a kid. He couldn't remember exactly what she had said or why he hadn't remembered it until now.

"Wow, that was pretty random," Simon muttered under his breath.

"See, that's what I'm sayin'?" Rich said, bringing Simon back to reality. "Thank you. Ridiculous."

"Well, ole' Jessie ain't the only one roaming around the school," Rob answered. "Adam's ghost is there too. People have seen him. They say *he's* going to choose the one who will end the curse."

"So, there are *two* ghosts?" Simon asked, tracking again with the ole wive's tale. By the time they had finished with the story, he was less than convinced of its validity. But, just for fun, he thought he'd goad the boys into pushing the issue. He always got a kick out of watching Rich blow a gasket. So, Simon took it a step farther, "How do you *know* Adam's there too?"

"There's two reasons," Rocky said getting off of his chair and walking around closer to Simon. "First, because my sister and her class saw him in the school."

"What?" Come on," Will said. "Even I can't believe that."

"Yeah, it's true," Rocky said. "She swore that when she was in fourth grade that the ghost of Adam came up from the stairs to the basement and into their classroom."

"Then what?" Rich asked, raising one eyebrow. He was mildly interested only because he had never heard this part of the story before.

"Then the whole class fell asleep," Rocky said.

"Then what?" Jez asked, totally engrossed in the story.

"What?" Rocky asked, acting like he was caught off guard by the question. "Oh, I don't know. I guess they just sorta woke up, like later." Then he took another drink of his beer.

After an expectant pause, the whole group suddenly burst out into laughter.

"What?" Rocky asked.

"That's so stupid!," Rich scoffed.

"Well, other people have claimed to have seen him too," Rocky said, once again a little hurt.

"Yeah, out at Potter's farm," Rob answered. "That's why the Satanic worshipers go out there and spray paint graffiti all over the house and barn. He's *not* the sandman at nappy-nap time for the fourth graders."

"Well, anyway he's haunting the school too," Rocky said.

"Oh brother!" Rich said. "Can we please talk about something else?" He grabbed the remote, pointed it at the flat screen TV on the wall, turned up the volume, and flipped through the channels.

"So, what's the other reason," Simon coyly asked Rocky. He saw that he had Rich on the brink of blowing up. It was so easy. He remembered that Rich could not stand for people to speculate about anything. He always loved raw data. Cold, hard facts. Things like RBI's, ERA's, and HR's.

"What?" Rocky asked.

"You said you had two reasons why you believed the legend was true," Simon said in a matter-of-fact tone of voice.

"Oh, the other reason is that I've seen the graveyard myself where they buried all them kids," Rocky said. "Adam's gravestone is there and Jessie Joseph's and eleven more. I know where it is. It's way in the back of a field, past the abandoned house. It's really spooky!"

"Oh, let's go out there now!" Jez said excitedly while clapping her hands. She took a swig of her drink and set it down. "Wouldn't that be fun? Let's go! I want to see it. Then we'll know if it's true."

Will, Rob, and Rocky looked at her with a blank stare.

"It might be kinda hard to find in the dark," Rocky said hesitantly.

"Why is it that they buried the kids out there in their own graveyard and not at the cemetery here in town?" Simon asked.

Rich suddenly turned from the TV. "Because they were all idiots like these guys here," he said pointing at Rob, Will, and Rocky. "And why would they bury Jessie Joseph, the murderer, in the same graveyard with…never mind. Stupid."

"Because, man, the town was horrified that all of this happened right under their noses," Rob said. "Some even thought that Adam was lying and Jessie was telling the truth, after the hanging. It became this big thing that loomed over the town. So, they decided to conceal it, put it out of their sight, and never talk about it again. At least, that's what Grandma used to say."

"Let's go," Jez said slapping her beautiful, tan knees with both hands. The sudden movement sort of marvelously jiggled her. "Simon, come on. You want to go, right?" As she slid off the stool, her blouse lifted revealing a tattoo on her lower back.

"I'm going, if you're going," Simon replied.

"Yeah!" Will said pushing away his empty beer mug. "Ah, man, how freaky. Let's do it."

"I'm in," Rob said. "I always wanted to see it."

"You goin', Rich?" Simon asked as he got off of his bar stool.

Rich had his arms folded while still clutching the remote control. Looking out of the corner of his eye with an air of disdain, "No, you kids go. Have fun."

As the four guys stumbled towards the front door, Rob said to Jez," You've gotta drive."

"Me? Why me?" she asked. "There's not enough room in my car."

"You've been drinking the least," Rob told her. "Thelma is probably working in her trophy shop. We had a little fun with her last night. If she sees any of our cars pullin' out, she's gonna throw the blue light on top of her car come after us. Don't worry, we'll take Rocky's dad's truck. Three of us can sit in the cab and two guys can ride in the back."

"Yeah sure, what do I care?" Rocky said with a shrug.

"All right," she said. "But who's riding in the back?"

"I don't mind," Simon said as he climbed into the bed of the Chevy.

It was a brilliant move on his part. Even though it wasn't premeditated, the indifference only seemed to fuel Jez's interest in him all the more. The chase was on.

* * *

Before long, they were winding their way down the dirt road that used to be the driveway to the old Potter place. No one had lived there for years, so the path was overgrown and rugged. Rocky and Simon bounced around in the back of the truck.

"Hey, take it easy up there, would ya?" Simon called out jokingly.

"Sorry!" Jez yelled back out the window. Simon looked longingly at the silhouette of her face in the green glow of the dashboard from the reflection in the side mirror.

The truck crunched along on the rocks and gravel as it made its way between the tall rows of corn. Simon could barely see them in the glow of the taillights, as they flapped in their wake. Finally, they came to a fork in the road. Simon poked his head up over the top of the cab as the truck came to a stop. To the right, at the top of the hill, he could see the old farmhouse, a dilapidated barn, and the remnants of a shed that had collapsed some time ago. Above the barn, on the other side of the house, there was a short path that led up to a windmill that was in bad disrepair. Beneath it, sat a flat concrete floor that looked like it may have been the foundation of another shed or small building or something.

"That's the old Potter place," Rocky yelled over the hum of the diesel motor. He seemed quite pleased with himself, like the host of a tour bus.

"Up there?" Jez yelled back to Rocky.

"No, no," Rob said rather pointedly. "To the left, to the left. Keep going!"

"I thought you'd never been here," Will said.

"Well, I've been to the Potter's place and that's all that's up there," Rob answered. He caught himself and made an effort to quickly regain his composure. But no one thought anything of it.

"No! Keep going," Rocky implored. "It's down by the creek."

They continued down the path for a few more miles. As they went, the path became even more overgrown and difficult to follow. Finally, they came to the end of the corn fields. On one side of the path there was an unkept pasture of wild weeds and bushes, while a tattered, old, barbed wire fence, and a row of trees lined the other side. It had been warm during the day, but now, around the stroke of midnight, the air began to cool. As a result, an eerie fog hovered over the pasture in the periphery of the headlights. The rugged trail tossed Simon and Rocky around like two sacks of potatoes. Due to their partially inebriated state, there were several times when they had to put their hands down to steady themselves. The field came to an end and nothing but trees lined both sides of the road towering high above them. The canvass blocked the stars that had helped to illuminate the night sky, and it became unsettlingly dark.

"A little farther!" Rocky yelled out to Jez. Then he turned to Simon, "This is awesome." As he spoke a puff of smoke escaped his mouth like tiny ghosts. "We gotta be getting near the creek, know what I'm sayin'?"

Suddenly, a terrible screech of metal cried out from the sides of the truck. The path had become so narrow that the limbs of the trees and bushes were scratching and scraping its sides. Jez slammed on the brakes while letting out a cacophony of profanity. Simon and Rocky were thrown into the back of the cab with a resounding thump.

"Sorry," she called back. "I am not scratching up your dad's truck! This is as far as I'm driving." Then she killed the motor.

"Come on," Rob said. "What are you doing?"

"No, that's okay, we can walk from here," Will said with a solemn tone.

The sudden silence held them captive for a moment, as the subtle sounds of the woods became audible. They let out a collective breath. Rob pulled out a flask, took a healthy swig, and held it out as a gesture to Will who gladly accepted. He took his own tug as he slid out of the cab. Rocky and Simon jumped out of the back while Jez forced open her door ever so slightly and wiggled her way out.

"So, which direction, Rocky?" Rob asked in a whisper.

"I don't know," Rocky said. He had evidently sobered a little from the ride in the back of the truck. "Look diff'rent ad night."

"Oh great," Rob said. "You don't know where we're going, perfect."

"Shhh, relax," Will said very deliberately. "We're close. Look. The fog gets more dense near the creek. We just need to split up a little and cover as much ground as we can. One of us is bound to run into it. Besides, it'll be freakier anyway."

"Are you crazy?" Rocky asked, breathing deeply into both of his hands for warmth.

Everyone looked at him for a brief moment.

"What?" Rocky asked.

"Stop being such a wuss," Will said. "I'll go this way. Rob can go that way. Spread out. Come on. Let's go."

Rocky and Rob started walking towards the thick foliage laden with fog.

"Dis is so scary!" Rocky said under his breath.

"Yeah, it's awesome," Rob said calling back over his shoulder. "Look out for cobwebs Jez."

"Nice," Jez said. "Thanks a lot."

She stood for a moment next to Simon shivering slightly with her shoulders pulled up towards her ears and clutching the truck keys in both hands. Simon had his hands in his pockets with his arms locked while also trying to stay warm. He looked at Jez and smiled.

"Cold?" he asked her.

She glanced over to see if the others were out of sight yet. Then she reached out, grabbed Simon's arm, and pulled him into the darkness.

"Whoa, where are we…?" Simon started to ask, hoping he knew the answer.

"Shhh!" Jez whispered as she held her index finger up to her pursed lips.

Simon could barely see the corners of her mouth raise up into a smile. After walking a few steps into the woods, she suddenly stopped and looked around in every direction. There was no way for them to know it, but she was taking him on the path that led straight down to the graves.

"Where are you going?" Simon asked. But he thought he already knew the answer. At least something in side of him hoped that he knew the answer anyway.

She contorted her face and wrinkled her nose as she looked around.

"Jez…, where are you?" Rob called out from somewhere in distance. "Wooo…" Then he laughed hysterically.

"Shut up, man!" Rocky called out from another direction. "You're freak'n me out!"

"You guys see anything?" Will called out to the others.

Their voices echoed off of the trees from somewhere out of the darkness.

"I've got an idea," Jez whispered with a wicked grin. She reached out and grabbed Simon's hand with both of hers, "Let's leave 'em."

"What?" Simon asked. He heard the words come out of his mouth, but he didn't know if he had been the one to say them. With the alcohol still coursing through his veins, everything slowed down like a narrow band of streaming video. His dulled faculties were going haywire. He wasn't tracking completely with the conversation because Jez's soft, cold hands cupping his own were far too distracting.

"Wouldn't that be great?" Jez asked. She pulled his face in close to hers in anticipation. They were so close now that the little ghosts bounced off each other's lips. She felt the callouses from his mysterious blisters on his hands, she asked, "What did you do to your hand?"

"What? Oh, I don't know," he answered, looking down for a brief second, before redirecting his attention to the proposal at hand. "You mean, just leave 'em out here?" Simon asked. Their eyes danced all over each other's faces, down to the lips, and then back again into each other's eyes. Again, he heard words coming out of his mouth, "They'd be so ticked. I-I couldn't do that to them."

Just then, Jez's dancing eyes stopped, she furrowed her brow, and moved in a little closer, gazing at his face.

"What's that on your cheek?" she asked as she reached out with her thumb to gently rub the spot. "Is it a bruise? I was meaning to ask you back in the tavern."

Suddenly, Simon remembered the Sharpie and the boys' artwork from the night before. His eyes narrowed to the middle and looked down as if he were trying to see the stain on his face.

"Okay, let's go," Simon whispered.

In an instant, they were back in the warm cab of the truck. Jez cranked up the engine and dangerously backed down the worn path at an alarming rate of speed. Simon wasn't quite sure if he could hear the yelling of his buddies down by the creek over the roar of the diesel engine. Even if not, he could certainly imagine it. The limbs of the tress once again raked the sides of he truck like tormented souls before it rumbled backwards into the open field. Jez cut the wheel, brought the tail end around, and jammed it into drive. Simon clutched the dash, while turning his head to see out the back window of the cab. He could hear himself yelling out of excitement, "Go! Go! Go!…"

Jez could barely see the road through her tears of laughter. She let out a shrieking cackle and then a snort as they bounced down the narrow driveway and jettisoned out onto the pavement. Simon thought that she must have been feeling the effects of the gin and tonic more than he had previously anticipated. She spun the wheel hard. The truck dipped to Simon's side and then righted itself again as they sped down the country road.

"Did you just snort, it was a snort wasn't it?" Simon said, laughing.

"No, no it wasn't," she answered while holding one hand to her mouth.

"Yes, yes you did, I heard it…" Simon went on.

They had only driven a short distance before Jez slowed down and pulled off the road onto a small clearing carved out of a cornfield.

"Where are you going?" Simon asked. Again he turned to look back behind them through the window of the cab. "Are we going back now?"

But Jez only grinned as she slowly pulled the truck around to the back of two corn silos that stood on the side of the ditch near the road. Bringing the truck to a stop, she cut off the lights. Seductively, she turned to face him in the soft greenish glow of the dash.

Meatloaf's classic hit single drifted through his mind as his eyes wandered down her cheek to the silky smooth curve of her neck. Suddenly, his eyes responsively darted downward as the tops of her shimmering thighs widened ever so slightly just below the hemline of her miniskirt when she moved gracefully toward him. Simon swallowed hard in anticipation. He was by all accounts a handsome enough guy, but nothing like this ever happened to him before. This was so wonderfully unexpected, and Jez was so beautiful. As she slowly drew near, she succulently licked her thumb and brought it up to his cheek.

"You never finished telling me about this," she said in a deep, sexy voice, "I can get it off for you."

In a matter of minutes, the windows of the truck were fogged up, and muffled sighs could be heard by a dark figure that stepped out of the cornfield behind the truck. The man wrapped the end of a long leash around his wrist, as he brought a lighter up to the cigarette that was dangling from his teeth. A Doberman stood poised with his ears straight up in the air and his eyes transfixed on the vehicle in front of him. Puffs of tiny smoke emanated out of the nostrils of the ferocious beast as he waited obediently for a command. In the orange glow of the cigarette, a smile crept over the man's face. He straightened again, twisted the leash around into the palm of his hand, turned, and disappeared into the abyss of cornfield.

6

WHAT MAKES THEM STUMBLE

Miss Passimons took a deep breath and then let out a sigh. She was doing her best to maintain composure and failing miserably. Standing at the chalkboard in the front of the classroom, she held a piece of chalk between her forefinger and thumb. With her back half turned to the class, she glanced over her shoulder with the coldest glare that she could muster. Over her twenty-six years of teaching 1st grade, she thought that she had seen it all. But, this new generation was the most disrespectful group she ever had the displeasure of trying to teach. And she thought their parents were bad when she taught them twenty years ago.

The boys and girls carried on just as before, unfazed by her theatrics. They yelled, giggled, argued, and frolicked about the room showing no signs of being intimidated by her empty threat. She looked over at her calendar that counted down the days to her retirement next May. Then she closed her eyes tightly and rubbed her temples.

"Don't make me write someone's name on the board during these last three days of school," she said, before pausing for effect. But, she was barely heard above the noise. Her eyes scanned purposefully around the room looking for any leverage at her disposal.. "I would hate to do that, but I *will* write your name on the board if I..."

The last words of her sentence were drowned out by a piercing yell from somewhere in the back of the room.

"Simon Adamson!" Miss Passimons shouted. "Keep your hands to yourself!"

"But, she started it!" the little boy protested, pointing a finger at the girl sitting next to him.

"I don't care *who* started it!" she replied on the verge of completely losing it.

Her crackling voice initially blunted the racket, but it was quickly swallowed up by a wave of laughter and mimicry. Miss Passimons turned back to the class after realizing that her tact was not having the desired affect. She robotically folded her arms and turned down her mouth quite forcefully. Half the class was out of their seats while some were wandering aimlessly about the room. She could feel her heartbeat pulsate in her temple as she thrust her arm into the air and held out her index finger. Still no reaction. Next came the middle finger, in "bunny ears" fashion. Her mouth twisted downward and her eyes volleyed back and forth from one side of the room to the other, revealing a hint of uncertainty. She couldn't send them all to the principal's office. Miss Harold threw a fit the last time she tried that one.

"The inmates are running the asylum," she thought hopelessly. Her eyes stopped suddenly on the closet door on the other side of the chalkboard. A grin curled up on one side of her mouth after the "aha" moment.

Miss Passimons raised her chin, narrowed her eyes, and waltzed over to the cart that was holding the TV and DVD player. She calmly unplugged the power cord from the outlet, folded it up nicely, and then proceeded to push the cart towards the closet. Just as she suspected, her actions went largely unnoticed until the cart stopped just beneath the American flag hanging at the front of the room. The bottom half of the red and white stripes draped over the top of the TV. Furtively, she slid around, walked over to the closet door, and opened it in dramatic fashion. Finally, a slight hush fell over the room as several of the more perceptive students realized what she was doing.

"No, Miss Passimons…" a few of them pleaded.

"Please don't…we'll be quiet. We swear."

Some of the more behaved students jumped back in their seats and shushed those still clamoring about the room.

"We'll be good. We'll be good. I promise. I promise," one of the sweeter girls in the front begged.

Miss Passimons did not respond even though she was ecstatic to see her ploy begin to have some effect. Instead of answering out loud, she again held out three fingers and pulled them down one by one, pausing again for effect. The sound of tiny sneakers squeaking back to their seats filled the room followed by the screeching metal chairs that scraped over the dusty wooden floor. Only one student remained standing defiantly at the back of the room.

Not daring to wait for complete compliance, Miss Passimons spoke her instructions in deliberate monotone.

"Sit down, Simon, or we won't get to watch the movie," one of the little girls whispered.

"The party for completing eighty percent of your homework assignments…" Miss Passimons started to say.

"What movie?" Simon asked in a whiny voice, so that the entire class could hear him.

"We will start the movie momentarily for those who have completed most of their homework this year. The rest of you will go to the tables at the back of the room and work on the assignments that are listed on the board," Miss Passimons said.

"What movie?" Simon asked, once again interrupting her.

"'Horton Hear's a Who'," she responded under her breath before turning back to the rest of the class. "When you are finished with your make up work…"

"That's a stupid movie!" Simon protested, folding his arms and scowling with disdain.

The comment drew a few chuckles from some of the other students. In a battle of wills, the teacher shot a look around the room to stomp out anyone who might be encouraging the defiant boy's behavior. Choosing to ignore his comment, she began again with the instructions. This time her voice was muffled by the metallic crunch of a stapler.

"*Simon!* What are you doing with my stapler?" she yelled in exasperation. "Put that back on my desk."

"*No!*" the rebellious child shouted.

"Put it back on my…" Miss Passimons demanded.

Simon smacked his hand with all of his force against the back of the stapler, sending yet another staple into the formica reading table.

"When are we going to start the movie?" Simon whined.

"You're *not* watching a movie," she answered. "You will be working on a long list of assignments at the back table." Then Miss Passimons decided to apply some peer pressure to bring little Simon under control.

"We will start the movie as soon as everyone has gone back to there seats," she threatened in an indifferent tone. The strategy only worked in part. On cue, the other students unmercifully blasted their classmate for his solitary rebellion. Much to Miss Passimons's dismay the attack only brazened the young boy's defiance, and a barrage of name calling ensued. Her plan had backfired.

"Well, you're stupider!" Simon yelled back at several students.

"Class. Class….*class!*" Miss Passimons shouted, feeling it begin to spiral out of control.

Simon wildly shoved a little girl out of her chair onto the floor. She burst into tears while Simon stuck his tongue out at her.

"That's it!" she yelled. "*Get over her this instant!*" When she made a move towards him, he rushed around to the other side of the desks.

Miss Passimons moved to the back of the room quickly for being in her mid-sixties and grabbed the little ruffian's arm. His face became red with rage as he took several swipes at the teacher. Miss Passimons squeezed harder, trying to control the unruly little boy.

"*Ouch!*" he yelled. "You're hurting my arm!"

"No, I'm not!" she objected, letting go of his arm.

"I'm gonna tell my mom," he threatened. "She'll sue you!" He let his legs turn into jelly and collapsed to the floor.

"*Get up now!*" she virtually screamed. When she realized that the other kids were all watching she tried to remember if she was paid up on her latest union dues. "Get up and go into the hallway," she said through gritted teeth.

Simon conjured up more tears and folded up his arms in defiance. Finally, he made his way towards the hallway with his head down.

Miss Passimons walked behind him pointing the way towards the door. After she made her way into the hall, she could hear her class.

"Uuummm," they chided in unison, and then they burst out laughing. As she closed the door behind her, she could hear chaos once again ensue. She was incensed and began to rain down her wrath on the unruly boy.

Her words echoed off of the old hardwood floors of the landing that connected the 1st and 2nd grade classrooms. Defiantly, Simon began walking towards the stairs leading down to the basement.

"*Simon!*" the irate teacher shouted. "You stop right there mister. You are in *big* trouble."

She bustled her way down the steps, crouched down to his level, and stuck a finger in his face.

"If you even say that I touched you…," Miss Passimons warned. "I never laid a hand on you!"

"Yes, you did!" he shouted back before turning his face towards the wall.

"Oh no, I didn't," she said once again between gritted teeth. "If I had touched you, you would have known it. You look at me when I'm talking to you!"

Just then, the door to the second grade classroom opened and a pretty, young teacher holding a large textbook in one hand stuck her head out the door.

"Miss Passimons?" Hope Wisemen asked with an expression of deep concern. "Is something the matter?"

Miss Passimons pulled the finger out of Simon's face, stood up, and tried to regain her composure. She panted heavily between words with her fist clenched and her face turning a deep red. Hope propped open the front door to her classroom with her foot, gave some instructions to her class, and then walked down to where Miss Passimons stood with the little boy. Listening intently to the more senior teacher's list of grievances, Hope guided Miss Passimons back to her classroom. She put her arm around the fuming teacher compassionately and whispered something to her under her breath. Simon thought he could hear her say something about only one more day.

"Oh no it's not, if he doesn't pass!" Miss Passimons objected. "He needs to get all of his make up work done! He *is* passing first grade, one way or the other. I will not live through another year with that monster!"

"Miss Passimons, he'll hear you," Hope said in consternation. "Why don't you give me the work that he needs to complete, and he can spend the rest of the day in my room."

"That's an excellent idea!" she replied. "It'll be a chance for you to get to know him. He's going to be your problem next year." She started to open the door back up to her classroom and then turned to say one more thing to the naïve, first year teacher. "Remember, we have that meeting tomorrow after school."

"Yes, thank you, I remember," Hope answered, praying that she would never get that jaded.

Miss Passimons shot one more angry look at Simon before returning to her room. After the door closed behind her, Hope looked in the direction of the problematic little boy. She walked down to where he stood on the steps. Simon turned away from her, leaned into the wall, and pressed his head against it. He furrowed his brow and tightened his lip, refusing to look at her. She began to speak to him in a calm voice.

"Simon," she said softly. "Won't you turn and look at me?"

He said nothing but took his finger and traced the outline of a rectangle on the wall where the paint had not faded as much as the rest of the wall. While she considered what she could do for the neglected child, Hope's eyes lifted to the corner of the rectangle for a moment. Then she knelt down next to him with the book in her lap.

"Would you like to come into my room and work on your assignments?" she asked tenderly.

He shook his head.

"Maybe we could work on it together," she offered.

"Leave me alone, you're stupid," he said without making eye contact.

At that moment, some fourth grade boys came around the corner of the stairwell and bounded down the first few steps.

"You looked like an idiot," the red headed boy said to a chubby boy with glasses, "when Ralph struck you out last night. You didn't even swing."

"It was inside, that's why, I didn't want it to hit me," the pudgy boy with glasses protested.

"Shut up, Porker, you're such a big baby," a second boy chimed in. "And man, your team is the worst."

"You shut up, Roger," the chubby boy said in retaliation.

"Both of you shut up," the fair-haired boy said, tired of the bickering.

Just then they noticed Little Simon Adamson and Miss Wiseman for first time. It was easy to make a quick assessment of the situation. In silence, they hopped down onto the landing, turned the corner, and descended a second set of stairs that led to the gymnasium; but not before glancing back several times to see the beautiful teacher. Hope waited for them to shuffle off out of earshot before she continued talking with the disgruntled student.

* * *

After the four 4th graders had pushed their way through the doors leading into the gym, the red headed boy said, "Oh man, that Simon Adamson is a little troublemaker! I wonder what he did this time."

"Well, whatever he did, I'm sure he deserved it," Parker said. "Miss Wisemen is so nice."

"Was I talkin' to you, Porker?" the red headed boy snarled. "You probably have a crush on her."

"Lay off, Jackson," the fair-haired boy said.

"Oh, come on, Ralph, he's such a twerp," Jackson said. "I don't know why you let him hang around."

"Hey, let's go back and spy on them and hear what she's saying to that little weirdo."

"Yeah, let's go," Roger said in agreement.

"No," Ralph replied. "We're taking garbage out to the incinerator, just like Mrs. Morrisette asked us to."

"You're such a goody-goody," Jackson said to his cousin with disdain.

"Shut up, Jackson! Ralph's not afraid of anything," Parker said, coming to his defense. "Are you Ralph? Besides, Mrs. Morrisette told us to be back soon."

"You shut up, Fatty," Jackson replied as he slugged Parker in the shoulder. "You guys are always afraid of gettin' in trouble."

"No, I'm not," Ralph objected. "My parents said they wouldn't let me play ball if I got into trouble. That's all."

Suddenly, Jackson realized that they were standing at the bottom of the stairs that led up to the chorus room. "So, you're not a couple of scaredy-cats?" Jackson asked with a challenging tone.

"No way," Ralph replied confidently.

"Well, prove it," Jackson said. "Let's go up to the chorus room and ride down the fire escape slide. Unless you're too big of a wimp."

Parker gulped, looking up at the dark, isolated room. "Dr. Al-Banna says, I can't get too excited on account of my asthma."

"Your *assmar* sucks," Ralph chided. He turned to Jackson. "At least, I'm not a wuss. I just don't wanna. If I get caught I won't get to pitch on opening day."

"No, I think you're scared," Jackson said with a heinous laugh. "What, are you afraid Jessie Joseph is going to get you?"

Ralph looked around at the other boys who looked back at him in silence. "What would I do with the bag of garbage?"

"Me and Roger can carry it out back for you," Parker quickly offered.

"Yeah," Jackson said. He shoved his bag into Roger's arms and began to ascend the darkened staircase. "Coming? Or are you chicken?"

Ralph plopped the bursting trash bag into the arms of the chubby little boy who teetered back and forth, before dropping it onto the gym floor and spilling all of the contents.

"Nice," Ralph said. "You can clean that up yourself."

"Ha! What a loser," Jackson said as he started up the flight of stairs.

Ralph ascended the creaky steps towards the infamous room. Halfway up the stairs, Jackson stopped on a landing and waited for Ralph before taking a sharp turn to finish the final ascent into the spooky room. Parker and Roger watched them make their way to the top before carrying the bulging bags out the door towards the incinerator. When Ralph and Jackson reached the top of the stairs, they looked at one another without saying a word. Jackson extended his arm, challenging Ralph to go first. As they inched their way down the short hallway leading to the chorus room, their bravado waned in the darkness. Their hearts were pounding, and they could audibly hear each other's labored breathing with each step into the darkness. Jackson who was right on Ralph's heels reached out and clutched the back of his cousin's shirt.

"The light switch has got to be here somewhere," Ralph whispered, sliding his hands over the smooth wall. Their eyes not having adjusted yet to the relative darkness, both boys groped aimlessly.

"Got it," Jackson said under bated breath. Ralph could hear the click-click, but nothing happened.

"What's the matter?" Ralph whispered.

"No light," Jackson replied.

"Whisper," Ralph said.

Jackson stood paralyzed for a moment peering into the darkened room. Though his eyes could have been deceiving him, he thought that he could see something on the floor of the room. He squinted hard and then opened them wide before realizing that he was seeing the reflection of the red exit sign for the fire escape on the shiny hardwood floor. Ralph, annoyed by the delay, pushed his way into the room. Jackson grabbed the back of his shirt once again and followed in tow.

"What was that?" Jackson whispered emphatically.

"What?" Ralph asked.

"I thought I heard something," Jackson said. "It sounded like footsteps."

They stopped for a moment to listen. All Ralph could hear was his own pulse pounding in his ears. His eyes began to adjust, and he could make out a dogleg at the far end of the room. He knew that it lead to a catwalk that ran high above the length of the stage below. The two boys made their way to the catwalk and peered down the long corridor to the exit light above the doors to the fire escape.

"I just thought of something," Jackson whispered. "What if somebody sees us come out at the bottom of the fire escape?"

"Afraid?" Ralph asked in an effort to turn the tables on Jackson.

"No," Jackson insisted.

This time they distinctly heard footsteps coming up behind them. They were getting louder and louder as they got closer.

"Go, Go, Go," Jackson said in a panic, climbing up the back of his cousin.

Ralph and Jackson raced down the catwalk, flung open the little doors to the fire escape, and slid down before shooting out into the daylight.

* * *

Watching from her kitchen window while washing dishes, Hannah Grace Rash was more than a little surprised to see a boy come flying out of the fire escape onto the school yard across the street from her house. She stopped washing the coffee mug for a moment, holding the washcloth in the mug just above the water.

"Oh my," she muttered with a look of concern on her face.

A second boy jettisoned out of the tunnel onto the first, and they both fell to the ground. Quickly, they sprang to their feet, brushed off their shirts, and sprinted towards two other boys who were tossing garbage into the incinerator that stood behind the gym. Once they saw their classmates, the boys by the incinerator dropped their bags and ran to greet their friends. The first two boys who had come from the escape gesticulated wildly while bouncing and pointing back at the school building from which they had just come. Hannah Grace couldn't help but follow the fire escape slide up to the chorus room.

A sad, empty stare came over her face. She wiped her trembling hands off on her apron and reached up to open a cabinet next to her for prescription bottle. After forcing it open, she spilled a tiny pill into her hand, leaned forward, and thrust it into her mouth before washing it down.

Without warning, the spring on the screen door at the front of the house twanged under the strain. The door recoiled and whacked the doorframe. Hannah Grace jumped, nearly dropping the glass of water from her hand.

"*Aunt Gracee!*" Sharon called from the front entryway to the house.

"I'm in the kitchen," Hannah Grace responded with one hand on her chest. She quickly returned the bottle to the cabinet, wiped her hands onto her apron, and turned to see her niece's daughter come bounding around the table in the dining room.

"What are you doing, Aunt Grace?" Sharon asked.

She flung her backpack onto the back of a dining room chair, walked into the kitchen, and gave Hannah Grace a big hug.

"Oh, I was just finishing the dishes," Hannah Grace replied. "I had forgotten for a moment that you would be here early today."

"Yeah, just had a half day today because of finals," Sharon answered still holding onto Hannah Grace around the waist. "I just got off the school bus and came straight here." She leaned back and got a good look at her great aunt's face. "What's the matter? You look like you've just seen a ghost?"

Hannah Grace searched Sharon's eyes. "Heaven's sakes, no. Nothing's the matter," she sheepishly replied. Hannah Grace looked closely into the young girl's face and shook her head with a grin. "You are growing up. You just get more and more beautiful everyday. Now what are you so giddy about?"

"What? Oh nothin'," Sharon answered, looking down in embarrassment and pulling away from her great aunt. "I'm probably just happy that it's almost summer."

"No, that's not it," Hannah Grace said. "I always know when you're not telling the truth, besides, you love school." She untied her apron and hung it up in the utility room.

Sharon shrugged her shoulders with a wide grin and said, "I don't know, I'm just happy."

"Just 'happy' huh?" Hannah Grace said, smiling back at her granddaughter. She walked hurriedly into the dining room, grabbed her jewelry off of the table, and proceeded on to the living room. Sharon skipped behind her humming softly. "But, why are you so happy? There's something else."

"You look like you're getting ready to leave," Sharon asked, trying her best to change the subject. "Are you getting ready to leave?"

"Yes," Hannah Grace replied. "Your great grandma Rash and I are preparing coffee and some snacks for a meeting at the church." Staring at her wedding ring that she had just slipped on, an intuitive thought suddenly crossed her mind.

With a blank expression, she turned to Sharon and said, "It's a boy, isn't it."

Sharon shrugged her shoulders playfully, picked up a picture frame off of the end table, and tossed herself onto the sofa.

"Oh, that is it, isn't it?" Hannah Grace asked expectantly waiting a reply. Temporarily distracted, she sat down on the edge of the couch. "My little Sharon has a boyfriend."

"Not exactly," she said a little uncomfortable.

Sharon glanced up at her grandmother and then looked back at the picture in the frame she was holding.

"Grandma, how did you and Uncle John meet?" she asked.

Hannah Grace leaned over to see the picture of her husband 'John.' "Oh, we met at an ice cream social many years ago. So who is this lucky young man? Is it Tommy Hughes? I've always like that boy."

"No, not him…I'm not tellin' you," she answered. "Why do you still wear your wedding ring?"

"Because I will always be married to your Uncle John," she said in a slightly melancholy tone as she got up and walked back to the kitchen.

"How old were you?" Sharon yelled.

"What?" Hannah Grace asked, half-listening as she looked for her earrings.

"How old were you when you met?" Sharon asked again.

Hannah Grace walked back into the living room wearing a light jacket.

"Let's see," Hannah Grace replied. "I was 15 years-old. Is it Billy Kirby?"

"*Aunt Gracee*, come on, Billy Kirby?" she whined.

"What? He's a nice boy," she said. Then she glanced down at her watch. "Oh dear, I have got to be going."

"How old was Uncle John?" Sharon asked at the same time that her cell phone rang out alerting her to a new text.

Hannah Grace was standing at the front door with one hand on the door handle. She was preoccupied with the thought of being late.

"I was...too young, and he was, uh', eighteen," she answered, grabbing a tupperware container.

"And how old were you when you got married?" Sharon pressed.

Hannah Grace purposely deflected the question. "We were too young," she answered. "Now I *have* to go. Will you be all right here by yourself?"

"Yes, ma'am," Sharon said, exasperated. "I'm going to be in high school next year, you know."

Hannah Grace opened the door and started down the steps, before something occurred to her. "Where is Shannon?" she asked. "I thought her mother said she was coming here after school today too."

"She didn't ride the bus today," Sharon answered, hating to lie. She looked down at a new message on her iPhone. Grateful for the distraction, she held it up to show Hannah Grace. "This is her now. She wants to know if it's okay to come over."

"Can she come over?" Hannah Grace repeated. "Why heavens, since when does Shannon Zeal ever ask if she can come over?"

"I don't know, she..."

Hannah Grace looked at her watch. "Goodness gracious," she said. "I have to go. You girls be good. There are some no-bake cookies in the kitchen. Bye-bye, I love you sweetie."

"Bye, love you too," Sharon called. She plopped back down on the couch, grabbed one of the pillows, and hugged it tightly as she hammered out a response on her cell phone. "Yes!"

Hannah Grace made her way onto the porch, paused, and looked back towards the house while digging for her car keys in her purse. Something about the conversation struck her, and she paused for a moment to contemplate what it might be. Finally, she thought better of it and made her way down the rickety steps onto the sidewalk. Hannah Grace knocked once on the front door of Mara's house before going inside.

Mara Rash was sitting on the ottoman when her daughter-in-law walked in. Quickly, she pulled a kleenex down from her face, sniffled, and placed an old, tattered photo album back onto the coffee table.

"Mother?" Hannah Grace asked knowingly. "What's wrong?"

"'Bout time you got here," Mara snarled as she popped up and limped her way towards the door. "Pastor is going to be wondering where we're at. Don't you have a clock over there?"

Hannah Grace said nothing as Mara passed in front of her and out the front door. Sometimes it was better to let it go. Hannah Grace rolled her eyes, grabbed the door handle, and pulled it shut behind her.

* * *

Pastor Cross wiggled a little in his seat, straightened up in his chair, and cleared his throat. His offer hung in the air for a moment while Mara began clearing the table. The Reverend Algood salvaged the last finger sandwich off of the tray just before Mara lifted it into the air. She shot him a disapproving glance out of the corner of her bifocals. Popping the whole thing into his mouth, he chomped down and squinted with delight.

"Ummm!" he said with his cheek bulging to one side. "Miss Mara, you have done yourself proud once again."

"It is not polite to talk with your mouth full…," was the nicest thing she could say in return. With a hand full of dirty plates, she turned and scooted off towards the kitchen.

"Mother Rash!" Hannah Grace exclaimed.

Mara glanced back over her shoulder before leaning back into the spring-loaded kitchen door.

"Please excuse her, Reverend Algood," Hannah Grace said. "She's just old and crotchety."

"Nonsense," the reverend said, licking his fingers. "She's a good woman. And one good cook."

At that, Father Rite shot a disapproving glance at Reverend Algood over the top of his coffee mug just as he brought it up to his face. He lowered it ever so slightly and began to rebuke the young pastor with the expensive suit. Recognizing that his little afternoon meeting might soon turn into a holy war, Pastor Cross spoke up before Father Rite could reprimand his contemporary.

"As I was saying, gentlemen," Pastor Cross said. "I would be willing to do the lion's share of the work. I would be happy to print flyers, prepare an itinerary…"

"Pete, I think it's great that you had us over here," Reverend Algood began. "It's a wonderful sentiment. And I, just as you, think the utmost of educating our youth. I do. But I have my reservations about the perception of the members of my congregation. You know, perception can be reality…"

"Pastor Cross, if I may," Brother Rite said, completely ignoring his brethren. "Our church has not historically meddled in such affairs. There's always been a certain protocol that the church follows in such matters. Historically, the Catholic Church has always done its level best to stay out of the political arena."

Mara returned from the kitchen with a pot of hot coffee, walked over to the table, and held it out towards Father Rite with a look of expectancy. When he failed to notice her, she deliberately cleared her throat.

"I…what?…Oh yes, please, Miss Mara…," Father Rite stammered.

"It was just a thought that I had," Pastor Cross said apologetically. "I thought it would be nice for everyone to come together on this issue. I think that it is important for folks to prayerfully consider the school referendum."

"No, No, Pete," Reverend Algood said when he saw the look on the Pastor's face. "I think it's a great idea." Distracted, he noticed Mara walking back towards the kitchen. "Oh, Mara, would you be a dear and top me off?" He raised his coffee cup up towards her with a Cheshire cat grin. Without changing expression, she paused momentarily before she reluctantly made her way back over to serve him.

"Thank you, you dear sweet woman," the reverend said. "Our situation is a little different from yours, Pete. That's all. Ya see, we're in the process of expanding our children's ministries. The building committee has expressed some concern to me that a land tax would discourage some of our primary donors from stepping up to the plate. You understand?"

Mara nearly dumped the hot coffee in the reverend's lap at his backhanded insult about Pastor Pete's shrinking membership, while gloating about the growth of his own prosperous ministry.

Defeated, Pastor Cross cupped his lower lip, looking down at his lukewarm coffee. "I see, Richard," he said. "But, surely you can understand how a new school would benefit the entire community."

"We all know the implications that a new school would have on Bethel," Pastor Rite replied. "But, have you considered that we are unduly influencing our members' votes and thereby infringing on the separation of church and state? We have always abided by that simple doctrine in the past."

"Gentlemen, how can we sit idly by, witnessing the decay of our education system?" Pastor Pete pleaded. "What kind of example are we providing for the community? Don't they look to us for leadership, for guidance? Now we have an opportunity to make an impact. Our silence gives the impression of indifference. Can we at least agree to devote a Sunday to a message on the importance of wisdom and knowledge from a biblical perspective?"

"Have you considered that in doing so, we actually might be breaking the law?" Pastor Rite asked. "Are you prepared to have the IRS pay you a visit, or better still, or are you prepared to go to jail? I, for one, am not."

"We all know what happened when we tried to do the 'Meet Me at the Poll' thing last fall," Pastor Algood said, between licking the egg salad from his fingers. "I'm still answering the e-mails."

Pastor Pete sat back in his chair, defeated at the mere mention of emails. He nodded contemplatively. After a short pause, he had a thought. Sitting forward again, he said, "I just feel like we need to *do* something. How about we simply try to drive voter participation, not even take a side or anything?"

"Like setting up a table on Main Street and helping people register?" Pastor Rite asked, as he warmed to the idea. "Now, that we've done before."

"Yes, like voter registration," Pastor Pete said.

"Who would run the booth?" the Reverend Algood asked, as Mara and Hannah Grace came from the kitchen carrying a large covered dish, four small plates, and some forks. All three of the local ministers looked to the women.

"Mara and I would be glad to help in any way that we can," Hannah Grace said out of a strong sense of duty.

"Great! Now that that's settled," Reverend Algood said with glee, clapping his hands together, "Miss Hannah Grace, I'd give my right arm for some of that famous coffee cake of yours."

Mara clanked the dishes onto the coffee table one by one. She was none too happy with her daughter-in-law for volunteering them yet again.

Meanwhile, Pastor Cross sat back in his chair, folded his legs, and rested his elbows on the arms of the chair, disappointed with his feeble concession. He clasped his hands together, while his index fingers formed a "steeple." Sullenly, he looked at the "people" inside and robotically wiggled his fingers. Submissively, he turned his head to look outside the window through the thinly veiled curtains of the parish to the decaying façade of the old school building. Out of the corner of his eye he noticed a young man walking down the sidewalk in front of the school across the street. The young man seemed completely raptured in bliss. Enviously, he stared directly into a face that didn't seem to have a care in the world.

* * *

As Simon made his way down the sidewalk, a multitude of sappy love songs reverberated in his head. They had never seemed so rich in wisdom or made so much sense to him as they did today. Making his way along the front of the school with its boarded up window and flaking paint, he considered the job opportunity that Will had mentioned. To his own surprise, he actually was entertaining the idea of staying in Bethel a little while longer. After all, there was no telling when the interview would be in Jersey. He fumbled through his pockets before pulling out his phone and checking for any new messages. Nothing. At the moment, he wasn't upset about not hearing from his Uncle Joe. In fact, he was a little relieved that he *hadn't* called. As Simon stared contentedly at the soft, powder puff clouds hovering in the blue skies high above the grain elevator, his mind kept coming back to the one thing and one thing only...Jez.

After passing the school on the opposite side of the road from the church, Simon made a halfhearted attempt to catch another glimpse of his old house. Unfortunately, a large pine tree in the corner of the churchyard obstructed his view. He did notice, however, the same rusted out beater of a car parked on the street a few doors down just as it had been the day before. Suddenly, he remembered the scrawny youth director.

"What was his name again?" he thought to himself. "John? No. George? No. *Jeremy*! That was it, Jeremy. Poor kid, couldn't coach his way out of a paper bag." He laughed at the thought; but, quickly remembered how Jeremy's players *did* seem to really like him, despite the beating they received at the hands of Rich's Yankees.

"They did do a few things well," he mused, "and a couple of those kids might actually be pretty good with a little coaching." By the time he had thought of a few pertinent hitting and fielding drills that might help them out, he found himself standing in front of the First National Bank of Bethel.

Simon held the door open for a frail, elderly woman with a walker. Scooting by at a snail's pace, she looked him in the eye, smiled, and nodded. "Thank you, young man," she said.

Simon smiled in kind and replied cordially, "You're welcome."

After she made her way out the door, he slid by her into the bank.

"Uh-oh, here comes Mr. Popular," Will said sardonically from behind the counter.

"What?" Simon asked, weaving his way through the lines of ropes. "Oh yeah. Last night. Sorry about that. I guess you could say I was 'convicted' to leave you guys for dead in the middle of nowhere."

"Oh, I get it," Will replied, while counting out a fist full of singles. "You were exacting your revenge. Is that it? I suppose I can understand that." He abruptly stopped counting, looked up at Simon with a grave expression, and said, "I guess you haven't heard then."

"Heard what?" Simon asked.

"Those guys never came back last night," Will whispered.

Simon's face went flush as he considered the implication.

But Will couldn't hold it in any longer. He busted out laughing.

"Oh, that's funny," Simon replied.

"Ha, had you going, buddy," Will answered. "You deserved that."

"Okay, you got me," Simon admitted. "So, what time did you guys get back into town?"

"'Bout one in the morning," Will said indifferently, placing the stacks of cash neatly back in a drawer.

"So, you're not ticked off?" Simon asked, surprised.

"Nah, man," Will replied. "Come on! Jez? You're only human. I think any of us would have done the same thing had we been in your shoes. Besides, the long walk gave me a chance to sober up before facing Rachel anyway. Now, Rocky and Rob might feel differently. But, oh well. They'll get over it. Hey, we all got home, eventually, and the sharpie stain is finally gone from your face. So, we'll call it even."

"That's good," Simon said. "Jez *is* something else, isn't she?"

"Oh, she's something else all right," Will answered before artfully changing the focus of the conversation. "Don't worry about the guys. Rob was just ticked that we never found the graveyard, and then he had to listen Rocky complain the whole way home about how his dad was going to kill him. And Rich, he was already mad at all of us. Don't worry about it. The guys have probably already forgotten all about it by now. So, what brings you to the bank, how can I help you?"

"I just need an ATM to get some cash," Simon said.

"ATM, ha, that's a good one," Will replied. "Soon, but not yet."

"No ATM?" Simon said. "Well, I'm getting a little low on money and need to take out a cash advance on my credit card." As Will took care of him, Simon looked down at the table behind the counter. There was a textbook of some kind with a notebook and a pen sitting next to it.

"Doing a little studying?" Simon asked.

"Finance," he replied. "It's tough. I've only got one more semester then I'll be done with my associate's degree and ready to start my undergrad." Will quickly counted out the money.

"That's great man," Simon said, reaching for the cash, "then what?"

"I don't know," Will answered. "Mr. Helrigle, the bank president, has been very supportive, allowing me to work while going to school. They're telling me that if I get a finance degree, they'll start training me as a loan officer."

"Oh, I met that guy at the ballpark yesterday," Simon said. "He seems pretty intense."

"Always," Will said, "but, without him there's no way I would be able to save for this wedding and pay for tuition at the same time. He gave me a pretty sweet deal on a loan."

"Yeah, about the wedding," Simon said, slightly embarrassed, "I didn't mean for Rich to put you on the spot like that. It was pretty rude of him."

"Dude, no," Will interrupted, "that's just Rich being Rich. It's cool. Rachel can deal with it."

"You sure? That's great," Simon said. "Man, I really hate to ask..."

"Let me guess, you want to bring Jez?" Will asked with a laugh. "Yeah, that'd be *awesome*. I wouldn't have it any other way. Speaking of which, you are coming to the bachelor party Friday night at the town hall aren't you? Rocky is throwing it together. Dude, you *have* to come now."

"Yeah, I'd love to," Simon said.

While Simon was putting the cash into his wallet, a door opened to his right at the far end of the bank. The nameplate on the door read, "Wilson B. Livingood, vice president." A young, married couple made their way out the door. The mother was cradling her baby daughter who was peacefully sleeping in her arms. She was followed by her husband and Mr. Livingood. Simon didn't recognize him at first in his suit and tie with no ball cap on his head. But then, Simon could see the strong resemblance to Wilson B. and his son, Ralph, who pitched brilliantly for two innings during the scrimmage. They both had very athletic frames, square jaws, and a thick head of blond hair.

Wilson shook hands with the husband and wife, exchanged pleasantries, and saw them to the door. Simon overheard him saying, "We should know by tomorrow what you're pre-qualified for, and then Mrs. Helrigle can get to work finding you a great starter home."

They thanked him profusely and made their way out the door. When Wilson turned, he recognized Simon and made his way over to him.

"Simon, was it?" Wilson B. asked, putting out his hand.

"Yes sir, that's right, Simon Freeman," he answered.

"Oh, Freeman," Wilson repeated, with interest. "You used to live here in Bethel. Yes, Rich was telling me about you. Said you played at TCU. I think I remember watching you play ball when you guys were in little league."

"Oh really?" Simon replied. "Yes, we used to live in Bethel for a while before moving to Texas."

"Yeah, I remember your dad," Wilson B. replied with a sympathetic expression.

But before Simon could answer, Lexus Helrigle walked up to the counter from a room in the back.

"Lexus," Wilson B. said, "you remember Simon from yesterday's game?"

"Yes," Lexus said, "how are you doing, Simon?"

"Played ball at TCU," Wilson B. added, raising his eyebrows.

"I didn't really play," Simon interjected. "But, yes, I was on the team for a couple of years."

"Is that so?" Lexus replied.

Simon could see the wheels turning in the president's head. He seemed like the kind of guy who was always working on an angle of some kind.

Lexus Helrigle was a tall, solid man with slick, red hair and freckles overlaying a pale complexion. He was wearing a sharp three piece suit that was neatly pressed and expensive Italian shoes that had been freshly shined.

"You did a really nice job yesterday," Lexus said lifting his chin with his eyes down as though he were measuring Simon up. "We can always use good umpires who know the game."

"Simon's just passing through," Will said. "He just graduated from college, and he is on his way to New Jersey for an interview for a sales position with a pharmaceutical company."

"That's fantastic," Wilson B. said with sincerity. "I had a buddy in school who tried to get me to interview for a job in that field a long time ago. Which company?"

"Biotherapeutics," Simon replied.

"Oh yeah, great company!" Wilson B. said. "What was your major?"

"Elementary education actually, but I never completed my student teaching," Simon answered sheepishly.

"Elementary education?" Lexus repeated. "You sure you don't want to stay in Bethel for a while longer? As it so happens, we have a first grade teacher who is retiring next year. Instead of raking in all of that money, you could teach a bunch of farmers' kids for next to nothing."

"I already told him that he could pull down some serious money this summer cleaning gum off the bottom of desks," Will joked. "But he flat out turned it down. Can you believe that?"

Lexus forced a grin, put his hand in his pocket, and said, "Well, it's good to meet you. If you do end up hanging around Bethel for some reason, you're always welcome to call some games. Best of luck with the pharma thing." He reached out and firmly shook Simon's hand before returning to his office.

"So, when is the interview?" Wilson B. asked.

"I'm not sure exactly," Simon answered rather embarrassed that he didn't have any more details. "They're launching a new drug, but it was delayed by the FDA. So, they put the interviews on hold."

"Oh yeah, I think I saw something about that in the Wall Street Journal," Wilson B. said. "FDA has been clamping down lately. Well, that was Lexus's cue to get back to work, so it was nice meeting you. Maybe I'll see you down at the park a couple more times before you take off."

"I hope so," Simon replied, shaking Wilson B.'s hand. "As a matter of fact, I'm heading down there now to help Rich out with practice."

"Ah, Rich," Wilson B. said, wagging his finger at Simon as he back-peddled towards his office. "You need to keep an eye on that guy. He's a bit of a salesman himself. If he thinks you can help out his baseball team, he will be scheming a way to keep you around a while."

As Simon turned and headed toward the door, he thought, "There's only one thing that would keep me in Bethel a little while longer." Instinctively, he looked down at his cell phone to see if Jez had returned any of his calls. Still nothing.

7

SIX THINGS THAT ARE DETESTABLE TO HIM

The American flag flapped wildly in the late afternoon wind that gusted from the South bringing with it a surge of warm air. The delightful weather only served to accentuate the warm feelings rising up in Simon. It permeated his entire being and pulsated through his body with each beat of his heart. While he stood at the corner of the baseball park, the entire series of events that had unfolded over the course of the last seventy-two hours played over and over in his mind. Was he really thinking of staying in Bethel? The opportunity in New Jersey was everything that he had ever dreamed of. Above all else it offered him something that he had never had before in his life; financial security and upward mobility. He would finally be somebody. Even now, as he checked off the long laundry list of reasons to leave for Jersey, a wonderfully extraneous thought that defied all logic and sound judgment would force its way to the forefront of his mind. It was a mental picture of Jez in a miniskirt. It was all he could think about. Every now and then, he looked down at this phone to see if he had somehow missed any texts or voice mails. Still nothing. It was driving him crazy. He wrestled with the notion of reaching out to her once again but was afraid that he would scare her off.

Unexpectedly, the door to the concession stand opened and a boy stepped out into the light of day with his head down. After him followed Jeremy Warner, the youth minister, with his right hand on the young man's shoulder. They walked very deliberately as Jeremy spoke to the boy. Simon was still some distance from them and therefore could not make out exactly what was being said, but by the look on Jeremy's face it seemed to be of great importance. The boy nodded intermittently at whatever it was that the scrawny youth pastor was saying to him. Simon recognized the young man as one of the Padres' woeful outfielders.

While trying not to bring any unnecessary attention to himself, Simon also made no deliberate effort to conceal himself either. He simply waited for his presence to be discovered. When Jeremy did finally glance up, he was visibly caught off guard to find someone standing at the end of the bleachers next to the backstop. It was obvious that Jeremy did not recognize Simon at first due to the look of perplexity on his face. Then it came to him and his demeanor changed instantly.

"Oh, hey," Jeremy said, as he dropped his hand off of the boy's shoulder. Glancing around awkwardly, he took whatever he had been carrying in his left hand and laid it down on a counter just inside the door of the concession stand and pulled it shut behind him.

"Hey," Simon replied as he quizzically looked on.

"You're Rich's buddy who helped umpire our scrimmage yesterday, aren't you?" Jeremy asked with a smile as they made their way towards one another.

"Yes, I am," Simon answered. "In fact I'm meeting him here in a few minutes. I'm Simon Freeman."

"Well, I'm Jeremy Warner, oh, and this is my good friend Randy," he said, putting both hands on the shoulders of the 10-year-old boy standing in front of him. The boy put out his hand and squinted up at Simon.

"Nice to meet you guys," Simon said, shaking the boy's hand.

"Does Rich have practice today?" Jeremy asked.

"I guess so," Simon replied. "He'll be here in about fifteen minutes."

There was an awkward pause, and the look on Jeremy's face revealed a hint of embarrassment. "I wondered if anyone had the field. My bad. I always forget to check the website," he said. Then he turned and spoke to the young boy. "Hey, uh, Randy why don't you head over there into the dugout, grab a bat, put on a helmet, and jump into the batter's box?"

The boy began to protest, "Do I have to?"

"Come on now, we talked about this," Jeremy said, holding up his scrawny index finger. "The only way to get over your fear is to face it. Head on."

Reluctantly, the boy dropped his chin to his chest and shuffled off in the direction of the dugout.

"I didn't want to say anything in front of Randy," Jeremy began. "He's been beaned a couple times and now he's scared to death of the ball. I thought maybe I'd try to help him get over his fear."

"I can understand that," Simon replied. "I've been plunked a few times. It's not much fun."

"So, you've played then?" Jeremy asked barely concealing his delight.

"A little," Simon answered, cautiously, "why?"

"Well, I haven't," Jeremy admitted. "I'm not much of a pitcher, and I don't have the greatest accuracy. I'm afraid that I might only make things worse by trying to pitch to Randy myself."

Simon could see where the youth pastor was going with this. Rich was right. Jeremy had never played baseball before. No wonder his team was so bad. Still, there was something Simon liked about the scrawny, little youth minister. He seemed genuine, like there were no pretenses about him. Simon got the impression that with Jeremy, what you see is what you get, and he liked that.

"Have you ever pitched?" Jeremy asked humbly.

"Some," Simon replied.

"I wouldn't want to impose, but would you mind tossing a few?" Jeremy asked. "I would be very grateful. Randy's got some other things going on at home. His parents are getting divorced. And, well, I just thought that if he could get over this fear, it might really boost his confidence, ya know?"

Simon looked up at the boy on the other side of the fence. Randy was in the batter's box, taking a few wild practice swings. His feet moved all over the place, he dropped his hands, and pulled his head as he took another hack. While he was able to diagnose the boy's problems immediately, he also knew there was no immediate solution to fix them. It would take weeks if not months of practice and repetition. It might even take a miracle.

Simon turned and looked at Jeremy. He was a plain, unassuming looking sort of fellow. His cheeks were slightly sunken highlighting a long pointy nose and a protruding chin. Still, there was something unique about him, like a vitality. It was something in his eyes- a sparkle almost. Simon couldn't begin to try and guess how old he was, but decided that he couldn't have been more than twenty even though he seemed like an old soul.

"I don't know that I could do any better," Simon said. He could barely choke out the words. Still, he typically wasn't one to get involved.

Jeremy didn't say a word, but only responded with an expectant grin.

"But, I can give it a try, I guess," Simon said, finally.

Jeremy breathed a deep sigh of relief. "Oh, man, that would be great," he said appreciatively. "You don't even know what a big help that'd be."

Simon saw Jeremy's team yesterday, so he had a pretty good idea. Digging his foot into the dirt in front of the rubber on the mound, he was overcome with the feeling of being 10 years-old again. It had been over three years since he last threw a baseball, and it felt really good turning it over in his hand.

"Are you ready, Randy?" Simon hollered. "Here it comes." Purposefully, he held out the ball to the boy so that he could get a look at it. Simon couldn't believe how nervous he was. It had been ages since he tried to throw a pitch, and there was a fair to midland chance that he would hit the poor kid.

The pathetic looking batter slumped into the batter's box with the big-barreled bat resting squarely on his shoulder and an oversized helmet falling down over his eyes. Randy lifted his chin slightly in an effort to see Simon under the lid. His feet were out of kilter and to make matters worse his hands were reversed on the handle.

"All right, let's get this over with," Simon thought. He gripped the ball, feeling again the hardened blister on his hand. He came set and began his pitching motion. But, before the he even let go of the ball, Randy dramatically bailed out of the batter's box. Simon stopped abruptly and turned to look at Jeremy in centerfield with a glove on his left hand that was almost comically too large.

"That's Okay, Randy!" the youth pastor yelled, his voice cracking. "You're doing great! Stay in there buddy! He's just got a little bit of 'fear-factor' going on." He gave a thumbs-up to Simon who turned back at the batter.

"What is he doing in the outfield?" Simon thought. "This kid couldn't hit off of a tee."

He dropped his head and sighed, trying to decide if he should just throw a bucket of balls and be done with the whole mess or if he should begin the massive undertaking. He looked up at the sky, sighed deeply, took off his glove, and walked towards the boy to begin the much needed batting lesson. Simon didn't have the heart to just go through the motions.

When Rich pulled up to the field a half-an-hour later, he smiled as his old friend wound up and delivered a strike. He quickly surmised the situation when he saw Randy batting and Jeremy Warner cheerleading from centerfield. Rich shook his head. To his surprise, on the next pitch the boy brought the head of the barrel around and roped a hit in the direction of left-center. Like a silent film, he saw Jeremy jumping up and down before bounding into the infield to hug the batter just after Simon gave the boy a high five. Sitting for a moment in his car, Rich looked on with great interest. Here's something he hadn't figured on. He bit onto a pen, pulled it from the cap, and jotted a note down on his lineup card. A broad smile swept over his face. He got out of the car to unload the equipment for practice.

"That was awesome!" Jeremy yelled excitedly to Simon. "Did you see that?"

"Yeah, that a' boy, Randy," Simon said. "He did great. Just keep that back foot still, hands high, head still..."

Jeremy managed to pick the boy up and swing him around in a circle. Randy's face beamed with pride. Simon was feeling pretty satisfied himself, tossing another baseball up in the air and then catching it. When Jeremy set the boy down, he immediately raced out to Simon on the pitcher mound and gave him a warm hug.

"Whoa, ok, big guy," Simon said, not knowing what to do. After a few seconds, Randy let go of his grip around Simon's waist, turned around, and raced for the dugout. Rich's team had begun to show up one by one, and Jeremy suggested that it was enough for one day. Simon had never coached before. He was overcome with how it made him feel to play a part in someone else's success. It was almost like *he* had hit the ball right along with Randy.

"That was great," Simon said. "Good for him. Once he got his foundation firmly set, that helped. With some work, he might actually be pretty good."

"Yeah, that was incredible!" Jeremy said. "What a dramatic change. A 'firm foundation', huh? I like the sound of that. Well, I can't thank you enough. That was really great. Really. You don't even know what that means to him."

"No," Simon said, "it was my pleasure. I really had fun. It had been ages since I threw BP to anyone. It was good of you to take some time to bring him out here and give him a little extra work."

"Well, I definitely think that it was by divine intervention that you were here," Jeremy confidently said. "Otherwise, my misguided instruction would have only made things much worse."

"Well, it looks like Rich is ready to get started with practice. He's giving me his look. And I have to be somewhere right now, anyway. But, are you going to be around a little later? I'd like to talk to you a little more about that 'firm foundation' stuff."

"Yeah, uh, I guess so," Simon replied, looking down at his silent cell phone again. "Looks like I don't have anything going on."

"Well, I've got this commitment," Jeremy said, "but after that I would love to ask you a few questions."

By this time, Rich had approached the two of them talking on his field. He shot a look of apology to Simon from behind Jeremy's back.

"Hey guys," Rich said.

"Hey Rich, are you working tonight?" Simon asked.

"Tonight, tomorrow night, the next night after that," Rich answered playfully.

"I'll probably just be hanging out at the tavern with Rich later if you wanna come by," Simon said.

"Cool," Jeremy said again looking down at his giant watch. "But I've gotta' run. I'll try to catch up with you later at the tavern. See ya." He spastically hurried off the field towards the dugout.

"Strange cat," Rich said, watching Jeremy trip over the lip of the dugout, "so, what's that all about?"

"He just needed some help coaching up one of his players," Simon said. "I think he just wants a few tips or pointers. I don't know."

"Coaching tips?" Rich asked, watching the nerdy youth pastor drive off in his old clunker. "Huh, maybe, but I doubt it.

"Anyways, uh, do you want to help me with a small chore that I need to take care of? There's a catfish dinner and some cold beer in it for you."

"Catfish, huh?" Simon answered. "Now how could I turn that down?"

"You can't," Rich said as he handed Simon a hard hat.

"What's this for?" Simon asked, as he turned the hard brimmed, metal lid over in his hand.

"We need to change out some of the light bulbs," Rich said, pointing his beefy index finger to the sky.

Simon glanced up at Rich and raised his eyebrows. "You're kidding, right?"

"No, 'fraid not," Rich replied, as they made their way to the storage closet of the concession stand. "We always keep a gross spare bulbs here in the back. For some reason, we go through a ton of them during the season. Must be bad wiring or something. Can you grab the twenty-foot ladder? It's on the wall there next to all of those extension cords. Yeah. No. By the box of extra fuses. Yep."

"Twenty-foot ladder?" Simon asked, taking it off of the wall. "That's hardly going to do it."

"Oh, that's only to get up to the first rung on the pole," Rich said matter-of-factly. "You shimmy up the rest of the way using these." He pulled out gaffs, hooks, and a belt.

91

"Are you serious?" Simon responded. "But, you're terrified of heights."

"I know," Rich said, walking out the door, "but, you're not."

* * *

"Well, if it's not the intellectual hobos," Rich called out from behind the bar as he lifted a tray of dirty dishes and carried them back into the kitchen. "How was the destruction and devastation wrought by the tornado, boys? Was it everything you hoped it would be?" His words dripped with sarcasm.

George followed Joey through the dense crowd of patrons. Awkwardly, they parted the sea of people, lugging their backpacks over their shoulders.

"It was an amazing experience," Joey said. "Shiloh was completely desolate and deserted- totally leveled like it was never there. Creepy." Sporting a do-rag and unshaven face, he bumped his overstuffed pack into several people waiting for a table near the bar. "Sorry, excuse me," he said with an air of superiority. Dramatically, he swung his backpack off of his shoulder and hoisted it onto the counter.

"It was so awesome!" George echoed, following closely in step. "We slept on the slab of a house that had been swept away, bathed in a hose at the local McDonald's, and ate scraps out of a garbage can."

"Sounds delightful," Rich said mockingly.

"You see, George, that's the kind of ridicule I would expect from the small minded people of Bethel," Joey said, haughtily. "People like Rich just don't get it, and never will."

George nodded in agreement, throwing his backpack onto the bar next to Joey's.

"No, no, no!" Rich snapped, while continuing to clean up the dirty dishes from the bar. "What do you boys think your doin'? Get that gear off the bar, man. We're busy tonight. Besides, you guys reek."

"Well, where do you want me to put it?" Joey asked, dismayed.

"That's a very leading question," Rich replied in a booming voice so that he could be heard over the din of noise. He picked up the large, gray plastic container full of dishes and swung around towards the kitchen. "See, the small-minded group of people find that very funny, pointing to the patrons sitting around them. Now, go sit with Simon and Rob and those guys way in the back by the pool table. These people are waiting to eat, and your 'homeless-cologne' is ruining their appetite."

"What'd he say?" George asked Joey over the noise of the large crowd.

"He said he's a narrow-minded Neanderthal," Joey yelled into George's ear, "and he wants us to go sit in the back with Simon and those guys."

"Simon's still here? Cool," George said.

"Guess so," Joey replied . "Let's go tell him all about our adventure. He's an educated man; he'll at least appreciate it."

Slowly, Joey and George made their way through all of the people standing near the bar. When they reached the pool table, they saw Simon, Rob, and Rocky all sitting at a small round table under one of the LCD's in the corner of the room. Having been there since Happy Hour, they were sharing a good laugh about the events that had transpired the night before out at the old Potter place.

"So, you never found the gravestones?" Simon asked with a smile.

"Na," Rocky replied. "It was so freaky, know what I'm say'n? I thought we wuz dead. I ain't never goin' out there again!"

"You guys forgive me or what?" Simon asked.

"Yeah, yeah, I guess," Rob replied, "but just remember. What goes around, comes around."

"Oh, come on!" Simon said with a laugh. "I thought we were all even after the Sharpie incident."

"Hardly," Rob said lifting his mug up to his lips while Rocky shook his head. "Leaving us for dead in the middle of nowhere, while you slink off with some hot chick does not even come close to even."

"Okay, but take it easy on me, would you?" Simon asked. When Rocky and Rob offered up no sort of affirmation, he decided not to push his luck. Wisely, he changed the subject. "Are we hanging out here all night or what?"

"Cain't," Rocky said with a look of disgust. "Ole lady Harold called my daddy and told him about our little joy ride the other night in his new truck. So, he said I had to be in early tonight. He's got me roof'n one of our rental properties at the break of dawn. He told me that I need to get my rest, cause 'morrow was going to be brutal."

"How old are you?" Rob asked. "Daddy's got the purse strings. Gotta do what Daddy says or he may take away your allowance."

"Shud up, man," Rocky retorted angrily. "Like you'd do any differ'nt, please. Shhh."

"Wish I had some kind of inheritance coming my way," Simon joked.

"Psssttt. Thank you!" Rocky said in agreement as he slid off of the stool.

"What about you, Rob?" Simon asked. "Are you going to hang out for a while or what?"

"No, I've got an appointment with Mrs. Silverson," Rob said. "I can't miss this one. She ripped me a pretty good one for standing her up last night."

"Hey fellas," Joey said as he approached the three of them, "what's up?"

"Look who's back from saving the world," Rob said, sarcastically.

"Well, how was it?" Simon asked, slapping Joey on the back before he noticed how filthy they were. Subtly, he wiped his hand on his pant leg. "What was it like?"

Rob and Rocky rolled their eyes at one other after Simon asked the question.

"You are going to love hearing about what we did!" Joey said, as he dragged another small table over. "You learn so much about the world when you go and do something like that. And you learn a lot about yourself too."

Simon nodded politely, as Rob poured everyone a beer from the pitcher.

"See, that's what I like about you Simon," Joey said, "you're educated. You get it! These guys don't want to hear it. They'd rather wallow in their ignorance. And that's too bad, because the more you experience things, the better chance you have of understanding how the universe works and…"

"Did id' look like a war zone?" Rocky asked. "I bet id' was like a war zone."

"Yeah, yeah, devastation like you wouldn't believe," George said excitedly. "It was like the set of a movie or something. The really weird thing is that it just seemed so random. The towns on either side were completely untouched, while Shiloh was just about completely wiped off the face of the earth. We were digging through mounds and mounds of debris, trying to find any signs of life."

"But man, these people were so happy that we were there. You've never seen people caring for one another and doing whatever they could to help each other out. After a while my arms got so tired I couldn't even lift them over my head. Got splinters all over my hands…"

"So, what about you Joey?" Simon asked. "Got any splinters?"

"Actually, I hurt my arm catching the train," Joey said. He stuck out his right arm and rubbed it. "I couldn't lift anything even if I had wanted to. The people just looked a little lost and confused. They didn't seem real smart if you know what I mean? So I just took charge and started directing, telling them where to go and what to do. Kind of orchestrating the search and rescue. They seemed reluctant at first like 'who's this guy?', but then they kind of all fell in line, like sheep."

"Oh, man, but you wouldn't believe what we saw," George said. "There was this dude, what was his name?" George asked Joey. "Anyway, he and his wife were so grateful that they fed us and everything."

"Oh yeah, Bill, he was so cool," Joey said in agreement. "Get this, the guy's there with his family. They lost their home, their farm, everything, right?…"

For the next hour and a half, Joey and George basked in the attention of telling the story of how they came to the rescue of the desperate, ignorant people of southern Illinois. They may have even embellished a little for effect every now and then. But, even if they had, it wasn't likely that Rob, Rocky, or Simon would have caught on. For the first twenty minutes they did their best to feign interest. Then as the stories wore on, they made less and less of an effort, often yawning and looking around the room as the tables turned over at the tavern.

The guys had long since forgone courteous smiles and knowing nods. They found that any such act only served to fuel the spinners of yarn and encouraged them to continue. Undaunted by the obvious disinterest of their listeners, Joey and George bounced stories off of one another, like hosts from Entertainment Tonight. Simon resorted to conversation survival mode and did the best he could to observe the various TV monitors around the room, while Rocky began to nod off several times leaning his cheek against a fist that was propped up by an elbow on the table. Conversely, Rob did not even bother to conceal his disinterest and spent the majority of the time texting on his phone. Every once in while, someone would interrupt them asking for the pitcher to be passed their way. It was brutal by all accounts. Neither of the two do-gooders picked up on any of the non-verbal signals to bring an end to the never-ending commentary.

But Joey and George had lived it, so they loved it and were quite sure everyone else loved it too. For they were the heroes in this epic tale against insurmountable odds and forces of nature. Consequently, they were more than willing to share what they had learned, without ever bothering to confirm if it were actually true. Finally, Simon saw his chance to bail out of the conversation when Will walked through the door still wearing his work clothes from the bank.

"*Willy!*" Simon yelled. "What's up?"

"Will, come on back here," Rob and Rocky called out in earnest mimicry.

"Hey guys, how's it going?" Will asked. "Well, if it isn't the wonder twins. Save the world yet?"

"Own the world yet?" Joey replied sharply.

"Working on it," Will replied.

Will continued past them, grabbed a chair, and pulled it up between Rocky and Rob. "Did you boys take Simon here to task for ditching us at Potter's last night?"

"Last night, at Potter's?" George asked. "What happened last night?"

"Nothin', long story," Rob said curtly. "Nah, we're over it. Besides, it was for a good cause. He saw his chance to get a little and took it. Now we see how he is. He just needs to watch his back."

"Who? What?" Joey and George were both dying to know.

Simon said nothing. Instead, he took another drink of his beer before revealing a Cheshire cat smile.

"Jez," Rocky intimated proudly.

"*Jez-a-Bell?*" they said in unison as though it were forced out of their mouths with a gush of air.

From behind Simon's back, Will sat up in his chair and made a gesture as though he were waving off Joey and George from saying anything further.

"Yeah, we kind of connected," Simon said with a smug expression.

"Da's my boy," Rocky said shaking Simon's arm.

Rob bit his bottom lip while Joey and George stared blankly.

"Don't be so modest, Simon," Will said as he poured himself a beer. "He's bringing her to the wedding on Saturday."

Joey and George were speechless, looking back and forth at the other guys before finally catching on.

"Tell us, Simon," Joey said, "when are you going to see her again?"

"I'm not sure," Simon said. "She said she's got to work every night this week. I think she even said something about closing the next three nights. That's cool. I don't want to scare her off. Press too hard, you know? I'm just going to play it cool."

"I could take you to see her," Rob said.

Rocky, Joey, and George looked up at Rob in surprise while they waited for Simon's response. Discreetly, Will gave Rob a sharp kick to the shin under the table.

"Ouch…what the…?" Rob grunted, as he rubbed his leg.

"You could?" Simon asked with interest sitting up in his chair. He wanted to play this thing right. "No, I don't want to come across as desperate or overly anxious."

"Suit yourself," Rob said.

The guys let out a collective breath and looked around at one another.

"You're coming to Will's bachelor party Friday night, aren't you," Joey asked, expectantly.

"Oh, he'll be there," Will said.

"Whoa, look at the time," Rob said. "I've gotta get going."

"I'm out too, dog," Rocky said mournfully. "Been out too much lately, know what I'm say'n?"

"Yeah, you're right about that," Will regretfully uttered under his breath.

"You're just trying to avoid going home to the soon to be ball-and-chain," Rob said to Will.

"Man, I'm lucky she let me in the house after last night," Will said. "She's been sick and irritable all of the time, and she's about to drive me crazy."

Just then a skinny arm came out of seemingly nowhere and set a leather bound book down on the small table in front of Simon.

"Hey guys," Jeremy said enthusiastically.

Rob muttered under his breath profanely.

"Hey there Jeremy," Simon answered. "Uh, what's goin' on, man?"

"Jeremiah!" Joey said condescendingly. "How's the brainwashing of the local youth going?"

"Actually," Jeremy replied, unfazed, "you wouldn't believe how God has been at work. We're busting at the seams. It's an awesome thing to witness. Of course, we could always use a couple of new Sunday school teachers."

He reached over to the bowl of pretzels and grabbed a handful. As he attempted to toss them into his mouth, his hand didn't quite reach far enough and some fragments fell down the front of his freshly starched shirt. Jeremy wiped them away and brushed off his tan pants.

"Are you the youth leader at the church across from the grade school?" Simon asked.

"No, actually I'm with Pastor Algood at the new church just outside of town," Jeremy said.

"Oh? I thought you were with Pastor Cross," Simon said.

"Pastor Cross, a.k.a, 'The Sandman'," Joey said to George sarcastically.

Jeremy gave a disapproving glance over to Joey and then said, "No, but I do know him pretty well. He's a good man."

"What brings you to the tavern tonight, Jeremiah?" Rob asked, tiring of the idle chit-chat. "Isn't it some kinda sin, you being in a bar and all? You don't want to tarnish that halo of yours."

Simon shifted in his seat and sat up as though he could guess the reason. He looked at Jeremy, proudly waiting for his response. Simon was certain that he had made the effort to come down to the tavern to ask him about getting some coaching tips after the miraculous success they had had earlier in the day with Randy.

"Now that you ask, I came down to talk to Simon here about a firm foundation," Jeremy said with an air of humility.

Simon didn't even feel his chest slightly puff-up.

"You mentioned earlier that I might find you down here," Jeremy said to Simon. "I would love to sit and chat with you for a few minutes if you wouldn't mind."

"No, I mean 'yes', of course, that's cool with me," Simon answered, knowingly. It was after all nothing short of a miracle that he was able to get Randy's feet squared away in one afternoon. Before he even threw the first pitch, Simon realized that the boy had a poor foundation, and that if he did not have a solid foundation then nothing else mattered. Any instructor worth a grain of salt knew that. Fortunately, Simon already had been mulling over a few ideas for how Jeremy could make some major strides in a relatively short period of time, and he was ready to share his expertise.

"Do you want to go over to a booth or to another table?" Simon asked politely. "I could get a pen from Rich and some napkins to take notes."

"Uh, okay," Jeremy answered, somewhat confused.

"No, No," Joey piped up. "Pull up a stool, have a seat. We always love to hear what you have to say, Jeremiah."

With the effects of Happy Hour now beginning to take hold of Simon's faculties, he relished the opportunity to share his knowledge and impress the entire group.

"Yes, sit, sit," George implored in earnest.

"Do you care, Simon?" Jeremy asked.

"No, I don't care," Simon said, putting out his hand in a gesture for the youth pastor to take a seat at the table with him.

"All right," Jeremy said as he looked around for something to sit on. All of the taller bar stools designated specifically for the little round tables had already been taken. So, Jeremy walked over to the bar and grabbed a shorter stool and dragged it clumsily over to the table. The guys watched him struggle under the weight of the chair. When he got it over to the table and sat down on it, he was a full foot shorter than everyone else with his shoulders barely reaching over the table. After sitting, he reached over and grabbed the leather bound book that he had set on the table earlier. For the first time, Simon noticed what it was. Simon's state of confusion bore on the countenance of his face as Jeremy leaned forward over the book with his forearms resting on either side of it. He clasped his hands together. With his head down, he said nothing for what seemed like an eternity. As Simon looked around the table at the other guys in bewilderment, he wondered what any of this had to do with baseball. Rob shook his head and leaned back to take a swig of beer. Joey waited respectfully in silence, while Rocky took off his cap, leaned forward, and closed his eyes. Finally, Jeremy sat up and spoke softly.

"Simon, I will get straight to the point. I..."

At that moment, Rob's cell phone rang. He looked down at the number and saw that it was Jack Lawless.

"Ah, too bad, I usually enjoy listening to 'Billy Graham Jr.'s' pitch," Rob said as he reached for the phone and picked it up. "Hello. Oh no! You're not interrupting anything important," he said getting up from the table. "I'd be glad to meet with her earlier than scheduled." He rose from the table, grabbed his jacket off the back of his stool, gave the sign of the cross in mockery across his chest, and walked off."

"Go on," Simon said to Jeremy, anxious for the baseball coaching tutorial to begin.

"As I was saying, I am going to be brief and to the point," Jeremy started again. Suddenly, the inflection in Jeremy's voice changed to that of a more somber monotone. Simon glanced over at Joey who nodded as if he knew what the youth minister was about to say. Jeremy looked directly into Simon's eyes as if searching his soul.

"Simon, do you *know* your Lord and Savior Jesus Christ?" Jeremy asked with humble sincerity.

Simon was dumbstruck. "I, uh-well," he stammered. Obviously, he didn't even consider that the youth pastor had come to the tavern to talk about anything other than baseball. Not that he had a problem with it. But, he had never been asked point blank in front of God and everybody, if he knew Jesus- whatever that meant. "I know who Christians claim he is, if that's what you mean," Simon said, expertly reciting the rhetoric of political correctness he had been taught in college.

Jeremy waited intently while Simon looked at the faces around him more confused about the purpose of the meeting. Without thinking Simon heard himself say, "I mean, I know some of the stories about him from Sunday school when I was a little kid."

The youth pastor grimaced slightly before gathering his thoughts. He began to speak again, choosing his words very carefully. "That's good. So many people haven't heard anything about him. But do you *know* him?" Again, Simon looked around for some kind of clue from the others.

Joey was more than happy to interject, "He wants to know if you are a Christian."

"Like, I'm a Catholic or like Jeremy goes to The First Community Church or somethin'?" Rocky asked, completely engrossed in the conversation.

"You idiot, Catholics *are* Christians," Joey said with a putrid expression on his face. Joey and George shared a look of incredulity.

"What?" Rocky asked defensively.

"Catholic is your denomination, Rocky," Jeremy explained lovingly. "It is your particular religious sect. Catholics do consider Jesus to be the Christ. Both of our denominations believe that Jesus is our Lord and Savior. We believe that he is the Christ or Messiah. So, we are brothers in Christ even though I worship at the community church, and you worship at the Catholic Church.

Jeremy then turned back to Simon and said, "The reason that I came here tonight is that I want desperately for you to know your Lord and Savior, Jesus Christ, before it's too late. I want you to *know* Him like He knows you. I want you to have an intimate relationship with Him."

"What do you mean by 'relationship', Jeremiah?" Joey mocked. "Are you telling me that Jesus talks to you or something? I'm starting to worry about you if you're hearing voices. You're not schizophrenic or something are you?"

"Is he talking to you now?" George asked with a sarcastic tone, picking up on Joey's lead. The joke elicited a chuckle from Rocky and Joey. "I mean if you're best friends with him and all, maybe you could ask him where I lost my last set of car keys. I'm just razzing you Jeremy. You know I respect all religions."

"As a matter of fact, I do believe that He speaks to me when I am willing to listen," Jeremy answered patiently. "And 'no', to answer your other question, he is not speaking to me at the present moment; however, I hope and pray that the Holy Spirit is using me as a conduit to speak to you right now.

"But I'm not talking about religion. I'm talking about a relationship, like Father-to-son, or friend-to-friend. That's one of the things that separates Christianity from all other world religions.

"God is love. He created the world, including the human race. He gave us free will. But, He made our relationship very intimate when He came Himself in the person of His only begotten son, Jesus Christ, to die on the cross in order to save us."

"Let me play devil's advocate for a minute- all pun intended," Joey said, feeling cocksure of himself. "You make the assumption that there is a God. Can you prove his existence? How can you even prove that we exist?"

"Don't get so educated that you become stupid," Will said, frustrated with Joey's contrite questions.

"Well, I know that I exist, and I am just as confident that God does too," Jeremy said meekly. "He gave us three ways to know that He exists. He gave us an awesome and orderly universe that speaks to an intelligent creator. Secondly, He gave us the Bible that reveals His true character. Lastly, He gave us, His creation, a soul and a conscience inside each one of us that is pre-wired to recognize its Creator."

"Seriously though," Will said, glossing over Jeremy's assertion, "I'm pretty sure that something created the universe. I mean, come on', it doesn't take a rocket scientist to understand that something can't just come from nothing. But, even if I buy into the whole Jesus-is-God thing, there's something that I never get. People always say, 'You need to get saved'. Saved from what?" He held out his hands and looked around the room.

Rocky sat forward and anticipated the answer with interest.

"That's a great question," Jeremy said, nearly coming out of his seat excited by the genuine interest. "We need to be saved from spending an eternity in Hades. That is where we deserve to go as punishment for our sins. You see, when Adam sinned, we all inherited that sin. Yes, God is a righteous God. But because of our sin, we are unrighteous and in direct opposition to God. Ultimately, the punishment for sin is death. So, that's what you need to be saved from. Not the first death which is a human death that no man can escape. But, the second death which is an eternity in Hades."

"But what kind of a God would make humans, his own creation, a bunch of sinners?" Will asked bitterly. "For that matter, what kind of a God would even make evil in the first place?"

"Now, that is a very important point that is often overlooked," Jeremy said. "God didn't create evil or make us sinners."

"Hear it comes," Joey said. "He's going to draw upon an analogy so you can understand."

"Anala- what?" Rocky asked.

"A simple story, so that the simpleminded, such as yourself, can understand," Joey answered.

With great humility, Jeremy continued, "God is Love. God did not create sin. But, He created man with free will, or the freedom to choose. He wants us to choose to love Him, obey Him, and follow Him."

"Wait, I'm confused, a choice between what?" Rocky asked, fascinated by the exchange and momentarily forgetting his newfound dialect.

"A choice between following God, which is righteousness, or following something else, which is unrighteousness," Jeremy answered. "Any time that we do, or say, or think anything that is unrighteousness, we sin. When God made Adam and Eve, He made them perfect and sinless, but He gave them free will. He gave them a choice. They had to choose whether or not to eat from the tree of knowledge in the Garden of Eden. They chose whether or not to be obedient to God."

"I knew it," Joey said slapping his knee. "You think that's literal. Ha!"

"Even though God instructed them not to, Adam chose to eat the fruit of knowledge," Jeremy continued, choosing to ignore Joey's statement. "When he did so, he not only became unrighteous, he also passed along his unrighteousness to all of the generations that would come after him."

"Kind of like a faulty gene?" Simon asked now starting to track the conversation.

"Something like that," Jeremy conceded. "I guess that you could look at sin as kind of like a disease that we are incapable of healing or cutting out of our own bodies. And we all have it. God being perfectly righteous disdains the presence of anything unrighteous, or this 'gene' as you called it. So, He had to cast it out of his presence. Therefore, the punishment for this gene, or disease, is death. As it is explained to us in the Bible, we needed to be saved from this disease. As a result, God sent a Savior who was a completely righteous substitute to take on our sin for us and be punished in our place in order to pay the penalty for us. God is the only being who is completely righteous, so He Himself came to this world in the flesh, chose to live a perfectly righteous life, and voluntarily died on the cross in our place. When He did, He paid the price for all of our sins through grace. It was a pardon if you will. After three days, He rose from the dead, appeared to the disciples and five hundred others, and now sits on at the right hand of God the Father. And if that weren't enough, He shares a part of Himself with the believer in the person of the Holy Spirit. Someday He will return to earth again. All of that being said, we still need to choose to be saved before it is too late.

"Isn't it great! After all of that, He still allows us free will. And anyone who accepts Jesus as their Lord and Savior, confesses their sins, and repents will be saved from Hades and receive eternal life in Heaven. In fact, it is the only way to Heaven. When you choose to receive the free gift of salvation through Faith, it begins a personal relationship in which you really *know* Him. It is the *beginning* of your journey to become like Christ through obedience to Him."

When he finished there was silence. Each person tried to take in and digest what Jeremy had told them. After first being blindsided by Jeremy's message, Simon's heart was softened by the young man's conviction. He pondered the message and evaluated its veracity.

"Dat's what I'm talking' bout!" Rocky said, basking in his newfound identity as a Catholic-Christian who was someday going to heaven. "Preach on bro', know what I'm say'n'!"

"I don't get it," George admitted.

"It's pretty simple really," Joey said. "I learned all about all of this in college this year. Almost all religions and cultures have shared a similar story to explain what Jeremy refers to as God, good and evil, all that stuff. It's just one of many myths or folktales to know the unknowable."

"So, *you* believe that Christianity is just a story that man made-up to explain the universe?" Jeremy asked thoughtfully. It wasn't a new concept to him because he was battling a form of that agnostic philosophy within his new church.

"Yes, but more than that," Joey smugly continued. "I think that Christianity is the most insidious myth of all. And Catholicism might be the most dangerous interpretation of the most dangerous myth."

"What?" Rocky shouted in protest. Several patrons in the restaurant stopped their conversations and turned to look at the table in the back of the room. "What are you talking about?"

Even Thelma Harold stuck her head out from around the poker machine at the bar to see what the raucous was all about. After making a quick study of the situation, she turned back to the machine and hit the "draw" button.

Rich happened to be nearby after bussing a table when he noticed Jeremy sitting with the guys. "What's going on here boys?" he asked. "Jeremy, this better not be what I think it is. I warned you about talk'n religion in here…" One of the waitresses called for him from the bar. Rich lifted his head to signal that he was coming. "Change the subject." They all nodded in agreement. Then he moved on.

Simon was a little taken aback. He wasn't used to this kind of conversation. Some of it he had heard before and had even contemplated himself. But, a great deal of what was being said was new to him, and he wanted to hear more.

When Rich had moved completely out of ear shot, Joey leaned forward and said, "Let me ask you this, Rocky. Which religion has started the most wars, huh? The problem is that your religion claims to have cornered the market on absolute truth. But, the church's history is rife with hypocrisy, hatred, racism, and violence."

"What? I don' even understand you half the time," Rocky said getting defensive. "What do ya mean? 'Rice'… what does rice have to do with anything?"

"'Rife' means…never mind," Joey started to answer in disgust. "Catholics claim that their little story explains all that we need to know about God and the universe. If that's not bad enough; then they say that there way is the only way to heaven. When in fact, if we take even a cursory glance at history, it reveals how Christians- and above all Catholics- used religion to kill, destroy, and conquer."

Rocky said nothing as his blood began to boil at Joey's accusations.

"No wonder we can't just all get along," Joey snapped. "Just look at Rocky's face. Catholics, and all Christians for that matter, are intolerant to any other possible beliefs or the slightest criticism about what their religion teaches. That means that, according to Christianity, every Muslim, Buddhist, or even Jew is going straight to Hades. Isn't that right, Jeremiah?"

"Well, I don't get the final say," Jeremy confessed with great compassion. "But, what the Bible teaches is that,unfortunately for them, if they deny Jesus Christ as their Lord and Savior then, 'yes'. Amazingly, he did not bat an eye, and he did not get defensive. His tone was void of superiority and his expression was of slight anguish. "That's why it is *so* imperative for Christians to…"

Simon looked over at Joey whose demeanor had changed significantly.

"That's the problem with you Christians," Joey said with great disdain. "I mean, I believe certain aspects of your story does reveal some truth about the universe. And I grew up in a Christian church, but that's just the way I was brought up. That's how I know all about what you call God and creation and all of that stuff.

"Suppose, however, I was brought up as a Buddhist in India or a Muslim in

Egypt. According to you, I'd be eternally punished just because I was unfortunate enough to be born and raised a different way. Meanwhile, anyone who sucks down some grape juice or chokes down a wafer goes through the pearly gates. That kind of mentality has started more wars and killed more people than anything else in the history of the world."

Rocky's fists clenched.

Jeremy looked at Joey and said, "I have heard that it has been said, 'We can all be wrong, or one of us can be right, but we cannot all be right.' God wants all of His children to be saved before it is too late. He is just, and right, and fair. And His salvation is available to everyone. That is exactly why everyone needs to hear the truth and have the opportunity to meet Jesus personally. That's why I came here tonight."

"You mean to know your truth," Joey retorted, raising his voice again. "The arrogance, unbelievable! So narrow minded. That's why we all can't get along, why we can't have peace in this world. It's because people like you who don't allow it. Where do you get off having a monopoly on truth? If you guys would just let people believe what they want to believe," he continued fervently. "No wonder the rest of the world hates Christians. If you guys would just take it for what it is- which is just a story- keep your beliefs to yourselves, and let everyone else believe what they want to believe, then our world would be a much happier place. Instead, you've got the whole thing so muddled-up to a point where some goofy-looking white guy in a funny hat claims to be infallible."

"That's it!" Rocky said reaching for Joey across the table and knocking over a few beers. The tavern went silent as people strained to get a glimpse of what was going on.

Rich came barreling around the corner of the bar. "Whoa, whoa, whoa!" he yelled. "What on earth are you doin', Rocky?" He reached out his big paw, grabbed Rocky by the shoulder and slammed him down into his seat as he glanced back around toward the room full of silent onlookers. After signaling to everyone that he had the situation under control, he spoke through clenched teeth to Jeremy, Joey, and Rocky. Simon marveled at how fast the whole thing spiraled out of control.

"Jeremy, what did I just say to you guys?" Rich asked, perturbed. He pointed his meaty index finger towards a small sign on the wall just to the right of the Beer Bong behind the bar. "What does that sign say?"

"No religion. No politics," Jeremy answered in an apologetic tone. "But, it was not my intent to talk about religion."

"Are you telling me you came in here tonight without wanting to talk about religion?" Rich asked pointedly.

"No, I honestly had no intention of talking about religion," Jeremy said. "I came to talk about a relationship with Jesus."

"That's it," Rich said. "All you guys gotta go! People have been complaining to

Jack about you, Jeremy. He's breathing down my neck about it. He said, 'Absolutely, zero tolerance.' Now, because you had to raise your voices and knock some bottles over, everyone in bar is waiting to see what I do, and word will get back to Jack. I guarantee it. I have no choice. This is a family establishment and the last thing we need is people talking about religion and politics. Folks come here to relax and eat in peace. Not get all emotional and stuff."

"What?" Will and Simon asked in unison. "Are you kickin' us out?"

"Sorry boys, but you're guilty by association," Rich said. "I told you, everybody's watchin'. Anyone who discusses politics, or religion, or Cubs vs Cardinals has got to go. That rule goes for everyone. Come on. All of you, let's go."

"Are you kidding me?" George asked.

"No, I'll get in deep with Jack if I don't do what he says," Rich said. "I'm telling you. Jack will hear about it this. He always does. He's in charge, and he makes the rules. If he makes a rule, then I don't have a choice, I've got to enforce it. If Jack said, 'No religion,' then that means 'No religion.' End of story. I'm not about to lose my job over something as ridiculous as this." He still had Rocky by the scruff of the neck. "And you. You come with me and calm down. The rest of you just go home."

Simon sat stunned for a moment. He thought that surely Rich was joking at first, but then he quickly realized that he meant what he had said. Obediently, Jeremy got off of his short stool and dragged it back where he had gotten it. After that, he picked up his Bible and offered the customers an apology.

"Sorry Rich, sorry boys," Jeremy said in earnestness. "I didn't intend for anyone to get in trouble. Simon, if you are still interested in talking some more about this later just give me a call." He reached into his pocket and pulled out a business card and handed it to Simon who was still in shock by the unexpected series of events.

"Yeah, uh, thanks," Simon said reaching for the card. He didn't know exactly what had just happened. Never had he actually witnessed two people argue so passionately about religion.

Rich escorted them towards the door, while Rocky went to cool off in the back room.

"I'll call you guys later," Rich said under his breath to Will and Simon.

Once they were out on the street, Joey said cheerily, "Wow, we've been banished. What a great story to tell everybody."

"That was pretty weird," Will said. "Oh well, I need to go home and study for that test anyway."

"Really? You're taking off?" Simon asked. Before Will could answer, Simon's cell phone rang. He flipped it open to see that he had already received a text from Rich. It read, "Sorry man...Come back around closing time." By the time he looked up, Will was already making his way towards his car.

Will called back to Simon, "Hey Simon, I almost forgot. Rich wanted me to make sure that you were going to be at the bachelor party Friday night. I've got classes the next couple of nights, so I might not see you before then. 6:30 sharp at the town hall, see ya there." He climbed into his old, rusted out BMW and drove off.

Simon heard the roar of a diesel engine and turned in time to see Rocky hanging out the window of his dad's shiny, fully chromed out Chevy Silverado. He pulled his shades down to the lower part of his nose, kissed his first two fingers and waved them into a peace sign before chugging down the road. As Simon breathed in the fumes, he watched the truck drive off. While he contemplated the series of events that led up to being kicked out of the Bethel tavern, he noticed again the prodigious grain elevators over the top of a late blooming maple tree that was just on the verge of sprouting its buds.

Joey and George pulled up in front of Simon. "Hey, man," Joey said. "That was wild wasn't it? I can't wait to tell the guys back at school. They'll think it's hilarious. What are you doing now, man?"

"I don't know," Simon answered. "Will and Rocky just went home."

"Jump in," Joey offered. "You can hang with us for a while."

He checked his cell phone for any messages from Jez, and then looked back to the tavern. Not having any better prospects, Simon climbed into the back of the massive Lincoln Continental. "So, what do a couple of great thinkers such as yourselves like to do for fun on a Friday night?"

8

SHUN EVIL

Simon scanned the vast array of movies from which to choose. Walking past the conquering hero action movies, the heart-warming romantic comedies, and the Disney feel-good family features, he meandered his way in-and-out of aisles perusing the selection. His mind was still distracted by what had transpired earlier at the tavern. He couldn't get Jeremy's words out of his head.

Meanwhile, Joey and George had already scattered throughout the video store hunting down a short list of classics. As Simon waited for them to locate their favorite movies, he made his way down the aisles. His random wanderings first took him down the row of video game rentals. With each step, the covers clamored for his attention with their bright colors, crazy fonts, and eye-popping artwork. Methodically, he strolled past the blood thirsty kill em' alls, the wacky beat the watchamajiggers, and the win at all costs sports-be-gods. But, he was disappointed to find nothing new under the sun. Sauntering around the corner into the next aisle, his eyes met The Teletubbies holding a birthday cake. With an abhorrent expression on his face, Simon sidestepped the row of kiddy flicks and ducked into the next aisle over. Before his naked, steaming eyes was a whole section of self-indulgent covers. Beneath a picture of a buxom young lady, a "Girls Gone Wild" video beckoned to his more temporal senses.

"Simon, what do you think?" George asked from several rows over.

Simon lifted his head up and squinted at George who was holding six movies in his hands.

"'Star Wars', man!" George said enthusiastically.

Simon gave an apologetic expression and slowly shook his head.

"You sure?" George asked, disappointed. "Oh man, but it's so awesome. We could stay up all night and watch the entire series."

"No, not that again," Joey bemoaned from the back of the store. "Every time we come here, you grab 'Star Wars'. Give it a break. How about 'Slacker Uprising,' that flick by Michael Moore?"

"No thanks," Simon replied, still perusing the low budget, shag carpet selections.

Undaunted, George and Joey bombarded Simon with timeless masterpieces like "Supersize Me" and "Lord of the Rings." Yet, they were unable to reach a consensus until they reached the last shelf. There, lining the entire back wall, was nothing but blood, guts, and gore. Joey and George looked at one another with gleeful approval.

"Oh yeah," they uttered in unison and high fived.

Even though Simon didn't share in their enthusiasm, he was tiring of the search.

"How about this, we turn it into a drinking game?" Joey said. "Each time somebody gets slaughtered, we each have to chug a beer."

"Yeah!" George answered while Simon raised his eyebrows with uncertainty.

"Get one with a high body count," George said.

"It's got to be classic though," Joey said, searching with his index finger.

"'Invasion of the Body Snatchers'?" George suggested.

"What are you, my grandpa?" Joey replied in disgust.

"No, I just have an appreciation for the oldies," George answered. "As a future director, I love watching the evolution of the horror films and how they progressed over the years. Even though certain elements overlap, they keep progressing, getting better and better as time passes."

"Here," Joey said moving deftly around a small child gripping his mother's hand.

"Excuse me, buddy," Joey said, smiling down at the little boy. The child, completely oblivious, didn't hear a word. His wide eyes were locked on a terrifying cover while his mom read the back of a romantic comedy on the shelf behind them.

"'Friday the 13th Part II'!" Joey said excitedly as he moved around the petrified child. "A definite classic with a high body count and a little gratuitous nudity. There's something for everyone to enjoy."

"Perfect!" George said in agreement.

"Oh man," Simon said. "That movie really freaked me out when I was a kid. I was about eight or something like that when I saw it for the first time. I was watching Nickelodeon one Saturday morning and flipped the channel down one to USA just in time to see this dude in a hockey mask drive a spear through this naked guy and girl 'wrestling'."

"Pretty scary, huh?" George chuckled.

"Oh yeah," Simon said. "I turned it back to the "The Munsters," but I couldn't help myself. I just had to flip the channel over to see Jason and his chainsaw. After that, I slept with my light on for like the next five years."

"Awesome!" Joey exclaimed. " 'Friday the 13th' it is. Besides the special effects are hilarious."

Clutching their highly acclaimed feature film, Joey and Simon made their way to the checkout, while George paused to see if they had the latest version of 'Grand Theft Auto'. Much to his dismay, it had already been checked out.

"Man!" George lamented. So, he made do with the next best thing.

Joey waltzed up to the counter, placed the movie next to the register, and then casually stepped back out of the way, looking at Simon expectantly. Reading his body language correctly, Simon reached into his pocket to retrieve a few crumpled up dollar bills.

"Hey, after we watch the movie, we can get online and let some 9-year-old on the West Coast kick our butts in 'God of War,'" George declared, holding the video game high in the air.

Without a word, Simon reached into his opposite pocket to scrounge up a few more dollars.

* * *

The killing rampage took its toll on the three of them as they struggled desperately to keep pace with the bludgeoning and the beers. Joey, who had obviously seen the movie multiple times, would tip off the next killing by preemptively declaring, "This is awesome, watch this! Watch this!" Then he would lip synch the last line just prior to the hacking and cackle with approval over the shrieks of terror. Failing to match their passion for multiple homicides, Simon would smile congenially and nod when the boys looked over to get his reaction. Joey and George's pleasure in the carnage was a typical reaction for a couple of teenage boys, but it reminded Simon of how terrified he was as a kid watching scary movies at sleepovers. It freaked him out to see the frenzied, euphoric state that other boys were whipped into watching masses of people being horribly mutilated. It was a very disturbing thing to witness. For some time, he declined invitations to spend the night at friends' houses. Now he was merely annoyed when they kept stopping the movie to go back and watch the carnage over again in slow motion. He was getting tired, and it was giving him a headache.

By the time the movie had ended, the three of them had each had more than their share of discounted liquor as evidenced by the degree of difficulty George had swapping out the movie for the XBox. As he swayed in front of the big screen TV while deliberately starring at two different remote controls, a Barbie-like anchor woman from CNN gave an account of a young girl being abducted in Tennessee. The network flashed several still photos of the beautiful teenager several times during the sensational story as Joey looked on, unfazed. Just as the talking head previewed the next segment on the War on Terror, George randomly pressed a button and 'God of War' popped up on the screen.

"Yes!" George said. "Got it!"

"It's about time," Joey snapped.

"Shut up! Grandma's system is a little different from ours," George replied.

Sifting through the shrapnel of discarded Keystone Light Beer cans, Simon would pick one up, shake it, look forlornly with the squint of an eye into the dark abyss, and toss it onto the coffee table. Nothing. From empty can to empty can he went, hoping against hope that he might discover a full one. He had understandably grown tired of watching the other two guys battle a couple of middle schoolers from Malibu. While George read the instruction manual out loud to Joey who was trying to master a finishing move; suddenly, his opponent picked Joey's guy up and ripped him apart.

"Whoa!" George proclaimed.

"No, he didn't!" Joey said and let out a forced laugh bringing his fist to his mouth. "Cool, I didn't even know you could do that! Flip to the page that tells us how to do that move!"

"Well, I don't mean to be an alarmist, boys," Simon began, "but, we are completely out of beer."

In truth, Simon's restlessness could be more attributed to yearning for Jez's company than that of his friends' ineptness at virtual killing. And it wasn't long before Joey and George became tired of Simon's drunken stupor monologue of his complete devotion to his new love. So, they made a mutually beneficial decision to hit the pause button and go on a beer run; not because it was early, but because they were young. So, Joey impaled one more enemy before turning off the game. The news popped on the screen just in time to catch another CNN anchorman giving an expressionless, anecdotal report of a spectacular homicide in Boston before giving a tantalizing tease about the most recent lottery numbers.

"Oh wow!" Joey said.

"What?" Simon and George asked simultaneously, looking back and forth from Joey to the newsman.

"I forgot to check the numbers on my lottery ticket," Joey said pulling out the piece of paper. "It was up to 225 million."

* * *

A long way from Easy Street, Simon and the two global warming alarmists squeezed into the front seat of George's grandma's 1988 Lincoln Continental that was parked in an alley next to the convenience store. Passing a forty ounce in a brown bag back and forth, Joey and George began to surrender to their most basic urge. Instead of going back to George's grandma's basement, they drove through the streets of Bethel past old girlfriends' houses, hoping against hope to see a light still on in a bedroom window. Their prospects diminished precipitously with each darkened house and unanswered text.

"Hey, what did you guys think of Jeremy tonight?" Joey asked out of the blue. "Is that guy unbelievable or what?"

"Unbelievable," George agreed. "He's always talking to us like we're complete idiots."

But Simon didn't respond. Instead, he was lost in the lyrics of Linkin Park and thoughts of Jez.

"What did you think, Simon?" Joey asked, picking up on his silence.

"Think of what?" Simon asked in sleepy haze.

"Of Jeremy, putting you on the spot like that?" Joey asked. "I thought that was so uncool, but what else can you expect from ole Jeremiah Warner. That's why I went after him so hard; then that simpleton, Rocky, got all bent out of shape."

"Oh," Simon said trying to recall the conversation, "I guess I hadn't given it much thought."

"Are you kidding?" Joey asked. "The guy's basically saying that you're going to Hades because you don't know Jesus Christ; whatever that means. And you don't take offense to that?"

"Wow, do you really think that's what he was saying?" Simon asked genuinely surprised. He hadn't personalized the argument like that.

"That's exactly what he was saying," Joey said. "That little dweeb is so closed minded, it's unbelievable. He's beyond drinking the Kool-Aid. He's sprinkling in the powder and stirring the pitcher. My philosophy professor at Harvard would have a field day with him."

"I'd love to see that," George said.

"Yeah, you will really get an indoctrination when you get to Modesto Junior College in the fall," Joey said.

"Modesto Junior College?" Simon said to George.

"Yeah," George proudly replied. "Hopefully, I can transfer to either UCLA after that to study cinema photography."

"Cool," Simon replied somewhat impressed.

"Anyway, the guy just doesn't get it," Joey continued on his rant. "He needs to lighten up and not take things so literally all the time.

"Who?" Simon asked.

"Who do you think, 'Who?' Joey said exasperated. "That dweeb, Jeremy."

"I really kind of thought he was asking me a pretty harmless question," Simon said.

"Oh, man," Joey said. "I need to get Rob on the phone so he can sell you one of his bogus life insurance policies. Everything he's saying is so exclusionary. Think about it. What percent of the earth's entire population would actually be going to heaven according to him? First, you would have to exclude anyone who never even heard of Jesus Christ. Then you would have to whittle down any alternative religions such as Islam, Buddhism,..."

"Liberalism," George added as he took another tug off of the bottle in the paper bag.

"Liberalism?" Simon said with a chuckle. "That's not a religion."

"...Judaism," Joey continued, annoyed at the interruption, "not to even mention like Native American religions and stuff like that."

Cruising listlessly through the darkened streets, George said, "Whatever, you knew what I meant."

"He wants to deny…whoever, from any other world religion, from going to heaven," Joey said angrily. "Even that's not enough. You would have to leave out the ancillary Christian religions like the Mormons and the Jehovah's Witnesses. Is he done sending people to Hades after that? No way. Even the Christians who are in the 'right' denominations who don't have Christ 'in their hearts' are denied. I just can't believe it. If there is a God, I sure hope he is a more loving God than that. 'And the greatest of these is love', right? Or something like that."

"You got that from an Alan Jackson song," Simon said in jest, starting to catch a second wind. "You have no idea where that comes from in the Bible, do you?"

"And I suppose you're some kind of Biblical scholar, Freeman?" Joey challenged. "Well, I know it's in there somewhere, isn't it?" he asked, still a little uncertain.

"Oh, I think it is," Simon said. "Yeah, it is. Don't ask me where though."

"But, you see what I mean?" Joey asked.

"Yeah, I never really thought about it like that before, I guess," Simon admitted.

"Tell him what you think God is really like," George said to Joey.

"I think that it's more like an 'it' than a 'he'," Joey gladly shared. "I think that this Being or Power that created the universe used to make itself known to man in ancient times. For instance, the story of Christ is like a metaphor of how that outward Being moved inward, and yet became more distant and mysterious at the same time. It's more like a common consciousness that we all share. And all these ancient religious legends are mere metaphors about us discovering and tapping into consciousness from unconsciousness. So, each of us is on a journey of discovery. Every single experience needs to be valued for what we learn from it. That's how we slowly unravel the unknowable and make it, or him, or whatever, knowable. That's why we can't criticize anyone else's experience, because they are very unique and tailor-made for each individual. I think that we each start our journey from our own particular geographic location and particular heritage and move from not knowing to knowing."

"Explain it to him like you explained it to me," George said. "That's how I was able to best understand it."

"Okay," Joey agreed. "Let's say everyone living in these small towns wanted to go to Chicago. You got your Mormonville, your Buddha Town, your Islam City and this Being, or God if you will, is going to give them all a very specific map to get to their ultimate destination. Don't you think that 'it' or 'he' is going to give each of them a unique map to find the road that leads from their town to Chicago? If there is a pervasive being in the universe, and he's supposed to be all about love, I think he would be more about making it easy to find the right road to 'it' or 'him'." Joey paused for a moment and turned to the back seat in order to see if Simon was tracking with what he was saying.

"I get it. Rand McNally is God," Simon said, having some fun at their expense. "Why didn't this being of yours just give us each a built in GPS that speaks to us directly? Or, even better, just start us all in Chicago from the very beginning?"

"Funny," Joey said wryly. "Okay, you make fun, but that's exactly my point. He wants us to learn from the journey itself. We need to cherish things like dead end roads and wrong turns, because we learn so much more from them. So, ultimately, no turn is a 'wrong' turn. They are all right.

"Because down each and every road we uncover more and more knowledge. And if we move far enough along the journey, we can become as educated and knowledgeable as the being itself. In effect, we too become apart of the great common consciousness."

"I think I know what you're saying!" Simon said. "It's like how I feel about Jez right now…"

Immediately, Joey and George both groaned.

"No, I'm serious," Simon said. "It's like the way that I feel when I think about her beautiful face. Are you telling me you can't learn more about this being or god you're talking about when you see beauty like that? And you can't tell me that life isn't supposed to be more about that feeling or at least a feeling like it." The car turned a corner and started down Main Street with the grain elevators in the foreground. Simon's eyes automatically ascended its walls to the metallic pinnacle. "It's…hard to put a finger on it. It's…"

"No, it's not hard to put a finger on it, it's in your loins," Joey said, as the three of them burst out laughing.

"No, no," Simon tried to say, but was having a hard time being heard over the sophomoric cackling.

Suddenly, from out of nowhere flashing lights exploded in the rearview mirror and a siren screamed.

"Oh man!" George said as his heart leaped from his chest. Quickly, he dropped the brown bag to the floorboard. In a panic, he looked for a place to conceal the undeniable evidence. George obediently bore slowly to the right hand side of the road, throwing the nearly empty bottle into the glovebox before bringing the car to a stop.

But instead of pulling in behind the old Lincoln, the flashing red and white lights shot around them, accelerating at a tremendous speed. Before they could fully comprehend their almost certain apprehension, they saw the ambulance screaming down Main Street and racing for the highway.

"An ambulance! Ah, man," George sighed in relief. "I couldn't get another ticket. My mom would have killed me."

"Go after it!" Joey said. "Let's see where it's going."

"Good idea," George said as he pulled back onto the road and laid down the accelerator of the powerful V-6. "I bet it's an accident."

"He's heading for the highway!" Joey said excitedly. "Catch up to it!"

As they attempted to narrow the gap between themselves and the ambulance, Joey and George speculated wildly as to where it was heading. They could see it clearly off in the distance over the flat fields and fledgling crops. Suddenly, it made a turn off of the slab onto a country road.

"Oh, man," George said, "I wonder if it's a car wreck. It looks like he's heading for Route 36."

"Could be, could be anything at this point, or anyone for that matter," Joey said, excitedly. "Could be the curse. Jessie Joseph strikes again, right?"

Simon turned his head from the flashing lights and stared at the back of Joey's head as his words hung heavily in the air. He again considered the veracity of the old folktale that Rob and the other guys had regaled. Without warning, the ambulance made another turn almost doubling back. Based on the direction that the ambulance turned, it narrowed the list of potential families and farmhouses that would more than likely be effected by the crisis.

"I'm betting it's a fire or something like that. Isn't the Silverson farm out this way?" Joey asked. "Hey, I have an idea. We'll head him off. Take the next right onto that dirt road."

Joey's plan seemed to work to perfection as they approached the speeding ambulance before it made yet another turn.

"Oh man, you're right. It is heading towards Mrs. Silverman's farm," George said enthusiastically. "I know a short cut." They wound their way around several back roads, turning to the right and then to the left until there was only one possible destination for the EMT. As the car approached from the back of the property, they drove onto a gravel road through a small cluster of trees. When they emerged, they could see the farmhouse, barns, and silos on the Silverman's property.

"It's Mrs Silverman's all right," Joey said smugly. "I knew it. I hope it's nothing lame like a heart attack or something."

"It still could be the curse," George said optimistically. "She does have grandchildren. Hey, wasn't Rob supposed to meet with her tonight?"

"I thought he was meeting with Jack," Joey replied. "Well, if it's something boring like a stroke then it's definitely not the curse, but if it's one of the grandkids, it'd be more than coincidental."

Simon couldn't believe the calloused nature of the conversation. He marveled at their detached, cold analysis of the situation. His heart was up in his throat as he looked towards the house with the flashing red and white lights reflecting off of the barns, sheds, and trees.

The car moved down a broad back road that appeared to dip around a bend before making its way up to the house. Each of the boys peered through the darkness trying to see anything sensational.

"I knew we could get here from that short cut," George boasted. "There are a ton of ways that we could have taken to get here, but there's only one that actually gets you through the gate at the driveway. I don't know why the ambulance went the way that they did. We know all of these roads like the back our hands. We go cruising all of the time."

Just as George finished his sentence, they turned a corner only to find two huge orange and white barricades adorning a sign that read "Bridge Out." There was no way to circumvent the creek. They would have to return from whence they came and make their way back around to the front of the house just as the ambulance had done.

"What?" George and Joey crowed at the same time with a barrage of profanity.

"There may be a 'ton' of roads that get *close* to the property, but only one that gets you inside the gate," Simon observed wryly.

They turned around trying not to get the big Lincoln stuck in a ditch before driving all of the way around to the access road and up the long driveway. By the time they retraced their steps, a sea of police cars, rescue vehicles, and fire trucks had made their way up to the house. The bright lights were almost blinding.

"Whoa!" Joey muttered. "Looks like this could be big."

When they had gotten as close as the barricades would allow, they noticed that none of the police officers, firemen, or paramedics seemed to be rushing around. Instead, they were standing in small clusters around the old, two-story farmhouse. Joey rolled down the window and got the attention of one of the volunteer firemen who casually walked over to the car and leaned down.

"What's going on?" Joey asked impatiently.

"False alarm," the young fireman replied. "Some old lady thought she was having a heart attack, but it's probably just a bad case of GERD."

"GERD?" George asked.

"Heartburn," the fireman replied.

"Oh," Joey and George said simultaneously, not bothering to conceal their disappointment.

"Any of you guys related to her?" the young volunteer fireman asked.

They all shook their head negatively.

"Then you guys need to be moving on," he instructed them. "We have to keep this area clear."

"Thanks for the info," Joey said as he reached down to roll up the window. The fireman gave a wave and headed back toward the rest of his buddies.

"Man, heartburn, what a bummer," Joey said in disgust. "Have you ever been so disappointed in your whole life?"

* * *

Rocky's father had fulfilled the promise that he had made to him regarding the severity of his punishment for breaking house rules. Like a thief in the night, his father stole into his room at 4:30 a.m. and roused him rudely from his peaceful slumber. Shortly thereafter, the calculated torture began. Long before breakfast,

Rocky had slopped the pigs, cleaned out the stalls, and watered the cows. Purposely, his father delayed the roofing of the rent house until the heat of the day.

Kurt Fields was a hard-hearted man who was unwavering in his firmly held beliefs. He prided himself in having a meticulous appearance. For as long as Rocky could remember, his father wore neatly ironed, short sleeve shirts, stiff, dark blue Wranglers, and steel-toed boots. Even though his livelihood consisted of dust and dirt, he kept himself spotless on the outside. Often after toiling in the soil, he would take out his handkerchief and work over his hands until they were completely free of any unseemly smudges. Being a practical man, he always had a pen, a notepad, and a tire pressure gauge in the pocket of his button-down shirt. Anytime he stepped outside he habitually donned a green, mesh John Deere hat that sat high on his head; for he was a creature of habit and as predictable as the setting of the sun in the West.

Every inch of the his property from the tractors and combines that he leased from First National Bank to the three thousand acres that he managed reflected his appearance. It was as meticulous and well groomed as the man himself. He had worked hard to portray a certain image to the public that would elicit the kind of respect and admiration that he had desired. And it had worked. For the most part, he was considered a highly influential, upstanding member of the community. As a part of that image, he demanded the same degree of perceived perfection from his dutiful wife of twenty-six years, and his one and only son who would supposedly carry on the family name. It was a heritage that had made them a very wealthy and influential family. Kurt Fields had exponentially grown the farm through investments, networks, coalitions, and shrewd dealings.

The shame of it all for Kurt Fields was that his only heir to all that he had amassed was an undeniable idiot and a major disappointment. In his mind, Rocky lacked the essential qualities that had been passed down from generation to generation, like cunning diplomacy, or grit, or just plain old horse sense. To Kurt, his son was as lazy as the day was long, and as dependent as a colt sucking at his mama's teat. It was a fault that he blamed on both Rocky's mother and her genetics. Mrs. Fields's primary goal in life was to keep her baby from ever experiencing struggle, trials, adversity, or confrontation. It was a dream that to date she had managed to fulfill. And her unbridled compassion for her baby left him virtually disabled.

Never once had it occurred to Kurt Fields that Rocky's lack of accountability might be attributed to his father never having enough confidence in him to give him any real responsibility, or that his son's lack of initiative might actually be due to his circumstances. The boy had always been provided with just enough to keep him satisfied with his present condition; thereby, robbing him of any drive or self-sufficiency. It is true that Rocky's ignorance combined with his reliance on his parents' provision made him easier for his father to control and manipulate, but it also made Kurt begin to wonder if his son would ever move out of his basement.

Long ago Kurt Fields had resigned himself to the fact that his son would never be the man he wanted him to be. And lately, with this new "Rapper" fad his son was into, it had gotten to the point that he could hardly stand to look at him. As a result, he pulled some strings and got Rocky a job spraying weeds for Monsanto for mere peanuts, so he wouldn't have to be around him all day long.

Rocky continued to desperately seek identity and approval from anything or anyone who would give it to him. He was not as big of an idiot that his father made him out to be. After all, he knew he would always be the black sheep of the family, even though it was his own father who urged him to skip Community College and go straight to work on the farm. It was merely the image of the perfect family that Kurt Land wanted to convey to the community. When it was useful, he would parade the family off to church, or the county fair, or a trade show, but, Rocky knew that he would never be as polished as his daddy's new baby; the Silverado.

What was he going to do? Would he ever dare trade the certainty of having his basic needs met for the rest of his life for the risk of venturing out to either succeed or fail on his own- merely for the *possibility* of having something more? Rocky paused the DVR as he looked around the basement that had been transformed into a makeshift apartment replete with kitchen, bath, big screen TV, wi-fi, and his own data plan. No. Even though Rocky had no equity, he would rather feign contentment, forgo his free will, fight off hopelessness, and accept his meager wage, all the while drowning in a sea of wealth. The small paycheck and sparse allowance would come like clockwork every month, regardless if he ever lifted a finger on the farm or sprayed a single row in the field. Most of his contemporaries would kill for that kind of security, but there was a reason he played the lottery religiously. Rocky was a slave with no shackles and prisoner with no walls. Even worse, Rocky was complicit in perpetuating his current circumstance. As long as his father was alive, Rocky would always sleep in the basement while Kurt Fields rested comfortably in the master suite.

By the time Rocky collapsed onto his futon in the basement, his blistered hands stung, his back ached, and his battered feet throbbed. He didn't even bother taking off his boots, let alone his clothes. It was a feeling his father wanted to impress upon his son. Rocky could here his father's words still reverberating in his ears "Work is hard", "You've got it pretty good here," "Don't we provide for you everything you need?", "Besides, where would you go? What would you do?" That illegitimate fear above all else gripped him as he aimlessly scrolled through the three hundred Direct TV channels.

He tried desperately to think of *what else he could do*, but it was of no use when he couldn't even imagine what he didn't know. Fortunately, Rocky's passive nature only left him disillusioned. A man prone to violence would have already burnt the farm down. Most of the time, Rocky did not consider his circumstances but accepted them for what they were. "It just is what it is," was his favorite mantra. However, something Jeremy Warner said at the tavern made his heart yearn for something more. Eventually, Rocky drifted off to sleep with wet streams cutting rivers of despair through the grit and grime embedded in his cheeks. He was stricken by comfort, robbed of self-worth, enticed by commercialism, and convinced of entitlement.

* * *

The bachelor party turned out to be just as Simon had imagined. Rob went to all of the trouble of reserving the Town Hall, providing several kegs of beer, and buying some pretzels. Outside of that, there wasn't much to it. The boys played cards, ate pork rinds, and puffed on Swisher Sweets from the local gas station.

To this point, the highlight of the evening for Simon was winning several hands of no-limit Hold'm Poker that Rich had seen many times on ESPN. Otherwise, it was about as lame as any event he had attended in quite some time. As the witching hour approached, Rob broke out the Lord Calvert and demanded everyone's participation in draining its contents. That was especially true of the bachelor who took a great deal of ribbing from Rich the entire night, starting with his gift of a gross of Trojans with an instructional video. Someone else had brought a shot-gun as an impractical joke. And there were over-and-unders on the number of years that the marriage would last.

To his credit, Will took it all in stride. He seemed more like a man being called to duty than one entering a blissful union. Until now, the events were very pedestrian. Outside of the change of venue, it could have been any other night at the tavern. Still, Rob adamantly promised his good friend a night to remember. From what anyone could gather from his inebriated slurring, he had placed several phone calls earlier to procure some "entertainment."

As the night wore on, Rob would excuse himself for a moment and then return to make a very dramatic announcement about the ETA of his personal gift to Will. The excitement increased as the alcohol took effect. Rumors circulated regarding the possible implications of the term "entertainment," but most were in agreement that there was a high likelihood that it involved nudity, dancing, and single dollar bills. When the party started all Simon could think about was Jez, but as the evening wore on and the spirits took their hold, even he began to share in the collective anticipation.

When the big moment arrived, Rich set up fold out chairs in rows facing a makeshift stage bearing a solitary chair that faced back towards the crowd. Rocky and Rob escorted the blindfolded man of the hour to center stage and plopped him down in the seat of honor. While Rich made a halfhearted, impromptu toast, Rob dimmed the lights, and Rocky set the iPod on some hip-hop ditty that nearly blew out the speakers of the archaic PA system. The town hall rocked while the young men clapped excitedly out of rhythm. A great clamor of whooping, hollering, and whistling persisted as Rob made his way with great fanfare over to the side door of the building. By now most of the young men were in a wild frenzy, and even Simon felt a grin creep across his face under the weight of his most basic instincts.

Rob shoved the door open before the first girl came out dancing through the doorway. She was scantily clad in a see-through nighty and little else. Simon held a cigar in one hand as he waved a wad of cash in the opposite hand. In a drunken stupor, he produced an ear-splitting whistle.

Suddenly, his hands slowly dropped to his sides as the entertainment, Ms. Jez Bell, sauntered her way over to Will, swirled her hair around a couple of times, and began her "dance". A flash went off in Simon's face before Rob put the cell phone down to his side, nearly falling over himself laughing. Amidst all of the noise of the cat calls, Rocky put his arm around Simon's neck and rubbed his head. Casually, Rob waltzed over and leaned-in to whisper into Simon's ear.

"Now we're even," he said smiling.

II

THE WAY

"Enter through the narrow gate.
For wide is the gate and broad is the road
that leads to destruction, and many enter through it.
But small is the gate and narrow the road
that leads to life, and only a few find it."

Matthew 7:13-14

9

THE BEGINNING OF WISDOM

Shannon, Sharon, Sean, and Mike danced in a group on the parquet floor while the other guests looked on. Playing to the crowd, the teenagers spun, twirled, and laughed hysterically, even though no one really took much notice. Lexus Helrigle and Wilson B. Livingood drew fielding drills on napkins, while Jackson and Ralph arm-wrestled at the kids' table. Next to them, Roger pretended to be shooting the flower girl with his index finger while Porker sifted through a bowl of mints, trying to find all of the blue ones. In the corner, Joey and George hovered guardedly over the keg of cheap, domestic beer.

To their right, Mara and Hannah Grace sat with Pastor Pete at a nearly empty table. They had been discussing the results of the meeting with the other clergymen in town, and they debated how to go about working the voter registration table Monday on Main Street.

Neither Mara nor Hannah Grace had listened very intently to what Pastor Pete had been saying. Instead they both were thinking back to Hannah Grace's wedding, one with nostalgia and the other with bitterness.

"Well?" Pastor Pete asked, always keeping himself busy with the duties of the church.

"Well, what?" Mara asked snidely. "You know, I can't hardly hear you over all this background noise!"

"What do you think of what I said?" Pastor Pete asked again politely, enunciating his words.

"Oh, I think that would be nice," Hannah Grace said with a forced smile, still not fully engaged.

"What did he say?" Mara replied in frustration. "I can't hear a dad-blum thing over this racket!"

"So, you'll do it?" Pastor Pete asked Hannah Grace with an expectant smile on his face.

"*Do what?*" Mara asked, leaning towards him with a pained expression.

"Of course, Pastor," Hannah Grace sputtered. "We're always up for an opportunity to serve."

After getting the confirmation that he sought, Pete turned to watch the newlyweds walk to the dance floor. When he did so, Hannah Grace dropped the veil of happiness, revealing her true feelings.

"*Help what?*" Mara asked, her voice crackling in anger.

"With the voter registration table on Main Street!" Hannah Grace replied, cupping her hand and yelling into her mother-in-law's ear.

As Mara stewed, a lovely young lady came up behind Pastor Pete and touched him on the shoulder. He turned first the wrong way and then the other. When he realized who it was he took the napkin out of his lap and began to stand. Mara looked at Hannah Grace with a very disapproving expression after being volunteered for yet another thankless chore that no one else would do.

"Now mother, please don't give me that look," Hannah Grace said almost apologetically.

"Well, if it's not our very own Hope Wiseman!" Pastor Pete said, reaching out to shake her hand. "It is nice to see you, as always."

"Oh, please sit, Pastor," Hope replied. "Looks like I will be joining you at this table."

"That's wonderful," Pete said, helping her with her chair.

"Ladies," Hope said with a beaming smile.

Hope looked over at Mara and Hannah Grace who offered their usual, polite nods.

"Are you and the girls all set to leave tomorrow?" Pastor Pete asked.

"Yes, it looks like the final number attending summer camp this year will be seven," Hope answered.

"That's two more than last year," he said with feigned optimism.

Hannah Grace and Mara strained to hear the conversation over the DJ blaring a bunch of clap-trap.

Mara leaned in to Hannah Grace and said, "I hear she made quite a scene at the faculty meeting yesterday, raising all kinds of cane about nothin'. 22 years-old, huh. And ain't all them others been there for years. Why, they probably got girdles older than her."

"Mother Rash, quiet," Hannah Grace replied, "she'll hear you. Besides, you know how young people are. They always think they can change the world. I wish I still thought that way. She'll learn soon enough."

"What she needs to learn is respect!" Mara chided.

Luckily, the loud singing to "YMCA" drowned out their conversation.

"So, you leave for summer camp right after church?" Pastor Pete asked Hope.

"Yes, from what I remember it takes about four to five hours to get there," Hope replied. "That should give us plenty of time to get settled in before dinner."

Across the room, Simon sat at his assigned seat, staring blankly at his bottle of Bud Light while picking at the label. He thought Jez might be the one he had been searching for his whole life. And now the euphoric feeling was gone only to be replaced by one equally intense but diametrically opposed to the first. He had been unceremoniously dropped from the heights of the heavens and now lay in an emotional chalk outline.

On the VFW dance floor, Will and his new bride danced to their first song as Mr. and Mrs. Will Thornchuk.

"Ah, homey'," Rocky said compassionately to Simon. "Don't take' id' so hard, know what I'm sayin'? Any dude would have fallen for her. Her body is smokin' hot. No doubt about it."

"Naaa," Rich slurred, pointing his beefy index finger at Simon over a small forest of empty Bud Light bottles sitting on the white linen table cloth. "That wadn't right. Not right at all. And ya know what...?

Simon looked over at him and lifted one eyebrow.

"...I'm sorry. I'm gonna make it up to you," Rich finished between swigs. "I mean, I feel bad...ya know?"

"Uh," Rob sputtered as he sat straight up in his chair. "Oh yeah, man. I mean, we all feel bad. You fell hard. Real hard. But, man, you should have seen your face! Wanna see your face? Look, I got it right here on my phone."

"Yeah," Simon replied. "I got the group text you sent out, remember?"

"I just can't believe that you didn't remember her from the strip club that first night you were in town," Rob said laughing. "You must have been snookered!"

"Yeah, I mean, I really thought I knew what you liked," Rich said, as he accidentally knocked over several long-neck bottles, prompting all of the guests to momentarily look over at their table.

"E-z, big fella," Rocky said as he righted the bottles. "Maybe you should slow down. Don't you gotta give a speech here in a sec'?"

"Shut up, maybe I do," Rich said as he surveyed the room and assessed the talent like a major league scout. "It's s'pose to be your speech anyway. But, hey, I gotta take care of Simon first, he's hurtin' real bad."

"No, no, no..." Simon said, concerned with Rich's insinuation, "I don't need anybody setting me up with any girls."

"Yes, yes, yes," Rich replied. "Jez just wasn't your type. I gotta find a good, wholesome girl..."

"No, don't do that," Simon objected. "I'm heading to Jersey tomorrow anyway."

"What? No! Why?" the guys objected in unison.

"Why?" Simon mocked. "I'm sitting at a reception in the back room of a V.F.W.- while the bar is still open out front to the general public mind you, with massive college loans,...penniless, with no job prospects, watching an old friend trying unsuccessfully to dance cheek-to-cheek with an extremely pregnant girl-who I'm not sure he even loves- who looks like she swallowed a beach ball."

They all laughed at Simon's rant as a smirk inched its way across his face .

"See, it's not *that* bad," Rich said, consoling his best friend.

"Yeah, besides," Rob chimed in, "you had no idea Jez was a...'professional'."

"Ah-man," Simon groaned, dropping his forehead to the table in shame.

"You just might want to make an appointment with Dr. Al-Banna to get checked out before you go to New Jersey," Rob quipped. "You don't need anything flaring up on the long drive."

"Great!" Simon moaned. "I'm gonna spend my last hundred dollars of still rolled-up singles on a co-pay to see if I might flare soon."

The entire table busted out laughing.

"There she is!" Rich practically yelled, careening his neck to see over the crowd of tables.

"There's who?" Simon asked with great trepidation.

Rich made a feeble attempt to straighten up his bow tie as he scooted back away from the table. "What you said is not completely true," he said to Simon. "Yes, you are at the Bethel V.F.W. watching a human tragedy play out before your eyes, but you do have several job prospects for some easy money- umpiring baseball games and working for the school district this summer. You got fantasy baseball, men's softball league, your best friends in the whole words- I mean world-, and an open bar.

"Besides, there's someone I want you to meet." He stood up, bumped the tabled, and knocked over the remaining empties.

"Uh, Rich," Rocky said, "I think they're calling you up to do the toast now."

"Come here, Simon," Rich slurred while trying to tuck-in his shirt tail.

"Oh wow," Simon said mortified, as the spotlight shone on their table. "What are you doing?"

"Get up, I want to introduce you to someone," Rich insisted.

Simon sat still and looked over his shoulder to give an apologetic grimace to the expectant crowd. "No, I'm serious," Rich said with a scowl through clenched teeth.

"But, Rich, I..." Simon started to say before remembering that Rich was a very large, intoxicated man.

"Ok, I'm up, I'm up," Simon said sliding away from the table.

"I'm gonna make this up to you, no one should feel like you're feelin'...no one," Rich said as he put his arm over Simon's shoulder and guided him across the dance floor. The spotlight followed them as the silent crowd looked on, confused. "I'll make it up to you. She's really cool. Don't get me wrong, she's not nearly as hot as Jez, but who is? We've all seen that..."

Simon looked at him sideways.

"...Anyway, she's cute, real cute," Rich continued. "You're gonna love her."

Rich stopped at the very edge of the dance floor in front of Hope's table with his arm still draped over Simon's shoulder. Mara gave them a disapproving once over and grunted.

"Hope Wiseman," Rich said, swaying unsteadily as Simon stared at the floor with his hands in his pockets. "I want you to meet someone. This here is one of my best friends in the entire world, Simon Freeman."

Hope sat with her mouth ajar in total shock. She lifted her hand up over head to shade her eyes from the intense spotlight, but all she could make out were two dark figures.

"Simon, this is Hope," Rich said, guiding him to a chair next to the completely mortified young lady.

"No, I really…okay," Simon stammered as Rich forcefully guided him by the shoulder into the empty seat.

"You two talk," Rich insisted. "You both majored in education for some stupid reason. Now, I've gotta go make a speech." Finally, he turned and teetered off in the direction of the stage.

"I am so sorry," Simon said, as Rich took ahold of the microphone and pulled out a crumpled napkin with scribbled lettering. "I had no idea he was going to…"

When Hope turned back towards Simon, he saw her face for the first time. She had the most beautiful big blue eyes that sparkled in the glow of the V.F.W. disco light.

"I have never seen Rich like this," Hope said as her eyes danced across Simon's handsome face for the first time.

Guests clanged their spoons on the sides of their glasses. Obligingly, Will and Rachel leaned towards one another and awkwardly kissed. Rich dropped the microphone to his side and rolled his eyes. It looked like a ballpoint pen in his giant hands. "All right, all right," he said with his lips too close to the microphone. "That was natural."

"How do you know Rich?" Hope asked Simon.

"Actually, I grew up in Bethel until I was ten," Simon replied, "but, I don't remember you. Have you lived here your whole life?"

"No, I moved here after graduating from college to teach first grade at the elementary school," she answered with a warm smile. "So, you're a teacher too?"

"Well, not exactly," Simon replied. "I never completed my student teaching."

Just then, an ear piercing screech came over the PA before Rich turned and took a few steps away from the speaker, awkwardly holding the microphone out before him.

"Whoa, that got your attention," Rich said followed by a series of expletives. "Sorry."

"You've never seen him drunk?" Simon asked Hope.

"Not like this," Hope answered. "He said he doesn't like getting drunk because he likes being in control, but he is in bad shape tonight."

"Ohhh," Simon answered, just now realizing that he had never seen Rich like this either.

"So, the best man's supposed to say somethin' at these things I guess," Rich said. "Ya always see in the movies and stuff that they have a hard time figurin' out what to say, but not me, I got plenty to say. Here…," he said as he lifted his napkin to his face. "Oh yeah. First, I have known these two my entire life. Will and I are best friends…no brothers…we're brothers. I don't remember not knowing Will. Me, Will, Shane, and Simon did everything together for the first ten years of our lives.

"I guess Rachel was around somewhere then," Rich said indifferently, "but, she was kinda invisible till we got some hair on our legs. Ha! Am I right, boys?" Rich said, turning to look at Will who smiled and nodded. "Completely invisible, till puberty hit. So, I guess you could say I've known Rachel ever since certain things, uh, developed," Rich motioned to convey his point, "know what I'm sayin'?"

With her teeth clenched, Rachel muttered something under her breath to Will who was smiling stupidly.

"Oh, Rich," Hope sorrowfully said under her breath.

"This isn't going well, is it?" Simon whispered to Hope.

One of the dad's stood up at one of the tables and started for the stage, but Rich had none of it.

"If you think you're man enough, Tom, come and get this microphone," Rich said with a scowl as the dad slid back into his seat.

Rachel glared angrily at Will who shook his head, "No".

"As I was sayin', I know these two people really well," Rich said. "Will was my brother- is my brother- and will always be my brother. That is why I agreed to be the best man. I wanted to show that nothing will ever come between us.

"And Rachel, well Rachel, I know her so well that I always knew her first dance with her new husband would be to that Jack Johnson song…what was it…oh yeah, 'Better Together.' Cause, yall know Rachel and I dated forever- all through middle school and high school. And I think it's the perfect song for her. To quote the immortal Jack Johnson, ah-hum:

"Love is the answer
At least to most questions in my heart
Like why we are here? And where do we go?
And how come it's so hard?
It's not always easy,
And life can sometimes be deceiving…"

To Simon's surprise, Jeremy Warner's message fleetingly ran through his mind as he heard Rich read the lyrics off of the napkin.

"'Deceiving', huh?" Rich continued. "But, but,…in the immortal words of Ms. Tina Turner, "…What's love got to do with it?…

"Am I right? See in other countries, at other times and other places, there have been many traditions and many ways to get people hitched," Rich said, stumbling on his words and swaying. "Arranged marriages, dowries, courtships…whatever, but in this great country of ours we have this wonderful tradition to date a little, have sex, then find out if you love the other person! Oh yeah, ain't that great? Yes, it's true. Pleasure trumps marriage in America!

"And ya just kinda keep swapping out partners until ya find the right one, or get tired of looking, or get too old, or too comfortable, or...somebody gets pregnant. Awesome, right? What a system. No potential problems there that I can see, except when, hypothetically, one person falls in love with a second person who leaves that person to go roll in the hay with a third person. That leaves the first person like that dude on "Indiana Jones and the Temple of Doom" who gets his heart ripped out with it still pumpin'."

Rich made sloshing, guttural noises as he mimed the scene.

"While the second person now has a baby with the third person," he continued, "and then afterwards they have to figure out if they can actually stay married during the times they don't *feel* attracted to one another anymore."

The wedding guests were frozen from shock.

"By all accounts, our current system of identifying a potential spouse is lousy. The divorce rate in this country is about fifty percent," Rich said as he turned to Will and Rachel raising his glass. "It'd be great if it were a batting average, but not so great for marriages. I don't know, maybe you two...excuse me, three...you three crazy kids can make it." He turned back to the guests and shouted, "Here's to being right fifty percent of the time!"

"To fifty percent!" Rob called out from his table in the back of the room. There were a few raw hand claps and then silence.

Rich drained his glass of champagne, dropped the microphone to the floor, kissed his fingers, motioned a "peace-out" sign, and stumbled towards the restroom.

"Oh no," Hope said with a pained look on her face. "That was terrible. I feel so bad for Rachel. And yet, at the same time, I feel awful for Rich too. Losing his high school sweetheart to his best friend can't be easy."

"Yeah," Simon agreed, suddenly feeling stupid about getting all torn up over a girl whom he only had known for a week.

"Yep, they dated nearly nine years, but she couldn't compete with the other love of Rich's life-"

"...Baseball," Simon said, shaking his head.

"Yeah, he was off at some tournament when they..." Hope said. "...You know... It's just small-town U.S.A. kind of stuff. You probably think we are just a bunch of hayseeds."

"No," Simon replied reassuringly. He paused. "What is a hayseed anyway? Maybe I can get you a drink and you can explain that one to me."

Hope cocked her head to the side, grinned, and then nodded affirmatively, "Diet Coke please."

Simon and Hope talked for hours on end through the dollar dance, the throwing of the bouquet, the slinging of the garter belt, and the showering of bird seed. Completely lost in conversation, the crowd slowly dissipated around them while they shared stories and laughed over common experiences in the education departments at their respective universities. Finally, as the DJ began to tear down, they realized that they were the lasts guests in the reception hall except for Rich who sat at a table by himself in the back corner of the room. He was slouched down in a fold out chair with his jacket off, sleeves rolled up, and tie undone. His bottom lip was filled with Skoal and his hands rested in his lap, one still holding onto a beer bottle that now doubled as his spit cup.

"Oh, Rich," Hope said with great compassion for the big-hearted giant.

Simon followed her gaze over to Rich. He was obviously ripped out of his gourd with disheveled hair and a far away look on his face. Simon and Hope made their way over to him.

"What's goin' on, big-guy?" Simon asked kneeling down in front of him and carefully taking the nasty bottle out of his hands. "Why the long face?"

"Let's get him home," Hope said, searching the table for a napkin so that he could spit out his chaw.

"Hey, guys," Rich slurred under his breath with dampened, bloodshot eyes. "You are the best two people I know in the entire world."

Simon and Hope looked at one another with sheepish grins as they put his massive arms over their shoulders helping the gentle giant to his feet.

"They're gone," Rich said wearily.

"What?" Simon asked as they made their way out the front doors of the V.F.W.

"They're gone," he repeated with his eyes nearly closed.

"You mean Will and Rachel?" Hope asked. "They'll be back."

"Yeah, they're just up the road at the Super 8 in Tuscola, I think," Simon added.

"Nah," Rich objected, "physically, they'll be back, but the people I knew- the two people who I loved more than anyone else in this world- left the day I heard what they had done behind my back, and they ain't ever comin' back."

Simon was staggered for a moment by the depth of Rich's pain.

Somehow, they managed to drag him over to the car and get him into the passenger seat. They stepped back, observing their friend who reminded them of a large, wounded beast.

"I'd better get him home," Simon said to Hope. "He's had a rough night."

"You'll never get him into bed by yourself," she said. "I'll come with you."

"I don't know, you sure?" Simon asked. "I'd hate to see you get yacked on or something."

"I'm a second grade teacher," Hope answered. "Do you really think that I've never been yacked on before?"

"That's probably true," Simon admitted. He started to shut the passenger door, but suddenly Rich caught it with his hand and whispered to them under his breath.

"Ya know what?" Rich asked. "Promise me, you two will never left me…left me?..leave me… like that." Then he leaned his head back against the seat and closed his eyes. Simon and Hope gazed at one another, sharing a moment.

As Simon started to close the door, Rich stopped it a second time.

"And promise me…," Rich continued, bringing them out of an awkward, intimate moment. They leaned in expectantly to hear his hushed words. "...to roll the window down for the drive home, cause I don't feel so good." In a flash, Simon moved quickly as possible to get the window down, but it was too late.

* * *

After they had gotten Rich into bed with a trash can resting near him for any foreseeable emergencies, Simon and Hope made their way to the front porch swing and sat down. It was a beautiful, peaceful night as the moths frolicked freely in the streetlight high above the sidewalk. From where they were sitting, they could see the now silent town of Bethel in all of its glory. The old house sat at the far end of Main Street catty-corner from the schoolyard. Behind the school in the background, Simon noticed, for the first time, the steeple of his old church rising high above the treetops. Without being too obvious, he glanced over at Hope as they slowly swayed on the swing.

"I don't know what Rich was talking about," he thought to himself. "She's really cute, but more than that she's also very, very cool."

"What?..." Hope started to say breaking the silence and making Simon jump. She giggled and said, "I didn't mean to startle you."

Simon grabbed at his heart jokingly, "No, that's all right. As a licensed public educator, I trust that you know CPR?"

"Is that what you need- CPR?" she asked softly. They looked into each other's eyes for a moment, until Hope smiled brightly.

"Maybe," he replied.

"I *am* trained in CPR," she joked, "but, I am very judicious about whom I administer it to."

"What do you mean?" he said playing along. "I thought you were legally bound to help. So, even if I were choking or something, you wouldn't perform the Heimlich on me?"

She shook her head no.

"Nice," Simon replied coyly, "so, I'd have to throw myself onto the back of the closest chair or something?"

"Well, I might bring you the chair," Hope answered with a laugh.

"That's cold," Simon replied. He was beginning to like this girl.

"What time is it?" she asked.

Simon looked down at his watch, and answered, "It's a quarter till three," he said. "Wow, it's late. And you've got to leave tomorrow, right? Wasn't that what you were saying earlier?"

"Yes, after church," she said regretfully. "Besides, daddy always says, 'Nothing good happens after midnight'."

"I would have to respectfully disagree," Simon thought to himself as he looked at Hope's delicate features.

"Do you run?" Hope asked unexpectedly.

"Only when chased," Simon replied, wincing at his own cliché answer.

"That's too bad," she said. "I was thinking it might be nice to have some company when I go in the morning. Hey, I have an idea, why don't you come to church with me after I run?"

"What? Where?" Simon asked.

"Right there," Hope said, pointing to the steeple rising up behind the school.

"Pastor Pete's church?" Simon asked. "That's where my family used to go. Well, sometimes. At least on holidays."

"Then you should know the way," Hope said.

"Yes, but I haven't been in years and…" Simon started to say.

"You aren't afraid of a little church'n are you?" she asked. "The worst thing that can happen is a little singing off key, or sitting in someone else's seat, or falling asleep during the sermon. Pretty harmless stuff really."

"No dancing with snakes?" Simon joked.

Hope shook her head, laughing.

"And what's the best thing that can happen to me?" he asked.

She just shrugged her shoulders playfully.

"I don't have a problem with church," Simon said. "I just haven't been in a while. That's all."

"Great, it's a date then," she said with a laugh. She jumped out of the swing turned around and put out a hand to help Simon up. He looked down at the hand and reached his out to accept the offer.

"It's late," she said. "I need to get going, but I will see you tomorrow just before ten on the church steps." She made her way down the porch and out to the street.

"How can I resist such an offer?" Simon asked leaning against one of the pillars of the porch.

"You can't," Hope said, before giving a most pleasant wave goodbye.

Simon stood on the porch in the stillness of the night and watched her car drive off. "She's really something," he thought, as he scanned the tiny, quiet downtown.

Suddenly, he heard the deep, guttural heaving sound coming from the house and cringed.

"Ah, man…!"

* * *

When a ray of light finally made its way across the room with the rising of the morning sun, it momentarily rested on Simon. He rolled over a couple of times, smacked his lips, and repositioned his pillow before the clanging of a bell struck a cord. Like a human rocket launch, Simon shot up out of bed and reached for the alarm clock. He was still wearing a pair of industrial, plastic gloves. The clock read 10:00 a.m. Letting a few expletives slip out, he showered, shaved, brushed his teeth, and rushed out the door.

By the time he raced up the steps and flung open the front doors to the tiny white church, the members of the congregation had just bowed their heads for a moment of silence. Simon paused in the doorway for a second before the creaky old door flung back and hit him in the shoulder.

Still with her head down, eyes closed, and hands clasped, Hope smiled and slid over a spot. After returning a few glances of indignation with a pained looked of apology, Simon spotted Hope. He stealthily tiptoed over to the pew and made an attempt at a soft landing. Just as he hit the pew, the pastor asked the congregation to rise. Hope could barely contain her laughter as Simon's face revealed his awkwardness. While the organist led into the intro, Simon leaned over and whispered in Hope's ear.

"I'm a little out of practice, give me some cues or something would ya?" he said with a grin.

"Fake it until you make it," she whispered back.

Simon had looked a little worse for the wear from the previous night, but when Hope turned towards him, she seemed full of life and vitality. She sang beautifully, while Simon mouthed the words a half-beat behind and slightly off key. Hope shook her head still smiling that radiant smile as she held out the hymn book in front of him.

By the time Pastor Pete had begun the sermon, Simon finally had a chance to survey the old church he had visited sporadically as a child. As he looked around, he was a little surprised that many of the faces seemed vaguely familiar to him. Some had not changed, or even moved, since he was there last. However, the crowd had thinned out. It was a sparse congregation of maybe twenty-five or so people in all. But, the memories flooded Simon's consciousness. A warm feeling swept over him, and he was glad that he came until Pastor Pete began his sermon.

It was titled "Working Out Our Own Salvation." It was as dry as butter-less, burnt toast and as long as a wait at the DMV. It wasn't long before Pastor Pete's monotone voice and didactic rhythm lulled him into a deep, inward cave of contemplation about everything accept what the man was saying. He could see the pastor's mouth moving without hearing a single word. Simon looked to Hope. She was not only listening intently, but she was also doing the unthinkable- scribbling notes on the church bulletin.

"Of what?" Simon thought with a puzzled look. "Maybe it's a packing list."

Over the course of the eternal twenty-minute sermon, Simon found himself continually looking back to Hope. When the sermon was over, he was the first to blurt out, "Amen." As the congregation began the last song, Pastor Pete told them to stand and take the hand of the person next to him.

"That's a good idea," Simon thought, as he looked over at Hope and then down at her delicate hand. She placed it deftly into his. Then she leaned forward, looking past him and subtly raising her chin. Finally, Simon got the message and looked to his right across the aisle at a frail, ancient woman who looked a little like a mole in a children's book. He took the hint and stepped sideways out into the aisle. The woman looked up through thick glasses and beamed from ear to ear. Taking her hand off of her cane, she slowly reached out for Simon's hand. He smiled politely, while inside he winced at the unpleasant feelings of her dry, wrinkly skin.

Reading the situation, Hope said to Simon in a hushed tone, "Be nice. She has dementia."

Through a gravely voice, the senile, old woman looked up at Simon and said, "So, you're the one."

Immediately, Simon's awkward grin fell completely from his face and his blood ran cold. He leaned back as the room spun. Suddenly, he was 8 years-old again, looking into the very same prune-faced woman with thick, bottle glasses. She had been the one who said the exact same words to him so many years ago. It was the very same memory that flashed through his mind the night Rob told about the legend of Jessie Joseph. His mind reeled while the congregation sang "...Oh no, you never let go, every high and every low, oh no, you never let go of me..."

When the song was over, Hope tapped him on the shoulder and made her way past him to the frail, elderly woman. She leaned down to the invalid and gave her a kiss on the cheek and said, "Mrs. Potter, I'd like to introduce my friend. This is Simon Freeman."

"Potter?" Simon thought.

"Simon Freeman," Pastor Pete called out from behind him. "I'm sorry I didn't recognize you last night. You've really grown, my goodness. It has been a long time I suppose."

Simon, still dazed, mechanically shook the Pastor's hand, "Yeah, uh, hello pastor. It has been a while."

"How is your mom?" the pastor continued. "I haven't seen or heard..."

Before the conversation could get any traction, Pastor Pete was whisked away by an elder who wanted to talk to him about the song selection for the service. Pastor Pete raised his hand apologetically as he was dragged away.

"You'll have to excuse me," Pastor Pete said as hurried off, "maybe, we can get caught up later."

Then Hope saddled up along side of Simon, slid her arm around his, and guided him out the front door.

"Were you worried that I wasn't going to make it?" Simon asked, trying to regain his composure.

"No," she said.

He feigned a disappointed expression.

"I had faith," she added as a matter of fact, "although, you were late."

"Well, you know how it is," Simon said. "I had to babysit Rich half the night..."

"Yeah, yeah, yeah," Hope replied. "Excuses, excuses…"

"Well, and I suppose you got your little run in this morning?" Simon asked accusingly.

"Yes, I did as a matter of fact," Hope answered.

"Oh yeah, how far did you go?" Simon asked playfully.

"Six," Hope answered.

"*Miles?*" Simon repeated.

Suddenly, Simon's phone rang.

"Oh wow," he said. "I forgot it was on. I am so glad it didn't go off in church."

"Yeah, it might have woken you up during the sermon," Hope joked.

"Ha-ha," Simon said encouraged by the thought that she had noticed him during the service too.

"Oh, it's Jeremy Warner," Simon said, "do you know him?"

"Of course, I have known Jeremy for about a year now," she said. "He's one of a kind, that's for sure. But how do you know him?"

"We met out at the ballpark a couple of times, and now he wants to get together with me," Simon answered. Feeling the need to further explain, he added, "I think he just wants a few coaching tips for his little league team or something."

"Yeah, uh, doubt it," Hope said. "If I know Jeremy, he's got something else in mind. Be careful with him. One conversation with Jeremy Warner might turn your whole world upside down."

Before she could elaborate, six giggling teens clutching cell phones came running over and surrounded Hope. They pleaded with her to get her things into the church van, so that they could leave for camp. She ushered them away but not before they took the opportunity to tease their summer counselor about her new "boyfriend".

"Girls, where's Sharon?" Hope asked, ignoring their playful banter after she noticed that they were still one short.

A little girl made up of mostly knees, elbows, and braces brashly answered, "She said she's not going to camp this year cause she didn't wanta hang out with a bunch of kids."

"Really? She turned in the permission slip," Hope said under her breath. She looked around and realized that Sharon hadn't been in the service either.

Unsettled at the discovery, Hope surveyed the crowd for Mara or Hannah Grace to get some sort of explanation before Pastor Pete made his way over to them.

"Oh, Pastor Pete, have you seen Mara or Hannah Grace Rash?" Hope asked.

"No, I'm afraid Hannah Grace was having one of her spells this morning," he answered with a grave expression.

"Oh, that's too bad," Hope said. In resignation, she turned back to Simon and said, "Oh well, we can't wait for her; we need to get going." She looked at the van now full of hyperactive girls before turning back towards Simon. "Thanks for coming this morning. Maybe you can take notes from the sermons, so you could get me up to speed when I get back."

"Maybe," Simon answered. "It's a definite 'maybe'. Will I be able to get in touch with you at camp?"

"It won't be easy," she said. "We have a very strict 'No cell phone' policy, but we do have phone privileges on weekends though. And we can write."

"Write? Like letters?" Simon asked. "So, what you're saying is that we can talk on weekends then."

"Or we could do that," Hope said rolling her eyes. "Maybe I could even make a trip back here. The counselors take turns working weekends throughout the summer. But being the head counselor, I have to stay at camp the first few weekends to deal with all of the homesick girls. Oh, but, here, let me give you my cell number."

They exchanged numbers before Simon walked her over to the cliché sixteen passenger church van. Hope leaned in and gave Simon an innocent hug. Still, it was enough for the girls on the bus to cover their mouths and shriek with glee. As they drove off, Simon waved thinking to himself, "She is so awesome." And it dawned on him that Hope could be a really good friend. "Strange," he thought. He had had plenty of girlfriends but never a girl who was a close friend.

He punched a text into his phone. It read, "Be advised, any incomplete notes from Pastor Sandman's sermons may be the result of pew induced narcolepsy. Just a warning."

Maybe Simon would look into that job at the elementary school and do a little umpiring on the side after all. He pulled out his cell phone to give Rich a call. When he did, Jeremy's text was still on the display. Indifferently, Simon responded, "Sure. See you then."

* * *

Rich's text was a little cloak and daggerish. It only said, "Be at the ballpark at 5:00 p.m. sharp," and nothing more. Simon had no idea that he was being roped into playing centerfield for Rich's church league team. How could he have known? After all, Rich didn't attend any particular church. It just happened to be the best thing going in Bethel for those clinging on to the sport that they loved so dearly. And Pastor Algood's fast growing church had the best talent around. So, it only made sense that Rich would lend his big bat to their noble 'outreach mission'. Rich in his usual manner had sold the team on Simon's skills and the potential he had to help their team win the league trophy. He had no way of knowing that by the time they took the field to beat down the Philo Presbyterian Church that Rich had already sown up a deal with Thelma Harold for Simon to work at Bethel Elementary.

They were to meet at 5:45 a.m. the next morning on the front steps of the school. Of course, Rich orchestrated the whole affair and wasted no time in securing Simon a spot in the umpiring rotation for their little league as well. By the fourth inning, Rich had called Rob, who had contacted his buddy Jack Lawless, to find Simon a place to rent. As luck would have it, Jack had just evicted someone the day before and agreed to show Simon the apartment that night around nine o'clock.

Even though he hadn't played in years, Simon lived up to the hype. Call it a gift from God, but you can't teach speed and Simon had plenty of it. He filled the gap, made a couple of diving catches, and even roped a triple down the line. The game proved to be more competitive than Simon had imagined. Initially, the concept was to evangelize to nonbelievers through something everyone enjoyed doing, 'meet them on common ground', but after two near brawls and one ejection, the only message Simon heard from Rich was, "Don't bring that weak stuff in here," after he hit a monster home run into the cornfield in right. When the game was over, Simon realized how much he missed the game he had dedicated so much of his life to playing. He could definitely see the allure of keeping it going a little longer. He was feeling good and had nearly forgotten all about the meeting with Jeremy, until he saw the scrawny youth director sitting in the bleachers waving wildly in his direction.

Up to this point, Simon had completely ignored Jeremy's text messages, but now he reasoned that if Jeremy was a friend of Hope's then maybe he was worth getting to know.

Rich was ready to celebrate the victory at the tavern when the game was over. It was a tradition that Rich had established in which the losing team bought the winning team a round of beers. Not surprisingly, it didn't take much prodding to convince the other players of its sensibility. After all, it was in the name of fellowship of course. Rich wasn't happy with Simon's request for a rain check, but he didn't have time to press the issue because the Cardinals and the Cubs were playing on Sunday Night Baseball.

After the crowd had dispersed, Jeremy wasted no time in getting to the heart of the matter.

"Where are you going, Simon?" he asked awkwardly, leaning back in the bleachers with his hands clasped beneath his right knee.

Simon looked around for a second and then looked back at Jeremy. His eyes gravitated to the drops of mustard and BBQ stain on Jeremy's shirt. "Uh, nowhere," Simon answered, confused.

"No, I am mean where are you heading in life?" Jeremy asked intently.

"I'm not exactly following you," Simon answered, "New Jersey, I guess."

"What's in Jersey?" Jeremy continued with his unorthodox line of questioning.

"A pharmaceutical sales job, money, an apartment or condo, a new car, I guess," Simon answered, perking up at the mere reciting of those prospects.

"I see," Jeremy said. His eyebrows furrowed slightly. "Do you think that is your purpose?"

"Purpose? " Simon asked.

"Yes, do you think that is God's purpose for your life?" Jeremy asked.

The question caught Simon off guard. They were two distinctly different things. Weren't they? Wasn't God a little busy keeping the whole world spinning and all to worry about what Simon was doing?

Then without any provocation, Old Mrs. Potter's words flooded his consciousness…"So, you're the one." The uninvited thought was followed by Rob's story about the curse, the hand on the cellar door, and the supposed haunting of the school.

Before Simon could comment, Jeremy asked a more pointed follow-up question, "Do you really think that it was an accident that you ended up here in Bethel after all of these years?" The question rocked Simon. Jeremy could see his expression change and realized that he must have hit a nerve.

Simon felt a tingle sweep over his entire body and the hairs stand up on the back of his neck. "The curse," he thought, looking down at the dust and dirt. Suddenly, the entire conversation about the town's old folktale replayed in his mind. As much as he wanted to, he couldn't dismiss what Rob had told him about the pattern of tragic deaths. And how a 'chosen one' would come and end the cycle. Could that be what Jeremy was talking about? He looked back up at Jeremy with his mouth slightly ajar and a perplexed expression on his face, wondering if he could trust in the youth pastor enough to confide in him. It was a crazy thought, but for some reason, it was not easily dismissed.

Jeremy, having had his own experience with revelations, read the situation and continued, "I don't think it's an accident at all. I don't believe in accidents. I believe in God's perfect will. In fact, I believe that it was predestined that you would not only come to Bethel, but that you and I would also be having this very conversation in this specific place at this specific time. God has a purpose for your life and he wants you to know what it is before it is too late."

Simon's face was flush. Jeremy's words were inescapable. He couldn't deny them. Simon had no choice but to meet them head on and address them. "What if it were true? What if it wasn't an accident that I came back to Bethel? What if I had been chosen for…something?" he thought. With his heart pounding in his chest, he asked Jeremy a question, "How can I know for sure if what you're saying is true? How can I know for sure that God has a purpose for my life? It all sounds so hard to believe."

Jeremy smiled and said, "That's what I've been trying to tell you. God wants desperately for you to seek him. 'For he who seeks will find.' And it's not as hard as you would imagine. His handprint is all around you, as well as within you. There is any emptiness inside you that only God can fill. You can feel it, can't you? It's undeniable. You know what I am saying is true. I can tell by the expression on your face."

"But, I must also tell you that if you're going to New Jersey seeking to fill that void with money, houses, car, women or anything else apart from God's will, then you're sadly mistaken. Those things will not make you feel important."

Jeremy's words cut to the bone. Simon couldn't express what had come over him. He had never experienced anything like he was feeling. It was like Jeremy had pried open the cover of his chest cavity and was reading off of the pages of his very soul.

"But, there's so much I don't get," Simon managed to say. "I don't understand. It's not a simple thing to just decide. I still have so many questions."

"Are you going to wait until all of the answers are revealed to you, before you seek what you already know to be true in your heart?" Jeremy asked, putting a hand on Simon's back. "Listen, God doesn't show us the plan all at once. That would rob us of faith. It would rob us of choice.

"You just graduated from college. You know that the proctor of the test wouldn't be able to find out anything about you, if he gave you all of the answers to the exam beforehand. No, there's only one way to live that is fulfilling. It starts with losing your life to find it. It's about serving and worshiping your Lord and Savior, Jesus Christ. Only then will you be able to begin to answer all of your burning questions."

Jeremy lost Simon on that one.

But before Simon could even articulate his question, Jeremy elaborated.

"As a follower of Christ, I don't profess to have all of the answers to all of the questions. In fact, there are many things that I don't fully understand myself. Maybe I never will. Maybe I'm not supposed to, but I do have the answers to the most important questions. There is nothing that we need to know about salvation that he hasn't revealed to us in God's inerrant word, the Holy Bible. He designed you and everyone else who is to be saved with an internal compass, so that when you read or hear his word with an open heart and open mind, that Truth will be revealed to you. And then you will know."

There was something moving within Simon. He was drawn to what Jeremy was saying and longed for it to be true, but still something else inside of him begged him to hold back, to doubt, to speculate, to second guess.

"Do you have any idea what you're asking me to do?" Simon pleaded in turmoil. "It's crazy! It doesn't make any sense. How can I be absolutely sure that if there is a God that he's calling me to do *anything*?"

"All you have to do is talk to him," Jeremy said. "If you want to know Him, you need to talk to Him like a son would talk to a father, or a friend to a friend, and that's what I'd like to do with you now before it's too late."

"Here?" he asked, looking down at his filthy clothes, and the unpretentious surroundings of the Bethel ballpark. "Now?"

"There's no better time or place than this time and this place," Jeremy replied, searching Simon's eyes. "Simon, I want to introduce you to your Lord and Savior Jesus Christ." The sun was setting in the West, and a soft orange glow reflected off what few clouds drifted through the soft blue skies. Both young men were sitting side by side, leaning forward with their forearms resting on their knees and their hands clasped. "Are you ready?" Jeremy asked. "He's been waiting anxiously for you to talk to Him and wanting for you to come to Him. Let's go to Him now in prayer." He reached out with his left hand and placed it on Simon's hands, bowed his head, and closed his eyes. Simon followed Jeremy's lead in awe and wonder of what was taking place inside of him.

"Dear God,…" Jeremy began. But before he could continue, a panicked voice called out to him from off in the distance.

"Jeremy! Jeremy!" called a voice off in the distance.

Both of the young men turned to see a middle-aged, woman hurrying towards them. She was carrying a flashlight in one hand and holding her chest with the other. Behind her followed a small group of adults and children alike walking side by side. Each of them held lanterns and flashlights that danced in the twilight as they moved in their direction like a giant wave.

"Mrs. Kirby, what's going on?" Jeremy asked, startled by the inflection of fear and trembling in her voice.

As she approached them, they could see her pained expression.

"It's Randy, he's wandered off," she said, trying to hold down her tears. "Have you seen him? Have you seen him anywhere?" Jeremy and Simon shook their heads.

"Randy?" Simon asked. "You mean, the little boy I pitched to the other day?"

"Yes," Jeremy replied.

"Oh, that was you?" the woman asked. "Thank you so much. He was so excited. It was all he could talk about. Now we can't find him and I'm getting worried. We've looked everywhere we can think of. He's been gone for hours. He was playing with the dog in the back yard. And the next thing I knew…"

Jeremy climbed down from the bleachers and put his arm around the panicked mother while the search party continued, calling out his name. After talking with her for another moment, they understood her to say that someone had seen a young boy playing with a dog near the Embarras River. The search party had made its way through town and was moving towards the creek, thinking that he might have gone there exploring.

"We'll be glad to help," Jeremy assured the distraught mother. "Don't worry, everything will be all right."

Simon was already jogging towards the concession stand to get the flashlight that sat on top of the fuse box. He handed it to Jeremy and they joined the search.

Once they arrived at the creek just a mile or so down the road from the ballpark, the sun had set completely, and the moon had not yet risen. The group started at the bridge crossing the creek where a little boy had been spotted earlier. They split into two groups in an effort to cover each bank of the winding creek. The two groups then formed a long line at an arms length from one another. Carefully, they moved along with their flashlights reaching out into the darkness and calling the boy's name. Several men even waded into the shallows of the creek that alternately narrowed and widened. At some points along the way, the men from the two different banks could almost touch hands. Other times, there was nearly twenty yards between them.

As the search continued without a sign of the boy, the family began to panic. Those searching muttered to one another about the possibility of a drowning. After the group had made it nearly a half of a mile from where they started, the foliage thickened considerably, so much so that the people in lines were forced to separate and make their own way. As it turned out, Jeremy and Simon were walking side by side still in earshot of one another. Simon ducked under and then climbed over branches, using one arm to hold back the limbs while he held his cell phone out as a lantern in the other.

"*Randy!*" Jeremy called out with his hand cupped around his mouth. In the coolness of the evening, puffs of smoke, like tiny ghosts, rose from his lips and disappeared into the darkness. There was no reply.

The brush before Simon became so thick it almost formed an impenetrable wall. He put his arm over his head for protection, turned his back slightly, and backed into it with his rear-end. Forcing his way through, a cobweb covered his head. Simon quickly snatched at it, blowing out a breath of air. When he did, he tripped over something that was about knee-high and awkwardly stumbled into a small clearing.

"Nice," he said aloud wiping the cobwebs from his cheeks.

"What's the matter?" Jeremy called out, hearing branches crack and break to his right. He made his way towards the sound and came out of the woods into the open area as Simon brushed off his shorts and shirt.

"Whoa," Jeremy said, shining his flashlight all around. The narrow ray of light revealed a half-fallen iron fence that Simon had tripped over. Simon held out his phone, leaned forward, and squinted to search the expanse. As soon as his eyes adjusted, it became clear to him that they were standing in an old, unkept graveyard. The weathered tombstones of different shapes and sizes leaned awkwardly in the tall weeds.

"It's an old cemetery," Jeremy said, stating the obvious.

Simon's heart began to race. "It's the Potter graveyard!" Simon said in almost a whisper.

"The what?" Jeremy asked.

"I heard that the Potters had a small graveyard out here, but I had never seen it until now," Simon answered.

"Oh," Jeremy said, as he shone his flashlight all around at the various tombstones. Most of them were small and unmarked. But there were two that stood taller than the rest. They were large rectangular towers with a point on the top, not unlike a tiny version of the Washington monument.

"*Randy?*" Jeremy called out, carefully making his way to the other side of the cemetery. "There's no one here. We'd better catch up with the rest of the group. Their voices are getting further off into the distance. Coming?"

"Yeah, I'm right behind you," Simon said while trying to keep his voice from quivering. His mind raced at the implications of the discovery. "It did exist. Those guys weren't lying," he marveled. Suddenly, he thought of the curse again and the conversation he just had with Jeremy in the bleachers. And now a child was missing. Jeremy had said that there were no accidents. Was Simon really destined to return to Bethel to end a curse?

Jeremy continued into the brush, calling out for Randy. But Simon had to take a closer look at the graves. There were eleven unmarked, smaller stones and the two taller ones that appeared to have some words etched into them. Uneasily, Simon lifted his phone in front of his face and slowly moved towards the relics. His eyes were wide open and his heart resonated in his ears. Leaning down to look at the first stone, he nearly passed out while he processed the implications of what he read. "Adam Potter, 1932-1937." Simon staggered backwards. His head was spinning. The words of Rob, Old lady Potter, and Jeremy all collided in the forefront of his consciousness. He took in a deep breath and made his way to the second stone and read, "Jessie Joseph, 1918 to –". The stone had been chipped and crumbled where the last date should have been written.

Then he heard Jeremy's voice in the distance, "Are you back there, Simon?"

Simon was awakened from his trance. "Wha', yeah! I'm, I'm on my way!" he replied. With his mind clear for a moment, he thought of Potter's abandoned house. "Of course," he said under his breath. Simon took one last look around at the tiny, decrepit cemetery, shuddered involuntarily, and headed off in a direction tangent to the creek.

Having found the way to the path that he, Jez, and boys had driven down less than a week ago, he followed it to the abandoned farmhouse and the dilapidated barn. Just as he came around the tree line, a figure jumped out of the shadows and grabbed Simon from behind. Simon nearly collapsed in fear, letting out a muffled cry through the stifling hand that covered his mouth. Laughter resonated in Simon's ear.

"I don't believe it," the voice said. "Dude, you should have seen your face."

Immediately, Simon recognized Robin Ateitup's voice who was by now holding his stomach, bent over in laughter.

"Rob!" Simon exclaimed, while dropping several obscenities. "You nearly scared me to death! I thought I was a goner," he added giving a swift kick to Rob in the rear end. "What are you doing out here? Are you looking for that lost kid too?"

Rob gathered himself, "What? Oh yeah, of course. Looking for the kid."

"Hey, I saw the cemetery," Simon said, his face beginning to regain some color.

"What'd I tell you?" Rob replied. "I wasn't lying."

"No, I'm beginning to think that you weren't," Simon admitted.

"Were you with the rest of the search party coming down the river?" Rob asked.

"Yeah, then I stumbled upon the cemetery and thought of the old Potter place," Simon answered. "Were you heading there too?"

"Yeah, it was the first thing I thought of when I heard about the kid," Rob intimated. "Where's the rest of the search party?"

"They moved on down the creek," Simon said. "I'm sure they'll double back at some point. But, let's go check out the house."

"Tell you what," Rob said. "The house is kinda dangerous. You know, fallen' apart. I used to play in it all the time as a kid. Why don't I check out the house while you look in the barn?"

"Sounds like a plan," Simon said. "I'll bet he's hiding out in one of those two places."

The two of them walked up the driveway together. Once at the house, they split up. As Simon approached the run down, old barn he noticed the four boarded up windows running down the side of the building and a set of stairs that led to the entry. He soon realized that it must have been an old, converted church. It was comprised of only a sanctuary and simple choir loft that someone was now using to store bales of hay.

Simon called Randy's name a few times, turned around, and headed back towards the house. With the moon creeping up over the trees and providing a little illumination, Simon suddenly heard a muffled cry. He jerked his head around in every direction trying to get a feel for where the sound was coming from. Turning towards a rusty, old windmill at the top of a small hill standing opposite the barn and the house, Simon heard the sound again.

"Rob!" Simon called out towards the house. Quickly, Simon climbed up the embankment. When he reached the top the hill, he found a flat, rectangle of cracked concrete slab. Just beyond the windmill there was a slightly elevated square of cement blocks with boards running over the top of it.

"The well!" he said aloud. "*Rob!* I think I found him! He's in the well. Randy! Is that you?" Simon raced over to the platform, pushed back a couple of boards, and fell to his knees. Holding his insufficient cell phone over the small aperture, he moved his head around trying to see into the abyss. He alternately widened and squinted his eyes several times, trying to get them to adjust. The cries were more audible now. Finally, after holding the phone at just the right angle, he could see the top of a little boy's head.

"Randy!" Simon called. "Don't worry, we'll get you out!" He tried to figure out a way to climb down, but the hole was too small in diameter for him to squeeze into.

Panicked, Simon called down to the figure, "I'll be right back, Randy. I've got to get help." The figure raised its head, and Simon could partially see a face. He jumped up and ran as fast he could down the hillside towards the house, calling out to Rob.

As he neared the house, Rob made his way out a side door.

"Dude, they found him!" Rob yelled to Simon who was sprinting towards him. "I just got off the phone with Jack."

"What? No!" Simon said, panting. He grabbed Rob's arm and pulled him towards the well. "No, man! He's up there! He's in the well! We've got to get help." Simon was dragging Rob across the yard towards the hill.

"No, no," Rob said as he tried to stop Simon. "They found Randy on his neighbor's porch, asleep on some patio furniture or something."

Simon stopped for a minute. He tried to process what Rob was telling him. "That may be, but some other kid is stuck in the well then!"

"Dude, don't try to freak me out," Rob said coolly. "I know I got you with jumpin' out of the woods and the whole Jez thing, but this isn't going to work."

"I'm serious," Simon said with a pained expression. "I'll show you. Come on, we're wasting time." He climbed the hill as fast as he could. Rob obligingly followed him. But, when Simon got back down on his knees and peered into the well, he couldn't see anything. *"Hey! Hey kid!"*

"Very funny," Rob said after having finally reached the top of the hill.

"I'm telling you, he was there!" Simon exclaimed. "I saw him."

Rob leaned over and flashed his light to the bottom.

"Well, what do you see?" Simon asked with great interest.

"Nothin'" Rob said. "Jokes over. Come on, Jack said he wants to show you the apartment. I'll drive you."

Simon snatched the flashlight out of Rob's hand and fell to the ground on his belly over the opening, "I'm telling you. It was a little boy! I saw his face." When he shone the light into the well, all he could see at the bottom was dry dirt, crumpled papers, and some other garbage.

Rob began to sense that Simon was either sincere with what he was saying, or he was an amazing actor.

"Maybe it was a coon or an opossum or some other animal," Rob said with some concern while he leaned over Simon's shoulder, looking at the bottom. "Whatever it was it's not there now. Come on. Let's go."

Simon searched his mind over and over again for a reasonable explanation. He knew what he saw and what he saw was no animal. It was a boy. A dirty faced little boy. Then he looked back in the direction of the cemetery, trembling with deep labored breaths, wondering if he was completely losing his mind.

"Adam?..."

10

DID HE REALLY SAY?

Very little was said on the car ride back into Bethel. Rob texted back and forth with Jack, while Simon stared out the window. His own reflection in the window looked down over him as he tried to sort things out through the darkness. The car meandered through the streets across the railroads tracks to the far end of town opposite the ballpark.

Finally, they pulled into the driveway of an old house that appeared to have been converted into several different apartments. A brand new GMC Sierra 3500 sparkled in the headlights of Rob's car. Simon leaned forward, his eyes tracking an exterior staircase up to the second floor where a dark figure stood in the shadows on a landing. The flicker of his cigarette glowed beneath an orange face. The man was leaning on the railing as he looked down at them. Simon immediately thought back to his first night in town and the man standing outside of the Bethel tavern.

"That's Jack," Rob said, putting the car in park. "Now I told him about your situation, and he's cool with it. He's a good friend of mine, and a good guy to get to know if you're going to be in Bethel a while. I put in a good word for you, so he's going to cut you a break on the rent and let you go month-to-month."

"So, he knows that I'm a little cash poor right now?" Simon asked.

"Yeah, I told him," Rob replied. "He's assured me you guys can cut some sort of deal. I'm telling you, he's cool. But I can't stay, I've got to go run an errand. There's some business I need to attend to for Jack. If you need a lift back to Rich's to get your stuff, Jack said he'd help you out. All right?"

"Yeah, thanks. See ya," Simon said as he got out of the car and made his way up the rickety steps to the apartment.

"Simon Freeman?" Jack asked as Simon reached the top of the stairs.

"Yes, you must be Jack," Simon replied. "I think I may have crossed paths with you before."

"There's no doubt," Jack said through the smoke of his dangling cigarette. "Let me show you what I have to offer you. Follow me."

He took one more deep drag and flicked the cigarette over the ledge into the bushes below. Once he hit the light switch, Simon walked in and looked around the tiny apartment. He was pleasantly surprised that it was completely furnished. There was only a living room that doubled as the bedroom, a tiny kitchen, and a bathroom. Dirty dishes sat in the sink and the place was riddled with trash and soiled clothes.

"Sorry, I didn't have a chance to have it cleaned up before showing it to you," Jack said, "but, my boy, Rob, said he felt like you wanted to get into your own place before Rich's parents came home from Florida. Is that right?"

"Yeah, that's right," Simon said.

"I know it's not much, but my understanding is that this is just a temporary thing until you head out east for a job interview of some kind," Jack said.

When he turned, Simon saw his face for the first time in the light. He had dark hair peppered with gray, striking blue eyes, deep grooves in his cheeks, and a thick goatee. His clothes were very unassuming and commonplace considering that Rob said that he was the most influential man in the entire county. He was neither tall or short, large or small. Everything about him was ordinary and familiar, except his hypnotic eyes. As Simon followed Jack through the paltry accommodations, a suffocating, insidious stench overwhelmed him. He held his hand over his nose, as Jack turned on the light in the bathroom. When he did so, Simon noticed Jack's gaudy gold watch and an equally gaudy chain link bracelet.

"Awe, man," Jack said. He reached down, pulled the lever on the toilet, and closed the door behind him. "Renters," he bemoaned with a disgusted look on his face. Then he grinned joyfully revealing the origin of the deep grooves in his cheeks. "People are amazing aren't they?"

"Uh, yeah, speaking of which," Simon said. "The place is fine. In fact, it's about exactly what I expected. But, did Rob fill you in on my financial situation?"

"Ha, you mean, did he tell me that you don't have any money?" Jack replied as he moved towards the kitchen, kicking garbage out of his way as he went. "Don't worry about it. Rob said you were good for it. We'll work it out. There's always a way. You've got a job at the school, right?"

"Yeah," Simon replied. "You sure know a lot about my situation."

"My friend, you are in a small town, my small town in fact," he said, peering through mere slits for eyes. "Ain't nothin' that happens in this town without me know'n about it." He opened the door to the refrigerator. "Jackpot. You'd be surprised what people will leave behind when they are in a hurry." Pulling 5/6's of a six pack from the fridge, he continued, "God bless them. Bunch of deadbeats. Every now and then they're good for something. So, we got a deal or what?"

"A deal?" Simon asked, not tracking. "What's the deal?"

"Well, you live here as long as you like and pay me when you can," Jack said with a booming laugh.

"Sounds too good to be true," Simon mused.

"Then it probably is, ha!" Jack said. He burst out in laughter again and slapped

Simon on the shoulder. "Come on. Let's let this place air out while you and me finish off this beer."

They opened all of the windows before heading out the door. Simon glanced down at his watch as they descended the stairs. It was already 9:15 p.m., but he felt obliged to humor the old guy after he had been so gracious. In his heart of hearts he knew it would be best for him to get some rest. 5:30 a.m. would come early.

"Worried about gettin' some shut-eye?" Jack observed. "Thelma has always liked to get goin' at the crack of dawn. Woman never sleeps. Or can't. Who knows?

"No worries, you'll be fine. You have to take time to enjoy yourself a little in this life. After all, you only get one shot at it."

"You know, she always did intimidate me a little," Simon admitted, recalling his early school days.

"Who, Thelma?" Jack asked. "Ha, she's a tough old bird all right. I have had my share of run-ins with her over the years. Show up on time and you'll be fine, it's her pet peeve."

Coincidentally, two lawn chairs sat in the backyard of the house facing a cornfield. Stalks of corn stood no more than two feet off of the ground in perfect rows, flapping and fluttering in the warm breeze. The field declined at a subtle grade for miles, fading off in the distance into a small valley. There were no trees to obscure the view, revealing a clear, brilliant sky with billions of twinkling stars and a half moon that was just beginning to rise in the East.

Jack lit another cigarette, took a deep breath, and asked Simon, "Shall we?" He held the pack of beers up by the empty plastic ring and extended his opposite hand. "After you, my boy."

Simon walked over to the chairs and sat down as Jack handed him a cold Miller Lite. The sploosh of the can, echoed off the back of the house.

"That's pretty awesome," Simon said looking out at the horizon to the lights from the grain elevators and water tower of the closest town that was nearly ten miles away.

"Ha! Do you want it?" Jack said with a boisterous laugh. "I'll give it to ya. As far as the eye can see. I own it all; well, at least for all intents and purposes I do."

"Really?" Simon asked. "You must do pretty well then."

"Better than most," Jack said proudly. "A man can do well in a small town if he is shrewd enough. Why a smart young guy such as yourself could do quite well.

"In fact, you remind me a little myself when I was just startin' out- ready to take on the world and all."

Jack took a long look at Simon who sat unassumingly sipping on his beer while taking in the scenery.

"Life can be pretty simple, you know?" Jack said. "People have a tendency to make it so complicated. Take your friend Jeremiah for instance..."

"Jeremy Warner?" Simon asked. He'd almost completely forgotten about

Jeremy and what had taken place earlier in the evening. Seeing the apartment had been a nice diversion from all of the confusion and turmoil that had been organizing inside of him like a violent storm. "Funny," Simon thought, sitting here with Jack drinking a beer, the issues that had been so vitally urgent earlier now seemed virtually inconsequential."

He suddenly felt a little silly and embarrassed having been swept away by his emotions. That wasn't like him at all.

"That little guy, God love him, makes mountains out of mole hills," Jack said. "In fact, he makes Chicken Little look like he's on Prozac. I swear he gets more people all riled up and frettin' about nothin', including himself. And busy, goodness gracious, he's busy!"

"I know what you mean," Simon intimated. "I was just talking to him tonight."

"Oh yeah?" Jack asked, raising an eyebrow. "Did he give you his pitch?"

"His pitch?" Simon asked.

"Yeah, just about everybody's pitching you somethin'," Jack went on to say. "You know, he ain't much different from our pal, Rob, sell'n his life insurance, which he's pretty good at by the way, least better than you'd think. He's starting to really get it!

"But, Ole Jeremiah, ha! Before you know it, you're begging to buy everything he's sell'n. It's a thing of beauty really. He takes it to another level. It's his passion, something Rob can't manufacture. It's innate, somethin' you're born with. Oh, I've been trying to get Jeremy to come work for me for years and years. So, did he give you his pitch?"

After listening intently to Jack's every word, Simon felt a little ashamed of how naïve he had been earlier. "I guess he did," he answered sheepishly.

"And were you buyin' it?" Jack asked.

Without answering him directly, Simon glanced at Jack out of the corner of his eye.

"Ha! I bet you was," Jack said, hardly able to contain himself with glee. "I suppose he told you that he knew exactly how you was feeling and all'. It's a wonderful tactic, selling 101 really. It's a little ruse called empathy, ya know."

Simon nodded slowly. He felt like someone was showing him how a card trick worked.

"Ah, don't take it so hard, son," Jack said. "Many a person, some even more heady than yourself, have fallen for such a ploy. I 'spose he was telling yah' about the meaning of life and happiness and all that?"

Simon nodded again, confirming Jack's suspicions.

"And he had you, hook, line, and sinker?" Jack said letting out his familiar bellowing laugh. "No, there ain't no shame, no shame at all. We all want to know how to be happy. And he was gonna give ya the secret, right?"

"Yeah, something like that," Simon said. "He said there was a void in my life that I was trying to fill with money and possessions and stuff."

"Did he really say that you wouldn't be happy if you had a little money?" Jack asked, leaning towards Simon with a raised eyebrow. "What's wrong with makin' a little money? What's wrong with being successful and enjoying yourself? That's the American way! No, son. There ain't nothing wrong, in my opinion, course, with setting a goal for yourself, work'n hard, and goin' for it. Find out what you're all about, test your mettle, ya know? See what's inside of you. To..to compete, to conquer your opponent, to win. Ha!"

Simon nodded in agreement. Jack was making a lot of sense to him. That's exactly why Simon left everything in Texas. And it was why he was traveling across the country to New Jersey. He wanted his slice of the American dream. Not that Simon had ever had money himself, but other people seemed to be doing just fine with it. He knew what life was like to be dirt poor, now he wanted to know what it was like to be filthy rich. Besides, the competition was what he loved most about sports, finding out if you were up to the task, and could do better than the next guy. It suddenly occurred to him that Jack had evidently competed and won an awful lot in the financial realm.

"Jack, what do you think happiness is then?" Simon asked, having finished off his first can of beer.

Jack pulled another one off of the plastic ring and handed it over to Simon without provocation. "Ah, now that's a good question," Jack answered, wiping down his goatee with his hand and looking off in the distance. "Ya ever see that movie with Billy Crystal where he's having a midlife crisis and goes with his buddies on a cattle drive?"

"Oh, uh, 'City Slickers', yeah, that's a classic," Simon said with a smile.

"Do you remember the part when he's on the cattle drive and Jack Palance tells Billy the meaning of life?" Jack asked, making sure that Simon was following along. "That one thing. It makes a lot of sense to me. I think life is finding that one thing that makes *you* happy and doing it.

"But it's different for each person. Everybody, whether they know it or not, is looking for that one thing. Some people just don't know it or have forgotten it. They get in a rut and stop look'n. We've all got dreams, just some people are on a journey to realize them and others are sittin' on the side of the road while life passes them by. That's why I think you're gonna be just fine, Simon. I can tell. You got that fire in your belly just like I had in my youth. People like you and me thrive on competition. We play to win. Not just win, but dominate."

Simon listened intently, because it was exactly what he wanted to hear. "What's your one thing, Jack?" Simon asked.

"What?" Jack said lighting yet another cigarette.

"What's your one thing that makes you happy?" Simon elaborated.

"Oh, that's easy, I love making deals," Jack answered, being mostly truthful.

* * *

147

With the sun barely rising above the grain elevators in the East, Simon stood on the front steps of Bethel Elementary School looking up at the grand, old building that was in complete disrepair. The front door was propped open by a curled up doormat. Simon took a deep breath, grabbed the metal handle and walked inside. Reeking of mildew, the entryway bore the mark of antiquity and decay. On either side of the front door, there was a carved out nook with a chipped concrete floor desperately in need of repair. The paint on the cracked walls had faded unevenly. Simon followed one of the cracks all of the way up the wall to the fifteen-foot ceilings. Water stains peppered a false ceiling.

In front of him, a broad staircase led up to a modest sized landing. To the best of his recollection, the first and second grade classrooms could be accessed from there. On the opposite side of the landing another set of stairs led down to a second landing. From there a right turn would take a person down a long hallway to the gym, while a turn to the left led to a stairwell into the basement. Simon shivered when he thought about the boiler room in the basement.

On either side of the first landing, two separate staircases ascended to the third and fourth Grade classrooms on the third floor of the building.

Simon was filled with emotion due to the memories from days gone by. Even though it was much smaller in scale, everything was just as he had remembered it from the coat closets to the water fountain. It was all wonderfully preserved in structure but horribly decayed in appearance. He wondered if the building was that bad when he had gone to school there, and he just hadn't noticed. Or, had it really deteriorated that dramatically over the past ten years. Either way, Simon could understand the call for the referendum to build a new school.

With a slight sense of youthful trepidation, he resigned himself to the idea that this was as good of way to make a little money until the FDA approved the new drug and he was summoned to New Jersey for an interview. There was no sense in living out East where everything was far more expensive, and he didn't know anyone. He would work at the school, umpire a little baseball, and hang out with his old friends before he moved on with his life. Simon took in a deep breath, resolute with his plan.

Even though he heard nothing stirring from within, someone had to have propped open the front door. Simon decided to take a look around and find his old principal, Thelma Harold. She must have been milling about in her office waiting for him to arrive. As he walked up the creaky staircase, he lifted his eyes to the floor of the landing and saw a small black object, like a crumpled up cloth or rag lying on the dull hardwood floor. Feeling an obligation to begin his duties as a "custodial engineer", he bent down to pick up the object. Abruptly, he stopped and jerked his hand back when he realized that it was a small, dead bat curled up on the floor!

His heart skipped a beat before he calmed himself by confirming that the hideous creature was actually dead. He looked around and saw a broken, chewed up pencil under the water fountain. Simon picked it up and walked back over to the dead baby bat. Just as he reached down to lift up one of the wings, Thelma bellowed from the bottom of the stairs leading to the boiler room.

"Freeman!" she said gruffly.

Simon nearly jumped out of his skin.

"Right on time," she mused. "I like that. Follow me to my office so we can talk."

Dutifully, he dropped the wing of the bat from the end of the pencil and hurried after the aged principal who was already hobbling her way towards the office. She lifted what appeared to be a walky-talky of some kind up to her ear and spoke in a muffled voice.

"One of the janitors, Mr. Gettby, will be joining us momentarily," Thelma said, turning to look at Simon. She was even more hunched over and decrepit than he had remembered. He was nearly a foot and a half taller than the woman who used to terrify him. Her face was old and withered, her eyes hazy, and her hair so thin that he could make out the shape of her scalp. Following her into the office, he marveled at how she could have been such an imposing figure to him as a child. They marched through the front office past the secretary's desk into to the principal's office. It was a place Simon dreaded as a student, and because of that healthy fear, he never even once gave a teacher a reason to send him there.

Thelma turned and pointed her bony index finger at him. "Sit," she commanded in a scratchy voice.

Simon flung himself quickly into the uncomfortable, wooden chair sitting in front of her desk, "Yes, ma'am."

"How's your mother doin'?" Thelma asked, as she took off a thin jacket and placed it on a hook behind the sturdy, oak desk. The entire room was littered with pile after pile of manila folders and stacks of papers. The walls were lined with a faux wood paneling from the seventies and dusty, crooked pictures of teaching staffs from the beginning of time. And there directly behind her large, green, vinyl chair hung the primary instrument of fear from his grade school days. It was the infamous wooden paddle with a handle that was taped for a better grip and holes drilled into the business side of the instrument.

It didn't even occur to Simon until now that Thelma was probably the principal at Bethel Elementary when his mother had gone to school some thirty odd years ago.

"Fine," Simon replied. "She lives in a small town in Texas with my aunt…"

"Norine," Thelma said, finishing his sentence. "Yes, I remember. I won't even ask about your dad. I know all about that sordid affair too. He never did keep his promises. Here's what I always tell the kids whose deadbeat fathers skip out on em'. He's the one with the problem, not you."

"Yes, ma'am," Simon replied, once again the pupil. He was thoroughly impressed by how lucid Thelma was despite being an institution in her own right.

She was nearly as old and decayed as the school building itself that she had resided over for the past half of a century, or more. Now she looked more like a gargoyle perched over her desk than an administrator.

"That's the problem theses days…" she began to say before Mr. Gettby entered the room carrying buckets, rags, and cleaning materials. "Oh, Mr. Gettby, this is Simon Freeman. Simon, Mr. Gettby. He has been a janitor here for six years now. You probably remember Mr. Cross. Goodness, he's been here nearly as long as I have. Gettin' old. Anyhow, they'll be your supervisors. You'll report to them primarily. After today, I'll be on vacation for a short spell and then spend the rest of the summer over at my trophy shop. Mr. Cross is working on the boiler over at Philo Elementary till he gets the dad-blasted thing fixed. Seems he's the only one who knows how to bring 'em back to life every year. Calls em' his babies. Anyway, until he gets back, it'll just be you and Mr. Gettby here in Bethel. Got that Gettby?"

"Yes, ma'a,," Mr. Getty replied flatly. He was considerably younger than the seasoned principal. Simon guessed that he was in his early to mid fifties. Befitting for his line of work, he wore a filthy, buttoned down light blue shirt, tattered blue slacks, and dark brown boots smattered in flecks of paint. Moreover, he had one of those bowling pin body shapes in which his hips were so low that he constantly needed to tug at his pants just to keep them up. It didn't help matters that he had a massive key ring hanging from one of his belt loops.

Bending down to set the bucket and cleaning supplies on the floor revealed a serious need for a belt or suspenders. When he stood up again, Simon got a good look at his face. He had fat cheeks, a double chin that jiggled when he nodded, and thinly greased hair that wrapped around his head. Not surprisingly, the man reeked of heavy cigarette smoke and sawdust.

As Thelma outlined the job description along with her expectations Gettby looked on, expressionless. He offered only "Yes, Ma'am," and "No Ma'am" at appropriate intervals. Otherwise, he revealed no sort of emotion or personality through his flat affect.

"And Freeman," she continued. "Every now and then I might need you to run to the bank for me to make a deposit or two. Can't have that insurance policy lapsing while I'm gone. I'll leave the instructions in my desk along with the envelopes. Here's the key to the drawer."

"Yes, ma'am," Simon replied, as he slid the key into his pocket.

"Now there is one special project that I want you boys to take on this summer," Thelma snarled. "It hasn't been done in ages and long overdue. I want the storage area in the basement cleaned out. Throw away or burn anything that we don't need no more. When it doubt, throw it out. Got it?"

"What's all in there?" Gettby asked with a slight inflection of agitation in his voice.

"Heaven only knows," Thelma answered. "I think that might be the source of our little infestation problem. All I know is it's packed to the gills, and it hasn't been cleaned out in years."

Gettby shot Simon a quick glance. Simon knew immediately what he was thinking and dreaded its implication. He had no desire to crawl around in a crusty old basement to clean out a room that was the probable source of any kind of "infestation".

"Thanks a lot, Will," he thought. "Easy money, huh?"

After Thelma had finished, Mr. Gettby turned for the door, and Simon took it as his cue to leave. Before he could get out the door, Thelma charged him with one last bit of advice.

"Now don't go at this thing like you're kill'n the snake," Thelma scolded. "Know what I'm sayin'?"

Both Gettby and Simon nodded obligingly, even though Simon hadn't the foggiest idea what she was talking about. After they left the office, the inhospitable janitor pulled out a cigarette and escorted Simon down to the creepy, old basement to check out the storage room. Simon could feel his skin crawl descending the steps to the damp and musty boiler room.

What exactly had she meant by 'infestation' to the school? Bats? Mice? Or even worse...*snakes*? The room was poorly lit with only a couple of bare bulbs. As a result, his head was on a swivel, peering about the far corners of the room for anything lurking in the shadows. Gettby tried a number of keys to the storage room before utilizing a pair of lock cutters that easily bit the clasp in half. The door scraped over the gravel floor as Gettby forced it open. He felt the walls for a light switch, but it was of no use.

"Probably some string ya gotta pull somewheres back in there," Gettby muttered, "but, you'll have ta' get through all this clutter to get to it first." He pulled a small flashlight out of his back pocket and shone it into the dark expanse, revealing a long narrow room that was jam-packed with all different kinds of unmarked boxes and unidentifiable junk. "Goes back there a ways. Room's probably twenty or thirty feet deep. I don't care what Harold says, we gotta get the school ready for the fall first. You can get to this when ya can."

Simon was trying to see around Gettby into the sarcophagus like room, replete with ancient spider webs, but Gettby shoved it shut before he could get a good look. Truth be told, he was more than happy to follow the Weeble Wobble of a janitor up to the 1st grade classroom.

"You can start here," Gettby grunted. "Take all these desks outside to the hose at the bottom of the fire escape and clean em' up. Here's a bucket, a rag, and some cleaner. I'll check back with ya round noon."

"Do you want me to get all of the graffiti off of them?" Simon asked with a smile, tracing his finger over a jagged carving in the top of a desk.

"It don't matter," Gettby replied, "Cross will probably clean 'em all again anyways. I'll be in the 7th and 8th grade rooms on the other side of the gymnasium if you need me for anything. Now, it's like Harold said, 'Don't go at it like you're kill'n the snake.' Take your time, plenty of breaks. It's a marathon, not a sprint."

Gettby wobbled off again leaving Simon alone to figure out what they meant by "kill'n the snake." He looked around his tiny 1st grade classroom in the soft light of the brilliant summer morning sun. Simon glanced at his watch. It was barely 6:30. Letting out a deep breath, he picked up the first desk and carried it out the door. One by one, he dragged all twenty-five desks outside, filled his bucket with hot water and soap, and got to work scrubbing them down. It was a disgusting job with thirty years worth of gum, dried glue, melted crayons, and streaks of magic marker. Determined to impress Miss Harold, Simon went to the task with fervor, scrubbing each desk inside and out until it shined like new. It was harder work than advertised, but by midmorning, he had finished every last one of them. Soaked from head to toe, Simon stood up, flung a towel over his shoulder, and surveyed his work with an air of satisfaction.

Just then, Mr. Gettby caught a glimpse of Simon out of the fire exit door to the seventh grade classroom.

"Hey, what do you think your doin'?" Gettby yelled with a deluge of profanity.

Simon looked around in confusion and then back at Gettby who wobbled quickly over to him like a hurried penguin.

"I was just cleaning the desks like you told me to," Simon replied in amazement.

"'I was just…I was just'," Mr. Gettby mimicked unkindly. "You was just working us out of a job was what you was doin'."

"What do you mean?" Simon asked, put-off by what he thought was a gross overreaction.

"You college boys; just bunch of idiots," Gettby snapped. "Are you paid by the hour or by the job?"

"By the hour," Simon answered a little defensively.

"Then why in God's name would you kill yourself cleaning all of these desks before lunch?" Gettby asked. "What are you supposed to do this afternoon and tomorra', huh? Didn't think about that, did ya? At this rate, your gonna be done in about three weeks and make about eight hundred bucks. No, no, no sir! And what-a we gonna do next summer? Huh? Ever think of that smart guy? You go and get it all done in three weeks and that's what they'll expect every year. Pretty soon they'll get ta' think'n, they only need one janitor! You gotta lot to learn, boy. Go to lunch and stay at lunch for the rest of the day! Got it?"

"Well, that doesn't hardly seem right, I…" Simon started to object.

"Got it?" Gettby asked again, shaking his head in disgust.

Simon could see that the old guy was about to blow a gasket. So, he resigned himself to follow the instructions of his immediate supervisor; after all, it was Gettby's school to maintain. Simon was only there for a summer at best and thought it wise not to buck the system.

"Yeah, okay, I got it," Simon said, dumping out his bucket of dirty water.

"No, you ain't got it, you're still work'n," Gettby said, as he yanked the pale from Simon's hands. "Go on, get. Go get lost. I gotta figure out what I'm gonna do with all of these clean desks." Gettby put one hand on his waist while he scratched his bald spot with the other.

Thelma watched through the blinds of her office window as Simon handed over his rag and schlepped off to the tavern with his tail between his legs. She held the blinds open with her raisin-like hands for a few minutes longer. Thoughtfully, the sage, old woman turned to look at the paddle on the wall before her eyes gravitated to a book sitting at the bottom of a large stack of manilla folders on her desk.

* * *

Simon couldn't wait to tell Rich about his morning, but when he entered the tavern, his buddy was nowhere to be found. After scanning the room, he noticed Will sitting by himself at the far end of the bar. Will waved him over just before taking a bite of a frog leg.

"What's goin' on, man?" Will asked before choking down his food. He pushed the sports page out of the way to give Simon a little more room. "The last time I saw you, you were drowning your sorrows at the reception. Now, word has it that you are Bethel's newest resident."

"Yeah, I guess a lot has happened over the last couple of days," Simon said pulling up a stool. "What about you? I'm surprised to see you here. I thought you would still be on your honeymoon."

"Na, we don't have any money for a real honeymoon," Will said flatly. "We just spent the night in Tuscola, walked around the outlet mall, and came home. Besides, I've got to work and get ready for the summer semester at OCC."

"OCC?" Simon asked.

"Olney Central College," Will said before taking a bite of sandwich, "and," he started to say before wiping his mouth with a napkin, "I hear you took that job at the school after all."

"Yeah, I started this morning, but you wouldn't believe what happened," Simon said.

After Simon explained the events that had transpired, Will laughed, picking up his last french fry and slopping it in Ketchup. "I told you, man," Will said. "It's a cush job. They don't want you to work hard. It's called job security. You know, it's all about supply and demand. The work at the school is in short supply. If you do too much too soon, there will be no demand for summer help, and you will be out of a job."

Wiping his mouth off one last time, Will threw ten singles on the bar and got up to leave. "Dollar dance," he said. "Get you something to eat, hang out here a while, and watch some SportsCenter. Besides, you need to get caught up on your major league baseball."

"Why's that?" Simon asked.

"Because now that you're staying, Rich is going to want you to permanently take over the vacancy in our fantasy baseball league," Will said. "If I were you, I would run by the grocery store, pick up the latest fantasy league magazines, find a quiet place in the school, and just chill out."

"Hey, speaking of Rich," Simon said. "Where is he?"

"Oh, he's running around like a chicken with his head cut off," Will replied, making his way to the door. "It's the opening day ceremony tonight at the ballpark."

Simon picked up his cell phone and texted a message to Rich.

Rich responded, "In Charleston right now, picking up fireworks. Can you umpire tonight?"

Simon pecked back his response, "Of course I can. But, fireworks? What, no 'fly over' by the Blue Angels? After all, it is Little League baseball."

* * *

After spending two hours at the tavern, Simon couldn't take watching the same episode of SportsCenter for the third consecutive time or eating another plate of greasy fries. With several new magazines in hand, he made his way back to the elementary school building by early afternoon. Simon was a little apprehensive about Gettby catching him back at the school, but he decided that he should at least be in the building until the official workday was over at three o'clock. It's not as if he had anywhere better to be or anything else to do anyhow.

When he turned the corner around the grocery store and crossed over the alley, he saw that the desks were not on the blacktop where he had left them. Tiptoeing through the halls of the school, he made his way up the first landing. As he approached the door of the 1ˢᵗ grade classroom, he could hear a group of teachers arguing with one another and Principal Harold. Simon peaked through the slight gap in the doorway, but the desks were nowhere to be seen. He took a quick glance around trying to imagine what Gettby had done with them until he heard Miss Harold's voice.

"Like I said, Miss Passimons," he heard Thelma say. "Hope had a prior commitment. She can't be hear to explain her side of it. There's no sense belaboring the point."

When he heard Hope's name, Simon saddled up closer to the room out of sight. Miss Passimons walked up to the front of the room with her grade book in hand. There were five other teachers sitting on fold out chairs in the nearly empty classroom facing Miss Passimons who began writing students' names on the board.

"As I was saying, we would be doing ourselves and our students a huge disfavor by having such a large failure rate," she stated. "So, I have taken the time to categorize the names of students who we need to consider moving on to the next grade level."

Another teacher spoke up, "If I could just piggyback on that," she said to Thelma who was perched at the edge of the teacher's desk with her arms folded. Miss Harold rolled her eyes and then motioned for the teacher to continue. "A child's self-esteem is so fragile. We need to do everything in our power to keep them with their peers of equal age. What good would it do to hold them back? Destroying their self-worth could possibly cripple them for the rest of their lives."

"Yes, Yes, self-esteem, got it," Thelma replied sharply. "But, how can you feel good about yourself if you can't read or write?"

A male teacher held up his hand. Thelma seemed annoyed by his formality. "Yes, Mr. Minor?"

"There's an even greater issue that we need to consider," Mr. Minor said. "With this high of a failure rate, we will most assuredly affect our Report Card from the state. We may have to go on a plan of some kind. We might lose state funding. And some teachers who are not tenured could even lose their jobs."

"Let's not get crazy," Thelma said irritated. "But nobody's going home until we get this thing figured out."

Miss Passimons continued writing the names on the board. Simon could hear the squeak of the chalk as she began to speak.

"The first student that we cannot afford to leave behind is Simon Adamson," she said with a tone of disdain.

"The boy can't add without counting on his fingers!" Thelma protested.

"Miss Harold, he is perfectly capable of learning anything he sets his mind to," Miss Passimons said. "Another year in first grade is not going to give him the proper instruction that he needs because that is not the problem. The problem is that he is undisciplined and without parental guidance. That's not going to change with another year in my classroom."

Mr. Minor raised his hand again.

"Bill, would you please stop raising your hand for pitty-sakes," Thelma said wryly.

"Oh, ok, well," he said. "Looking over the list of failures, it just occurred to me that if we hold back all of the students who are capable of learning but just not trying, then we will have extremely large class sizes. I don't think the school district has the funds for another teacher. Each of us could have thirty students in a classroom! How are any of the students going to get the individual attention they deserve? Not to mention that will virtually double the number of kids with learning disabilities and, by the way, the amount of paperwork that goes along with it."

Several of the teachers gasped and each of them began to speak at the same time.

Having heard as much as he had wanted to hear, Simon slinked his way back down the stairs to the landing that led down to the basement, but then thought better of it. He turned and stared down a hallway that led to the gym, remembering the small chorus room above the stage.

On the heels of that thought, he suddenly remembered Rocky's story of the mysterious footsteps, the sink that kicked on by itself, and Jessie Joseph. Without prompting, he again considered the graveyard on Potter's property and what it was that he saw in the well. "This is ridiculous," he thought, shaking off the series of strange coincidences. Resolute, he made his way to the secluded room where he would be out of sight and out of mind. Besides, it was the only room in the entire school with a window air conditioning unit.

Slumping down into a comfortable teacher's chair at the front of the room, he began perusing the stats, facts, and figures of the major league players. He leaned forward and pulled a folded up piece of paper from his back pocket. It was a list of the teams from Rich's fantasy league, which included a full roster of players who had been drafted. From there, he went to work.

Time passed quickly as he poured through the numbers in the remote confines of the quiet chorus room. When he looked down at his watch, he was surprised to see that it was well past quitting time. Simon closed his magazines, folded the piece of paper back up, and placed it in his pocket. He made his way to the door and turned out the lights, pleased by his findings in the research and confident in his strategy to formulate a team strong enough to challenge Rich's mighty fantasy league franchise.

* * *

Opening night proved to be an amazing spectacle. Simon could hardly believe his own eyes. It was a scene straight of out of the movies. The weather provided a perfect backdrop of azure skies and a picturesque sunset. Residually, people came out in droves, packing the bleachers, and sitting four deep in lawn chairs around Rich's little league mecca. The fence had been adorned with red, white, and blue festive half-rounds of bunting, reminiscent of the days of the "Gas House Gang". There were no Blue Angels, but somehow Rich had arranged for a parachutist to drop in from twelve thousand feet with the game ball.

Simon was more than a little jealous watching the four teams from Bethel take the field in their brand spanking new uniforms. The Yankees, Devil Rays, Angels, and Padres lined each of the base paths to the theme music from Field of Dreams, along with their coaches in full managerial garb. Simon had felt a little foolish when Rich gave him his official umpiring uniform, but he as he looked on at the lavish ceremony, he was glad to not be in cargo shorts and a t-shirt as he had previously planned. When the PA announcer read a player's name and number, the boy would step out and wave his hat to the crowd before returning to the base path.

Simon took a sneak peak at Joey and George standing behind home plate facing Old Glory flapping proudly in the breeze high above the ball field. Everyone stood as a barbershop quartet wearing red and white pinstripe jackets, white slacks, and boater hats began The National Anthem. The players held their hats over their hearts and most of the crowd followed suit. Jeremy Warner had to wipe a tear from his eye as the beautiful harmony rose to a triumphant pinnacle, signing the words Sir Francis Key penned, "...oh say does that Star Spangled Banner yet wave, o'er the land of the free, and the home of the brave."

Simon had to hold back the overwhelming flood of emotion. "Lot of dust floating around out here," he said to George and Joey over the enthusiastic applause of the massive crowd.

"I know it," George said, wiping his own eyes.

"Yeah, right," Joey said to them before bellowing out the most exciting words in English language. "*Play ball!*"

As the Padres prepared to bat and the Angels took the field, small children scampered in and out of lawn chairs playing tag, hide n' seek, and hot box. The smell of popcorn, hot dogs, and cotton candy permeated the park, and Simon was sure that he had died and gone to heaven.

The Angel's flamethrower, Ralph Livingood, took the mound and fired the first pitch to Little Randy Kirby of Jeremy's hapless Padres. Thanks to Simon's tutorial, Randy managed to get the barrel of the bat around in time to get a piece of a two-seam fastball and fouled it off over the backstop. Amid the cries of "Heads-up" Sharon and Shannon screamed and covered their heads. The ball caromed harmlessly off of the bike stand where the girls had been sitting.

Sean and Mike doubled over in laughter at the overreaction of the two young girls. Shannon waltzed over and gave Sean a hard slap on his chiseled bicep. He grabbed for her as she ran playfully around the bike stand in her Daisy Duke shorts and spaghetti strap blouse.

Mara looked on disapprovingly from her lawn chair behind the dugout down the third base line. She nudged Hannah Grace who was cheering on the underdog Padres. Hannah Grace ignored the entreaty at first, but Mara stubbornly persisted.

"What, Mother?" Hannah Grace finally asked, looking in the direction of her mother-in-law.

"Get a load of Sharon's friend, Shannon," Mara said with a sour expression. "Just like her mother. I'm telling you she is not a good influence on Sharon. And those boys look like trouble to me."

"Oh mother," Hannah Grace replied. "You know that Shannon has been Sharon's best friend forever. They practically live at my house. She's a sweet girl. And those boys... Well, they're boys."

"Exactly," Mara snapped. "And if you ask me, Shannon looks like a red hot tart."

"Well, as it so happens no one *is* asking you," Hannah Grace responded with a mortified expression. But then she stared forlornly at the young teens as though she was looking back through the worn out photo albums of her own memories. Hannah Grace gave a second glance over her shoulder to see her sweet Sharon leaning against the bike stand next to a boy who did appear to be quite a bit older. Nonetheless, it seemed perfectly innocent to her. She shook off the impulse to intervene and turned in time to see another Padre dragging his bat back to the dugout in shame.

Shannon yelled as Sean tried to put an ice cube down her shirt. She raced behind Shannon and grabbed her by the arms using her friend as a human shield. Sean overpowered the both of them and slid the ice cube down the back of Shannon's shirt. She shrieked and grinned cunningly. To Sean's delight, she shook out the ice cube from her shirt and threw it at him.

Mara was just about to get up out of her chair and take matters into her own hands when Pastor Pete walked up beside her.

"Hello ladies," Pastor Pete said to Mara and Hannah Grace. "Enjoying the game? It's such a beautiful night."

Mara glared at him with contempt as Hannah Grace politely answered, "Oh, hello, Pastor. Yes, it's a lovely evening."

"How did things go with the registration booth today?" Pastor Pete asked with a degree of guilt due to his absence. "Did anyone get signed up?"

"We actually had three register today," Hannah Grace said while still watching the game.

"Three in five hours," Mara said in a huff. "Hannah got sunburned."

"She did?" Pastor asked, genuinely affected.

"Oh mother, just a little," she said embarrassed. "I just got a little color. It's not a big deal."

"Oh yeah, I can see you got a little bit of sun," Pastor Pete acknowledged, as the crowd roared after a big hit by Ralph. "I meant to come up and check in with you, but I was trying to pick out some new music for next week's sermon. Evidently last week's..."

Hannah Grace nearly jumped out her seat trying to follow the path of the ball to the fence. "Get it Randy, get it back in!" she yelled.

Jeremy was jumping up and down in front of the dugout, imploring his outfielders to stop fighting over the ball while Ralph raced around the bases. As he crossed home plate, Joey gave an obligatory safe motion with his hands before brushing the dust off of home plate with a hand broom. Four runs scored, and as predicted, the game was looking like it would be decided by the mercy rule. Those prognostications came to fruition as Ralph sizzled through four innings with nine strikeouts. The last was a backwards K' of his classmate Parker. With a tear streaming down his cheek through the dust on his face, Parker walked to the dugout as the Angel's celebrated gleefully on the pitcher's mound. The parents of the Padres clapped out of devotion while the parents of the Angels cheered out of pride. Wilson B. Livingood picked up his son Ralph and swung him around in a circle for his dominant performance.

On one side of the field, Jeremy consoled his beleaguered boys, bowed his head, and gave thanks to God for the opportunity to play the game. Meanwhile, in the other dugout, Wilson B. started his postgame talk with a quote from Yogi Berra, "You can't win them all unless you win the first one."

Observing the scene, Simon felt a surge of adrenaline just by being a part of the game that he loved so dearly. It had been a long time since he had felt that way. By the time he had finished playing, baseball had become a job, and in the end, a major disappointment. But now, being on the field opening day with all of these young boys he once again remembered the fundamental pleasure of playing the game. He smiled and took in a deep breath as the Devil Rays took the field for the second game.

The second game of the doubleheader proved to be as good as advertised. Rich's Yankees may have been the reigning Champions, but the Devil Rays had a tall, left-handed fireballer of their own in Jackson Helrigle. Just before the first pitch, Joey called Simon and George in for a little conference.

"Let's stay sharp," Joey insisted. "This one might get pretty heated."

His words proved to be true as the game went back and forth through six innings. Each team had scored two runs and were deadlocked going into the last inning. The tension built over the course of the game with several close calls being argued from both sides. Joey even had to warn Coach Helrigle at one point for his belligerent criticism of the balls and strikes. Moms sat on the edge of their seats rubbing their hands together while the dads paced about the fence like caged animals. The players in the field chattered incessantly as the first of the Yankees came to the plate to start the seventh. Jackson put his hat back on top of his sweaty, red hair, and rubbed the ball in his bare hands before slipping on his glove.

The anticipation was gripping as Jackson proceeded to mow down the first two batters. With the intensity mounting, the Yankees' cleanup hitter strode to the plate with his big barrel bat draped over his shoulder. As the batter took a deep breath and dug his cleats into the dirt, the pressure was almost palpable. Joey diplomatically held his hand up towards Jackson until the batter was ready, and then he motioned for the ace to deliver the pitch. Sweat poured down his face and his heart pounded in his ears. Jackson glanced at his dad in the dugout over the top of his Mizzuno glove, and nodded. The crowd was nearly frantic as Jackson fired the pitch. He let out a grunt as it flung from his hand. The ball sizzled high and inside, just under the Yankee slugger's chin as he spun wildly out of the way. Several mothers jumped out of their chairs in protest while a wall of dads clutched the chain link fence and also made their displeasure known. Joey clicked his indicator and smugly scanned the incensed crowd.

Once again, Jackson looked over the top of his glove at his father standing in the dugout. He nodded, wound up, and delivered another fastball under the batter's chin. The fans went berserk. Rich, who was coaching third, came halfway down the base path, complaining to Joey who had no choice but to give Jackson a warning.

After a short meeting between the managers and the umpires, Jackson retook the mound and looked to his father one more time. This time he fired the ball over the outer portion of the plate. It looked as if they were trying to intentionally walk the Yankee's cleanup hitter. Unfazed by the brush back, the batter leaned far out over the plate and somehow managed to hit the ball with the meat of the bat. As it lifted high into the air, the crowd rose with it in anticipation. The home run cleared the fence by a country-mile and landed several rows deep into the cornfield. The bomb electrified the Yankees who swarmed their hero after he jumped on home plate, giving them a three to two lead.

After the next Yankee batter struck out, the Devil Rays had their chance to rally in the bottom of the 7th inning. The pitcher who had been in command through the first six innings now seemed to be tiring. After walking the last three batters at the bottom of the Devil Rays roster, the Yankee's hurler dug deep and struck out the lead off batter. Now with bases juiced and just one out, the Yankee ace faced the second batter at the top of the order. With the crowd at a near frenzied state, the two-hole hitter popped up a lazy fly ball to the first baseman. Now there were two outs. With the bases loaded, Jackson strode to the plate. Lexus walked down from the third base line and put his hands on both of his boy's shoulders, giving him some last minute instructions. Then he patted his boy on the butt and sent him to the plate. Joey could barely be heard above the noise of the crowd as the first two pitches just missed outside. With the count 2-0, the pressure was on the weary pitcher. After the catcher tossed him a new ball, the pitcher kicked the dirt in front of the mound and looked to Rich in the dugout for the signal. The pitcher nodded and got set to throw. The change-up drifted over the inside corner of the plate and Jackson crushed it off the barrel of the bat. The ball whizzed down the first base line just over Simon's head like a bad slice. The crowd exploded as Jackson sprinted towards first. But, Joey came running down the line giving the indication that the ball went foul, overriding Simon's call. Coach Helrigle nearly came unglued as he charged at Joey. At the same time, Simon came running down the first base line towards the cocky, young umpire.

"What are you looking at?" Helrigle bellowed. "That ball was fair!"

"Sorry coach, it had already curved foul over the top of first base," Joey said matter-of-factly as he started to put his mask back on.

"Whoa, whoa," Simon said, stepping in between the angry coach and the arrogant umpire. "No, it was fair. I saw the chalk fly into the air when the ball hit the ground. Besides, that really wasn't your call to make."

When Rich heard Simon's claim, he ran out of the dugout.

"Are you sure?" Joey asked, dropping the mask back down to his side. He was obviously miffed at Simon's challenge to his call.

By now, George had jogged down from his position as third base umpire. "It definitely looked foul from my angle," George said in support of Joey's assertion.

"No, I'm one hundred percent sure, it was a fair ball," Simon said.

"What?" Rich said angrily. "The call was already made. It has to stand as a 'foul ball'."

Joey looked at George and then back to Simon.

"Let's go take a look," Simon said, sure of what he had seen.

"Yeah, let's take a look," Coach Helrigle said in agreement.

"All right," Rich agreed.

The four of them walked down the first base line, kneeled down, and took a close look at the chalk. Thanks to all of the effort that Rich had put into his immaculate field, the foul line was straight as an arrow. It only took Simon a second to scan the white chalk line on the lip of the infield to find the spot where the ball hit. Clearly, there was an indentation on the line just as Simon had maintained all along. It was undeniable. No more evidence was needed.

Joey stood up and motioned fair ball and called the game. The Devil Ray players and parents went wild, while the proud Yankees cried and gnashed their teeth over the injustice that had befallen them. Lexus Helrigle patted Simon on the back and then ran to his team in adulation. He picked up Jackson, hoisted him up on his shoulder, and paraded him around the infield.

"Good call, 'blue'," Rich conceded to Simon still looking down at the mark.

"Game of inches, right?" Simon said as he put a hand on Rich's shoulder.

George was at a loss for words. All he could do was nod in agreement. He was completely baffled by how his eyes could have deceived him.

Meanwhile, Joey seethed with anger and burned with embarrassment for the blatant usurpation of power even though he had no right to make the call as it is in the by-laws of the rule book.

11

JUST DYING TO KNOW

It had been nearly three weeks since Simon had chanced upon the town of his childhood. And it had already been over a week since he took the job at Bethel Elementary School. Since that time he had gotten into a comfortable routine while waiting for the call from his uncle. In the morning, he would lazily perform some menial task that Gettby had given him and then retire to his secluded hideout, above the stage in the scandalous chorus room. Thelma was out of town visiting her sister in Indiana, and Mr. Cross had yet to fix the boiler at the Philo Elementary School.

As a result, Simon was completely unsupervised. Consequently, he spent his afternoons tweaking the lineup of his fantasy league team, catching a quick cat nap, or reading about the latest news on the school referendum in the local paper. After work, he would head straight to the ballpark either to help with Rich's practices, prep the field, or play in his own slow-pitch softball game. Afterwards, he and Rich would make their way to the tavern. Usually, the entire gang would reconvene at their usual perches at the bar watching baseball, arguing about their fantasy teams, and consuming large quantities of beer. Each night, Simon would close down the joint with the boys, customarily singing Frank Sinatra's classic mantra before stumbling his way back to the tiny apartment. It was all becoming very familiar.

The money was far from flowing, but it was enough to sustain his current lifestyle while he waited for his ship to come in. In the beginning, he was impatient and often edgy about the job in New Jersey- constantly checking his voicemail only to find messages from his mother or his aunt. But, as the days went by Simon resigned himself to the fact that things would happen when they were supposed to happen and not a moment sooner. He hadn't even bothered to explore what had led him to such a conclusion. Instead, he unconsciously chose to aimlessly drift through this new life and take things as they came to him.

Simon had also found himself thinking more and more about Hope who was still calming the fears of the homesick teenagers at church camp in southern Illinois. Over the past two weekends they had texted back and forth several times with quick bursts of playful banter. On Sunday night she chastised him in a long e-mail for not coming through on his promise to take notes from Pastor Pete's sermon. In the same correspondence, she asked him about whether or not he had met with Jeremy and what, if anything, had come of it.

He chose to ignore the latter question because he was still unsettled about that particular issue. It wasn't that Simon had purposely avoided Jeremy. It just so happened that Jeremy's teams were often annihilated in the first game of a twin bill, and by the time that the second game was over, the youth pastor was nowhere to be found. As it turned out, Jeremy was every bit as busy as Jack had suggested, so it was merely a matter of coincidence that they had not crossed paths since their last conversation. Still, Simon did promise Hope to record the minutes from Pastor Pete's next sermon, and that weighed on his conscience. He thought it would be more fun to provide her with his own interpretation of the sermons instead, just to keep himself awake. Hope was delighted to get Simon's commitment to start going to church either way and looked forward to receiving his notes.

Simon put down his phone after re-reading one of Hope's cleverly written messages. As he leaned back in the comfortable teacher's chair in the infamous chorus room, he dropped his cell phone to his lap and glanced up at the clock. He was only halfway through the morning and had already taken the garbage to the incinerator, painted over the doorway to the main entrance, and installed a new ceiling fan in the teachers' lounge.

Without warning, large raindrops pelted the window to the chorus room.

"Might not be any games this weekend," he thought, despondently looking out at the dark skies. Habitually, he picked up one of his baseball magazines. After thumbing through the pages, he found himself bored. Simon had already gotten in trouble once today with Mr. Gettby for working too hard. As the prospects of another long "workday" began to set in, Simon restlessly looked about the room for something to do. Void of purpose, he got up out of his chair, lazily made his way over to the window, and sat down on top of some bookshelves that had been built into the wall. Looking through the water-warped window, he decided to try and text Rich again. Just as he took the phone out of his pocket, it slipped from his hand and fell to the floor.

Simon cursed as he bent over to pick it up. When he leaned down to get it, he glanced at the textbooks lining the shelves beneath him. Wiping the dirt off the phone onto his shirt, he reached down and grabbed a 5th grade science book and began to thumb through the pages. After reading several sections, he realized how much he didn't know.

"Are you smarter than a fifth grader?" he mused out loud. "I guess not."

Then he made his way back to his favorite chair with the book in hand, sat back down, and continued reading. Surprisingly, he found it fascinating. The information was supplied in broad, simple terms that were very easy to comprehend and digest. As a result, he read through several units rather quickly before arriving at the chapters on the Big Bang Theory. He tried to imagine for a moment how a dense point of matter could spontaneously combust to create an entire universe, but he simply couldn't wrap his head around the notion.

Out of curiosity, Simon made his way back over to the bookshelf to see what else he could find. Thumbing through a 6th grade science book, he was again struck by his lack of knowledge regarding the Theory of Evolution. He tried the best he could to muster enough faith, but somehow he just couldn't rationalize the gaps in the hypothesis. Consequently, he flipped the pages back and fourth from a picture of a mitochondria to a picture of Darwin without seeing any family resemblance. Disinterested, he tossed the book back onto the shelf and exchanged it for a 7th grade history book.

Grabbing the world history book off the shelf, it didn't take long before he was completely engrossed reading the extensive biographies of Marx, Nietzsche, Freud, Lenin, Stalin, Mao, and Hitler. That killed most of the morning.

After reading short excerpts on Joan of Arc and Winston Churchill, Simon swapped the book for an 8th grade U.S. history book. By the time his ancestors had killed off the Indians, enforced slavery, dropped the atomic bomb, messed up the Bay of Pigs, and sold arms to the Egyptians, Simon's stomach protested adamantly; so he skipped the brief excerpts on William Bradford and George Washington and headed off for lunch.

As he replaced the book on the shelf, he peered through the streaks of raindrops running down the window and noticed a young couple briskly pushing a baby stroller down the sidewalk. He thought they looked familiar and then recognized them as the same couple that had been doing business with Wilson B. Livingood at the bank when Simon went in to get a cash advance. The man held out the umbrella over the stroller as his wife maneuvered it through the front door of one of the businesses next to the bank on Main Street. Above the entrance the sign read, "Helrigle Real Estate."

"Huh, Lexus Helrigle gives the loans at the bank, and Mrs. Helrigle sells the houses," Simon mused, "nice little racket. Keep it all in the family."

* * *

The young mother wiped her feet on the mat at the door while her husband shook out the umbrella. Before the door shut behind them, a secretary came bounding around her desk to greet them and get a look at the baby.

"Oh my, is she asleep?" the older woman asked while clutching her hands under her chin. "How old is she? Oh, she's just precious. What's her name?"

"Thank you, her name is Pearl, and she's eight months old," the mother said proudly, as she lifted back the cover to the stroller. "We were up half the night, so she's taking a little nap right now."

"Pearl, oh, how precious," she said again with admiration.

"We're here to see Claire Helrigle," the young lady said. "She's going to show us some houses today. Oh, I am Susan Cain, by the way, and this is my husband, Dan. Is she in?"

"Yes, yes, of course," the secretary said, rushing back to her desk. "I'll let her know you're here."

Behind the secretary's desk a beautiful woman in her mid-thirties emerged from her office to greet the virgin homeowners. She was well dressed in a smart business suit, high heels, and flashy jewelry.

"Mrs. Helrigle, this is Mr. and Mrs. Cain and their sweet baby girl, Pearl," the secretary gushed.

"Yes, hello Mrs. Cain, please call me Claire," she said as she shook their hands. "I spoke with you on the phone. You have a lovely family."

"Oh, thank you very much, ma'am," Dan replied. "We're really excited about getting out of our tiny apartment and into a house."

"Well, I pulled down a number of listings for us to take a look at today based on the amount that the bank approved you for," Claire replied, motioning for them to come back to her office.

Within the hour they had arrived at a simple farmhouse on the outskirts of Bethel. The gravel drive popped and grind under the tires of the black Mercedes as Claire handed each of them a piece of paper with a full description of the property.

"It's definitely a fixer-upper," Claire told them as she put the car in park. "No one has lived here for years. I mean it could be a real steal at this price if someone were willing to give it a little TLC. Not only could be a great starter home, but it could also be a nice investment."

Just then the baby let out a bloodcurdling scream. Slightly embarrassed, Susan did her best to calm her down quickly.

"Sounds like someone's hungry," Claire said turning to get a look at Pearl's face. "I remember when my Jackson was that little. He was hungry all the time- still is in fact. Seems like yesterday really. They can't talk back to you at that age. Just wait till she's ten. Oh brother."

"She shouldn't be hungry already," Susan replied with a slightly concerned expression. "I'll just let her suck on her paci until we get back in the car."

To say that the old house was in disrepair was a gross understatement. By the looks of the yard, no one had even stepped foot on the property in months. As Claire got the key box open, Dan and Susan looked at each other skeptically. Entering the foyer, it became readily apparent that the inside was in worse condition than the outside of the house. The entire interior was in shambles with dirty, cobweb-ridden sheets covering old pieces of furniture, holes in the floorboards, and giant cracks in the ceiling. Susan and Dan were nearly in tears trying to contain their laughter as they concluded their tour in the kitchen of the house. Before Claire could even say anything, Susan was already shaking her head while she bounced Pearl softly up and down.

"Don't you even want to take a look upstairs?" Claire asked. "They say that at one time this house was the most prominent in all of Bethel. And the land is highly coveted.

"Huh, I didn't notice this before, but there does appear to be a lean on it. I can ask Lexus about that if you'd like."

"Still, no thank you," Dan replied after he got himself back under control. "I think we've seen enough."

"Now before you say no," Claire said, getting out some papers. "this is a very fair price, but I think you could go even lower. I happen to have some insider information that the owners are feeling a little financial strain. Remember a big part of real estate is location, location, location. And this is a fantastic property with about two and half acres that butts up against the Embarrass Creek very close to town. You could either use the money you save in the purchase to restore this historical landmark to its original glory, or tear it down altogether and build your dream house. So, what do you think?"

Pearl cried all the way back to the car as Susan rummaged through the baby bag to find her formula. While Claire put the lock box back on the front door, Susan and Dan climbed into the SUV and burst out laughing.

"If you think I'm going to let our baby spend one night in that house, you're crazy," Susan said with a smile over Pearl's wailing, "and what is that thing up on the hill? Some kind of old church or something?

"No, there's no steeple," Dan replied. "It's either an old one-room school house or a barn, I think. But, I don't know, with my 'mad' skills, we could bring that place back to life and flip it," Dan said with a cheesy grin on his face. "I bet in its hay-day it was the envy of the entire county."

"Uh, yeah, I think I have more skills than you do," Susan joked. "Remember when you tried to put that lattice up in the rental? Besides, I don't see how even the best carpenter could resuscitate that. It's 'DOA', honey."

"So, I guess that's a definite 'no'," Claire said as she climbed into the driver's seat. "That's okay. We've got plenty more to see today. I just wanted to give you a sense of what's out there and what you can get for your money. My husband said that you guys are pre-qualified for $200,000, but I thought we would start with the lowest listings and work our way up."

Pearl's screams carried over a rolling meadow and echoed off the waters of the creek.

* * *

"Did you hear that?" Shannon asked dramatically as she scooted closer to Sean.

"Yeah, it's probably Adam Potter, wooo!" Sean teased as he baited the hook.

"Don't talk about stuff like that, you'll freak me out," Sharon said, lifting her bobber to see if she had anything.

"What are you afraid of?" Sean asked. "You've got Mikey to protect you."

Mike shot Sean a disapproving glare while he re-tied a knot. "It's probably a coyote or wild dog," Mike said confidently. "There's nobody around here. This is our secret fishin' hole."

"Oh, so we should be so privileged that you invited us," Shannon said, putting her hand to her chest purposefully. Abruptly, she kicked water at Sean, screamed, and took off running towards the field.

"No you didn't," Sean said. He dropped the pole, turned his hat around backwards, and took off after her. Sharon watched the two of them run around in the field before they made their way off into the underbrush.

"They're crazy," Mike said shyly.

"Yeah," Sharon agreed, not daring to look at him. She sat on a fallen log, hunched over with her knees together while clutching the fishing pole in both hands. After an awkward moment of silence, Sharon lifted her eyes towards the woods listening for her loudmouth friend who left her with this guy who for all she knew could be some kind of goon or something.

While Sharon searched the dense shrubbery with her eyes, Mike took the opportunity to get a good look at her. She was definitely young, but anyone could see that she had a cute face and the promise of a figure. Once developed, she would be as hot as anyone in school. He thought of the girls in his own class who considered themselves out of his league. Most of them, he remembered, looked like Sharon when they first started high school. There was no doubt in his mind that Sharon was special. He could see that. By the time she was a senior, she would be the most sought after girl in school, but for the moment, he was the only guy around. Nervously, Mike decided to take a chance and talk to her.

"So, you and Shannon are pretty tight, huh?" Mike asked.

"What? Oh, yeah, we're BFF's," Sharon replied. "That was so dumb," she thought. "He must think I'm such a kid." She made a feeble attempt to recover and said, "That's what we call ourselves, BFF's." "Ugh," she thought, scolding herself while rolling her eyes back in her head. "I bet he really thinks you're an idiot now," she thought.

There was another awkward pause before Sharon tried again to make a connection of some kind.

"What I mean is that we've known each other so long that we know exactly what the other one is thinking without saying a word," Sharon said, now beginning to feel a little more confident. "We're like identical twins, you know? Well, not identical. She's obviously prettier. All the guys think so anyway."

"I don't think so," Mike said, seizing his opportunity.

They shared a glance for a moment before Sharon looked away in ecstatic embarrassment.

"Oh, hey," Mike said, excitedly pointing at her bobber. "Set the hook, I think you've got one!"

From sitting on the hood of his dad's new truck on top of a bluff off in the distance, Rocky could see two tiny specks of people through a clearing. They appeared to be wrestling with a fishing pole. The deep thump of the bass from his rap music exploded out of his iPod into his ears as he stopped bouncing his head around long enough to take another swig out of his Coleman water jug. He was covered in dried dirt from head to toe having waded through muddy row after muddy row in his dad's bean field pulling weeds.

The old man was still putting it to him over his "lack of respect" after having found scratches down the sides of the new truck. Rocky put the jug down, scanned the weed-ridden field, and shook his head in disdain. His dad was obsessed with keeping his fields neat and clean, even though it hardly mattered at harvest time. What it really came down to was his passive-aggressive feud with Frank Moore and their self-described title for tidiest property. Often, his dad swore that Mr. Moore came in the middle of the night and sowed weeds just to antagonize the old man. Ironically, Mr. Moore made the same claims privately about Rocky's dad.

Rocky slipped his filthy gloves back onto his hands, swung his feet over the edge of the truck, and jumped down. "This is ridiculous. I could run back into town, get my sprayer, and take care of this field in twenty minutes," he mused. As the rain resumed, Rocky looked to the sky in anger. He kicked his cooler with all of his might sending its contents reeling. Then he took his gloves off, pulled open the door to the truck, threw them inside, and fired up the engine. "Forget this," he muttered profanely.

* * *

After lunch Simon was ascending the steps to the chorus room when the deep throttle of a diesel engine shook him to the core. He arrived at the window just in time to catch a glimpse of Rocky's funky sprayer contraption bouncing down Main Street at a high rate of speed.

Simon reached once more for the US history book, flipped open the cover, and looked for a date of publication, the publisher, and name of the author. The book was "American Destiny" written by Carnes and Garraty. It was published in 2002 by Longman Publishing. All during lunch something had nagged at him about what he had read earlier. It wasn't what he remembered learning in school as a kid. There were many major events that seemed to be absent from the contents. As he flipped through the pages, a hand grabbed his shoulder from behind causing Simon to nearly jump out of skin. The book went flying from his hands. Stumbling to the floor, he turned to see the figure standing behind him.

"Whoa, there," the stranger said. "I didn't mean to frighten you. You look like you just seen a ghost." The man reached out his hand to help Simon up off the floor. "I'm Andy Cross. And you must be Simon Freeman."

"Yes, I am," Simon said trying to regain his composure, "nice to meet you."

He wiped the dust off his pants as Mr. Cross reached down to pick up the history book that Simon had dropped.

As he stooped down to get it, Simon got a chance to get a look at the short, barrel-chested janitor. He appeared to be in his mid to upper seventies. His hair, dyed jet black, was smartly greased and pulled straight back. Simon took note of the stark contrast between the unkept Mr. Gettby and the tidy appearance of Mr. Cross with his neatly pressed, brown, buttoned-down shirt and freshly ironed tan slacks.

While Mr. Cross bent down to pick up the book, he had evidently spotted some smushed gum on floor. Quickly, he wielded a putty knife from his pocket and pried it off the hardwood. When the man stood up with the book in hand, Simon could see that he was a stout man, with a thick head, flappy, hound dog cheeks, and a slight gap in his front teeth.

"Here you go," Mr. Cross said thoughtfully, "I saw the light was on and thought you might be up here. They all make their way here eventually."

"They who?" Simon asked confused. Grabbing the book from the man's thick, calloused hands.

"The summer help," Mr. Cross said flatly. "Only air conditioner in the whole building besides Miss Harold's office, but don't nobody wants to go hang out in there, you know."

"Yeah, well, I..." Simon began to stammer looking around the room for a plausible explanation as to why he was there.

But before he could say another word, Mr. Cross held out his hand. "I just came to tell you, if you need me, I'll be in the 1st grade classroom doin' the floors. Gettby's over in Sidney gettin' some paint, but he'll be at the Philo Elementary building rest of the summer."

"Oh," was all that Simon could get out of his mouth. The guilt of his languid behavior overcame him. "Can I do something for you? Do you have a job for me?"

"No thanks," Mr. Cross said, looking around the room aimlessly. "If I need you, I know where to find ya. I've been gettin' this school ready every summer for nearly forty-seven years. Got my own little formula for doin' it, so, you know."

While Mr. Cross spoke, he seemed to have a restless, nervous energy about him.

"I'd be glad to do my part," Simon said. "Just let me know what you want me to do."

"That's mighty nice of ya," Mr. Cross said through the gap in his smoked stained teeth. "I might could use ya for an errand or two to the hardware store. Other than that, I don't need much help. As I say, I been at Bethel Elementary a long spell. Well, I gotta get goin'. Gotta get to them floors, ya know."

Awkwardly, he turned towards the door and hurried down the stairs.

"See you later," Simon said, dumbfounded.

But there was no response.

"That's an odd fellow," Simon thought to himself. It was funny how Simon hadn't remembered much about him from his old school days. Sure, he knew the name. He even recalled a few times when he was summoned by the teachers to fetch the janitor from the spooky, old basement. But, in his mind's eye, he could only recall a blurred, faceless figure that spoke little and grinned a lot.

Simon didn't know what to think of their meeting. Nor did he know what to do. After all, he was being paid to work at the school. Yet, no one, including Mr. Cross, gave him any work to do. He scowled and slid the history book back on the shelf. When the rain once again pelted the window, he looked outside to the street below where a woman wearing a business suit scrambled out of a black Mercedes. Using a briefcase to cover her head, the woman shut the door of the SUV with her hip before quickly shuffling in her high heels to the front door of the real estate office.

* * *

Pearl pouted and begrudgingly sucked on her pacifier as her mother desperately tried to comfort her baby girl. The child's almost mournful eyes danced while she scanned the features of her mother's face. Spontaneously, Pearl reached her tiny fingers up to grasp at her mother's chin.

Susan Cain paid her little attention. Mindlessly, she grabbed the baby's fingers and kissed them, swaying a little back and forth. Her attention was focused on the piece of paper that her husband was holding up in the front seat that described the next home on the realtor's list.

"It seems a little more reasonable," Danny Cain said with a raised eyebrow, "at least, it's right here in town."

"And built within the last 200 years!" Susan said with a laugh. "Who could live in that last house? There is no way I'd ever even consider moving into that ghost motel. So primitive. I wonder if it even had indoor plumbing or electricity. Seriously."

"I think it had one small bathroom downstairs," Danny said with a smile. "I totally agree with you. No way. But, hey, the next house is over 1,800 square feet with one and a half bathrooms."

Susan pulled the comp from his hand. "We'd all have to *share* a bathroom?" she stammered.

"Okay, but at least it is the right price," Danny said. "I just thought we'd get a little more for our money in a small town."

"Danny, the sheet says the house is eighty years old," Susan said exasperated, dropping the piece of paper to her side.

"Well, maybe it's been completely renovated," Danny responded optimistically. "Does it say anything about granite countertops or stainless steel appliances?... Oh, here comes Claire."

* * *

Hannah Grace blankly stared out her kitchen window. She was watching a young woman in a business suite scramble to her car through the rain on Main Street. The distraught old widow didn't even give it a second thought. Tears streamed from her eyes in concert with the rain outside. Lately, it had become a regular thing, but it hadn't always been that way. There was a time when she glowed vibrantly and her heart swelled. Most days she was able to control her pain. But, when the weather was dreary, it was dreary in her soul. She pulled down a glass form the cabinet and filled it with water at the sink before reaching for her prescription bottle. Hannah Grace dabbed her eyes with a Kleenex before prying open the bottle and shaking a small, pink pill into her wrinkled hand. When she tossed it into her mouth, she caught a glimpse of the picture sitting on the end table next to the couch in the living room.

After washing the pill down with a drink, she slowly made her way over to it. With her hand shaking, she picked it up and sat down on the edge of the couch. Hannah Grace's watery eyes searched the black and white photo of her husband, John. Although he had been gone six years, the circumstances of his dark demise still pierced her heart. She dropped her head and recoiled under the strain of sobs. Through her tears she looked towards her phone with slight trepidation- then thought better of it. Another moment passed before she caved in. She made her way to the door, grabbed a rain jacket, held it over her head, and shuffled out the door to Mara's house.

Mara jumped when she heard the front door of her house creak open. Quickly, she slid the photo album off the top of the coffee table and hid it underneath an old, dusty book. Before her daughter-in-law could see her, Mara hurried off towards the kitchen to dispose of her glass of "Angel's Envy".

Sensing something amiss, Hannah Grace raced to the kitchen. "Mother Rash," Hannah Grace said. "What on earth are you doing?"

"None of your business!" Mara replied angrily.

"You know what the doctor said," Hannah Grace pleaded.

"Who, that kook, Dr. Al-Bammy?" Mara asked perturbed.

"Dr. Al-Banna," Hannah Grace said correcting Mara while checking the sink for evidence. After licking the bourbon off of her index finger, she folded her arms and scowled expressing her obvious displeasure.

"Mother Rash, what am I going to do with you?..." Hannah Grace started to say. Tears burst forth once again. "Oh, I know mother."

"You don't know nothin'," Mara retorted sharply, wiping her eyes with her apron.

"I know what day it is," Hannah Grace said moving slowly towards Mara and trying to give her a hug.

Mara shoved her arms away. "He's gone," Mara snapped. "And that's that! Ain't no good cryin' about it or carrying on like some kind of dad-blasted fool!" She turned towards her kitchen window just in time to see a black Mercedes go racing by.

* * *

"Now, I think you're really going to like this house that we're about to see," Claire said to Danny and Susan. "Remember, the first house was significantly less than this one. So, you're going to get more house and better amenities. Not to mention the convenience of living here in town close to the school. It's just around the corner here next to the church. It's a two-story Victorian style home. As we drive by you can see how our local physician Dr. Al-Banna has remodeled a similarly styled house. Uh, right there." Claire slowed the car to a crawl and pointed at the pink house with the white porch and Saturday Evening Post picket fence.

"Oh, that's beautiful!" Susan said. "They did an amazing job."

"Yeah, they did," Danny agreed. "Wow. So, he's the one who owns the family practice that you see from the highway coming into town?"

"Internal medicine," Claire replied. "They came here from somewhere in the Middle East about six years ago. He and his wife are such nice people- *very* religious. Everybody just loves them. I'd highly recommend him as a family doctor. And here is the house that we are going to take a look at."

Susan and Danny were still looking back at the lavish home of the good doctor, and when they turned expectantly to see the house, they were sadly disappointed to see that it was in need of renovating. The overgrown, weed-ridden yard and decaying home were straight out of a horror movie. Startled, Susan gasped.

Danny's eyes searched the old house with the faded paint, a missing shudder, and a collapsed porch.

"This is the house?" Danny asked. "At the price we were talking about?"

"Yep, this is it," Claire said. "Now keep in mind appearances can be deceiving. Like I said before, real estate is location, location, location. The house is in a great neighborhood smack dab in the middle of town. It also has twice the amount of square feet than the first one I showed you if you include the unfinished basement."

Susan wasn't sure she wanted to get out of the car, looking at the ugly house. Danny again glanced over his shoulder at the doctor's house.

"It's so...so...ugly," Susan said with a forced laugh.

"But, keep in mind," Claire began to say, "a great deal of what you see are merely surface issues that can easily be corrected with a little landscaping and some paint."

"What about the porch?" Danny asked while looking at the drooping structure.

"That will have to be replaced," Claire admitted, "but you can find some reasonably priced…uh, ethnic… workers who would do that for next to nothing. And it would make such a difference, really. Come on, don't let the outside fool you. It's what's on the inside that counts."

They stood looking at the comps on the linoleum counter in the outdated kitchen. Susan bounced Pearl over her shoulder with a concerned expression on her face.

Danny ran his hand through his hair and let out a gush of air. "So, this house *is* right at the price that we were hoping to spend on our first home," he said in shock, "I just can't believe it. I thought we would get so much more for the money."

"Yep," Claire replied.

"What do you think, Susan?" Danny asked contemplatively.

"What do I think?" Susan said looking around at the run down house. "I don't think it has half of the things that we had on our wish list. It has only one full sized bathroom, no playroom or fenced-in yard. It has a thirty year-old roof, radiators, no central air, and no marble countertops."

"Now, Susan," Claire said calmly, "in your price range you're going to have to compromise a little."

"Claire," Susan said, getting a little agitated, "this kitchen doesn't have a pantry or even a decent sized place to put a kitchen table. My parent's house had three and a half bathrooms. It had a finished basement. It had a three-car garage. It had a pantry!"

Claire Helrigle raised her eyebrows, smiled, and cocked her head. "Dear, you're buying in a seller's market," she said diplomatically. "If you want a house at a great value, then I would suggest finding the one that best meets your needs with the greatest potential for resale value. With a little money and a little work, you can fix many of the things that you don't like about the house, but you cannot improve the location. It's in a great spot."

Danny thought it would be a good time to ask a question. "Okay, so the house is at the 'right' price, but it needs a little fixing up," he said. "How much money would it take to get in the condition of say, the doctor's house down the street?"

"You would probably be talking sixty to seventy-thousand dollars," Claire said while Danny and Susan's hearts sank, "but guys, you're young. You have time! More than likely you will only be in the first house you buy four or five years."

Danny and Susan looked around in silence at the cracked linoleum floor, the faded wallpaper, and the stained ceiling.

"Come on, guys," Claire exhorted, "don't look so glum."

"Surely there are more houses on the market in our price range that you can show us," Danny said trying to see a silver lining.

"Sure there are," Claire said enthusiastically.

Danny looked at Susan and smiled.

"But this one is the best for resale value because of how close it is to Main Street and the elementary school," Claire replied.

Danny's face drooped again.

"That's why I showed you this one second," Claire said. "It won't be on the market long. I'm thinking in terms of retaining value over time. In four or five years, when you guys are making more money and have expanded your family, you'll probably want to move into a bigger, nicer house. Then you will have to sell your house. You will want to have made a profit to use as a down payment on the next one. This house has the best chance of doing that for you."

"What about the first one?" Danny asked.

"Same thing, that much land in central Illinois at that price is a bargain," Claire said. "You wouldn't even have to live in that house. You could get that old well working again and put in a trailer..."

Susan tried to fight back her tears, but she couldn't help thinking of the gorgeous house that she grew up in.

"Oh honey," Claire said. She walked over and put her arm around Susan and said, "there is another option that I haven't even considered until now."

Susan blew her nose into a piece of toilet paper that Danny had gotten for her from the bathroom.

"Which is?" Danny asked.

"The whole idea is capitalizing on a smart investment," Claire said calculatingly, "so, you could spend a little more and get everything that you are looking for right now. It might be a little tighter on your budget, but like I said, your income will keep growing. And over time the house will keep gaining more and more value. If you stay in the house a long time, then the property itself serves as a kind of 401K. After you've raised your family and the kids move out, then you sell the house and make a *huge* profit."

"Huh," Susan said starting to feel better, "you mean we could get a great house that we really love right now?"

"And, if we stay in it over a long period of time, it will eventually be a great thing for us financially?" Danny asked, seeing dollar signs for their retirement.

"Yeah, more or less," Claire said mirroring the excitement of her young buyers. "As it so happens, my husband, Lexus, and I have a subdivision at the edge of town that we are developing. We actually live in it now."

"Really?" Susan asked in anticipation.

"Yeah, we are just putting the finishing touches on a beautiful house just around the corner from us," Claire said, placing both hands on her cheeks. "You would absolutely love it. It has everything on your wish list and more. Of course, it is a little more than what you are qualified for, but I could call Lexus. He can run the numbers again. I'm sure we could make you some sort of deal. Do you want to go just take a look?"

Carefully holding Pearl's head, Susan nearly ran over Danny getting out the door of the fixer-upper.

"I guess that's a 'yes'," Danny said with a laugh.

Even though the rain turned into a sprinkle, Susan covered Pearl's head with a blanket, ran to the Mercedes, and hopped into the back seat. Danny followed along. As they watched Claire lock the front door, they again looked across the disfigured eye-sore of a house with disdain.

Claire punched some numbers into her cell phone and then squeezed it between her cheek and shoulder while fumbling for the lock to the old rickety house. "Lexus, the Cain's want to see the house that we were talking about," she said cunningly. "Yes. Have Wilson B. run the numbers again. See what you can come up with. I'll call you in a few. Love ya, bye."

* * *

As the Mercedes' front wheels turned towards the road, a rusted out old beater of a car sped past them and stopped in front of a house a few doors down. Jeremy jumped out, ran around to the back of the car, and popped open the trunk. He was whistling joyfully while struggling to gather the grocery bags up in his arms. With a tremendous amount of grunting and groaning, he shoved the trunk closed with his elbow and raced up the front walk. The youth pastor ascended the steps and knocked on the screen door with his foot.

The same young girl with dark hair and blond streaks slowly made her way to the door. Jeremy gave a rousing greeting that was returned only by a grunt. Swinging the screen door open, the indifferent young woman leaned against it while she put a ponytail holder in place. Jeremy started to walk in before the girl stopped him abruptly. She turned and called loudly into the house. In a moment, a little boy made his way out onto the porch. With some effort, Jeremy managed to hold the bags in place with his bony knee as he reached out to rub the young child's head before making his way into the house.

To Pastor Pete, who watched the entire scene from the window of his office at the parish, the boy seemed to protest adamantly. The young mother held the door open with her foot as she scolded the young child. From that distance, Pastor Pete couldn't read her lips, but he could tell that the little boy was getting an earful. In a flash, the boy rushed at her and stomped his shoe onto her bare foot. The girl quickly yanked it away. With a face full of rage, she raised her hand back as if she were about to strike the disobedient child. Pastor Pete put both of his hands on the arms of his chair and raised his body off the seat, but before he could get any farther, the girl reached down to her foot, and rubbed it as the boy ran down the stairs of the front porch.

The pastor rose completely from his chair, moved towards the window, and looked through the blinds at the car parked on the street in front of the house. He knew the car for sure. It was Jeremy Warner's. There was no mistaking it. Pete held the blinds open with two fingers for a minute before looking down at the floor. He started to move towards the door of his office and then thought better of it.

Instead, he made his way back to the desk and sat back down in his chair. Picking up his mug of green tea with both hands, he brought it carefully up to his mouth and carefully sipped while reading the last few sentences of Sunday's sermon. He squinted and mouthed the words inaudibly regarding Adam's original sin.

After he had finished the last line, he gave a disgusted look and set the mug back down on the coaster. Pete rubbed his face with both hands, sat forward, and hammered away again at the keys, but it was of no use. The words were not coming to him. Letting out a deep sigh, he looked to a small iron cross on the wall of his office. When he looked back at the computer the icon on the bottom right of the screen beckoned to him. He valiantly staved off the urge several times before submitting to the power that it had over him. Once again, he reached for the mouse, pulled down the curser, and obediently clicked on the icon. The images, as they had many, many times before, flashed in the reflection of the bifocals covering his anguished face.

When it was over, he pulled his glasses off his face and sat back in his office chair completely disgusted with himself. Chewing on the end of the frames, he leaned on his right elbow and stared off in the distance towards the school. The rain had completely stopped even though the clouds still loomed overhead. Pete looked back to the computer, reached out his hand, and held down the delete button and watched the words of his sermon disappear. Out of the corner of his eye he noticed a light in a window to a room above the gymnasium. As he turned to give it his full attention, the light suddenly went out.

"Huh," Pete muttered, "that's strange."

* * *

After Simon turned off the light to the room, he made his way to the 1st grade classroom only to find Andy Cross working his fingers to the bone, stripping the floor. He couldn't take it anymore. Most American's would kill for a cush job like his- sit around and do nothing but wait for a paycheck. Nonetheless, Simon found himself overcome with feelings of boredom, guilt, and worthlessness.

"Uh, excuse me, Mr. Cross," Simon said.

The determined janitor was working so fervently on the stubborn floor that he hadn't heard him. Simon watched in wonder as the sturdy, old man grunted and groaned under the strain of his work. He worked like a man possessed, wrestling with the floor as if it were an old adversary.

Simon cupped his hand over his mouth and yelled, "Mr. Cross!"

"Huh, wha'?" Mr. Cross stammered. He pushed his glasses back up to the bridge of his nose as he looked towards the doorway where Simon stood.

"Sorry to bother you," Simon said still a little embarrassed after being caught goofing off earlier. "Can I help you with anything?"

"Wha? No, No, I think I got everything under control, ya know," Mr. Cross replied using the back of his hand to wipe his forehead. Simon could see the beads of sweat on his upper lip, and the old man's breathing was labored.

"Well,…okay," Simon said. "I was just checking in." There was an awkward moment of silence before Simon continued. "Miss Harold mentioned something about cleaning out the storage room in the basement." Mr. Cross said nothing but only nodded. "I think I'll go down and get started on that."

Again, Mr. Cross did not respond. "Ok then, I'll see ya. Call me if you need anything," Simon said and he clumsily backed out of the room.

Just as Simon was out of sight, Mr. Cross lifted his hand and waved. "Ok, then." He put his hands on his hips and stared at the door for a moment before mustering his strength to attack the floor again.

"Oh brother, what a weirdo," Simon thought, making his way down the steps to the infested basement. He had half-hoped that Mr. Cross would have stopped him and given him some other task to complete. Instead, Simon stood furtively on the bottom step and leaned into the darkness while groping with his hand for the light switch. As soon as the lights came on, Simon heard the scuffling of feet to his left in the direction of the boiler. His heart skipped a beat as he jerked his head around to discover the origin of the sound. When he did, he caught a glimpse of something out of the corner of his eye. Whatever it was moved quickly behind the ancient, cast iron boiler.

Simon's pulse pounded in his ears as he deftly made his way towards the boiler. He held his hands up as though preparing for combat. Suddenly, he heard a booming clang of metal slamming on metal when he saw something on the ground. There were two socked feet laying behind the boiler.

Simon's eyes widened in horror. His heart was in his throat and his legs felt like Jello. Just then Simon saw a large industrial flashlight lying on the floor next to the furnace. He reached over stealthily, grabbed it in his sweaty palms, and held it high in the air ready to strike. When he got within a short distance, one of the feet moved, and he heard a groan. Simon jumped around the corner ready to deliver a violent blow with the heavy duty flashlight.

To his surprise, Mr. Gettby was laying flat on his back holding one arm over his eyes. Simon looked for any sign of trauma. Seeing the janitor lying on the floor of the basement, Simon was certain that something had gone terribly wrong. But there were no signs of foul play. That was when he noticed Mr. Gettby's head comfortably laying on a folded up towel laid over a pair of galoshes. Suddenly, the man's chest rose, and he gave a fitful snort. In the process, he woke himself from his nap only to see Simon standing over the top of him holding a flashlight high in the air.

"What the…?" Mr. Gettby called out. While raining down a series of curses on Simon, he rose quickly grabbing his galoshes. "What are you doin' with my flashlight? Are you crazy?"

Simon dropped the flashlight to his side and took a few steps away from the irate janitor. "I thought you were hurt or something?" he sputtered.

"And I s'pose you was gonna finish me off ?" Mr. Gettby said angrily as he grabbed the flashlight out of Simon's hand. "If I was dead, why would you need to hit me with a flashlight?"

"I don't know," Simon said defensively, "there was a loud crash and then I saw something out of the corner of my eye. And I thought you were in Philo..."

"I thought, I thought...," Mr. Gettby replied mockingly. "Don't think, would yah? I mean to say, a feller can't even catch a wink or two without somebody scaring the snot out of 'em."

Still in a fit of rage, he struggled to get his dirty galoshes back on his feet.

"I just came down to start clearing out the storage room and..," Simon said. But, he quickly realized that no explanation was going to appease Mr. Gettby.

"Well, have at it!" Mr. Gettby said with a new flurry of cuss words. "Stupid college boy. I don't have to put up with this. We'll see what old lady Harold has to say about it."

His last words trailed off as he ran up the stairs. Simon watched him go in bewilderment.

"What just happened?" Simon asked.

He looked around the room for what he could have possibly seen running away while Mr. Gettby lay snoozing on the floor. Unless his eyes were playing tricks on him again, whatever it was must still be down there. He turned on the flashlight and deliberately walked three quarters of the way around the furnace but saw nothing extraordinary. He remembered the baby bat that he saw on his first day and thought again about the 'infestation'. After an involuntary shiver, he made his way back over to the door of the storage room on the opposite end of the musty basement.

Simon took a deep breath, lifted the flashlight next to his cheek, and reached for the handle to the door. As he pulled back on the handle, Simon shone the light through the tiny aperture and leaned to his right. There was nothing but a wall of junk in his immediate view. Moving the light about, he couldn't see much past the initial stack of desks and chairs that obstructed the entryway.

"Why on earth would anyone keep all of this stuff around?" Simon thought, fanning the dust in the air away from his face.

Most of the items that he pulled out needed to be taken to the massive trash bin sitting in the alley next to the school. One by one he took the discarded chairs and broken down desks up the stairs, out the door, and into the alley. After taking six desks and eleven chairs out of the storage room, he found large trash bags covering unidentified objects that were stacked one on top of the other. Wiping off the cobwebs, Simon pulled down the trash bag from the top of the pile. He set it on the floor, untied the knot, and shone the flashlight down into the bag.

Impulsively, Simon jerked his head back. Then he slowly leaned in closer to get a second look. It was a red mask of some kind with two horns sticking out of the top of it. Confidently, Simon ripped the top open, finding it to be full of Halloween decorations. He picked up the mask and directed the light at plastic devil's mask. Amused by the discovery, he dropped the mask to the floor of the basement and picked through several other costumes and party favors.

"I'll let Mr. Cross decide what to do with all of this stuff," Simon thought.

He picked up the heavy bags two at a time and carried them to the opposite end of the basement where there was enough room to pick through the junk. After Simon pulled four bags from the pile, there was a round metal object laying over the top of one of the last trash bags. In the poorly illuminated room he squatted down next to it and leaned in closely to examine the object. Picking it up, Simon realized that it was a small metal basin of some kind. It was maybe three feet in diameter and a foot deep with handles on each side.

"Why would they keep this thing?" Simon thought, shaking his head. "Maybe Cross or Gettby will want it for something."

Dutifully, he carried it to the other side of the room and laid it with the other decorations. When he made his way back into the storage room, he picked up the flashlight to search the depths of the densely packed room. The light sporadically danced over the arbitrary piles of junk and then stopped on an unidentifiable rectangular object leaning against the wall. His curiosity aroused, Simon walked over and took a closer look. The wooden structure was probably two feet wide, three or four feet long, and a foot or two deep.

Simon put his flashlight in his mouth as he lifted the wooden object off of the floor. He hugged it tightly and tried to stand it up, but it was caught on something. After hard tugs, the wooden piece came free. Simon spun wildly and slipped to the floor. To catch himself, he had to let go of the object. It fell to the floor with a great crash as a cloud of dust rose into the air. Coughing, Simon wafted the air with his hand and squinted to keep the dirt from getting into his eyes. With the back of his index finger, he carefully wiped his watery eyes. When he looked up again, he immediately recognized what he had pulled from the storage room.

It was a small wooden coffin. Simon jumped to his feet and stared in disbelief at the horrific sight. Immediately, his stomach turned as the details of the story about Jessie Joseph flooded his consciousness. With bated breath, he picked up the flashlight and slapped the side of it with the palm of his hand several times before it came back to life. Simon tentatively crept towards the small coffin. His pulse raced as he gently lifted the lid. As soon as he saw that it was empty, he let out a gush of air. Suddenly, a small black object shot out of the back of the tiny room and flapped wildly all about his face.

Simon dropped the lid of the coffin, raised his arms up over his head, and scrambled up the stairs. In a flash, he was out the front door of the school and heading for the tavern. He made it to the end of the alley next to the grocery store before his intellect kicked in. Bent over gripping his knees and panting uncontrollably, Simon realized how crazy he would sound to the guys.

"What would I tell them?..." he gasped. "...That I saw a vampire?"

* * *

Susan ran her hand over the smooth marble countertops in the lavish kitchen as a broad smile crept across her face. Holding her precious Pearl, she approvingly scanned the cherry cabinets and tile floor while Danny stood on the other side of the bar in the living room. He was busy planning out the exact location of the big screen TV.

"So, you like it?" Claire asked, even though she didn't have to.

"Like it?" Susan gushed. "It's amazing! Did you pick out all of the cabinetry yourself?"

"Lexus and I have picked out everything, from the wide open floor plan all the way down to the chandelier in the entryway," Claire said proudly. "It's been our little project. Well, that is until baseball season started. Now it's my little project."

"You've done a great job," Danny said, looking out the back window to the half acre dirt lot, "it's like something straight out of Extreme Home Makeover."

"And this is the subdivision that you live in as well?" Susan asked as she opened the stainless steel refrigerator.

"Yes, we do, and we love it here," Claire replied. "That's our house right over there." She was pointing out the window in between two monstrous brick homes. "It's the one with the iron fence around the in-ground swimming pool."

"With the fiberglass basketball hoop and batting cage?" Danny asked, covetously.

"No, oh, I guess several of them have the iron fence around the in-ground swimming pool," Claire said. "It's the one with the Cadillac SUV in the driveway and the ski boat in the third garage. I'm going to have to get on Jackson for leaving that door open again. Huh, boys. What are we going to do with them?"

Danny surveyed the perfectly manicured lawns just as the Helrigle's sprinkler system kicked on.

"What's the price of the house?" Susan asked, the smile temporarily disappearing from her face.

"Well, that depends," Claire said, mirroring the expression of her client. "Follow me."

When she turned to walk out of the kitchen, Susan caught Danny's arm. Her face was beaming with delight. He nodded and looked up at the vaulted ceilings with a hint of worry in his countenance. Dutifully, they followed Claire around the corner of the kitchen to a short hallway that opened up into the master bedroom.

"Amazing!" Susan said holding her hand up to her mouth. "It's huge!"

"Yes, it's a good sized room," Claire acknowledged without any fanfare. "All the bedrooms are really. However, there is a little one across the hallway."

"There's a bedroom across the hallway downstairs?" Susan asked excitedly looking down at her little Pearl.

"Well, it can be either a bedroom or large office," Claire answered knowingly.

"The other four bedrooms are all upstairs. We did that purposely so that if a couple has a newborn, they can have the baby…"

"…close to them," Susan said finishing Claire's thought. "Then as they get older you can just send them upstairs."

"Precisely," Claire said, patting Susan on the shoulder, "you're so savvy. Maybe we should consult with you on the next one we build. Yes, the kids move upstairs and the parents get a little privacy. Then the next baby comes!"

They all burst out laughing.

"But that's not what I was referring to when I said the price of the home still has not been established," Claire continued after catching her breath.

With great affect, the wily real estate agent sauntered over to a set of double doors coming off of the bedroom and flung them open. "The exact price will be determined by what we end up doing with the bathrooms and walk-in closets.

"Do you see this?" Danny asked, amazed. "It's as big as our apartment!"

Claire laughed and said, "Yes, we took some liberties with the size of the master bathroom. It has a shower and a Jacuzzi, but we haven't decided whether or not we will go with granite for the countertops and the floors. And I'm still up-in-arms about whether or not we should do custom, built-in shelving in the walk-in." She reached over and pulled open the door to the cavernous closet.

"Wow!" Susan said, bouncing Pearl on her hip. "Look at all of this room for my clothes, and shoes, and accessories."

Danny looked a little pale as he considered the amount of apparel it would take to fill it. "So, the exact price has not been set, but surely you can give us a ball park figure," he said, trying to curb the momentum Claire had garnered with Susan.

"And Pearl could be just across the hall," Susan mused. "Oh, it's perfect. We just want the best for her. You know, give her all of the advantages."

"Of course," Claire said rubbing the baby's head. "Yes, Danny, I can give you a rough estimate. It's going to be between…oh wait! I didn't show you the other major factor that will determine the price tag. Where is my mind today?"

Hurriedly, she led the young couple back through the short hallway to a door just off of the living room. Danny looked forlornly at his exuberant wife who had clearly taken a liking to the luxurious home. Claire opened the door and stood off to the side.

"Danny, you probably want to go first just in case there's anything sitting on the stairs," Claire said, indicating she was wearing high heels.

"Oh, of course, is it dangerous?" Danny asked as he slowly descended the staircase to the basement.

"No, no, the guys have just been doing some work down there, and they sometimes leave their tools or nails or things laying around," Claire replied. "We've talked and talked with them about it, but…"

Danny did not hear the rest of what Claire was saying as he reached the floor of the unfinished basement. It was so expansive that the only words that came to Danny's brain was "Man Cave."

"There are just so many possibilities down here," Claire said. "We haven't decided whether or not we will finish it off or just leave it. If you finish it off, you would add about another 1,500 square feet of living space. I mean, Danny, you look like you keep in good shape. This could be a great workout room. We finished ours off and have never had any regrets. It's just kind of Lexus's and Jackson's hideout. I don't even go down there anymore. I just send them to the basement, shut the door, and let them play their air hockey or pool or whatever while they watch the game."

"I guess I *could* ask the boss for a little overtime," Danny said under his breath while picturing where the pool table would go.

But now Susan was the one who was starting to have some reservations.

"Hey, I just thought of something!" Claire said, disingenuously. "If you guys were interested in the house, we could leave it undone. That would do two things. First, it would curb your initial price some, and second, it would give you some future equity for resale value if you were able to do it yourself later on down the road. With the basement finished, we're probably talking between $400,000 and $425,000. But, without it, you're looking somewhere between $350,000 and $325,000- very reasonable."

Danny and Susan were stunned. "Uh, that's about twice as much as we were hoping to spend," Danny said disappointedly.

"And about $100,000 more than what we are qualified for," Susan added.

"Well, of course this would be more of a permanent home, something you would be in a long, long time," Claire said offering something to else to consider. "Like I said, this would be a really secure long term investment. It'd be like living in your own little nest egg for retirement."

"You would save some money from moving all the time," Danny said trying to justify his desires. "The values of homes do keep going up, and if we did ever finish off the basement we could add a lot of equity to the home."

"I don't know," Susan said trying her best to keep a level head, "I mean, it sounds like a moot point really. After all, we're not even qualified." As her words hung in the air, she dreamily recollected the chandelier in the entryway and was unable to suppress the thought of what her friends would say when they came through the front door for the first time.

"Oh, honey," Claire said with a pouty face. "We're the builders. Lexus and I set the price. I just want you guys to be happy. If you really want this house, we'll run some more numbers. As Lexus always says, 'where there's a will, there's a way'. We'll find a way to work out a deal."

As the three of them ascended the steps, they talked of possible financial options to get them into the home. Claire put the lockbox back on the door and thought, "Like fish in a barrel." When she turned to walk to her car, she saw Angie

Livingood getting the mail from across the street. Angie gave a friendly wave as they backed the Mercedes out of the driveway.

"That's my sister, Angie," Claire said, "she's a sweetheart. Her husband Wilson B. is the vice president at the bank, and they also have a 12-year-old named Ralph. Hey, I just thought of something, after you guys move in, Angie can have a Southern Living party for you."

"Southern Living?" Danny asked. "What's that?"

"It's like really cute stuff for your home," Susan said tightening up Pearl's seat belt.

"Oh, yeah, it's all the rage around here," Claire said. "Angie has like twenty people underneath her. She does very well. Better than me some months. Makes me think I need to quit what I'm doing."

"You mean a pyramid scheme like Amway?" Danny asked innocently.

Susan shot him a look.

"No, it's a little different," Claire said. "It's network marking. Susan you'd be great at it. Say, that might be a nice way to bring in a little extra income each month."

"Well, how much could she make?" Danny asked stupidly.

Susan opened her eyes wide, burning a hole in the back of his head. "Danny!" she said through gritted teeth.

"No, that's okay," Claire said. "That's what it's all about, right? It's about the money. I know. Did you see that pool in their backyard?"

"Yes," Danny said. "It looks awesome."

"Angie paid for it all herself last year, nice huh?" Claire said.

Longingly, the young couple turned and looked back at the large, beautiful house.

"I guess I could do some parties after you get home from work," Susan intimated.

"And what would we do with Pearl?" Danny asked in all sincerity.

"You'd watch her of course," Susan chided.

"You sound like Lexus," Claire said with a laugh.

12

THE FRUIT OF ENMITY

As Simon dug the shovel into the sand sitting in the back of the mule, he contemplated the distinct possibility that Jessie Joseph, Adam Potter, and the curse might actually be true. How could he possibly deny the mounting evidence that pointed to such an irrational conclusion? First, he was more certain now than ever that he had in fact seen a hand pull down the cellar door of the school the first night he arrived in Bethel.

Simon dumped out the load of sand near the standing water at second base. Rich had called earlier begging for Simon to do his level best to patch up the infield for their softball game that was scheduled for seven o'clock. His old friend would have done it himself but had to hold down the tavern.

Pulling the rake from the passenger seat of the 4-wheeler, Simon furrowed his brow and tried to organize his random thoughts. Second, he and Jeremy had unquestionably stumbled upon the forgotten graveyard on Clay Potter's property. The gravestones confirmed the names of the occupants who rested below. More than that, Jessie's stone had no date to mark his death. Why would that be?

He fervently raked the sand in an effort to absorb the large puddle of water. Suddenly, he stopped and leaned against the rake, recalling the night when they helped the search party look for Randy. Thirdly, there was little doubt in his mind now that he did in fact see a boy's face at the bottom of the well near Potter's farmhouse. If only Rob had seen it too.

"Is there anyway on God's green earth that could have been Adam Potter?" Simon thought.

A shiver coursed through his body and he quickly dismissed the ridiculous proposition. There had to be a more plausible explanation. Finally, there was the hand carved child sized coffin in the basement of the school. That reality couldn't be denied.

"Didn't Rob say that one boy had gotten away but it was a couple of days before they found him hiding out in Potter's barn?" Simon thought as he dug into the sand. "That certainly would explain the extra hand carved coffin. Obviously, they thought that there were going to be twelve dead children. Then when the boy was found, there was no need for the coffin. An empty coffin. Rob said Jessie vowed to exact revenge on the people of Bethel by filling the empty coffin with the children of future generations. Until…until…"

Simon stood for a moment as he had a dreadful, inescapable thought. There was the incident at the church on the day that he visited with Hope. When the old senile woman asked him if he was "the one" it resurrected a memory buried deeply in his psyche. Old Mrs. Potter used to say the same thing to him as a boy. "The One," he thought, "might actually refer to his destiny to stop the cycle of tragedies that had gripped the community for generations. But, why me? And how? How could I bring an end to a curse?"

He stopped and leaned against the rake with his right hand while his left rested on his hip. "This is stupid," he scolded himself. "A curse. How dumb." He started to rake again and then came to the realization that his efforts were futile. There would be no games this Friday night. Rich had told him that it had been an extremely wet spring and that the water tables were high. Instead of being absorbed into the ground, the rain gathered on the surface before flowing to lower ground and taking the precious topsoil with it. Evidently, the irritated farmers had been complaining about the situation for over a month now. No one knew when the rains would let up.

The distraction was only temporary as Simon's mind quickly returned to the topic at hand. He was unable to suppress the thought that he was brought to Bethel for a specific reason just as Jeremy had suggested. "I wish there was someone I trusted enough to talk to about all of this," he thought. "Rich and the guys would think I was crazy. I could drive down and see Hope." Then he thought better of that. "She would think I was some kind of nut job and probably never talk to me again."

Just then the door to the concession stand unexpectedly opened. Jeremy walked out with his skinny arm draped over one of his player's shoulders. Neither of them spotted Simon, as they walked with their heads down. Jeremy was talking into the ear of the boy and was holding a book of some kind in his other hand. Before they made their way completely out of the doorway, Jeremy turned as though suddenly remembering something. Carefully, he placed the book back on a shelf in the room, turned out the light, and pulled the door shut behind him, wrenching the handle to make sure that it was locked. The boy waited next to the bleachers with his head down, writing his name in the dirt with his foot. Jeremy walked over to him, knelt down, and put both hands on his shoulders as if he were giving some kind of instructions. Just as Jeremy pointed towards the boy's face with his index finger, he glanced to the side and caught sight of Simon standing at second base.

Jeremy smiled and waved wildly to Simon who returned the gesture. Standing to his feet, Jeremy put his chin into his chest, closed his eyes, and mouthed some words. As soon as Jeremy let go of the chubby boy's shoulders, the boy walked off towards Main Street. Jeremy turned and made his way over to Simon. Strangely, Simon could feel that same familiar feeling of acceptance come over him as the scrawny little youth director approached. For some odd reason, despite all of Jeremy's eccentricities, Simon really liked the guy.

"Do you think if Noah had been a baseball fanatic, he would have tried throwing down some sand first before building the ark?" Jeremy asked jokingly with a broad grin.

"Ha," Simon said with a laugh, "you haven't been hearing anything lately from the big man upstairs about gathering animals have you? According to the farmers at the tavern, doomsday is upon us."

"No," Jeremy replied shaking hands with Simon. "He hasn't said anything to me about it. Of course, He doesn't usually consult me about…anything."

"Doing a little one-on-one instruction?" Simon asked, pointing towards the concession stand.

"What? Oh yeah, that," Jeremy said sheepishly. "You caught me in the act again. Yeah, Parker has been going through a tough time here lately. He reminds me a lot of myself, a little dorky, little bit of a bookworm, awkward, and hopelessly unpopular. Kids love to weed out the weak from the herd."

"Do you really think it's a good idea to have those sessions with no one else around?" Simon asked rather pointedly. "I mean these days anyone can raise accusations about anyone, and it would only be your word against his."

"And whom would be my accuser?" Jeremy asked knowingly.

Simon mistook Jeremy's inference and replied, "No. No, I'm not saying you're doing anything wrong or anything like that."

Jeremy laughed and said, "Of course not, you don't strike me as one who would raise an accusation against the innocent. Besides I know my accuser. Do you know yours?"

Simon's face revealed that he was still lost.

"Never mind, we'll get to that," Jeremy said with his own unique style. "I appreciate your concern, but there is no need to worry. Besides, I never meet with the boys by myself."

"Oh, no?" Simon asked, looking over Jeremy's shoulder towards the concession stand. Then he looked back at Jeremy who was pointing skyward.

"Oh yeah, of course," Simon said uncomfortably.

"By the way, have you given any more thought to the conversation that you and I had a while back?" Jeremy asked. "I've tried to catch up with you a few times since then."

"Yeah, I'm sorry," Simon mumbled. "I've been a little busy."

"No, hey, my apologies," Jeremy said sincerely. "I should have made more of an effort. I've had quite a bit on my plate here lately. Anyway, enough of my excuses. Back to my original question. You seemed to be trying hard to sort things out the last time we talked. Have you come to any kind of resolution?"

"Yes, and no," Simon stammered. "Yes, I have thought a good deal about our conversation, and no, I haven't come to any sort of conclusion."

"Is there anything that I can help you with?" Jeremy offered. "Maybe there's something you'd like to ask me, ya know, before it's too late."

Simon looked into Jeremy's expectant face as he debated as to whether or not he could confide in the young youth pastor.

"Maybe there are a couple of things I'd like to ask you," Simon timidly admitted.

"Well, would you like to step into my office?" Jeremy asked, extending his hand towards the bleachers.

While walking towards the dugout, Simon received a text. He pulled his cell phone out of his pocket and read the message.

"It's Rich," Simon said to Jeremy. "He wants to know if we're on for tonight or not. Let me shoot him back a quick message that we are definitely off. Sorry." He punched in the cryptic message as he and Jeremy sat down on the bench of the home team dugout.

"Okay," Jeremy said after waiting patiently for Simon to finish up. "What can I help you with?"

"Well, I guess for starters," Simon said, choosing his words carefully so as not to offend, "I'm not sure about the whole Jesus thing. My life is going pretty well right now. I think I'm finally heading in the right direction."

"Oh," Jeremy replied with a confused expression on his face.

Just then, a compact car came tearing around the intersection just behind right field. The Ford Escort was coming from the country and heading towards town. Both Simon and Jeremy looked on as the tiny car leaned heavily to one side of its eighteen-inch wheels, barely making a sharp turn. They could hear the heavy metal music blaring from the speakers, and they could hear the four passengers singing along as they zoomed past the concession stand. Careening around the intersection behind the back stop, rocks flew from the spinning wheels. As the car sped past a yellow sign that warned drivers to slow for children playing, Jeremy got a quick glimpse of the four teenagers. An older boy was driving with a very young girl in the passenger seat while another couple snuggled together in the back seat. Jeremy had definitely seen them around town before and thought he may have even known one of the girls. For a moment, he reflected on the way in which the teenager drove so recklessly with a total disregard for the warning signs.

"That's ridiculous," Simon said in frustration. "Do you know them?"

"I think so; it's a small town," Jeremy answered. "It won't take much leg work to find out who they are."

"Yeah, they were driving pretty crazy," Simon said. "Luckily, there weren't any kids around."

His off-handed comment gave Jeremy an idea. "Did it appear to you that those four teenagers seemed to be having a great time cruising- not a care in the world- just kinda having fun?" he strategically asked.

"Yeah, I guess so," Simon answered. "But, there's a reason the sign's there. They need to slow down."

"Why?" Jeremy asked.

"Why?" Simon retorted in a disgusted tone of voice. "Because they could kill themselves or somebody else. They wouldn't be having a very good time then would they? It would be tragic if they put themselves or some kid in the grave out of sheer ignorance."

"Obviously, the warning signs are there to protect the pedestrians, right?" Jeremy asked pointedly. Simon nodded in agreement not sure of where the conversation was going. "And it would be fair to say that they are also there to protect the driver as well. In other words, you would be doing them a disservice to not track them down and warn them about what might happen if they continue to drive so recklessly even though they were having a great time and no one was hurt by their actions. The driver might even be pretty offended by your meddling in his life, right? I mean he probably wouldn't thank you. Let's put it that way."

"I suppose not," Simon said, "but, do you have to wait until they actually do run over somebody or smash their car into a tree before saying something to them?" Suddenly Simon caught on. "I mean, I don't plan on tracking the kid down if that's what you're getting at. After all, that's why we have cops."

"True, but there aren't any policemen around," Jeremy challenged. "Anyone could see that they were putting themselves and others in imminent danger due to their reckless driving even though they were completely oblivious to their perilous situation."

"Do you think that you and I have to be perfect drivers before we can say something to a teenager who is endangering himself as well as others even though that's not our vocation?" Jeremy asked. "Have you ever heard of a guy named Ryan Dobson? He gave an account of a barge hitting a bridge on the Arkansas River in Eastern Oklahoma..."

"I get it, I get," Simon rudely interrupted. "You want me to go track down that driver to tell him to slow down."

"Yes, but no," Jeremy answered, his face turning very solemn. "People who don't know Jesus Christ as their Lord and Savior are just driving down the road without any worries. They think they have all the time in the world not having a clue that they in danger. Someone needs to tell them before it's too late."

Simon's smile erased from his face. He turned from Jeremy and looked out at the pristine baseball field.

"Things may seem to be going great for you right now in a worldly sense," Jeremy said, "but, there is an imminent danger on the horizon for each of us. Death is inevitable, and it is as undeniable as your birth. Once you acknowledge those two facts, there are several natural questions that you have to contemplate. Where did you come from? Why are you here? What happens when you die? And they're all connected."

Like an arrow piercing his heart, Simon leaned forward resting his elbows on his knees with his hands clasped together. His cell phone ringer went off, but he chose to ignore it.

"Millions of people have come up with millions of different answers to those three questions," Jeremy said, "but, the Bible, the living word of God, gives us the only definitive answer to each of them. The one God, the triune God, has always existed. He created us. He knitted you in your mother's womb, Simon. He made you to serve and worship Him. You have a divine appointment, a destiny. He made you with a specific purpose in mind, a job that only you can do..."

Simon jerked his head and stared intently at Jeremy. "But, how do you know that for sure?" Simon asked, suddenly alarmed. The hairs were standing up the back of his neck and his heart raced in his chest. Again, his cell phone rang incessantly, but once again he ignored its entreaties.

Jeremy smiled, reached out, and put his hand on Simon's shoulder. "All of the signs are there," the youth pastor mused, "could it be simply that you have been ignoring them? I did for some time myself before I started praying, reading the Word, and listening. Now I know the truth in my heart, in my soul, and in my mind. You will die one day and there are only two possible answers as to where your soul will go for all eternity. And there is only one way we can get to Heaven, and it's through Jesus Christ."

"But, how do you know that is the truth?" Simon asked. "Why would God do that? Why would there have to be only one way? Why would he send so many people to Hades? And even if it were true, why would he give us a purpose and not tell us what that purpose is?"

"Let me do my best to answer those very important questions," Jeremy said. "The answers are actually intertwined. God loved us enough to give us free will, to choose whether or not we will follow Him or our own desires. Evil is the necessary byproduct that resulted from giving us a choice.

"Even then, God did not originally expose man to evil. Adam and Eve lived with God in paradise. And they could have lived there for all eternity. But, He gave them a choice. And Adam chose to sin. Unfortunately- or fortunately- for all of us, the price of sin is death. We should be so glad that a righteous God cannot tolerate anything unrighteous in His presence. As a result, he was forced to evict Adam and Eve from paradise. God is just. He cannot deny himself. He must exact justice on those who choose to do the wrong thing. Otherwise, anyone could do anything to anybody else and there would be no repercussions. That would not be fair. That would not be justice.

"And so, sin is passed down through man from one generation to the next, like DNA. Now we have a very serious problem. The entire human race is unrighteous and unable to pay the debt ourselves. We need a Savior, and fortunately for us, God already knew that because He is the Alpha and Omega, the beginning and the end. God knew He was going to give us a choice, and He knew that we would choose poorly. As a result, God planned long ago to send Himself in the person of His son Jesus to fulfill the law and the prophets in order to become the perfect sacrifice. Jesus died in our place on the cross. We receive salvation by faith through grace. Jesus was resurrected and ascended into Heaven where he sits on the right hand of God the Father. If that weren't enough, God shares Himself with us through the Holy Spirit, so that He can transform us into His image, so that we will one day be like Jesus for His glory. And one day He will return to judge humanity."

"Okay," Simon replied. "Even if that's true why wouldn't He make that obvious to everybody? Why does He let so many people go to Hades? That does not seem right for a completely righteous God."

"I believe that is greatest sticking point for people to believe in and worship Him," Jeremy answered with his eyes welling up with tears. "So, let me try to put it in as simple terms as I can. True love requires a reciprocation born out of choice. God equipped humans with an intellect, an inner conscience, and an ordered universe that testifies to a creator. Even after man sinned, God continued to communicate in the spoken word through the prophets for a period of time. He provided us His rules for living. He left open the lines of communication for everyone through prayer. He predicated His coming and fulfilled it as evidence to His authenticity. He came and saved us. He gave us great miracles and many signs and symbols. He allowed a select group of witnesses to see Jesus ascend into Heaven and empowered them with the Holy Spirit to take the message to the world. Then He even recorded all of it in the Bible and gave us preachers and the testimony of fellow believers to teach us the truth and show us the way.

"God wants everyone to go to heaven. He doesn't want anyone to go to Hades. But at the end of the day, He still has to leave us with a choice. Either we believe or do not believe. Otherwise, He would have had robots who could not choose. And if man was not given a choice, he could not choose to reciprocate God's love. That would only leave Heaven incomplete, unrighteous, and imperfect."

As Simon listened, he could once again sense something moving within him, something that gravitated towards Jeremy's words.

"And as far as sending people to Hades," Jeremy said, "as tragic as it is, people make their own choices in life. But, that's where our purpose comes into play. God wants a relationship with us. He wants us to have some accountability. He wants us to seek, to knock, and to find Him. God wants us to interact with Him.

"When we do that, He most assuredly lets us know our purpose- eventually. I don't know everything, but I do know this. Each of our purposes has everything to do with our relationship with one another. Our purpose involves reaching as many people as possible in order to tell them the Good News about the free gift of salvation."

Simon sat in silence trying to absorb all that Jeremy said before saying, "That's a lot to think about. I need some time. I mean when I hear what you are saying it definitely strikes a cord. But, I just need to sort it out."

"What else do you need to know?" Jeremy asked.

"Well, okay..." Simon said as his heart began to pound in his ears. He was still worried about sounding crazy, "About my purpose. You won't believe this, but I have been thinking..." Suddenly, his phone buzzed one more time, announcing that he had just received another text. Still, Simon chose to ignore it.

"Somebody really wants to get ahold of you," Jeremy said, looking down at the phone.

"It's Rich," Simon said, rattled by what he was about to share with Jeremy. "He can wait. I'll call him back when I get a chance."

"I think it's like that!" Jeremy offered with a smile.

"What's like what?" Simon asked.

"It's like God is constantly trying to get ahold of us, but we refuse to pick up the phone, promising to get to Him when we 'get a chance'," Jeremy answered. "If you ask Him with a pure heart and listen with open ears, He will make your purpose clear. It may not be audible, but He will make it clear. The question is how can God tell anyone anything who isn't listening?"

Simon laughed looking down at the phone and said, "I guess I just need a sign of some kind, you know, to be sure."

"Blessed is he who does not see and still believes," Jeremy said spontaneously.

But, Simon did not know exactly what he meant.

"Have you asked Him what you should do with your life and actually expected an answer?" Jeremy inquired.

The question struck a nerve with Simon, and he felt himself get a little defensive. "I've asked that question about a billion times," he objected.

"Yes, but are you really paying attention?" Jeremy inquired. "Maybe His message is not so much in words but in the circumstances or signs or symbols. Maybe it's just a swelling of your heart."

Suddenly, Rich's car came flying around the corner. He barely paused at the 4-way stop before turning the corner and charging up the road behind the dugout where Simon sat with Jeremy. Slamming on the brakes, Rich brought the car to a screeching halt.

The behemoth bartender rolled down the window and yelled, "*Simon!* Come quick, it's an emergency!

"What is it?" Simon asked with great concern, getting up from the bench.

"Just come quick!" Rich demanded, while beckoning for Simon to come to the car.

"I'm sorry, I better go," Simon said to Jeremy.

"Yeah, go, sounds serious," Jeremy responded. Then he called over to Rich, "Is there anything I can do?"

"No, Jeremy, we've got it, thanks!" Rich quipped.

Worried, Simon ran around to the passenger side and jumped in. Jeremy looked on as they tore down the road, made the turn at the next intersection, and headed back towards Main Street.

"What is it?" Simon asked. "What's going on?"

"We've got to get this trade in before the deadline tonight," Rich said holding up a piece of paper.

"What?" Simon asked, confused.

"The trade you offered me earlier today," Rich said, slightly agitated. "I've been trying to get a hold of you for the last hour. All trades have to be in before the first pitch of the first game of the night in order to have their stats count for their new teams. It's in the by-laws."

"You've got to be kidding me," Simon said throwing his head back into the headrest of the passenger seat.

"No, I'm not, those are the rules, and if you don't read the rule book, then it's going to be total chaos," Rich chirped as they pulled up to the tavern. "We have to both sign a trade agreement in front of a witness.

"Jeremy of all people, huh. You should have known he was going to hold you up. That guy'll talk you to death if you let him. Why didn't you pick up your cell? Never mind, it doesn't matter. Come on, let's get in there. We only have a few minutes."

Rich put the car in park, jumped out, and trotted towards the front door. Simon just sat there, flabbergasted. Realizing that his friend hadn't gotten out of the car, Rich stopped, turned around, and motioned for him to hurry up.

"You're killing me Freeman!" Rich declared.

* * *

Simon felt a little self-conscious sitting by himself in a pew near the front of the church. He could feel the weight of the stares on the back of the neck. Had the snooze alarm not gone off for a third time, he would have missed the sermon completely. As is, he barely made it before the greeting. With no more than twenty-five or thirty members in attendance, it was quite the anomaly to have a guest, especially one who was under the age of sixty. It was fairly commonplace to have someone in their twilight years take a new found interest in religion, and it was even fairly commonplace for one of the senior members to have a grandchild or nephew at a service to celebrate Mother's Day, or Christmas, or Easter. But to have a young, single man attend church by himself of his own volition creates quite a stir in a small town.

Ignoring the idle chatter of the good Pastor, several men speculated what the young lad might have done, while a row of elderly women sitting in the back row wondered openly whether he might be gay. Mara dropped her hand from her mouth, looking out the corner of her eye towards Simon.

"Oh mother, please," Hannah Grace whispered in a hushed voice.

Mara leaned in closer to Hannah Grace's ear and raised her hand over her mouth again.

"How am I supposed to know?" Hannah Grace said just as Pastor Pete repeated his proposition for the third time.

"...though hearing not hearing and though seeing not seeing..." the Pastor said in a monotone voice.

Because Mara's hearing wasn't what it used to be, most of what was said could be heard by just about everyone without much straining. Nonetheless, Simon didn't mind. He was busy playing stenographer for Hope.

"She's going to be shocked," Simon thought, as a smile crept across his face. He raised his eyes to Pastor Pete who was extolling the virtues of living with integrity. In the margins of his bulletin, Simon made his own clever commentary for Hope's benefit. He loved her sense of humor and thought that she might enjoy some of his play on words. Simon wrote Pastor Pete's title, "Integrity- the Core of the Christian" at the top of the outline and added his own subtext "...the missing attribute to a bad apple." At least he was amusing himself.

Really, the idea of taking notes served two distinct purposes now for Simon. Of course, it would give him an excuse to call Hope. But more than that, something inside of him wanted to be in church and to hear more about what he had discussed with Jeremy. He thought that he might even talk to the Pastor after the service and ask him a few questions. Even though Simon had good intentions, Pastor Pete Cross's delivery reminded him of his eight o'clock Poli Sci class at TCU, where merely staying awake proved to be a daunting task. Simon pulled out all of the stops to combat his drowsiness, including sitting straight up in the pew, periodically stretching his neck, and fervently blinking. At one point, he even pulled some of the hairs out of arm, but it was of no use. The onslaught of yawns crashed upon the shores of his consciousness wave upon wave, completely drowning his intellect.

When the torturous boredom came to a merciful end, Simon was less than inspired to approach Pastor Pete about the questions still lingering in his mind. He was already apprehensive about confiding in anyone about the outrageous thoughts that had occupied his mind since his last meeting with Jeremiah Warner. Now that everyone was beginning to exit the pews following the service, he was certain that it was a bad idea. In a panic, Simon turned to make a quick exit, but it was too late. The swarm of blue-hairs met him in the aisle each one thinking it their duty to thank him for coming and invite him back for the next Sunday. Old women with walkers and men with canes slowly approached and corralled him into a corner of the sanctuary. Each of them took him by the hand, smiled warmly, and bombarded him with trite questions.

Simon did his best to be cordial while discreetly looking for a path to the door. Just then, Mara and Hannah Grace approached him. Hannah Grace spoke first, "Hello, my name is Hannah Grace Rash and this is my mother-in-law Mara Rash. It is very nice to meet you." She smiled sweetly while Mara looked him over with a skeptical eye.

"Hello, I'm Simon Freeman," he said shaking their hands, "it's a pleasure to meet you as well."

Hannah Grace's face fell.

"Is something the matter?" Simon asked.

"Freeman you say?" Hannah Grace asked. "We knew some Freeman's from a while back. Are you from here?"

"Yes, as a matter of fact," Simon said for the hundredth time, "I lived in Bethel with my parents until I was 10 years-old."

Before Hannah Grace could level another question, Pastor Pete stepped in and saved him.

"Simon, so nice of you to come," Pastor Pete said, taking Simon by the elbow. "Can I walk you to the door?" The pastor whisked him away. "Sorry about that. They're not accustomed to having visitors. You looked like you needed a little help."

"Thanks, I appreciate that," Simon said. "I didn't want to be impolite, but I…"

"…Wanted to actually leave sometime today?" Pastor Pete asked. "I understand." They walked out the door and stood at the top of the steps to the church. "We'd love to have you back again, and I'll do my best to hold back the legion of greeters." He reached out to shake Simon's hand with a warm smile.

As Simon shook the pastor's hand, he tarried long enough that Pastor Pete got the impression there was something else. "I don't know if you're going to be in town very long, but I would love to get together and chat a little more."

Simon lifted his eyes to meet the pastor's, still hesitant to leave himself vulnerable. "Sure, maybe," Simon benignly answered.

"Well, great," the pastor commented, "that'd be just great. Drop by anytime, and let me know if there is anything that I can do for you in the meantime."

Just then an elderly man walked up next to the pastor. "Pastor, you gotta minute? I'd like to talk to you about the roof. I seen some shingles that came off during the last storm. I'm afraid we may have a leak."

"Yes," the pastor said to the gentleman. "Take care, Simon. Maybe I'll see you around."

"Maybe, thanks Pastor," Simon said shyly.

When Simon turned to leave, he nearly tripped over an elderly woman sitting in a wheelchair waiting for her ride. He immediately recognized her as Mrs. Potter, the invalid who asked the question that had haunted him for the past two weeks. Embarrassed, he smiled and nodded at the old senile woman who was hunched over holding her purse in her lap.

"Oh, excuse me, I'm so sorry," Simon managed to say, "Are you all right? I didn't see you there."

Looking up at Simon, she beamed with a wide grin, accentuating the deep wrinkles in her cheeks and forehead. In her gravely voice she asked, "Have you begun?"

* * *

A nervous, sick feeling welled up inside of Simon as he scrolled to Hope's phone number in his list of contacts. Impulsively, he rubbed the sweaty palm of his right hand on his shorts and waited for her to pick up. He had been looking forward to this diversion after having grappled with his dilemma.

It had been a week since he and Hope spoke last. And while they had been exchanging texts periodically during the week, it wasn't quite the same. He found himself longing to hear her sweet, soft voice while they joked and laughed about everything and nothing.

Still, their relationship was so new that Simon anxiously wondered if the next conversation would be as familiar as the last. Or would their initial connection lose its luster over time due to the distance between them. He couldn't help but wonder why she had not tried to call him. Unsuccessfully, Simon tried to pretend that it didn't bother him. Now he waited in anticipation for her to answer the phone.

"Hey, you," Hope said warmly on the other end of the line.

Simon's heart nearly leapt from his chest at the sound of her voice.

"Hey yourself," Simon said with a cheesy grin, "how's the head honcho of the happy campers doing?"

"I'm fine thanks, but not all of the campers are happy," Hope said. "I was wondering if you would call today."

"That's funny because I was wondering if you were going to call me, but I wasn't willing to take that bet," Simon said joking.

"Oh, I might have gotten around to it," Hope replied, deliberately torturing him.

"'Might have', really?" Simon said, feigning offense to the statement. "Are you insinuating that hanging out with a bunch of 12 and 13-year-old girls would be just as intellectually stimulating as conversing with me?"

"Well, in man years you are at the same level of maturity, so..." Hope said in jest.

"You're probably right," Simon replied with a laugh. "Do they think that disgusting body emissions are vile and hilarious at the same time?"

"In fact, they do," Hope said laughing. "When they're out in the wild these dainty girls joyfully belch and pass gas like a bunch of frat brothers."

"As it so happens, I didn't pledge so I wouldn't have the slightest idea what you are referring to," Simon said in a playful tone. "I just hung out with a bunch of baseball players. I won't tell you what they do. But now, I am beginning to value tact and civility in all manner of passing gas."

"Oh, is that so?" Hope replied. "How refreshing. You are mature beyond your years. So, what do I owe the pleasure of a call from such a suave and somewhat civilized suitor."

"Suitor is it?" Simon said. "That's pretty presumptuous. As it so happens, I am merely fulfilling a promise that I made."

"I see, and what promise would that be?" Hope asked.

"I have before me a categorically, and somewhat accurate account, of Pastor Yawn's sermon today," Simon said.

"Is that so?" Hope asked.

"Yes, ma'am," Simon replied.

"Will wonders never cease?" she said. "Well, what are you waiting for, let's hear what revelations of truth the good pastor conveyed today to his congregation."

"Okay, but before I get started, I am obligated to read to you a disclaimer that all facts, figures, and quotes are a mere representation of the actual sermon and may or may not be completely authentic," Simon said trying to contain his laughter. "Any inaccuracies, gaps in context, and/or tangent commentary are permissible and in fact highly probable. Therefore, any false conclusions drawn by the listener cannot be attributed to the messenger rendering him void of any liability or legal action."

"How official," Hope mused.

"Yes, and there's more," Simon said. "If the said listener in this case- i.e. you- would like to hear a completely accurate, untainted version of one of Pastor Pete's sermons she will have to come to Bethel and hear it for herself."

"Is that an invitation?" Hope asked.

"Maybe," Simon answered.

"Then maybe I'll come home...sometime," Hope said with a laugh.

"Oh, that hurts, a little teaser," Simon said. "Okay, hear goes the sermon. Are you ready? I edited this a few times, so here it goes... "Integrity- the Heart of the Christian," subtext- "And the vein of the Politician's Existence. Get it? I used vein kinda like bane making it go with the whole heart thing?"

"Yeah, yeah, I get it, real clever," Hope said mockingly. "Still not laughing yet."

The hours that they talked seemed like minutes to both of them. Hope found Simon's humorous take on the sermon to be very entertaining. By the time he had finished, the crooks of their arms hurt, their ears were sore, and their voices dry. Still, both of them kept manufacturing reasons to stay on longer until they simply had nothing left to say.

"So, you'll text me later?" Simon asked.

"I thought you were texting me," Hope said.

"Oh come on now, I was the one to call today, so..." Simon said.

"Okay, maybe I can find some time this week to shoot you a quick text," Hope replied.

"What about coming home this weekend?" Simon asked, pushing his luck.

"Sorry, not likely, we had six homesick girls this weekend," Hope said with an apologetic tone. "Next week it will probably be three and then one the week after that. Maybe, I can come home in three weeks."

"Sounds like a date," Simon said.

"Then it is," Hope said just before ending the call.

After ending the call, Simon laid the phone down next him and slid down onto the couch in his tiny apartment. He had thought several times during the conversation about telling Hope all of the things that were going on inside of him. Even though she never asked about talking with Jeremy, he suspected that she knew the zealous youth pastor well enough to know how the conversation went. But, they were having such a great time that the topic hadn't come up. Hope made him feel so comfortable.

He just wanted to give his personal struggle a rest for a while. Besides, would she truly understand? Simon was sure that Hope would have plenty to say about his conversations with Jeremy. But, how would she take hearing about what he thought his purpose might be? She would probably think he was some kind of liar or lunatic.

"Who knows?" Simon asked. "Maybe I am."

Lost in thought, he didn't hear the truck pull into the gravel driveway just below his apartment. It was only when a door slammed shut that it roused him from his contemplative state. Simon leaned over and glanced out the window.

"Jack?" Simon thought.

He walked over to his door, opened it, and stepped out into the warm night air. There was no one coming up the steps. Simon looked at the shiny, new truck parked in the driveway, but there were no signs of his landlord. Without bothering to slip on a pair of shoes, he made his way down the steps. Behind him, he heard the same familiar sploosh of a beer can being opened. Simon turned towards the backyard where he saw a dark figure sitting in a lawn chair.

"Jack?" Simon asked, walking towards his unannounced visitor. He could see the cigarette smoke drifting in the evening breeze as he approached.

Jack looked up over his shoulder. He pulled the cigarette from his mouth and said, "Simon, my boy, how have you been? Here, pull yourself up a lawn chair and grab a cold one." Lifting the plastic that held five cold Bud Lights high into the air, Jack grinned with delight through his well-groomed goatee.

"Thanks," Simon said a little taken aback. He glanced over his shoulder at the apartment. "I, uh, I haven't received my first paycheck yet from the school district."

"What? Oh, ha, you thought I was comin' for the rent," Jack said, taking another drink of beer. "Nah, I know you're good for it. Sure is a beautiful night, isn't it?"

Simon took a look out at the dark, sprawling fields that stretched to the horizon off in the distance with a million stars shining brightly in the sky above.

"Yes, it is," Simon said as he took a seat next to his hospitable landlord. "What brings you by tonight then if not for rent?" Simon asked opening the ice cold can and taking a sip.

"Makin deals," Jack replied, placing the cigarette deftly back into his mouth. "Just doin' some business, ya know."

Simon nodded, uncertain.

"I was thinkin' bout our last conversation you and I had out here the other night," Jack said, leaning towards Simon, "you and me was talkin' about opportunity."

"We were?" Simon asked innocently.

"Course we was, ha!" Jack said followed by bellowing laughter and profanity. "Son, I like you. You and me were talking about purpose and finding what makes you happy. I'm all about making people happy. Seems to me that you've been pretty happy here in Bethel the last couple of weeks. Would that be an accurate statement?"

"Yeah, I guess so," Simon confessed.

"Well, son, if life is about doing what makes you happy, then why on earth would you want to go all the way to New Jersey to find what is right in front of your face, follow me?" Jack asked.

"Not completely," Simon replied.

"There is something here that's not in Jersey," Jack said with a wide grin.

"And what would that be...?" Simon asked with the hairs starting to stand up on the back of his neck.

"...Hope, of course," Jack answered before taking a long drink of beer.

Simon nearly choked on his Bud Light. He looked around at the lights of the grain elevator from the neighboring town of Philo off in the distance. "Hope?" Simon asked trying to be dismissive.

"Yes, Hope Wiseman," Jack reiterated. "Why, the whole town knows 'bout you two hooking up after Will and Rachel's wedding reception."

Simon was quick to set the record straight, "We didn't 'hook-up', we talked..."

Jack waved him off while taking another drag on his cigarette. "Hmmph," the shrewd businessman scoffed, "I don't really care. Don't make no difference to me what you two did, but word has it you two been keepin' in touch ever since. That true?"

"Yes, but, how do you know that?" Simon asked.

Jack ignored the question and slapped Simon on the leg several times and said, "Business, son. Just business. And what's in Jersey that's not here?"

Simon gave Jack a look that revealed what a stupid question he thought it was. "Well, the job of course," he replied, "and money...uh...and..."

"...What if I was to tell you I had an equally lucrative offer for you right here in Bethel?" Jack asked candidly.

"Well, I guess I'd say, 'What's the opportunity?' " Simon said, starting to take an interest in Jack's entreaties. "It'd have to be pretty lucrative to be comparable to pharmaceutical sales."

"Ha, son, don't you beat all?" Jack said smashing his beer can, tossing it to the ground, and pulling another one from the plastic. "Straight to the chase. I like that. Comparin' my offer to a job you ain't got yet. Ha! Well, son, you'd be surprised at how much of a market there is here in the sticks. There are a few different capacities I could see you serving me in. Wouldn't be much different from what you're looking for out East. A sharp young guy such as yourself. Got a good head on your shoulders. Handsome. Likable. You could do very well here." Jack paused, leaned away from Simon, and squinted his eyes as though sizing him up. "Let's not define what role just yet. I have several new enterprises that I am working on right now that you might be cut out for."

"Really?" Simon said after swallowing the last of his first beer. "What are they?"

Jack handed him another beer. "Easier to show you than tell you," Jack answered. "Tell you what, how about I have my newest understudy pick you up tomorrow night. You don't have any plans do ya?"

Simon shook his head at first. Then he remembered something. "Oh, yeah, I've got to umpire two little league games tomorrow night," he said.

"Those'll be over around eight," Jack said knowingly. "How bout after that?"

"Yeah, I guess that could work," Simon answered.

"Ha, good then," Jack replied. "I'll have my assistant text you a time and place to meet. He can give you a little insight into a couple of our projects, and I can catch up with you afterwards. You and me can chat. See what you think. How does that sound to ya?"

"Sounds good," Simon said, wiping his mouth with the back of his hand. "Who's your new understudy?" Simon asked as he spilled a little beer down the front of his shirt.

"Robin Ateitup," Jack replied.

Simon stopped wiping his shirt for a moment and looked at Jack. "Rob?" he stammered. "Really?"

"Yes, sir," Jack said, "absolutely fearless. What is it they say bout them great free throw shooters at the end of a big basketball game? Oh yeah…they have no conscience. He's got no conscience just ice in his veins. Yes sir, he's got a bright future that one."

13

HOW GREAT IS THAT DARKNESS?

Morning came early as Simon fumbled for the alarm clock in an attempt to put an end to its incessant buzzing. Still feeling the effects of his beer buzz, he managed to force one eye open. When he did, he immediately realized that he had overslept. It was almost six in the morning. He was going to be late. Fortunately, he had passed out on the bed in his clothes. Scrambling for his toothbrush, he did his best to rake the putrid taste from his tongue, but his breath still reeked of alcohol. Simon hadn't remembered saying goodnight to Jack, or making his way up the stairs, or crashing into bed.

"Strange," he thought. "It was only three or four beers. You'd think I would learn my lesson about drinking on an empty stomach."

Simon sped down to the school. As he jumped out of the car, he could see a light on in the classroom that he had been painting the day before.

"Oh great," Simon said under his stale breath. "First, the whole thing with Mr. Gettby and now I'm late. They're going to fire me for sure."

As Simon ascended the steps, he could smell the rich aroma of a freshly brewed pot of coffee wafting through the air. Entering the classroom, he looked past the scaffolding, drop clothes, and paint cans to see Mr. Cross leaning against the windowsill. He was sipping on a mug of coffee while watching the sun come up in the East.

"Good Morning, Mr. Cross," Simon said sheepishly, "sorry I'm late, I overslept. It will never happen again!"

"Well, good morning Simon, my boy," Mr. Cross replied with a warm smile.

He didn't appear to be bothered in the least by Simon's tardiness. In fact, it was the most relaxed he had ever seen the old man. During the past few days, Simon had closely observed the odd janitor who worked feverishly at getting the school ready for fall. His work ethic and diligence had impressed Simon, even though his efforts were often scattered like some sort of mad scientist. It was a stark contrast to that of Mr. Gettby.

"Thought ya might like a little warm brew this mornin'," Mr. Cross said, walking over to the coffee maker sitting on the teacher's desk at the back of the room. "You drink coffee?"

"A little," Simon said, just beginning to fully appreciate his apparent clemency.

"Can I get you a cup?" Mr. Cross said holding the pot up in the air. "Monday's can be tough sometimes."

"Sure, thanks," Simon replied, reaching for the piping hot mug, "sorry to keep you waiting for me."

"Oh, I wasn't waitin' on ya," Mr. Cross said. "Been here since five. Already stripped the floor in the 2nd grade classroom."

"Really?" Simon asked, following Mr. Cross back to the open window where the brilliant glow of the morning sun shone brightly, "are you trying to get out of here early today or something?"

"What?" Mr. Cross asked with a confused expression. "No, just another day."

"You mean you normally start that early?" Simon asked.

"Sometimes," Mr. Cross answered as he watched the long, narrow shadows from the grain elevator recede from the school yard.

"If you come in early, then shouldn't you be entitled to leave a little earlier?" Simon said. "What are your normal hours."

"Don't really have 'hours'," Mr. Cross said with a grunt and a smile.

"But, you get paid by the hour don't you?" Simon asked.

"Suppose so," Mr. Cross conceded, "but I work when there's something that has to be done. And there's always something that has to be done at an old school."

He looked down at the floor and noticed another old, smashed piece of gum. He set his coffee down, reached into his pocket, and pulled out his trusty putty knife. Simon watched him as he went at the piece of gum zealously as though it were a blight on his personal character.

"I don't sleep a whole lot," Mr. Cross said in between grunts. "Hadn't been able to for a long time. Ah, gotcha'. See here?" he said holding up the gum. "I come in all hours and do this and that."

"Wow, isn't that something," Simon said, taking a sip of wonderfully hot coffee. "How long have you been janitor here?"

"Over fifty years," Andy said picking his mug back up.

Simon nearly spit out his coffee, "Fifty years? That's a long time. Are you planning on retiring soon?"

"Retire?" Mr. Cross said with a laugh. "I ain't ever gonna retire. What would I do? Ain't got no wife, no family to speak of- except for my brother Peter. The school's all I got. The school and the kids. That's what keeps me goin'."

"But fifty years!" Simon said in wonder. "I bet you've seen some changes around here."

"Oh sure, I remember way back in the day," Mr. Cross began to say, "before we had the fancy boiler furnace we got now. We had coal furnaces. And it'd get so cold that we had to keep it runnin' all night. So, I'd set my alarm to come in at two or three in the mornin' and shovel coal."

Simon looked at Mr. Cross, completely aghast. He thought the old man would have a look of bitterness or disdain, but instead his face beamed with pride and nostalgia.

"I hope they paid you a little overtime," Simon said.

"Nope," Mr. Cross replied, "don't do it for the money."

"Well, I bet the union threw a fit," Simon mused.

"Ha, unions," Mr. Cross muttered, before taking another sip of coffee.

Simon's face revealed his confusion, but Mr. Cross didn't expand on what he meant. Then Simon turned and looked out the window at the beautiful town cast in a radiant golden glow of the morning sun. For a moment, he listened to the hush of the wind rustling the leaves in the trees, the chirping of the birds, and the dull hum of the grain elevator. The fresh air danced in his hair, brushed his cheek, and stirred his senses. Suddenly, Simon couldn't help but think about his conversation with Jeremy regarding purpose and his other conversation with Jack regarding opportunity. He thought of Hope, Mrs. Potter's question, and the curse.

Simon snapped out of his trance and asked Mr. Cross, "Haven't seen any ghosts around here in all those years have you?"

Mr. Cross jerked his head around and studied Simon's face, "Ghosts? What kinda ghosts?"

Simon could see that the question completely changed the old man's demeanor. Mr. Cross looked at him expressionless waiting for a reply.

"No, uh nothing, just ghosts, you know like we used, uh, think that the school was haunted," Simon said with a nervous laugh.

"Haunted?" Mr. Cross repeated, tossing the rest of his coffee out the window onto the schoolyard below.

"Yeah, you know like ghost stories," Simon said trying to recover. "We used to say Jessie Joseph and Adam Potter haunted the school. Of course, I don't believe it, but I will admit I was a little freaked out when I found that small coffin last week in the storage room..."

"You found a coffin?" Mr. Cross asked with a stern expression. "Where is it?"

"It's still in the basement, must have been some kind of Halloween decoration or something," Simon said jovially. "Miss Harold wanted me to clean the storage room out when I got a chance. So, I started on it last week but didn't get very far. There's a lot of stuff down there. I threw out the obvious garbage, but I kept a stack of other items for you to look through."

"A coffin in the storage room in the basement?" Mr. Cross asked with a pained expression.

Simon nodded, "Yeah, I just piled it all up in the far corner of the basement for you or Mr. Gettby to look through and see if anything was worth keeping."

"Let's go take a look," Mr. Cross said decidedly heading for the door.

Descending the steps to the basement, Simon got an uneasy feeling that Mr. Cross's mood had dramatically changed. He tried to reassure himself that it was probably due to Miss Harold giving him one more chore to do and getting him off of his set schedule. When they reached the floor of the basement, Mr. Cross reached over and flipped on the light switch.

"Where's the stuff that you was talk'n about?" Mr. Cross asked.

"It's on the other side of the furnace," Simon said, leading him around to it. He ducked his head to avoid the low hanging duct work. "I just put it over here thinking there would be more room to sort it all out. I'll be glad to take anything you don't want out to the incinerator…"

Just as Simon turned back towards the janitor, the pile of junk unexpectedly crashed to the ground. His legs went weak and blood rushed from his face. The lid had fallen off of the coffin and was laying on the floor beside it. Even more startling, the small door behind the furnace had swung wide open.

* * *

Simon, still affected by what he had seen, now stood with Joey and George next to the back-stop while Rich's ace pitcher warmed up on the mound. Joey held the rulebook in his hand, studying it carefully.

"What are you looking up?" George asked.

"I was just checking on the number of warmup pitches allowed," Joey answered. "I gotta make sure we're spot on with this one cause it's going to get heated."

"Oh yeah?" Simon said, lost in thought.

"Why's that?" George asked.

"Are you kidding me?" Joey asked with a frown. "Rich can't start one and two. He'll implode. So, if his team's not playing well, he might pull an Ozzie Guillen on us out there. Here it is. It's article 2.1.A. Just as I thought, 'A pitcher shall be allotted ten warmup pitches to start a ballgame and then eight pitches at the advent of each inning thereafter.' Then he strode towards the mound with his chin held high and yelled, "Coming down, boys!"

"Surprised, you had to look that one up," George said.

"Oh, I already knew it," Joey said pulling his mask down over his face. "You just can't be too sure, that's all," he said instructively to George. "Study your rule book religiously. That way when you are in the heat of battle, it'll just come to you. You don't even have to think twice about it."

Joey's words once again proved to be prophetic. Things were about to heat up. The Angel's were throwing their ace, Ralph Livingood, against the Yankees. He was the most dominating pitcher in the league, more so than Jackson Helrigle even. Whereas Jackson mostly threw fastballs and pitched by intimidation, Ralph was becoming a masterful artist, changing speeds and painting the corners. Even at age ten, he was completely in command of his stuff.

Now he walked around the mound, took his cap off, and placed it under his arm. He wiped the ball with both hands while shooting a quick glance over to his dad who was standing in the doorway of the dugout.

Wilson B. smacked his hands together several times giving fervent exhortations to his son who was about to start the biggest game of his life. Fans packed the bleachers and the lawn chairs were stacked several rows deep down the first and third base lines. Simon could feel the tension in the air as he walked past Rich who was standing in the first base coach's box.

"Good luck, coach," Simon said under his breath as he walked past the Yankees skipper.

But, Rich didn't say a word in response. Instead, he simply scowled and spit some of his chaw towards the fence. Clearly, he was in the zone. Expectations had been running high at the beginning of the season for the reigning champs, and Rich was feeling the weight of the world on his shoulders. He had lost several key players from last year's team that went all the way to regionals before bowing out of the tournament. Now he was faced with the unenviable task of replacing his ace pitcher and number three, four, and six batters in the heart of the Yankee lineup. After the narrow loss to Helrigle's Devil Rays, a few of the parents were already beginning to grumble. In a small town, there is very little chatter that doesn't eventually stir in the ear of the accused. And Rich knew all too well which parents were more than likely to be causing all of the trouble.

Coldly, he stared at two dads who stood at the fence next to the dugout. One was bending the other's ear as Ralph took the mound. Rich clapped his hands to get the batter's attention before going through several signals. When finished, he clapped his hands again, turned, and walked back several steps towards right field.

The lead off man dug into the batter's box as Ralph nodded at the catcher, began his wind up, and fired the first pitch.

Joey bellowed, "*Strike!*"

Rich frowned at Joey who returned his glare. Simon waited for one of them to look away. Finally, Joey was forced to look back towards the mound as Ralph prepared the second pitch. This time the ball appeared to be slightly outside.

Once again Joey gave a very animated signal for a second time and yelled, "*Strike!*"

"Come on, Blue!" Rich yelled from the coach's box. The Yankee fans clamored for justice amidst the Angel's fans' cheers of approval.

Joey clicked his ticker before looking down the first base line a second time towards Rich who angrily chastised the umpire. Deliberately, Joey held up his fingers indicating the 0-2 count.

Simon looked from Joey to Rich and then back again, suspecting he knew what was going on here.

Once again Ralph looked to his father in the dugout. All of the extra time they had spent in the batting cage was starting to pay off. Wilson B. knew that his son had talent because he had the very same kind of talent when he himself was a kid. He also knew that Ralph would get all of the opportunities that he never had gotten. His son, the fair-haired boy, was special, and everybody knew it.

"If he keeps his head on straight and stays healthy, he might go all the way to the big leagues," Wilson B. thought.

The tall flame thrower once again came set. He looked for the signal, nodded, and wound up. This time the Yankee batter dove out of the box into the dirt. As he gave an animated signal, Joey yelled, "*Strike three!*"

Wilson B. pumped his fist in the air, while Ralph's mother shrieked with excitement.

Rich violently grabbed his cap off of his head and walked halfway down the baseline yelling at the ump, "WHAT? You've got to be kidding me! He had to dive out of the box, Joey!"

Simon glanced over to George who had a concerned expression on his face. The crowd on both sides had already been whipped into a frenzy. Joey looked down the first baseline and gave a warning over the clamor. "Better settle down coach!" he threatened.

"Let him have it, Rich!" one of the dads standing next to the fence shouted.

"Yeah, don't let him get away with that," another demanded. "Show a little backbone."

Rich pivoted, spit on the ground, and folded his massive arms in protest as Ralph made short work of the next two Yankee batters, ending the top half of the first. From that point on, the intensity only continued to escalate with each new inning. After establishing his authority, Joey maintained control of the game from behind the plate by relying on the rulebook. Even though there were several close plays and contested calls, all disputes eventually succumbed to the weight of the rules.

George and Simon were glad to have Joey's encyclopedic memory of the exact page numbers and specific articles to reference in defense of several close calls that could have gone either way. At different points during the contentious game each of the umpires' calls were challenged by the respective coaches while the crowd protested adamantly. And yet each time it was Joey who bailed the crew out by citing the precedent for the decision, thereby rendering each coach powerless to press the issue any further. Ultimately, both the coaches and the parents of the players were satisfied with the way in which Joey managed the game. The result was a well-played contest between two little league juggernauts.

In the bottom of the fifth inning, the Angels finally started getting to the Yankee ace whose arm was beginning to tire. After the first batter had reached on a walk, Ralph brought him around to score with a scorching line drive to the gap in left center. The Angles' fans exploded off of the bleachers and out of their lawn chairs with wild screaming, clapping, and whistling, while the Yankee parents festered and stewed. Having lost several of his key pitchers from the year before, Rich went with his gut and stuck with his starter. The ploy worked and the Yankees were able to get out of the inning with only having given up a single run. And that is where the score remained until the seventh and final inning.

Rich gathered his players around him in the front of the dugout and gave a rousing speech in an effort to ignite a rally. "Listen guys, this is what champions do," Rich exclaimed. "When their backs are to the wall and they're facing adversity, they rise to the challenge. By rule, Ralph can only pitch to four more batters. If we can get two guys on, then they'll have to bring in somebody else to pitch."

Charged by the passion of their coach, the first Yankee batter made little effort to get out of the way of a wild pitch that plunked him, sending him to first base. Wilson B. and the Angels' parents bellowed once again in protest, but their accusations fell on deaf ears. Joey merely looked down at his clicker and held up a fist indicating that there were no outs. The next batter laid down a perfect bunt. Ralph raced to the ball, picked it up, and turned to throw. When he did, his right foot slipped out from under him causing the ball to rise above the first baseman's head. The crowd erupted while Rich violently waved the runners on to the next base. The Yankees now had runners on second and third base with no outs.

The drama being played out was heart wrenching for parents, coaches, players, and umpires alike. No one was sitting down. Parents lined the field anxiously clutching the fence, while the players could barely hear their coaches' instructions over the noise of the crowd. Simon was loving it all- the environment, the noise, the intensity. He took a moment in-between pitches to look around the ballpark. He wanted to take it all in.

This, after all, *was* the great American past time. In the big scheme of things, the game meant nothing, but the kids didn't know that. To them it was everything. This is what Simon missed about baseball as he had gotten older when it became more of a chore or a job. He missed the purity and innocence of the game that he once experienced as a kid right here at the very same ball field.

True to his competitive nature, Ralph bore down and struck out the next two Yankees before exiting the game to wild applause. His dad gave him a big bear hug and patted him on the back before bringing in the closer.

To Rich's delight, the Angels' big lefty was having trouble finding the strike zone under the intense pressure. Consequently, the pitcher fell behind 0-2 in the count. Then he made a fatal mistake and lobbed a softball over the heart of the plate, and the Yankee batter made him pay for it, sending a shot down the third base line. Again, the noise was deafening as two base runners crossed home plate. Regaining his composure, the Angels' pitcher was able to get the final out, but not before the damage had already been done. They now trailed the Yankees one to two.

Going into the bottom of the last inning, Rich was faced with the same dilemma that plagued his adversary. His ace could only pitch to two more batters. Under extreme duress, the hurler got the first two Angels to ground out. Now there was just one out between Rich and a much-needed victory. But, when he went to his bullpen, his closer had the same jitters that had bedeviled the Angels' pitcher. He was all over the place walking two straight batters before Rich called timeout and headed to the mound.

"You've got to get this kid out," Rich said towering over the 10-year-old boy. "Cause if you don't, Ralph Livingood is up next and there's no place for him to go. We can't walk in the tying run. Now, let's go!"

The little boy nodded with a determined expression. He peered over the top of his glove and fired a strike, but the batter rose to the challenge and battled back. With the count full, the Yankee pitcher set to throw and delivered the next pitch. For the first time all night, Joey paused before making the call and signaled for the batter to take his base. Rich nearly came undone. He threw his hat into the dugout and mumbled a few choice words.

Now with the bases juiced and Ralph coming to the plate, the crowd was beside themselves with anticipation. Ralph turned towards his dad down the third base line who gave several signals before clapping decisively.

Lexus Helrigle and his Devil Rays looked on with great interest from behind the right field fence where they had been warming up for the nightcap against Jeremy's woeful Padres.

With the pitcher trying to keep the ball down in the strike zone, the count went to 3-0. Ralph put the bat over his shoulder and took a deep breath before stepping back into the batter's box. Meanwhile, Rich paced up and down the dugout like a caged lion, sorting through his options. He knew Ralph was a great hitter, maybe the best he had ever seen from Bethel. As his pitcher stepped onto the rubber, Rich got his attention and gave him the signal to intentionally walk the slugger. The two dads at the fence were nearly beside themselves.

Ralph saw the signal and knew its implication. He crowded the plate as tightly as possible, but much to Rich's dismay, the Yankee pitcher looked to the left of the dugout towards his dad standing at the fence. The disgruntled father was motioning for him to go ahead and pitch to the batter. The pitcher looked back and forth between the his coach and his dad before beginning his windup. To Ralph's surprise, the ball was heading straight down the middle of the plate as he unleashed his Easton and hammered the pitch deep over the fence in right, sailing high over Lexus Helrigle before bouncing into the cornfield.

The game winning home run elicited a wild celebration for the Angels and their families as Ralph touched all the bags before stomping on home plate and being engulfed by his teammates. Rich could only look on with frustration at the blatant defiance of his pitcher.

After the teams finished shaking hands, Simon made his way over to console his friend who was already planning his postgame speech and the inevitable conversation that he was going to have to have with one of the parents.

"Hey, man," Simon said, grabbing Rich by the arm. "Tough loss. Your kids played a great game. You should be proud of them."

Rich looked at Simon with a baffled expression. " 'Proud of them'?" Rich repeated in disbelief.

"Yeah, both teams played an amazing game," Simon said a little taken aback.

"That doesn't mean jack!" Rich retorted. "There are winners and losers. That's it. There's no such thing as a moral victory."

Simon was speechless as Rich made his way over to his team and pulled up a bucket to sit on. It looked like a funeral. Players were balling, fathers looked on with set jaws, while mothers bore solemn expressions. Conversely, the scene was in direct contrast to the Angels' side of the field where the coaches handed out game balls to the euphoric players.

Between games Joey, George, and Simon all congregated at the back-stop, where George gushed over Joey's knowledge of the little league rules.

"Man, how did you know about the interference rule with the donut on the on deck circle?" George asked in amazement. "That could have been ugly. I thought Rich was going to totally lose it!"

"That's what I've been trying to tell you," Joey said smugly. "The more you study the rule book the less likely anyone will oppose you. They can argue with you all night, but it doesn't matter as long as you are on the right side of the rules. It makes life behind the plate so much easier when they are right at your fingertips. The game runs more smoothly when the fans, coaches, and players all submit to your decisions because you have a stronger command of the letter of the law. I mean, there's a reason somebody takes the time to write them down, right? They cover every situation you will ever run into. In fact, that's the only way to do it. I don't know how anybody could umpire without knowing *all* of the rules."

George and Simon nodded mindfully while Joey sucked on a couple of ice cubes. It all made perfect sense to Simon who was scheduled to be behind the plate for the second game of the twin bill. While he reflected on Joey's assertions, he surveyed the crowd outside the field of play and contemplated his own ability as an arbitrator.

Suddenly, he recognized two older women sitting in lawn chairs down the third base line as the two women who had greeted him after church on Sunday. And he again thought of the words of old Mrs. Potter. At that moment, Hannah Grace happened to look up and make eye contact with Simon. Before he could turn away, she waved to him. Politely, he waved back.

"Flirting with the ladies?" Joey asked mockingly.

"Funny," Simon replied. "No, I know them. I mean I met them the other day at…I can't remember where it was." Simon certainly didn't want to bring up going to church to Joey of all people.

"Probably at the voter registration table in front of the bank," Joey said incredulously as though Simon should have known. "Duh!"

* * *

"Look Mother, the young man whom we met at church is one of the umpires," Hannah Grace said with outward enthusiasm. "He just waved to us."

"Hmmph," Mara responded. "No, I didn't see. I was too busy keepin' an eye on your pretty little niece. Cause if you ain't gonna, then I gotta."

Hannah Grace turned toward the bike rack where Mara had been staring. She gasped at first thinking that Sharon was Shannon who was sitting in a much older boy's lap as he held her a little too tightly.

"Oh, Shannon," Hannah Grace said with great disapproval.

"No, not that one," Mara said agitated. She pointed to the other end of the bike rack where Sharon was playfully wrestling with another older boy.

"Oh, mother, they're just…" Hannah Grace started to say while closely observing her innocent niece.

"They're just…They're just…" Mara mimicked. "Well, you was 'just' with my John not long ago yourself and look what happened to the two of you."

Hannah Grace's face dropped at the deliberate jab. "That was different," Hannah Grace sputtered. "We were a little older than that."

"Huh, not much!" Mara said. "What a year or two?"

"Anyway Sharon's got a better head on her shoulders than that," Hannah Grace said with a tone of uncertainty. "Besides, they're not serious. I don't even know who that boy is." But, Mara was not listening. She was leaning against her hand that was propped up on the arm of the lawn chair and staring off in the distance.

Hannah Grace gave a worried glance back over her shoulder to her precious Sharon. The young girl was smiling and laughing while half struggling to free her hands from the older boy who was acting like he was going to put an ice cube down her shirt. Playfully, she yanked one hand free, accidentally popping the boy in the nose. They both stopped for a moment. Sharon had a look of shock on her face while the boy rubbed his nose. Then they busted out laughing as he chased her around the bike rack again.

"I wasn't much older, was I?" Hannah Grace said, conceding the point.

* * *

The next game between the Devil Rays and the Padres was not to have nearly the drama of the first contest. It was a beat down from the first pitch. Lexus showed no mercy in starting his son Jackson against the hapless Padres. Consequently, Jeremy was having a hard time even keeping his players in the batter's box. Jackson had been groomed in the mold of a Bob Gibson type pitcher who came with high, inside heat, then worked the lower, outside corner of the strike zone. The strategy was working to perfection as Jackson logged backwards K' after backwards K' into the scorebook. Even so, Lexus was mercilessly riding his son, criticizing even the slightest imperfections whether it be on the mound or at the plate. Simon could only guess that he was somehow affected by the earlier game, because the Padres were certainly posing no threat through three scoreless innings. In the meantime, Jackson had driven in five runs on his own, pushing the lead to sixteen as they neared the mercy rule.

True to his nature, Jeremy took the beat-down in stride providing his players with support and exhortations to try their hardest and have some fun. Several times, in between innings, Simon made small talk with Jeremy who responded in kind. Nothing was said of their conversation several nights earlier, even though Simon had had a hard time pushing it out of his mind. There was something that he wanted to ask Pastor Pete before losing his nerve. But even now the timing didn't seem right. Jeremy seemed distracted and not himself. After the fourth inning came to a close Simon decided to check in with the scrawny youth pastor and see if everything was all right.

"Jeremy," Simon said walking over to the Padre dugout.

"Hey, Simon," Jeremy said looking over his shoulder while helping to get the gear on his catcher.

"Can I have a word with you for a second?" Simon asked while George and Joey looked on disapprovingly.

"Uh, sure, what's up?" Jeremy asked as the two of them strolled toward left field.

"I just wanted to make sure you were okay," Simon said. "You don't seem yourself tonight, anything the matter?"

"Oh, no," Jeremy replied with his face looking flush.

"That's good," Simon replied. "I was just making sure. Well, if that's the case, I thought that maybe if you had a second after the game I could ask you a couple more questions that have been nagging me."

"Tonight?" Jeremy asked. "Yeah, I suppose. But, I can't talk long because I have something important that I have to do later."

"Oh, well if tonight's bad for you…" Simon started to say.

"No, no, it'll be fine," Jeremy answered once again coming to his senses. "I just can't talk long that's all."

"No, that's okay, really," Simon said. "I have somewhere I've got to be too. There's just one thing I wanted to ask you."

"Simon!" Joey called from behind home plate, pointing at his watch.

"Well, okay, I'll talk to you after the game," Simon said with a smile. "I guess we're starting up again." But, Jeremy had already started walking back towards the first base coach's box.

Jackson was on his way to a no-hitter going into the fourth and final inning. Lexus put his hands on both of Jackson's shoulders and gave him some final instructions. Adamantly, he wagged his finger in his son's face before turning him loose to take the mound. Simon called, "Batter up!" before he noticed little Randy dragging his bat towards home plate. Simon thought back to the day when he and Jeremy worked with him on getting his feet set.

As Jackson reared back and let the first pitch rip, Randy took a loading step. The pitch was high and tight, but somehow Randy managed to get the barrel of his bat out in front. To everyone's surprise, he put the head of the bat on the ball, drilling it into left field and ruining Jackson's dad's precious no-hitter.

Lexus went crazy in the dugout, yelling at his son for letting it slip through his fingers. In a rage, he slammed the row of helmets and knocked over some of the bats. Jackson looked to the dugout with a hurt expression on his face while Jeremy ardently congratulated Randy at first base. The little boy's face beamed with great satisfaction.

Simon couldn't help but feel happy for Randy, and he swelled with pride for the small part that he played in helping him get a firm foundation. Meanwhile, Jackson snapped his glove down as he caught the ball from the catcher. He walked around the mound, rubbing the ball with a look of bitter anger on his face. When he finally looked up again, he saw his old buddy "Porker" apprehensively stepping into the batter's box. Jackson's lip curled with a devilish grin. Before the first pitch even left Jackson's hand, Parker was bailing out of the batter's box as an act of self-preservation.

"Stay in there Parker," Jeremy yelled from first base.

Meanwhile, Lexus was still berating Jackson for losing his focus. And when Jackson's mother tried to come to the boy's defense, it only made matters worse. Jackson gripped the ball hard and came set on the rubber, knowing what he *had* to do. Digging deep, he threw the two-seamer with everything he had. Parker didn't have a chance of getting out of the way. The dull thud of the ball hitting the hefty boy between the boy's shoulder blades echoed off of the concession stand as the crowd moaned. Jeremy came running from first base as Simon kneeled down next to the boy who was writhing in pain on the ground and gasping for air through gritted teeth.

Without compassion, Jackson looked over to his father who was leaning on the doorway to the dugout. Lexus first looked over at Parker who was still trying to regain his breath, before giving his son a nod of approval for retaliating after giving up the precious 'no-no.' His boy might has what it takes after all.

* * *

After Jeremy helped Parker into the front seat of his parent's car, he leaned forward with his eyes closed for a moment and muttered a few words before shutting the door and bidding the family goodnight.

"Is everything all right?" Simon asked from over Jeremy's shoulder.

"What?" Jeremy asked.

"Do you think Parker will be all right?" Simon asked again troubled by Jeremy's strange behavior. He didn't exhibit the same boundless energy and annoying optimism. But, what was most alarming was that the warm smile that normally adorned Jeremy's face was noticeably absent.

"I don't know," Jeremy said flatly as he watched the car drive away.

"Hey, I know you only have a second," Simon said while taking a look at his watch, "but, there's something that you might be able to answer for me."

"I do need to get going soon, but go ahead," Jeremy said, "what's your question?"

"Well, okay," Simon said as he tried to muster the courage to broach the subject. "You know how you talked about having a purpose for our lives?"

"Yes," Jeremy replied.

"Well, I am beginning to think that I may know what that is for me," Simon said.

At that, Jeremy's expression changed and a broad smile swept over his face. "That's awesome!" Jeremy said. "So, what is your question?"

"It's kind of a stupid question actually," Simon admitted, "do you...do you believe that there could be such a thing as a curse?"

"A curse?" Jeremy repeated with a forced laugh.

"Yeah, it's stupid," Simon replied, shaking his head while looking down at the ground. "I know. Never mind."

"Of course, I do!" Jeremy said with a dire expression on his face.

Simon could feel the hairs on the back of his neck standing up . "You do?" he asked desperately.

"Yeah, I mean, 'Does a mother cry out in pain during delivery? Is the ground difficult to toil and work? And does the snake crawl on his belly?" Jeremy asked rhetorically.

Simon looked on with a blank expression, having no idea what Jeremy was referring to.

Jeremy peeked at his watch and said, "Look, can we talk about this later? I've really got to get over to the town hall meeting about the referendum, and it started five minutes ago."

"Yeah, sure, no problem," Simon answered, still rocked by Jeremy's response.

Jeremy started jogging to his car as he called back over his shoulder, "Cool, thanks. I'm really sorry. I'll catch up with you later. Where will you be?"

"I don't know, I'm meeting with Rob about a potential opportunity to work for Jack Lawless," Simon yelled back.

Jeremy stopped dead in his tracks and turned to face Simon. "Jack Lawless?" Jeremy repeated.

"Yeah, he says he might have the perfect opportunity for me," Simon intimated.

"We really need to get together later," Jeremy said, walking a few steps back towards Simon, "put my number into your cell phone."

Quickly, Simon dug into his pockets and pulled out his cell. Just as he was about to punch in Jeremy's number, he saw that he had missed a text from Rob to meet him at the town hall at 8:00 p.m. As Simon was about to put the phone back into his pocket, it slipped out of his hand and smacked against the pavement sending the battery flying.

He let a few expletives slip before picking up the cracked phone and retrieving the battery. After putting it back together, he tried to turn it on, but it was of no use. It was dead.

"So it goes," Simon muttered under his breath. "Great. What if Uncle Joe calls…or Hope…or Rob?"

He didn't even consider the most important call he would be missing later that night.

* * *

Trying his best not to make a scene, Simon worked his way through several rows of farmers before finding a seat next to Rob, Joey, and George. Somehow they had managed to save him a spot even though the hall was completely packed. Simon was still in the lurch about why Rob wanted to attend the meeting. He suspected that it had something to do with one of the ventures that Jack had alluded to the night before.

George and Joey sat up and moved their legs to the side as Simon made his way past them to the empty chair next to Rob. Simon started to say hello, but before he could do so, Joey put his index finger to his lips and then pointed to Miss Harold who was just finishing with her assessment of the general condition of the school building in Bethel.

"Where've you been, man?" Rob whispered.

"Sorry, I didn't see your text until just a few minutes ago," Simon replied.

"What are we doing here anyway?" Simon asked.

Rob mouthed the word "Jack". He motioned towards the members of the school board sitting at a foldout table in the front of the room. Each member had a microphone in front of them with wires streaming to the floor with one notable exception. There was one conspicuously empty fold out chair sitting at the end of the table where the president of the school board normally sat. A podium with its own microphone stood at the front of the room facing the school board members.

Thelma sat hunched over a piece of paper reading through a pair of bifocals. As she ran through the building's extensive list of maintenance needs and deficiencies, Simon listened intently. He still had no clue as to why they were there. Even more surprising, he didn't expect to find George and Joey sitting with Rob at the meeting. Jack hadn't mentioned anything about them. Feeling slightly threatened, he wondered if they too were being recruited by the shrewd businessman.

"Surely not," Simon thought. "They probably were just taking an interest in the local politics." He wouldn't put it past them to be lobbying for something or other.

With Thelma droning on and on about inadequate ventilation and statewide mandates, Simon glanced at Joey and George to try and ascertain their reason for being at the meeting. When he did, he caught a glimpse of Mr. Cross standing next to the wall at the far end of the room. The old janitor held his hat with both hands in front of him, expressionless, as he listened with great interest. Then Simon caught sight of another figure over Mr. Cross's shoulder lurking in the shadows. It was none other than Dr. Al-Banna.

Unexpectedly, Simon suddenly heard Jeremy's voice over the antiquated PA system.

"What a dweeb," Joey said in a whispered tone to Simon and Rob. "Can you believe this guy?"

Simon ignored the derogatory remark. Instead, he sat forward as he strained to see over the sea of John Deere and International mesh hats only to find Jeremy standing behind the podium. His hands shook as he laid out his notes before him. Awkwardly, he grabbed both sides of the podium as if to steady himself. Raising his fist to his mouth, he cleared his throat a couple of times before leaning down to speak into the microphone.

"Ladies and gentlemen, I appreciate the opportunity to speak to you tonight about the referendum on building a new elementary school," Jeremy said with a quivering voice. "We have all heard the extensive list of items that need to be fixed just for the current building to meet codes and fulfill state regulations. That's not even mentioning bringing it into the twenty-first century with computers or wiring the building for the internet. And we all understand the tremendous financial burden that building a new school would incur for our community..."

"Mr. Warner," Thelma said, interrupting the nervous youth pastor. "We don't need to take up everyone's time stating the obvious." There were several snickers and a few people who clapped, including Joey. "Do you have a point?"

"Yes, ma'am," Jeremy said swallowing hard before continuing, "an investment. The school is not a cost to our community. It is an investment. I was not born in Bethel. I am not from here. Many still consider me an outsider, but I feel as though over the past couple of years that I have been somewhat adopted into the community. And during that time, I have developed an attachment for the people here..."

"Is he for real?" Rob said under his breath to Simon.

"...Especially the children," Jeremy continued. "The founders of Bethel made an investment when they originally built the grade school over a hundred years ago. I know there is a large price to pay to build new schools, and I know that the farmers would have to shoulder most of that burden under the current proposal, but a long time ago the founders of Bethel paid a great price. Why? Why would they do that? It had to have been a major financial burden for them too. After all, the building has stood the test of time. But, they did it. They did it because they saw it as an investment for their children's future and the future of their community. For an educated citizen is a better citizen."

There were several groans from the audience, and Simon could see that out of the one hundred or so people in attendance the vast majority seemed to be in direct opposition to Jeremy.

"Our freedoms come from wisdom and knowledge and understanding," Jeremy passionately insisted. He was overcoming his nerves and now spoke earnestly with strength and eloquence. "The churches and the schools are the heart of a community. The school and the fine people who work there shape and mold the minds of our future citizens who will eventually lead us on into the 21st century and beyond. How can we stand idly by while the rest of the world overtakes us? How can we handicap our children by not equipping them with the tools necessary to perpetuate the ideology of the American Dream? There is a sentiment that things will always be as they have been, because it is all that we have ever known. But I submit to you that there are no guarantees when it comes to our freedom or even the future of this great country. There is no such thing as entitlement. And there is no such thing as freedom that goes unchallenged. As Ronald Reagan once said, 'An informed patriot is what we want'."

Simon could feel Jeremy gaining steam. Looking at faces around him, he could see some of them begin to soften. A few of the spectators even unfolded their arms and sat forward.

"There are people in this world who want to take what we have," Jeremy said with passion, "and mark my words, they will do anything- and I mean *anything*- to get it.

"Where were you on 9/11? What were you doing that day? How did you feel as terrorists flew those planes into the Twin Towers and the Pentagon?" Jeremy paused for a moment as tears welled up in his eyes, and the eyes of many people in the audience. Even Simon had a lump in his throat as Jeremy made his final plea. "We have an obligation...an obligation to our children to prepare them for the unprecedented challenges that lie ahead. Yes, our liberties are based on the wisdom of our founding fathers, but wisdom comes from..."

Abruptly, there was a high-pitched squeal over the PA before it went completely dead. Men and women instinctively covered their ears in response to the horrible screech.

"Sorry," Rob said, looking down at an unplugged extension cord. "Sorry!" He held it up and then plugged it back in, causing a second violent screech to rip through the speakers.

Thelma shot Rob a disapproving glare before speaking, "I'm afraid your two minutes are over Mr. Warner," she said apologetically, "thank you."

"I-I just urge people to vote in favor of the children and their future," Jeremy said nervously in a feeble attempt to garner support.

"Thank you," the old principal said apologetically.

As he stepped back from the podium, several people clapped including Simon. Rob put his left hand over Simon's hands and shook his head dismissively.

"Is there anyone else who would like to say anything?" Miss Harold asked. She looked to Lexus Helrigle and Wilson B. Livingood who sat with their arms folded in the front row. Then she glanced at Mara and Hannah Grace who sat properly with their hands clasped on their laps. Next, her eyes met with Pastor Pete who looked away before turning to Mr. Cross who was standing in silence with his head down. No one came forward.

Mara leaned forward in her chair and looked past Hannah Grace to Pastor Pete who sat in silence. She shook her head in disgust and then sat back in her seat. Hannah Grace was still wiping the tears from her eyes after Jeremy's passionate speech.

"All right then," Miss Harold said, "is there anyone in dissent of the referendum who would like to speak?"

A stream of land owners got up from their seats and formed a long line behind the podium. Some held a piece of paper in their hands while others spoke extemporaneously. Seeing the flood of opposition, Jeremy dropped his head and made his way out the door into the sultry night. Nearly two hours later the last of the dissenters finished his final remarks. His words merely echoed the sentiments of the other farmers who spoke of the economic strain and financial burdens that they faced. A common theme was this year's particular crop that had been threatened by the over abundance of rain that had fallen in the spring.

Even though they spoke with great expertise about the potential economic crisis that they faced, Simon couldn't help but side with Jeremy. More than that, he was so impressed by the courage that the young man displayed in addressing a mob of people who were obviously in direct opposition to him. Surprised by his own emotional response, Simon realized that he had been deeply moved by the words of his friend.

"Friend?" Simon thought. "Is Jeremy a friend? I mean, I suppose he is." He once again considered the enlightening conversations that the two of them had had over the previous few weeks. He thought about Jeremy's compassion and understanding. His kind words and sincere concern. "What am I thinking? Of course, he's a friend."

Just as Simon came to that realization, Rob surprisingly stood up, straightened his tie, and made his way to the podium.

"Yes, Mr. Ateitup?" Miss Harold said. "We have already given everyone the opportunity to express support and opposition to the referendum."

"Yes, ma'am, I understand that," Rob said pulling some documents from the inside pocket of his suit. "I am neither. I am merely here to convey a message on behalf of Jack Lawless."

The crowd hushed as Miss Harold looked up from some notes that she had been jotting down, glanced down to the empty chair at the end of the table, and frowned. The board members looked down at the old principal and gave nods of approval.

"All right, you may speak," Miss Harold said.

"Mr. Lawless apologizes, but he regretfully had a prior engagement which could not be avoided," Rob said.

Simon was impressed with how smooth and polished Rob came across. He was far from the hapless drunk he was used to seeing carousing at the bar in the tavern, and he now understood why Jack touted his potential.

"Ladies and gentlemen, for the record, Mr. Lawless would like to publicly profess his position of neutrality on the issue of the referendum," Rob began to say, thereby eliciting some murmuring around the room. "He of course favors innovation and progress and has always been an advocate for education and the pursuit of knowledge. Obviously, a new building with all of the advances in technology would allow great opportunity for our youth to access *all* that the world has to offer right at their fingertips.

While Mr. Lawless wholeheartedly believes that the rich should pay their fair share of taxes, he also worries that the building of a new school would only jeopardize the economic stability of the community. Therefore, Mr. Lawless has come up with a pragmatic solution that would benefit the whole of society. In cooperation with the president of the First National Bank of Bethel, Mr. Lexus Helrigle, Jack would like to extend a most generous offer. He is willing to match any voluntary donation, dollar for dollar, towards the repairs and modifications necessary to bring the building up to code and fulfill the state's requirements. While he realizes that such a renovation will not provide the school with all of the latest technological advances, he is certain that it will relieve most of the unnecessary financial strain on the local landowners and businessmen."

"Just how much are we talking here?" one of the farmers called out from the back of the room.

"Jack did not put a cap on the grant," Rob said contemptuously.

The small murmur rose to a clamor before Thelma quieted the crowd with the authority of the gavel.

With an expression of great concern, Thelma once again leaned into the microphone. "Exactly how would such an arrangement work?" she asked.

Rob folded up the piece of paper and slipped it back into his coat pocket. Confidently, he smiled at the old principal and spoke, "Come on, Thelma. You know Jack. With only a few minor concessions and stipulations, he is ready to make a deal."

Once again, the people enthusiastically demanded that the board accept the unknown terms of the contract even before reading it.

The beleaguered principal's face turned pale and the corners of her mouth turned down as she slowly sat back in her chair.

"So that's how you buy a public institution," she muttered under her breath in disbelief.

* * *

Joey slid his hand into the ice cold cooler, retrieved four Bud Lights, and began to distribute them to everyone in the car. He tapped the can on Rob's shoulder. Taking one hand off of the steering wheel, he blindly reached back and grabbed ahold of the beer.

"Thanks man," Rob said, looking back at Joey in his rearview mirror.

"Here you go, George," Joey offered as he handed over a can to his protege sitting next to him in the back seat. George greedily grabbed for the can and made short work of getting it open.

"Simon?" Joey asked, resting the cold can on Simon's shoulder in the front passenger seat.

Simon glanced at the beer over his shoulder and instinctively reached for it before catching himself.

"Wait," Simon said. "Where are we going? I thought you were going to show me some of Jack's latest business ventures."

"We are," Rob replied flatly before taking a long swig from the shiny aluminum can.

Simon waved off Joey.

"No thanks," Simon said, "where are we going anyway?"

"You'll see," Rob said.

"What?" Joey chided, "you're not drinking?"

"No," Simon said plainly. He wanted to be sharp if he was going to be contemplating a job offer from Jack, especially if it had the potential to be as lucrative as the sales job in pharma.

"Not feeling well?" George asked.

"Come on, have a beer," Rob said. "It's no biggie."

Still, Simon held his ground.

"What are you some kind of 'Mary'," Joey remarked snidely over George's laughter. "Do you want me to get you a skirt to put on?"

"Funny," Simon replied, "I just want to have all of my faculties together if I'm going to be talking business. That's all."

Rob and Joey shared a glance in the rearview mirror before busting out in laughter as they drove out of Bethel towards the interstate.

"What?" Simon asked, getting slightly agitated.

"Nothing," Rob said before sliding an "Eve 6" CD into the car stereo and cranking up the volume. The words from "Inside Out" exploded through the sound system. Joey, George, and Rob sang fanatically to the lyrics, "...I would swallow my doubt, turn it inside out, find nothing but faith in nothing, want to put my tender heart in a blender, watch it spin around into a beautiful oblivion..."

When Simon tried again to ask about their destination over the earsplitting music, the only answer he received was a repeat of the chorus. Rendered dumb from the thumping bass, Simon merely sat back in his seat and took in the scenery that had been illuminated by the full moon rising high above the fields. Watching the corn and bean stalks rush by out the window, he speculated as to where they could be going or whom they might be seeing at nine o'clock on a Monday night.

As they neared the on ramp to the interstate, Rob rolled down the window and threw out his empty beer can before motioning to Joey for a refill. The car slowed down as Rob flipped on the turn signal. Simon looked at Rob and then peered out into the darkness, searching expectantly. Simon thought that they were going to turn onto the on ramp of the interstate. Instead, Rob jerked the wheel and turned the car into the parking lot of an old, abandoned gas station. Confused, Simon reached over and turned down the deafening music.

"Ah, come on!" George said, "I love that song."

Ignoring his comment, Simon asked Rob, "What's this, some kind of joke?"

"Nope," Rob replied evasively.

"It's an abandoned gas station," Simon said in disdain as the car came to a stop under the overhang.

"Sometimes looks can be deceiving," Rob said getting out of the car.

Simon, George, and Joey followed his lead.

"So, Jack wants us to open a gas station?" Simon said with a nervous laugh.

"From pharma to the big oil companies, man, you'll get in bed with anybody Freeman," Joey said sardonically.

"Nice, first I'm a janitor at the school and now you want me to pump gas," Simon joked. "I can see why you were being so mysterious. This is a big opportunity all right."

"Actually, it's not a gas station," Rob said digging through his pockets to find a key.

"It's not?" Simon asked. "Well, of course not, it's nothing. It's an abandoned building by the interstate."

"No, it's our ticket into a billion dollar a year industry," Rob said, holding a key ring up to the moonlight. "Simon, can you grab me the flashlight out of the trunk?"

"Sure," he said having his interest peeked. "Are we really talking about the oil industry?" he asked making his way over to the trunk of car.

"No, not quite," Rob said as he pulled a cigarette out of his pocket.

The dim light from the trunk came on as Simon excitedly lifted it up. He groped around with his hands.

"What is all of this junk, Rob?" Simon said with a laugh. "Ever think of cleaning this thing out once in while?" He felt the handle of a baseball bat and pulled it out under the light.

"Odd," he thought. Then he leaned around the back of the car and held the bat up to Rob, "I didn't know you played."

"I don't play," Rob said, lighting his cigarette while Joey reached for the pack. "The flashlight's probably by the tire iron...and rope. Next to the gas can."

Simon smiled, shook his head, and started to put the bat back down before he noticed the end of it. His heart began to race as he raised it up in the light and leaned in close to it. The end of the Louisville Slugger was covered with red blotches and tiny hairs that were stuck to it. His head spun as he remembered his blood splattered jeans and the unexplained blisters that he had on his hands for the past couple of weeks.

Suddenly, Rob came around to the back of the car and snatched the bat out his hands. "What are you doing?" Rob asked with a flurry of expletives. "You haven't found that thing yet? Here it is? If it was a snake..."

Simon stood back with his mouth agape. Rob flicked the switch, but nothing happened. He hit the end of the flashlight a few times before it flickered and came to life. Then he held it under his face, giving it an orange, ghoulish appearance.

"Walk this way," Rob said still carrying the bloody baseball bat. "Come on. I got the key. Let's go check it out." He wrenched open the door and made his way inside before waving for Simon, Joey, and George to follow him.

"Cool," George said excitedly as he walked through the door.

"It's about time," Joey said taking a drag on his cigarette.

Furtively, Simon swallowed hard before following them through the cobwebs into the dark room. His mind raced in an attempt to recollect what had happened his first night in Bethel while hanging out with Rob and the boys.

"There," Rob said just as the lights came on. He leaned against the bat and put out his hand, "Ta-da!"

"Ta-da?" Joey said. "It's a wreck! Look at this place. It's going to take a bunch of money just to get it cleaned up."

"Go ahead, Simon, ask me," Rob implored.

"Ask you what?" Simon replied unsurely. He was still fixated on the baseball bat and the matted blood.

"Yeah, ask me what we are standing in," Rob said.

"Okay, what are we standing in?" Simon asked solemnly.

"Bethel's first Adult Time Super Store!" Rob said as Simon's face contorted.

"Awesome!" Joey said.

"You're kidding," George stated in disbelief. "Nobody'll believe this."

"Whoa, you can't tell anybody yet," Rob threatened. "We're still in negotiations for the property. What do you think, Simon? Jack wants us to manage it for him. He puts up the capital, and we just rake it in."

"A *video* store?" Simon asked.

"No, not just a video store," Rob said like a kid in a candy shop. "I mean, yes, there will be a novelty store component. It's going to be like one-stop shopping. The Walmart of pornography, if you will. It'll be the biggest gentlemen's club between St. Louis and Chicago."

"You mean strip club," Simon said still trying to latch on to what he was hearing. "Jack wants me to give up a great job in pharmaceutical sales to manage a strip club?"

"Yes," Rob said. "But, that's just the tip of the iceberg. The gentlemen's club is more of a store front. It's a way to generate some income so that we get into the big money market."

"Which is what?" George asked.

"Let me ask you something," Rob said, "what limits a strip club's ability to drive clientele?"

"That's easy," Joey said. "Discretion. People are afraid of what other people think."

"Exactly!" Rob said. "So, how do you get fine upstanding citizens like Lexus Helrigle or Wilson B. Livingood, or your buddy Jeremy Warner to become a regular customer?" Rob was so excited that he couldn't wait for their answer. "You take it to their homes through the internet. That's the big ticket! Simon, we can make millions, I'm telling you. You can have anything and everything that you've ever wanted."

"By selling porn?" Simon asked.

"Who cares?" Joey asked.

"Yeah, what difference does it make?" Rob asked. "Whether it's selling blood pressure medicines, or Viagra, or Valtrex, or the morning after pill, it's all about making money. I'm not selling insurance my whole life. I'm going to sell life. It's brutal trying to sell people things that they need, but they don't want. Trust me. That's how pharma is going to be. So, how do you make money? Sell things that feed people's vices! Sell them what they crave. What they can't live without."

"Wait a minute," Joey said before Simon could respond, "isn't this the land that they are talking about putting the new school on?"

Simon looked at Joey dumbfounded.

"Yeah," Rob said, "but, the referendum doesn't have a snowball's chance to pass. It's too expensive. These farmers aren't going to go for another tax hike. Not to mention, nobody in Bethel wants to consolidate with Philo. Besides, Jack is working out all of those details. It's part of the under the table negotiations for the grant."

"Aren't people going to throw a fit when they find out they are about to have a strip club in their community?" Simon asked naively.

"Also a part of the negotiations my friend," Rob said. "It's all being taken care of, man. Jack has thought of everything. Once he makes a deal, that's it. We're in, and there's nothing they can do to get out of it. His contracts are binding. I mean, dude, he has a Harvard law degree for crying out loud."

"I don't know," Simon said looking around the shoddy building.

"Come on," Rob said walking over to the front door with the flashlight showing him the way.

"Where are we going now?" Simon asked with his stomach beginning to turn.

"We're going to see Jack," Rob replied.

* * *

The car made its way back towards Bethel with Joey and George going on and on about the prospects of the new Bethel Adult time Super Store. Rob wearily answered as many of their questions as he could about the project. Despondently, Simon stared out the window while Joey pulled out a few more celebratory Bud Lights. Joey hospitably tapped Simon on the shoulder with the shiny silver can. But, Simon once again waved him off.

"What in the world, Freeman?" Rob asked, taking exception to his downcast expression. "I offer you the chance of a lifetime, and you act like somebody ran over your dog."

"What?" Simon asked. "Oh, no, I know it's probably very lucrative. I just never saw myself doing something like that."

"Like what, making people happy?" Joey said. "I'd be all over it! Besides, if they don't get it there, they'll just get it somewhere else. So, why not make some money off of it?"

"Yeah, entertaining people, distracting them from their wretched lives," Rob said as he turned off of the main slab and made his way down a country road.

"I don't know," Simon said feeling sick to his stomach.

"Well, I do," Joey said. "If he's out, then I'm in. Tell Jack, or I'll tell Jack myself. It's a gold mine."

"Maybe," Rob said, "but, Jack's not asking you. He's asking Simon." He turned to Simon and asked, "What's the deal, you think you're too good for us or something?"

The car made several more turns as it drove further and further back into the sticks. Simon's mind was all over the place. He couldn't concentrate on any one thing. First, he thought of the job in New Jersey, then he thought of Hope and Jeremy, before thinking about Jack and the offer. It wasn't like he had never looked at pornography in his life, but something did not feel right. The debate raged within him. It wasn't just about money, was it?"

"Am I so above everyone else that I can't do that kind of thing?" Simon thought. "People look at that junk all of the time. What's the harm? Who cares what other people do? Live and let live, isn't that what I've always said? Besides, it's not my responsibility to be the morality police." But no matter how much he reasoned, something inside of him kept going back to Jeremy and Hope.

As Joey and Rob argued about the business opportunity, Simon tried to sift through what it was that was giving him pause. A part of him tried desperately to shake his conscience, thinking about all of the money he could make. But it was no use. There was no denying it. Jeremy's words reassured him with the truth while Hope's voice was an antidote to the vile temptation he was facing. When he thought of Hope the pain in stomach subsided momentarily, and he knew what his answer would be.

"Are you afraid of ending up like us, living in this little hick town with us hayseeds?" Rob asked hotly. "Well, I got news for you, buddy, you're already one of us!"

Suddenly, Rob slammed on the brakes while wrenching the steering wheel. He let out a series of expletives as the car swerved to avoid a small animal in the road.

"What are you doing?" Joey asked looking out the back window and wiping the beer off of his shirt.

"Sorry, man," Rob said, "it just came out of nowhere."

"What was it?" Simon asked.

"Opossum!" Joey answered. "I can't believe you swerved to miss it. Back up! Back up!"

Dutifully, Rob put the car in reverse and hit the gas. The car swerved again wildly backwards down the country road. He hit the brakes, threw the car in park, and jumped out. Joey and George followed closely behind.

"Whoa, what are we doing?" Simon asked fearfully. He turned around in his seat and saw the trunk fly open and heard the guys laughing excitedly.

Simon made his way cautiously to the back of the car. In the red glow of the parking lights, he saw Rob handing out baseball bats to George and Joey.

"Come on, Freeman," Rob said, offering him a baseball bat. Joey and George were already in the high grass of the ditch looking for the opossum.

"What are you doing?" Simon asked.

"There he is!" George said as the hideous creature darted back onto the road.

Before Simon fully realized what was happening, Rob rushed at the defenseless animal. It was a horrible, graphic scene. Simon nearly wretched as the desperate, helpless animal squealed for mercy. As Joey and Rob took swing after swing, Simon reached a hand over his mouth and turned towards the ditch.

A few moments later, George, Joey, and Rob slid back into the car where Simon was already sitting with a pale, green complexion. George got in first and moved quietly to his seat in the back. Then Joey jumped in celebrating the carnage, followed by Rob who grinned with great satisfaction.

"Ah, man, that was awesome!" Joey yelled, charged by the experience.

"I know!" Rob acknowledged, "did you hear how loud he was screaming? Sounded like a baby."

"Oh, I know!" Joey said wiping the blood off of his face. "I've got it all over me. What a rush!"

"Look at Freeman!" Rob said laughing. "You all right buddy?"

"You guys are sick," Simon said with disgust.

"Is that right?" Rob asked.

"Yeah, getting your jollies off of beating some poor, defenseless animal," Simon said with an air of condescension.

"Funny," Rob said with his brow furrowing. "Your first night back in town, you didn't think so. In fact, you were the one we had to pull off of it. You just kept swinging and swinging and swinging…"

Suddenly, Simon remembered the blood splatter on his jeans and the blisters on his hands, and he dropped his head in disgust and self-loathing.

"Simon got some last time?" Joey asked rubbing Simon's head. "There's nothing like the first time. I remember my first time." He looked forward with a sinister grin. "Oh, don't take it so hard Simon. It's like I said. Everything is an experience that brings you further into consciousness. Once you have taken life, you learn so much about life and yourself, and the universe. Look! I'm still shaking!"

"All right," Rob said. "Simon's not feeling ya."

"I just wonder," Joey said, his eyes dark. "What it would be like to take a human's life. You know. I wonder what *that* feels like. That kind of power. It must be amazing."

"Okay, stop trying to be funny, Simon's already thrown up once, and I don't want him getting sick in my car," Rob said reaching into his pocket. "time to chill out a little."

"No, I'm serious," Joey continued. "I wonder what it would be like to commit the perfect crime. I've thought about that a lot before. That must be such a rush."

"Yeah, like the rush of twelve thousand volts racing through your body from the chair," George said with a laugh.

"You joke, but that might be the ultimate experience actually," Joey pontificated. "What a way to go. Being absorbed into the consciousness of the universe and moving on to the next experience in the journey. That would be cool too, but that's not what I'm talking about."

Still shaken from the brutality that his friends had displayed and the elation that they expressed, Simon was even more astounded by Joey's musings. He hadn't felt that way in a long time, and it sickened him like when people tell a racist joke or make fun of someone who is disabled. As if horrific violence as entertainment wasn't enough, these guys had taken it to a new level by acting on the brutality. What Simon couldn't fathom was that he had evidently eagerly participated in such a gruesome bludgeoning. If that was the case, what else was he capable of doing?

Joey continued with his supposition, "I mean there are some individuals in this world who people would be thrilled to be rid of, right?"

"You mean like Stalin or Hitler or Mao or Castro?" George asked taking another drink as the car drove on into the night.

"Whatever!...More like Dahmer or Bundy," Joey said, "nobody would be upset if one of those guys got whacked."

"Maybe so, but what are you going to do, track down a serial killer or rapist?" George asked with a laugh.

Rob said nothing. Evidently he was deep in thought, holding onto the steering wheel with his right hand while leaning on his left arm that was propped up against the window.

"Still, I think you can kind of predict which kids will end up being public enemy number one so to speak," Joey said wistfully. "Like I've got this cousin, Roger, who's a huge pain in the butt. He's one of those only child, spoiled brats. Kid's a freak, I'm telling you. He's got that look. And one time, I saw him tie firecrackers to a stray cat. Sadistic. I don't think anybody would miss that little psycho."

"Come on," George said, playing along with the game, "he's an only child. His parents have spoiled him because they love him. They'd be beside themselves with grief. You'd have to find someone who...someone who..."

"...Who had no one, almost invisible, someone who you'd almost be doing society a favor by knocking them off," Rob said chiming in out of the blue.

Simon looked at him in disbelief, but Rob was staring off into the distance beyond his headlights.

"I've got it!" Joey said with excitement.

Just then, Rob's cell phone rang wildly, nearly stopping Simon's heart cold. He glanced down at the text just as they pulled into the parking lot of some dive out in the middle of nowhere. Simon leaned forward to look up at the sign as they pulled into one of the last parking spots in the crowded lot. It read, "Westville's Adult time Superstore."

"Jack wants me and you to go straight to his office so we can talk a little business," Rob said to Simon as he slid the phone back into his pocket.

"What about us?" Joey asked, feeling slightly insulted.

"He said he's got a table for you two up by the stage, free booze all night," Rob said flatly.

"That's my boy!" Joey said, while high fiving George.

"All right!" George wailed.

Once inside, the bouncers waived Rob and the guys through without paying for a cover. They weaved through the dense smoke and sea of faceless men as scantily clad girls walked past them carrying trays full of bottles, shot glasses, and pitchers.

"See, Simon, this is what I'm talking about!" Rob yelled over the earsplitting club music. "Look at this place. It's packed on a Monday night out in the middle of nowhere. Think of the money these guys are dropping in here. Basically, they go out and work all day to make money for us."

He stopped near the stage and pointed to an empty table with a sign that read "VIP." Joey and George nodded and made their way to the table watching the near naked dancer spinning around the pole on the stage. Rob waived for Simon to follow him back to a door just to the left of the small stage. Meanwhile, Simon tried to keep his eyes looking straight ahead, fighting the urge to sneak a peak at the dancer.

"Ha, boys, there you are!" Jack said, getting up from behind his desk where he had been counting out stacks of money. "How was the drive, 'bout fifty minutes, right?"

"Yep," Rob confirmed as he reached out to shake Jack's hand.

Simon pretended not to notice all of the succulent money sitting on the desk that beckoned to him.

"Should be a good enough distance as to not compete, ya know?" Jack said with a broad smile as he put his arm around Simon's shoulders and showed him the way to two chairs in front of his desk. "Now what can I get you boys to drink?"

"Gin and tonic," Rob said before he plopped down in the leather chair.

"Nothing for me, thanks," Simon said with a blank expression.

"Ha, nothing?" Jack said. "You feelin' all right? Don't look so good."

"Long story," Rob said.

"I'm fine," Simon replied.

"Well, Simon, did Rob here show you the place and lay out the plans for ya?" Jack asked after ordering Rob's drink through an intercom system on the desk.

"Yes, sir," Simon said.

"Well, what do you think?" Jack asked. "There's a lot of money to be made from traffic off the interstate! Enticing opportunity, huh? I back it, you manage it, and we share in the profits. Unbelievably good deal!"

Rob shared a smile with Jack and then looked over to Simon expectantly.

"Yeah, well, I really appreciate your offer," Simon said, trying not to look directly into Jack's penetrating eyes, "but, I think I'm just going to stick to the original plan. You know, stay on the path. Head to New Jersey when the call comes and take my chances there."

Rob was beside himself in disbelief at Simon's reply to the more than generous offer. He started to speak before Jack stopped him.

"You know the deal," Jack said to Rob. "Man, has to make his own decision." Then he spoke directly to Simon. "That's a shame," Jack said with his face turning dark, "I thought for sure you'd be all over this. It's obvious that you have a burning desire to be successful. You have nothing to lose in this deal. Virtually, no risk. And the money, wow, I'm telling you, you could get whatever your heart desires. Ha, our purses will be overflowing with money." As he finished, he waved his hand over the stacks of cash. "No?"

"I'm afraid not," Simon said decidedly. Rob was shaking his head in disgust.

Suddenly, there was a knock at the door and a scantily clad brunette waltzed into the room holding a tray of drinks. Simon didn't bother looking back at the door. He didn't have to. He knew what he would see if he did.

"Thank you, my dear," Jack said with a smile. "Oh, where are my manners? Simon, my boy, this is the lovely Jez Bell. Just a little stage name I came up with," he added with a wink.

Simon jerked his head around and saw the enchanting face of Jez smiling back at him.

"Hey, baby!" Jez said seductively.

At once, he was nearly overwhelmed with an unwanted yearning for her, and a dense fog of blurred memories permeated his mind. Her words dripped like honey and her speech was smoother than oil. Mercifully, the strength came from an unknown source to finally turn away. When he did, the more familiar part of him condemned his fleshly urges, and he was able to suppress the cascade of hormones that had triggered the momentary uprising in his soul.

"Ha! My goodness, I completely forgot that you two already know each other," Jack said as he pulled out a cigarette and lit it.

Simon shrunk back in his chair.

"I was wondering when you'd come to see me again," Jez said as a deliberate entreaty.

"Now get, darlin'," Jack said. "Can't ya see we're talkin' bidness, ha!"

Obediently, she turned and sauntered away. When she did, Simon noticed that Rob's eyes followed her hungrily out the door.

"Well, I wish you the best of luck," Jack said. "I've dabbled in the pharmaceutical industry myself. There's a lot money to be had there as well. In fact, we have a couple of animal farms that we manage for some of the big companies out here in the boonies. Have my hand in a little bit of everything ya know."

Before Simon could say another word, the door flung open and one of the bouncers hurried around the table to Jack and whispered in his ear.

"Afraid the meeting's over boys," Jack said abruptly. "Rob, there's a matter that you and I need to attend to. A chance for you to earn your stripes ya know, ha! It may take some time.

Simon, you and I have a little bit of a debt to settle, am I right?"

Simon swallowed hard and nodded.

"Right. I'm callin' in a little favor," Jack said with a stern face. "I want you to just kinda hang out here a little while with Joey and George at the table out there by the stage and enjoy yourself. Enjoy yourself and think hard about my offer. Drinks are on the house."

Simon breathed a sigh of relief.

"Well, I really should...," Simon replied.

"Great!" Jack said walking him to the door that led back out to the bar. "One thing you'll learn about me, Simon, I am relentless when I get a man in my crosshairs. I like your resolve. Channeled in the right direction, it can be a great asset. I can't make you do anything. Wish I could. But, I can only offer the opportunity. Still, I believe you have a great deal to offer our little enterprise, so don't think we're done here by any means. All right?" Then Jack turned to Rob and said, "Let's go put out a fire."

They made their way into the noisy club. Not having a ride home, Simon begrudgingly took his seat next George and Joey who were finishing off the last of a pitcher in between acts.

"Well?" Joey asked. "Did you cut a deal or what?"

Simon fell into the chair and shook his head negatively.

"What? Why not?" Joey asked.

To Simon, it was a very good question. Even he was somewhat perplexed at having such an inexplicable objection to the extremely lucrative offer. Unable to pinpoint its origin, he thought of Jack's idea of success- the one thing that makes you happy. Obviously, the opportunity that he had just been given shared many of the attributes that drew him to pharmaceutical sales- money, nice cars, a big house, vacations, women...status?..."

"Status...that must be it," Simon thought. "I must find it objectionable how other people would see me. There must be something inside me that demands that I earn all of those things in a more respectable industry like pharma or banking. Like Helrigle and Livingood. Those guys have all of the offerings that people would admire and hold in high regard and they've got it all on top of that."

"Oh man, I just can't believe it," Joey said loudly over the music, shaking his head. "Don't know you know that there is more money made in the porn industry each year in America than all of the sporting events combined."

George reached over and slapped Simon on the knee. "That's okay man, I get it," he said more insightfully. "We make our own beds and then lie in them, right?"

"Yeah, but he could have been lying in them with girls who look like Jez for the rest of his life, like my hero Heff," Joey said regretfully. "Being the owner of a gentleman's club has other fringe benefits, you know."

But, Simon said nothing. He just blankly stared off in the distance. There in the back of the room, he saw Jez being whisked away by a large, burly man wearing stained Carhartts and a dirty mesh hat. The grotesque man led her to a tiny room directly in Simon's line of sight. It looked like a voters booth or changing room with the curtain pulled back. With a fist full of singles, the unshaven, husky man who looked to be in his mid-fifties pulled her into the room. She turned to pull the curtain closed, but then made eye contact with Simon from across the room. Purposely, she winked at him and left a gap in the curtain. His stomach turned as she gyrated. Simon's stomach turned and he marveled at his self-loathing and shame. Suddenly, sirens went off in his head, and he remembered Rob encouraging him to get checked out by Dr. Al-Banna.

The lights in the general admission cut off and a spotlight shone on a corner of the stage at a dark curtain. Impulsively, the crowd of men started to clap in unison to the beat of the music. Lights flashed and a whirl of smoke rose from the front of the stage, as a dark haired young lady wearing a sleek, full bodied leather suit strode onto the stage to the wild roar of the crowd.

When Simon caught a glimpse of the girl's face, he recognized her immediately. It was the same young girl that Jeremy Warner had taken the armful of groceries.

* * *

Simon leaned his head against the window of the car as it made it's way past the rows of corn and beans in the ghostly glow of the midnight moonlight. His head pulsated under the pressure of a migraine headache. Still contemplating the strange series of events that had transpired over the course of the evening, his heart longed to talk to Hope. Obviously, there were some details that he might inadvertently leave out. He looked down at his lifeless phone, hoping against hope that he could somehow revive it.

Jack and Rob never did return to the club. Unbeknownst to Simon, Rob had had the foresight to leave his car keys with Joey who conveniently forgot to tell Simon until he was ready to leave. Seeing that Simon was miserable, George talked Joey into cutting out early and heading for home. As Joey and his understudy cut-up in the front seat of the truck, regaling in their latest adventure, Simon sat behind them in pensive silence.

"Head's killing you, isn't it?" Joey observed, looking at Simon in the rearview mirror. "Tell you what always helps me when I get a migraine." Reaching into his pocket he pulled out a joint and offered it to the distraught passenger. Simon pushed Joey's hand away.

"Suit yourself," Joey said, slipping the blunt between his teeth and lighting it. "Don't mind if I do."

Simon shook his head and leaned against the window. "Do you have to do that right now?" Simon asked, agitated.

"What?" Joey asked. "I don't just do it to get 'high'."

"Yeah, right," Simon muttered.

"So closed minded," Joey mused, as he exhaled a plume of smoke. For your information, marijuana has medicinal benefits. Early American Indians used cannabis and mushrooms for enlightenment…

"…In fact, have you ever heard of Harvard professor Timothy Leary?"

"Leave the guy alone," George interrupted. "Can't you see the guy's hurting. Besides, you never told us 'who'?" George said, interrupting Joey.

"Who what?" Joey said randomly bursting out in laughter.

"Earlier, when we were talking," George continued, "you never told us who'd be the perfect victim of the perfect crime. Was it Jeremy Warner?"

Immediately, Simon turned to George with a look of distain.

"Jeremy? No," Joey said. "But it's a thought. The guy's such a geek, and he's so self-righteous!"

"I thought you respected anyone who was 'spiritual'?" Simon chided.

"Oh look who's up!" Joey said. "Yes, I do as a matter of fact. I respect his passion, but I despise his small mindedness and intolerance to new ideas. You see, I believe that the greatest limiting factor in experiencing the universe and understanding the great, common consciousness is Christianity and the Ten Commandments."

Simon furrowed his brow and leaned to the side in order to get a look at Joey's face. He wondered if he were joking. But, his expression revealed no such sentiment. Baffled as well by the statement, George also looked at Joey for the first time with skepticism.

"Are you kidding?" George said.

"No, I'm dead serious," Joey said. "When you take some philosophy classes, or religion classes, or better yet, if you study some American Indian folklore you'll begin to understand what I'm saying. Here's my theory." He took another drag before turning down a lonely country road. "As I said before, God, or what I refer to as the great, common consciousness used to make himself known to the people in the ancient world. Then he turned inwards as described in the myth about Jesus and now we can only know him through our experiences. You see, it's so obvious. Antiquated laws like the Ten Commandments only limit what people feel that they can freely experience. Even if people do break the laws, they don't get the full affect of the experience due to the guilt. It's like dulling your cosmic senses."

When he finished, he took another long drag on the joint. Simon's eyes searched the darkness as he tried to fully grasp the full magnitude of such a philosophy.

"The commandments are a line in the sand, dork!" George objected. It was the first time that Simon had ever heard the young contemporary defy Joey's counsel, and he was glad to hear it.

"Yes, it's a line!" Joey said zealously. "It is a boundary. A limiting boundary of knowledge."

"It's a boundary all right," George said, remembering his up-bringing. "It's a boundary between good and evil!"

"That's just it, man!" Joey argued. "That's the great lie. There's only experiencing or not experiencing! There is no such thing as evil!"

Without warning, red lights exploded in the rearview mirror. Joey and George let fly a flurry of profanity looking for a place to put out the still burning blunt. George slightly slid down the window, wafting the tainted air out of the confined cab. Inexplicably, the county sheriff shot around them as Joey pulled off to the side of the road.

"Wow!" Joey said, putting his hand on his chest and exhaling deeply. "I nearly had a heart attack!"

"What are you doing?" George said. "Follow him, see where's going. The guy was flying."

"No, come on guys, don't," Simon pleaded. "I just want to get home and get to bed. I've got to be at work in four short hours."

"Oh, come on, Freeman," Joey said taking advantage of the teachable moment as they drove away from the grain elevators of Bethel. "See, this is what I've been talking about, man. You're limiting your opportunity to experience something. You never know what you're missing."

Just as he finished speaking and came up over a bluff, they saw it in the valley below. It was a scene unlike any other that they had ever witnessed before in their lives. So many lights flashed and spun on the horizon that it was reminiscent of something out of a movie. A small sea of ambulances, rescue vehicles, fire trucks, and police cars lined a tiny dirt road just at the edge of Potter's farm. The boy's stared in wonder, but not a word was uttered. Intuitively, they knew it was bad, whatever it was, and the hairs stood up on the back of Simon's neck. For the first time in a while, the words of the song on the radio could be heard playing in the background, "...sing for the laughter, sing for the tear, sing with me, if it's just for today, maybe tomorrow, the good Lord will take you away..." Simon shuddered as they approached a state trooper guarding the familiar yellow tape.

"Wow, what happened here?" Joey excitedly asked the officer.

"I'm not at liberty to say," the unwavering policeman warned holding up his hand flatly. "You boys need to head on down the road."

"Come on, man," Joey pried.

There was shouting and confusion as EMT's and policemen furiously scrambled about. Hoses ran all over the ground from the trucks to a large group of firemen congregated together in a ditch about a hundred yards off in the distance.

The trooper spoke more sternly due to their lack of cooperation. "This is serious police business. I'm going to kindly ask you to turn your vehicle around and move out," he said through clenched teeth.

"Just tell us, if it's a fire, or car wreck, or what?" Joey pressed, as he put the car in reverse.

"Maybe you're not hearing me, given your 'condition'!" the man snarled, getting even more agitated. Then he paused for a moment when he saw Simon's face. "Hey, wait a minute, I know you."

"You do?" Simon said surprised.

"Sure, you're the kid from Texas I met at the Bethel Tavern a few weeks ago," the policeman said with his face softening a little. "Yeah, the ball player, how are you doing?"

"Good, I'm good," Simon replied awkwardly.

"So, can you clue us in?" Joey asked cautiously. "What's going on?"

"All right," the officer said leaning closer to the window, "but if I tell you, you gotta leave. Okay? It's a body."

"A body?" George echoed.

"Shh!" the young cop said looking over his shoulder. "You didn't hear it from me."

"Cool," Joey murmured. The cop looked at him strangely.

"Is it a man or a woman?" George asked.

"...Or a kid?" Joey asked with great fascination.

"Can't tell," the officer confided.

"Why not?" Joey asked with his eyes ablaze.

"Burnt to a crisp," the officer whispered. "Now time to move on."

"Car wreck?" Joey asked, trying to peer over the large man's shoulder up the road.

The officer shook his head slowly as he guided them back to where they came from.

"A murder? Was it a murder?" Joey asked nearly beside himself now.

After a short pause, the man lifted his shoulders up to his ears and told them without telling them. "Now, don't make me tell you again. Keep moving."

"Whoa!" George said almost in shock.

"Jessie Joseph strikes again!" Joey said slowly backing down the road.

"What?" Simon asked as his stomach turned.

Joey's flippant assertion throttled Simon, because it's probability was undeniably in concert with what he had already decided to be true deep down in his heart.

"The curse!" Joey said. "The curse is alive and well in Bethel."

Jeremy's words echoed in Simon's head, "I don't believe it was a coincidence that you came back to Bethel."

As the boys turned to make their way back towards the giant grain elevators that towered over the dimly lit town, Simon tried in vain to derive at an answer to the ultimate question... "Why?"

III

THE TRUTH

"Don't you believe that I am in the Father,
and that the Father is in me?
The words that I speak are not on my own authority.
Rather, it is the Father, living in me,
who is doing His work in me."

-John 14:10

14

AT ONCE AND IMMEDIATELY

"Wow, this is big!" Joey said fumbling for numbers on his cell phone as he drove back to Bethel. "Can you believe that? A murder? Right here in Bethel!"

"He didn't actually say it was a murder," George said soberly.

"And he didn't say that it wasn't, either," Joey said, putting the phone up to his ear. "People don't just spontaneously combust." He looked down at his phone in frustration. "Man, isn't anybody going to pick up? Did you see his face when I asked him if it was a murder? Dude, he all but told me that it was."

Simon looked over his shoulder to the small band of flashing lights off in the distance and searched himself for some way to come to grips with how his world was unraveling. Again, he picked up his cell phone attempting with futility to get the battery to work one last time. Longingly, he wondered if he had written Hope's number down anywhere else. Racking his brain, he tried desperately to remember the last two digits. Suddenly, it occurred to him that he could be missing calls from any number of people who might be trying to get ahold of him.

As he raised his eyes towards the heights of the massive grain elevator, Joey dropped the phone to his side.

"What?" George asked expectantly.

"I just talked to Will," Joey said with a great energy about him. "The news is saying that it's Jeremy Warner!

"What?" Simon said, leaning forward. His head was spinning and he felt like someone had just punched him in the gut, like the air was knocked completely out of him; and he struggled mightily to regain his breath.

"The news reported that some teenagers out joy riding came upon a fire on the side of the road in the country," Joey said. "From a distance, they thought it was some kind of animal, but as they got closer, they realized that it...well...wasn't. They called for the authorities, and it's just been confirmed that it was Jeremy."

"Oh man, I can't believe it. That's horrible," George said as his face went pale.

Simon was speechless, stricken with grief. His eyes danced and fluttered as he rubbed the tops of his jeans with both hands. "How could they know that quickly?" he thought. "You'd think they wouldn't be able to identify the body without an autopsy. Maybe it wasn't him. Maybe it was a case of mistaken identity." The random thoughts exploded in his consciousness like napalm, and he tried to take comfort in the peculiarity of the surreal news as inaccurate and unsubstantiated.

"Oh Jeremy," Simon said absentmindedly under his breath, his eyes beginning to water.

"Who would do such a horrible thing?" George speculated. "In Bethel of all places."

"I don't know," Joey said shaking his head and biting his lip, "but Will said he was at the tavern with Rocky and Rich. They want us to meet them down there."

* * *

The guys sat at the bar watching the news and waiting for more word, but there was nothing; just the typical, mindless late night programming. Furiously, they each texted and phoned whomever they could think of to get more information. Rich set a towel over his shoulder as he leaned down against the bar with one hand and listened intently to the voice on the other end of the line.

"That was Rob," Rich said hanging up the phone. "He said a couple of guys who are members at the club are volunteer firemen, and they were able to give him some of the details. They found Jeremy's car..."

Simon could barely listen to the details. He closed his eyes hard and cringed. As much as he tried to fight them back, tears welled up in his eyes, and he bit down hard on his lip as he quivered in pain. Still, no one noticed. They were too enthralled with the sensational bits of news that Rich was repeating.

"They said there was no doubt that he had been set on fire, his clothes were drenched in gasoline," Rich said.

"Wow," Rocky said between the bits of chaw on his lips.

"It's unbelievable," Will added, stunned by the news.

"Yeah, incredible," Joey said hungry for more details.

"What could possibly be the motive?" Will asked. "I mean he was youth director at a church for crying out loud."

Simon's eyes watered, and he choked a little on his words as he spoke, "He was a good guy."

"Yeah, I mean he was a little different, but a good guy all in all," George said.

"I don't know, looks can be deceiving sometimes," Joey said contemplatively.

"What are you talkin' about?" Rich asked, noticing Simon's face for the first time.

"He ticked off a whole bunch of people tonight at the town hall meeting," Joey said matter-of-factly.

"No," Rich said. "That's ridiculous. Nobody would do something like this over some stupid Town Hall meeting."

"Huh," Joey objected. "Ever watch *Dateline*? There were also the rumors going around about what he might have been doing with his baseball team," Joey said in speculative tone of voice.

Suddenly, Simon thought of the two times he saw Jeremy walking out of the concession stand with his arm over one of his player's shoulders.

"Oh, come on," Will said, agitated. "That's crazy."

"Is it?" Joey asked. "He was always sneakin' off with kids, getting them alone, off by himself. I know if I found some wacko messing with my kid, I'd do something about it...I'd...Oh man! I just thought of something." He snapped his fingers and then paused for affect. "It's just like Jessie Joseph! Doing unspeakable things to little kids. A trusted guy in the community who nobody would ever suspect."

"You're being stupid," Rich snapped. "That's pretty irresponsible, making accusations with no proof. I mean the poor guy's been dead for a couple of hours, and you've already decided he was some kind of pedophile who deserved all of this. The least we could do is have some respect for the people who knew and cared for him."

Suddenly, it occurred to Simon that Hope might not know.

"Any of you guys know Hope's phone number?" Simon asked, dismissing Joey's heartless accusations.

"Hope Wiseman?" Joey asked incredulously. "Yeah, right. We talk all of the time."

No one had any idea how to get ahold of her. Desperately, Simon racked his brain to think of the number. Then something occurred to him.

"Hey, what's the closest truck stop off the interstate?" Simon asked getting off of his stool.

"What? I dunno, Mattoon maybe," Rich said reaching for the remote control to the television.

"My battery is dead on my cell phone and I need to get a new one, now!" Simon said insistently.

"They prob'ly got 'em dare," Rocky said cupping his mug with his hand. "Truckers always be on their cell."

"What? Don't go anywhere at this time of night," Rich said thoughtfully. "There's nothing you can do right now anyway. It's almost two in the morning. Sit down. We can have a beer or two and just chill a little bit. You'll feel better. I think I've even got Baseball Tonight Tivo'd."

"Not me," Will said moving towards the exit, "I'm heading home to Rachel. She's probably worried about me." For the first time in his life, he hoped that were true.

"Did anybody hear how the Cubbies did tonight?" Joey asked settling in at the bar while looking at the LCD.

George looked at his mentor sideways. His face was contorted as though there was a bad taste in his mouth.

In a flash, Simon was charging out the door and heading for his car. Tears rolled down his cheeks as he made his way in silence down the highway. There was only the roar of the engine and the hum of the tires on the road as the conversations that he had had with Jeremy played over and over in his head.

Capitalism was thriving at two o'clock in the morning at the truck stop in Mattoon where life went on indifferently. Simon was able to find a battery for his phone. Ripping the package open with his bare hands, he accidentally flipped it out of the case onto the hard ground of the parking lot. Quickly he picked it up, popped it into the phone, and called Hope. He paced like a caged animal waiting for her to pick up. No answer. When Hope's recorded voice came on, it coursed through his body like a much needed shot of novocaine. Impatiently, he pleaded for her to answer.

"Come on," he muttered, waiting for her to pick up. After her short message, the phone beeped. "Oh, uh, Hope, it's Simon. I really need you to give me a call when you get a chance. It's urgent. Something has happened that you need to know. Uh, thanks. Call me."

He quickly dropped the phone from his ear and looked down to see a missed text alert. It was from a number that he didn't recognize. Still thinking it could be Hope, he scrolled and clicked. The message was from Jeremy! Simon's heart raced and his breathing became heavy. His eyes danced over the words as he read a message that had been left earlier in the evening.

"Hey, saw you at meeting," the message began. "I've been thinking about your question. Yes, I believe in curses… as much as I believe in blessings. I also believe that God either causes or allows both of them into our lives with the purpose of bringing us closer to Him in order to be more like Christ for His glory. The problem is sometimes that we cannot tell which one is which until much later, but either way they are meant to shape or mold us in Jesus's image. Hope that helps. Also, thought more about the question you have been struggling with. Call me. We really need to talk about Jack. God bless."

"…Other question that I've been struggling with?" Simon thought. "How could he have known?"

Simon jumped as the phone vibrated and rang wildly in his hand. He looked down and saw that it was Hope's number. Quickly, he answered her call.

"Hey, yeah, sorry to call you so late," Simon said leaning down and covering his eyes with his hand. With great effort, he was finally able to speak. "I've got some terrible news…"

* * *

They held their embrace for a few moments before Hope finally let go of Simon. The feeling of her arms wrapped around him gave him a sense of comfort that he hadn't even known was possible. He didn't want to let go but knew he had to. It was only the second time that they had ever been together in person although they had faithfully corresponded back and forth ever since she left for summer camp. But the tragedy hung over their meeting like the darkness that had descended on Bethel since Jeremy's murder, making it surreal and awkward. She moved away from him wiping her eyes. They were puffy and red as though she hadn't slept.

"How was the drive?" Simon asked, not knowing what to say.

"Fine, long," Hope said. "I must look like a mess." Then she let out a nervous laugh.

In truth, Simon had never seen anything more beautiful in his entire life. Words could not express how glad he was to see her. "No, not all," he sputtered, thinking it inappropriate to express how he really felt given the circumstances.

"I just can't believe it," Hope lamented. "How can something like that happen? Anywhere? Let alone in Bethel. And to Jeremy of all people."

"I know," Simon replied with great compassion. "I think the whole town is reeling from the shock. It's the first official murder investigation since..." Then he thought better of it.

"Have the authorities found out anything else?" she asked desperately.

"No, the papers are still insinuating that it looks like a drug deal gone bad," Simon said in disgust.

"Drug deal?" Hope said. "I don't believe that for a minute! I mean, come on, Jeremy? No way."

"I don't believe it either," Simon agreed, "but they did say that it had all the ear marks."

"And do they know if he was definitely dead before they...?" Hope dared to ask.

"In all honesty, I can't see how they could know," Simon said with a trembly voice, barely getting out the words. "They just said that he was shot..."

"It all just makes me sick," Hope said clutching her stomach with both arms. "But, what did they say about his broken fingers? Was he trying to fight back?"

"A friend of Rob's on the volunteer fire department said that they were probably trying to torture him in order to get information out of him or send some kind of message," Simon said despondently. "Are you sure you want to do this now? We don't have to do this."

"What time is the vigil at the church?" Hope asked, looking down at her watch.

"It starts at six o'clock," Simon answered.

"Well, I can't just sit around crying, waiting," Hope said, wiping tears from her eyes. "That's torture. I'm angry and I can't shut my brain off. I know it sounds stupid, but if I just sit then the pain consumes me, and if I try to distract myself, it's worse. When I need to clear my mind, I run." She paused before continuing. "I know it sounds dumb, but I have to get some of this out of my system."

"A run?" Simon asked, not having anticipated such an odd response to dealing with pain and suffering. But somehow, at the same time, nothing made much sense right now. As a former athlete, he could appreciate the value of displacing anger, pain, and emotion into physical activity that could purge the soul and clear the mind.

* * *

"Are you sure you want to go with me?" Hope asked. She was very serious as though she were trying desperately to harness her emotions. "How long has it been since you ran?"

"It's been a little while," Simon admitted. Actually, he hadn't run since his last off-season workout at TCU before the elbow surgery. Looking at his spindly, little running mate, he felt confident that he could keep up. Prior to quitting baseball, he worked out all of the time. It wasn't unusual for him to go out and run five or six miles, no problem. Awkwardly he did some twisting and bending. "No, this will be good for me...." Even though it was the last thing in the world that he thought he would be doing that day.

Hope glanced up at him without saying a word. The pain in her intense expression said it all.

As the two of them started walking towards the countryside from the ballpark, Simon asked, "How fast do you typically go?"

"About seven minute-mile pace, something like that," Hope said flatly. "Although, when I'm really stressed I sometimes push it a little harder."

Simon raised his eyebrows as Hope took off running. It wasn't long before his breathing became labored. A side stitch developed in his side, and he could feel the balls of his feet begin to blister around the four mile mark. Unfortunately for him, it was a humid June afternoon and the stalks of corn, now about waist high, choked out the air. Sweat poured from his brow, as he fought hard to keep up. Meanwhile, Hope vented her feelings while exerting little effort. Mostly, Simon could only muster a nod or grunt in response.

"You-you've been...doin' this for a while, huh?" Simon managed to ask.

"Yes, I'm training for Twin Cities Marathon in St. Paul," Hope said plainly.

"Oh great, great!" Simon said sarcastically. "You could have shared that a little earlier."

"Do you want to go back?" Hope asked.

"No, no," Simon said, "this actually is therapeutic."

"Well, I am glad you came," Hope said, allowing herself a fleeting smile for the first time since she heard the news of Jeremy. "Normally, I like to run by myself."

"Doesn't that get pretty boring?" Simon asked, through bated breath.

"Listen, I teach twenty 7-year-olds; silence is bliss," Hope said. "Besides, it gives me a chance to pray as I run and spend some time with God."

"Yeah, I can see that," Simon said as he worked hard to hide a developing limp. "I started praying a few miles back." Oddly, the running really was helping. At the moment, his emotional pain was overcome by a more intense physical pain.

Suddenly, Hope's face turned sour as the pace noticeably slowed. "That's what I love the most about running," she said with a graven face. "If you push hard enough, you invariably get to a point where you can no longer rely on yourself. It breaks you and humbles you, and eventually, you have to rely on God. It's like a microcosm of life. The harder it gets, the more we need Him."

Before Simon could comment on the interesting observation, Hope stopped running altogether. Gratefully, he followed suit and stumbled around some before stopping. Gasping for breath, he bent over and leaned on his knees. When he looked up, he saw that Hope had walked about twenty yards down the road away from him to a black patch of wild prairie grass in the ditch on the side of the road. While he had been struggling to keep pace with Hope, he hadn't noticed all of the twists and turns that they had taken down the back country roads. It looked completely different in the light of day. It had now become obvious that Hope wanted to see the place where Jeremy's body was discovered.

Trying to regain his breath, he watched her bow her head. Respectfully, he left her alone, not daring to interrupt. For some time, she stood over the site in reverence. There were a couple of times when Simon could see her shoulders bounce up and down, and he wondered if he should go to her and comfort her for the loss of her friend, but he rightfully refrained choosing instead to give silent support. Then she stood up, turned, and walked back to him. Her eyes were red and swollen.

"I just had to see it for myself," Hope muttered. "To process that it really happened…or..or..for closure, I guess…I don't know…maybe I shouldn't have…"

"Are you okay?" Simon asked, empathetically.

"No," Hope said with tears streaming down her soft cheeks.

Simon put his arm around Hope's shoulder doing his best to comfort her. They turned around and began the long walk together back towards the massive grain elevators of Bethel.

Not even in that moment did Simon realize how a shared traumatic experience could expedite a new relationship or galvanize an emergent conviction.

* * *

Simon could not believe how long the line was to Pastor Algood's newly built church that stood some distance from town amongst the fields of beans, corn, and hay. It started at the doors of the metal shed of a building, curled around to the side of the structure, and circled the parking lot. While the vigil was to take place in the evening, a small service celebrating Jeremy's' life was to be conducted later in the week. A funeral was to be planned in his hometown after all of the results of the autopsy were gathered.

"I never knew he had touched so many people's lives," Simon said to Hope, taking a little consolation in the hoards of people who had turned out to pay their respects.

"Hmmph," Hope said with her arms folded and a scowl on her face, surveying the individuals who waited in line.

"What?" Simon asked picking up on her skepticism.

"Nothing," She said grimly. "There's no way for me to search each person's heart, so I shouldn't be so cynical, but this is what we do in a small town when somebody dies. This is what is expected. Half of them have been gossiping all over town about…never mind. I just want this to be about Jeremy tonight. That's all. Not for the sake of appearances or theater."

Simon turned and searched the line behind them for faces that he might recognize. Throngs of people milled about in line, speaking in hushed tones. There was Rich, and Rocky, and Rob a few yards behind them. Further down the line behind them, he spotted Joey and George deep in ravenous conversation. Towards the very back, he recognized Lexus Helrigle and Wilson B. Livingood standing amongst their families with their hands in their suit pockets while the mothers draped their arms over their boys' shoulders. Behind them was a group of four teenagers that Simon recognized from the ballpark.

Looking to the front of the line near the doors that remained closed, Simon noticed Pastor Pete with Hannah Grace and Mara Rash wearing their mourning clothes. Their faces were solemn as Mara whispered something into Hannah Grace's ear. Only a single figure stood between them and the doors to the church. The man wearing a dark suit had his head bowed. His arms were straight down and his hands were locked in front of him. Simon ducked his head around the cluster of people in front of him trying to get a better look at the gentleman. He seemed very familiar and yet out of place. Then it came to him.

"Jack?" he thought. "He's the last guy I expected to see here." For the first time, he considered how much Jeremy would have opposed the business affairs of Jack Lawless especially the 'Bethel Adult time Super Store'. Even though Jack expressed his admiration of Jeremy's passion, the young youth director had to be a constant thorn in his side according to Hope.

Simon shook his head in disgust at Jack's tacky gesture. Suddenly, he was overwhelmingly embarrassed that he had ever even entertained the notion of working for a guy like Jack. Unprovoked, images of Jez's naked body dancing at the club exacted an assault on his mind within mere tenths of a second. Before he could even begin to fend them off, the frames of images in his mind rapidly eroded to the night he hungrily groped her body. The memories were like cords of desire holding fast. A shiver came over him, and he felt incredibly dirty and disgusted at himself. Wrought with shame and guilt, he fended off the desire that burned in his heart and desperately began burying the memory of his night with Jez. With a pained expression, he looked to Hope who was wiping her tears of grief with a wadded up Kleenex.

"What would she say if she ever found out?" he thought with a strong sense of regret.

Unexpectedly, Hope looked directly into his eyes and spoke, staggering Simon for a moment as though she could see the darkness in his heart through the window to his soul.

"Do you know what is really infuriating to me?" Hope asked in confidence through tears and gritted teeth.

Simon shook his head slowly.

"People," she said. "People who put on a front of decency when I would venture a guess that many of them are only here because of the sensationalism, like this is some kind of event that they wouldn't want to miss. I know I shouldn't feel that way, but I do. There's no way of knowing by looking at their somber faces or listening to their polite words. Most of them have no clue what Jeremy was really all about."

Simon thought for a moment about his encounters with Jeremy and realized that Hope was right. He was special, and yet Simon's own friends treated him as some kind of sideshow or circus act, never really taking him seriously. Simon turned and once again searched the faces in the crowd. The murmuring began to steadily grow louder as the crowd continued to trickle in.

"Do you know what many of these people are saying about him right now?" Hope asked, shaking with rage. "They're saying that he was a junky. That he was a meth addict and that he regularly solicited prostitutes. Some of them are even speculating about his relationship with his baseball team!"

Simon immediately knew the source of that allegation and looked back at Joey who acted as if he were standing in line at the movie theater. George on the other hand looked genuinely remorseful with a grim expression on his face. He blankly stared off in the distance as Joey filled his ear with empty rhetoric.

* * *

A praise and worship band finished the last stanza of a new amped up version of the old gospel hymn, Harvest time, before Pastor Algid made his way to center stage to address the packed house. For a moment, Simon had to remind himself that he wasn't watching the midnight show on a Carnival cruise. To his surprise, a charismatic preacher wearing loafers, faded blue jeans, with a loud, buttoned down shirt that was untucked in the back ran onto the stage pumping his fist into the air. The smell of Starbucks coffee brewing permeated the auditorium as the stylish preacher with moused bleach hair and trendy spectacles began to address those who were paying their respects.

There was a picture of Jeremy's beaming countenance on a large easel off to the side surrounded by flowers that filled the stage.

The pastor clapped wildly with a broad smile across his face as the praise and worship team put down their electric guitars and exited the stage. Once off the stage, Pastor Algood turned to his audience.

"Hey, now, why the long faces?" the pastor said purposefully. "This is a celebration! A celebration of life. You will hear no dirges here tonight, am I right?" Then he clapped his hands hard and rocked his head back and forth, exhorting the crowd who followed his lead with awkward clapping, faulty whistling, and even a few random cheers.

Simon turned to Hope who was sitting to his right in the pew. Her heart seethed with anger while her stomach wrenched in agony, doing her best to maintain her composure.

"We welcome you tonight on this special occasion," the pastor continued with a bright smile. "For those of you who are visiting "Bountiful Meadows" for the first time, this is how we do it. We are not your typical place of worship. In fact, we discourage using the "C" word around here." Dramatically, the pastor put his hand flatly up to the side of his mouth, leaned towards the congregation, and darted his eyes about the room. "That's "Church" for those of you who maybe grew up with the same boring, dry experience that I had. At "Bountiful Meadows," we take a different approach. We do everything in our power to steer clear of all of the stereotypical ritual that turns so many people off. For that reason, we put God at the center of worship. We're not here to judge you or criticize you. God wants us to come as you are. Whether it's in jeans," he said pausing to point at his designer, stone-washed jeans, "or a suit and tie or a smock, or a hijab, we don't care, and we don't think God does either."

Several people clapped as Simon and Hope shared an undecided glance. "This was Jeremy's church?" Simon thought, a little troubled at the notion.

"We're not your fire and brimstone type place of worship," Pastor Algood continued. "We believe that there are enough negative things in people's lives today that we don't need to hear about more doom and gloom. I'm here to tell you that God is not like that. He wants to be your friend, and we're here to help you get to know him, whatever that may mean to you. If you feel like standing tonight, then stand. If you feel like kneeling then kneel. If you feel like dancing in the aisle, then dance. Because we are here to celebrate the life of a beautiful young man who lived life on his own terms, who knew God in his own personal way, not caring about what others thought of him. Jeremy dared to be Jeremy, and we loved him for it. In a moment, I am going to lead us in prayer, and then we'll get the praise and worship team back up on stage to do what we like to call "Rock'n on the Rock." Because we value and respect all different forms of religion, we are going to have a moment of silence and you can talk for a few moments with God as you know him. Then I let the band do their thing. After that, I will come back up on stage and say a few words about Jeremy."

As Simon looked around the room not sure of what he was supposed to do, Pastor Algood bowed his head and closed his eyes. He was amazed that this was the same church that Jeremy served as a youth pastor. It was nothing like Simon had expected based on his conversations with Jeremy that were so filled with substance.

After what seemed like an eternity, Pastor Algood began his prayer, "Dear God, or Allah, or Shangdi, or Bhagwan…or whatever other name you go by," the pastor paused to make eye contact with Dr. Al-Banna who sat near the front of the room, "we, your children, come to you tonight to pay our respects to the life of Jeremiah Warner as we knew him here on earth and to bid his farewell and safe travels on to the next life. May your presence fill this room tonight and may we tap into your bountiful spirit. We also ask that those responsible be brought to justice, so that our beloved community can move beyond this present darkness. Amen." Intently, he lifted his eyes, smiled brightly, and jogged off the stage as the guitarist struck an earsplitting, shrill note on his whammy bar, before a cleanly choreographed quartet graced the stage under flashing lights and a burst of smoke.

Many people stood and clapped, periodically raising their hands to the ceiling and waving them back and forth. On the big screen behind the stage, a slide show full of pictures of Jeremy flashed to the rhythm of the rock music. Baffled, Simon looked over once again to Hope who was sobbing uncontrollably into her hands. Impulsively, he reached over and put his arm around her. When he did she leaned into his shoulder, and he could feel her tears begin to dampen his shirt. As Simon watched the images on the screen, he was struck how they seemed to be in direct contrast to the performance at the altar. The slide show portrayed Jeremy as Simon knew him. All of the pictures were all of him ministering to widows, to children, to cancer patients, and even to inmates at the county jail. The pictures depicted a self-deprecating life of servanthood. And Simon took great comfort in the undeniable truth they told of a legacy that superseded all of the grandiose showmanship.

The congregation's ears were still ringing as Pastor Algood walked back onto the stage with his arm draped over the shoulder of a boy. The young man had his chin buried in his chest, and he clutched a piece of paper in his hands. When he looked up, Simon recognized the boy immediately as the one whom he had seen walking out of the concession stand with Jeremy only a week before.

"This is Parker Godsell," the pastor said looking down at the chubby boy with glasses. "He and his families are members of 'Bountiful Meadows'. Parker also happened to be a part of Jeremy's youth group and baseball team, the Padres. He asked me if he could say a few words tonight. So, I said sure, I think that'd be great. So, Parker, the floor is yours. Just say whatever's on your heart, buddy."

He handed the boy a microphone and moved off to the corner of the stage. The house lights came up, and it was a completely silent for a moment. Shaking, the boy bit his lip and held the paper close to his face as he spoke down into the microphone.

"I, uh, I wanted to say somethin'," the 10-year-old muttered. "Mr. Jeremy was my youth leader and my coach on my baseball team. And, well, we have a pretty bad team. But, I like it, even though I'm not any good. See I wouldn't even be a part of a team if it wasn't for Mr. Jeremy. Like I said, I'm not good enough to get on any other team. When I got cut from one team, I was really sad and I told Mr. Jeremy why. And he said he didn't know anything about baseball, but he would coach a team so me and guys like me could play too." In the stillness of the room, void of stage lighting, stage effects, screaming guitars, and slideshows, the little boy's words jerked at the heart of even the staunchest cynics. Tears welled up in his eyes as the boy spoke the truth.

Hope sat forward in the pew while Simon recalled some of the counsel that Jeremy had given him. He remembered Jeremy's two unavoidable truths that everyone has to grapple with, as sure as everyone was born, everyone will die. Then he thought of the three questions that arise from that assertion: Who or what created us? Why are we here? And what happens when we die? Something inside of him began to stir, and he thoughtfully considered the answers that Jeremy offered to the questions soundly resonating in his heart before he considered another nagging question.

"What is my purpose?" he introspectively asked himself, suspecting he already knew the answer. He thought of the legend, the school, Jessie Joseph and Adam Potter's gravestones, the face at the bottom of the well, the words of the senile woman, and of course, he thought of the curse. Never had he been more certain of anything in his life. His eyes lifted as the courageous boy continued to speak.

"So, anyway," Parker said, "we've never won a game or nothin'. Most games we don't even score a single run. Last game, we got killed by like twenty-six runs or somethin'. I wanted to quit, but Mr. Jeremy wouldn't let me. He asked me a question. He says, 'How do you know when you win or lose?' I kinda looked a him funny, and said, 'duh, by the scoreboard at then end of the game'. Mr. Jeremy asked me if I felt like I was a loser, and I said yes. And Mr. Jeremy, well, he asked me somethin' that made me think a lot. He asked me, 'Do you think when Jesus was on the cross people said he was a winner or a loser? 'A loser, I guess', I said. And Mr. Jeremy said that that's what a lot of people thought at first, even the disciples, because they all thought the game was over. Then he asked me if that was the end of the story for Jesus, and I said no, course not. Cause everybody knows Jesus rose from the grave. Mr. Jeremy, then he asked me, 'how can we tell if *we* are winners or losers?' I just kinda shrugged my shoulders. I said I didn't know. He asked, "Is it by how popular we are, or how much money we have, or if we win a lot of baseball games? I nodded, cause it sounded good to me. But he said no. Then he asked me, what if there is a scoreboard behind the scoreboard that only God can see? What if he is keeping a different score that truly decides the winners and losers? He said, maybe people pay too much attention to the wrong scoreboard.

Then he told me a secret. And I want to tell you, tonight, because, well, even though I'm sad, I'm not as sad cause I know the secret and cause I sorta think he would-a wanted me to tell it to you. He said that everyone needs to find out the truth before it is too late because most people are too busy tryin' to win the wrong game."

The only way to know if you are a winner or a loser, whether you've won the prize or not, is when you die and you meet God face to face for the first time and He says to you..."

When Simon heard Jeremy's secret, he was jolted by the gravity of the words of the child. He was bewildered by the profound insight and marveled at how he had never before even contemplated the possibility. It was contrary to all that he had built his life upon, to anything that he had ever heard, or read, or seen, or had been taught. And he was overcome with the suspicion that he had been subject to a great lie. If so, it was greatest lie of all. If he was right, Simon had been given a glimpse of what was behind the curtain.

No! Even more than that. If he was right then the curtain had been completely torn in two and there would be no way to ever put it back up again. Simon searched the depths of his soul for confirmation of the veracity of the boy's words. Stunned by the magnitude of such an assertion and the ramifications it would have on his life, he was sickened by the potential depths of his foolishness up to this point. If it were indeed true, it would not only be his "one thing", it would be everyone's "one thing." Immediately, he wanted to share it with Hope. But, when he turned to her, he could tell that she was completely enamored by the young man who was just now finishing his speech.

"...So anyway, that's how I know Mr. Jeremy is the biggest *winner* of us all because he was focused on the right game all along," he stammered. "I wanted to say that, cause, like I said, I think Mr. Jeremy would like that, that's all."

Parker dropped the microphone to his side and it squealed with feedback over the PA drowning out the silence. Pastor Algood rushed to the boys side and picked up the microphone to save the audience from the horrible screech. The boy unceremoniously walked off the stage as Pastor Algood turned on his own microphone.

"That's right!" Pastor Algood said beaming. "Wow. Thanks Parker, that took a great deal of courage. You can't tell me he did that on his own. I would say the spirit has been moving here all night. You see, if you have the faith of a child you too can tap into the spirit. When you do it will empower you in each aspect of your life, your family, your work, your friendships. There is no limit to what the spirit can do for you. He will fill your storehouse and your cup will overflow. And you will prosper beyond your wildest dreams!"

When the vigil was over, Simon followed Hope through the chaos, out the doors to the front of the church. He couldn't wait to talk to share his epiphany with her. Reaching out his hand, he grabbed her gently by the arm and pulled her off to the side away from the crowd.

"I need to talk to you!" Simon said, trying to contain his excitement so as to not draw unwanted attention.

But, Hope was only half-listening as she searched the faces in the crowd.

"Hope, did you hear me?" Simon asked, expectantly.

"Yes, I am listening," Hope said, "but, I was looking for Parker. I wanted to tell him how impressed I was by his courage to stand for the truth. Jeremy would have been so proud of him. But, I don't see him."

"That's exactly what I wanted to talk to you about!" Simon said with great excitement. "The little boy's words. Well, they, they made me realize something."

Hope stopped looking for the boy. She turned her swollen, red eyes to Simon and searched his bright, beaming countenance. Now he had her full attention.

"There's something I want to tell you," Simon said through a bright smile and misty eyes.

"Yes?" Hope asked, anticipating his words.

"I have been wanting to tell you for some time, well wanting to tell anyone really," Simon said as Hope's expression changed. "Jeremy and I have talked several times about having a purpose in life. That God gives people a specific purpose." She was nodding, tracking his words carefully. "Until I heard the little boy talking, I was too afraid to tell anyone, but I think I know God's purpose for me…"

Just then, Rich reached them through the crowd that was now spilling into the parking lot. "Hey guys, I didn't mean to interrupt, but everybody's heading over to the tavern," he said, before realizing that they were having an intimate conversation. "I just wanted to let you know. Okay?"

"Oh, yeah thanks," Simon said. He waited for Rich to get completely out of earshot, before resuming his conversation with Hope.

"Sorry about that," Simon said as he took Hope's hands into his own and looked deeply into her eyes. "I know this is going to sound crazy. It sounds crazy to me too. But, I think that God wants me to…"

"Hey kids," Jack said between his lips that were deftly holding a lit cigarette. "Not interruptin' anything here am I? Ha. Terrible, terrible thing 'bout Jeremy."

The hairs on the back of Simon's neck stood on end, hearing the hollow words.

"Kept try'n to get him to come work for me," Jack continued. "Shame. The boy had so much potential."

"Is there something that you wanted, Mr. Lawless?" Simon asked with a tone of disdain and resentment.

"Mr. Lawless? Ha! Why so polite, Simon?" Jack asked, exhaling smoke as he laughed. "Oh, oh, I see, try'n to put on airs," Jack said looking knowingly to Hope who was standing behind Simon with a downcast expression and her arms folded tightly. "Where are my manners? You two look like you wanta be alone. So be it. I was just wondering if this weren't yours?" Jack asked, holding a ratty wallet between his fingers.

Simon looked at it quizzically, "No, what would make you think it's mine?"

"Jez found it in one of the little side rooms at the club the other night, and she thought it could have been yours," the cunning businessman said smugly. "No? All right then. Leave you two love birds alone then." He dipped his head towards Hope. "Ma'am." And then he casually walked off, whistling.

Simon's face went flush and there was a horrible feeling in the pit of his stomach. He jerked his head back around to look at Hope. Her mouth was ajar and her eyes filled with tears.

"Why would Jez think that it might be *yours?*" Hope asked with a pained expression.

* * *

In the back of the church, behind a row of large bushes and trees, Jackson sat on Parker's back while pushing his face into the dirt and forcing his arm behind his shoulder blades.

"You yell out one more time, and I'm gonna break your arm, you fat loser," Jackson said through gritted teeth.

"*Ouch,*" Parker cried. "Get off of me! Get off."

"You are such a dork, Porker," Jackson said with a laugh.

"You're hurting me, get off," Parker squealed. "I'm going to tell on you. You are going to be in big trouble."

"Ohh, I'm so scared!" Jackson said. "Who are you going to tell? One of your daddy's?"

"Where's my glasses?" Parker said through spit and tears. "I can't see nothin' without my glasses."

Roger stepped out of the shadows with a giant cross on the metal building gleaming in the uplighting just above him. He reached down, picked up the thick glasses out of the dewy grass, and put them on his face.

"Look at me, Jackson!" Roger said. "I'm a fat dork. I am a 'Weiner' in God's eyes."

Jackson laughed and reached out his hand for the glasses with one hand, while the other held Parker's hand behind his neck. Just then, Ralph came around the corner looking for Jackson. When he saw what was happening, he ran to Parker's defense. Roger stuck out his foot and tripped him, so that he hit the ground with a thud.

"What's the big idea?" Ralph said angrily. "Get off of him Jackson, let him go! Your dad sent me to find you so we can go home."

Jackson put the glasses on his face, and imitated Parker just as Roger had done, "I'm just a big loser. I can't even defend myself..or hit a baseball."

"I said get off of him," Ralph said threateningly as he rose to his feet. "Or else."

"Or else what?" Jackson asked sarcastically, while Roger looked on the ground for a large, fallen branch.

Ralph clenched his fists and moved towards Jackson who got up off of Parker with one last shove.

"Saving your girlfriend?" Jackson mocked.

Parker rolled over awkwardly, his face dirtied with mud and tears. Through his panting breath, he yelled at Jackson. "Give me my glasses back, you big bully!"

"Yeah, give him back his glasses," Ralph said sternly.

Roger was holding a large stick like a club at his side. He now stood directly behind Ralph waiting to see how the scene would unfold.

"Fine, here you go you fat Piggy!" Jackson said, tossing the glasses at Parker's chest.

Quickly, the hapless victim picked the glasses up and put them on his face. Scrambling to his feet, he was about to level a fury of insults at Jackson. Suddenly, the red-headed bully cocked his arm back and punched Parker in the stomach with all of his might. The chubby boy stumbled backwards grabbing his gut and gasping for breath. Ralph reached out and grabbed his arms before he fell again to the ground. Over his shoulder, Roger burst out laughing as he and Jackson darted off towards the front of the church.

After a few seconds, Parker stood back up. He stood, desperately trying to catch his breath. When he did, he swore bitterly at Jackson. Ralph picked his glasses up a second time, dusted them off, and handed them to Parker.

"Th-thanks, Ralph," Parker said, wiping his muddied face with the back of his hand.

"Shut up, Parker," Ralph said in disgust as he turned to walk back around to the front of the building.

Parker followed slowly behind him with head down, hair matted, and his shirt untucked.

* * *

Simon had finished his explanation and now waited for Hope to say something, anything. She sat in the passenger seat of his car with her arms folded tightly, blankly staring with a furrowed brow at the dashboard. With a Kleenex clutched in her right hand, she began to speak through quivering lips.

"So, you didn't know what the job opportunity was beforehand?" Hope asked skeptically.

"No, I had no idea," Simon replied in earnest. "I thought Jack was a farmer or something. He talked about how he owned most of the land around here. Nobody said anything to the contrary. I didn't even know where Rob was taking me." He paused waiting for Hope's reply. "I-I know that ignorance is not a very good excuse. I should have asked. I should have looked into it more. I know that now."

He was filled with regret and anguish because he could see how the indiscretion affected Hope. She looked out of the corner of her eye at him. Her expression was one of disappointment. It killed him to see her this way, and he longed for the night that they had joked and laughed on the porch at Rich's house after the wedding. Now his choices and his actions had changed all of that at least for the time being. Sitting together in the front seat of his car under a streetlight on Main Street, he wondered if she would ever look at him that way again. His heart burned in his chest as he turned from her and glanced up at the giant grain elevator looming high above them.

"And there's nothing else?" Hope asked, unexpectedly.

"Nothing else?" Simon repeated sheepishly.

"I mean, did anything else happen at the club that you need to tell me about?" she asked with a pained expression.

"Like what?" Simon asked, trying as best he could to fain surprise and ignorance.

"Like why would Jez think that a wallet left in a little 'side room' be yours?" Hope said choking back tears through clenched teeth.

"I have no idea," Simon replied. "I was never in any side room with Jez or any other girl at the club for that matter."

"I just need to know the truth," Hope insisted. "I have to trust you. I can't *be* with anyone that I can't trust. Were you with Jez or not?"

When he searched her teary eyes, he understood all that was riding on his answer. He couldn't lose her now. That would be too devastating just as he was beginning to figure things out and get a sense of direction in his life. His feelings for Hope were growing day by day. Simon thought about her question, and then gave a very calculated answer.

"No, I was not with Jez *that* night," he answered truthfully in his own mind. "Like I said, I didn't have a ride back to town. So, I had to wait for Joey and George to get a ride."

He could feel something dark inside of him like a stain on his heart, and the more he scrubbed at it, the more it smudged, making it far worse than it was to begin with.

Hope shook her head slowly, looking down at the floorboards of the car. After a few minutes, she looked up at him and relinquished an uncertain grin that hinted at forgiveness and conveyed understanding.

"Okay," she said through a few sniffles. "I believe you. I just need you to be honest with me. That's all. I think that I know you, and that I would like to get to know you even more."

Simon sat up in his seat, feeling a great weight momentarily lifted. "I feel the same way," he responded.

"Good," she said turning towards him with a look of relief while taking his hands. If that's the case, then we should be able to tell each other anything. That's what I want."

When he felt her hands, a shot of adrenaline coursed through his body, and his heart swelled. He wanted nothing more than to continue to build upon what they had started.

"Me too," Simon agreed with great sincerity.

"Good, that's good," Hope said. "So now, what is this purpose that God has for you? You said that it had to do with Parker's speech."

Simon looked up from Hope's soft hands to her expectant face. Having expended so much time and attention to damage control, he had nearly forgotten the conversation that they were having prior to Jack's calculated intervention. After a moment, he fumbled clumsily for the words and conviction that he had at the church after listening to Parker's testimony. Now he wasn't as sure of himself. He wondered if it might be a terrible mistake to divulge the epiphany he had had in that very emotional moment.

"What?" she asked softly. "I thought you were about to tell me something very important."

"Yes, I was," Simon answered, recalling his promise. "Okay, here it goes. I think God wants me to end the curse." The words were out of his mouth now and he couldn't get them back, no matter how desperately he wanted to after seeing her expression change.

"End what curse?" Hope asked confused.

"The curse of Jessie Joseph," Simon heard himself say as he felt Hope pull her hands back.

"Jessie Joseph?" Hope asked with disgust.

"I know it sounds crazy," Simon said, talking fast. "but, it's like what Jeremy said. People thought Moses was crazy, or Noah, or…."

"You're comparing yourself to Moses and Noah?" Hope asked, disturbed by Simon's words. He wasn't making any sense to her.

"No, not like that," Simon said. "Look the curse is…well, you see…a long time ago, this guy named Jessie Joseph…"

"Yeah, I know all about the legend," Hope said shaking her head. "I teach at the school, remember? Kids tell the story of Jessie Joseph around the schoolyard to scare each other."

"Then you also know that Jessie has come back to Bethel to take the life of some young person every six years for the past seventy-two years," Simon said, getting more than a little defensive. His worst fears of sharing his feelings with Hope were coming to fruition, but there was no going back now. He was in the middle of it, and his mind raced to articulate what he really meant. "Don't you see? Jeremy's tragic death is six years after the last one in Bethel." He paused trying to piece his random thoughts together.

"That's it?" Hope asked, devastated. "That's your purpose? That's all you got out of talking to Jeremy all of that time? You're going to put an end to a ghost story, basically."

"No!" Simon said. "Well, yes, but, that's not *it*. A lot of things have happened since I came here. I don't think it's *just* some ghost story. Hope, I saw the graveyard. I saw Clay Potter's hidden graveyard with Jessie Joseph and Adam Potter's tombstones and eleven other unmarked graves."

He knew that he sounded more and more like a lunatic with each word that fell out of his mouth. Hope put her hands to her face and looked away from him out the window of the car. Simon could see her shoulders bouncing up and down, and his heart ached.

"There's more," Simon heard himself say.

But, Hope put her hand up for him to stop.

"Hope," Simon said, "it's like what they say; someone has to put an end to the curse, to the tragic deaths. I think it's me. I think *I'm* that someone."

"Just take me home," she said, not bothering to turn away from the window.

"Hope, I can show you..." he didn't even bother finishing the sentence.

"Why are you doing this?" she asked through gasps of breath. "Please, I can't take anymore of this right now. I just want to go home." She reached for the door handle.

"Wait, no, I'll take you home," Simon said in a conciliatory tone. "Let me take you home at least."

He turned the car on, put it in reverse, and slowly backed out of the parking spot. They drove in silence as he searched for the words to say to make it all better. But the words didn't come as they pulled up in front of her parent's house. As soon as the car came to a stop, Hope reached again for the door handle. Impulsively, Simon grabbed her arm. Hope swung her head around and looked at his hand with a pained expression.

"Please, let me go," Hope almost pleaded.

"Hope, I know I sound like some kind of wacko," Simon said. "I'm not coming across the right way...I am not articulating my thoughts very well. Tonight was not a good night to talk about this. We both just lost a good friend.

"I-I want you to know that I really like you. I don't want to make things worse. And I made things worse. A lot worse. I mean, I *really* like you." She winced and turned away. "Maybe you could find it in your heart to forgive me for being so insensitive and clumsy. It was just really bad timing. If you can forgive me, I'd like a second chance to explain it the right way."

Hope pulled her arm back, and Simon let her go. "Good night, Simon," she said as she closed the car door behind her. Without looking back, she ran up the walk, ascended the steps, and went inside. Simon threw his head back into the seat. His chest felt like he had swallowed a bag of nails.

* * *

Simon dragged himself up onto a bar stool as Rich finished a dissertation on the practicality of choosing at least one new prospect early in the fantasy league baseball draft. Still, the rest of the guys paid no heed, opting instead to listen to Skip Carey and time McCarver's commentary on the first two innings of the 2004 World Series on ESPN Classic. Their eyes were lifted to the mesmerizing picture of the bright LCD, while they clutched their icy beer mugs like pacifiers.

No one noticed Simon slip in and sit down next to them over the state of the art surround sound.

"See, that's what I'm sayin'," Rich continued. When he turned back towards the guys at the bar, he noticed Simon for the first time.

"Hey man!" Rich said, reaching for the remote and turning the sound down. "I didn't hear you come in. Let me get you a beer!"

Rocky, Will, Rob, Joey, and George each grunted or nodded a nondescript greeting, but Simon didn't bother returning the gesture. As Rich poured his beer, he observed Simon's downcast demeanor.

"Sorry about Jeremy," Rich said to Simon as he set the frothy mug in front of his old friend.

Still, Simon said nothing. He stared at the streaming bubbles in the yellow glow of the lager as a piece of ice slowly slid down the side of the glass.

Hearing Rich's offer of condolence, Joey leaned back in his stool and looked at Simon.

"Jeremy, Jeremy, Jeremy," Joey said, coldly. "What did that guy get himself into?"

Rob glanced at Joey out the corner of his eye while slowly draining his glass of beer.

"Shut up, Joey," Rich said, through clenched teeth.

"No, I'm just saying," Joey continued disrespectfully, "you just have to wonder. I mean you think that you know someone."

"I said, shut your mouth," Rich repeated. Trying his best to change the conversation the only way he knew how, Rich said, "Hey, while we're all here, I've got the latest standings for the league. Let me pull it up on my blackberry. It'll be a nice little distraction from everything, ya know?"

There were several groans, before Will slid off of his stool and said, "No thanks, I've got a finance quiz tomorrow. So, I'm going to call it a night."

"Oh, come on," Rich said holding his hands up in the air.

Will didn't even acknowledge Rich's absurd ploy. Instead, he patted Simon on the back as he made his way out the door.

Not thinking, Rocky absentmindedly asked out of the blue, "So, they think id' was some kinda drug deal gone bad? I just can't believe it."

"Rocky!" Rich said, giving him a stern look and motioning towards Simon.

"What? Oh," Rocky muttered, still confused.

"I know, right," Joey replied, ignoring Rich's inference. "That's what I'm saying. You think you know someone. There goes that wholesome image he was putting on, right?"

"Just give it a rest, Joey," George said, losing some more respect for his mentor.

"No, no, I won't," Joey replied. "We can either talk about it and learn from it, or we can just sweep it under the rug and miss out on a teachable moment.

Here the guy gives all of this holier-than-thou rhetoric while he's out shooting up, sleepin' around, and who knows what all else."

Simon jumped out of his chair so fast it flipped to the ground, banging like the recoil of a .45. Before anyone could stop him, he had slammed Joey's head to the bar spilling beers in every direction.

"Hey!" Rob said, jumping up with his slacks soaked.

Just as Simon drew back his fist, Rich grabbed it with his massive hand.

"No, no, no!" Rich said. "Easy big fella!"

The swirl of the ceiling fans was all that could be heard above the silence. A lonely drunk at the end of the bar looked on expressionless as Rich struggled to hold Simon back.

"That's it," Joey said angrily, his face still pressed against the bar drenched in sticky beer, "resort to violence instead of using your brain and talking about it."

"*Shut up, Joey!*" Rich said. "I wouldn't be running my mouth right now if I were you."

Simon's face was three shades of red as he fought hard to drop his fist to his side. Finally, he tore his hand away.

Showing a great deal of self-restraint, Simon turned and walked away.

"Don't tell me, you were buying into that garbage from Jeremy!" Joey called out, wiping off his wet face. "Come on. Come back and sit down, Simon."

But Simon never turned back. He shoved the door open and made his way towards his car.

"Man, what was that?" Joey asked, trying to regain his composure. "If he wants to ignore the facts and live in some kind of fantasyland, then whatever! Forget him!"

"Dude, you are so lucky I didn't let him go," Rich said. "Now just *get out of here*. Go home."

"What? Really?" Joey asked in disbelief. "Come on, George, we don't need this."

But, George didn't budge. After a moment of indecisiveness, he finally slid off of the stool and followed Joey out the door.

* * *

Simon wrenched the key to the ignition one more time pleading with it to start. Nothing. Fueled by raw emotion, he slammed both hands against the steering wheel before resting his head on it. His mind raced. Jeremy's words echoed in his mind, as he tried to shake the expression of Hope's face when he decided to confide in her. He thought of his conversations with Jack and the promise of a job in Jersey. His head throbbed. He had reached his breaking point.

"What job?" he thought, letting out a flurry of profanity. "There's no job!"

The pressure had built and built inside of him like a raging tempest of uncertainty, despair, regret, and confusion. Overwhelmed by a dark feeling of hopelessness, he poured himself out of the car and stood on Main Street. Simon slammed the car door and looked high above the moths fluttering around the streetlight to the towering grain elevators that hummed incessantly in the humid, summer night air. Spontaneously, he slowly walked towards them, drawn by a magnetic force and an undefined yearning. Now he stood at the base. His eyes scaled the cold concrete to the heights of its summit. Like some surreal out of body experience, he needed to know what was at the top that beckoned to him. He reached for the cold rung of the iron ladder and began his ascent. With each step, he climbed higher and higher above the tiny town of Bethel like a man possessed. What was it about the prodigious elevators that had tormented him ever since he returned to his hometown?

No well formulated thoughts or notions were able take root in his consciousness. The darkness and deep despair defrayed even a glimmer of sound reasoning. All wisdom and discretion had been filtered out. Instead, he was consumed with fleeting snippets of negative thoughts; the interview being delayed; the tragic death of his friend; the rejection of Hope; and of course, the curse.

Simon deliberately moved up the side of the man-made mountain until he found himself nearly 200 feet off the ground. Pausing for just a moment, a silent slight breeze roused his consciousness. He shook the cobwebs from his head and cleared his mind. Suddenly, he looked down and realized the peril that he had put himself in.

"What am I doing?" he thought as though waking from a trance.

At once, his palms began to sweat and his heart raced while looking down at the tiny buildings and toy cars below. Carefully, he took his foot off and reached down the ladder for the next rung that would lead him once again back down to ground zero.

Thankful to be safely back on solid ground, he looked back up to the dangerous heights from which he had inexplicably found himself.

"Stupid," he said under his breath, wiping his damp palms on his slacks. "How could I have been so stupid? What was I thinking? That could have been bad. Thank you. Thank you." He said instinctively, but to no one or nothing in particular.

As he walked away from the twin towers with his hands in his pockets, he began to really think for the first time.

"Thank what?" Simon thought with a furrowed brow. "Or who?" The question plagued him.

As he set out walking with no particular destination in mind, he glanced back again to the heights of the tower cast against the heavens. Captivated, he began to contemplate the billions of dazzling stars for a few moments before casting his eyes downward again towards the elevators. He had no doubt that he had been compelled to do what he did. But, for the life of him, he couldn't figure out why. As he searched for answers, he made his way aimlessly through the streets of Bethel until he found himself standing at the entrance to the new subdivision on the edge of town. He read the words proudly chiseled into the stone, "Prosperity Estates."

Simon considered for a moment the beautiful, landscaped, stone bulwarks, and iron gates. Amidst the rhythmic swishing of the automatic sprinkler system, he made his way through the refreshing mist and gazed at the impressive, new luxury homes. A fleeting warm feeling came over him. And his heart yearned. This is what he had wanted when he set out from the university. This had been the primary driving force in his life up to this point. Three car garages, swimming pools, manicured lawns, and chromed out SUV's. This was success. These were the winners, or so he used to think. He had always thought that once he gained the summit of that mountain, then finally everyone would know, including himself, that he was somebody.

As he walked along admiring the modern identifiable marks of accomplishment, he couldn't shake the words of the courageous young man at Jeremy's visitation. Before he came to his own understanding of the message, he heard a metallic "tink." Then he heard it again, "Tink." Drawing near to the source of the peculiar sound, Simon picked up on a muffled voice that almost barked in bursts. The sounds grew louder and louder the closer he got to the biggest, most beautiful house in the entire subdivision. And it wasn't long before he could make out Lexus Helrigle's voice giving forceful instruction to his son Jackson. As Simon made his way a little further down the street, he could see the bright lights above the batting cage in the backyard.

"Jackson Michael Helrigle!" Lexus yelled, followed by a flurry of profanity. "That's pathetic! You know that? What kind of effort is that? How many times do I have to tell you? Inside out, inside out! If you think you're going to the bigs with that kind of effort you're sadly mistaken, mister."

Simon could hear the beleaguered boy talking back to his father.

"My hands hurt!" Jackson cried out, resting the Easton on his shoulder.

"'My *hands hurt*'!' " Lexus mocked sarcastically back at this son. "Be a man. Suck it up." Then he loaded another ball into pitching machine.

Glancing down at his watch, Simon saw that it was nearly 10:30 at night. Only just a few hours ago, Simon would have applauded that kind of drive, work ethic, and determination to reach such a worldly goal. Now he didn't know how he felt about it.

"Wasn't that what this country was built on?" he asked himself. He ducked his chin into his chest and moved further on down the road.

"What is success?" he challenged himself. "How do you know when you've actually achieved it? What's it measured by? Could Parker have actually been right? What are we all really doing here? What's the point of it all?"

Looking back at the exclusive community, he felt that burning desire inside of him. He felt the pressure to achieve, to gain, to conquer, and to accumulate. Wasn't that drive? Wasn't that the fuel of success? And he remembered why he had wanted to go into pharmaceutical sales in the first place. It was a path like an opportunity.

"We're in the Land of Opportunity, right?" Simon asked out loud. "Life, liberty, and the pursuit of happiness, all that. That's all I want is to be happy. Is it too much to ask? It's…it's…like what Jack said," Simon thought, making a slip in his own defense of a life aimed at achievement. "…'Like Jack said'…," he thought with less enthusiasm. His head throbbed under the weight of the turmoil brewing within.

Again, he was unable to shake the words of the innocent child and his testimony. After walking a few more blocks, he found himself standing behind the backstop of Rich's mecca to little league baseball. Even under the dark cover of night, the impressive condition of the field was obvious. He clutched the fence and stared at the freshly cut grass and carefully manicured infield. Simon leaned back and looked up to the American flag softly waving above the backstop. Again, he read the proud proclamation of champions, doing his best to convince himself of their significance.

"That's right!" he said forcefully. "Everybody loves a winner. All I want to do is roll up my sleeves, put my nose to the grindstone, compete,…and win. So, why do I feel like such a loser?"

Suddenly, he was confronted by the demons of his failures on the diamond that culminated in his ultimately quitting the Horned Frogs baseball team. He seethed with shame and regret. For a moment he desperately wanted to go back and change history. Like a man drowning in his own failure, he wildly grasped a hold of the memories and clung to them for life. Knowing what he knew now, he wanted to go back and shake that stupid teenager who quit the team, quit on himself, and quit his lifelong dream. A dreadful feeling of finality swept over him and a big part of him cried out to keep it alive. Like a horrible ache that tortured his very soul, he struggled deep inside to reach the source of it and find relief from the disturbing feelings of inadequacy and failure. But, another barely audible voice inside of him warned of what lie deep beneath the surface.

"I just need to learn from it," he said through gritted teeth. "Use it as fuel to take myself to the top!" Suddenly, he remembered the last words of his college baseball coach. They were stupid, and cliché, and …painfully true. "Quitters never win, and winners never quit."

They echoed in his head until he turned from the field to the dugout where he and Jeremy had talked so intimately just a few days before. When he did, he found a moment's rest from the demons that haunted him from his past. Jeremy's own words gave him solace and comfort. It was then that it occurred to him.

"By society's account," Simon thought, "Jeremy and Parker would undoubtedly be considered losers. But, what was it about Jeremy's words that made him think positively? And what was it about Parker's courage that made him feel secure?"

How could a 20-year-old scrawny youth director of a small church be so wise, and an awkward 10-year-old with bottleneck glasses be so strong? Confounded, he didn't know what to make of it all. It threw a monkey wrench into his whole understanding of the world and how it worked: competition; capitalism; have's and have not's; survival of the fittest; and, yes, winners and losers. May the best man win! He understood that world. What he didn't understand was why he so highly regarded a skinny little geek who made pennies and some overweight, nerdy kid who continually bailed out of the batter's box for fear of getting hit by the pitch, could make such an indelible impression on him. What was it that made them different? Instead of finding peace, it only heightened the confluence of thoughts and emotions that were swirling about inside of him.

Turning from the field, Simon made his way back to Main Street. Propping himself up against the solid pillars of the First National Bank of Bethel, Simon considered the allure of the beckoning neon lights of the revamped tavern. As he observed the wretched condition of the other buildings lining Main Street, he remembered what Jack said about money and opportunity. It was then that he noticed Thelma Harold in the window of her trophy shop. She was working feverishly late into the night on a large order for baseball trophies, plaques, ribbons, and rings.

Business had been booming for nearly a decade. Miss Harold could have easily retired from her position as principal and supplemented her income entirely by her little enterprise. Ironically, it was her position as principal that gave her a front row seat to a developing trend in which people began to hold self-esteem in higher regard than achievement, wisdom, or discipline. And so, after years of fighting it, she decided instead to profit from it, even though she knew all of the plastic, ribbon, and synthetic wood in the world couldn't cover the mediocrity and ineptitude that all of the empty praising perpetuated. Not that she would ever leave her position at Bethel Elementary. If it had ever been all about the money, she would have never gone into education to begin with. But, you can't eat or drink ideals, and they won't keep you warm in the cold of winter.

Simon watched her for a few minutes wondering why she wasn't perched on her stool in front of the poker machine at the tavern like she usually was at this time of night. Little did he know that she always worked when she was hopelessly distraught.

"What makes her tick?" he wondered. "What makes anybody do what they do for that matter?"

Again, he thought about his conversation with Jeremy about purpose. There was something burning inside of him to do *something*. Did it have anything to do with the stupid curse? Was it sales? Was it Hope? The pressure mounted. A single spark was about to ignite, and he was on the verge of total combustion.

"If not those things, then what?" he thought, grappling with the question as he made his way past the shops and stores to a row of houses opposite the school. His shoulders raised and his jaw set as the tension continued to build. "What am

I supposed to do? Why am I here? Why did I ever come back to this God forsaken town, anyway? And why don't I just leave? Just get in the car and go. What's keeping me here?"

The restlessness inside smoldered just beneath the surface as he continued wandering through the streets of the tiny community that had obviously been rocked by the most recent calamity. Even though it was eleven o'clock at night there were more lights on than usual in the windows as even ordinary folks tried to reckon with the deepest of questions. Unequipped to draw upon any truth and untrained to tap into wisdom, they wrung their hands and ineffectually tended to old scars freshly opened by the latest tragedy.

Mara was no different, sitting in her home of nearly sixty-five years. With an angry expression and clenched fists, she rocked back and forth with the ghosts of the past swirling all about her. Fuming, she set the photo album back under the table on top of an old, dusty book. Her venomous desire for vengeance shunted from her heart and pulsated through her veins, gripping her very being. Now she stared over her empty glass next to the bottle of Hennessy waiting in vain for the sweet release of sleep that would never come.

Meanwhile, next door, Hannah Grace's hands shook so much that she could barely read the instructions on the side of her medicine bottle. Through uncontrollable tears, she searched to see how often she could take the potent antidepressants. After only a few hours, the last pill that she had taken had already lost its affect. Now, standing over the sink in the kitchen, she wreathed in pain. Deciding it would be worth the risk, she popped opened the bottle, dumped a pill into her hand, and looked around for her glass of water. She found it in the living room on the coffee table next to the stacks of black and white photos taken out of shoeboxes that had been strewn about. As she cocked her head back, the record player popped and crackled out Vaughn Monroe's *Ghost Rider's in the Sky*.

Simon never noticed her silhouette through the curtains in the front window of the old Victorian house. He was too consumed by the terrible ache inside of him that was nearing its boiling point. Like the storage room at the elementary school, there were things buried deep in the recesses of his mind that he had locked away a long time ago. Now with tensions mounting, he unlocked the door and dragged them out one by one into the light. They were filled with anguish, shame, and grief from all of his failures and shortcomings. Tears filled his eyes as he bit his bottom lip in order to defray the hurt.

Before he knew it, he found himself standing again in front of his old home. Staring at the refurbished house through watery eyes, all of his feelings of inadequacy and rejection boiled over. From out of nowhere, a small car sped around the corner and darted past him, providing him a merciful distraction. Laughter and singing could be barely heard above the blaring Doppler effect of the stereo and the roar of the engine. For a brief moment, Billy Joel's lyrics hung in the air, "…Sooner or later it comes down to fate, I might as well be the one…" As the car zoomed past, the dome light afforded him a snapshot that lingered for a moment in Simon's mind. The driver was a teenage boy holding onto a silver can in a red coozy, while a young girl was pulling a new CD out of its case. Void of inhibition, both were singing at the top of their lungs while another couple in the back seat made out. The car was long gone before Simon was able to make the connection. It was the same car he and Jeremy had seen driving wildly by the ballpark. So much had changed in such a short period of time.

Pastor Pete heard the commotion, but never even bothered to look up from the computer in his office. He was too captivated by the images. The blue light of the screen reflected in his bifocals as shadows of the venetian blinds grew, expanded, and moved across the room from the headlights of the passing car. Robotically, he moved and clicked the mouse repeatedly until that all too familiar feeling of self-loathing gripped him once again. Finally, he closed the file, returned to the document that he had been working on, and began to delete the title of his sermon, "The Six Things that God Hates." He sat back, slumped in his chair, and rubbed his face with both hands. In so doing, he failed to notice the figure across the street standing on the sidewalk or the one passing back and forth in the window of the chorus room of the old school. Instead, he got out of his chair to go dust the pews and vacuum the sanctuary.

Pausing for a moment in the shadow of the church, a rage came over Simon as he contemplated the beautifully remodeled pink house and white picket fence as all that had been buried, but never far from him, came to a head. He dragged the ugliest of all hurt out of the deepest recesses of the compartments of his mind. Reluctantly, he pondered the abandonment and the rejection of his father.

"What! We weren't good enough for you!" Simon thought, shaking with resentment. "Ha! What a joke," he bitterly cursed. "Why did you leave us? This was supposed to be *our* home." He said through an anguished face, looking at the tire swing at the end of the rope of the old oak tree. "We were a family, and you took it all away from us. You said you would come back! You said you would! I waited for you and you never did. You never did…Oh God help me!" he bellowed as tears poured down his cheeks.

Was that the giant void that he was trying desperately to fill in his life? Through deep, convulsive breaths, he was no longer able to hold back the flood of tears. Simon fell to his knees on the hard concrete and wept, completely broken.

"God, dear God, please help me. Please!" he pleaded.

Out of desperation, Simon raised his hands to his forehead and clasped them together. With his eyes shut tight, he went to the Lord with sincere remorse and begged for mercy. Rocking back and forth, he prayed for the first time in many, many years. He started admitting all of the things that he had done. One by one, he confessed all of his sins from the greatest to the least. Pleading for forgiveness, he recalled the words of Jeremy and declared Jesus Christ as the Lord and Savior of his life.

With all of his heart, he began to fervently thank God for all of the blessings that he had been taking for granted in his life. Instinctively, he humbled himself and leaned forward with his face to the ground. Then he did something he would have never thought possible. He found himself actually thanking God for the trials and tribulations. When he did, Simon suddenly felt a physical presence, a spirit, lift him off of the pavement.

In that moment, a weight was also lifted from him and a peace came over him unlike any other he had ever before felt in his life, so complete and whole. His shoulders relaxed and his countenance changed. It was as if God had his arm draped over his shoulder and was leading him down a new path. An indescribable kind of warmth filled his inner being. More than some temporary, contrived numbing of the pain, it was a permanent promise of assurance. In that moment, his life had changed forever because his eternal destiny had been secured. And he knew it. He knew it in a way that was irrefutable. He had had an encounter with Jesus Christ and his life would never be the same!

A broad smile spread across his face as he turned to look back at the house from his past. He shook his head, marveling at the awesome simplicity of it all. Suddenly, all Simon wanted to do was praise God for His infinite, unconditional love.

His feet barely touched the ground as they made their way around the corner. Simon continued his conversation with the Creator of the universe. He was experiencing a joy he had never before known possible, and he thought of Jeremy. This is what Jeremy had been trying to tell him, an intimate relationship. God had been waiting for him all along.

Without realizing it, Simon was led to sit on a fire hydrant next to a yellow, children's crossing sign in front of Bethel Elementary. He was amazed at all that had happened. Like a switch that was suddenly flipped.

What had he been waiting for all of this time? A sign? He prayed for forgiveness for his rebellious heart and willful stubbornness as he gazed at the stars. The same Being that had fixed securely the Heavens above had spoken to Simon, and he gushed in reverence and thanksgiving. In awe, he leaned against the fire hydrant and folded his arms in wonder of it all.

"Jeremy was right," he said aloud, "that is what it is all about!"

Never having considered the perfect designs of his redeemer, Simon stared at Pastor Pete's church across the street with visions of a hope and a future, for which he could only praise his Lord and Savior, Jesus Christ. Giddy, Simon laughed out loud at his own doubt and foolishness that had held him captive for so many years.

"You were there the whole time," he said aloud. At that moment, the light of the marquee came on in front of the church. Beneath the time for Sunday's service, there was a message, "Come, follow me."

Simon nearly fell off of the fire hydrant, trying to stand to his feet. Never had he ever imagined in his wildest dreams that when he had asked for a sign, that God would literally give him one.

15

THE PLANS I HAVE FOR YOU

Simon bounded through the doors of Bethel Elementary at 5:19 a.m. Still energized by the truth that had been revealed to him, he was wide awake. He wanted to tell the world about the good news, but at midnight in Bethel he didn't have much luck. After countless failed attempts to get ahold of Hope on her cell phone, he finally went to her parent's house only to discover that her car was not there. He could only guess that she had decided to return to the summer camp in southern Illinois after he had dropped her off. Finally, he resigned himself to leaving Hope a message, begging her to call him back.

Undaunted, he tried to contact Rich, and Rocky, and Will, and Rob. But, each of his calls only met impersonal voice mail messages. Finally, he called his mother in Texas who received the news with skepticism and worry. At first, he was surprised by her not sharing in the excitement. Quickly, he became annoyed with her. When she finally realized that no one had died or been seriously injured, she chastised him for nearly giving her a heart attack. After trying in vain to assure her that he was not on drugs, he hung up the phone.

Next, he searched in vain to find a Bible to read. With none at his disposal, he spent the remainder of the night and on into the wee hours of the morning recording his experience. He wanted to remember every single, solitary detail. Just before dawn, he jotted down Parker's testimony at the visitation, and he thought of Jeremy's horrific death. His heart ached for his friend as he pondered the circumstances that surrounded the murder. Simon wished more than anything to talk to his friend. He wanted him to share in the revelation that he had played such a large role. More than that, he had so many questions to ask him now. If he closed his eyes and listened, he could hear the youth director's words.

Simon wrote them down on the yellow pages of an old notebook. "Purpose! God has a *purpose* for my life." He sat back on the couch and chewed on the end of the pencil. Quickly, he leaned forward and began writing again. "I think my purpose is to end the curse of Jessie Joseph!" Then he deeply exhaled.

"But, how?" Simon wondered, realizing that everything had not been revealed to him yet.

Rather than trying to rack his brain by calculating the incalculable, he continued with his own personal testimony. Simon knew God would reveal what to do, when He wanted to do it, at the perfect time to do it, and not a moment before. He would pray, listen, and wait. Until then, he finished out the last few paragraphs of his incredible experience as the sun broke over the face of the horizon.

Now he stood with a full cup of coffee, leaning out the second story window of the school building, watching it rise above the grain elevators of Bethel. The blinding light kept him from looking directly at the peak of the elevators, but he could plainly see the words written on the water tower.

"Bethel, the Center of the Universe," Simon read before relinquishing a laugh.

Suddenly, Simon heard the shuffling of feet in the hallway just outside the door of the third grade classroom. He jerked his head around expecting to see Mr. Cross. Instead, he saw a small, shoeless foot and the frayed cuff of a ratty pair of jeans. His heart skipped a beat as a bevy of thoughts challenged his reasoning. Then he heard the slap of feet scurrying down the steps.

"Adam!" Simon spontaneously yelled as he scrambled after the specter. With his heart pounding in his chest, he quickly descended the first ten steps before jumping to the landing with a thud. With his eyes darting about the room, he stopped to listen. In the silence, he could hear the slapping sounds of bare feet heading towards the basement.

Simon sprinted down the steps gasping for breath, as adrenaline shot through his body. Reaching the last step, he flicked on the lights to the basement just as he heard the scrape of a wooden door against the dirty concrete floor behind the boiler. Nearly slipping to the ground, Simon caught himself before gathering steam. When he made his way around the old furnace, he saw the small door in the wall slowly recoil, exposing a small, dark tunnel. Cautiously, Simon tiptoed towards it as his eyes groped about the room to assess the legitimacy of the swaying shadows from the bare bulbs hanging from the I-beams. Kneeling down at opening of the door, he peered into dark expanse of the tunnel wondering where it led. The aperture was no more than four feet high and three feet wide. Inside, there were a multitude of pipes and vents covered in dust and cobwebs lining its walls. Simon could feel a cool, damp draft coming out of the opening. It appeared as though it were some kind of utility tunnel connecting the oldest part of the building to the newer section that had been built much later. He looked for some kind of light switch, but found none. His heart raced as he debated whether or not to step into the darkness.

Abruptly, he heard heavy footsteps above him on the floor to the entryway of the school. With his hand shaking, Simon closed the door and pulled it tight, before backing slowly away and moved furtively back up the stairs to the 3rd grade classroom. Uncertain of who or what he might find, he cautiously inched his way through the doorway. To his relief, he found Mr. Cross filling a mug of coffee from the teacher's desk at the back of the room next to the window sill.

"There you are!" Mr. Cross said, "Mornin'."

"Uh, good morning," Simon said, deeply troubled by his encounter with a spirit.

"What's the big idea, anyway?" Mr. Cross said. "Gettin' here early and makin' a pot of coffee?"

"Huh, uh, well, you always do it for me, so I just wanted to return the favor," Simon said, wildly looking about the room. "Hey, uh, you didn't happen to see anything peculiar when you walked in, did you?"

"Peculiar?" Mr. Cross said indifferently, pouring a pack of Splenda into his coffee. "Like what?"

"Like a...little boy?" Simon asked sheepishly.

Mr. Cross looked up from his mug at Simon, "Little boy? No. Why?"

"Because I saw him...or it...just a few minutes ago," Simon said gravely, "I chased him..."

"You actually saw him?" Mr. Cross pressed, dropping his coffee mug to his side.

"...his foot, I saw his foot," Simon continued, "I chased him down the steps to basement..."

"The basement?" Mr. Cross said, his eyes searching the floor as though he could see through it.

"Yeah, I chased him down to a tiny door in the wall," Simon said excitedly. "Do you know what I'm talking about? The one behind the boiler."

Mr. Cross slowly nodded.

"Do you know where it leads?" Simon asked.

"Yeah, it goes to the annex, the one boiler heats both buildin's," Mr. Cross said walking slowly to him, "but you know for a *fact* you saw a boy?"

Simon nodded, "I mean I saw a foot, but, yes, I think so."

"And you're a thousand percent sure it went to the basement and not out the front door?" Mr. Cross asked, cunningly.

"Not a hundred percent, but ninety-nine percent sure," Simon answered defensively.

"Could ya be mistaken maybe? Cause when I drove up, I saw somethin' running through the bushes," Mr. Cross said. "Coulda' been a dog or cat or somethin'." Simon was shaking his head. "Cause they get in the school all the time."

"No, no way," Simon said, unconvinced. "I saw a barefoot and a tattered pant leg to an old pair of ratty jeans. And the door to that tunnel was open. More than open. It was still moving when I got to it!"

"Oh, oh, well, that's probably my fault," Mr. Cross explained. "I was down there work'n on it over the weekend. I probably accidentally left it open. Ya know, forgot to latch it shut. There's a strong draft that comes through there and moves that door all over the place. I'll just go down and latch it shut."

Simon followed the grizzled old janitor down the steps to the basement. Mr. Cross latched the door and slapped a padlock on it.

"Don't need nobody mess'n around down there," Mr. Cross said. "There's all kinds a' junk to get into."

"Like what?" Simon asked, still shaken.

"Everything from power circuits to phone lines to…snakes," Mr. Cross said with a gruff laugh as he turned to head back up the steps.

"Oh, so that's what Miss Harold meant by an infestation in the basement," Simon said, now cautiously looking around the floor of the basement. By now he was completely freaked out.

Mr. Cross jerked his head around and stared at Simon, "What?"

Startled, Simon sputtered with his head spinning, "Yeah, she told me she wanted to clean out the basement because there was an infestation. Is it snakes? It's funny because she said not to go at it like I was 'killin' the snake'. It's funny, because in Texas they have that expression, but they say, 'like you're killing snakes'. I thought that was what she was trying to tell me, without telling me."

"Oh, yeah, nah, it's just an expression," Mr. Cross said as he put one hand on the railing and his foot on the first step. "Guess I should get started on them floors. They ain't gonna strip themselves."

"No, I suppose they're not," Simon said, overcome by all that had just transpired. Mr. Cross grunted and started to ascend the steps before Simon even had a chance to say anything to him about his encounter with his Lord and Savior. All night he tried to tell someone, anyone, about his life changing experience. And now when he had the opportunity, he balked. On impulse, he called out to Mr. Cross, "Hey, can I help you?"

Mr. Cross stopped, ducked his head to survey the basement, and said, "Na, thanks." Seeing Simon's disappointed face, he added, "You could keep clean'n out that storage room, like Miss Harold wants. Call me if you need anything." Then he began up the steps once more.

With his opportunity slipping away, Simon called out again awkwardly, "I met Jesus Christ last night. I mean I gave my life to Jesus Christ last night." Simon winced as soon as the words left his mouth.

They hung in the air for a moment as Mr. Cross stopped on the step. After an excruciatingly long pause, he said, "Okay."

"Okay, then," Simon said rubbing the sides of his shorts with both hands. "I just wanted to tell you that."

"Hey," Mr. Cross replied.

"Yes, sir?" Simon asked with great anticipation.

"Don't forget to take the garbage to the incinerator," Mr. Cross said flatly before continuing up the steps.

Simon stood for a moment reflecting on his inability to express the amazing truth he had come to know. It wasn't nearly as easy as he had imagined it to be. Pensively, he replayed the exchange in his mind, hoping to articulate it much better at the next opportunity. Simon knew what he had experienced was real, and he wanted to share it with everyone.

Just as he knew that he *had seen* a little boy in the doorway of the classroom. He was not buying Mr. Cross's explanation. The old janitor might be able to rationalize away the meaning of it, but he couldn't dispute what Simon had seen. Even though he was still shaken by the experience, he decided that it only confirmed to him God's plan for why he was there. In a strange way, it was almost comforting. If the curse were true, and he was where God wanted him to be, then what other amazing things could he expect to see? He closed his eyes, bowed his head, and mouthed a few words. For a few minutes, he stood still in the middle of the basement, almost numb by all that had happened. Not knowing exactly what to do next. he did what he could do, and got to work.

* * *

After a half an hour, he had made his way through nearly a quarter of the large storage room. While dragging out old, damaged desks and pulling down broken chairs, his face was shrouded time and again in cobwebs. Every now and then he had to flick a nasty spider off of him onto the floor and smash it with his foot.

Reaching under a large piece of canvas, Simon felt something made of plastic. It was maybe two feet tall and yet it was extremely light. Digging it out from under the covering, he realized that it was a plastic figurine. Curiously, he flipped it around to see the front side and found himself looking into the face of Mary.

"Oh, wow," Simon muttered under his breath.

She was on her knees, bowing her head with her hands clasped and her eyes shut. It was one piece of a large, plastic nativity scene. Simon considered the solemnity of her angelic countenance as he brushed aside the cobwebs and dust from her face. Carefully, he carried the object out of the storage facility in search of a rag and some water. He cleaned it off and set it down on the floor of the basement. Returning to the canvas cover, he retrieved several more figurines. First, there were the shepherds, then the wise men. Then he found Joseph and a few of the barn animals.

One by one, Simon gently scrubbed the plastic pieces clean, setting them up around Mary at the far corner of the basement near the small door next to the furnace. Once again returning to the dark storage room, he pulled back the covering, exposing the three-walled stable. Simon dragged the large wooden frame over to the diorama and set it all up as he remembered it at Christmas time in front of the school as a child. Returning one more time to the dark room, he found the manger with the tiny baby Jesus lying in swaddling clothes amongst a bed of straw. With reverence, Simon carried Him to the stable and placed the Baby in the center of the nativity scene. Slowly, he stood up and backed away with a lump in his throat.

"This was *not* a coincidence," he said to himself marveling at God's perfect timing. Even though he didn't know exactly what it meant, he knew it was a sign of some kind that he was at least on the right path. In awe, he bowed his head and said another short prayer of thanks. As soon as he was done, he began to think about what he was supposed to do, but the more the he thought, the more confused and unsure he became. After some time, he returned to his task, frustrated by not being able to decipher a plausible answer.

Grabbing a dusty box held together with electric tape, Simon struggled to pull it free from the top of the pile of the junk in the storage area. He gave it one more hard tug before it was set free from the wreckage. Simon stumbled backwards awkwardly, holding fast to the heavy box that pressed against his cheek. When he did, a large, hairy spider landed on his face. Panicked, Simon wildly swiped at the spider. The box slipped from his grip, falling to ground, and spilling its contents. Angrily, Simon stomped at the fast moving six-legged creature that was scrambling for its life. Finally, he caught it square with the ball of his foot. On impact, a thousand tiny, baby spiders were sent scurrying away from their mother. Over and over again, he pounded the ground with the sole of his shoe until each and every one of the unwanted intruders was annihilated.

Simon sat back for a second, caught his breath, and took a quick body count. "Maybe that's the infestation," he thought, before looking at the seemingly inexhaustible piles of unidentified items he still had to sift through. "Better than snakes!"

He looked down at the contents of the box that had fallen out on impact. Tossing the loose books and papers back into the container, he reached for an old, dusty book that was lying upside down on the ground. It was open with the pages folded back. Simon picked it up, turned it over, and looked at the cover. It was a yearbook from 1935. Out of curiosity, Simon held it up to the dim light of the naked bulb and flipped through the black and white photographs. He stopped on one of the pages and pulled it close to his face. All of a sudden, a powerful sensation came over him. And Simon was certain that he had discovered something that might explain what he was supposed to do.

In another moment, he was racing up the stairs and standing in the doorway of the 4th grade classroom where Mr. Cross had been stripping the floor. The stocky janitor cut the motor to his machine, tugged at his slacks, and walked over to where Simon was holding open the brittle yearbook.

"Hey, look what I found down in the storage room in the basement," Simon said excitedly as he extended the book towards the slightly annoyed custodian.

Mr. Cross frowned as he took it out of Simon's hand and studied the pages. After a few seconds, he flipped it over to get a look at the cover of the yearbook.

"Ah, yeah, an old yearbook," Mr. Cross said unimpressed, "how bout' that?"

Simon quickly reached to take the book back out of Mr. Cross' meaty fingers before he lost the page.

"No, I know that," Simon said, trying to slow down and articulate his thoughts, "but, look at this picture of this 3rd grade class." He slid over next to the burly janitor and pointed at the photo. "Don't they look like they're standing on the steps to the entryway downstairs?"

"Yeah, they are," Mr. Cross said with a confused look on his face. "So, what of it?" he asked while wiping his sweaty forehead with a red handkerchief.

"Look!" Simon said pointing to an object behind the last row of students. "Is that a chandelier?"

"Oh, yeah," Mr. Cross said taking the book back into his hands with a slight grin, "Uh-huh, sure is."

"A chandelier?" Simon asked.

"It's a beaut', isn't it?" Mr. Cross said with pride.

"Yes, it is," Simon answered.

"It hung up there above the first landing for nearly fifty years before the state determined it to be a safety hazard," Mr. Cross said with a look of melancholy. "Oh, the school used to be a real beauty. That panel'n you see down here," he said pointing off to one side of the students on the steps in the picture, "that was real oak. It had a real nice stain to it. Pretty."

"Oh yeah, I can see it," Simon muttered, pulling the yearbook up close to his face. "Wow!"

"Now look at it," Mr. Cross lamented, pointing to the lower half of the wall of the classroom.

Simon had never even noticed it before, but the paneling was still there. It had just been painted over so many times that it had sadly blended into the wall now. Simon glanced back down at the black and white photo to get another look.

"Oh man, look at the intricate ornamentation on the ceiling there," Simon said, "but Mr. Cross was already making his way back to his noisy machine.

"Yep, they put in them false ceilin's to keep the heatin" bill down in the seventies," Mr. Cross said blandly.

"It is very impressive," Simon said.

"What is?" Mr. Cross asked dully with his finger on the start button.

"How regal the school used to be," Simon said. "How much money that must have cost back then."

"That's just the way they made things back then," Mr. Cross said, starting to get a little annoyed.

"No, I don't think so," Simon said. "I mean, with all due respect, they could have just slapped up some wooden A-frame. But, they didn't. They didn't just do the bare minimum."

"I guess," Mr. Cross answered.

"You guess," Simon objected. "At one time, this place was a work of art!"

"Maybe folks just cared a little more about things back then," Mr. Cross answered. "Look, I gotta get back to work."

"Hey, I have an idea," Simon said, ignoring Mr. Cross's inference. "With Miss Harold's permission and your help, I would like to kind of fix it up a little."

"Fix what up?" Mr. Cross asked with a sideways look.

"The entryway," Simon said, thinking of Jeremy's speech at the town hall meeting. "I think that it's a shame that the community doesn't take enough of an interest in the school or education to vote for that referendum to pass. You know, to build a new state of the art kind of school to give the kids around here a chance to make something of themselves."

"So?" Mr. Cross said, shrugging his shoulders.

"So, I think that maybe if we clean up the entryway, kind of getting it looking like it used to, maybe it would generate enough interest and excitement to get people to vote in favor of a new school!" Simon said passionately holding the picture out for Mr. Cross to see it again for affect. With a huge smile on his face, he waited for Mr. Cross's reaction.

"You're crazy," Mr. Cross said as he fired up the noisy machine.

"Yeah, I'm starting to think so," Simon admitted.

"And what do you know about carpentry or renovations and such?" Mr. Cross yelled over the growling motor.

"Well, nothing," Simon shouted. "I thought maybe you could…"

Mr. Cross kicked back on the noisy scraper and turned his back on the college boy.

Stunned by the old custodian's abrupt rejection, Simon watched him for a few seconds dumbstruck. Then he turned the picture back around and scanned it one more time.

"But, I think that's what I'm supposed to do," Simon mumbled under his breath. "*Marble?*" he yelled over the noise of the motor to Mr. Cross. After the janitor glanced up disapprovingly, Simon turned and made his way out of the room. "Man, marble floors!"

* * *

Standing at the approximate spot where the picture had been taken, Simon held the yearbook out in front of him with both hands. He was trying to imagine what it must have looked like in color. Undaunted by Mr. Cross's lack of enthusiasm, Simon introspectively considered how restoring the school would make perfect sense as to why he was brought back to Bethel. First he thought about the legend and the role that the old school played in it. Then he thought about the little boy in the well, the gravestones, and the barefoot and tattered jeans.

"So, just maybe, if I restore the school and get the referendum passed, it will end the curse?" Simon thought with great optimism. "Maybe that's the purpose God has in store for me that Jeremy was talking about!

"I can't bring him back, and I can't do anything about the investigation or the rumors; but I can honor his memory by living out my faith." After all, there are many ways to deal with grief.

Sullen, he thought about the conversations that he had had during his brief friendship with the vibrant youth director. Could it have been a coincidence? Jeremy told Simon that it was no accident that he came to Bethel on the very night that they stumbled upon the hidden graveyard. Moreover, it was no accident that he heard Jeremy's moving speech at the town hall meeting. Then there was the encounter with God and now the nativity scene that he had just come across in the basement. And now the yearbook picture. He was certain that it was not by chance. And what about Hope? Was it yet just another coincidence that she was a teacher at the school? No way. It was all starting to make sense.

"What a great way to restore the mess I made of things with her last night," he thought, amazed by how perfect the plan was. "She'll be able to see that this was all that I meant, accomplishing a specific mission that was given…by God." Simon winced again at how it sounded in his mind. He would have to think of a more polished way to say it to Hope if she would answer any of his calls. He dropped the yearbook to his side and set out to find Miss Harold to begin the work that had been started inside of him.

* * *

"You want to do what?" Thelma asked, looking up over her bifocals while furtively holding a trophy in her hands. She sat up, slipped off the glasses, and let them dangle around her neck.

Simon held the picture in the yearbook out to her.

"Where did you get this?" Miss Harold inquired, reaching out her hands for the book.

"I found it in the storage room this morning," he replied. "It fell out of a box and flipped upside down, open to this page. Look." He pointed to the picture of the 3rd grade class standing on the stairs in the entryway to the school.

Miss Harold held her glasses up to her face and carefully scanned the black and white photograph.

"I think that if I kind of fix it up a little…," he stammered sheepishly, "…you know, clean it up and put a fresh coat of paint on it. Make it look a little more like it used to. Then maybe we can get the local newspaper to do a story on it and turn the public opinion in favor of the referendum."

When he said the word referendum, Miss Harold shot him a look. With one eyebrow raised she asked him, "You think a little paint's going to do all of that?"

Simon paused for a moment wondering if he should tell her all that he had experienced since returning to Bethel, culminating in the revelation he had in the basement of the old school. Thinking better of it, he decided to take a more palatable approach.

"It's worth a shot," Simon said with a shrug. "If it doesn't work, then we're only out a little paint and some elbow grease."

Miss Harold chewed on the end her glasses for a moment. With a furrowed brow, she flipped the yearbook over to the cover. And then she turned back over to the picture inside.

"So, you're the one, huh?" Miss Harold asked.

"Ma'am?" Simon asked, feeling his legs turn to rubber as he immediately thought of the senile old woman at the church.

"The one who is going to provide the elbow grease for this little project," she asked, pointing the arm of her glasses at him.

Simon exhaled, and then answered, "Yes ma'am."

"I spose as long as it doesn't interfere with the rest of your work, you can give a go at it," she said.

Simon almost laughed when the old principal suggested that he might not be able to get the rest of his work done. "It won't interfere," Simon assured her. "I'll get my other work done first thing every day before I do any of this," he said holding up the picture.

"Okay then," Miss Harold replied, "here's what you do. You go across the street to the hardware store and get ya the supplies you need. Tell Bill to put it on the school's tab."

"I will, thanks!" Simon said with enthusiasm. "But how do I know what color of paint to get?" he asked looking down at the black and white photo.

"Pearl white," Miss Harold said without hesitation.

"Pearl white, okay," Simon repeated before heading towards the door.

"'Bout twenty gallons should get it covered," Thelma said as she slipped her glasses back on and picked up the plastic trophy once more, "but that building better be ready before school starts."

Simon grabbed the handle of the door to the shop, stopped, and turned back to the haggard and worn, old woman that he once feared as a child. "It'll all get done," he promised.

Thelma Harold raised her eyes and looked at him over the top of her horn-rimmed bifocals. "Hmmph," she grunted, "to get it all done before the start of the school year, you're going to have to go at it like you're kill'n the snake."

* * *

With a hop in his step like a man newly requisitioned for service, Simon looked both ways as he jogged across Main Street towards the hardware store that stood next door to Claire Helrigle's real estate office. Sliding in between two trucks parked on the opposite side of the street, Simon accidentally bumped the corner of Mara Rash's fold out table. She had been manning the voter registration table by herself today because Hannah Grace was in the throw's of yet another one of her spells.

"Oh, I am so sorry," Simon said as he reached down to pick up some of the papers and pencils that he accidentally knocked off the table.

"Watch where you're goin," Mara grunted. She slowly leaned down from her chair to pick up a couple of slowly rolling pencils.

"Let me get that," Simon said, coming around to the back of the table.

"Say, you're the young feller from church," Mara said in a matter of fact tone. "Always's takin' them notes."

"What?" Simon said, looking up at the crinkled face of the elderly woman. "Oh, yes, I guess I am 'hello'." After making the connection, he extended his hand.

Dutifully, she reached out and shook it. When she did, he could feel her age in the veins of her soft, weak hand.

"I'm..." before he could finish, Mara spoke.

"...Simon Freeman, I know, I know," Mara said annoyed. "I knew your father and your mother and your aunt."

"You did?" Simon asked, more than a little surprised.

"Uh-huh," she acknowledged. "So where you headin" in such a dad-blum hurry?" Mara asked, rubber necking to see what he had in his hands.

"I was on my way to the hardware store," he answered, slightly embarrassed. "I'm really sorry. I didn't see your table until I..."

"...Rammed into it?" Mara said dryly.

"Uh, yeah, I suppose so," Simon said with a laugh. "What is it for anyway?" he asked, making an effort to show some interest. "Are you selling something?"

"What I'm sell'n ain't nobody buy'n...even though it's free and paid for at the ultimate price," Mara said pointing with a bony finger to a sign hanging from the front of the table. "Nobody gives two cents about it anyways these days."

"Voter registration," Simon said, reading the sign aloud. It suddenly occurred to him. "Oh, for the referendum?"

"One in the same," Mara answered growing tired already of the conversation.

"That's funny," Simon said with a smile that was returned with a frown. "I mean, it's funny because that's why I'm going to the hardware store."

"Really?" Mara said with a spark of interest. "Do tell."

Simon paused momentarily, cupped his bottom lip, and raised his eyebrows as he considered just how he should answer the question. "Well," he stammered, looking down at the yearbook, "I'm working at the elementary school this summer."

"I already know all that!" Mara said impatiently.

"Oh, okay," Simon said a little puzzled. "So, I had this idea to kind of fix up the school in order to encourage people to vote. Kind of like what you are doing."

"Hmmph," Mara grunted cynically, trying to size up the young man. Observing the sincere expression on Simon's countenance, Mara redirected her criticism. "Well, that's more ambition than I've seen from anybody else around here," she conceded.

"Oh, thanks," Simon replied, a bit concerned by the implication. "So, you haven't had very many people register?"

Mara glared and said, "Everybody already knows what the results are going to be, so why bother, right?"

"Well, maybe someone can generate some enthusiasm," Simon said, sensing Mara's disgust.

"If you ask me," Mara said, "if certain prominent people in the community showed some backbone and voiced their opinion, then maybe 'someone' could."

Mistakenly, Simon associated Mara's outward disgust with Jeremy's plea for action. Drawing on Jeremy's words, Simon decided to confide in her a little. "I found this old yearbook this morning in a storage room of the basement at the school," he said, as he flipped through the pages to the picture that had captivated his imagination. Turning the book over in his hands, he showed it to Mara.

With great conviction, Simon guardedly shared his plan with the cynical elderly woman. At first, Simon seemed to have gained her support for the project. But, blinded by his enthusiasm, he failed to notice Mara's expression change as soon as she saw the old picture. Visibly shaken, she pushed the book away from her. It was then that he noticed the change in her demeanor.

"Is something the matter?" Simon asked, sensing that he had gone too far.

"Nothin's the matter!" she snarled.

"Is there something wrong with the picture?" Simon asked, looking down at the yearbook.

"Nah, ain't nothin' wrong with picture," Mara said snootily, "got a drawer full of yearbooks just like that one. My son went to school there from first through... well...just seen it all before. That's all."

When he heard her assertion, a thought came to Simon's mind. "Hey, you might be able to help me then," he offered.

"How's that?" Mara asked.

"Maybe, you can tell me how things were," Simon said. There was an awkward pause as Mara stepped back and folded her arms. "I mean, the photos are in black and white, so it's hard to tell what color things are in the picture," he said. Still, she said nothing. "So, maybe if I get stuck you can tell me how it once was."

"Oh, I know exactly how it was," Mara said through a curled lip with misty eyes.

After an awkward pause, Simon decided to move on. "Okay then," he said, "if I can't figure something out, I'll come find you?"

Mara nodded not daring to look the young man directly in the eye.

"Anyway, it was nice talking to you," Simon said. He gave a polite wave as he backed away from the table and made his way to the hardware store. In another minute, he had all but forgotten his brief encounter with the crotchety, old lady.

* * *

"Like I said, when we came over the bluff and saw all of the lights, I knew it was something big," Joey said, proudly regaling the story from the week before. "I knew the second that cop tried to give us the brush off that it was a murder. I just knew it, you know, like clairvoyant, or something. I just felt it in my bones."

The noonday lunch crowd was beginning to thin out as it approached one o'clock in the afternoon. The same conversation was on everyone's lips. There was no escaping the dark cloud that hung over the small midwestern town.

Will and George leaned in closer to hear Joey one more time recall the details of the events from that terrible night. Taking a long drag on his cigarette, Rob paid little attention as he focused in on the latest report from the local news station. Meanwhile, Rich was trying his best to ignore the conversation as he bussed the tables and cashed out the few remaining patrons.

"I can't believe Jeremy had ice in his veins," George said, having the audacity to interrupt his friend's tale.

"Ice?" Will asked.

"Meth," George replied.

"Oh," Will said, "is that's what the autopsy showed? I didn't hear that."

"Yep," George answered definitively, "and he had a bunch of cash hidden in the cushions of his car seat."

"I gotta hand it to him," Joey said, nonchalantly, "he was doin' more living than I ever gave him credit for."

"So, what did he officially die of?" Will asked.

"Officially?" Joey asked. "He was shot, but not until…after."

"After?" Will asked, completely engrossed in the details.

Joey raised his eyebrows.

"Horrible," Will said, sucking on an ice cube. "Why would they do something like that? Creepy. Whole town's completely freaked out."

"Send a message I guess," Joey answered in a matter of fact tone. "I don't think anybody'd be double-crossing those dudes anytime soon."

Rob glanced at Joey as he snuffed out his cigarette in the ash tray.

Will wafted his hand through the air to clear the smoke. "Why do you gotta do that in here?" he asked.

"Everybody does," Rob answered briskly, "it's a bar. Besides, Jack doesn't care."

Returning to the conversation at hand, George said, "What amazes me is how many people saw him go into that girl's house right in broad daylight, acting like he's bringing her groceries or something. Wow. What a cover!"

"Here we thought he was providing her a service, come to find out it was the other way around," Joey said with a laugh just as Simon walked through the front door of the bar.

"Hey, man," Rich said. "How are you doing? I've been texting you all morning."

Before he could answer, Joey slid off of his stool and started walking towards Simon with his hand extended.

"Hey, Simon," Joey said, conjuring up a solemn expression. "I just want to say that I was out of line the other night, and I hope that you can accept my apology."

For a moment, he stood with his hand extended, waiting. The guys sitting at the bar turned to observe the exchange while Rich readied himself to jump over the counter it necessary. Finally, Simon reached out his hand.

"Yeah," Simon said, "no problem. I accept your apology. Joey reached and placed his left hand under Simon's right elbow as they shook hands.

They all simultaneously exhaled.

"Cool," Joey said. "Have a seat, man. Let me get a stool for you."

"So, what's going on guys?" Simon said with an expression that revealed rejuvenation and purpose. Rich was the first to recognize it.

"You seem like you're doing better," Rich said, leaning against the bar. After the night of the vigil, Rich decided to let Simon have some space to get his head back on straight. Now he was convinced that his strategy had worked.

"I am," Simon replied, "in fact, I'm glad you are all here. Oh, wait a minute. Where's Rocky?" He asked looking around.

"He's been really busy lately," Rich said. "With all of the rain that we've had this spring, the weeds are sprouting like crazy in the fields. He's spraying night and day."

"Oh, okay," Simon said as he sat down on the stool. "I suppose I can tell him later."

"Tell him what?" George asked.

Simon thought for a moment about telling them everything from his prayer, to the marquee, to Adam's ghost, the nativity scene, the yearbook picture... But, in a brief lapse of intestinal fortitude, he opted for the soft sell.

"I've been thinking about this thing with Jeremy, and I can't get it out of my mind," Simon said with sincerity. "Even when I went to work this morning, it was all I could think about, you know. As I was mopping the gym floor, I was thinking about what Jeremy had said at the town hall meeting."

To this point, Rob had been half-listening, checking texts, and playing with his lighter. Now he was dialed in to what Simon was saying.

"I was thinking, 'What would be the best way to honor Jeremy's life?'," Simon said, looking down at his folded hands resting on the bar.

George and Joey shared a skeptical glance.

"Evidently, he doesn't have any family to speak of," Simon said. "And I thought, 'How will he be remembered? Or, will he be remembered at all? While I was working, I found an old yearbook with a picture of the entryway to the school, and it occurred to me. Jeremy was lobbying for this whole school referendum thing. And I'm there at the school getting paid to do virtually nothing. So, I thought I could kind of fix up the entryway. You know, make it look like it did back in the day."

"What good would that do?" Rob asked, confused.

"Well, I don't know," Simon admitted. "I was thinking that it might generate a little interest. Maybe the paper would write an article about it or something. It could possibly drive some support for the referendum that Jeremy was so passionate about. Because right now nobody seems to care."

Rob's face went blank as he said, "Huh, I don't know, man. I think that whole thing is kind of a lost cause. You heard all of those people at the meeting that night. Everybody's against it."

"Yeah, I know," Simon said, getting a little more animated, "but I really think I'm supposed to...I mean, I think it would be cool to... you know, do this for Jeremy. I think he would have really liked that. I think it would be a nice gesture."

"Wouldn't you have to get permission to do something like that?" Rob asked.

"Thelma's already given me the okay," Simon said. "What's the worst thing that could happen? The school's out a little paint. Which I picked up the other day. So, anyway, I was wondering if any of you guys might be interested in giving me a hand."

There was an awkward pause as they tried to absorb what Simon was telling them.

"I'm in," Joey said to everyone's surprise.

The rest of the guys turned and looked at him like he was crazy. Even Simon was astounded by Joey's enthusiastic response.

"Yeah, I like it," Joey continued. "It's a kind of a noble, chivalrous gesture. I mean, kind of a Don Quixote thing, but nonetheless it is a thoughtful gesture to honor a fallen...uh...acquaintance. I think it's the perfect tribute to Jeremy."

Suddenly, Will looked down at his watch. "Oh no," he said. "I'm late. I gotta get back to the bank." He got up from his stool, threw a few dollars on the bar, and quickly excused himself. "Simon, I like the idea. I mean I'm really busy with classes and work and all, but if you need some help, just let me know," he said, disingenuously.

"All right, thanks," Simon said, waving to Will as he exited the tavern.

George looked at Joey before saying, "Yeah, it sounds cool to me. It's about time people around here started having more of a regard for higher learning anyway. I could get behind it."

Rob, repulsed by the comment, shot a look of disgust at the young idealistic teenager's blind enthusiasm.

"What about you, Rich?" Simon asked, noticing that his friend had remained silent up to that point.

"I mean, it sounds okay, I guess," Rich said. "But when would you be doin' this thing?"

"I'm going back over there after I get a bite to eat…" Simon started to say.

"Now?" Joey asked. "Oh, we've already got plans tonight. Maybe tomorrow."

"That's okay," Simon said. "I've been working on it pretty late into the evening. Then I hit it again in the mornings right after I get my other work done."

"We'll come over to the school, first thing, after we roll out of bed," Joey said with certainty.

"Cool, that'd be great," Simon said. "Thanks."

"I'm not so sure that the community is ready to honor Jeremy, considering the investigation is still going on," Rob intimated. "I mean…"

"Look," Simon said with a sigh. "I get it. People who didn't know Jeremy might have the wrong idea about him based on rumors and circumstantial evidence. But, I know that wasn't Jeremy. He would never have done those things.

"I can't do anything about the investigation. And I can't dispel all of the rumors at this point. But, I have to do *something* because I know he was a victim of a horrible crime."

"Yeah, but…" Rob started to say.

Rich frowned at Rob and then spoke up. "I'd love to help ya, Simon," Rich said. "I don't see any harm in it or anything stupid like that." Rich shot a glance to Rob. "But, you know, my plate is really full right now. I go down to the ballpark in the morning to work on the field, practice in the afternoon, and then come back here to work until close."

"Yeah, don't worry about it," Simon said. "I really didn't know if you guys would want to help out. I mean it's great that Joey and George are volunteering. But, I mainly just wanted to let you guys know, so you don't wonder where I was or what I was doing. Oh, that reminds me though, I won't be able to help you with practices for a while. I'll be little busy with this project, I'm sure."

Rich, a little taken aback, stammered, "What? No, by all means, dude. I get it. I think we can get along without you." He was trying to be understanding of how people process grief differently, even though he was at a loss for how Simon could have been so affected by Jeremy's untimely death after knowing him for only a short period of time.

"Aren't ya a little creeped out working all alone in the school at night?" George asked perfunctorily.

"Na," Simon said, forcing a laugh. "What's there to be afraid of?"

16

AND THE TEMPTER CAME TO HIM

Susan tried shifting Pearl over to her other arm. However, nothing seemed to be working. She was mortified that her precious Pearl was creating such a fuss at the signing of the papers for their first house. Embarrassed, she apologized time and again to Wilson B. Livingood and Claire Helrigle. They assured her that it was not an issue. Having raised children themselves, they understood how kids had a knack for acting their worst at the most inopportune times. But Pearl was in rare form, especially for her. People often commented on what a perfect baby she was. Now Susan was using every trick in her diaper bag to get her baby to calm down.

"I am so sorry," Susan said, flustered by the ear piercing cries.

"Oh, honey, that's okay," Claire said, "she's probably just tired and ready for a nap. Here..." She picked up a tiny American flag that was in a stand on the large oak desk and waved it in front of the cranky baby, but she was only temporarily amused by the distraction before breaking out into more wild cries.

"Well, I don't think she's tired or hungry," Susan said above the wailing child. "She'll take her bottle for a minute and then just spit it out. Normally, if she's tired, I just give her her paci and she's out like a light. I don't know what's gotten into her."

"Poor thing," Wilson B. said, as he reached over to delicately rub Pearl's baby-soft hair. "Maybe she's just a little colicky. Ralph had that problem. Man, I thought we'd never get through that stage."

"She never has been before," Susan said, trying yet another position. "But, maybe you're right. I just don't know what's gotten into her today. She doesn't seem to have a fever."

Besides being embarrassed of the misery that her daughter was inflicting on the employees at First National Bank of Bethel, Susan was also a little concerned. She continually put Pearl's cheek against her own, checking for a temperature. Each time, she found her to feel normal. On one hand, she was relieved to find no outward signs of sickness, but on the other hand, she couldn't fix what she didn't know was wrong. Closing on their dream home was supposed to be a day of celebration, not one wrought with anxiety.

"Oh, I might have something she'd like," Claire said, getting out of her chair and heading for the door just as Lexus Helrigle was walking in. "I'll be right back."

Even though his wife's frustration mounted with Pearl's display of displeasure, Danny Cain wasn't going to let anything detract from his ecstatic state. When they originally saw the price tag on the luxury home, he thought there was no possible way for them to qualify for the loan, even though Claire was assuring them otherwise. Nonetheless, Danny was skeptical.

Somehow Lexus and Wilson B. made it happen. The monthly payments were right where they needed for them to be, as long as the overtime kept coming. There was no doubt that the mortgage was pushing the outer limits of their budget, but it was doable nonetheless.

Although Wilson B. articulately and concisely explained the details of the Interest Only mortgage, something was still very unsettling about it. He didn't even know banks did forty year loans. There were more than a few nights that Danny lay awake in bed, feeling the full weight of the sizable financial commitment. What Claire told them made sense. The house was an investment that would gain equity and value over time. Her point was that once their child or children had grown up and moved on, they could sell the house for a handsome profit that would be a good chunk of their nest egg for retirement. After all, real estate had always been one of the safest investments over the long haul. It had been even better than the erratic stock market. At least that's what the ambitious agent had told him.

Her words ran over and over again in Danny's mind, "It's like a 401K that you live in." When he thought in those terms, he often felt better. Still, it was that substantial monthly payment that gave him the most angst. The 'What if this happened?' and 'What if that happened?' kept plaguing him. Lexus sat expressionless across from Danny at the large conference table reading the young man's countenance while working a coin through the knuckles in his fingers under the desk.

"You know," Lexus said, "this is a great thing that you're doing. I remember when Claire and I bought our first house. So much anxiety. We kept thinking, 'Is this the right thing to do? Will we be able to afford it?' And things were tight at first," Lexus admitted. "There were even some months when we wondered if we were going to make it. But, as time went on, our incomes gradually increased. Then I got a promotion at the bank, and Claire's real estate business took off. That was about fifteen years ago now. We ended up selling that house, made a really nice profit, and used it to leverage our current home."

Danny listened with great interest to the comforting words of the bank president.

Suddenly, Claire came back into the room and flung herself down in the high back leather chair next to Susan who was rocking Pearl in her arms. "Bubbles!" Claire said as she opened the lid and dipped the plastic piece into the container. "All babies love bubbles," she said before cupping her lips and blowing gently.

In a moment, a bubble started to form. Gliding precariously over the mound of paperwork, Pearl looked on through puffy, red eyes.

"Claire," Lexus said disapprovingly.

"What?" Claire said. "Look, she loves it."

Pearl inherently reached out her tiny hand, groping wildly for the allusive treasure. Without warning it popped just above Danny's head as he dated the form, June 6, 2007.

But he paid no heed. His mind was otherwise occupied with thoughts of where he would hang the LCD. His pulse raced while Wilson B. went over each document page by page. Danny and Susan nodded in kind as though they completely understood all of the legal jargon. The only thing that became abundantly clear was when and where to sign or initial.

Any time Danny felt sick to his stomach, he reminded himself what Susan had said about tightening their belts for a while, making sacrifices in other areas in order to give their daughter all of the benefits and advantages that this world had to offer. If that meant giving up going out to eat a few nights a week or having basic cable TV for a while then so be it. In the long run, the benefits would far outweigh the temporary hardships.

"Like not having ESPN Classic is really a 'hardship'," Danny thought as he looked as his beautiful wife rocking their bundle of joy.

"Danny," Wilson B. said, pointing with his pen to a blank line at the bottom of the last document.

"Oh, sorry," Danny said taking a deep breath just as Pearl spit out her paci and gave a bloodcurdling scream. He leaned forward and signed and dated the last document with a shaky hand.

"And that's it!" Wilson B. said as a broad smile swept across his face. "Congratulations! You are now officially homeowners."

"Yeah!" Claire said with a clap of her hands up under her chin. "Here are your house keys."

Danny leaned in and hugged Susan over the crying baby. Then he gave his daughter a soft kiss on the top of her head.

"Oh, I nearly forgot to tell you," Wilson B. said, "because we're signing the papers today, your first payment won't be until the end of next month."

"You're kidding!" Susan said.

"Nope," Wilson B. said, collecting the documents.

"That's awesome," Danny said. "It just keeps getting better and better."

"And here is a little something from the bank," Claire said, revealing a bottle of champagne with a bow on it.

"Thank you so much," Susan said as she swayed back and forth in an effort to quiet the baby.

"And that's not all," Claire said in a sing-song voice, "there's a little something from me in the laundry room of your new home. You did say that you didn't have a washer and dryer, didn't you?"

"What?" Susan said, excited. "No, you didn't!"

Claire said nothing, but only gave an exaggerated nod with a wide smile.

"You didn't have to do that," Danny said, "thank you so much!"

The overzealous realtor gave each of them a big hug as she said, "Ah, it was the least I could do. You guys have been so great. We wish you nothing but the best. Besides, we're going to be neighbors. Welcome to Prosperity Estates."

"That's right, 'neighbors'," Susan said, through tears of joy. "We can't thank you enough!"

By the time Danny and Susan pushed the stroller out of the pleasant climate controlled bank air and onto the blazing hot sidewalk, they were in a state of shock. The surreal experience left them somewhat dazed as they strode past two elderly women sitting at the foldout table.

"Well, it's almost five o'clock," Danny said, looking down at his watch. "What do you want to do for dinner? You want to get something at the tavern to celebrate?"

"No," Susan said, holding Pearls cheek up to her own once more, "I can't get her to stop crying. I don't want to subject everyone in there to that. That wouldn't be fun for anyone. Besides, I thought we agreed that we'd have to cut back on going out to eat for a while, except for special occasions and things like that."

"I know, but come on," Danny said. "This is a special occasion. How about I go pick something up and meet you back at our *new* house?" Danny asked with great excitement. "Eat a couple of steaks, drink some champagne..." He raised and lowered his eyebrows a few times playfully.

"I thought Pearl's performance at the bank today might act as a kind of permanent birth control for you," she half-joked. "She's just been so fussy lately."

"What do you mean?" Danny asked. "I'm sure no one hardly noticed our precious angel acting like a complete nightmare."

* * *

Will paused for a moment, watching the young couple through the large plate glass window at the front of the bank. As they turned to go their separate ways, their faces beamed blissfully in the late afternoon sun. The young teller reflected for another moment before resuming his task of closing out his register for the day. He had just started to count out a large stack of twenties when Claire and Lexus emerged from the president's office. Lexus gave his wife a great big bear hug and lifted her completely off of the floor as he planted a long kiss on her lips.

"Woo hoo!" Claire yelled out spontaneously. Almost everyone had gone home for the day from the bank. Only Wilson B. and Will remained.

"What was with the whole washer and dryer thing?" Lexus asked with a scowl.

"Oh, get over it," Claire said. "I mean, did you see their faces? Don't you realize how happy we made them?"

"Well, I guess they'll pay for them when that bubble bursts on the balloon in five years anyway," Lexus grumbled.

"Oh, Lex," Claire said. "Money, money, money, money… You worry too much."

"One of us has to," Lexus replied, "because one of us spends it as fast as we get it. I saw that Tiffany's charge card statement."

"Wait till you see the one from Victoria's Secret," Claire said with a laugh before giving her husband a kiss.

"Oh, why didn't you say so," Lexus said, considering for a moment his premeditated investment on his wife's enhancements for her career. "I'll see you at home later then."

"Oh come on, let's go celebrate!" she said, making her way to the front door.

"I'd love to, but I can't," Lexus said. "I've got some things to tidy up here, and then Jackson has practice at seven."

"Seven o'clock *tonight?*" Claire repeated, disappointed.

"Yeah, Wilson B's team has the early practice, and we have the late one tonight," Lexus said.

"That's ridiculous," Claire responded as Wilson B. ran to the front door of the bank carrying his brief case and a ball cap.

"I agree, it is ridiculous," Lexus said. "That's why we've been in negotiation with Dr. Al-Banna to purchase some land for a park with a couple of practice fields. But, it is what it is for now. So, I'll see you later, okay?"

"Oh, I'll have to let you out, Mrs. Helrigle," Will said, putting down the stack of bills and making his way around the counter.

"We can still celebrate later," Lexus said, putting his hands into his suit pockets.

"All right, you boys have fun," Claire said with a wave. "Baseball, baseball, baseball…"

Will turned the key in the lock of the glass door and let her out.

"Women," Lexus said rolling his eyes as he started to help Will close out.

"Yeah, I'm starting to figure that out myself," Will replied as he made his way back around the counter.

Lexus picked up a wad of cash off of the counter of the bank. Playfully, he ran his thumb through the stack while holding it under his nose. "Ah, the sweet smell of money!" he said jokingly to Will.

"There's nothing like it," Will longingly admitted. "Maybe someday, I'll actually have some of my own."

"You will," Lexus said, "I have no doubt about it. You have that certain something. You remind me of myself when I was your age. I can see that hunger in your eyes. Never let it go away. That's the secret you know."

"Thanks," Will said proudly. "Obviously, you've never lost it. So, what's the trick? How do you keep that fire in your belly?"

"Here it is," Lexus said with a wry smile. "Are you ready? It's simple, but it could be the most important thing you ever learn. The way to stay hungry, the way to keep that edge, is to never be satisfied."

"How do you do that?" Will asked.

"It's pretty easy really," Lexus said. "Guys like you and me. We're wired that way. It just comes naturally. Once you make that first deal and score a little cash, you want that feeling again and again. Take that last deal for instance." The shrewd banker pointed towards the door.

"You mean the Cain's mortgage?" Will asked tracking closely with Lexus's every word.

"Precisely," Lexus said. "We just made a lot of money on that one deal. They bought a house that I built. My wife gets the commission on the sale, and the bank cashes in on the interest over the next forty years with a current interest rate in the fives that could balloon to nine or ten percent after five years! And if it falls apart, the Feds pick up the tab. It's a sweet little business model."

"Yes, it is," Will admitted, before his expression changed, "but there is one part of it that I don't quite get. They took out one of the highest risk loans on the market, right?"

"Hey, listen," Lexus said, "you can't get wrapped around all of that. Our job is to provide clients with solutions in their pursuit of the American dream. Claire showed them a half-dozen houses before they chose the one that they ended up with. The key is to show them a few lousy ones first. After a while, they're practically begging you to see the ones that are at the highest range of what they can qualify for. Once we help them find a house that they love, it's our job to get them into it any way that we can. It's not our job to counsel them on which direction to go or what loan to take out. It all comes down to numbers like down payment, payments per month, credit history. Bottom line is we got them into the house that *they* wanted with the monthly payment *they* needed. Besides, they can always refinance later on down the road when their credit score is better."

"Oh, I don't have a problem with any of that," Will replied quickly.

"Whew," Lexus said, "otherwise, you'd have a serious problem reaching your goals like Wilson B. His conscience gets in the way a lot of the time. He starts thinking, 'what about this?' and 'what about that?' I know he's my brother-in-law and all, but honestly he wears me out sometimes.

"Look, we didn't create the system. We don't write the legislation. Our sole purpose is to optimize the economic environment in a way that will produce the greatest ROI. Sometimes that means operating in the gray. But, once you learn how to work the system and understand how the game is played, then you maximize it to reach your own personal goals. It's no different from what Pastor Algood preaches every Sunday about tapping into the positive energy of the universe.

"But, if you waste your time worrying about 'what if the customer can't make the payment?' or 'what if the market collapses?' or 'what if the loans go south?'... what if, what if, what if. Who cares? That's somebody else's problem. Just lock in and do what you got to do. Simple. Do you have a problem with any of that?"

"No," Will replied, "nothing is going to get in the way of my career. But the thing that I don't get about a high risk mortgage is the potential jeopardy that it puts the bank in. I can kind of understand Wilson B's concerns if the client can't make the payments and forecloses because of the effect on the bottom line. Wouldn't we have to absorb that hit?"

"That's why I like you, Will," Lexus said, patting his young protégé on the back. "You're always thinking. No, it doesn't effect our bottom line. That's where good ole Uncle Sam comes in. We sell the loan to Fannie Mae or Freddie Mac, so that we're off the hook. If the house goes into foreclosure, then the government bails them out. Believe me, we come out ahead either way in the end. We never just absorb the loss. We're First National. The economy needs us. For that matter, the entire country needs us. We're too big to fail!"

Will nodded even though he was still a little fuzzy on the explanation because it belied what he was learning in his macroeconomics class at the local community college.

"What's the matter?" Lexus asked.

"Oh nothing," Will said. "It's just that my idiot professors don't have a clue about any of this stuff."

"Just get the degree," Lexus said. "All you need is that piece of paper. I'll teach you everything you need to know. When do you finish up?"

"Soon, I hope," Will said. "Trying to pay for school and take care of a new wife and kid is tough."

"I imagine," Lexus said, "but what doesn't kill you makes you stronger. Pretty soon you'll be a self-made man just like me. Nothing feels better than knowing that you did it all yourself."

After a short pause, he stopped what he was doing and turned again to the Will. "Oh, and can I offer you some more free advice?" he asked.

"Of course," Will said.

"About the wife and kid thing," Lexus said, "you know I love my family, right?"

"Yeah, anybody can see that," Will said, surprised by the sudden turn in the conversation.

"And I'm not saying that this would ever happen or anything," Lexus said, preempting his next statement, "but, you never know how things will go. Who can predict the future, right? Only about fifty percent of all marriages last. So, if I were you, I would start preparing a contingency plan just in case, God forbid, you ever get divorced."

"What do you mean, contingency plan?" Will asked.

"I know it sounds terrible," Lexus said, "but, I see it every day in this line of work. Things start off great and pretty soon two people who once loved each other want to rip each other's throats out."

Will thought of his own parents and nodded.

"So, if I were you, I would start setting aside some money and put it somewhere safe, somewhere that only you know about, where it's only in your name," Lexus said. "Once again, it's about understanding the game, creating a plan, and working it."

Will knew better than to ask if Lexus had done the same thing himself. "You mean like open my own savings account?"

"More like a money market account overseas," Lexus said. "It'd just be a little nest egg for you in the event that anything should ever happen. I mean, I can't think of a single frat brother who's still married outside of myself and Wilson B."

"Yeah, I get what you're saying," Will said. "Just an emergency stash."

"Exactly," Lexus said. "I even dip into mine every now and then to get a little cash for this or that. Sometimes you have to look out for number one, cause if you don't, nobody else will."

"That sounds good, but I just don't have any extra cash right now," Will said dully.

"Well, after you finish up school and get that diploma, I will strongly consider promoting you to loan officer," Lexus said. "You can get your feet wet there and start making a little money. And I'll teach you everything I know."

"Thanks," Will said as he reflected for a moment on his promising future when another thought occurred to him. "You really know your stuff," Will commented, "that's for sure."

"Oh, I didn't come up with any of this on my own," Lexus said. "Ha, are you kidding me?"

"No?" Will replied. "Then who was *your* mentor?"

"Jack," Lexus replied. "The guy has more money than God, is older than dirt, and he's never satisfied. That's how he stays hungry. It's never enough. More, more, more. That's the trick. That's how he keeps the fire burning inside of him. That's his one thing.

"Hey, that reminds me. Jack and the rest of the bank's board of directors have expressed an interest in your buddy, Simon Freeman."

"Really?" Will asked "What do they want with him?"

"They seem to think that he also has a lot of potential," Lexus said. "I only know him from little league umpiring, but he seems like a pretty heady guy. Good work ethic. Confident. Presents himself well. Articulate.

"They were just spitballing some ideas. Keep this to yourself, but we might be opening another branch in Philo. If that's the case then Wilson B. would probably become the president, and we would need someone to fill his shoes like with one of our young, ambitious loan officers."

Will's ears perked up at the insinuation.

"And then we would need someone to fill your position, someone like Simon,"

Lexus said. "Do you think you can talk to him and feel him out? Nothing formal, just kinda feel him out, you know."

"Yeah, I could do that, no problem," Will said. "I think he might consider it. After all, why else would he be going after that sales job in Jersey, unless he shared our ambition?"

"Well, we'll find out, won't we?" Lexus said as he counted out stacks of one hundred dollar bills.

* * *

Hannah Grace was late. Fumbling for her earrings, she frantically raced through the house looking for her car keys. She was a little more flustered than usual. As was their custom when there was a funeral in Bethel, Mara and Hannah Grace had prepared a meal. Only this time there was no family to take it to. So, they did the next best thing, deciding to take it to Jeremy's youth group at Pastor Algood's countryside church who were meeting for the first time since the tragic death. Although Hannah Grace loved children, being around them also was a painful reminder of her and her now deceased husband's barren home. Without her own little ones to coddle, Hannah Grace redirected her motherly instinct to every other child she came into contact with in an effort to fill the emptiness inside of her. But, at the end of the day, they were still someone else's kids, and she went home alone to a large, empty house. That's why she loved having Sharon over. She was the closest thing to having one of her own. And even though Sharon's youthful exuberance often manifested in an infinite cacophony of chitter-chatter and pointless questions, Hannah Grace loved and treasured every inane minute.

"Honey, have you seen my car keys anywhere?" Hannah Grace asked, frantically turning over the cushions to the couch.

"Aunt Gracee," Sharon said, picking through a bowl of apple cobbler, "what am I going to do with you?"

"Oh, child, you sound like John," Hannah Grace said as she pushed the cushions back in place. "He used to always say, 'you'd lose your head if it wasn't attached to your body'."

As Hannah Grace bent down to look under the end table, Sharon plopped herself down onto the old couch.

"Your Great Grandma Rash is going to kill me if I don't get going," Hannah Grace muttered. When she rose from behind the end table, she accidentally knocked over the familiar black and white picture.

Sharon put her spoon down, reached over, and set it back up. Carefully examining the photo, a question came to mind that had never occurred to her before.

"What year were you married, Gracee?" Sharon asked nonchalantly.

Distracted, Hannah Grace blurted out, "1947. Oh, I bet they're on the stoop. I set them down when I was bringing in the groceries."

With her eyebrows furrowed in deep thought, Sharon licked the final dab of ice cream off of the spoon, made her way to the front door of the house, and opened it.

"*Aunt Gracee!*" Sharon gleefully yelled out. It was just as she had suspected.

Hannah Grace quickly made her way through the dining room to the foyer. "Heavens to Betsy, I left them in the door!" She said grabbing her head with both hands. "Must be losing my mind, thanks darlin'."

Sharon was so excited that she nearly choked on her apple cobbler. "No, not that! You were only three years older than me when you got married!"

"What?" Hannah Grace asked as she searched her beautiful young niece's face.

"You are 77 years-old, you were born in 1931, and you were married in 1947," Sharon said excitedly pointing the spoon at her aunt.

Hannah Grace quickly turned her back on Sharon and headed for the kitchen in an effort to avoid any further discussion of the topic. "Gotta get the covered dishes to the car," Hannah Grace mumbled.

But, Sharon who wouldn't be deterred that easily was right on her great aunt's heels. "Oh, you are so busted!" she said with a laugh. "I can't believe it. Just three years older than me! It'd be like me getting married to Mike during my junior year."

Hannah Grace stopped and turned abruptly to Sharon who was holding her hand up over her mouth.

"Who?" Hannah Grace asked with great surprise.

"Nobody, I mean, uh, Mike," Sharon said, trying now to backpedal. "The point is that you got married when you were 16 years-old!"

Hannah Grace paused for a moment with one hand on her hip. "Well, things were different back then!" she argued. "John was about to be stationed in the Pacific, and we were in love." Trying her best to recover, she changed her tack. "We were young and stupid and that's all there is to it. Don't go getting any crazy ideas."

But, Hannah Grace was very unsettled by the dreamy look in her great niece's shining blue eyes.

"Sharon," Hannah Grace said, putting the covered dish back down on the table as soon as she realized that 'don't do as I do, do as I say' is a poor platform for preaching. She put her hand under Sharon's chin and looked directly into her eyes. "Promise me you'll never do something as dumb as I did. You are so young, and you have your whole life in front of you."

"You may have been young and dumb and all of that, but it obviously turned out all right," Sharon said. "You are still wear your wedding ring even though Uncle John has been gone for almost six years now, and you still keep that picture in the living room. Obviously, you loved him? Duh."

"Of course, I did," Hannah Grace admitted, her eyes tearing up, "I still do."

"And maybe that was how they did it in the old days," Sharon continued, "but don't you always say that folks used to get married and stay married in the old days. So, maybe that's how it should be."

"But, Sharon, you don't understand *why* we got married…"

Just then the phone rang. Hannah Grace tried her best to ignore it even though she knew it would be Mara wondering where she was.

"Now you listen here young lady and you listen good," Hannah Grace said. "I should have waited until I was older to…to…." The phone rang again.

"But, you were in love like a real life 'Romeo and Juliet'," Sharon said dreamily.

"Life isn't like the movies Sharon," Hannah Grace said picking up the tray once again. "This is serious. I have got to get going, but you and I are going to talk about this later."

"I know life's not like the movies, or a fairytale, or anything like that," Sharon said as she turned and followed Hannah Grace to the door, "but you were married for over like fifty years! I'd say that's 'Happily ever after'." She said doing the math over again in her head. "Yeah, fifty-five years."

Hannah Grace stopped with one hand holding the dish and the other one on the door handle. "Oh, Sharon," she said exasperated as her face turned pale, "yes, we thought we were in love, but we got married because we *had* to! That's not a fairytale. It's a nightmare."

Sharon stood frozen with a look of shock on her face, dropping the spoon to her side as the back door shut.

* * *

Mara reached forward and flicked away the air conditioner vents in the car and hugged herself, rubbing her arms for warmth.

"Heaven's sakes, you got it cold in here," Mara snarled.

But, Hannah Grace paid her no attention. She was busy replaying her conversation with Sharon over and over again in her mind.

"Did you hear me?" Mara said raising her brittle voice.

"Yes, I heard you, mother!" Hannah Grace said sharply.

Mara stared at her daughter-in-law for a moment. She figured Hannah Grace was just under one of her spells again. They came with such frequency now that Mara had long ago lost her compassion for them. They merely annoyed her like everything else in this forsaken world.

"And what in the devil's name took you so long to get out of the house?" Mara said disdainfully while looking out the window at a field of corn. The stalks were nearly waste high now and swayed lazily in the light of the fading sun in the West. But Hannah Grace offered no reply.

Relentless, Mara continued, "Never seen anyone in all my life, who was always late everywhere they went. It'd be a wonder of all wonders if you showed up early somewhere. Heaven forbid!"

"That's enough mother Rash," Hannah Grace said doing her best to bottle up her emotions. She reached over and dug through her purse as she drove.

"What in sam hill are you doin' now?" Mara snapped.

"I'm trying to find my pills," Hannah Grace replied, as the old familiar feeling of intense grief began to creep in.

Mara rolled her eyes and said, "Always them durn pills. If you ask me, they're the problem. Don't they give you them nightmares?"

"Mara," Hannah Grace said agitated. "You know what gives me nightmares."

Mara always knew when she had crossed the line with her daughter-in-law. Feeling a twinge of regret, she tried changing the subject.

"Don't know why we're doin' this," Mara said. "Ain't none of them kids going to appreciate it anyways."

"We said we'd bring them dinner, and we are going to bring them dinner," Hannah Grace said through gritted teeth. "It's…it's what we do."

Mara lifted the corner of her mouth in disapproval. There was something different about her daughter-in-law's demeanor. Normally, her spells only made her sad and languished.

"What's eating you tonight?" Mara finally asked.

"The past," Hannah Grace said bitterly.

"You're not the only one who thinks about him every day," Mara said, "but, you don't see me shedding any tears or reaching for some medicine that that quack put you on."

"It's not that," Hannah Grace said, "I think Sharon is dating a much older boy."

"The one we seen with her at the ballpark?" Mara asked, leaning towards Hannah Grace.

"I don't know, but probably," Hannah Grace said. "She was asking all kinds of questions about John and me. She was asking me a few weeks ago how old we were when we got married."

"Oh brother," Mara interrupted. "I hope you didn't…"

"No, I avoided the question," Hannah Grace said, "but this time she asked the year. And I wasn't thinking…"

"You told her, and she figured it out," Mara said. "Huh, a couple of dumb kids."

"That's what I told her," Hannah Grace said, "but she said something about a boy named Mike and 'Romeo and Juliet' and a bunch of nonsense."

"Mike Cook?" Mara asked.

"Mother, he's old enough to be her father," Hannah Grace said.

"Oh," Mara said, searching the recesses of her memory. "He had the pancreatitis?"

"Yes, he had the pancreatitis," Hannah Grace said, "ten years ago." After a short pause, Hannah Grace spoke again. "I just hope she's too smart for that."

"It's not about smart," Mara said. "Girl doesn't even have any hips yet. Now that friend of hers, Shannon- that's a different story.

"Kid's are always romanticizing. Livin' in a dream world. Take that boy who was in church the other day. I spoke with him at the registration table, and you won't believe what he wants to do."

"Can you tell me later, mother?" Hannah Grace asked, becoming a little more civil as they parked the car in front of Bountiful Meadows. "We need to get this chicken in there before it cools."

* * *

"She said that?" Shannon asked, looking at the picture in the frame at the end of the couch.

"Yep!" Sharon said as she chewed on her fingernail.

"What do you suppose she meant?" Shannon asked. "They didn't have any kids, did they?"

"No, not that I know of," Sharon answered. "That's what I'm saying. But, why else would you say, 'we *had* to get married'."

At that moment, the doorbell rang. The girls sprang to their feet, ran their fingers through their hair, and scrambled for the door. Shannon beat Sharon to the foyer as the two almost fell over each other trying to get the chain unlatched. Illogically, they burst out laughing as they fought to get it open.

"Whoa, what's going on here?" Sean asked with a wide grin, holding a brown bag in his right hand. "A little women's wrestling?"

"All right!" Mike said, pumping his fist.

"Yeah, right, you'd like that wouldn't you, ya pervert?" Shannon said, before she threw herself into her boyfriends arm's and gave him a wet, sloppy kiss.

Sharon rolled her eyes and looked away while pulling the bangs out of her eyes with her index finger.

"Hi there," Mike said sheepishly to Sharon.

"Hi," she said with a nervous grin.

The boys made their way into the kitchen and put the six-pack and wine coolers in the refrigerator.

"You sure she's not going to be home anytime soon?" Sean asked skeptically as he pulled out two bottles from the bag.

"Oh yeah, I'm sure," Shannon replied. "They are serving dinner and cleaning up for an entire youth group. So they shouldn't be home for hours. What's this?" She asked taking one of the bottles out of Sean's hands.

Sharon's eyes bugged out of her head. "Shannon," she said between gritted teeth.

"For you," Sean said. Then he held one out to Sharon who shook her head.

"My aunt would kill me if she knew we had alcohol here," Sharon said, suddenly getting upset.

"Come on, be cool," Mike said. "It's no big deal!"

"It is to me," Sharon replied.

"Maybe they're too young after all, Mike," Sean said to his friend who was already going through the food in the pantry as had the last several times they had come to Hannah Grace's house. He turned to Shannon and said, "Maybe we should just go."

"No!" Shannon said, as she grabbed Sharon by the arm and dragged her into the dining room.

"What are you doing?" Shannon asked emphatically.

"They brought alcohol into my aunt's house!" Sharon shouted. Mike and Sean listened in from the kitchen as they shared a bag of pretzels.

"What's the big deal?" Shannon asked.

"It's not right," Sharon pleaded.

"It's not like we're throwing a big party or somethin'," Sharon said. "They're just having a couple of beers and watchin' a movie."

"Still, it's just not right," Sharon insisted, "they didn't even ask. They just barged in like they own the place. Watching movies when Hannah Grace isn't here is one thing, but drinking is a whole different thing altogether."

"Oh, so you'll like, have no problem gettin' in a car with them and riding around while they're drinking, but you won't sit and watch a movie with them?" Shannon asked. "That doesn't make any sense. Look, don't you like Mike?"

"Well, yes," Sharon admitted.

"Then don't mess this up," Shannon pleaded, "be cool. It's no biggie. Look, it's not like you have to drink anything."

"Are you going to drink?" Sharon asked, mulling over her options in her mind while she chewed on her fingernails.

"Maybe a little," Shannon said with a giggle.

"Shannon!" Sharon said, slapping both of her hands down at her side.

"Relax, they're just wine coolers," Shannon said. She stepped towards her friend and grabbed both of her hands while giving her best hound dog expression. "*Please*. Live a little. What will it hurt? Just this one time. For me?"

"All right, but they need to get it all out of here before Aunt Gracee gets back," Sharon said.

Shannon jumped up and down with excitement. "Yes! You're the best!" she squealed. Excitedly, she grabbed Sharon by the hand and dragged her back into the kitchen just as Sean was finishing off his first can of Coors Light.

"What's the movie tonight?" Shannon asked as she bounded back over to her boyfriend.

"'American Pie'," Sean said while handing her a Citrus flavored wine cooler.

"Oh, I love this movie!" Shannon mused.

Sean and Mike shared cheshire grins.

* * *

Simon had no idea how long it had been since he began working on his newfound project. He was completely absorbed in his work and hadn't bothered to look at the clock. Naively, he had opened his first can of paint and laid down his drop cloth at the bottom of the stairs of the entryway. Thinking that he would simply just start painting, he dipped the old brush into the virgin bucket. When he purchased the paint, he had forgotten to get new brushes. Thelma said that there were already plenty of painting supplies in the janitor's closet. He had found them just as she had described, sitting in a bucket under the workbench next to the cleaning supplies. But he hadn't bargained on the brushes being coated with lacquer. Now after dipping it into the fresh can of paint only for a second, the lacquer dispersed throughout, irreversibly contaminating the entire bucket of paint.

He did his best to pour out the vast majority of the vile lacquer, but it was in vain. After cleaning out the brush with paint thinner and rinsing it thoroughly, he made another attempt. Simon dipped the brush into the can and soaked it thoroughly. Carefully, he gave it one stroke along the baseboard. Satisfied, he sat up and admired the clean, new paint. It felt good to be acting on what he believed he had been called to do. But when he dipped the brush back into the can a second time, he noticed that there were tiny flecks of dirt and grime floating in the paint can.

"What in the world?" he said, looking confused. He lifted the brush up in front of his face and saw all of the debris in the paint in the bristles. "Huh?"

His eyes searched the wall for an explanation. Taking his finger, he raked the top of the baseboards to find a thick coating of dust and dirt.

"Great," Simon said as he followed the baseboard with his eyes around the coat closet, up the stairs, and onto the first landing. Putting down the brush, he went to get a bucket, some soap, and a rag.

The entire night had unfolded much in the same manner as Simon's inexperience with handiwork time and time again reared its ugly head. By the time he had finished cleaning all of the baseboards, it was nearly nine o'clock at night. Not to be deterred by his little setback, Simon took another stab at the paint brush. This time, however, presented a new problem. There had been so many coats of paint applied to the walls over the years that there was no longer a well-defined ledge to the baseboard. Residually, there was a rounded, smooth continual slope where there once was a hard ninety-degree angle. Each time Simon tried to apply the brush to the wall, drips would run down the side of the baseboard onto the floor.

Upon closer examination, Simon could see that the baseboards had been painted the same color as the wall and wondered if that had always been the case. If so, he would follow suit and just paint over the banged up baseboards. To be sure, he decided to consult the old black and white photo. But strangely, the old yearbook was nowhere to be found. After twenty minutes he decided that it must be some kind of sign and gave up the search. Frustrated and exhausted, he decided to quit for the night.

"It has to be around here somewhere," he said with his hands on his hips, baffled by the disappearance, "books don't just get up and walk away. Unless…"

* * *

As Simon made his way out to the front of the school, he noticed a car in the driveway to one of the old houses across the street. The dome light revealed two elderly women slowly getting out of the vehicle. They appeared to be bickering about something. Suddenly, he recognized them from church. And he recalled the conversation that he had had with the older one while she was sitting at the voter registration table in front of the bank.

"What was her name?" Simon thought. "Mary, Martha, no…Margaret?"

He remembered how she had told him that she had several yearbooks with pictures of the interior of the school.

"I'll be fine, goodnight," Mara said, gathering up a few things from the backseat.

"I'm walking you to your door," Hannah Grace insisted.

"That's ridiculous," Mara grunted. "It's no more than ten yards down the street!"

"Fine, suite yourself," Hannah Grace replied, exasperated by her mother-in-law's stubbornness. "Goodnight, Mara." Then she opened the door, walked up the to the front stoop, and entered the house. The older woman slammed the car door shut, clutched her bags, and turned to walk home.

"Oh yeah, 'Mara'," Simon said under his breath.

As she turned, one of the bags slipped from her hands to the ground. On impulse, Simon walked towards her to help out. Crossing the street, he heard the sound of a car spinning rocks before grabbing pavement from the alley behind Hannah Grace's house. Simon turned just in time to see the same, by now familiar, compact car careen down the street. Mara turned as well only to see a dark figure standing in the street.

Startled, the elderly woman cried out, "Who's there?"

"Oh, hello!" Simon said, embarrassed. "It's me, uh, Simon Freeman."

"Who?" Mara said, squinting into the darkness.

"Simon Freeman," he repeated as he took a couple of steps towards her. "I spoke with you the other day in front of the bank."

"Oh, well, what do you want?" she said, angrily.

"I don't want anything," Simon said with a broad smile. "I was just coming out of the school and saw that you had dropped one of your bags. Can I give you a hand?"

"No, I don't need no help from nobody, thank you," Mara replied. "What in tarnation are you doing in the school at this time of night?" she asked suspiciously. "You vandalizin'?"

Simon was picking up the items on the ground and putting them back into her bag. "No ma'am," he said. "I was working on that little project that I was telling you about, painting the entryway."

"Hmmph," Mara grumbled. She was unimpressed and leery of Simon's motives. "Well, ain't got any money in my wallet."

"Okay," Simon said, taken a little aback. "I just thought you needed some…" He could see her shoulders rise to her ears and her face scrunch up. "I mean. I know you don't need any help, but it would be a great honor if I could do you the favor of carrying these bags for you."

"Are you drunk?" she asked without flinching.

"No, no ma'am," Simon answered, picking up the bag and extending his hand for the other one.

"Okay then, I guess," she said. "But don't smash the bread!"

"Yes, ma'am," he said.

After they ascended the steps to the front porch, she turned and spoke to him as she bent down to get the key into the keyhole. "Don't see so good on account my cataracts."

"Can I help?…" he started to say before catching himself. "I would love to do that for you."

"If you must," she said, handing him the keys.

He opened the door for her and moved out of the way to let her in before setting the other bag on the floor just inside the doorway.

"Well, thanks and goodnight," Mara said, shutting the door behind her.

"Uh, ma'am," Simon heard himself say, "you mentioned that you had several pictures like the one I showed you the other day in the yearbook, and I was wondering if I could borrow one of them."

"What?" Mara asked. "Why do you need it?"

"I guess I've sort of misplaced the yearbook that…," Simon started to say, slightly embarrassed.

"You mean you lost it," Mara said.

"No, I mean, I probably just set it down somewhere," Simon said timidly.

"Then you can probably just find it, now good day," Mara said, once again pushing the door shut.

"Okay, I may have lost it," Simon admitted as he leaned in and spoke through the crack in the door. "And I really need the picture for the project. Please."

Mara stopped pushing on the door for a moment while Simon waited for her answer. "Just a minute," she snarled, "you wait there." Then she closed the door. He could hear her putting the chain on the clasp. In a few moments, she returned, cracked open the door, and slid a picture through the opening.

"Here," she said with a frown.

Simon took it from her hand and glanced at the black and white photo. Even though it was a different picture from a fourth grade class in 1937, it was taken from a nearly identical vantage point.

"Thank you so much!" Simon said, holding out the photo. "I'll take good care of it and get it right back to you."

"All right, all right, now get off my porch," Mara replied slamming the door. He could hear the bolt being slammed shut.

Turning away from the house, Simon examined the photograph more closely. It was almost identical to the first, but not quite. Somehow the picture seemed to be taken a few steps further back exposing more of the walls on either side of the staircase. To the left, there was the corner of some kind of dark picture frame that could not be seen in the other yearbook photo, and he wondered for a moment what could be hanging on the wall. Suddenly, the porch light was turned off, and he was left standing in the dark. Simon could take a hint, so he descended the steps, armed with a vision and inspired by a cause.

* * *

Simon pulled into the driveway leading to his tiny apartment. Exhausted, he climbed out of the driver's seat and made his way to the stairs. Just as he was above to ascend the steps, he noticed what appeared to be the outline of a dark figure sitting in one of the lawn chairs in the back yard. Uncertain as to whether or not his eyes were playing tricks on him, he leaned forward and squinted. Whatever it was had not moved a muscle, but it wasn't just his imagination. There was definitely something there. Simon warily moved towards the unidentified object.

"Hello?" Simon uttered guardedly with his head cocked to one side.

Still, there was no response. As he approached the figure sitting in the chair, he was almost certain that it was a person.

"Excuse me…, hello," Simon said, now standing almost even with the back of the chair. He stretched out his neck to get a look at the face when a puff of smoke floated into the air from a small, hot orange circle.

"Jack?" Simon asked, widening his eyes to absorb as much light as possible.

Looking straight ahead, the man spoke, "Simon Freeman."

"Jack, man, you nearly gave me a heart attack," Simon said, letting out a gush of air. "What are you doing out here?" He pulled his cell phone out of his pocket and looked at the time. "It's late."

"Oh, I was just out for a little stroll and thought I'd pop in," Jack said flatly.

Simon noticed that he wasn't bubbling over with the same vigor and enthusiasm that he usually displayed. He was much more composed and introspective.

"Pull up a lawn chair, my boy," Jack offered, gesturing to the empty chair next to him. "Can I offer you a beverage?" he asked holding up a brown bag that clanked.

"No thank you, I need to get up early to get in a run before work," Simon replied.

Jack shot him a disapproving glance. Simon understood the inference and slid into the chair next to his landlord.

"Is everything all right?" Simon asked.

"Ha, that's a tricky one," Jack said taking a drag from his cigarette. "If there was only the present, or the past, I would say that I am better than all right."

Simon leaned back and looked at the outline of the dark figure, perplexed by the odd behavior and strange statement. He wondered if Jack wasn't drunk.

"But, we don't live in a vacuum, do we?" Jack said, whimsically.

"How do you mean?" Simon asked.

"Take a look around," Jack said, waving his hand about in the air. "If this moment were all that we experience, focused on, thought of, then life would be perfect wouldn't it?"

Simon looked around and thought for a moment about the serenity and peacefulness of the blanket of darkness. As his eyes began to adjust, he could make out the horizon against the dark, star studded sky and felt as though he understood what Jack was driving at.

"Unfortunately, so many people don't live in the moment," he continued, "they live in the past, present, and the future all at once, know what I mean?"

There was something about Jack's tone that drew Simon in. He thought about the old man's assertion, realizing its validity. Often, Simon's own actions were dictated by events that had happened in the past, like his father leaving or Jeremy's murder, and yet, at the same time, he was motivated by the promise of his future, like a relationship with Hope.

"It's a shame really," Jack said. "People would enjoy this life a whole lot more if they weren't burdened by the regret of the past or the worry of the future. If they could just live for the moment, in the moment, ya know? They'd be so much happier. Take you for instance."

Simon shot him a bewildered glance.

"Given a chance a share a beer with a friend on a perfect night such as this, most of the time you wouldn't hesitate," Jack continued, "but your current actions are affected by the past like how tiring your day was, and by the future, like what time you have to get up and go to work tomorrow. Oh, I understand, believe me. When I allow my mind to drift to the past or contemplate what the future holds, it overwhelms me, like an emotional tidal wave that presses down, holds you on the bottom against the rocks, and leaves you gasping for your final breath." Simon nodded as if he understood. "In the meantime, we miss out on the present. Look around at what's happening presently. What could be more satisfying? More serene?"

Then he looked down to his cigarette. "Take smoking for instance. If I think about the past like how healthy I felt before my first light or the future when I'll be hacking up blood, then I'd never enjoy the simple pleasure it brings me."

"Yeah, but come on, Jack" Simon mused. "You know that stuff can kill you. Can it be *that* good?"

"Ha, at the present time, yes," Jack said looking down again at the Pall Mall dangling from his stained fingers. "You don't smoke do ya. Too smart for that, huh?" Jack looked over to Simon and smirked. "Ah, but if you only knew how sweet it is, how it satisfies such a deep craving, how you think about having one even when you're just lying in bed at night or first thing in the morning when you wake up, then you might think about it differently. If I could only impart it to you..." Simon grinned and looked into the darkness with an air of superiority. "Oh, wait a minute. I think I know what it would be like for you." Surprised, Simon looked over to Jack.

"Oh yeah?" Simon scoffed. "What's it like?"

"It's like Jez!" Jack said abruptly.

The hairs on the back of Simon's neck stood up, and his blood ran cold. "But, I didn't..." Simon started to say before Jack waved him off. "Please, my boy, we're only human," Jack said. "Come on, have you not seen her? Oh, what am I say'n? Of course you've seen her. You can probably see her right now in the soft glow of the dashboard light right now."

Simon, though he tried mightily, could not push away the images that assaulted his consciousness and captivated every fiber of his being.

"The soft, smooth skin..." Jack shook his head. "Gettin' myself all bent out of shape here just think'n bout it."

Like cords binding him tight, Simon struggled to free himself from the burning images indelibly imprinted on his mind.

"That's what it's like," Jack said, holding up the cigarette to show Simon. "You probably lie in bed awake, thinking about that night, no doubt." He looked over to his gaunt young companion. "Oh, I know, nobody wants to think of their mistress as a, uh, dancer. Ruins the effect, thinking about all those guys watching her." Simon felt sick to his stomach. "But, ha, that's what I'm sayin' brother," Jack said excitedly, leaning in towards Simon's chair, "if you could only just enjoy it in a vacuum as just one moment in time separate from all others, free of guilt, free of repercussions. If you could have Hope and think about Jez all at the same time, have your cake and eat it to sort of thing." Simon jerked his head around, suddenly seething with anger and burning with shame. "And why not?" Jack continued.

"Why does it have to be any other way? Why does there have to be rules in the first place?

"After all, we're just men. We conquer, we pillage, we plunder. It's what we do. Said another way, we set goals, we form a plan, we execute it, we achieve, and we win! It's the American Dream! I mean what is a man apart from money, fame, and fortune? Are we to be condemned for our achievements? Are we to be ashamed of our most exhilarating experiences? What kind of messed up world it is when men are criticized for being men. That's called *success*. Bottom line, we should be applauded for it.

"And what about you? Why should you deny yourself all of the simple pleasures in life? You only get one shot at this thing. Do you know how many guys would kill to be in your shoes? First, you and Jez and now got yourself a shot at the last blessed virgin in Bethel. Ha! Why not take your shot at it, squeeze out every ounce you can, live in the moment, not waste one precious second. Go for it. No regrets," Jack said finishing with a flurry of profanity. He shook his head and took a long swig of beer.

"I mean, haven't you ever dreamt of doing something big only to let it slip through your fingers?" Jack asked pointedly, as he motioned throwing a baseball.

Simon looked down at the scar on his elbow and thought of his dream of playing in the majors, and his lost opportunity to finally be somebody.

"Cause if you have, you'd know what I'm talking bout'," Jack insisted, taking another drag. "Yes sir, if there's something you want out there, don't waste any time. I say, go for it. And don't let nothin' distract you or stand in your way."

Simon sat speechless. Jack's words pierced his heart and tugged at his very core. He couldn't articulate how he felt. Simon never had anything. He never knew comfort or luxury or status. The old man's words spoke to Simon's insecurities. They spoke to the void inside of him. To the thing that had driven him before his encounter. It was the thing that would not let him rest. The thing that kept him hungry for success.

Charged by Jack's passionate words, he once again remembered why he had started out on this trip in the first place. "What is wrong with that?" Simon thought, feeling suddenly discontent. "Why shouldn't I have that kind of lifestyle? Look at Helrigle, look at Livingood, look at Jack. They're no better than me." Simon had never had anything, except a brain and some ambition. "But isn't that all anyone needs in the land of opportunity?" he pondered. "Take those two simple qualities and parlay them into making something of yourself, of being somebody. Wasn't that what this country was built on?

"What am I doing? I have a college degree, and I'm a janitor at a grade school. What on earth am I doing here? I have gotten distracted. I have strayed off course. What's the matter with me? Do I have some kind of sick, self-destructive tendency or something?" Suddenly, he was questioning everything.

The two of them sat in silence for a few minutes before Jack looked down at Simon's hand. "What cha' got there?" Jack asked.

Simon had forgotten that he was holding Mara's photograph of the entryway to the school. "What? Oh, this?" he said holding the picture. "It's just an old yearbook photo."

"Ha, really, may I?" Jack asked, holding out his hand.

"Sure," Simon said feeling empty and defeated.

Jack took out his lighter and flicked a flame. "Oh yeah, I remember this," he said with a laugh.

"You do?" Simon asked, surprised.

"I mean I remember the way the school looked back in the day," Jack said. "Where'd ya get it?"

"Long story short, the first one I found was in a storage room in the basement of the school," Simon said with a worn out voice.

"Didn't see any ghosts in there did ya, ha?" Jack asked with a deep, resonating laugh.

Simon was once again at a loss for words. He just sat there, astonished.

"No? Ha!" Jack said. "You don't know that story?"

Taking a deep swallow, Simon stared blankly with glazed over eyes.

"The terrifying teacher who murdered his entire class?" Jack continued. "Jessie Joseph? Nothing? Adam Potter? The whole curse thing? Come on, I thought you was from here. Doesn't ring a bell, huh?"

Simon didn't move a muscle. He was numb. Instead, he stared straight ahead into the darkness.

"Just a silly old folktale that kids around here love to tell," Jack said as he sat back and took a long drink. "Never mind all that. Curses, huh!" he said under his breath. "Ridiculous. My only curse is that we are presently out of beer, and I have other work to attend to."

Slowly, Jack rose from his chair, stretched, and walked off leaving Simon alone clinging to a photograph, searching for answers, and nursing a bruised ego. More than anything, he was ashamed that one discouraging day and one conversation with Jack could bring about such deep-seated doubt.

17

SHALLOW SOIL

By the time Simon slinked in through the front doors of Bethel Elementary, it was almost ten o'clock in the morning. His conversation with Jack Lawless had taken its toll on him. He lied awake half the night, tossing and turning. Simon had his head down as he started to ascend the first stair.

"There he is!" a familiar voice said from the landing up above. "I was beginnin' to worry 'bout you," Mr. Cross said with his hands on his hips, looking down the staircase.

"Uh, yeah, I was...," Simon started to say, "...I'm late."

"No kiddin'?" Mr. Cross said with a laugh. "Figured you might a' overslept, considerin' all of the work that was done here last night."

"The *work* that was done?" Simon repeated, not thinking.

"Well, if it wasn't you then a bunch a' pixies must a' come in here last night, cleaned the baseboards, and started puttin' down tape," Mr. Cross said with a laugh. "Come on. I got somethin' to show ya." He waived his hand for Simon to follow him to the top of the stairs.

After reaching the landing, Simon found Mr. Cross leaning proudly against a scaffolding. "Beauty, ain't she?" the janitor said with a chuckle, before noticing the dumbfounded expression on Simon's face. "Oh, I know she ain't much to look at, but she'll do."

"Do what?" Simon asked. Before he could answer, Mr. Cross had already bounded into the second grade classroom and re-emerged with a piping hot cup of coffee.

"For reaching the thirty-foot ceilin', 'course," Mr. Cross said as he handed him the cup. "You missed a dandy of a sunrise this morn'n. Come on let's get goin', no time to dilly-dally."

Still half-dazed, Simon started to paint while Mr. Cross continued to work on taping around the edges of the room. Encouraged by the old janitor's sudden change of heart, Simon took to his work with newfound purpose. In just a short amount of time, he was already feeling better. They had no sooner finished a large portion of the wall that could only be reached from the towering scaffolding when Thelma Harold appeared at the top of the stairs.

"Well, looky here," Mrs. Harold said with great satisfaction.

"Hello Miss Harold," Mr. Cross said as if tipping an imaginary hat.

"Good morning, Miss Harold," Simon said with a slightly forced smile.

"Freeman," Thelma retorted flatly as she surveyed the work that had been done.

"Yes, ma'am?" Simon said holding a wet paint brush deftly in the air.

"Well done," the grizzled old veteran muttered before returning from whence she had come.

"Thank you," Simon said. He was more than a little surprised at how good those words made him feel.

And by the time he and Mr. Cross had moved the scaffolding to a new spot, they had a couple more visitors. Mara and Hannah Grace carefully made their way up the steps carrying fresh baked cookies and refreshments. Having finished exchanging pleasantries and partaking of a few delicious chocolate chip cookies, the women left them to continue their work on the noble task. As Mara and Hannah Grace turned to go, Mara, who hadn't so much as cracked a smile or given any indication of their chance meeting the night before, suddenly stopped and turned around at the top of the staircase.

"Don't go loos'n my picture, I want it back," she snipped. After which, she turned to make her way gingerly back down the steps while clutching the railing.

"Yes ma'am," Simon said as he watched them leave. "That was awfully nice of them," Simon said to Mr. Cross, still wondering what would compel the elderly women to do such a thing.

"Yep, them's a couple of real nice ladies," Mr. Cross said absentmindedly as he continued to work on the task at hand.

Lunchtime came and went without either of them taking so much as a potty break. And even though they had made noticeable progress, there was still much that needed to be done. Finally, it was Mr. Cross who had to excuse himself for a moment.

"Prostate," was all he said as he climbed back down the scaffolding and headed for the restroom.

Just then Simon's cell phone rang. Holding the dripping brush in one hand, he fumbled for the phone in his pocket. On the third ring he wrestled it free from his keys and checked the caller ID.

"Hope!" Simon said aloud. He punched the button to pick up the call, but it was too late. "Oh man, come on," he said as he set the brush down and quickly dialed Hope's number, but he only got her voice mail. He pulled the phone away from his ear and looked down to see that she had left a message. time and again he dialed and redialed her number, but it was to no avail. Anxious and frustrated all at the same time, he dialed the number one more time just to hear Hope's heavenly voice on the message.

"Hey, it's me," she said softly. "You must be working or something. I just wanted to say sorry for how I reacted. I was just caught off guard by...anyway...I really want to talk to you, so when you get a chance give me a call. Oh, and I heard through the grapevine about what you're doing at the school, and I think it's great. Bye, uh, call me."

A shot of adrenaline coursed through his body and he tried once again to return her call, but each time he was met by the pleasant message of her voice mail.

"What is the deal?" he said, slightly annoyed as he hit send again. "Hey, how are you? It was great hearing your voice. I just missed you somehow." He sorted through his mind trying to find the right words to express himself before he continued, "I'm sorry too. I should have told you about the club and the whole Jack Lawless job offer thing, and it was stupid of me to try to tell you about, or uh, to...I didn't really articulate very well what I was trying to say." He winced as he heard the words come out of his mouth. "Bottom line, I really want to talk to you too, so I'm just going to keep trying until I get ahold of you. Bye."

Simon punched end and held the cell phone under his chin as a wave of optimism came over him. He looked around at the work he had started and thought about the work that had been started in him. Then he retrieved his voice mail again just to listen to Hope's voice.

Her call changed everything. Simon was obviously thrilled to hear from her after the train wreck that was their last conversation, but it was more than that. After his conversation with Jack, he wrestled with his doubt into the wee hours of the morning. Before coming to work, he had all but convinced himself to say his goodbyes and head out East anyway. Now, in the light of day, he was more confused than ever. The experience he had seemed so real, and yet his answers were not definitive. Instead, they came to him as if it were a code he had to decipher in his heart. He longed for answers to the questions in his mind. Simon thought about the conversation that he had with Jack that made him question everything, but now he, more than ever, wished that he could talk to Jeremy again.

"What would he tell me?" Simon said under his breath. Then he suddenly remembered the invitation that Pastor Pete had given him to come by anytime to see him.

Swiftly, he climbed down from the scaffolding, raced down the stairs, and bolted out the front doors into the bright sunshine. After the doors closed behind him, Mr. Cross emerged from the bottom of the stairs, drying his hands on a paper towel.

"How 'bout we get some lunch?" Mr. Cross asked while rubbing off his hands. When no one answered, he looked around the landing. "Freeman? Freeman?"

* * *

When no one had answered the door to the parish, Simon made his way to the front of the church. Wondering if he was doing the right thing, he took a glance at the marquee in front of the church and remembered the message, "Come, Follow Me." Simon smiled knowingly and turned back at the aging, white church, and it's highly recognizable steeple rising high above the trees.

Resigned to find answers, he ascended the steps and pulled on the handle to the large wooden door. Surprisingly, it was unlocked. Simon quietly moved through the vestibule, listening for any signs of life. The obnoxious hum of a vacuum cleaner could be heard in the sanctuary. Peering through the crack in the doors, Simon saw the pastor holding a cord in one hand, while he pushed the noisy vacuum cleaner with the other. Apprehensively, Simon stepped backwards towards the exit. After regaining his resolve, he lowered his head, closed his eyes, and pushed his way through the spring-loaded doors into the sanctuary.

"Pastor Pete," Simon said with his hands cupped over his mouth as he walked towards the oblivious man. "Excuse me, Pastor!" Simon said louder, but was still unheard.

He reached out his hand and touched the pastor on the shoulder. Both of them jumped as the pastor wheeled around towards his assailant. As soon as he recognized Simon, he closed his eyes and took a deep breath. Quickly, he flicked off the switch to the vacuum.

"Ahh!" Pastor Pete said, placing his hand over his heart.

"I am so sorry," Simon said. "Are you okay? I didn't mean to startle you like that."

"No, no," Pastor Pete replied, trying to get his breath. "I just…I was just…" he sat down on the closest pew and breathed in deeply. "It's all right. I just wasn't expecting anyone."

"I could come back some other time if you like," Simon said. He was half-hoping that the pastor would take him up on the offer.

"Don't be ridiculous, I'm fine," Pastor Pete replied. "I clean when I'm having a hard time with a sermon. Now, to what do I owe the pleasure of your visit, Simon?"

"Well, I don't know exactly where to start," Simon hesitantly answered.

"Why don't you try the beginning?" the pastor said.

"It's kind of complicated," Simon said, delaying.

"Okay, then why don't you begin at the end and work backwards?" Pastor Pete suggested.

"The thing is, it's not over, I'm kind of in the middle of it," Simon muttered, looking down at the carpet.

The pastor took a deep breath and then said, "Then how about just getting to the heart of the issue."

Simon looked up from the floor to the cross on the podium at the front of the church. "Okay, Pastor. Here it goes. Do you believe in curses?" he asked, cutting to the chase.

The pastor sat back in the pew and forced a smile. "Oh, I get it," he responded. "Simon, my boy, I think that we all feel cursed sometimes. Things don't seem to be going our way, a stroke of bad luck, hard times, but I can assure you that things are never as bad as they seem..."

"No, I know, but that's not what I'm talking about," Simon said.

"Is this about the referendum and renovating the lobby of the school?" the pastor asked perceptively.

"How does everyone know about that?" Simon asked, amazed.

"It's a small town, Simon," the pastor replied. "Hannah Grace Rash called me this morning."

"Oh," Simon said. "That makes sense. Indirectly, my question does have to do with that, but I wasn't referring to bad luck or hard times. What I mean is, 'Do you believe that there are curses beyond that like..." he was recalling his conversation with Jeremy..." Adam and the Eve and the forbidden fruit and stuff like that?"

Pastor Pete's face fell as he began to feel the weight of the loaded question, "Well, yes, of course," he sputtered, now choosing his words carefully. "The Bible has a great deal of references to curses.

"Is there one in particular that you are referring to?" he asked, fearing that he might already know the answer.

"I'm not talking just about the Bible," Simon said, leaning forward on his knees with his hands clasped. "I mean, do you think that someone or something could be cursed?"

"Like a town?" Pastor Pete said, reflexively before trying to play it off. "Uh, I mean, the farmers around here are always saying that they're cursed. Either there's too much rain or not enough rain. This particular spring it's been too much, of course. But next year...only God knows?" He finished with an awkward, forced laugh.

"No, that's not exactly what I mean either," Simon asked excitedly, sitting up straight and looking the pastor in the eye. "Can a town like Bethel be cursed for something that happened in the past?"

Catching himself, the pastor sat back and dug his chin into his chest and acted as if he had never explored the idea before. After a moment, he shook his head slowly and replied, "I can't really say."

Simon leaned forward resting his elbows on his knees. "No?" Simon asked.

Pastor Pete searched Simon's pained expression. "What makes you ask?" he heard himself say.

"The referendum just got me thinking," Simon replied candidly, disappointed by the pastor's lack of insight. "Bethel, it's just... you know I haven't been around here in a while, but it seems like everything stays the same. Outside of the ballpark, the tavern, and the bank there doesn't seem to be any progress.

"You would think that a town that had seen better days would jump at the chance to, ya know, get a fresh start. I mean most of the businesses on Main Street are shuttered, the factories have closed, and most of the houses are falling apart. Does anyone care?"

"Ah, you mean like the referendum?" the pastor asked relieved. "A new school. Better education. New opportunities. Jobs. Quality of life. That sort of thing?"

"I don't know exactly, maybe," Simon said, unwilling to fully disclose everything swirling around in his head.

"Yes, you would think that people around here would jump at the chance to better themselves and give their children a better future," the pastor said in all sincerity, relieved to have avoided the ultimate question. He too leaned forward and rested his elbows on his knees. "People are sometimes shortsighted or apathetic, but I don't know that I would go so far as to call a lack of progress a curse."

"Yeah, right," Simon said as he reflected on the words of the pastor.

After a brief moment, the pastor sat up and spoke, "But sometimes all they need is someone to show them the way. Give them a vision and inspire them to action. I think that what you're doing at the school is a great thing!" he said with genuine enthusiasm and admiration. "I would just stay the course if I were you."

"Thanks," Simon replied.

"Is there anything else that I can do for you?" the Pastor asked.

Simon chewed on his bottom lip, contemplating whether or not he should elaborate any further. "No, no, that's it," he said solemnly.

"I mean it," the pastor said, now thinking that the young man merely needed some encouragement, "if I were in a position to, I would help out myself, but..." He thought for a moment before continuing. "Say, you know Ms. Hannah Grace wasn't the only one who called me this morning about you and your little project."

"Really?" Simon asked, intrigued.

"No, Hope Wiseman also gave me a call," Pastor Pete said as Simon sat straight up and smiled. "She was very interested in what you're doing from a purely educational perspective of course." The Pastor grinned, put his hand on Simon's arm before standing up and leading him to the front doors.

Invigorated by what the Pastor had told him about Hope, Simon was ready to tackle the daunting task of renovating the entryway again. Even though the mystery of the curse and his part in it was foggier than ever, he was certain about one thing. He knew how Hope made him feel.

Pastor Pete stood at the top of the steps to the church with his hands in his pockets as he watched the young lad make his way across the street, jump into the front seat of his car, and drive off. But, after Simon's old beater was out of sight, his mouth turned downward. He dropped his head to his chest and made his way back to the vacuum cleaner, greatly disturbed by his young visitor's burning question.

* * *

Simon stood in line at the counter of the hardware store holding an armful of new brushes, a putty knife, and a can of paint thinner. Inspired by Hope's inquiry and the endless possibilities inferred by its meaning, his mind drifted dreamily while waiting his turn at the counter. He had hardly even noticed the young man in front of him until the items in Simon's arms ached, having held them an inordinate amount of time. Snapping out of his trance, he leaned around to see what the hold up was all about. When he did, Simon saw all of the lawn care materials lying in the overstuffed cart next to the cash register. There were hoses, fertilizer, sprinklers, grass seed, gloves, and a rake.

The man behind the register spoke as he punched his index finger onto the buttons of the antiquated cash register. "The straw is out in the back," he said, looking over the top of his glasses. "If you just drive around the block and come up the through the alley, we'll throw it in the car for you. Your total comes to $324.63. Will that be cash or credit?"

"Oh, wow," the young man standing in front of Simon said. "I had no idea it would be that much. Let me see," he replied, as he thumbed through his wallet. He picked out his debit card and looked at it for a moment contemplatively, while the man behind the counter whistled softly, tapping his fingers on the counter. Then he shook his head and returned it to the sleeve in the brown leather wallet before grabbing a second card. "Credit," he said slightly embarrassed as he looked around for the machine to slide it through.

"All righty, then," the man at the checkout said while punching away at the old register once more. "Oh, I've got to take it and run it through the machine in the back. Sorry."

Taking the card, the owner of the store made his way to the back room. Suddenly, he turned and snapped his fingers. "Oh, I'm sorry, but can I see some ID?" he asked apologetically. "Folks at the bank have been harp'n on the whole identity theft thing."

"Of course, here you go," the young man said, diving his fingers once again into his wallet.

The elderly worker rubbed his bifocals on his red vest before placing them back on the end of his nose. "Stinks gettin' old. You'll see someday," he joked, holding the card out at arms length while digging his chin into his chest and cupping his mouth downward. "Danny Cain," he said out loud reading the driver's license. "You aren't by chance related to Tom Cain are ya?"

"No sir, not that I know of," Danny said with a laugh.

"Uh, good, he's a no good, low down scoundrel anyways," the old man joked. "Been best friends with him for years. I'll be right back." As he walked through a curtain that led to the back room, he yelled out, "Judy! Get off the phone, got a credit card I need to run."

Simon's arms were nearly numb by the time the man behind the counter returned.

"Here you go," he said between whistling, "if you'll just sign here."

While Danny signed the piece of paper, the old man asked him, "Are you from around here or just move'n in?"

"Move'n in, actually," Danny said as he handed the piece of paper back to the man. "My wife and I just bought a house in the new subdivision at the edge of town."

"Oh, well, Prosperity Estates, fancy neighborhood," the man replied. "That explains all of the yard supplies."

"Pardon?" Danny said, curiously.

"Isn't that a part of the restrictions?" he asked.

"Oh, I didn't know I was under the gun to get the yard going," Danny joked putting his hands on the cart.

"Yes sir," the man said, matter-of-factly. "It's pretty strict out there, pretty strict in deed. Might want to think about putting in a sprinkler system. Saves time and money.

"Well, you have a good day sir and come back and see us soon."

"Will do, thanks a lot," Danny replied, failing to fully grasp the insight he had been given by the kind storeowner about his HOA. He turned, made his way to the front of the store, and pushed the heavy cart out the door as the bell clanged above his head.

"Well, if it isn't Simon Freeman," the old man said with a smile as he dropped his bifocals from his nose. "Judy!" the man unexpectedly yelled to the back room over his shoulder. "What can I do you for, son?"

"I'm just getting a few more paint supplies," Simon said. "Miss Harold said it'd be okay to put them on the school's tab."

"All right, sir," the old man said. "Happy to do it. *Judy!*" he yelled again over his shoulder. He turned back towards the counter and began filling out a piece of paper as he spoke, "We heard all about what you were doing at the school over there."

"You did?" Simon asked. He shouldn't have been surprised by how fast word spread through Bethel by now, but he was.

"Yes, sir," the man replied just as Judy appeared from the back room.

"What are you yell'n about, ya old goat?" she asked playfully before she saw Simon. "Oh, it's you."

"That's what I've been trying to tell you, woman," the man said. Then he spoke again to Simon. "We think it's just great what you're do'n."

"You do?" Simon said, genuinely struck by the man's sincerity.

"Yes, we do," Judy said with a smile. "It's about time someone around here had enough gumption to do something about the school. You have our full support."

"Whatever you need, just let us know," the man said with a smile as he put his arm around his wife. "You're all set. Best of luck, Mr. Freeman."

"Well, thanks, I really appreciate that," Simon replied. He gathered his bags from the counter, waved, and headed to the door. Somehow the kind words of strangers affected him deeply, and he began to wonder if he had misjudged the potential far-reaching impact that his idea might actually have on the community. "This might actually work after all," he thought as the bell clanged obnoxiously overhead.

Simon had no sooner stepped out into the heat of the day when he felt the thumpity-thump of a deep bass reverberate in his ears and pound his chest. Just as he looked up, he heard the roar of a powerful diesel engine and saw the Mercedes emblem proudly adorning the hood of Rocky's weed spraying contraption. It bounced up and down seemingly in concert to the music as he drove down Main Street.

Rocky stuck his arm out the window and yelled, "*Freeman!*" over the Eminem's lyrics, ..."you only get one shot. Do not miss your chance to blow this opportunity comes once in a lifetime yo..."

Simon gave a wave as he moved his head from one shoulder to the other in step with the music. With a broad smile, he bounded to his car, jumped in, and headed back to achieve his objective.

Mouthing the words to his favorite song, Rocky paused at the four-way stop on Main Street, made a left, and headed for the country. Animated, he pumped his fist to the chorus while the sprayer bounded past the ballpark where Rich was dragging the infield. Rocky tugged on the horn several times, but if Rich heard him, he didn't bother to acknowledge it. Over his shoulder, Rocky watched his friend leaning out the side of the mule and looking down at the oversaturated infield.

Rocky pulled down on his flat billed Yankees cap and shook his head. After the song ended, he reached up onto the hood and pulled down his iPod, scrolling through his play list for the next tune. Placing the device back down at his side, he glanced over at his GPS to make sure he was heading to the right field before retrieving his Blackberry from his pocket. With one eye on the road and the other on the tiny screen, he rolled his thumb expertly over the nearly worn out track ball to check for any e-mail messages that he might have missed. He stopped on one that caught his attention and clicked on it. It was from Rich. The urgent message was titled, "Mandatory Fantasy League Meeting."

At a crossroads, the soft voice of the TomTom spoke, "Turn right in 300 feet." Rocky glanced over at the screen just in time to see himself crossing over the bridge to the Embarrass River. Obediently, he put his foot on the brakes, turned the wheel, and guided the lumbering oversized three-wheeler over a culvert and into the grass between a line of trees and a bean field. It was already his fifth field of the day. Ever since the heavy spring rains, his sprayer had been in high demand, and as a result the cush job that his dad had set him up with was proving to be quite profitable after all.

Rocky brought the machine to a stop, pulled down some paperwork, and ran some numbers. Excitedly, he picked up the Blackberry once again and hit the speed dial.

"Yo," Rocky said gleefully into the phone. "Yeah, I know you don't like that. Sorry. I'm sorry, dad. Okay." With his enthusiasm slightly dampened, he continued. "I just wanted to tell you how much I made this month already," he continued proudly, longing desperately for his dad's approval. "No. What do you mean. Rent? Half?" The smile swept away from his face. "That doesn't seem fair. I mean, I've been working hard…well, I've been out here spray'n since five o'clock in the morning. I didn't have time to do that…" His face soured as he listened to his dad's rant. "I'll feed them when I get home. I'll do that too. Oh, wait," he said remembering Rich's e-mail. "I've got something tonight…just *something*. No, I don't want to live somewhere else. No, I don't want to make my own truck payment." His eyes rolled back in his head. "Yes sir. Okay. Yes, sir. Bye."

He put the phone back down and stared with a downcast face off into the distance. A look of disgust swept over his face. Dejected, Rocky picked up the phone and called Rich as he climbed out of the cab. While he waited for the commissioner of the fantasy league to answer, he scaled a ladder, stood up on the top of the giant tank, and began prepping the machine for the work at hand.

"What's up, G'?" Rocky said dispassionately. "Na', can't. Can't make it. Just can't…!"

Distracted by the conversation, he didn't even notice the four teenagers off in the distance through a gap in the tree line fishing on the shore of the creek.

Sharon sat on a flat rock next to Mike with her fishing pole in her hand while her toe dipped lazily into the warm waters of the shallow creek. The water level had been high from the spring rains, but had since began to level. Dreamily she looked over tat Mike who was tying on a new hook. Not far from them, Shannon sat in between Sean's legs, resting her forearms on his knees. The brawny senior-to-be held his arms around her with his chin resting on her shoulder. Together they held the pole. Even though the fish were not biting, it couldn't be said that there wasn't any action at the secluded little fishing hole.

Until now, the torrential rains had caused the water to crest in the creek, muddying the waters, and creating perfect conditions for catching catfish. But as the four of them sat idly by, the clear water of the creek provided little cover. If that wasn't enough, the exceedingly hot temperatures stymied the appetite of finicky fish. And so, after several hours of trying, they had been skunked.

"This sucks," Sean said. "Where are all of the fish?"

"The water's too clear," Mike said, perturbed.

"No, it's just too hot," Shannon replied.

"It is hot," Sharon agreed flatly.

"Will you two quit?" Sean asked playfully. "You've complained about how hot it is ever since we got out here."

"Well, it is, and I'm bored," Shannon said, leaning forward while turning to look into Sean's face. When she did so, it produced a slight gap that did not escape the eyes of her hormone crazed companion.

Suddenly, Sean had a terribly, wonderful idea. "If you're so hot," he said, "then jump in the creek."

"We didn't bring our suits," Sharon innocently responded.

"Yeah, dummy," Shannon replied cunningly, turning her face back to the creek while she reached for the large class ring dangling from her necklace. "What are we supposed to do?"

"Just jump in," Sean insisted as though it were an obvious solution.

Sharon swung her head around and looked at the two love birds.

"With our clothes on?" Shannon asked playfully.

"No, I mean skinny dipping, uh, duh," Sean answered challengingly.

The corner of Mike's lip curled, and he looked out of the corner of his eye to see Sharon's reaction.

"No way!" Sharon said mortified. Unfortunately for her mom and dad, Sharon's reaction had more to do with her being self-conscious about her lack of development than her purity. It was a fact that would have even surprised herself had she actually taken the time to think about it.

"Sean Patrick," Shannon said, feigning surprise and disgust. Actually, the idea was far less offensive to Shannon who had been conditioned by cable TV and pop culture.

"Not naked, or nothin'," Sean said, shrewdly. "In your underwear. You got underwear on don't ya?"

"No," Shannon said purposefully.

"What?" Sean exclaimed, excited by the mere assertion. "What's the difference between underwear and a swimsuit? I mean really, if you think about it?"

There was an awkward pause. Mike kept his head down with his eyebrows raised, looking back and forth from Sean to Shannon to Sharon.

"I'm just say'n," Sean prodded, "you two have been complaining nonstop about how hot it is, and you have an ice cold creek to jump into. What's the big deal? Nobody cares. In fact, there isn't anybody around. It'd almost be silly *not* to." This time he paused for effect. "Unless you're too scared or something."

Sharon gave him a look of contempt and rolled her eyes. When she looked back, Shannon was standing up with her arms crossed in front of her, grabbing at her blouse. Sean smiled, elated at the prospect, while Mike's jaw dropped to the ground.

"*Shannon!*" Sharon yelled in disbelief. "What are you *doing?*"

"I'm jumping in," Shannon said steely. She threw the shirt at Sean. Quickly, she proceeded to shimmy off her Daisy Dukes. Once down around her ankles, she stepped her left foot out of one hole and used her right foot to kick the shorts into her boyfriend's beaming face. In a flash, Shannon jumped off of the rocky ledge into the cool water.

Aghast, Sharon spontaneously stood to her feet in complete shock. The three onlookers from the shore were dumbstruck. In a splash, Shannon popped up out of the water with her head back. When she stood, the water came up to just beneath her waist just like she had seen on shampoo ads and in the movies. Calculatingly, she reached up with both of her hands over her head to pull her hair back for added effect. As the glistening water streamed down her body, it suddenly became quite clear what the difference was between a swimsuit and underwear.

"Now, who's afraid?" Shannon said, trying her best to imitate her role models on "Desperate Housewives."

Still at a loss for words, Sharon looked over to Mike who stared longingly at her best friend's hourglass figure. Burning with jealously, Sharon glanced down at her shapeless frame. It was hard to believe looking at Shannon that only two years ago she was still playing with Barbies.

A smile crept across Mike's face. Then he turned towards Shannon. Behind him, Sean nearly killed himself trying to get his cargo shorts off, before jumping into the clear creek water.

From a distance, Rocky had witnessed the entire scene play out from the top of his sprayer. Nearly forgetting himself, he brought the phone back up to his ear. "Oh, G'," Rocky said to Rich. "You ain't gonna believe what I jus' seen. How old's your sister?..."

* * *

Simon had no sooner climbed to the top of the scaffolding when Joey and George came bounding up the stairs. He glanced down at his watch before wiping the sweat from his brow.

"Whoa, dude, check it out," Joey said, holding his arms straight out and spinning in a circle on the landing. "You really meant it!" he said as though surprised. He flipped his hat around backwards and clapped his hands together. "You've actually got quite a bit done, my friend."

"Thanks," Simon answered, "Mr. Cross was helping me earlier, but he got called over to Philo Grade School. There's still a lot to do. It's more work than you'd think. I thought you guys were coming after you rolled out of bed."

"We did," George replied, rubbing the sleep from his eyes.

"It's one o'clock in the afternoon," Simon said, glancing at his watch.

"Yeah, we were up all night last night," Joey replied. "We rented 'Grand Theft Auto: Chinatown Wars.'"

"It was awesome!" George added. "Dude, in one part, there's this scene where a car is rocking back and forth, and...!"

"...And oh, oh...and this dude killed this other dude," Joey said, simulating the act with his hands. "It looks so real! Sick graphics."

"Nice," Simon said thinly trying to mask his disapproval.

"Yeah," George said, smiling with his hands on his hips.

"So, you guys came to help out or what?" Simon asked, changing the subject.

312

"You bet," Joey said, "we're all about doing our part for the greater good, man. Then we'll tell those slackers all about it down at the tavern tonight."

"Okay," Simon said, uncertain of what that meant exactly.

"Dude, grab a brush and pan," Joey said to George. "We better get to work."

Over the next half an hour, Simon and George worked while Joey expounded on a variety of subjects ranging from Asian philosophy to the works of James Joyce. In between, he managed to sloppily paint a small section of a wall.

"Man, it's hot in here," George said, wiping his forehead with the back of his arm.

"Yeah, there's no air moving in here," Joey agreed. "Oh, hey, look what time it is. I almost forgot, we need to get online for the Phish reunion concert. Dude, we gotta go," Joey said to George.

"You go get the tickets and I'll stay here and keep painting," George said without looking up from the swath he made on the wall with his brush.

"But dude, I need your credit card, remember?" Joey asked, annoyed.

"Ah, man," George said dropping his brush to his side and turning around to look at his granola friend. "I told you, you need to get your own card."

"And I've told you I don't believe in them," Joey responded. "Besides, Mom said I can't use hers anymore."

Simon paused for a moment to look down from the scaffolding.

"You wanted to go, right?" Joey said.

"Yeah, I guess," George replied.

"Then you can either drop your credit card down to me, and I order the tickets, or you can come with me, and we can order them together," Joey said.

"Why don't I just go, and *you* help Simon," George said, marveling at his friend's lack of resourcefulness.

"No, no, no," Joey said. "That won't work for me. I need to see where the seats are."

George looked at Simon and shook his head. "Dude, I'm sorry," he said as he set his brush down in the tray.

"Yeah, for real," Joey said. "See ya. I can't wait to tell everyone about what we're doing."

"Okay, uh, thanks for coming?" Simon said as he continued with his work.

The two wanna be drifters were down the stairs and out the door before Simon could ask them what time they'd be back. He really just wanted to know if he needed to clean out their brushes before the paint dried, but he suspected that he already knew the answer.

Hours passed, and even though Simon worked tirelessly, he had barely covered one section of one wall of the landing to the entryway. Dinnertime came and went, and there was still no sign of Joey and George. Simon wasn't expecting their return any time soon. Holding the brush covered in the pearl white paint, Simon looked at all of the work that was still to be done and let out a deep sigh. Digging into his pocket, he pulled out his phone once more. He hadn't heard from Hope all day. And now his battery was dead.

"Ugh," Simon grunted. "I forgot to plug it in last night! Stupid, stupid, stupid."

Suddenly, he heard steps coming from the basement stairs that led to the landing. Simon held his breath and his heart skipped a beat as he looked expectantly in the direction of its source.

"Man, an' I thought I's hard on myself," Rocky said with a smile as he came around the corner of the stairwell.

"Oh, Rocky," Simon said, leaning his head back and shaking his head.

"Who you expectin'?" Rocky asked wearily, looking around the room with slight trepidation.

Simon chose to play it off. "Not a ghost wearing steel-toed work boots and Carhartts, if that's what you mean," he scoffed.

"Dat's exactly what I meant," Rocky said, turning to make sure nothing was behind him. "How can you stand work'n here? Place creeps me out. Know what I'm say'n?"

"You'd get used to it," Simon answered.

"Huh," Rocky uttered.

"So, what brings you down here?" Simon asked.

"Rich sent me over," Rocky replied, "we was spose to have a meet'n tonight."

"Meeting? About what?" Simon asked as he climbed down from the scaffolding.

"A fantasy league meetin'," Rocky answered, rubbing his arm uncomfortably. "Said he tried all day to get a hold of ya but your phone was dead."

"Oh, yeah," Simon said. "Hey, that reminds me. Can I borrow your phone?"

"Yeah, why?" Rocky asked, fumbling through the pockets in his overalls. "Oh, na', wait, I left it on the bar at the tavern."

"That's all right," Simon said as he looked at Hope's 2nd Grade classroom. "Hey, can you tell Rich I won't be able to make it to his meeting? I'm just starting to make some real progress here."

"Dat's cool," Rocky said blandly, "I don't really care neither. My team's twenty games out anyways. Know what I'm say'n?"

Simon noticed that Rocky wasn't his normal, enthusiastic self.

"Is something wrong, Rocky?" Simon asked, rubbing his hands with a rag.

"Na'," Rocky said, looking down while placing his hands into the back pockets of his overalls while running the toe of his boot over the floor.

"You sure?" Simon asked. "You seem like something's bothering you. Why don't you have a seat in my office?" he joked, opening his hand towards the bottom step of the staircase.

Rocky flopped himself down onto the step, and Simon sat down beside him.

"It's my dad," Rocky said dropping his dialect, "he's been on my case."

"Yeah, about what?" Simon asked with genuine concern.

"Everything," Rocky said with tears welling up in his eyes.

"Why?" Simon asked.

"I think he's ashamed of me and always has been," Rocky said, choking back the words.

"No," Simon said, with his smile disappearing from his face. "Hey, hey, big guy, easy there."

Rocky turned his head and rubbed his eyes with his hand. Not ever having been in a position to counsel someone else, Simon tried to find the words to comfort his friend. Inexplicably, he was suddenly able to draw upon his own recent experience to ease the pain of a hurting friend.

"Hey, you know, I've been going through some stuff here lately too with Jeremy's death, and Hope, and...stuff," Simon confessed.

"Really?" Rocky said, trying to regain his composure.

"Yeah, but let me tell you what God has done for me," Simon said, deciding to guardedly tell the story of his divine appointment. Remembering the words of Pastor Pete, he started at his present circumstance and worked backwards. Simon told Rocky about the night he prayed and felt the presence of his Lord and Savior Jesus Christ and saw the message on the church marquee. Simon tried to capture the heart of Jeremy's words. As he quoted his recently deceased friend, the irony of the situation began to sink in. Now he was ministering to another friend simply by telling him about his own experience. He had a powerful testimony about what God had done for him. He was able to share with another human being about how God had forgiven him. He was able to say how God had given him the strength to press on, how He had given him a purpose to honor Jeremy by doing the work at the school. As he spoke, Rocky's entire demeanor changed.

Simon wasn't completely forthright about his testimony, thinking it best to leave out all of that stuff about the curse. He decided that it might only cloud the core message about the free gift that Jesus Christ offers to all who believe in Him. Even when Simon talked about his conversations with Jeremy, he only accentuated the positive. He simply felt Rocky needed to be uplifted by the message and not dissuaded by every sordid detail regarding the fall or judgment. And if the end result were any indication, Simon's calculated decision to censor his testimony seemed to have its desired effect. Unexpectedly, Rocky pulled off his Yankees cap, kneeled down on the floor of the landing, and asked Simon to help him pray.

Stunned by the request, Simon hesitated at first. He was unsure of his authority, but then he decided to do his best to accommodate his friend's request.

Rocky had always called himself a Christian having grown up in the Catholic church. But when they had finished praying, he decided that things were going to be different from now on. He was ready to receive God's blessings.

Beaming with a bright smile, Rocky wiped a few tears of joy away before giving Simon a warm embrace. Pulling his gold chain from over his head, he descended the steps, promising that he would return to help Simon paint the school. But first, he wanted to go tell his father what he had done. Simon bid him farewell as Rocky excitedly ran down the stairs and out the front door.

His friend's reaction was different from his own. Rocky had been a little more animated and vocal about his excitement, but that was him. That was his personality. He wore his emotions on his sleeve, but what Simon had not anticipated was the feeling that welled up inside of himself at having been the person to lead someone else to salvation. He stood tall at the top of the stairs completely enthralled at the wonder of it all, swelling with pride.

* * *

It had already been quite a day for Rich even before his cell phone rang just before the evening news came on. He had agonized all day about what to do to get his beleaguered little league team back on track. Since claiming the championship the previous season, expectations had been running high. Sure they had lost some key players from that team, but the kids that he had thought would fill those shoes were simply not getting the job done. It had been gnawing at Rich for weeks, but it all came to a head when they lost to a mediocre team from Tolono. Now players and parents alike were beginning to lose faith as well as their patience with the fiery coach. No one questioned his methods when his team was on top, but now that they had fallen to the middle of the pack, the criticism came in waves. And the pressure was beginning to mount.

If that wasn't enough, he received the play-by-play from Rocky about the activities of his kid sister at the creek. He had no choice but to call their mother and nark on her. After all, it was for her own good. It's what big brothers do. They look out for the best interest of their younger siblings, even if it wasn't appreciated.

Now Sharon wouldn't even speak to him after she was grounded and no longer allowed to see Mike. All she kept saying was how they didn't understand, how she hadn't done anything wrong, how she was in love, and how there was nothing they could do to keep her from seeing the high school senior. It was at that point that Rich offered to pay the young man a visit himself.

More often than not Rich had to take on the roll of disciplinarian, because their father was a contractor who traveled a great deal for his job. Around and around the three of them went until Sharon finally ran to her room crying and slamming her bedroom door in protest.

What's more, only three of the members of his beloved fantasy league bothered to show up for the meeting at the tavern. There were some serious problems that needed to be addressed before the whole season got completely away from them. Rich's team was running away with the title which meant that the other guys were no longer actively participating. Apathy was beginning to breed inactivity. Guys were keeping players in their lineup even when they were on injured reserve for crying out loud! The net result was that Rich no longer had a challenge, and it was taking the fun out of the whole thing.

To cap it all off, his best friend, the only guy who was making it interesting, had gone crazy, spending most of his time at the school these days.

When Rich first heard about Simon's plan, he was less than enthused but thought that it was just his way of dealing with his grief over Jeremy's murder. Rich thought it was a phase that would pass quickly, but it hadn't. Instead, there was a buzz around town about his little project to commemorate a guy who couldn't coach his way out of paper bag. Rich missed Simon being around. He certainly couldn't bounce his ideas about the team or the fantasy league off of Rob or Will. Now Rich wasn't even sure that he could pencil Simon into the top of the lineup of his church softball team. So, when the phone rang he was fully expecting it to be his old friend.

"Hello," Rich said, "Oh, yeah, high time. No. I realize he didn't pitch last week. Yes. Well, that's something I'm considering…uh-huh. Well, what we're doing isn't working. He might keep playing short or I might give him a try in left. I know we don't have anybody right now, but I've got my eye on a kid from one of the other teams whose really coming around with his swing."

Rich had to hold the phone out away from his ear as the irate parent blasted him with hateful criticism laced with profanity. The parent didn't even give him an opportunity to respond. Instead, he hung up after the long tirade. Perturbed, Rich brought the phone back down from his ear. Against all hope, he scrolled anxiously to see if he had missed any calls or texts. Nothing. Just then Rocky came crashing through the front door of the tavern. His customary Yankees hat and gold jewelry were strangely absent along with his urban dialect. With a wide grin, Rocky raised his hands to the air, and declared to the few patrons still milling about, "Jesus Christ is my Lord and Savior!"

"Oh, God," Rich muttered, as he looked up to the ceiling before dropping his chin to his chest. "From Eminem to Benny Hinn. Lord help us!"

18

A GHOST OF A CHANCE

In a matter of only a few days, the support had become somewhat overwhelming for Simon. His plan to drive votes in favor of the referendum by repainting the entryway of the school was gaining steam. First, it was Lexus Helrigle who made a calculated decision to openly support the efforts of the little reclamation project. For some time, he had toyed with the idea of running for a political office, maybe even mayor. Jack had often encouraged him to do so, because he said he was tired of the responsibilities. Knowing that the referendum was a foregone conclusion, Lexus and Jack thought that it would be a great opportunity to win the support of the bleeding hearts and green-people for whom things like education and the environment were important. Not only that, but it was directly in step with the promise that he made at the town hall meeting to provide the necessary funding to get the old building up to date on the latest codes. It was a no-brainer as far as Jack was concerned. Let the referendum fail and get credit for trying to save it.

Unaware of any of their schemes, it was a great shock to Simon when Lexus donned the doors of Bethel Elementary one evening to lend a helping hand. The bank president even brought along his wife Claire and his son Jackson albeit against his will.

Wilson B. and Angie Livingood who had volunteered their time based on their convictions were even more surprised by Lexus's sudden interest in education. What did not surprise Wilson B, however, was to find the ambitious young bank teller, Will Thornchuk, working a roller while Lexus glad-handed the other volunteers. Will thought it more profitable to spend his time in this way than toiling through yet another paper on economics, and he was right. Butt-kissing was not a prerequisite, but it was a very pragmatic elective. It pleased Lexus greatly to see his young understudy's shameless attempts to gain favor. Nor would it go unnoticed by Jack either who was constantly turning over rocks trying to find "good" people.

The fact that Mara and Hannah Grace Rash brought in refreshments each night was also not surprising. They were well known throughout the community for their willingness to serve when needed. It was almost expected because it had become second nature for them to do so. In an act of solidarity, the three local pastors agreed to make an appearance. Pastor Pete showed up first, making the rounds while extolling the workers with words of encouragement. As he was standing with his hands behind his back admiring the work, he noticed an unattended paintbrush sitting in a tray of paint on the floor. Pete looked around cautiously before reaching down and picking it up. But before he could act on his impulses, Pastor Algood and Father Rite walked through the front doors. Their bipartisan appearance just so happened to coincide with the distribution of Mara's famous apple pie.

"Well, look here," Pastor Algood said, reaching out for a slice of pie. "timing's everything."

"What are you blabber'n about?" Mara snapped. "Ain't we here right on time, like I told you when you called?"

Slightly chagrined, Pastor Algood commented on the progress that the group had made in between bites of food and sips of coffee. Still hampered by the overriding sentiment of political correctness, neither he nor Father Rite dared take part. Pastor Algood joked that he didn't look good in orange, but secretly he worried about the status of his church's 501C3 tax exemption status and the popular opinion of some of his most loyal tithers who also happened to own a good bit of farm land.

Several teachers made their way to the school, wanting to make a difference. A few were less than enthusiastic about being in the building in the summertime, and there were a few notable absentees including Thelma Harold and Miss Passimons. Oddly enough, Mr. Cross who had been so enthusiastic when he first set up the scaffolding for Simon was nowhere to be found once there were more than enough helping hands to go around. Simon thought that Mr. Cross would be all the more encouraged by the support, but lately he had been coming up with more and more excuses to work at the Philo Grade School instead. He was an odd, little man who almost seemed happier when there was more to be done. Not having time to examine the janitor's motives more closely, Simon shrugged it off, surmising that all of the help must have given him time to complete his extensive punch list that needed to get done before the beginning of the new school year.

On the other hand, one of Bethel's most prominent citizens was greatly moved by the public display of community solidarity. Dr. Hassan Al-Banna brought his wife Sawda and his three children, Mohammed, Fatimeah, and Abdul to take part in completing the project. Dr. Al-Banna proved to be just as personable and gracious as everyone had said. And just like everyone else, the good doctor rolled up his sleeves and went to work, even taking part in the more mundane tasks such as washing out the brushes. Though no one could match Rocky's zealousness, Dr. Al-Banna did more than his fair share of the work. Because Sawda spent a great deal of her time tending to their small children, she wasn't able to do as much of the labor. Nonetheless, she managed to pick up a paintbrush here and there, doing what she could when she could.

Simon rather enjoyed their company. He found them to be a delightful family. And it made him happy to think that they were living in his old, refurbished home.

Simon thought about the renovations that Dr. Al-Banna had made to his old homestead. Then he recalled seeing Sawda and the children his first full day back in Bethel. After a few hours of working side by side with the prominent physician, Dr. Al-Banna made Simon feel extremely at ease, often praising him for taking such initiative for such a worthy cause. Completely disarmed, Simon divulged that he grew up in the Al-Banna's house for the first ten years of his life.

"Isn't that something," Dr. Al-Banna said with a smile as he reached down to move his paint tray.

"Of course, it didn't look anything like it does now," Simon admitted as he laid on another coat of pearl white paint.

"Ah, no, it was in pretty bad shape when we first moved in," the doctor mused, "but with a little time and a little work, we were able to fix it up. It took more than a can of paint I can assure you."

"I would say so," Simon said in all sincerity. "I would have never dreamed it could have looked like that. Honestly, I hardly recognized it."

"But, you know," Dr. Al-Banna said, "it is no different from what you are doing here, my friend, only more so. The death of that young man rocked this community. And you have been able to ease the suffering of an entire town by having them help repair a building."

The statement struck a chord with Simon. He stopped painting for a moment and turned to the good doctor, thinking what he said just might have something to do with ending the curse.

"No, I mean it," the good doctor continued. "It takes a certain kind of charisma to lead people. Believe me, I know. This community needed something after the…" he paused and the two of them shared a look of understanding. And Simon once again thought of Jeremy's horrific death.

They continued to paint in silence for a few moments. Neither of them dared to verbalize what they were both thinking. Simon reflected on the loss of friend, never before considering the impact that the murderous act had on the people of Bethel. Dr. Al-Banna was probably right. Many of the volunteers were there to feel better. They were there to feel safe. To verbalize it would only serve to detract from the sentiment. Judiciously, Simon decided to change the subject.

"Dr. Al-Banna, I've actually been thinking of coming to see you," he confided.

"Yes?" Dr. Al-Banna replied, "About what?"

"I've got a couple of sores around my mouth that have been really bothering me," Simon said, sticking his chin out to the doctor.

"Yes, I noticed those," Dr. Al-Banna said. "You should come in. Just call to make an appointment, and we'll get you in."

"Well, I've been kind of waiting it out to see if it would just go away," Simon said, sheepishly. "I don't have any insurance and to be honest, I'm a little cash poor at the present time."

"Don't worry about that," Dr. Al-Banna said with a laugh, "after all you are painting my Mosque, the least I could do is comp you a visit."

Simon smiled, failing to comprehend what he heard. He paused awkwardly for a moment and turned to the doctor again as though waiting for a punch line, but none was forthcoming.

Dr. Al-Banna stopped painting for a moment, turned to Simon, and said matter-of-factly, "Besides, Herpes Simplex is no laughing matter."

So much for living in the moment with Jez, Simon thought. Contrary to Jack's musings, there is a past, a present, and a future after all.

* * *

In a little less than a week the project was finished. A reporter from the local paper had been contacted. He showed up to take some pictures and interview Simon, Lexus, Dr. Al-Banna, and a few of the teachers. Simon told the disinterested reporter all about Jeremy's town hall speech, and how the project was intended to gain votes for the referendum to honor his memory. Afterwards, the reporter took a picture at the bottom of the stairs from almost the exact spot that yearbook pictures had been taken in 1937. Everyone who had helped stood together proudly on the steps holding out their paintbrushes. At first, Simon stood in the back row off to the side until it was insisted that he move front and center amidst a flurry of applause. When asked, the less than enthused reporter said that the article would probably run on the front page of next week's edition of *The Bethel Chronicle*.

After the photo was taken, there was much patting one another on the back for what they had accomplished together in such a short period of time. It became the talk of the town and one of the nicer feel-good stories, in the wake of the terrible still unresolved investigation. Simon looked around proudly at the fresh paint and surmised that people need a cause as much, maybe even more, than they needed hope. Many people came over to shake his hand as they admired the work that had been done. Unbeknownst to Simon, the small sampling of enthusiastic townspeople skewed his perspective on the impact that it actually had on the bedroom community. From where Simon stood, surrounded by the cheery group of supporters, it appeared as though Dr. Al-Banna might have been right. Maybe his being called to repaint the school did have a lasting impression on the people of Bethel.

"Maybe that was it," Simon thought. "Maybe the tragic event and positive outpouring of support was just enough to pass the referendum and finally put an end to the curse once and for all."

It was soon decided that a celebration was in order. Someone suggested that they should all make their way over to the tavern, get a bite to eat, and enjoy one another's company. Simon first declined their entreaties with an aw-shucks expression that contradicted his self-congratulating inner voice that now began to once again dominate his conscious. After only a little cajoling, he acquiesced.

"Okay, okay," he said to the group that had congregated around him. "I'm just going to take care of a couple of things, and then I'll be right over."

After the crowd had dispersed, Simon and Rocky were left to tidy things up a bit. It didn't take long to discover that there wasn't much that needed to be done. Rocky had taken care of the majority of it while the reporter took the pictures and completed the interview with Simon.

"You weren't in the picture?" Simon asked.

Rocky stood up after having put a lid on a can of paint. When he turned to face him, Simon noticed for the first time a gold cross hanging around his neck. It drew his attention because he had become so accustomed to the Mercedes emblem that Rocky had so proudly worn there before.

"No, I didn't deserve to be in any picture," Rocky said, flatly.

Simon, struck by his friend's new vernacular, failed to process the comment at first.

"Oh, the necklace," Rocky said, following Simon's eyes. He picked it up and kissed it. "Nice, huh?" he asked, admiringly.

"Yeah," Simon said, snapping out of his meditating on the tiny gold cross. "It's really...shiny."

"You were right, Simon," Rocky said as he resumed folding up the drop cloth and putting it away.

"I was?" Simon replied proudly pulling some stray pieces of tape off of the walls, "about what?"

"About all of the things God can do *for* you," Rocky said. He offered up a smile and slapped Simon on the shoulder before closing his eyes and mumbling a prayer. After which, he lifted his eyes and headed for the door.

Simon gave a sideways glance to the new believer while turning Rocky's assertion over again in his mind. "Yeah, but it's not just all about what God does *for* you..." he started to reply.

"You coming or what?" Rocky asked. "Man, I'm starving!"

"Yeah, I'm right behind you," Simon said. "Let me just get the lights." He quickly jogged over to the far wall to hit the switch, but just before he turned them off, he noticed something. At the top of the wall was a small patch that somehow had gone unpainted. He tried to ignore it at first, but the longer he looked at it, the more it stood out like a black eye. For a split second, Simon considered moving the scaffolding.

"Freeman, come on," Rocky called, after sticking his head back in the door.

"Okay, coming," Simon replied, deciding to take care of it later.

* * *

No one was happier to see Simon come through the front doors of the tavern than Rich Land. Now that this ridiculous little project was behind them, everything could get back to how it was before.

When his friend walked in, there was clapping and whistling. Rocky stood behind Simon, placed both his hands on the man of the hour's shoulders, and guided him through the throng of people who had participated in the school project. They were lined up so close on either side of Simon that he couldn't see past them to the other hundred or so taxpaying patrons sitting at tables who were looking on with great disdain.

The volunteers smiled at Simon as they walked by shaking his hand and patting him on the back. Slightly embarrassed by all of the attention, Simon couldn't put a finger on exactly how he felt at that particular moment. It was an odd compilation of exhilaration, relief, and self-satisfaction. The crowd parted as he made his way to the bar where Joey, George, Will, and Rob were seated. All but Rob greeted him warmly, pulling up a bar stool and insisting that he take a seat. Obligingly, he dropped his head, held up his hands, and sat down.

"Well, it looks like the guest of honor has arrived," Rich said leaning on both of his massive hands against the bar with a towel draped over his shoulder. He was so glad to have things back to normal that he impulsively yelled out, "Beers on the house!" before he remembering who his boss was.

"Yeah, that's what I'm talking about," Joey said, excitedly.

"Not for you, jerk-wad," Rich snarled with a furrowed brow, "for the man of the hour." Then he turned to the rest of the crowd and yelled, "Beer on the house, only for the man of the hour!" After which, there was a collective groan of disappointment.

"But, hey, we were the first two to go down there and help out," Joey said proudly pointing at himself and George. "Nobody went down there until we did. Then everybody came after that."

"Shut up," Rob said leaning forward on the bar with arms wrapped around a bottle of beer.

"I didn't see you over there," Joey haughtily replied.

Without thinking to ask, Rich had dropped a tall, frozen mug of beer in front of Simon.

"Rocky?" Rich said, pointing a meaty index finger towards the born again Christian.

"Just a water for me, please," Rocky replied.

"A water?" Will repeated.

"Don't worry, he'll tell you all about it, just ask," Rich said with a sardonic expression. Then his face lit up again as he turned to Simon. "Hey, you must be starving. I'll be right back." He bustled off in the direction of the kitchen to get some Italian beef that had been simmering all day in the crock pot.

While Rocky shared his "testimony" with the guys, Simon thought about how much he had accomplished and how good it made him feel. "I did it," he thought, taking a long swig of beer and wiping the froth from his mouth. The entryway to the school looked better than it had in years.

By no means was it identical to the picture in the yearbook, but it had certainly garnered the attention of a lot of people. The paper was going to cover the story and voters would go to the poles next week with a whole different take on the referendum. After reading the article, maybe people would realize that it was really a tribute to Jeremy and what he was all about.

And then there was Hope, of course. The project had once again restored her faith in him bringing them closer than ever. He dreamily smiled at the thought as he unknowingly ran his index finger over the disturbing bump on his lip.

"Jeremy was right," Simon mused. "God did bring me here for a purpose and now it's done. He wasn't making me choose between Bethel and my dreams. It was just a detour. Maybe even a test of some kind." He chuckled to himself thinking of how simple it was and how much he had agonized over the whole thing. Taking another swig of beer, he realized that there wasn't anything supernatural about it. It was just organizing the community to rally around a cause. The past few days had been such a whirlwind that he hadn't even had time to go for a run, read the Bible, pray, or even think about getting down to the basement to clean out the storage room. But now his task was complete. Raising the glass to his lips, he took a big swig before lowering it again to the bar. He was beaming with pride. With a frothy upper lip, he hadn't realized how parched he had been, until now. "Maybe it was just a stray dog after all...like Mr. Cross said."

"...Isn't that right, Simon?" Rocky asked, suddenly bringing him out of his daydream.

Simon looked up from his beer to see all of the guys looking at him expectantly. "Yeah," he replied as if he had a clue as to what they were talking about. Satisfied with his response, Rocky continued.

Just then, Rich barreled through the spring-loaded door, emerging from the kitchen with a handful of plates covered with piping hot Italian beef. The amazing aroma filled the air and tantalized the senses.

"Okay, man," Rich said, leaning in closer to talk over the noise. "Now that you're done with all that junk, I need your help with my team. We're really struggling, man. Okay, here's the thing..."

Simon listened attentively as he hungrily devoured the juicy meat and consumed the ice cold beers. Time and again Rich was called away to tend to the needs of other patrons, but each time he returned quickly picking up the conversation in stride as though there hadn't been any interruption at all. They talked about how to fix the Yankees, Simon's umpiring schedule, the problems with the fantasy league, and the upcoming softball schedule.

When Rich was called away to swap out a keg, Simon glanced down at his phone after realizing that he had received a text. He was disappointed at first to see that it wasn't from Hope; but, he almost fell off of his stool when he realized it was from his godfather. The message simply read, "Looks like we'll be moving forward again. Take a look at the attachment. Hope all is well and I'll talk to you soon." Simon scrolled down, opened the attachment, and skimmed its contents. It was an article about how well the new drug had been doing in other markets around the world where it had already been approved. Everything seemed to finally be coming together.

Simon smiled after re-reading the word "hope". His smile quickly faded as he wondered if she would ever consider moving to the East Coast. Suddenly, someone nudged him on the shoulder. Simon turned to see Will standing next to him holding a shot glass in each hand.

"Come on, man," Will said. "You earned it, dude."

Simon looked down at the shot of jagger and shivered convulsively. Each of the guys lifted their own shot of whisky high in the air.

"To Simon and his whacked out idea," Will said to everyone in earshot, "salut!"

Not wanting to make anyone feel bad, Simon obligingly closed his eyes and knocked back the hard liquor that sent a burning fire through his body. He shook his head like a wet dog and winced repulsively. Following his lead, Will slammed his empty shot glass on the bar, leaned down, and whispered into Simon's ear.

"Can I talk to you for a minute in private?" Will asked excitedly.

"Yeah, sure," Simon replied, intrigued by the secrecy.

They made their way through the crowd to the back of the bar. It took a little while because they had to stop every few feet for someone else to express their admiration and gratitude to Simon. Finally, they reached a table in the back of the room and sat down.

"You're pretty popular these day," Will said, beaming from ear to ear.

"I guess so," Simon admitted, puffing-up a bit, "so, what's going on?"

"How would you like to come work at the bank?" Will asked. "Now before you answer, you would start as a teller just to get your feet wet at first. But, pay your dues and you can quickly climb the ladder. Here's the thing, you didn't hear it from me, but there's talk of buying out the Philo Exchange Bank which would mean plenty of opportunities for advancement in the near future. What do you think?"

"I don't know," Simon said, caught off guard by the offer. "It's all pretty sudden. I mean, is there an opening right now?"

"Yeah, well, I think so," Will answered as if considering it only for the first time. "It sounds like they would probably just create a position for you or something for the time being."

"Who's 'they'?" Simon asked.

"The board of directors," Will replied. "Dude, look at how well Helrigle and Livingood do. Have you seen their houses, their cars…their wives?" he added raising his eyebrows. "And they barely work a forty hour week. Banker's hours, man!"

"I don't know," Simon said, flattered by offer. "I just got a text that the interviews for the sales position in Jersey are probably going to start up again soon."

"Man, you must be livin' right," Will said, before remembering what Lexus coached him to say. "Oh yeah, that's great and all, but what about Hope?"

The smile fell from Simon's face as he contemplated again the likelihood of her following him to New Jersey after only knowing each other for such a short period of time.

"Tell you what," Will continued. "You think it over and get back to me in the next couple of days. It's an incredible opportunity. I'm just say'n."

Simon nodded just as Rich made his way through the crowd.

"There you are," Rich said carrying a full pitcher of beer. "Man, for a minute there I thought you took off. When this place clears out, I want to talk to you about practice tomorrow. I got a few ideas. Okay?"

Simon nodded in agreement as Rich replaced his empty mug with a fresh, frozen one.

"Bethel, huh?" Simon thought to himself as he looked at the ice rolling down the side of the mug.

Rocky was making his way around the tavern telling anyone who would listen about what the Lord was doing *for* him. Many members of Pastor Algood's church concurred with him. They were also quick to tell of all that the Lord had done for them too and invited Rocky to come to Sunday service at Bountiful Meadows to learn more about the secret to prosperity.

Meanwhile, Joey and George had had all of the love fest that they could stand for one night and decided to join Will and Simon at the table at the back of the tavern. Their conversation was spirited and the beer flowed freely as they talked about everything from movies, to music, to sports. Several lively arguments erupted over top ten action flicks of all-time, best albums, and most dominating pitchers in major league history. The crowd had taken much longer to disperse than Rich had anticipated. People were either too geared up from the school project or still too afraid to return to their isolated, vulnerable homes. Whatever the reason, most of the guys were three sheets to the wind by the time Rich joined them at the back table. All had had their fill except for Rocky who claimed to be filled with living water.

"What has gotten into you, Rocky?" Rich asked, annoyed.

"I'll tell you what's gotten into me," Rocky said with a smile, pointing to his inebriated friend. "Tell them, Simon. What happened at the school was totally a 'God-thing'. Tell them, Simon. He'll tell you all about it. This is awesome. You gotta hear this."

"Oh really?" Joey asked with great interest. "Do tell."

Simon looked up from his fantasy league lineup that he had been scribbling down on a napkin. The room spun and Rocky's face went in and out of focus before he realized what in the world they were yakking about.

"Oh-oh, yeah!" Simon said excitedly, looking through glazed-over, slits for eyes. "Yes! That's right. God has been at work doin' his thang' right here in Bethel." He finished by tapping his index finger into the table several times.

"Really?" George asked.

"Oh yeah, big time!" Simon replied, with slurred speech.

Rocky had a look of concern on his face as he realized for the first time that Simon was completely wasted.

"Let me tell you something," Simon said. "I met Jesus."

"No kidding?" Joey asked, egging-on the inebriated, hometown hero.

"Well, he means he had a very intense experience in front of the church," Rocky said trying to cover for Simon.

"Yes…no!..I know what I means. I *met* Jesus," Simon said emphatically. "And he gave me a purpose."

"That a fact?" Joey asked sarcastically. He sat forward and snuck a peak at the other guys who were sitting around the table.

Rich jumped in to keep Joey from having his fun at the expense of his close friend. "All right buddy," Rich said getting up from the table. "Maybe, it's time to get you home." He grabbed Simon by the arm and lifted him off of his seat.

"Wait, wait a minute," Simon said through slurred words. "I wanna tell them this. Jesus told me to fix the school up to get ref, refrend…"

"Referendum?" George said with a laugh.

Rocky looked on with great disappointment.

"Okay lets go," Rich said. "Will, watch the bar for me, would ya? I'm taking him home."

After a few steps, Simon pulled his arm away and wobbled back towards the table. "No," Simon said. "God wanted me to get all the people to vote for the new school. And it worked! I fixed the school, I got Hope back. *I* saved him," Simon said, pointing back at Rocky. "Cause, you know what else?"…

"No, what?" Rich said, taking Simon by the arm.

"I'm the one," he whispered.

"That's right, Freeman," Will yelled out in a drunken stupor. "You da' man!"

Rich stared at Will for a moment. "On second thought," he said, "George, watch the bar for me for a minute while I take Simon home."

Embarrassed, Rocky took the gold cross hanging from around his neck and slid it inside his shirt. Simon nodded proudly before bumping into a chair and knocking it to the floor. Rich quickly reached out to catch Simon to keep him from falling.

"Okay," Rich said. "Easy, here we go." Once again, they started for the door.

"Oh, and you know the best part?" Simon called out over his shoulder.

"No, no, no, ssshhh," Rich said into his ear as he guided Simon away from the table. "I think you've said enough for one night. Let's take you home now."

"No," Joey called back, playing to the crowd who had now gathered around. "What's the best part?"

"There's no curse, no mo'!" Simon said, happily.

Joey, George, and Will busted out laughing while Rocky sat in silence feeling utterly foolish.

"Whew! That's a relief," Joey said just as Rich dragged Simon out the front door.

Once out in the humid, night air, Rich dug in his pockets for his keys while Simon looked over at his burly friend and smiled.

"I love you, man," Simon said.

"Yeah, I love you too, buddy," Rich said absentmindedly. "Now what did I do with those stink'n keys?" Rich propped Simon up against the car for a moment in order to search through another pocket.

"Don't let them write on me...promise me you guys won't write on me," Simon muttered with a pained expression.

"No, never," Rich mindlessly replied, rummaging through his pockets.

"No, I mean it," Simon said. "I love you, I love Hope...not in the same way. But, still...I love this town. I love everybody." Just as a morning dove descended from the grain elevator, Simon broke free of Rich's grasp, stumbled into the street startling the graceful bird.

"Woe, look out," Simon said as he spastically ducked his head and flailed his arms over his head. He lifted his eyes to watch the bird wildly flap its wings, ascending away from Simon past the bright light of the street lamp towards the heights of the grain elevator. When the bird reached the pinnacle of the massive concrete cylinder, it came to rest on top of a curious, steel structure. Simon cocked his head and squinted as he took a step in the direction of the elevator.

"Hey!..." Simon said with a graven face, pointing to the metal structure.

"That's it!" Rich said. "Got 'em. Come on, man, time to take you home."

Perched high above Bethel on the man-made mountain rising up off of the Midwestern plains, the benevolent bird looked down on Simon as Rich poured him into the car.

* * *

It had actually been two weeks longer than the reporter had said it would be before the article on the school made the front page of the local paper. Each time the paper came out, Simon would run down to the gas station to get a copy only to discover that it had been bumped for another "more important" story. First, there was the article on the recent heat wave that was threatening to blunt the growth of the crops. The next week they ran a story on the little league baseball tournament that Bethel hosted, "Bringing fun and much needed revenue to local businesses," as the tag line touted. Irritated, Simon finally called the editor to register a formal complaint. Voting on the new school was now only a few days away, and support was waning since the initial fervor of the community project.

During that time, things had otherwise pretty much gone back to normal. The town had resorted to what it had always done before in the midst of a tragedy such as Jeremy's. Outwardly, the people were eager to dismiss the entire incident and sweep it under the rug, while privately spreading unfounded rumors and accusations. Right after the shocking murder, attendance at church services soared, even in Pastor Pete's congregation, but it wasn't long before the nagging questions drove people to alternative resources to find answers. People greedily speculated and grossly exaggerated in confidence, while inwardly raging against God.

The people of Bethel weren't the only ones who had fallen into their old ways. After fulfilling his purpose, Simon had little to do but return to his old routine while awaiting his promising future. With Simon's help, Rich's Yankees had rebounded to win the big sixteen team Bethel tournament, temporarily appeasing the rabid parents. In the process, Simon had even made a pretty decent amount of money umpiring the games alongside George and Joey, whose extensive knowledge of the rule book time and time again kept the crew out of trouble. Two potentially promising job opportunities eminently loomed on the horizon, and his long distance relationship with Hope continued to progress, albeit at a slower pace than he would have liked.

As much as she would have loved to dismiss it, Hope was still wary of Simon's assertions the night of Jeremy's funeral and his admission about his night with Jez Bell. But, with each passing day, the fire that had been dampened by Simon's bizarre remarks and social indiscretion, was being rekindled by the slow burning embers in her heart.

Even so, life was in a bit of a holding pattern. While waiting for something to break loose, either the job in Jersey or the one at the bank, he had returned to his regular routine at work being content with the task he had already completed. Thelma Harold went to Des Moines to nurse one of her sisters back to health after a minor surgery while Mr. Cross was running himself ragged between Bethel and Philo. As a result, Simon often found himself back in the chorus room above the gym, sitting in front of the window air conditioning unit to get out of the brutal, July heat while perusing magazines or catching an afternoon nap.

In his spare time, Simon helped Rich maintain the baseball field, tinkered with his fantasy league team, and played some church league softball. With all of his evening activities, he was finding it hard to get up for Sunday morning church service. He and the boys often closed down the tavern, carousing into the wee hours of morning, and the previous night had been even later than most. Just as they were about to call it a night, Rich cycled back through the 370 channels and came across the start of "Major League." He declared it sacrilegious for them to not watch it in its entirety. And there were no dissenters.

As a result, Simon had been dragging around all day before finally plopping down into the comfy, high backed leather chair in the chorus room. He had actually spent more time than usual helping Mr. Cross with refinishing the gym floor. The old janitor somehow seemed happier now that all of the extra help had returned to their mundane lives, and it was just the two of them again.

With a little more than an hour to go before he called it a day, Simon sat idly watching each tick of the clock. Rubbing his bloodshot eyes with the heels of his hand, he looked around the room for anything to pass the time and noticed once again the textbooks on the shelf beneath the window next to the fire escape that were feeding the young minds of Bethel. He grabbed a fourth grade science book and thumbed through the pages before momentarily pausing to study an illustration depicting Darwin's evolution from monkey to man. For the first time in his life, he seriously considered the term, "*Theory* of Evolution". Curious, he went back to read the details of the infamous scientist's DNA'less assertions, but some pages had been torn out, leaving large gaps. His naked eye absorbed the content of the pages of disconnected ideas that were difficult to digest. Impervious, he put it back on the shelf and grabbed a sixth grade history book. After reading about Marx's Communist Manifesto, Simon perused a chapter on Hitler's gas chambers, Stalin's Gulags, and Mao's Great Leap Forward. He then read a very short excerpt on D-Day before shelving the textbook altogether. Out of curiosity, he reached for an eighth grade literature book that contained Voltaire's "Zadig", Nietzche's "The Birth of Tragedy", and the lyrics to Lennon's "Imagine" in a section of the poetry unit.

Disenchanted, he set the book down and pulled out a fifth grade health book titled "It's Perfectly Normal." Randomly, he read a few pages, glancing at the clock every now and then only to find that it had virtually stopped moving. He returned his attention to the book that implored the students to have safe sex as it listed the different types of contraceptive alternatives as well as many illustrations that depicted various sexual acts. Completely disturbed by the notion of 11-year-olds reading such content, he glanced around the infamous chorus room and shuttered at the thought of what happened at the hands of Jessie Joseph. Before he could expound on the connection between Darwin's Theory and Thomas Huxley, he had another alarming thought. Simon stuck out his tongue, raked it along the sores on his lip, thought about Dr. Al-Banna's offer to make an appointment.

Disillusioned, he set the book back on the shelf and dug through some of the stacks of paperback novels. Simon was surprised to find classic novels that he had read in high school or college. There was Ayn Rand's "Fountainhead", J.D. Sallinger's "The Catcher in the Rye," and Thomas Moore's "Utopia."

Then he found something very curious. Sitting on the shelf amidst the paperback novels, Simon discovered a copy of the Quran of all things. Suddenly, he remembered Dr. Al-Banna having thanked him for painting his "mosque". Could he have been serious? Having never had read any of the Quran before, Simon flipped to the pages and perused a few random passages. The first was Surah 3:54. The verse read, "Allah was the best of deceivers." His curiosity aroused, Simon thumbed through the brittle pages to another passage, Surah 9:5. It read, "Kill the disbeliever wherever you find him…" While images of the plane striking the second tower flashed through his mind, he studied some more passages before finding Surah 48:28 which read, "It is he who sent his messenger with guidance and the religion of truth, that he may exalt it above every other religion…" Somewhat disturbed by the revelation, Simon pulled his phone out and googled the term "Jihad" that he had heard so many times before on FoxNews. After reading a few articles on the subject, he decided to dismiss the complex topic altogether and set the book back on the shelf. Even though he was somewhat disturbed by what he read, he found it much easier to pretend to not know. He had enough on his plate to worry about at the present time. Besides, solving the world's problems was slightly above his pay grade.

With still more than forty-five minutes to go before quitting time, Simon grabbed a copy of "Lord of the Flies" and took it back to the desk. Simon remembered the basic premise of the book from reading it in high school. Although his recall of the details were sketchy at best, he considered it a good book, but he made it only a little past the discovery of the conch shell before the cool air and steady hum of the window unit lulled him into a peaceful, languid state. Several times his head nodded involuntarily. To combat his condition, he would sit up and try to reposition himself before slipping back into a semiconscious state. With no intention of reading the entire book, Simon decided to flip through the pages to find the more noteworthy sections of the allegory. Just as he was reading about Jack impaling the severed sow's head onto a stake, Simon's eyes grew heavy, and he finally drifted off to sleep. This time for good. He was out cold and slept like the dead.

Hours went by before the sound of bare feet rapidly slapping against the hardwood on the staircase leading down to the gym floor roused him from his deep slumber. Dazed and confused, Simon stirred a little before stretching out his arms behind his head and surrendering a loud yawn. When he finally realized where he was, he launched himself forward in the chair, sending "Lord of the Flies" tumbling to the floor. He could hardly believe his eyes when he read on the clock on the wall. It was six o'clock at night. He had been asleep for nearly four hours.

"Goodness," he said with a yawn, "I guess it's time to go home."

When he turned to get out of the chair, he nearly knocked a newspaper off of the corner of the desk. Before he could even think about it, he reached out his hand and snagged the paper in the midair. Now holding the latest edition of *The Bethel Chronicle* in his hand, he noticed on the back page a black and white picture from the stairwell in the entryway of the school. He quickly surmised that Mr. Cross must have left the paper on the desk for him while he was asleep.

Slightly embarrassed, Simon turned his attention to the picture for a moment, scanning the many faces before fixating on his own likeness at the front and center of the photo. Beaming proudly, he read the headline to the article, "Locals Give School Entryway Much Needed Facelift." Simon folded the newspaper in half and sat back down in the chair to read the article. To his dismay, the reporter depicted the project as more of a community rally than any kind of political statement about changing public opinion about the school referendum. Annoyed, Simon read on. There was not even a mention of Jeremy Warner or Simon's motivation for spearheading the undertaking. It was if the writer of the article had completely disregarded Simon's answers to the interview questions and interjected his own editorial on the project. Simon was even misquoted as saying, "By painting the entryway, we hope to gain support for our schools." When in all actuality, he had said, "By painting the entryway, we hope to gain support for a new school building."

By the time Simon finished the article, he was furious. The poor excuse for a journalist took liberties and slanted the story to make it seem as though the volunteers' sole motivation for helping was to preserve the current school rather than usher in a new era of community support for education.

Sickened, he flipped over the paper to the front page and read the blurb beneath a large picture and nearly jumped out of his seat. The headline of the article read, "Citizens Unwilling to Pay the Price for Higher Education." The entire article focused on the financial strains that a new school would place on the shoulders of the average Bethel household. The reporter had even made a random, impromptu survey of 200 homeowners, concluding that over eighty percent of the people were going to vote against the referendum. At the end of the hatchet piece, the reporter then turned commentator and proceeded to rip the school board for endangering the proud history of Bethel by proposing a consolidation with another township and threatening to leave a large carbon footprint on the environment with all of the new construction.

Seething with anger, Simon violently kicked the teacher's desk. The loud bang and streaking metal on wood resounded out the doorway of the chorus room and echoed off of the gymnasium floor. Biting his bottom lip, he scanned the picture again. It just didn't make any sense. Simon wondered why God would make his purpose so clear to him if it was all just a moot point anyway. Why did he spend all of the time and effort for nothing? With a furrowed brow, he carefully analyzed the events that had transpired. He definitely was supposed to fix up the entryway. That much was clear. It was supposed to honor Jeremy. He was sure of that. Hope was definitely behind it. People came and volunteered their time. All of those things were good, right?

"So, what happened then?" Simon wondered. "What was the point of the whole thing if it was only going to fail to reach the ultimate objective?"

Pensively, Simon stared at the picture in the newspaper. It wasn't long before he was standing at the base of the stairs where the photograph had been taken. He held out Mara's picture from 1937 in one hand and the newspaper in the other. For a few minutes, Simon looked back and forth between the photos and the freshly painted walls of the entryway.

It was obvious that the old entryway was far more impressive with its vaulted, tin ceiling, oak paneling, and brilliant chandelier. But, that went without saying. Since the time that picture was taken, many changes had been made to bring the old building up to code. The vaulted ceiling was impractical and the chandelier was probably an electrical hazard. The oak paneling had been there from the beginning, even though it was virtually unrecognizable under the thick layers of paint that had been sloppily applied over the years. Still, there was no way to get things back to how it was before. Was there?

Simon leaned in closer to Mara's old picture of the third grade class and noticed again the strange unidentified corner of a large frame on the wall to the left of the students standing on the steps. Its absence was obvious when glancing back and forth between the old and new photographs. Simon sighed deeply, dropped the photos to his sides and raised his head towards the ceiling, muttering his first prayer in over a week. When he did, the patch of wall that had somehow gone unpainted caught his attention again. Simon snarled at the insolent blight.

As though possessed, he marched out the doors to Mr. Cross' maintenance shed. Piece by piece he carried the dismantled scaffolding back up the stairs and onto the landing that connected the first and second grade classrooms. In little over an hour, he had rebuilt the metal framework that nearly reached the heights of the false ceilings, placing it strategically in front of the portion of unpainted wall. After retrieving the paint, tray, and brush, Simon now stood at the top of the scaffolding, determined to complete the work that had been begun in him. Not having taken the exact measurements, Simon had to crouch down to keep from hitting his head on the tiles of the false ceiling.

In no more than twenty minutes, he had completely covered the eyesore with a fresh coat of paint. When he finished, he stood up to admire his work. Unmindful, he accidentally stood straight up and put his head through a section of the false ceiling, lifting it into the air. Before he realized it, his eyes were peering through the darkness of the vast expanse between the false and original ceilings of the entryway. As Simon pushed back the tile, the light illuminated the dark abyss and revealed an ornamented tin ceiling no more than another eight feet above his head. Instantly, Simon knew in his heart what he had to do.

Just as he came to the conclusion, a tiny voice called to him from beneath the scaffolding. Simon's heart skipped a beat as he ducked back under the tiles to see a gaunt, barefooted little boy wearing ratty overalls and a filthy t-shirt standing at the top of the stairs leading down to the basement. Simon's blood ran cold and the hairs stood up on the back of his neck as he stared, motionless at the specter.

"It's Adam Potter!" he thought, his heart pounding in his ears.

"Are you him?" the dirty faced boy asked flatly with a blank expression.

Simon could hardly believe what he was seeing. The room was almost spinning when he recognized the frazzled pant leg and dirty foot as the same he had seen a few weeks before.

Simon heard his own voice answer cryptically, "I don't know, *am I* him?"

The boy nodded slowly, standing stiffly with his arms straight down at his sides.

With a shaking hand, Simon furtively reached for the metal railing. Intuitively, he wanted to climb down to get closer to the…boy.

"I thought so," Simon said with a trembling voice. But, when he slowly reached for the rung to climb down, the boy darted off.

"No! no! no!" Simon said excitedly. "Stay there. Don't run!" He jumped from the scaffolding that was nearly seven feet off of the ground. When he hit the floor, he felt the sting of the recoil all the way to the top of his head. Undaunted, Simon raced down the steps towards the next landing. He stopped, turned his head slightly and listened, but all he could hear was his own bated breath. Quietly, Simon made his way over to the steps that led to the basement and stood for a few more seconds in silence. However, he heard no sound. In a heartbeat, he raced over to the hall that led to the gym, opened the door, and looked up at the steps that led to the chorus room. Still nothing. The figure had vanished just as quickly as it had appeared.

After searching the building and finding it empty, the gravity of what he had just experienced set in. "No, can't be…was that?" Simon said. "That was the ghost of Adam Potter! I just saw Adam Potter." Still somewhat in shock, Simon started to come to his senses. As the number into his phone, he quickly realized that no one was going to believe him. So, he dropped it back into his pocket.

"They'd all think I was crazy," he said. He dug his head into his chest and ran his hands through his hair, agonizing over what to do. Simon was visibly shaken from the visit of the little boy whose image and words replayed over and over in his mind.

"'Are you him'? Him who?" Simon asked to himself as he walked back up the landing where he had been painting. He looked up at the opening in the false ceiling. The light exposed the authentic ornamental tin ceiling. Reluctantly, he felt as though he already knew the answer. The curse was alive and well in Bethel after all, and he was indeed the one who was going to end it. Not by slapping a band-aid on the problem, but by gutting the entryway and making it *exactly* like it was before Jessie Joseph committed the unspeakable crimes against Adam Potter and his classmates in 1935. It wasn't meant to be just another fresh coat of white wash. It was meant to be a full restoration.

But he had to be sure this time. Wildly, Simon spun around in a circle looking for the picture he had dropped onto the steps that lead down to the front doors of the school. He clutched the photo in both hands and brought it up to his face to get a better look. After surveying the room, he noticed for the first time the faces of the children in Mara's old class photo.

"If only I could talk to...," Simon said before coming to a realization. Of course, how could he have been so stupid. He raced down the steps and headed out the front door to pay Mara Rash a visit.

* * *

By nine o'clock, Mara had already finished off her first glass of Angel's Envy while perusing the pages of the old photo album when she heard a brisk knock on her front door. She gingerly lifted herself out of her chair and slowly made her way to the front door. Simon heard several locks being undone before the door propped open ever so slightly with the chain still attached. Mara peaked around the door with almost a look of expectation on her face. But, her countenance changed to an expression of annoyance when she saw that it was Simon.

"Ah, it's you," Mara snapped.

"Were you expecting someone?" Simon asked, through labored breaths.

"Just the same dad-blasted demons that haunt me every night," Mara replied remorsefully. "What do *you* want?"

"I'm sorry to bother you," Simon said. "I know it's late, but I wanted to ask you a few questions about this." He held up the picture she had given him. With her eyes glazed over and her breath wreaking of cognac, Mara's face fell as she slowly reached out to take hold of the picture.

"Did you live here when it happened?" Simon asked expectantly. "You had a child in this class, didn't you? That's why you have this picture."

Suddenly, she snatched it out of his hand and tried to slam the door shut, but Simon stuck out his foot to keep from closing all of the way.

"Go on, get out of here!" Mara barked through tart cursing.

"You told me that you've lived in Bethel your entire life," Simon said excitedly. "I just need to ask you a couple of questions about a teacher named Jessie Joseph."

Mara once again pressed against the door. "Get your foot out the way!" she yelled.

"I need to know what happened!" Simon said, his voice nearly cracking.

"Go on! Leave me alone," she replied. "I got nothin' to say about that snake."

"Snake?" Simon repeated, remembering what Thelma had said about 'Killing the snake.' "Well, what about Adam Potter then?" Simon asked.

The old woman slammed her heal into the top of Simon's shoe.

"Mrs. Rash, I just *saw* Adam Potter tonight at the school!" Simon yelled desperately.

With that, Mara fell silent no longer pressing against the door. Cautiously, Simon pulled back his foot out of the doorway. The door slowly closed. Then he heard the sound of the chain being unsecured from the latch before the door slowly fell open as though of its own accord. Simon took a step into the house and looked up in time to see Mara walking with picture in hand back to her chair.

"So, you seen him too, huh?" Mara muttered in great despair.

The hairs stood up on the back of Simon's neck.

She guided herself down to sit, leaned forward, and picked the album back up. Simon closed the front door behind him, made his way over to the couch, and sat down. Without looking up at him, Mara thumbed through the all too familiar album and delicately returned the picture to its rightful spot.

"Yes, my son John Mark is in that picture," she said, barely choking out her words. "It was a picture of his 4th grade class. 'Cept in them days it was 3rd and 4th grade combined 'course."

"So, is the story about Jessie Joseph true?" Simon asked gravely.

"You know everyone just thought the world of that man," Mara began as she sat back in her chair and blankly stared off into the distance. "Jessie had one of them magnetic personalities. He'd never met a stranger. And them kids. Heavens to Betsy how they doted on him. Anytime I ever saw em' out in front of the school, they all clamored around him, trying to get his attention. Nobody saw *any of it* coming. Nobody!"

Simon sat on the edge of the couch and listened intently with his hands clutched.

"Well, he had us all fooled," Mara snipped reaching for her drink. "John was there the day Adam Potter died."

"What year was that?" Simon asked through a trembling voice.

"Fall of 1935," Mara said into her glass. Simon looked down trying to make the calculations in his mind.

"Seventy-two years ago?" Simon said.

Mara nodded with a scowl and a turned down mouth, "Seventy-two long years," she repeated. Simon looked down to run through some more calculations about the pattern of every six years when she continued, "He's been tormenting this town ever since."

Simon looked up startled and asked softly, "So, did it really happen just as they say?"

Mara spoke as if hypnotized, "John said at first that it weren't. That snake had gotten to them before John could talk to the authorities."

"Wait, so it wasn't Adam who went to the police?" Simon asked confused. "You're saying it was John?" His heart was pounding in his ears.

"It didn't take long to find out what was really going on over there," Mara snarled motioning towards the school. "The horrible things that happened to those precious babies in that room above the gymnasium. John was the first one to speak up against him. So, brave." She held her clenched fist up to her mouth for a moment and trembled. "Then it all came out. It weren't long before everyone found out." Mara turned to face Simon, "And you say you seen Adam Potter tonight over there at the school? Don't surprise me a bit. I've been seeing that boy's face every night for seven decades. Been seeing all them lights goin' on and off in the school late at night, shadows crossing the street in the wee hours of the morning."

Simon flopped back onto the couch and looked upwards, captivated by the words that he heard coming from Mara's lips. Resolute, he sat forward after a moment.

"So, it's all true?" Simon asked.

"Is *what* all true?" she snapped. "That Jessie Joseph killed Adam, and he tried to pin it on my John? Course, it's all true."

"What? No," Simon said, confused. "What are you talking about?"

The question sent Mara into a rage. She slammed the photo album onto the coffee table, knocking her glass to the ground and shattering it to pieces. Her words dripped with hatred and were laced with profanity.

"I'm talking about how that snake killed Adam and stole my little boy's innocence!" She screamed as she struggled to put the album back under the coffee table. Simon looked down stupefied just as she slid it over the top of an old, dusty Bible. "Now, get outta here!"

"But, I'm confused. Jessie Joseph *killed* Adam, wait, who died? I thought…" Simon blabbered as he jumped to his feet. The old woman was slapping him with both hands on the arm. "Where is John now? Can I talk to him?"

"I don't have to tell you anything. Who do you think you are anyway? Get out of my house," Mara said through clenched teeth. "Go on, get!" she yelled. "No more of your stupid questions!"

"I just need to know about the school what it was like back then, so I can..," Simon said as he was backpedaling towards the front door.

But Mara was having none of it. She pulled his arm towards the door and shoved him through the threshold. Simon was afraid she was going to have a heart attack or a stroke.

"All right, all right," Simon said walking voluntarily out onto the porch with his arms raised to protect his face.

"You don't believe me, just go and look it up for yourself!" Mara yelled right before slamming the door in his face.

Simon stood for a moment almost paralyzed by the confused ramblings of an old, intoxicated woman. He tried to make some sense of it all. According to Mara, Adam had died and Jessie was somehow responsible but put the blame on her son, John. Standing on the porch, his mind impulsively raced, and he shuddered at the thought of what "unspeakable crimes" might mean.

19

THE STAIN OF HIS GUILT

Simon had spent the rest of the night pulling back the false ceiling in order to reveal what was hidden behind it. To his dismay, he did not uncover the magnificent chandelier that once hung from the tin ceiling. There were only some old, dead wires dangling from where it once proudly presided, but the grand, ornamented ceiling was nearly completely intact beneath a few layers of paint. Using some oven cleaner and a putty knife, he managed to slowly uncover the shiny silver tin hidden beneath.

Completely driven by the task at hand, Simon attacked the project with fervor. Hours passed by quickly before the sun rose in the East. His back ached and the blisters on his hands burned as he stopped for a moment to look down at his watch. He suspected that the public library opened sometime between eight and nine in the morning, and he had every intention of being there when it did.

Now Simon paced back and forth in front of the library waiting impatiently for it to open. Having taken heed of Mara's challenge to look it up for himself, Simon knew that he had to find some definitive evidence to support his claims. He needed something concrete to take back to Hope. Otherwise, he had every reason to believe that her reaction would be the same as it was on the night of Jeremy's vigil, and he was not willing to take that risk. More than ever before, he realized that he needed Hope. And Hope would need something that would convince her that Simon wasn't losing his mind.

It was more than a little unusual to have anyone waiting for the doors to open at the Bethel public library. When the young librarian unlocked the front door, she was keenly aware of the hazards of being alone with a strange man, and Simon's appearance as well as his odd behavior made her uncomfortable. He had dark bags under his eyes, his hair was a mess, and his face unshaven. But it was the crazed look in his eyes that put her on edge. Cautiously, she directed him to the computers in the back of the room.

Simon searched the names of Jessie Joseph and Adam Potter with the off chance that something would pop up, but all of the information proved to be completely irrelevant. Suddenly, he got another idea. Taking a different approach, he searched for articles on the more recent tragedies that Rob had referenced while recounting the legend. In only a few clicks, he was able to find the archives for *The Bethel Chronicle*, and it wasn't long after that that he discovered an issue from September of 2001. Not long thereafter, Simon ran across a short article about an elderly man who died an untimely death. On September 16th, only a few days after 9/11, a longtime resident of Bethel plummeted to his death from the grain elevator. Foul play was ruled out. Authorities declared it a suicide. The man's name was none other than John Mark Rash!

"John Rash," Simon said under his breath as he ran his fingers through his hair. "Mara's son?" Then he remembered Mara bitterly claimed that *they* murdered him. Simon only assumed that she meant when John was a child, and when she referred to *they*, he naturally assumed she meant Jessie.

While the incident was tragic, it didn't completely fit the narrative of the curse. Clearly, John was not a child. However, an article pertaining to the death of a teenager, Michael Newdow, was more likely the next link in a pattern of tragic deaths. The discovery was enough evidence to confirm what Simon already knew to be true in his heart.

A few clicks later, he discovered a black and white photograph of a mangled car wrapped around a chain link fence with a massive metal pole crushing the canopy of the vehicle. His eyes hungrily consumed the picture before he read the caption, "Local teenager, Michael Newdow, was pronounced dead after his car veered from the road and caromed into a power pole." Hungrily, he read the details of the article. On Saturday, June 14th, Michael Newdow, a 16-year-old from Bethel, was found dead at the scene of an accident after his car swerved from the road, jumped a ditch, and smashed through a chain link fence before coming to an abrupt halt after hitting a large, metal flag pole.

Simon glanced back at the photo and was able to discern the corner of a tattered American flag at the far left corner of the photo, draping over the trunk of the nearly unrecognizable vehicle.

He continued reading the article. The accident took place around 1:15 am on Elk Grove Ave. when residents were awakened by a loud crash. Captain Chad Shipley of the County Sheriff's office who was first to arrive on the scene was quoted as saying the single car accident was the result of excessive speed and reckless driving.

It was irrefutable evidence that exactly six years before Jeremy's tragedy another young man's life was taken in a horrific accident. Could it be a mere coincidence?

Not long after, he found another article from June of 1996. The short piece described the strange death of an elderly, senile woman who was electrocuted while taking her dog for a walk on Virginia Avenue in Bethel. Authorities determined that Ruth Ginsberg was shocked to death after stepping on a manhole cover due to stray voltage. Once again, the tragedy didn't exactly fit the legend. Even though

Ginsberg was a a lifelong resident of Bethel, she was no spring chicken at the time of her demise.

Searching older editions of the Chronicle, Simon really thought he was on to something when he discovered yet another bizarre tragedy from June of 1992. The article established that Daniel Wiseman, while overly preoccupied with daily mundane tasks, forgot his 14-month-old daughter was still sitting in her car seat in the back of the car. The poor, innocent child died from heat exhaustion. Again, it wasn't exactly in line with the pattern of every six years, but it was a horribly tragic death of yet another child from Bethel nonetheless.

For the next two hours, Simon did in fact find a number of other deaths that further substantiated the veracity of the legend. Fueled by the stack of evidence that was piling up, Simon once again decided to search for articles pertaining to the original tragedy. With great fervor he clicked through link after link only to be disappointed time and again by his futility. Frustrated, he came to the conclusion that he needed to look for alternative resources. Once again, he approached the jittery librarian who was busily working behind the desk with her back turned toward him.

"Excuse me, Miss!" Simon said with desperation in his voice.

The young woman nearly jumped out her chair as she reached a hand across her chest.

"I'm sorry," Simon said, impassioned, "I just need a little help finding some information. I am looking for old newspaper articles from *The Bethel Chronicle*."

"Is-is there anything in particular that you are looking for?" she asked, still trying to regain her composure.

Simon hesitated as he contemplated how much he should divulge to her about his research. "Actually, I'm looking for information from 1935 or 1936…on Jessie Joseph," he said sheepishly under his breath.

The young lady gasped and held her hand over her mouth. "Wow!…" she said with a look of shock on her face.

"What? What is it?" Simon asked with great anticipation.

"Anything from 1935 would be on microfiche," she said. "No one ever uses the microfiche machine, and I've never been trained on it."

"That's it?" Simon asked as he deeply exhaled.

"Well, it's way back in the corner," she said still skeptical of Simon's intentions. "And like I said, I've never been trained on it. So,…"

Simon only needed to slightly press the issue before the young lady was on the phone with the regular librarian who was on vacation in the Ozarks. She walked the two of them through how to find the canisters that held the film with the old editions of the local newspapers. Simon's anxiousness bore on his face, and he nervously paced back and forth as the young librarian loaded a canister. Impulsively, Simon kept wiping his mouth with the palm of his hand as he waited for the girl to get the archaic machine to work. Cautiously, the young librarian continually glanced at Simon over her shoulder with a watchful eye.

"Hey, I got it!" she excitedly exclaimed before remembering herself and backing away from Simon towards her work station. "Well, there you go. If there is anything else that I can do for you, I will be at the front desk…talking to my boyfriend…who is a very big guy and lives right around the corner. So…"

"Uh, okay, thanks," Simon replied, puzzled by the irrelevant information.

Once the apprehensive librarian made her way back to the front desk, Simon anxiously scanned through the articles starting in January of 1935. *The Bethel Chronicle* was a weekly rag at that time filled with a great deal of mundane information about activities going on in the community. In less than an hour, he found an article that made mention of the infamous Jessie Joseph. There was no picture, but the article did authenticate that Jessie was in fact a new teacher at the grade school. It gave an account of a local food drive that Jessie was spearheading with the help of some students. Simon's heart raced as he leaned forward in his chair to read the details. Much to his dismay, the piece revealed very little new information other than Jessie was in his first year of teaching the first and second grade classes at Bethel Elementary.

Simon remembered Mara telling him that the class sizes were so small and that space was so limited at that time, that they actually combined two grades per teacher in each classroom. With even greater anticipation, Simon looked for a method to print the article. After failing to figure it on his own, he once again approached the nervous librarian who by now supposed Simon to be one of the local Meth junkies due to his appearance and erratic behavior. As he approached the front desk, she clutched a nearby 3-hole punch while speaking in hushed tones over her cell phone. Bringing the phone down just beneath her mouth, she forced a smile and said to him, "Yes?"

In another couple of minutes, they had the head librarian back on the phone. As it turns out, the machine was so old that it was incapable of producing copies of the text. Simon would have to simply jot the information down on a piece of paper. If Hope needed more than that, he could always bring her to the library to see for herself.

Fueled by the discovery of a sliver of evidence, he went back to the microfiche even more determined than before. It wasn't long before he discovered a second article. The small feature gave an account of a prominent local farmer named Clay Potter who had made a sizable donation to the school for books and supplies. There was little information to confirm the legend other than the fact that he was the father of Adam and Evelyn Potter who were 6-year-old twins attending first grade at Bethel Elementary. Beyond that, there was only a single quote from Mr. Potter. When asked why he made the donation, he replied that he had been inspired by a sermon in which he was reminded that Jesus had implored Peter to feed his sheep.

Even though the story made no mention of the events surrounding the terrible tragedy, it was something. Simon was on track. His heart raced as his eyes wildly danced over the pages of the old paper, scanning for any word that might reveal another piece of the puzzle.

"*Ha! I'm not crazy!*" Simon suddenly yelled out loud as he jumped up out of his seat.

The startled librarian jumped as well dropping the phone to the floor. She quickly picked it up, never daring to take her eyes off of the strange man standing in front of the microfiche machine. This time she actually dialed a number and chewed on her fingernail while she waited for someone to pick up.

The headline of the article declared on the screen read, "Tragedy Befalls Bethel Elementary." It was dated November 1, 1935. Excitedly, Simon's eyes danced over the page frantically for the article, but it was missing. There was nothing on the film, just a blank screen. Someone had removed it.

"What the...? *No!*" Simon yelled out with a flurry of profanity, slamming the desk with the palm of his hand.

Quickly, the librarian slid out from behind the desk and shuffled backwards towards the front door, clutching her phone.

Flipping the dials to the old machine with reckless abandon, Simon frantically searched for the missing piece.

"Where did it go?" he cried out.

Even though the rest of the paper remained intact, there was no sign of the article that the headline was referring to. It had been erased. Simon ran his hand through his greasy hair wondering what on earth had happened to the film. Quickly, he fumbled for the next canister and loaded the film. His hands shook as he poured over the archived newspapers. With each new edition of the paper, Simon's blood ran cold. There were articles missing from every issue of *The Bethel Chronicle* from November 1935 to April 1936. The documents appeared to have been tampered with after they were converted to microfiche. Simon couldn't help but wonder if it was a deliberate attempt to cover up the dark tragedy.

"But who would do such a thing?" Simon asked under his stale breath. "His mind raced with the possibilities."

Suddenly, a large hand gripped his shoulder from out of nowhere. Simon tried to get up out of his seat as he turned, but the firm hand shoved him back down into the chair. It was a state trooper.

"Everything all right here, son?" the iron-jawed officer asked, holding one hand on the butt of his revolver.

Simon looked around at the empty canisters and film that had been strewn all over the desk in front of him. And he realized for the first time what he must look like. He reeked of body odor and was covered in dirt, paint chips, and grime from head to toe.

"Simon?" the officer asked, as he leaned forward to get a good look at the potential perp.

It was the same state trooper whom he had met the first night he returned to Bethel while hanging out with his old friends at the tavern.

"Is everything okay here?" the trooper asked, concerned by Simon's grave expression.

"Yeah, fine," Simon replied. "Everything's fine." It was a lie of course. Nothing was fine. Simon was in the middle of something bigger than himself that he still didn't understand.

"I got a call that some lunatic was tearing up the library and causing a disturbance," the officer said with a laugh while removing his hand from his weapon.

The young librarian was standing behind her desk chewing on her fingernail as she expectantly watched the exchange.

"What are you up to?" the officer asked.

"Oh, uh, just doing a little research on a...a... project," Simon replied somewhat truthfully.

"Oh," the trooper replied, "are you all right? You look like you've seen a ghost."

"What?" Simon asked.

"You just look a little frazzled," the officer observed. "Actually, you look terrible to be honest. You're hair's all messed up, you haven't shaved, and you smell a little 'gamey', if you know what I mean. You boys been up all night partying again?" he asked with laugh.

"No, no, I'm just in the middle of a little renovation project at the school and didn't have a chance to get cleaned up before coming down here this morning, that's all," Simon said, regaining his composure.

"He's all right, Missy," the officer said turning to the librarian who had moved a few steps closer to the door. Then he turned back to Simon, "Next time run a comb through your hair or something. You scared the daylights out of the librarian. Okay?"

"Sure, sorry," Simon replied. "Sorry," he called out to the librarian. "I didn't mean to alarm you, ma'am."

"Hey, and get all of this cleaned up before you go, okay?" the officer said as he headed out the front door while speaking into the mic on his shoulder.

"Yeah, definitely," Simon replied, "no problem." Then something occurred to Simon as he turned to the still unnerved librarian. "Do have any other records archived from the 1930's?"

"Like what?" she asked apprehensively.

"Like obituaries," Simon said.

"No, but they might have those in the county records," she said. Then she thought for a moment. "But you probably have better luck trying the state records in Springfield."

Simon sat up and thought about it for a minute.

"Of course!" Simon replied, as he rushed out the front door. "Thank you so much!"

"Hey, wait a minute!" she called out to him. "What about the...?" Ugh, men! Always leaving behind a mess for someone else to clean up!"

* * *

In just a little over two hours, Simon found himself standing in front of the Illinois Department of Public Health building in Springfield. Consumed by the idea of finding something that would definitively support the authenticity of the legend and Mara's claims, Simon quickly ascended the steps of the government building even though he had not slept for the past twenty-four hours.

Now, as he poured over the information, the pressure building inside of him continued to mount. At every turn, he met yet another obstacle. Even after he finally found the right building, he soon discovered that there are eligibility requirements to access death certificates. The snippy, old woman behind the desk let him know in no uncertain terms that they were not public records. When asked, she suggested going to the state library and searching the obituaries in newspapers from larger towns within the vicinity of Bethel from the same time period.

Undeterred, Simon followed the directions of the surly woman working at the information desk and hurriedly made his way to the state library. With a little help from a refreshingly pleasant librarian, it wasn't long before he was once again searching through old papers on microfiche.

There were very few references to tiny Bethel, IL in any of the major newspapers. For hours and hours he scoured the antiquated films. Nothing. He felt sick. He hadn't slept. He hadn't eaten. And now discouraged, he leaned his head on the desk in front of him as the tears began to well up in his bloodshot, swollen eyes. He had to know if this thing was real, or if he was in fact losing his mind.

Unexpectedly, the helpful librarian approached him furtively holding a tray of films from *The Charleston Times-Courier*. It was geographically the closest town with a newspaper to Bethel that they had found up to that point. Simon heartily thanked the librarian for her hospitality. She answered in kind before warning him that the library would be closing shortly.

With a renewed sense of purpose, Simon immediately searched for editions from the November 1935. Then he found it. Just beneath an article on Adolf Hitler signing a decree authorizing the founding of the Reich Luftwaffe was Adam Potter's obituary. The nondescript obit stated that the Adam was survived by his father, mother, and sister. Otherwise, the only other detail that the article revealed was that the 6-year-old had tragically passed away *in the Bethel Elementary School building*!

"He died in the school?" Simon said aloud, confused by the contradiction to Rob's account of the murders.

Even more bizarre, there was no other account of any other child's death in Bethel from November of 1935 through the spring of 1936. Simon hypothesized that maybe Adam Potter only made the larger Charleston paper because his father Clay was such a prominent member of the community. The details didn't completely fit, but it was still enough for him to keep digging. Simon called for the assistance of the librarian once more to have her help him print the article.

She did so only after some pleading. Officially, the library had already closed fifteen minutes ago. As she reluctantly printed off the article from the archaic machine, the librarian was suddenly called away giving Simon a few more precious minutes to flip through a couple more editions of the paper.

Just as the lights were being turned off in the building, Simon ran across the article that he had been hoping to find. It was nothing more than a short op-ed piece on page two of the times Courier under one article describing Hitler's greatest peace speech to Reichstag, claiming he did not have the slightest thought of conquering other nations or people, and a second, parallel article describing the founding of the Aleppo branch of the Muslim Brotherhood in Syria.

Ravenously, Simon began to digest the contents of the article. The op-ed piece gave an account of a teacher, one Jessie Joseph of Bethel, IL, who was on trial for criminal activity on charges that included abuse and even murder. A chill ran down Simon's spine. Finally, he had something concrete to take to Hope. If he was going to do this, he needed her support. Surely, if nothing else, this would substantiate his claims. With the last of the lights being turned off one by one, Simon didn't have time to print the article. Instead, he was forced to quickly jot down the details on a scrap piece of paper. Just as he finished, the night watchman called out to him.

* * *

Once again, Simon found himself weaving his thirty-five hundred pounds of Detroit steel in and out of car seated infested minivans and Nodoz aided freighters. Only this time, his mind was unable to whimsically drift from ESPN to Cinemax. Instead, it was consumed by one driving thought. He wondered what Hope would say when he told her everything and presented the evidence. Anxiously, his extremities twitched and fidgeted with nervous energy. Invigorated with a great sense of purpose, every ounce of him readied for the requisition of the service that loomed on the horizon. As the sun began to set, Simon glanced down at his watch and then back again at his cell phone, but there was still no word from Hope. A brilliant green flash above the upper rim of the sun exploded in Simon's periphery, as he headed south on I-55 in the general direction of the undisclosed location of the all girl's Christian Summer Camp in southern Illinois. He still had at least another hour before reaching Carbondale. If he hadn't heard from Hope by then, he had no clue how he was going to find the camp.

While driving down the interstate in silence, he was also driving himself crazy in anticipation of his impending conversation with Hope. He replayed the hypothetical dialogue over and over in his mind, mimicking both sides of the exchange. But the more he practiced, the crazier he sounded, and the tension mounted.

What would he do without Hope if she rejected him again? He longed to hear her voice and see her brilliant smile. The epiphany surprised even himself. Just as the warm thought began to permeate his entire being, Hope's expression of disappointment the first time he tried to share with her his innermost feelings flooded his consciousness and shattered his fragile state of mind. He looked over to the seat next to him at the articles that he had printed off and notes he had copied from archives. Even though he now had a substantial amount of evidence, he wondered if it would be enough for her to believe him.

Exasperated, he tried to clear his head by turning on the radio. First, he attempted to find a meaningless sports talk station that would take his mind off of the looming conversation that he was no longer looking forward to. While the talk show hosts out of St. Louis lamented the hitting woes of the slumping Cardinals with Albert Pujols on the DL, Simon did his best to lose himself in meaningless distraction, but it wasn't working. Next, he fumbled for a rock station, but the implicit lyrics from "Centerfold" that in the past would have inspired his depraved imagination, now only served to remind him of his shameful night with Jez. And it seemed as if all that had once provided an intoxicatingly vivid escape from reality now only left him feeling hallow and empty.

Lost in that thought, he failed to notice that the radio reception began to spit and sputter with static. The clarity soon deteriorated to the point where a powerful voice from a second radio station out of Memphis wrestled with the rock station out of St. Louis for the same number on the dial. Just as the host began the intro to the program out of the Home of the Blues, Loverboy broke in with their song,... "makin' love to whoever I please, I gotta do it my way, or no way at all..." out of the station from the Gateway to the West.

A few minutes later the crackle of static gave way again to some pastor named Adrian Rogers, railing about the nature of sin. It was then that Simon snapped out of his trance and became aware of the conflicting transmissions being emitted over the stereo. With a scowl of displeasure, he reached out to turn the dial. When he did so, he noticed a cross on the side of the road, and he instantly recalled the night he felt God's presence and read the message on the marquee. But before he could explore any connection, he noticed a car off in the distance, sitting on the shoulder of the road with its hazard lights on. As Simon's car drew near, he recognized all of the telltale signs of a flat tire.

Suddenly, he felt a tug at his heart to pull over and help. In no more than an instant, two conflicting desires clashed. Obviously, there was a person stranded who might need the help of someone who wasn't a psycho. But, at the same time, he felt a strong desire to talk to Hope before he lost his nerve.

"Besides, what do I know about cars anyway?" he reasoned. "I know where the gas goes, where oil goes, and that the tires need air. Other than that, what help could I provide?"

He had a cell phone but didn't everyone these days? At the very least, he could let the person use his phone or give them a ride, a voice from somewhere deep inside of him countered. As soon as he came to that conclusion, another voice inside of him challenged that it could be some degenerate laying in wait for some unbeknownst do-gooder. In a matter of mere seconds, he came to the conclusion that the right thing was to stop and help, and that he would do just that if he wasn't in such a hurry to get somewhere. In another flash, he was up on the car and noticed a skinny, young woman with flowing black hair struggling to budge a tire iron.

"Poor girl," he said to himself, looking back in his rearview mirror, "I hope she'll be all right." He knew he should have stopped, but comforted himself by saying that it was definitely too late now. Wasn't it? Just then, his cell phone blasted and flashed in the twilight, and he saw that it was Hope's number on the ID. His heart skipped a beat.

"God, if you just help me with this, I will do whatever you say from here on out," Simon thought reaching for the phone. As he picked it up, he heard that same voice from deep inside of him say, "Just tell her the truth."

* * *

Hope's directions were spotty at best, but after a few U-turns and a little backtracking, he was now driving down a one-lane gravel road under a canopy of trees and heading in the right direction of the camp. Unfortunately for Simon, she sounded less than enthusiastic about his unannounced visit. But, unbeknownst to him, it had more to do with the rules of the Christian camp and the interpretation of impropriety than it did about her personal feelings for Simon. Truth be told, she could hardly contain her excitement to see him.

Nonetheless, there was the inconvenient issue of her being the head counselor and her obligation to be above reproach in all matters of decorum. But, more than just her feelings for Simon, she could also hear the urgency in his voice. In an act of great compromise, she just so happened to decide to go for a long walk off of the premises at the same time that he just so happened to turn down the road leading to the entrance to the camp.

Even though Simon was anxious to see Hope for the first time in weeks, he still anguished with the unavoidable conversation that he needed to have with her. It wasn't that he doubted what he knew to be true. It was that he also knew how crazy it sounded. He couldn't bear to have her react in the same way she did the night of Jeremy's funeral. His heart ached as the expression of her pained face flashed again before his eyes. As the painful memory crossed his mind, the gravel began to crunch beneath the tires of his slow moving car. Suddenly, he saw Hope just beyond his headlights walking briskly towards him on the side of the road with her arms folded. As soon as she recognized the car, a wide grin came across her angelic face and in that moment, he was certain that he loved her.

Simon rolled down his window just as Hope bounded over to the car and gave him a warm hug around his neck. His beleaguered body that had been operating only on heavy doses of truck stop coffee exploded with a rush of adrenaline.

After what seemed like an eternity, she let go, raced around to the passenger side, and hopped in. Slightly embarrassed by her own transparency, she smoothed back her long, blond hair and looked down at the floorboard of the car. It was the first time Simon had ever seen her flustered. Intently, she turned back towards him with a cheesy grin and said, "What?"

But, Simon was without the words to express how he felt. He couldn't take his eyes off of her beautiful face, and he realized just how much he had missed her.

"What?" she said again with her palms up. "I know I look terrible," she said before realizing that she sounded like her mother.

"Oh no, I think at this moment you're the most beautiful thing I have seen in my entire life," he said in all sincerity.

"Yeah, right," Hope said with an uncertain smile, her heart pounding in her chest.

As Simon contentedly gazed upon her beautiful countenance, Hope got a little uncomfortable and tried to break the awkward silence. She too felt the strong connection. But, she also knew the potentiality of revealing those feelings with a boy in a car on a deserted road in the light of the moon.

"So, I know you didn't drive all the way down here in the middle of the night to tell me that," Hope said, taking hold of her senses.

The statement brought him out of the trance, and he once again remembered why he had come.

"Is there somewhere we can go to talk?" Simon asked, sheepishly looking around at the darkened woods.

"Yeah, of course," Hope said, feeling the weight of his words and noting the sudden change in Simon's demeanor.

* * *

After he had finished telling Hope everything and showing her all of the evidence, he couldn't bear to look her in the eye for fear of rejection. Instead, he stared off into the mirrored reflection of the moon on the still waters. Picking at some paint chips of the weathered slats of the old dock, he waited with bated breath for her response.

"Wow," she said under her breath while looking at the copies of the old articles and scribbled notes. The giddy feelings had long since subsided, and she was able to properly process his words with wisdom and discernment.

After some time, she spoke. "So, why did you come here tonight, Simon?"

"Because," he responded, flicking the paint chips into the water still unable to look her directly in the eye. He was too afraid that he would see the same look of dejection and disappointment that haunted the recesses of his mind. "Because, I know in my heart that I have to do this. This is what I'm *supposed* to do it. Like Jeremy said, we each have a purpose, and I think ending the cycle of tragedies in Bethel is mine."

"You mean the curse?" Hope said for the sake of clarity.

"Yes, the curse," Simon replied. "I know it sounds…"

Then he suddenly stopped short.

"So, what then?" Hope asked, leaning closer to see his face buried in the crook of his arm that rested on his knee. She sensed that there was more to it than he was letting on.

"I need *you*, Hope," Simon said. "I know that I haven't known you very long, but I need you to believe in me."

"Why?" Hope asked with great anticipation dancing in her expectant eyes.

He looked up out of the corner of his eyes at Hope's delicate face and decided to take the risk. "Because I…because I think that I am falling in love with you."

"What makes you think that?" Hope asked, testing him just a little.

"Because I've never kissed you, but I want to more than anything. And yet, I don't want to until you want to just as badly as I do, because I don't want to ruin what we have. And I've never felt…"

Before he could finish, she leaned forward and kissed him delicately on the lips.

Somewhat shocked but mostly electrified by her profound gesture, Simon stammered, "So, you don't think I'm crazy?"

"Not really," she said with a laugh. "I don't think you're any crazier than Moses or Noah."

"Are you comparing me to Moses or Noah?" he asked as a broad smile swept across his face.

"Maybe without the long flowing beard," Hope replied. "I do think you're not any more crazy than anyone else who God has ever called to do anything crazy… like everyone probably thought of Noah before it ever started to rain."

"How long did it take him to build the ark? Like a hundred years or something?" Simon replied, dropping his head for theatrics sake. But he couldn't hide the smile from his face. Hope nodded with a smile, and they shared a laugh. 'Thank you,

God,' he said to himself as he looked deeply into Hope's sparkling eyes. 'Just tell the truth, and the truth will set you free, simple as that,' he thought. With her acceptance of his absurd assertions, a tremendous weight had been lifted off of his shoulders.

"So…," Hope said as she slid closer to him and took ahold of his muscular arm. "…I am willing to wait for the first drop of rain to fall if you are."

"Well, you have to admit that at least the clouds are darkening," Simon said, taking up on the analogy and looking down at the articles and notes in her hand.

"Maybe," Hope replied, coyly.

"Maybe?" he mimicked, jokingly. He was on cloud nine and feeling invincible. "What about these articles, or the lady from the church, or what Jeremy said, or the lights going on and off at night or…"

Hope shrugged her shoulders and said, "I think you really believe what you're telling me."

"Okay, but what about the gravestones and the boy in the well, I know what I saw that night," Simon said confidently.

Hope paused for a moment and frowned. "Yeah, about that," she said, "now how was it again that you knew the graveyard was so close to Potter's house the night you were looking for the lost boy?"

"What?" Simon asked, still basking in the glow of the reciprocation of his feelings for Hope.

"You said that you and Jeremy ran across the graveyard while looking for the boy, and then you remembered how close Potter's house was to the cemetery," she said inquisitively. "You said that that was how you figured the little boy might be at the abandoned house. How did you know you were close to the house?"

"Because some of us went out there the first week I was back in town," Simon said without thinking it through. He had become so intent on proving his case that he was completely blindsided by the next question.

"Why were you out there?" Hope instinctively asked.

"I told you this, remember?" Simon said. "We all got to talking about the legend at the tavern, and we then decided to go see it for ourselves."

"Who's we?" Hope asked.

It was then that Simon realized in his quest to convince Hope about the curse that he had painted himself into a corner. Just as he had discovered the value of telling the truth, he was about to feel the jagged side of that double-edged sword pierce the chamber around his heart, revealing the permanent stain. At first, he panicked and considered concealing the truth. Then he remembered how God had led him to tell Hope the truth about what he believed his purpose to be and how it all worked out in the end. Naturally, he had to have every reason to believe that God would do it again in this case too.

"Rob, Rocky, Will, and me, and…Jez," Simon said.

Hope scowled. "Jessica Bell? Why was Jessica there?" she asked, completely caught off guard.

"She just happened to be at the bar that night and heard Rob's story," Simon stammered. "She wanted to see it too, the gravesite I mean, she wanted to see the *gravesite*," Simon said, trying to backpedal. It was like he heard someone else talking and couldn't make himself stop. "Actually, it was her idea in the first place. Rocky said that he had seen the graves before, and Jez wanted to go. Everybody did. Well, everybody except Rich."

Hope sat back for a moment, letting go of his arm. Simon could see the wheels turning in her head, as he hoped against hope that she wouldn't press the issue any farther, but she did.

"Then how is it that you never saw the gravesite that night?" Hope pointedly asked.

Simon cringed. His blood ran cold, and his heart was up in his throat.

"Because when we got to Potter's property everybody jumped out of the truck and spread out to find the graveyard, except for Jez….and me," Simon heard himself say. "She thought it would be funny if we jumped back in the truck and left the other ones stranded in the woods. You know as a kind of prank."

"And did you?" Hope asked.

"Did we what?" Simon asked.

"Did the two of you leave them?" Hope asked. Her intuition was uncanny, and she was tracking with the story perfectly, all the while wishing she wasn't right.

"Yes," Simon said, regretfully.

"Just the two of you?" Hope asked.

"Yes."

"And where did you go?" Hope asked folding her arms.

"We parked…"

"I think I'm going to be *sick*," Hope said her face turning pale. Under the light of the moon, she saw right through him as though she were reading the story off of the pages of his soul. "You told me point blank that nothing happened between you and Jez! Now you're telling me something did?

"No, No, No" Simon said, turning to face her. It was like a wild fire furiously fanning out of control. Desperately, he reached out with both hands and held her by the shoulders. "I was not *with* her. Besides, what I said was, 'I didn't do anything with Jez *at the strip club*'."

"Oh, I see, " Hope said as she rolled her teary eyes and pushed him aside in order to get past him.

"Hope!" Simon said going after her. "I was not *with her, with her* anywhere at anytime."

She turned toward him, pained and enraged. "And how am I supposed to believe you Simon?" she asked. "Huh? Tell me that. How do I know that I am just not asking the question with the right semantics?" Tears were streaming down her cheeks.

"You can believe me on this one," he said without thinking. "I can prove it because…because she couldn't. Know what I mean?"

There was silence.

"That was the only thing that stopped you?" Hope asked, incredulous.

"Oh, come on," Simon pleaded. He was genuinely perplexed by Hope's reaction. He thought for sure she would be relieved. "I wasn't with her. Isn't that enough? Who cares what the reason was."

He was so busy trying to justify his actions that he failed to recognize the shear agony in her face.

"But you wanted to, right?" Hope asked accusingly.

"Yeah, I guess so, but what guy wouldn't? Besides, that was before I even knew you," Simon responded, suddenly getting defensive. Honestly, he was at a loss.

Hope shook her head and could barely get her words out, "If you *wanted to be with her* then I hate to tell you buddy boy, but you might as well have *been* with her. That's how it works. And for your information it does matter, because the guy I'm waiting for would never want to *be with, be with* anyone else. He would be saving himself. Because that's how it was meant to be. So, why would I give anything that is reserved for him to someone like you?"

With armed folded, she pivoted and stomped off of the creaky dock.

"Come on, that's not even being realistic," Simon responded, sealing his own fate. "I know I should have told you everything from the very beginning, but you're being irrational. No guy would be able to wait until they were…"

She stopped for a moment and turned back towards him with an angry scowl and said, "I hope you at least got a refund!"

"Refund?" Simon said with a perplexed expression. "But, she's not a…"

With that, Hope stormed off down the gravel road back towards the camp. There was nothing Simon could say or do at that point. Feebly, he called out to her, "Hope, *Hope*, don't walk away. Let me at least drive you back! Hope!"

But there was no answer. What had begun so perfectly was poisoned by the perpetual stain embedded in his heart that bled through his thinly disguised façade and poured out onto his sleeve.

Paralyzed from shock, it took a few minutes before what had just transpired began to sink in.

"Why are you doing this to me?" Simon asked through clenched teeth while looking up at the heavens.

* * *

His world completely shattered, Simon's four hour drive back to Bethel did nothing but further fuel the wrenching pain that ached in his gut. Like Chinese water torture, the conversation with Hope kept playing over and over in his head. He was drowning in his sorrow and self-pity while still trying to comprehend all that she had said to him. Simon honestly thought that he would have earned Hope's respect by following God's will and being completely open and honest. Instead, it had all blown up in his face. Did she really expect to find a guy who had never been with a girl before, let alone one whoever *wanted* to be with another girl? Was that even possible? The guy would either have to be completely unattractive or... Simon could hardly comprehend the other possibility, and its implication staggered him for a moment as if it had never occurred to him before. Was a it really a path he could have actually chosen to take? Or was he just a victim of his hormones like everybody else? Did she really expect to marry a virgin in this day and age?

Now both physical and emotional exhaustion set in like a suffocating blanket. He had alienated himself from the one person he cared most about in the entire world, and now he had to consider the distinct possibility that he was going out of his mind. There was no denying what he had seen and heard with his own eyes and ears at the school.

"Those things actually happened, right?" he asked, trying his best to convince himself. "They were real. Weren't they? Not just some psychotic hallucination or grand delusion!"

It was difficult for him to think clearly or formulate a complete thought. It had now been nearly two days since Simon had gotten any sleep. As he pulled into the driveway of his apartment, all he wanted was peace and rest, but it wasn't meant to be. Jack's shiny, new Sierra was waiting in the drive. Simon glanced down through tired eyes at his watch only see that it was nearly four o'clock in the morning.

"What now?" he asked under his stale breath.

As the car turned into the drive, the high beams revealed Jack standing with his arms folded leaning against the gate of his truck. When the car came to a stop, the shrewd landlord took his cigarette out of his mouth, tossed it to the ground, and smashed it with the heel of his foot. Casually, he made his way around to Simon's window.

"Jack," Simon said, flatly, "what's going on?"

"Ha, I was just look'n for ya," Jack said with a broad grin. "Thought I'd missed ya. Then next thing I know, here ya are. How bout' that ?"

"Is everything all right?" Simon asked, looking through swollen, bloodshot eyes at Jack's beaming face.

"'Fraid I need to collect the rent that you owe me," Jack said expectantly.

"Now?" Simon asked, glancing at the clock on his dashboard.

"I've always found it easier to collect my debts late at night," Jack divulged. "I find that folks are much more willing to cooperate when their faculties are compromised. Most times they give me whatever I want with the hopes of just gettin' rid of me. Ha!"

"Oh, Jack," Simon replied, "I didn't know. I mean, I knew we had a deal and that you were helping me out. But, I…"

"Correct me if I'm wrong," Jack said, "but didn't you say that you'd gladly pay *me* after you got your first paycheck?"

"Yeah, but…" Simon began to say.

"And did you not get paid this week?" Jack asked, dipping his head to one side and lifting his eyebrows.

"Yes, but I've only got three hundred dollars to my name right now," Simon protested.

"That's somethin'," Jack replied. "Tell you what, I'll make ya a deal out of the goodness of my heart. Give me half of that, and we'll call it even for last month's rent, but ya owe me one."

"I guess I can write you a check for a hundred and fifty," Simon said, hardly believing he was having this conversation at four o'clock in the morning.

There was one thing that Jack was right about. Simon was ready to do just about anything to get rid of him at this point.

"Perfect," Jack said, leaning both hands on the door of the car. " 'Scratch me out a check'. Ha, 'Scratch'," Jack said looking up to the stars. "That was kind of a nickname of mine back in the day. Ya know, before the days of debit cards, and Paypal, and what not."

"Oh yeah," Simon answered absentmindedly looking around his car. He leaned over to the glove box, pulled out his checkbook, and wrote a check in the amount of a hundred and fifty. "Okay, here you go." He ripped it out and handed it over to Jack.

"How do I know this is any good?" Jack asked, holding it up to the light.

"It's good," Simon said tiredly. "Trust me." He reached for the handle to push the door open, but Jack didn't budge. "Excuse me," Simon said, forcing the door open and crawling out.

"Oh sorry," Jack replied, "course. Head inside. Get ya some rest. Look's like you could use some shut-eye."

Simon gave a sarcastic grin as he walked past the wily old man and headed up the staircase.

"I don't know how you youngsters do it," Jack called out to Simon with a laugh. "Partying all night then gettin' up and go'n to work. You gotta be there in what, another hour or so? I'd be dead on my feet if I were you."

Simon gave a wave of his hand as he ascended the steps to his tiny apartment.

"Say, I just thought of somethin' you can do that'll make us even," Jack said with a snap of his fingers.

Simon stopped but didn't say anything. Holding the screen door open in his left hand, he leaned back and looked down at the nocturnal entrepreneur.

"You could knock it off with all that referendum business," Jack said as though he had just thought of it on the spot. "Yeah, causes a stir. Get's folks all worked up, ya know."

"No problem," Simon replied dully. "You don't have to worry. I'm through with all that."

* * *

At 5:46 a.m., the phone rang incessantly. Through the slit of a blood shot-eye, Simon looked for the phone at the edge of the bed. Even though he was wiped out, sleep had not come easy. All of the events of the past several days plagued him as he slipped in and out of consciousness.

"Hello?" Simon said through a gravelly voice. Before his brain could even begin to process the possibility, his heart longed for it to be Hope. Instead, it was Andy Cross who was so upset that he could barely put together two intelligible words.

"Uh, Simon, what are you…where are you at?" he bellowed into the phone. "The ceilin'! What did you do to the ceilin'?" Andy asked in a panicked voice.

For a moment, Simon's brain couldn't quite compute what the old janitor was yammering about. Then it finally dawned on him. Andy must have just now seen that Simon had taken down the false ceiling in the entryway to the school.

"Oh yeah, the ceiling, right," Simon replied with a gravelly voice as he squinted at the alarm clock. "I took it down."

"You did…why would you…who said you could…?" Andy stuttered.

"Nobody, I just did it," Simon said, swinging his legs over the side of the bed and running his hand through his matted hair.

"Well, why…I mean who do you think you are that you can just…" Andy sputtered as his voice cracked.

"Thelma gave us permission to restore the entryway, right? So,…" Simon started to say.

"No, no, no," Andy objected. "She said to just do a little painting, that's all, not…just get down here, we gotta fix it!" He hung up without bothering to say goodbye.

Simon pulled the phone away from his ear and frowned at it. He was beyond annoyed. More than that he soon discovered that the pain in his chest had not ceased to ache and his head throbbed.

After throwing some water on his face, he reluctantly headed down to the school. As his car pulled up to the front of the school, Andy came hurrying out of the building to meet him. He was frantic. The panicked janitor rushed to Simon's door, opened it, and grabbed Simon by the arm.

"We…we gotta fix this," Andy said with his blood pressure soaring. "I mean, Miss Harold gets back in town sometime tomorrow, so you've got to get it back to how it was before!" Andy pulled him out of the car and dragged him to the school.

"Relax, Mr. Cross, relax," Simon said slowly, in a halfhearted attempt to calm down the old janitor.

"I don't know what I'm gonna do," Andy said, standing just inside the doorway and looking up at the tin ceiling. "I gotta finish the floors in two more classrooms and the gym, and scrub the desks, and fix the boiler, and…I don't have time for this! School starts in a little over a month and I…"

"I got it, I got it," Simon promised. "I'll take care of it. Don't worry. Go do what you need to do."

Andy lingered a little longer in his panicked state before taking Simon at his word that he would return the ceiling to its previous condition. Simon ushered Andy to the gymnasium where he had been stripping the hardwood before returning to the landing.

Simon's heart was broken. He was a victim of his own…what? Honesty? Spiritual growth? One tiny indiscretion? He still had no idea why Hope was so upset. He was never *with* Jez, so he didn't necessarily lie about that. Besides, he and Hope didn't even know each other when he first arrived in Bethel.

"How can you cheat on someone you don't even know?" Simon pondered. He sat at the base of the stairs agonizing over that perplexing question. At this point, he was physically, mentally, and spiritually defeated. Simon was ready to give up the whole thing; Jeremy, Hope, Bethel, the curse, all of it. Jaded and disillusioned, he would wipe the past month completely out of his mind and move on to New Jersey with a fresh start. It was a brash sentiment that lacked steam. Little by little he gathered the aluminum frame, foam tiles, and hardware and began the task of reconstructing the functional, false ceiling.

However, it soon became apparent that putting the ceiling back together proved far more difficult than bringing it down. Nothing was congruous. On the contrary, none of the metal joists or trusses were matching up, and to his consternation, the anchors in the crumbling plaster had now been reamed out, providing little to no support. While wrestling with one particularly stubborn screw, Simon's Phillips slipped, raking the back of his hand against the metalwork. He let out a flurry of curse words before bringing his bleeding knuckle up to his mouth. Simon took it out and examined the deep gash in his hand before shaking it out and replacing it back into his mouth.

From his vantage point standing on the scaffolding high above the landing, he dropped his head and stared blankly at the floor. Without invitation, the memory of seeing Adam Potter's likeness forced its way into his consciousness. Simon scowled at the vivid recollection and the subsequent series of events that ultimately led him to his fallout with Hope. Recalling the series of unfortunate events that had since transpired, he came to the conclusion that this silly ghost story was ruining his life. After all, it was the whole reason he ended up alone with Jez in her truck that night in the first place. It was time to just let it go, push it out of his mind, and move on. He would put in his time at the school, hang out with his friends, do the umpiring thing, and head east when the call came to interview for the sales job. As he tried to muster up the resolve to carry out his new plan, Simon threw down his screwdriver, shimmied down the scaffolding, and hopped to the floor.

First, he would have to fix the ceiling. Simon came to the rightful conclusion that he needed to go to the hardware store to purchase some larger screws and anchors if he was going to put things back as he had found it.

Suddenly, his ringer went off. Simon fumbled for the phone deep in his pocket. It was his voicemail. Somehow he had missed several calls. While punching in the password, his head admonished his heart for daring to believe it could be Hope. It wasn't. It was his godfather, Joe, calling from New Jersey. "Even better," Simon told himself.

"Simon, hey," the voice on the message said. "Sorry I missed you. I tried a couple of times, but I keep getting your voice mail. Anyway, I wanted to tell you in person, but I've got some bad news. The FDA in their infinite wisdom has temporarily put the kibosh on the new drug. Evidently some monkeys developed a rash during one of the landmark trials for our drug," Joe sighed deeply before continuing, "anyhow, I don't know what to tell you, buddy boy. The FDA is asking for more safety data. It might delay us, it might shut it down completely, who knows. Just give me a call when you get a chance, and try to hang in there. There will be other opportunities."

Staggered by the message, Simon slowly guided himself down to sit on the stairs. "Can it get any worse?" he said aloud. He laughed, a wild disgusted laugh, and shook his head.

"Perfect, just perfect," he said, peppered with a bevy of perverse words.

The messages continued. The next one was from Rich, and he sounded pretty ticked off. "Freeman, where have you been, man?" the burly bartender growled. "Did you forget about umpiring last night? The least you could do is give me a call. Joey covered behind home plate, but we had to get some dad out of he stands. It was a nightmare. Not cool.

"Give me a call as soon as you get this. I need to know if you're going to do the game tomorrow night. And by the way, what in the world did you tell Rocky? Dude has been acting all holier-than-thou and says we have you to thank for it. He won't drink any alcohol, and he's dropping out of the fantasy league because he says it's 'like gambling'. He even got on Rob about his *language*. I liked him better when I couldn't understand him. Anyway, you're on quite a roll."

Simon didn't have to check the rest of the messages. They were all from Rich. He called at 5:45, 5:52, and 5:58 p.m. the night before. Deep in thought, he absentmindedly set the cell phone down on the step beside him. He chastised himself for letting Rich down, but even more for trying to offer Rocky spiritual advice. What business did he have telling anyone anything about religion or God? After a moment, he got up and made his way to the car. Annoyed at his recent series of gaffes, he put it in gear, punched the gas, and sent gravel flying. He didn't even know why. It was just something guys did when they were angry; probably some kind of declaration of power in an effort to compensate for his strong sense of inadequacy. But at this point, it was anybody's guess as to why anyone does anything. Simon was having a difficult time pinpointing his motivation for doing any of the things that he had done lately. He was hopelessly adrift, like a rudderless vessel without a compass. And a violent tempest loomed on the horizon.

* * *

Once he gathered the proper screws, anchors, and washers, Simon made his way to the front of the store carrying his bounty in both hands. When he reached the counter, a familiar looking young man stood before him in line pleading with the owner of the store.

"Mr. Cain," the storeowner said, standing next to a powerless, checkout girl, "I am completely sympathetic to your situation, but I don't see what I can do. It's not like we can just dig the sprinkler system back up out of the ground and refund your money."

Simon noticed for the first time the young man's distraught face. It looked as if he had not shaved in days. His hair was disheveled, and his visage bore a most desperate look of anguish. He closed his eyes as he tilted his head back and exhaled in exasperation. He cupped his lips and searched for the right words to state his case.

"Mr. O'Neill," Danny started to say, "here's the thing. My little girl is very sick. We're waiting for a call from Dr. Al-Banna about whether we need to take her to the emergency room."

By now, Mr. O'Neill's wife, Judy, had made her way from the office in the back and was listening to the story.

"Dr. Al-Banna is a good man and a fine doctor," Judy interjected. She was already sympathetic to the Cain's situation after hearing the details about the sick baby. Rumors circulated that their daughter was suffering from anything ranging from bird flu to Hodgkin's disease. "Your daughter is in good hands."

"Thank you," Danny said with his eyes beginning to tear up before continuing. "Anyway, as I was explaining to your husband, my insurance has not kicked in yet with my new company, and we're going to have to shoulder the medical expenses…" Danny paused and swallowed hard, looking down at the floor of the old hardware store. "You see we had to come to the closing of our house with more money than we had first anticipated. And then there was a fee for everything to be hooked up or turned on. I just had no idea…anyway, we're a little cash poor at the present time."

"As I said before, I don't see what we can do," Bill O'Neill replied. "You paid for the sprinkler heads, and the PVC pipe, and the labor. None of which can be returned."

"Mr. O'Neill," Danny said with an anguished face and tears swelling up in his eyes, "I'm begging you. Is there anything you can do?"

"Well, I…" Mr. O'Neill stammered.

"Of course there is, honey," Judy said, giving her husband a stiff elbow.

"Ouch," Bill said, rubbing his arm.

"Give the man back his money, Bill," Judy said with a scowl while holding onto her glasses that hung around her neck.

"But, Judy, the system is in the ground, what's done is done!" Mr. O'Neill said through gritted teeth while opening his eyes wide for affect. He thought she had clearly understood the threat that the current lull in the economy posed to their small business not to the mention the building of a new Walmart in Charleston.

"Here's what we'll do," Judy said, sympathetically. "I'll write you a check for the $3,343.43; the entire cost of the sprinkler system." Mr. O'Neill gasped. "We'll put together a payment plan with no interest that'll begin whenever you feel like you can make the first installment."

"Thank you, thank you so much!" Danny said passionately with tears streaming down his cheeks. "It's just my wife has been so upset. We didn't know where to turn. Pearl is running a very high fever and she can't keep any food down. Anyway, you don't know how much this means to us." He said while wildly shaking their hands. "Thank you! Thank you! We'll be forever in debt to you," he said making his way to the front door of the store.

"Oh no, you won't!" Bill called out to him as he the bell clanged on the front door.

"You're welcome, honey," Judy said, waving, "we'll be praying for you. Oh, and if you find that that isn't enough…"

Mr. O'Neill jumped in, anticipating the next words out of his wife's mouth. "… You might want to go see Jack Lawless," he offered. "He is well known for working out deals with desperate folks in times of distress."

Judy frowned at her husband.

"Oh, is that so?" Danny said, holding the door open. "I've met Mr. Lawless. Nice man. I'll have to keep that in mind. Have a great day and thanks again."

As Mr. and Mrs. O'Neill squabbled, Simon leaned down and dropped the contents of his aching arms onto the counter. In mid-sentence, with his index finger extended towards his wife, Mr. O'Neill turned to Simon and then looked down at the counter.

"Oh no!" Mr. O'Neill protested. "I'm afraid not, Simon."

"What?" Simon replied, confused.

"You've been cut off from the school charge account," Mr. O'Neill said steadfastly.

"Cut off?" Simon repeated.

"That's right," Mr. O'Neill replied. "The school board notified us this morning. So, unless you plan on paying for this stuff out of your own pocket..."

"Oh, Bill," Judy said, rolling her eyes. "You can't even talk to him when he gets like this."

"Don't 'oh, Bill' me," Mr. O'Neill said to his wife with his face turning three shades of purple, "this ain't some kind of charity that we're running here. If we're not careful, pretty soon we'll be the charity."

Judy looked at Simon and shrugged apologetically.

"Sorry, Honey," she said, regretfully.

Simon left the couple arguing and made his way outside to the sidewalk. Dejected, he looked to his right at the old school. He knew that there wasn't any way he could get the false ceiling back up without the hardware, but he also didn't feel like talking to Mr. Cross right now either. He took a deep sigh and looked at Miss Harold's darkened Trophy Shop across the street. Then he looked to his left at the lonely voter registration table where Hannah Grace sat crocheting.

Feeling hopelessly defeated, Simon opted for the company of friends. Taking a deep breath, he made his way across the street to the tavern. Maybe it was time to completely confide in Rich.

"Well, look what the cat dragged in," Joey said from his perch on a bar stool, clutching an ice cold beer. George peaked over his shoulder to get a glimpse, while Rich looked up from counting out fist full of dollars.

"Dude, we thought that you'd completely vanished," Rob said. "Where have you been? Rich is not happy with you at all."

"Something came up and I...something came up," Simon answered.

"You look terrible, by the way," Joey said, pulling out a stool for Simon to sit down on.

By eleven o'clock in the morning, the tavern was already beginning to fill up with the lunch crowd.

"Thanks," Simon replied, catching a glimpse of himself in the mirror behind the bar. He looked down at the empty beer bottles in front of George, Rob, and Joey. "It's not even noon."

"Yeah, we had a rough one last night," Joey replied with a smile.

"A little hair of dog," Rob quipped as he lifted the mug and grinned.

"Oh, it was wild last night," George said, "wait till you hear this story. We went out to Jack's and..."

Before he could continue, Rich walked over and stood in front of them to fill an empty basket with pretzels.

"Hey, man," Simon said sheepishly, but there was no response just a hard, icy stare as Rich moved around the bar to the other baskets.

"Dude, he's *not* happy," Joey said, "and thanks, by the way, for leaving me hanging last night. They had to pull Ray Stoltz out of the stands to do the bases.

It was horrible. The guy had no understanding of the rulebook. I don't know if he ever even played the game a day in his life."

Simon hardly acknowledged Joey as he got out of his seat and made his way over to Rich at the other end of the bar.

"Look, I'm sorry for putting you in a bad spot last night," Simon said, "but something came up."

"I'll say you put me in a bad spot," Rich snapped, "Stoltz blew two calls at second base that cost us the game!"

In the face of all that he had been through the past couple of days, Simon found it difficult to even feign sympathy about the game. However, he was acutely aware that he had let his friend down.

"What can I say?" Simon replied, "I'm sorry, man. But, it couldn't be helped. There was something that I had to deal with."

"Well, where were you..." Rich started to say as he turned and faced Simon. Seeing the worn appearance and empty expression of his old friend, he asked, "Dude, are you okay? Are you sick or something?"

"I don't know, maybe," Simon said flatly, referring more to his mental health.

"Well, are you gonna be able to do the game tomorrow night?" Rich asked still failing to understand the gravity of the situation. "It's a big game, Helrigle's Yankees vs Livingood's Angels for the first place in the standings. The winner will be in the driver's seat for the pennant."

"Yeah, I can do it after all I need the money," Simon said. Again, he felt the weight of the world on his shoulders. "Can I talk to you in private for a minute?" he asked, as all of the emotions that he had been suppressing finally rose to the surface.

"Sure, give me a sec," Rich said, a little concerned. "Joey! Take over behind the bar. We'll be in the storage room if you need me. And no freebees!"

Joey gave a thumbs up as he slid off of his stool. The two guys made their way to the storage room. Rich shut the door behind him and pulled up a CO2 canister of Coke to sit on. He motioned for Simon to sit down before folding his arms like some kind of giant genie. Simon looked around for a place to sit, before lowering himself down onto a stack of empty pallets. They awkwardly sat in silence for a minute as Simon debated how much he was willing to risk sharing with his long time friend.

"So?" Rich asked. "I've only got a couple of minutes. I can't trust Joey running the tap for too long."

"I don't even know where to start," Simon confided as he rubbed the tops of his thighs.

"I think I know what this is all about," Rich said, leaning down with his hands on his knees.

"You do?" Simon asked through swollen, bloodshot eyes. "No, I don't think so."

"Yeah, I think so," Rich countered. "I can see it written on your face. Come on, I mean I'm a bartender for crying out loud. It's a girl. It's Hope. Am I right? I'm right. Right?"

"Yeah, kinda," Simon admitted. "But, there's more to it than that, I…"

"They just rip your heart out," Rich said, reaching over and rubbing Simon's head. "I know man. Rachel and I dated all through junior high and high school. Then one day she says, 'I used to think that you loved sports more than you loved me, and that used to hurt, but now I know that's only because you love yourself more than you love anything else.'

"What does that even mean?" he asked, his voice trailing off as he stared at the concrete floor.

"I don't know, but like I was saying," Simon continued. "I think I'm going out of my mind."

"Chicks do that to you," Rich said, coming to life. "I remember after Rachel…"

Determined to get Rich's attentions, Simon blurted out, "I've been seeing Adam Potter's ghost in the school."

"What?" Rich said, standing up. There was a long pause as Rich stared at Simon. A smirk came across his face at first, but then quickly faded as he realized that Simon was not joking. "Ah, man, you've got to be kidding me! Come on!"

"Just hear me out," Simon pleaded. "Sit down. I've debated whether or not I should even tell anyone any of this, but I have to. I have to talk to someone."

Reluctantly, Rich sat back down, looking at his watch. "You've got ten minutes."

Simon started at the beginning and told Rich as much as he could about the events that had transpired since arriving in Bethel. But, due to the time constraints, his thoughts were disjointed and loosely connected, and he feared that he was not doing justice to the gravity of the situation in his hurried account.

Rich's expression of skepticism did not change. His chin was lifted and he looked down at Simon through sullen, haughty eyes.

"…And that's the reason why I thought God brought me back to Bethel to end the curse," Simon finished, letting out a gush of air. He had talked a hundred miles an hour trying to get everything in, and now there was dead silence. In the retelling of the story, Simon poured out his heart, recounting the very depths of his despair, the lost opportunity in New Jersey, the death of a new friend, the rejection of Hope, and the question of his sanity.

Just as Rich finally began to speak, the door opened and Joey peaked around the corner.

"What are you guys doing?" Joey asked. "There's like a hundred people out there."

"I'll be right there," Rich said coldly as he got up. "I've gotta get out there. We'll talk later." Then just as he started to close the door behind him, Rich turned around.

Simon looked up at his old friend in great anticipation.

"But, you are definitely going to be able to umpire the game tomorrow night, right?"

Simon nodded.

"That's good," Rich said. "Oh, hey, feel free to stay in here as long as you need to get yourself together."

Something in Rich's expression, or the tone of his voice, clearly indicated that he either did not or could not believe what Simon was saying.

For a moment, Simon sat alone, disillusioned and dejected. Then, something quite unexpected happened. Instead of delivering yet another blow to his already tender psyche, the conversation had quite a diametrically opposite effect. It made Simon angry.

Rich's look of skepticism and air of superiority only served to fuel his desire to defend what he had experienced. He was tired of apologizing for an undeniable truth that he no longer would oppose just because life would be easier if he hadn't. That truth, like a thorn deep in his flesh, had mercilessly gnawed away at him, and the more he worked at removing it the deeper it dug in. Now, it was so deeply embedded that any attempt to eradicate it from his consciousness would completely tear down the infrastructure on which he had built his understanding of reality itself. To dismiss this one experience because it wasn't socially acceptable or politically correct would compromise the integrity of all other experiences. Simon took what should have been a mortal blow to his ego and turned on it like a Greco-Roman wrestler.

Instead of spending all of his time, energy, and emotion trying to deny what he saw, heard, and felt, Simon decided to open up his mind to a whole new realm of possibilities. No longer would he be embarrassed or ashamed of his position. Form that time on, he would own it.

Maybe there were ghosts and curses after all! Maybe there always had been, and he had merely been blinded to that truth until now. Maybe it was like some kind of fourth dimension or something, that he had only now been privileged to see. At its core the seemingly benign paradigm shift only slightly altered the plumb line of his fundamental system of beliefs. But once extrapolated out to how he would process and evaluate all of his other experiences moving forward, it shattered previously impenetrable walls built with wheat-less bricks, destroying all preconceived notions of right and wrong.

To have all such boundaries dismantled is a very liberating and at the same time a tenuous proposition. What had been previously outside the realm of possibility was now possible. With his current state of mind, all bets were off. Everything he had once accepted as fact was now in question, and all of his fundamental beliefs were now negotiable. And for that reason, Simon would soon discover that he was capable of doing what was previously unimaginable. For now, that highly combustible power of doubt lay dormant just beneath the surface undetected and waiting to be ignited.

Without knowing exactly what to do about it, Simon opted for the modern day antidote for inactivity and boredom, escapism. Before the night was over, however, he would discover yet another kind of freedom. It was the kind precipitated from hitting rock bottom. For there is nothing else a person can lose once they've completely lost it.

20

DID HE REALLY SAY?

Joey threw back the shot without so much as wincing. The guys at the bar gave out a mighty roar as a fist full of singles changed hands. Simon, for once, had fortune fall his way. The uproar temporarily drew the disapproving glare of the tail end of the lunchtime crowd. And Rich was none too pleased that his previous warnings had gone unheeded. George, Simon, Rob, Joey, and Will were simply having too much fun to listen or care. Joey and George were perpetually celebrating being college students on summer break, while Rob was taking time out from the drudgery that was selling whole life insurance. Regretfully, Will, having only been on a lunch break, was unable to partake. Nonetheless, he was gratified enough by witnessing the free fall of his young friends into a midweek, early afternoon stupor. The rest of the patrons, however, were less than enthusiastic about the gross display of overindulgence.

Especially repulsive to the casual observer was the young man with unshaven face and disheveled hair that had not once but twice spilled the contents of his gin and tonic all over himself. The combination of a lack of sleep and an empty stomach would soon prove to be a recipe for disaster for Simon.

For the time being, he was still enough in charge of his faculties to diffuse Rich's fury. Just as the burly bartender was about to bounce the unruly bunch from the premises, Simon cleverly requested a list of fantasy league rosters and the official forms to post a trade. The strategic ploy worked masterfully. Completely disarmed by the newfound interest in the all but defunct fantasy league, the commissioner happily scrambled to the office in the back of the tavern to retrieve the documents.

Simon slapped half of his winnings onto the counter and sequestered the sports page from the end of the bar. Scouring the box scores, he was determined to change the entire DNA of his fantasy team.

This very much pleased Rich whose demeanor changed almost instantaneously. Even though the lunch crowd was still demanding a great deal of attention, he still somehow managed to oversee several landmark trades. In a matter of minutes, the inebriated team owners had made more fictitious trades than the previous three

365

months of the season combined. The brawny bartender was so happy that he failed to recognize the increasing volume and deteriorating speech of his intoxicated friends. And if there was one voice rising above the rest, it was Simon's whose senses were also in rapid decline. After one more round of shots of Jaegermeister, Simon made the irreversible transformation from innocuous to obnoxious. As his filter deteriorated so too did his vernacular which in turn gave rise to an unprecedented volume of vulgarity. At that precise moment, Rocky stepped out of the summer heat followed by his father and two other prominent farmers. They stood basking for a moment in the air conditioning while waiting to be seated.

"Oh great," Rob said, cursing, "here comes the Pope."

"What?" Simon asked as he spun around in his stool. When he saw Rocky, he slid off of his seat and stumbled towards the front door. "*Rocky*! Hey, what's goin' on brotha'?"

"Simon?" Rocky said horrified as he rebuffed a hug.

"So this is the guy who convinced you that you needed to be 'born again', huh?" Kurt Land asked sardonically, shaking his head.

Rocky was mortified.

"Tha's right, sir, and who, whom, who…and ha! Who you be?" Simon said, laughing, with his hand extended.

"Figures," Kurt Land said, ignoring the gesture before heading off to a vacant booth.

"Simon, what are you *doing*?" Rocky asked with a pained expression. "You're wasted."

"Daz righ', and soon you will be too my friend," Simon said, trying to put his arm around Rocky's shoulder. "Come on over here." Simon tried to lead the way, but Rocky would have none of it.

"No thanks," Rocky said, struggling to free himself from Simon's hand. He was bewildered by Simon's hypocritical behavior. "We just came in to grab some lunch."

"Ya sure?" Simon slurred.

"Yeah, I'm sure," Rocky replied. He was disgusted with Simon but even more so with himself. "I'd better go join my dad. I don't want him waiting for me to order. I'll see ya later."

"Suit yourself," Simon managed to say before stumbling back to the bar.

As Rocky slid into the booth, his father started in, "So, he's the do-gooder who spearheaded the painting of the school? The one that's three sheets to the wind?"

"Yeah," Rocky admitted, staring far off into his glass of water while absentmindedly stirring its icy contents.

"I suppose he's drunk on the spirit then?" Kurt Land said, precipitating a bellow of laughter from his contemporaries. "Rocky, it never ceases to amaze me how you seem to gravitate towards these nut-jobs. I hope you see what a waste of time all of that nonsense was."

"A bunch of people helped out with the school," Rocky said, halfheartedly trying to defend Simon's efforts.

"What did the paper say?" Kurt Land asked. "There were maybe seventy-five to one hundred people who showed up? I realize you're no math whiz son, but there's a thousand people in Bethel, most of whom make their living off of the land. There's no way they're going to vote to pay more taxes for a new school building when most of them don't even have kids there anymore."

Predictably, Kurt Land was only able to see the worst in his son, even when he was trying to do his best. Rocky wanted to melt into his seat. His father had the uncanny ability to make him feel as small and insignificant as any human being who had ever walked the planet.

As the conversation amongst the three farmers shifted to cursing the weather and bemoaning the decline in the value of pork bellies, Rocky scowled at his father out of the corners of his eyes. It was an odd relationship. He recognized that his father provided for him in so much as he gave him food, shelter, water, basic health care, a cell phone, and digital cable. And as Kurt Land's only son, Rocky would never have to go out and earn it for himself. It would all be provided for him. In return, Kurt Land only demanded respect while reserving the right of control. Rocky was loyal to his father due to his daddy's welfare-like provision. And his father loved and supported Rocky when it was convenient or when it was useful for achieving his political ambitions in the community. Otherwise, Kurt Land tolerated Rocky's strange antics and odd behavior as long as his son did what he was told and somehow managed to not embarrass him. Under the present dynamic, Rocky would be forever indebted to his father. He accepted it as his lot in life, even though he secretly stewed and festered for not having more than he was given.

Rocky had never fully examined the true nature of the relationship because it was all he had ever known. Instead, he worked tirelessly to gain the acceptance of his indifferent father while at the same time trying to discover his own identity. It never occurred to him that the two endeavors diametrically opposed one another. Rocky was blinded by the fear that all of the luxuries that his father perpetually dangled in front of him. That included his inheritance which might be taken away at a moment's notice. And maybe that was because Kurt Land always reminded him of that fact. The ever-present threat suspended Rocky just above the threshold of true fulfillment his entire life, leaving him just happy enough so as to be mostly miserable. Love contrived by acts and a sense of obligation is a bottomless well that leaves the soul thirsting for reciprocity. He was fettered by invisible chains and complicit in his subjugation. And so, day after day, Rocky went to work unscrupulously sowing weeds among the wheat only to turn around and charge the farmers to spray the very same weeds he had himself sown under the cover of darkness.

The Christianity that Simon offered was supposed to be different. Rocky thought that it would bring him all of the joy, and wealth, and prosperity his father only promised. For years, Rocky had slipped on personas like costumes in a novelty store, trying to fill a great hopelessness deep inside of him. The Christianity that had yet to fully take root was supposed to be the cure. The change was supposed to be on the inside rather than the outside. It was supposed to be real this time, but as he watched Simon slip off of his stool laughing uncontrollably while letting out a smattering of blasphemies, Rocky came to the conclusion that being a Christian was just another empty façade. Disenchanted and once again adrift, Rocky quickly dismissed himself a place at the table.

"Where you going, son?" Kurt Land asked, "I thought you were going to bless the meal," he added sarcastically before giving the sign of the cross. The other two farmers were beside themselves with laughter as Rocky stomped off towards the bar.

A Victoria Secret ad came on the LCD at the bar, prompting Simon to begin regaling his tale of his night with Jez. Even Rich, who had been overlooking Simon's unbecoming rhetoric, looked up from the new team rosters and raised his eyebrow with a pained expression. Just as Simon was about to get to the juicy part, Rocky reached over his shoulder and slammed his necklace onto the bar.

"Whoa!" Simon exclaimed with an over exaggerated laugh. "Hey! What's this?"

"You can keep it!" Rocky snarled through gritted teeth. "I won't be needing it any more."

"What the...?" Simon stammered, trying his best to process what had just happened, but Rocky was already making his way to the door of the tavern. Simon picked up the necklace with the cross hanging just beneath his clenched fist. "Rocky! Hold up. What's going on, man?"

The rest of the fellas at the bar looked on with delight.

Rocky stopped at the door, turned, and walked back a few steps towards Simon.

"You really had me buying it!" he snapped, his eyes beginning to well up. "I've been preaching to my old man all week about repentance, and purpose, and prosperity...and how we need to pass the referendum. Well, I've got news for you. None of it matters. I was an idiot to believe in you."

Then he turned abruptly and headed out the door. The entire tavern was by now completely silent waiting to see if any more drama might unfold. Disappointed, they returned to their idle, empty chit-chat.

"What?" Simon said still trying to comprehend what was happening. "Believe in me? I never said you needed to believe in *me*. I said you needed to believe in Him. I said to believe in Jesus!"

When Simon tried to follow in pursuit of his disgruntled friend, he wobbled and nearly fell to the ground before Rob caught him by the arm.

"Whoa!" Joey said to George while clapping. "Looks like someone has finally seen the light!"

"Dude, shut up," Rich said from behind the bar.

"What are you talking about?" Simon asked. The room was spinning and everything was coming in and out of focus.

"I'm talking about Rocky breaking free of the blinders that he's had on his entire life," Joey said proudly.

"What? You did this?" Simon said accusingly.

"No, no, no, my friend," Joey said smugly. "*I* didn't have to do anything."

Simon looked at George who immediately looked down at his bottle of beer, so that he wouldn't have to look him in the eye.

"All right, that's it," Rob said, tossing a few dollars on the bar. "I'm out of here. Too much drama for me."

"Yeah, I've got to get back to work," Will muttered before sliding off of his stool and following Rob out the door.

"What's that supposed to mean?..." Simon asked, perturbed. "...'I didn't have to do a thing'?"

"It means you're a hypocrite," Joey said smugly. "It means your words and your actions belie your beliefs. Haven't you read, 'A perverse tongue will be chopped off,' or 'You have heard that it was said, do not lust', or …'do not give in to drunkenness'…No?

"That's typical, most Christians don't know what's actually in the Bible. Thanks to your little display here today, Rocky was finally able to see right through you. And thanks to you he sees right through the whole Jesus myth too. Really, he should thank you. Now he can be free to move on and experience all of the richness that life has to offer."

"But, Jesus *is* real," Simon said with a look of consternation. "He's not some myth."

"Simon, he's no more real than Jessie Joseph, and the little ghosts you've been seeing at the school," Joey mocked, before he and George burst into laughter.

Simon's mouth dropped open as he looked at Rich, dumbfounded by his best friend's betrayal.

Rich shot Joey a dirty look, but didn't bother denying the impropriety. Instead, he just went back to washing glasses at the sink behind the bar.

"Oh, don't feel bad, lots of people have fallen for it," Joey said with an air of superiority, while George nodded in agreement. "It's not to be taken literally! It's a *legend*." He said in a condescending tone as if talking to a 5-year-old. "You create this impossible standard that no man can actually follow. You go around acting as if you have some kind of monopoly on truth. You tell everyone else that they're wrong and you're right, which by the way, I have news for you…there is no absolute truth…and then you proceed to break all of the rules that you yourself set forth in the first place. It's complete lunacy!"

"It's not about rules, it's about a…" Simon started to say.

"… a warm and fuzzy relationship," Joey finished holding up quotation marks.

"Yeah, yeah, yeah, I know, I know. How convenient. It gives you a really nice out for breaking the rules. No worries. Just go to church, ask for forgiveness, and wipe the slate clean; break the rules again and around and around we go. Think about it, Simon, 'Die unto yourself', 'Be born again,' do you really think we are literally to be born again? I mean, how is that even possible? How can a man be born again? Think about it, it's not to be taken literally. It's just one of many legends and folktales from ancient times to explain the Great Common Consciousness. Just like the American Indians, the Greeks, the Hindus, I could go on and on."

"Bu-bu-but…" Simon stuttered.

"'Bu-bu-bu'," Joey mimicked, "that's all you Christians have to say when faced with the truth."

"But, you have to have faith," Simon said almost in a whisper under his inebriated breath.

Joey nearly spit out his beer. "Faith!" Joey laughed. "Faith is awfully convenient isn't it? It's a fail safe for any question Christians can't answer. That's *why* legends are made in the first place. To explain the unexplainable. Go on, give me another." He extended his arm and motioned with his fingers.

Simon had nothing more to say. He just stood there completely stripped of any shred of dignity.

"Come here," Joey said while beckoning him with his index finger. "I know it's difficult at first to wrap your head around. It's tough when all you were exposed to growing up was going to church. Don't feel bad. I was the same way. Actually, it was Jack who first showed me the light. So, I can't take the credit for what I'm about to tell you. But, it is worth its weight in gold." Joey draped his arm over Simon's shoulder and spoke into his ear. "Once you comprehend this fact, it will change your life forever. There is no such thing as right and wrong! There is only the experience. Think of it. It will completely free you to tap into this world and everything that it has to offer; because the earth and everything in it *is* god, and that includes you and me."

"And that's why we have to protect it, 'go green' all that, you know," George said with a wink, bringing a Bud Light bottle up to his lips.

"Please, I'm talking here," Joey retorted, "the only absolute truth therefore is that there is no absolute truth. As our own gods, we all have our own truths based on our own individual experiences. Therefore, there is no self-deprecation, only empowerment, so it's completely contrary to your worldview. It is a totally wimpy worldview based completely on feeling guilty and making yourself lower than everyone else. Rise up, man! Go! Live!"

"So when you guys go out and do your good deeds, like painting the school to honor Jeremy's life, it's just about the experience for yourselves?" Simon dared to ask, trying to grasp what Joey was sharing.

"Do, not do," Joey said shrugging his shoulders. "What difference does it make?"

"Hey, you sound like Yoda," George said with a laugh.

Joey continued on, ignoring his young protégé, "It's just one more experience, a step closer to knowing what you refer to as God. And as far as Jeremy goes, who knows? Maybe he had more experiences than I ever gave him credit for. Probably not. But it doesn't matter because when we die we will all be swallowed up into the Great Common Consciousness anyway. There is no judgment, no Hades. And then we will all know everything, and nothing in this world will have mattered anyway."

When he finished his grand soliloquy, he beamed with pride at Simon as if he had just freed him from a prison of limitations to a world of infinite possibility.

But Simon was filled with great despair and felt sick to his stomach as he remembered everything he had said and done to turn Rocky away from God. He thought of his language and drinking, and he thought of his retelling the story about his night with Jez. Then he turned and looked at all of the patrons who had witnessed his depravity.

Abruptly, Simon struggled to free himself from Joey's arm and stumbled for the door as if suffocating. Once outside on the sidewalk, he made his way over to a tree lining the street. He reached out a hand and leaned against its trunk, gasping for air. After a moment, he looked up to the top of the grain elevator and was overcome with a desperate need to talk to Hope. He reached for his phone, but it was not in his pocket. It was still sitting on the stairs in the school.

Simon made his way to the school building and raced up the stairs to find the phone where he had set it down. After many unsuccessful attempts to reach Hope, Simon collapsed for a period of time in the chair in the chorus room. Still heavily intoxicated, Simon was roused from his deep slumber by a loud noise.

Suddenly, there was a flash out the corner of his waking eye, and he heard the slapping sound of tiny footsteps making their way down a flight of stairs. With his reaction time, slowed by his condition, Simon spun wildly around to catch only a glimpse of a small, shoeless foot making the turn on the next landing that led to the basement.

Before Simon could even process what he was doing, he charged after the shadowy figure with rabid determination. Unexpectedly, a wrath enveloped him. He tore after what he supposed to be Adam Potter. Not merely a ghost but an actual person. For the boy wasn't like a ghost or some sort of specter, it was far too real. Now he ran down the basement stairs in hot pursuit of the only tangible thing that could fully substantiate his claims and verify his sanity. Still heavily intoxicated, everything seemed to move in distorted, slow motion. The hollow echo of his own shoes against the stairs sounded muffled as if from a distant cave.

Spastically, he descended the last set of stairs and flung himself down onto the cool, concrete floor of the basement. Jerking his head around wildly from one side to the other, his eyes searched the long shadows of the room for any sign of movement. He stood motionless holding his breath. Nothing. With his pulse pounding in his ears, he tiptoed his way around the monstrous boiler. Like a lion hunting a jackal, he jumped around to the back of it, certain that he would find his prey lurking in the corner, but there was nothing there. Even more baffling was the strange little square door that led to the darkened, narrow corridor. It had been padlocked from the inside, making it impossible for anyone to have used it as an escape route.

Certain that the child had to still be somewhere in the basement, Simon examined every crack and crevice but still found nothing. Crazed from his futility, Simon clenched his fists and gave out a wild, bloodcurdling yell. Since coming to Bethel, he had lost everything. Rightfully, he attributed all of his pain and suffering to the impalpable legend and undeniable curse. Somehow even losing the job in Jersey felt linked to his misadventures in this forsaken town.

Now the one thing that could have exonerated him to Joey, Rocky, Rich, and even Hope had slipped through his fingers. But how? Where could have it gone? Out of frustration, Simon turned and kicked a plastic jack-o-lantern from the Halloween decorations. It ricocheted off of the wall and into the Nativity scene, striking one of the legs of the manger. The blow knocked it to the ground, spilling its contents. Simon stood up and took notice. There was straw and a blanket, but no baby Jesus.

Even ghosts couldn't carry things off. This he was fairly sure of. Simon looked over at the grinning, gap-toothed jack-o'-lantern resting beside an old, rusty shovel and wrongly interpreted it as an omen. With his judgment still clouded from the excess of spirits, an outrageous thought came to him. As Simon deeply heaved liquor-tainted breaths, it occurred to him again that Adam Potter might not be a ghost after all. Maybe Adam Potter was alive and well. Not alive in the same sense that a human was alive, but alive nonetheless.

And the highly combustible powder keg that had been simmering just beneath the surface suddenly ignited. What had once seemed impossible was now possible, what was unfathomable, fathomable. Simon grabbed the shovel and headed for the car not realizing that he was in search of the wrong grave.

* * *

Like a divining rod, the handle of the shovel pointed the way through the dense thicket down by the creek on Clay Potter's property to the abandoned graveyard. In no time, Simon was standing on the cusp of the dilapidated iron fence outlining the old, abandoned plot. Long shadows blanketed the crumbling stones wrought in moss as the sun began its descent in the West. The undergrowth was thicker than he had remembered from the first night that he and Jeremy had stumbled upon it. Somehow being at the gravesite while contemplating what he was about to undertake sobered him up a little. He glanced over his shoulder, searching the dark depths of the woods for any sign of life. There was something almost palpable in the air, like a presence. He couldn't quite put a finger on it, but it felt as though he was being watched.

Resolute nonetheless, Simon crawled over the half-fallen, ornamented fence and made his way over to Adam Potter's gravestone. With great conviction, he drove the spade of the shovel into the unforgiving ground. The overgrown weeds made it more difficult to dig than he had expected. Simon grunted as he drove his foot onto the top of the rusted spade while wriggling it back and forth. After no more than a half of an hour, he was standing knee deep in a sizable hole. His hands burned with fresh blisters and his back ached under the strain of moving heaps of earth. He poured out all of his anger and frustration into the endeavor. Beads of sweat dripped from the end of his nose, landing on the wooden handle. Breathing hard, he leaned against the shovel momentarily to wipe his forehead with the back of his hand. In doing so, streaks of mud smudged his furrowed brow.

When he took a moment to regain his breath, the strange feeling of being watched came over him once again. This time it was even more penetrating than before. Simon looked about him, turning his head to one side and then the other.

Frantically, he called out, "Who's there?"

But nothing stirred in the thick brush. There was only the sound of the breeze blowing through the leaves in the trees and the thumping of his heart in his chest. After comforting himself that it was merely his own imagination, Simon took to the task again, this time with even more fervor.

With each new shovel full of dirt, Simon acted like a man possessed. What had begun as a crusade to prove himself had morphed into something far more important. His own sanity was on the line. As he dug, he brooded over the past and all of the events that had led up to this moment. Without provocation, he unexpectedly thought of the dilapidated, white house where he was raised and the father who abandoned him.

It was then that the tip of the shovel struck something, making a hollow, wooden sound. Simon stopped for a moment, looking intensely through wild eyes. Quickly, he worked to free the small casket from the ground. In mere minutes, he discovered that it was not unlike the one he had found in the storage room of the basement at the school. Simon fell to his knees and began to wipe the rest of the dirt away from the lid with his filthy, shaking hands.

After a great deal of struggle, he hoisted the coffin from the deep hole and laid it on the ground next to the mound of unearthed dirt. Simon jumped out of the gravesite and readied himself for opening the lid. Once more, he looked wildly around, rubbing his hands on the top of his thighs. Steadfast, he reached down and timidly pulled the lid open. Jutting his neck out to one side, he looked out of the corner of his terrified eyes to see what was inside. With a gasp, the lid flopped to the ground. Simon slowly stood up while he hungrily inspected every inch of the contents of the coffin.

It appeared to be the decaying bones of a small child. If indeed this was Adam

Potter's remains, it defied Rob's version of the legend and the curse. Simon was vexed. The evidence completely contradicted his hypothesis. He had been so sure that he would find an empty tomb.

Simon cursed and spun around in a circle several times in a rage. How could it be? There was nothing there that gave any credence to his supposition. The only theory it substantiated was that he was definitely losing his mind. Infuriated, he replaced the lid on the coffin, lifted it off of the ground, and unceremoniously dropped it back into the hole. Angrily, he kicked the large pile of dirt back on top of the coffin. In only a matter of minutes, he had managed to fill a large portion of the hole.

Fueled by his intense disappointment, he now turned to Jessie Joseph's headstone. Like a raving lunatic, he took the shovel and retrieved large deposits of dirt from out of the ground. Simon dug and dug with reckless abandon. The deeper he dug the more he began to unearth the source of his feelings of inadequacy and inferiority. They were both buried in the same dark chamber of his heart that bore the memories of the last time he saw his father. Next, he thought of the pink house, and the white picket fence, and the happy family that now resided there.

"That was supposed to be my house, and my yard, and my tire swing!" Simon yelled out, no longer caring if anyone was watching or not. "Why did you leave us? Why didn't you ever write or call? Was I not good enough for you? Didn't you love me?" With each question Simon yelled louder and louder as his voice echoed through the dense woods.

Finally, he struck the top of something hard. With an orange flame of fire setting just over the tree line against the backdrop of a purple hue sky, Simon freed the top of a pine box. It was not as much a coffin this time as it was a rectangular shipping crate.

Wearily, Simon once agin dropped to his knees to wipe the surface clean of excess dirt and debris. Jessie's coffin wasn't buried as deeply as Adam's, but it was much larger than the first. Instead of struggling to pull it from the ground, Simon stepped out of the gravesite, turned, fell to his stomach, and reached for the lid. By now, the hold of alcohol had begun to dissipate. Covered in sweat and dirt, Simon labored to take a deep breath as he worked it open.

Suddenly, he heard something quickly moving through the brush in the woods behind him. Terrified, Simon jumped to his feet and spun around. Daring not to breathe, he listened carefully while his eyes danced, searching the shadows. Whatever it was sounded like it was alarmingly close by. Simon could sense the presence of something or someone just beyond the closest row of trees. Cautiously, he slowly bent down to pick up the rusty shovel.

He stood up and boldly called out, "Who's there? I know you're out there. Come on out!"

Nothing. It was completely silent. The sudden rush of adrenaline had a real sobering affect and now the gravity of his actions began to set in. After what seemed like an eternity, he turned again to the pine box. With less certainty this time, he fell again to his stomach and reached out for the cover. He could feel the rough texture of the wood as he worked the lid free. Simon's heartbeat pounded in his ears as his eyes fell upon the decomposed body that had been dressed in a dark, aged suit. Somehow the skeleton of Jessie Joseph did not horrify him as he thought it might. Instead, he blankly stared into the face of what he perceived to be the source of his suffering. After examining the corpse closer, he found no evidence to support a death by hanging. The neck did not appear to have been broken or otherwise compromised.

What Simon had discovered at the graveyard was disheartening. It didn't fully support the legend as told by his friends, but it didn't completely refute it either. He was more confused than ever. Simon was no closer to unlocking truth about the curse than when he started digging. While under the influence, Simon was almost certain he was going to find Adam's casket empty and some evidence of a snapped neck from Jessie's tired old bones. Now, almost completely sober, he simply felt sickened and ashamed. Sitting in the dark amongst the desecrated graves, Simon began to sob uncontrollably, before emitting a shrill, almost inhuman cry.

* * *

Off in the distance on the opposite side of the creek, Sharon practically jumped into Mike's lap while desperately clutching his shirt.

"What in the world was that?" Sharon asked with a look of terror on her face.

Even though Mike was equally terrified, he couldn't let it show. At eighteen years of age, he was supposed to be a man. And men weren't supposed to be afraid of anything.

"See, what'd I tell you!" Mike said, noticeably shaken. "That's what people say. If you come here late at night, you can hear the screams of the boys and girls who were drowned by Jessie Joseph in the creek."

More than being afraid, however, he was even exhilarated by being in such close proximity to his young girlfriend who clung to him tightly for protection. She was so close that he could feel the pounding of her heart in her chest.

"What was it for real?" Sharon asked, with a nervous laugh. Her eyes were darting all about the small car into the dark recesses of the trees lining the creek.

"I'm telling you," Mike replied, looking down into Sharon's soft blue eyes, "it's the cry of the eleven victims of Jessie Joseph."

"No," Sharon whispered, making a futile attempt to comfort herself. "It's probably just some kind of wounded animal or something."

"Then what was it we heard before that?" Mike asked, trying to fan the flames of her fear. "You have to admit that those first cries sounded like someone yelling."

It was all working just as Sean had suggested. The more frightened the girl, the closer she got. It was all going according to plan, except for the fact that they both had actually heard something very unsettling.

Sharon looked up into Mike's handsome face. Their lips were merely inches apart. This was the moment. Mike had to risk possible rejection and embarrassment. If he was going to make a move, it had to be now.

Mike was not about to let his window of opportunity pass him by. He leaned in slowly and closed his eyes. In an instant, he realized that Sharon was not backing away. Their lips touched as a shot of electricity coursed through Sharon's entire body, making her quickly forget her fears and inhibitions.

In a span of only ten minutes, the windows of the tiny car were completely fogged up. The two teenagers were being swept away by all of the sights and sounds and touching and caressing. As they fumbled awkwardly in the dark, a large shadowy figure stealthily approached the car.

The two young lovers were completely blinded as to the extent of their vulnerability when a massive figure violently yanked open the passenger door. Sharon screamed as Mike was dragged from the car like a rag doll.

* * *

By the time Simon reached his driveway, it was nearly midnight. A half-moon was ascending in the East just above the line of trees as he made his way to the stairs that led up to his apartment. He was completely exhausted. It took far longer to cover the plots than he had expected. Somehow there was a lot more dirt that came out of those two holes than he could ever put back in. It was a hard but necessary lesson to learn that once some things are dragged out into the light of day they cannot be put back no matter how hard a person tries. It's a fact that Simon was too tired to contemplate at the moment. And so, the two burial sites that crested with fresh dirt were witness to the exhumation. There was no denying the disturbance of the dead's repose. And it wouldn't be long before the entire town would wildly speculate about what it all meant, especially in light of Jeremy's horrific murder and the legend.

Simon wasn't thinking about the repercussions of his actions at the moment. With the undesirous effects of a hangover beginning to take hold, he only longed for a bottle of water, a couple of Tylenol, and the comfort of his bed. He was filthy, covered from head to toe in dirt, from his smudged face to his besmirched soul. As his first step hit the bottom stair leading up to his apartment, Simon felt the heavy weight of despair and hopelessness dragging down his very soul.

Alarmingly, he heard the distinctive strike of a match and turned to see the soft glow of a flickering, counterfeit light. The dark figure sitting in one of the lawn chairs in the backyard brought the hot orange glow up to his lips, temporarily eclipsing the flame.

Simon dropped his chin to his chest and dutifully dragged his tired body out to the backyard where he collapsed into the empty lawn chair next to his unannounced visitor. Jack didn't acknowledge his presence or extend an offer for one of the cold beverages dangling from the plastic ring. Instead, the two of them sat silently for a period of time under the canopy of darkness.

It was Jack who spoke first. "Rough night?" he asked indifferently.

Taking into account his awful appearance, Simon hesitated to answer as he considered the implications of Jack's question. "You might say that," he replied, never daring to make eye contact.

"You look like death warmed over," Jack mused before the familiar sound of a sploosh echoed off of the back of the house. "What have you been up to?"

"I've been working on a...a project," Simon answered tiredly. "Did you come to collect the rest of what I owe you? Because, I don't have it."

Ignoring the question, Jack said flippantly, "Ya know, it was a shame about them monkey's gettin' a rash and all."

Simon sat up in his chair, turned toward Jack, and scowled. "What do you know about that?" he asked.

"Oh, my boy, you still don't get it," Jack said with a smirk, "I know everything that goes on around here.

"Crazy business, pharmaceuticals, research, competition, regulation, and the scrutiny of the FDA. An $800 million investment hinges on a few primates getting a little, uh, chapped."

"But, *how* did you know about that?" Simon asked again, looking out the corner of his eye.

"Oh, I have my ways," Jack replied, coyly. Then he added, "Wall Street Journal."

"Oh," Simon said turning back to the expanse of fields lying off in the distance.

"What do *you* know about all of that is the question?" Jack asked pointedly.

"I heard the same thing you did I guess, that the monkeys..." Simon started to say.

"No, no," Jack interrupted, "I mean, have you ever actually asked your godfather what the drug does?"

Simon thought for a moment. It had never occurred to him to ask what it treated. All he had ever bothered to ask was how much money he could make and what kind of benefits he would receive. Embarrassed, Simon had to answer, "No, I can't honestly say that I know what the drug is for."

"It's a 'morning after' type of a pill," Jack said. "Yeah, crazy, state-of-the-art technology. It's like a biological eraser for having any undesired, messy bi-products. Big, big market." For the first time, Jack glanced over at Simon with his steely blue eyes to get a glimpse of his listener's reaction. "I wonder if it could have any other applications. I mean just think of it. It wouldn't matter if what you were doing was right or wrong, because there wouldn't be any repercussions. Be nice wouldn't it, a world without consequences, Ha! A drug like that would sell itself! I'd buy some."

Simon thought of Hope's words the night that he told her about Jez. "I don't think it really matters," Simon replied, "it doesn't sound like the drug is going to make it to market anyway."

"What will you do then if there is no job waiting for you in New Jersey?" Jack asked.

"There will always be other drugs and other opportunities," Simon replied wisely, through a grave voice and bloodshot eyes.

"Speaking of which, have you given any more thought to that position at the bank?" Jack asked, unexpectedly.

Simon jerked his head around surprised. "How did you…" he started to say, before catching himself. "…No, I haven't."

"Shame, it's a great opportunity," Jack replied. "I could put in a good word if you like. I happen to be the chairman of the board of directors at First National."

"First National of Bethel?" Simon asked, uncertain. "Or *the* First National in Manhattan?"

Jack merely raised his eyebrows.

Simon was beginning to understand. "If it's such a great opportunity, why don't you ask Rob or even Joey for that matter?" he asked.

"Ha, ya see? Jack candidly replied. "Rob has one particular skill set while you have another. No, I was wrong to offer you the position at the super store. I can see that now. No, you seem more suited for the world of banking like Lexus, or Wilson B., or even Will."

"You don't give up, do you?" Simon asked, his eyes becoming very heavy.

"'Fraid not," Jack admitted. "Once I get my sights on someone, I just keep coming at them until they cave. More times than not I get my man in the end."

"Do they normally put up a fight?" Simon asked, tracking Jack's insinuation.

"Sometimes, yes, but mostly, no, nowadays" Jack admitted. "Sometimes, it's like Joseph, er uh, Joey Campbell. They jump at the opportunity. While other times it's like Thelma Harold. I've been workin' on that ole gal for years. Stubborn as a mule, that one."

"What makes you think that you could ever get to someone like Miss Harold?" Simon asked.

"Oh, everyone has their price, their 'thing'," Jack responded. "Take your dad for instance…"

Slighted, Simon's face soured as he turned to look at Jack.

"…He was also very stubborn," Jack said. "I had to keep on him and keep on him."

"What was his price, Jack?" Simon asked bitterly.

"Strangely, it ended up being what it is for many men," Jack proudly replied. "It was freedom."

"Freedom?" Simon asked, confused.

"Ha! Not *real* freedom, mind you," Jack scoffed, "freedom of responsibility, freedom to come and go as he pleased, freedom to do whatever he wanted, whenever he wanted," Jack said before taking another drink.

"How did you do it?" Simon asked, trying to mask his pain and anger.

"Well, I started by fueling his discontent," Jack said, whimsically reminiscing. "I merely had to reinforce what he already wanted to hear. Like many discontented men, he wanted to be told that he was being robbed of something that he was entitled to."

"Entitled to?" Simon asked, naively. "Entitled to what?"

"Just entitled, ya know, like he deserved something that he was being denied. I told him he was being cheated out of real happiness due to his responsibilities. I may have even hinted that you and your mom were in the way of all of that," Jack said as though sharing how a magic trick works. "Then I fanned the flames a little when he was tired or frustrated…or drunk. I used those intense feelings to convince him that there was a tremendous void in his life. That he was missing that 'one thing'. After that, it got easier."

"How do you mean that it got easier?" Simon inquired while doing his best to keep his emotions in check.

"Well, at first he was perfectly content with you and your mother and the life you guys had on Washington Street," Jack reflected. "That kept me at bay for quite some time, but once I applied some weariness, a little economic pressure, and accentuated some of the basic miscommunication between husbands and wives. After that he caved. It was textbook really. Just kept whispering in his ear that he wasn't getting his basic carnal needs met. Then I waited for the perfect moment to introduce him to a pretty little thing down at the tavern and wallah!

"You see, he used to try and fill the void in his life with you, your mother, and his career..etc. But, you and I both know that wasn't going to ever do the trick. And so, I eventually was able to convince him that the thing that could make him feel content and happy was actually the thing keeping him from *real* happiness. In the end, he wanted to be free of rules and responsibilities like the burden of taking care of you and your mother. You could say I gave him the freedom to serve himself."

"Well, if he's free to serve himself, at least he's not serving *you*," Simon said, darkly.

"Ha!" Jack laughed. "See. That's why I like you, boy. That's the best part about it, when men serve themselves is when they're actually serving me the most. All I have to do is convince them that life is all about being happy. It's all about entertainment, vacations, money, sex, status, stuff- even retirement for that matter. Anything that inhibits working towards that endeavor is a major stumbling block for filling the emptiness in their lives. In the process, men will do, or say, or believe just about anything to justify what they do. It don't matter how illogical or sinister it is. Brilliant isn't it?"

"So, you deceived him," Simon muttered under his breath.

"What's that?" Jack asked, leaning in a little closer. "Oh yeah, well, here's the thing. If you're not in the right, if you don't have the facts on your side, or the majority on your side, or the authority, then you, uh…do what you have to do to reach your ultimate objective."

"Which is to destroy families," Simon stated, thoroughly disgusted, "by attacking the fathers."

"Oh no, not necessarily," Jack said, hardly able to contain himself. He was practically giddy now. "I'm an equal opportunity 'destroyer'! I show no prejudice when it comes to reaching my ultimate objective. The men are just sometimes easier to break because they don't have that built in maternal instinct. You want to hear something I figured out early in the twentieth Century?

"I started convincing women that they had no value unless they were equal to men in every way. Take for example the earning of money outside the home. Things like that. Ever since then, I've been working on this big worldwide 'unisex' campaign. I…get this…I convince some of the most educated men and women in the world that there's *no difference* between a man and woman. Ha! You would think that would be obvious, right? But, no. They can't figure it out! They're so confused. Amazing. Anyways, it took some time to really take root, but it's really gaining steam. It's just one dimension of a larger initiative to put sex above everything else. Quite effective for destroying families. Then it trickles down to the kids. The whole thing is going great! Couldn't be any happier about it."

Then Jack shot a glance over at Simon. "But, you didn't fall for any of that, did you, my boy?" he asked. "No sir. I needed to take a different approach with you. Most of the time, I am satisfied with men thinking that I don't even exist. I lead them to believe that there's life, and then death, and that's it; so, 'Hey, live it up while you can'. That sort of thing. For most people, the less they know the better. But, no, there's a smaller percent of the population for which the opposite is true. No, I had to show you who I am. I'm convinced of that now."

"How can you possibly benefit from any of that?" Simon asked through clenched teeth.

"Oh, that's an easy one," Jack replied willingly. "I'm selling every vice that a person thinks will make them happy from saturated fat to pornography to everything in between. And when they can't pay for what they bought, I am more than happy to lend it to them until I can collect at an undisclosed, uh, later date. Once they are indebted to me, they become my slaves. I own them, and I become their king."

"But, to what end Jack?" Simon asked almost pleading.

"To what end?" Jack repeated, getting a little agitated.

"Yes, what is your end game?" Simon asked, too tired to mince words.

"Oh, I see what ya mean," Jack said suddenly becoming dark and sullen. "Hate. My end game is hate. Well, hate and death, I guess, if you must know.

"You see, I know *my* fate. I know where I'm goin', but until then, it's all about how many others I can take with me. Cause, truth is, neither you or I or anyone else for that matter *really* know who's goin' where. For all anyone knows, it's a person's own choice. And so, I go after everyone with vengeance as my driving force and bloodshed as my fuel!"

Simon turned from Jack and stared off into the distance, wondering if he should push the envelope. After another minute, Simon boldly asked, "What's mine, Jack?"

"Your what?" Jack repeated, still seething as he meditated on his lot in life.

"My price, my 'one thing'?" Simon asked.

"Fear," Jack said dryly.

"Fear?" Simon responded, "but I'm not afraid of you, Jack."

"Ha! That's what I love about you boy!" Jack replied, the banter suddenly lifting his spirits, "but I didn't say anything about *me*."

Simon was staggered by the assertion. Even so, he was getting so tired that it was difficult to formulate his thoughts or even keep his eyes open. Annoyed by Jack's riddle and wrongly thinking the old man was referring to Simon's recent epiphany about his fear of failure, he decided to change the subject.

"What about Jeremy Warner?" Simon challenged, taking a different tact. "You never got to him."

"Is that how you heard it?" Jack asked.

"No, of course not, they're saying all kinds of terrible things about him," Simon replied, confident in who Jeremy was, "but you and I really know the truth don't we?"

"Jeremiah Warner, yes, that was a shame," Jack acknowledged as he got up from his lawn chair. "He had completely filled his life full of something that I could never take away."

"Maybe, I have that too," Simon countered as his vision was getting more blurry.

"No, when I look at you I see something entirely different," Jack replied, as he walked towards the darkness. "First, there was Jez, then there was the thing with Rocky. Oh, and how ya broke Hope's heart! Not to mention what you done to that poor defenseless opossum the first night you was here. But, tonight, you even surprised *me* with what you are capable of."

"I don't know what you're talking about," Simon defensively muttered. Now he was taking long blinks and rubbing his tired eyes.

"Was the ground hard?" Jack asked, ignoring Simon's question.

"What?" Simon asked, starting to blink uncontrollably.

"What I mean is did you feel a rush when you opened the caskets?" Jack said staring out at the vast expanse before him.

"But how did you...wait...you were the one watching me in the woods!" Simon said accusingly.

"And did you find what you were looking for at the bottom of those graves?"

Jack asked. "What about the smell of death? Will you ever be able to get that scent out of your nostrils or wash the filth from your hands?

"That's what I love about this war, ya know. Anybody can flip sides at any given minute, given the right incentive or circumstances."

Simon's head was cluttered with crazy, random thoughts. Frustrated, he suddenly blurted out, "Why don't you just kill me too like you did Jeremy and get it over with?"

"Ha! That's another reason I like you, boy, always straight and to the point," Jack said with his back still to Simon. He was surveying the endless fields under the umbrella of darkness. "It's true. The harvest *is* plentiful.

"No. You still have great potential. All you have to do is look at Rocky to know that. You're much more valuable to me alive than dead; at least for the time being anyway."

As Simon sank back into his lawn chair, he tried desperately to digest it all. Could this really be happening? Was it some kind of strange dream? Suddenly, he looked back up at Jack Lawless. The dark, shadowy figure gave him a wink and then turned his back to Simon. Without warning, his appearance morphed into that of a enormous red dragon with seven heads and ten horns and seven crowns on its head that flapped his giant wings and launched himself into the night sky.

IN

THE LIFE

"Very truly I tell you,
no one can see the kingdom of God
unless they are born again."

-John 3:3

21

MILLSTONES AROUND THEIR NECKS

By the time Simon woke up from a deep sleep, it was late in the morning. Until now, the peak of the roof on the old house had sheltered him from the intense sun. Simon scrunched up his face and dared to peak out of a squinty, bloodshot eye. For a split second, he had completely forgotten where he was. He half expected to see his wall of posters in his dorm room. It didn't take long before he realized he was still sitting in one of the lawn chairs in the yard behind his apartment building.

"Jack?" Simon said with a shudder as he sat up in his chair. Suddenly, the memory of the events from the night before came flooding back, and he tried desperately to discern fiction from reality. He lifted his hands in front of his face and turned them around. They were bloodied and dirty. Unbelievably, the digging of the graves had really taken place. It wasn't just a figment of his imagination or a snapshot of some bizarre dream. Ashamed, he sat up in the chair and looked down only to find that he was still wearing the same clothes from the day before. When he looked back up, his head throbbed in pain. Simon rubbed his eyes with the palms of his hands. Without provocation, he felt a strong urge to hurl. He sat forward with his head between his legs and took deep calculated breaths, trying to decide if he should fight or force the issue.

After the moment passed, he took the time to acknowledge that the sun had indeed come up. The earth had not stopped spinning. And as much as he might have wished otherwise, he was still alive. Now, he simply had to make a decision.

* * *

For the first time in a long time, Simon felt the need to begin his day in prayer. And after taking a long shower, getting some food in his stomach, and brushing his teeth, he had a completely new lease on life. Of course, all of the events from the previous night dominated his thinking. He was still trying to get his head around all that had taken place. It was especially difficult for him to grasp how much of it had really happened. Debilitated by intense exhaustion, sleep deprivation, and intoxication, the entire sequence was shrouded in a dense fog of uncertainty.

Even the exhuming of the graves seemed like some kind of intense nightmare, but the fresh blisters on his hands and the aching of his back gave testimony to the contrary. Of course, it was his conversation with Jack that was subjected to the greatest degree of scrutiny. If it indeed all went down as he had remembered, then it would be a gross understatement to say it was disturbing.

Amazingly, Simon was neither fearful nor anxious about the implications of Jack's true nature. Instead, he had come to a sort of peace about it. He had resolved to wait for the gift his Father had promised. He had come to the rightful conclusion that if it were true then there was nothing he himself could do about it anyway. If he ran, it would merely be a change in geography, not a change of circumstances. And if he had suffered some sort of drug induced hallucination or a form of psychosis then there was no escaping that either. Whatever the case, he decided to meet it head on. There would be no more running.

The thing that disturbed him the most, as he drove to the school in the mid-day heat, was Jack's assertion that Simon's 'thing' was fear. For the life of him, he couldn't imagine what he was supposed to be afraid of besides snakes. Intuitively, he thought that if there were anything in this world that he should be afraid of, it would be Jack Lawless. But he didn't feel afraid of him, and he was almost certain that it wasn't merely a false bravado. Obviously, Jack was a very dangerous individual who was capable of doing very heinous atrocities. Nonetheless, Simon garnered a great deal of strength from simply knowing what he was really up against. Even more significantly, Simon knew at least two people who had come under the same attack and yet never succumbed to the pressure. He came to the conclusion that he needed to find out how they were able to overcome Jack. How he wished he could talk to Jeremy again. There was so much he wanted to ask him right now, and he needed some answers.

When he finally entered the front doors of the school, he found Mr. Cross at the top of the scaffolding doing his best to reconstruct the false ceiling that Simon had struggled with the day before. It was a futile effort given the damage done to the anchors in the drywall. After watching the old janitor for a minute or two, Simon felt the undeniable urge to make amends by extending an offer to help.

Mr. Cross didn't even bother to look down at Simon. Instead, he simply grunted, "No thanks, I can get it from here." Much to Simon's surprise, Mr. Cross did not say it with even an ounce of accusation or sarcasm. Instead, he seemed completely content taking on the mundane task. It was as if Simon had accidentally stumbled upon a previously unidentified job that only Andy could do. For the first time, Simon observed Mr. Cross through a different set of lenses. He thought about what Jack said, "Everyone has their thing…" Now as he looked at the busy, old janitor he wondered what Mr. Cross's 'thing' could be.

"Are you sure?" Simon asked, "I would be glad to help. I tried to put it back up yesterday, but I couldn't get the screws to hold the framework. So I went over to the hardware store, but they had put my spending account on hold."

"Oh yeah, sorry about that," Mr. Cross said as he wrenched his screwdriver back and forth. "I didn't know what to do. I was just surprised by what you'd done is all. I needed time to think before ya went and done anything else that'd put us behind schedule. But, it's okay."

"So, no hard feelings then?" Simon asked.

"Na," Mr. Cross said between grunts. "No cry'n over spilt milk, we gotta get this ceilin' back up before the vote on the referendum. Their talkin' 'bout puttin' the booths up right here in the lobby on the landin'."

"But, there's not enough time!" Simon squawked. "Aren't they voting on that tomorrow?"

"Nope," Mr. Cross replied. "Been pushed back."

"Pushed it back?" Simon bellowed, "Why?"

"Somethin' about need'n more figures from the state or somethin'," the old janitor answered as he fought with another anchor, "just a bunch of red tape if ya ask me.

"Now they're say'n August 13th."

"Huh," Simon muttered as he considered the possible implications. Then he looked over his shoulder towards the office, "Is she back yet?"

"No, well, I mean she's back in town," Andy answered, "but she ain't been in her office if that's what ya mean. She should be by later this afternoon. Hopefully, I can get all of this put back together before then so she don't blow her top!"

"Well then, is there anything that I can do for *you*?" Simon asked. It was a simple question, but it had been one that had never been uttered from his lips. At least, if he had said it he hadn't felt it. But now it resonated deep down inside of him. What he suddenly realized is that it represented a significant shift in his mindset. It was like a fundamental switch had been flipped. And even though he couldn't say exactly how, Simon felt like that one simple statement encapsulated something far greater and more powerful.

"Na, there ain't nothin'….oh wait a minute, you could finish cleaning out that storage room in the basement," Mr. Cross offered, "that'd make the ole' gal happy."

"All right, sounds good," Simon answered enthusiastically. And so, he resumed the task of clearing out the treasures from the windowless room, knowing that it would please his supervisor.

The work gave Simon a wonderful sense of purpose and provided a welcome distraction. For a few hours, he pulled out a vast array of dusty, rundown school items before uncovering a large, wooden bunny from under a canvas. With furrowed brow, Simon examined the curious object. Then he realized what he was looking at. The bunny was some sort of Easter decoration. Along with the wooden display, he found hundreds of small woven baskets and about a thousand plastic, colored eggs. Looking down into one of the baskets, Simon noticed an ancient, discarded piece of candy cane stuck in the green, faux grass. Carefully, he extracted the curiously misplaced stocking stuffer. Holding it like a "J" between his thumb and forefinger, he contemplated the meaning of the red and white stripes for the first time in his life.

Intuitively, he turned to look at the nativity scene still standing in the corner of the basement and made the connection. As though drawn by some mystical force, he made his way over to the manger. There was still no sign of baby Jesus, but in His place now lay a tattered, old book. Simon looked around the room quizzically before lifting the antique from the bed of straw.

It proved to be a rare find. The book was an original New England primer. Fascinated, Simon held the book up to the light and gently thumbed through stiff, yellow pages.

"Wow, this thing's got to be over a hundred years old," Simon said in awe.

The book was filled with rhymes and poems that helped young students develop a firm grasp of the basics of grammar and arithmetic, but there was something wonderfully unexpected written in the moldy, creased pages. There were, of all things, Bible verses. And not just any Bible verses, but those that gave explicit instruction for living.

"All of the basics...," Simon thought. His eyes danced over the pages as he read the passages. Some were wonderfully familiar while others were brand new to him. "This is incredible! They were teaching the Bible in school?"

He had already heard that somewhere before, but now, looking at the actual primer, it was like a revelation to him. But, where did the book come from? It hadn't been there the day before when he accidentally knocked over the empty manger. Simon started walking through the basement, peering around corners and searching the dark recesses for some sort of a clue. Not being sure of what it was he was looking for, he couldn't be sure if he'd know when he found it, but something told him that it had to do with the tiny door behind the boiler. The clasped padlock still hung on the latch as it had before. Still, Simon was not convinced. He knelt down and examined the door more closely. The hinges were rusty and worn but the lock and the latch were brand new.

When Simon investigated further, he made a noteworthy discovery. The latch was not actually attached to the wall. Warily, Simon reached out and pulled on the small, rotting door. With only a slight tug, the door swung open revealing a darkened tunnel. Someone had rigged the door to give the appearance of it being secure. But who and why?

Simon charged up the two flights of stairs to the landing where Mr. Cross was still wrestling with the false ceiling. Surprisingly, he had made some headway in the relatively short period of time that Simon had been working in the basement. Again, Mr. Cross failed to acknowledge Simon's presence.

"Mr. Cross," Simon called out expectantly.

"Yeah," Andy replied through grunts and groans, not even bothering to look down.

"Mr. Cross do you know anything about the small door in the basement behind the boiler?" Simon asked.

"Yeah," Mr. Cross replied, glancing out of the corner of his thick glasses. "Wait, didn't we already talk about this?"

"Do you happen to know why there's a new lock clasped on a latch that is not actually attached to anything?" Simon asked as though he were interrogating a witness.

Finally, Mr. Cross stopped toiling, dropped his arms, and a let out a deep sigh. Simon waited with bated breath, anticipating his response.

"Yeah, as a matter of fact, I do," Mr. Cross answered, despondently.

"Well?" Simon asked, accusingly.

Mr. Cross hiked up his trousers and looked about the room as if he were about to divulge some very sensitive information. "I did it," he answered sheepishly.

"What? But why," Simon asked, bewildered.

"You can't tell anybody what I'm about to tell you," Mr. Cross said with a pained expression. He proceeded to tell Simon the circumstances surrounding the mysterious door. "You see, there's this 1st grade boy who lives near here. He's got a really bad situation at home. Everybody knows it. So, I unlock the cellar door so he's got some place to go."

Simon's head raced thinking of the implications of what he just heard. "Do you mean to tell me that there is a little boy who runs around the school?" Simon asked, calling up to Mr. Cross standing on the scaffolding.

"Ssshhh," Mr. Cross said, as he scrambled down to the landing where Simon stood. "Nobody else knows about it. Truth is, I could get in a lot of trouble if anyone ever found out."

"Wait a minute," Simon said, trying to fully grasp what Mr. Cross was saying, "you have some little boy hang out with you here in the school after hours and no one knows about it?"

"Ah, it ain't nothin' like that," Mr. Cross said, as though he just got a whiff of something putrid. "Like I said, the kid's got a really bad situation at home. His mom don't pay no attention to him. She's a dancer or somethin' out at Jack's place. Word has it she does drugs too. Why I've even heard it tell that she brings her work home with her, if ya know what I mean. I think that's why he sneaks out at night."

"He sneaks out at night?" Simon asked, shocked. "He's how old, and he's not afraid?"

"Six or seven, I s'pose," Mr. Cross said, emphatically, "and he's got a whole lot more to be afraid of at home than he does here, I can assure you."

"Still, you think he would be scared to death to go out alone at night," Simon said, almost as it he were talking to himself.

"Well, I asked him about that one time," Mr. Cross said. "He was sittin' in Miss Harold's office on a bench waitin' for her to come in. And I says, 'what are you doin' in here?', and he says, 'I bit a girl out on the playground'. Then I says, 'How come you went and done a thing like that?', and he says, 'Don't you know?' Finally, he leans in and says, 'Cause I'm a vampire.''

Immediately, Simon remembered the tiny bat that he had found on the steps during his first day working at the school. He spontaneously convulsed before shaking off the ridiculous notion.

"So," Mr. Cross continued. "I asked him, 'Well, you got somewheres to go when it's cold?' He said he'd been hidin' out at Potter's old house in the country."

Simon immediately thought of the well next to the concrete platform next to the barn.

"So, I told em'," Mr. Cross continued," I'd leave the cellar door unlocked, and he could hide out in the tunnel under the building. It is warmer there. But, then I got to thinkin' that if it got too cold, I could unlock the door to the boiler room. I knew he'd be fine there in the basement."

"What's this boy look like?" Simon asked, with great anticipation.

"Ah, he's just a regular look'n little boy," Mr. Cross said. "He's small, kinda pale...has a buzz haircut cause of lice. He usually wears ratty jeans and a dirty t-shirt and no shoes. Why?"

"I've seen him running around here," Simon said, his voice tailing off as he processed the information.

"Oh, I thought as much," Mr. Cross said, "yeah, that's a problem. I can't have him just runnin' all over the school. Course, I knew he was. People been say'n that they've seen lights comin' on and goin' off at night, and others been hearin' footsteps. People are startin' to think that the school's haunted or somethin'. Can you believe that?" Mr. Cross shook his head and chuckled at how silly people can be.

"Ha, that *is* funny," Simon said, somewhat humiliated. "What's this boy's name?"

"Actually his name is Simon too," Mr. Cross said, "Little Simon Adamson."

"Really?" Simon mused. "And where does he live, besides here?"

"He lives around the corner on Washington St.," Mr. Cross replied. "Little boy's got some pretty serious issues."

"Is that so?" Simon said, staggered by the revelation.

He couldn't believe what he was hearing. It was incredible, but then again the more he thought about it the more that it all made perfect sense. As he thought about it longer, he was also pretty certain he knew exactly where the boy lived. It very well could be the same house where he saw Jeremy delivering the groceries. The young girl with piercings, tattoos, and long black hair who answered the door was probably Little Simon's mother.

Simon was completely blown away by what he was hearing. It changed everything. He wasn't losing his mind after all. "This is great news!" he unexpectedly blurted out.

"It is?" Mr. Cross asked, confused.

"There's no curse!" Simon said, forgetting himself.

"Curse?" Mr. Cross repeated with a strange expression on his face.

"It's a long story," Simon said. Now he couldn't wait to get to his cell phone. He had an important call that he needed to make.

"So, anyways, I'd appreciate it if you didn't tell nobody," Mr. Cross said.

"No, I wouldn't dream of it," Simon answered, beaming.

"Thanks, I guess that makes us even," Mr. Cross said pointing to the false ceiling. "Hey, what's that you've got there in your hand?"

"This? Oh, it's a book I found downstairs," Simon replied. "I think it's an old New England Primer. Did you know they actually used to teach Bible verses during school back in the day?" He was delicately thumbing through the pages for Mr. Cross to see, but the janitor seemed disinterested.

"Oh yeah," Mr. Cross muttered, as he climbed back up the scaffolding. "We used to start every day with one. Our teacher would write a verse on the board, and we'd all have to recite it before we did anything else." While he spoke, he pointed towards the 1st grade classroom. "We'd say the pledge of allegiance, the teacher would say a prayer, and then we'd recite a Bible verse everyday."

"How about that," Simon said. "You'd never see something like that today."

"No, no you wouldn't," Mr. Cross said as he resumed his task. "As far as I'm concerned you can toss that thing into the incinerator with all of the rest of the junk down there."

"Junk?" Simon squawked. "Do you know how valuable this thing is?"

"No," Andy replied flatly. "Do you?"

* * *

Simon stood in front of the small door behind the boiler with flashlight in hand. Even though he had no reason to believe that Mr. Cross was not being completely forthright, he still wanted to see for himself. After taking a deep breath, he pulled open the tiny door with the unattached latch and shone the flashlight into the deep recesses of the tunnel. It was an old, worn out flashlight that barely penetrated the thick darkness of the musty corridor. It ran the length of the gymnasium to the other end of the school. Looking at the cobweb strewn pipes, Simon was amazed that a 6 or 7-year-old boy would not be terrified to hang out down there. With uncertainty, Simon ducked his head and moved along slowly, almost feeling his way. As he made his way, he heard something scurrying ahead of him, like tiny nails scratching on the concrete floor. He came to the conclusion that it was either rats or mice, and a convulsive shiver ran through his body.

"This must be one brave kid," he said under his breath.

Halfway down the tunnel, Simon came to a small carveout in the wall. As he shone the flashlight about the small rectangular space, he saw a dirty, torn blanket lying on the floor. A few magazines, a couple of army men, some banana peels, empty bottles of Aquafina water, and a small pillow were strewn about. Sure enough, it looked to be some sort of makeshift hideout. Simon worked his way down the remaining corridor to the cellar doors at the other end of the school and pushed them open. A flash of blinding sunlight pierced the darkness, engulfing his feeble flashlight. From the stairwell, he could see down the alley across the street to Pastor Pete's church. On the other side of the church was the house where he supposed Little Adam Simon resided. It all supported everything Mr. Cross had told him.

A tremendous weight had been lifted from his shoulders. Finding out about Little Simon Adamson changed everything for Simon Freeman. Now he could move on with his life. The remains of Jessie Joseph and Adam Potter were securely in their graves, and what he had imagined as a ghost was merely a frightened, little boy. Simon realized that Jeremy's tragic death was just an awful coincidence. It wasn't the twelfth tragedy in six year cycle. Besides, he never really felt like Jeremy's death matched up with the legend anyway. Jeremy wasn't even from Bethel originally. He had only moved to town within the last year or so. According to Rob, Jessie Joseph only took the lives of descendants from the original twelve students.

Sure there had been a car accident and a suicide six years ago, and a crazy electrocution six years before that, but what town didn't suffer from such maladies? At this point, it wouldn't surprise him if the whole thing had been made up. And as far as Jack Lawless was concerned, all of that could easily be attributed to exhaustion, or alcohol, or both. There certainly was depravity in Bethel, but not any more than any other town across the country. For a moment, Simon was comforted by all of the plausible explanations. Everything seemed to be turning out all right after all. That is, everything except for Hope.

Naturally, Simon thought of his own transgression with Jez Bell. That was only natural, right? When he thought of the hurt look on Hope's face, he remembered what she had said to him, the man she was supposed to spend the rest of her life with. Did she really expect to marry a *virgin*? As much as he tried, Simon could not get past such a ridiculous notion. After all, this was the twenty-first Century.

Simon was especially baffled by her reaction, given that he hadn't actually known Jez. Still, was that enough to break off everything that he and Hope might have had going? He was just a guy, and that's what guys do. Right? What guy wouldn't have done the same thing given the circumstances? Then it hit him like a ton of bricks.

"Jeremy wouldn't have," he said aloud, "that's who."

That knowledge quickly refuted his convenient defense of conventional wisdom. The truth cut him to the quick. There were better men out there who would have resisted Jez's entreaties. And Simon hadn't been one of them. Therefore, Hope might in fact be right. Simon might not be 'the one' for her because he might not be good enough for her. It was a realization that saddened him for what he had done in the past and what he had wanted to do with Jez, but there was no changing any of that now.

Subsequently, it stood to reason that there was no way that Jeremy had been doing meth or seeing prostitutes, despite rumors to the contrary. He was simply a better servant of Jesus Christ than that.

Simon carefully let the metal, cellar doors close and was immediately enveloped again by the darkness. Quickly, he turned the flashlight on and off trying to get it to work. He struck it a couple of times with the palm of his hand before it came back to life. Convinced by the overwhelming evidence, he moved back down the tunnel towards the boiler room. But when he passed the small enclave, he instinctively flashed the light once more into the recesses of the opening and spotted something that he hadn't noticed on the first pass. He reached down with two fingers and carefully lifted up a soiled magazine. Beneath it, he discovered the original black and white photograph of the entryway that he thought he had lost. Simon picked it up and reflected for a moment on the impact that the picture had had on him. Why did it make such a huge impression on him? Why did he assume it had anything to do with his purpose for being back in Bethel?

Suddenly, Simon thought of his conversations that he had with Jeremy, and the positive influence that the humble youth pastor had had on him in such a short period of time. Each time they had spoken, Simon had come away feeling as though he was hearing the truth. Talking to Joey or Rob or Jack never made him feel that way. More than that, the fruit of Jeremy's labor gave credence to what he said, including what he had said about purpose. Any facts supporting the legend of Jessie Joseph could be explained away by examining the evidence, but Simon was convicted by something that could not be explained away. It was something that substantiated all of Jeremy's claims on a level of truth that superseded tangible evidence or mere intellect. It was his own personal encounter that he had with Jesus Christ. There was no doubt in his mind that Jesus spoke to him through the marquee at Pastor Pete's church, that read "Come, Follow Me." And now, looking at the photo in his trembling hand, he felt that same overwhelming presence inside of him. But why?

The longer Simon stared at the picture, the more he longed to talk to Jeremy. He was confused and needed answers. Even if he wasn't seeing ghosts, there still was a vote forthcoming on the referendum. It stood to reason that there still might be a purpose involving a full scale renovation. And then there was something else. He was still madly in love with Hope.

Simon desperately needed to confide in someone, and so he decided that the most logical would be to pay Pastor Pete another visit. Maybe this time he would have the answers to some of his most pertinent questions. At the very least, maybe he could lend Simon a Bible.

* * *

While standing on the porch of the parish, Simon could see Pastor Pete sitting at his desk through the blinds of his office. The soft, blue glow of the computer screen flashed and fluttered on the pastor's sullen face. Simon wildly waved his hand, trying unsuccessfully to get Pete's attention. Whatever was on the screen had the pastor completely captivated.

As it turns out, it was the same thing that always tormented him. It was the folder at the bottom right hand portion of the screen. Just as he had done time and time again, Pastor Pete caved under its hypnotic allure. His eyes hungrily danced about the screen, even though he had read them hundreds of times before.

After realizing that he was having no luck getting the good pastor's attention, Simon rang the doorbell, but there was still no visible reaction from the pastor. The pastor was consumed by something that held him in its grip like a powerful addiction.

What Simon couldn't see was that Pastor Pete had once again opened a folder on his desktop entitled "Grievances". The email he was reading now was sent from a former member of his church in response to a sermon that Pastor Pete had given following 9/11. Like many clergymen, the events surrounding the largest terror attack on American soil forced Pete to search for answers to the question everyone was asking, "Why? Why would a loving God allow something so terrible to happen?"

And like many pastors at the time, Pastor Pete came to the conclusion that it very well could be God's judgment on our country for our blatant disobedience and for forsaking our covenant by worshiping and serving other gods. In the sermon following that infamous day, the good pastor identified plausible explanations for how God could allow an unprovoked attack like that on *our* country.

Pastor Pete eloquently outlined a series of far reaching transgressions that the people of the United States of America had been perpetrating for the better part of the past seventy years. How we, the people, had succumbed to haughtiness, deception, the shedding of innocent blood, wicked schemes, evil acts, and dissension.

He supports position by citing many verses of scripture such as the reasons for Moses and the elders never having reached the promised land, Sodom and Gomorrah's destruction, and of course, Jehoiakim, son of Josiah king of Judah, being handed over to Nebuchadnezzar. There was precedent, to be sure, for blatant defiance and its residual consequences. The message was a difficult one for Pastor Pete to deliver. It was the first time in years that he had dared to broach such inflammatory topics. However, it must have been even more difficult to hear for at least one member of the congregation.

The pews in churches all across the country were filled with Americans that day, many of whom had not been to church for a long time, if ever. They all wanted to know one thing, "Why does God allow bad things to happen to good people?"

And Bethel was no different. Pastor Pete's small church was busting at the seams with men and women in great despair, searching for answers.

The good pastor anticipated his opportunity to reach the unsaved. He knew that there would be an initial heightened interest that would wane as time passed. And so, he prepared his own heart to receive the message from God.

Like for so many others, the Sunday following 9/11 had been the first time in years that John Rash had attended church. Knowing the depths of John's affliction and long suffering from the trauma he endured as a child, his mother, Mara Rash, and his wife, Hannah Grace Rash, regularly invited him to join them for Sunday service. Until that fateful day, he had always declined their entreaties. It took the largest attack on American soil for the sardonic, alcoholic John Rash to accept their long-standing offer. Pastor Pete knew that he might only get one shot to bring some of the strays, like John Rash, back into the flock.

Normally, under such conditions, Pastor Pete would do his best to compose a message that would be agreeable and inviting so as not to offend or drive away would be converts. However, this time was different. Empowered by the gravity of the American tragedy, the pastor did his best to be a conduit from God to the congregation. It was a charge given to his position to which he had never deemed himself worthy of.

Ironically, such feelings of inadequacy stemmed from the same horrible incident that had so adversely affected John Rash. While John had been driven to drink, Pete Cross had been driven to the cloth in hopes of one day making recompense for the part he played in it. Pete never was able to forgive himself, fueling his own doubts about his worthiness to speak on behalf of God.

But this was different. Something about the attack brought about a sense of urgency for people to connect with God, so much so that even Pastor Cross dared to avail himself to God as his own personal messenger. Therefore, he did not have the luxury to compose a sermon of political correctness. Instead, he spent a great deal of time that week on his knees. Prayerfully, he labored over a message that cut straight through to the heart of the attacks and what, if anything, they meant. Emboldened by his newfound duty to seek what he thought was God's will, Pastor Pete pulled no punches in his observations and criticisms of the depths to which our great country had fallen after years of backsliding and blatant rebellion. He challenged those in attendance to take the opportunity to search their souls and closely examine their own transgressions compared to God's standard of perfection.

Pastor Pete mouthed the words of his sermon as he read them off of the computer screen, "Brothers and sisters in Christ, there is evil in this world. This sinister attack, carried out by adversaries who want nothing more than our complete and utter destruction, is merely a glimpse of a war raging all around us, even within us, between good and evil. The terrorists who hijacked those planes were merely instruments of our ultimate enemy.

What makes this particular attack so striking is that it hits us close to home. The images on the TV are so stark and vivid. We see the terrifying images, and we hear the horrific sounds. And we are confronted with the reality that Satan walks about like a lion, seeking whom he may devour.

But I am hear to tell you that Satan carries out unobserved attacks every day on our souls that are every bit as lethal to our eternal lives as the attack on the Twin Towers. The Prince of Darkness will use any means necessary to capture our minds and destroy our bodies. He wants nothing more than to sift us like wheat.

And yet, physical and emotional suffering are not even the devil's most effective instrument for achieving his ultimate goal, because it often times has an undesired, counteractive effect. Because suffering often wakes us up, puts us on alert, and even drives us back into the loving arms of God.

No, I am afraid tell you that our enemy uses an even more sinister weapon than bloodshed. Listen carefully what I say to you today, the devil's most effective weapon for dragging our souls to the very pit of Hades is indifference and apathy. I contend that the devil preoccupies the hearts, and souls, and minds of those who claim to be Christians with the temporal things of this world as a distraction to what is truly important and what is eternal. I ask you, do we really seek God in the midst of prosperity and contentment?

After a lengthy pause, the pastor concluded his controversial sermon in this way, "Many have expressed to me that they simply cannot understand how God could allow such a terrible thing to happen to innocent men, women, and children. I am not God. I cannot pretend to definitively know why He does what He does or allows what He allows. But as I seek answers to these questions in the Bible, it becomes clear that there is a precedent for other nations throughout history who suffered far worse calamities at the hands of God. After reading about the circumstances of those disasters, the fundamental question does not become 'how can God allow this to happen?', but rather, 'Why do we time and again turn our backs on Him?'."

"America has historically been a Christian country founded by Christians and built upon Judeo-Christian doctrines and principles. Christians are followers of Jesus Christ. All who hate Jesus, hate the triune God. All who hate the Trinity, hate America. Not the America that we know today, but the America at its conception. Naturally, then, our enemies hate the freedoms that have been endowed by our creator. Not a freedom to do whatever pleases us, but a hallowed, inalienable freedom for all men and women. True freedom has been defined by the Ten Commandments and purposely crafted into our founding documents by the framers of the Constitution.

"There is no doubt that we have strayed far from the ideals of the original argument at the hands of original sin. And as much as we might want to blame God for the attacks, we can reasonably conclude that the Islamic Extremists who are carrying out Jihad, the atheists who actively work each day to divorce our country from God, and even the Christians who have stood by idly and allowed it to happen, are far more culpable.

"Follow me on this one, our country was only exceptional because God blessed American because the vast majority of our people acknowledged His son as our Lord and Savior and lived their lives accordingly. And because Jesus Christ was the cornerstone of our society. But, as we have 'progressed' we have moved farther and farther away from Him. It is not a stretch then to consider the possibility that what happened in New York, and Pennsylvania, and Washington D.C. earlier this week is the result of His judgment on us. We must consider the possibility that God has poured out His wrath as a result of our great disobedience. As I mentioned, it wouldn't be the first time in history. God has raised up enemies against His own people before as a harbinger as to what will come if we do not repent and turn from our wicked ways.

"But God is more than just. He is also merciful. God has not chosen to wipe us completely off of the face of the earth, or allowed an enemy to occupy this great land. At least He hasn't yet! Instead He has given us a second chance to return to Him, to return to whom we once were. We can once again be that city on a hill. As great a tragedy that befell our country on Tuesday morning at 8:46 a.m. EST, it doesn't have to be the beginning of the end for this once great nation. The greatest tragedy would be ignoring this warning and going about our lives as if nothing ever had happened.

"Loved ones, do not let our fellow Americans or your fellow brothers and sisters in Christ die in vain. Do something about it! Now is the time. We citizens of this chosen nation need to confess the error of our ways, ask for forgiveness, and repent of our sins. God forbid that we may further kindle His wrath, for each action, each word, each thought is either a declaration of devotion or an act of rebellion. As for myself, I am going to recommit myself to a life of serving and worshiping Jesus Christ."

The pastor's controversial words ignited a great discord that erupted among those in attendance that day. Even as Pete stood leaning with both hands on the podium while catching his breath, the naysayers shouted their dissent over the applause of those in agreement. As many people were offended as were inspired by the remarks of the pastor on that day. And the impact in the community was profound for an all too short period of time.

Now Pastor Pete sat back in his chair, pulled his bifocals off, bit his bottom lip, and contemplated his own hypocrisy. All of the passion and momentum brought about by the events on that fateful September day quickly dissipated in the community, the congregation, and eventually his own heart. In no time, the people of Bethel had grown tired of manna and demanded meat. And the demons of doubt regarding the Pastor's worthiness returned sevenfold, leaving him only with the hate mail wrought by his controversial words.

In the aftermath, the Pastor was left second guessing where the authority came from to compose such a divisive sermon. Judging by the results, he could not help but come to the conclusion that the offensive words that day were his own. He then reasoned that God could not use him because of his past. As a result, he took full responsibility for turning away a significant number of people that day, and he vowed to never make the same mistake again. It was a thought that crippled his ability to teach the entire Gospel. From that time on, Pastor Pete chose to give only very benign sermons that steered clear of the more controversial passages of the Bible. He focused only on the goodness of God and the promise of heaven. The change in philosophy must have been very agreeable to the twenty or thirty people who now regularly attended Sunday services for there were no more complaints other than song selection, or the temperature in the sanctuary, or the arrangement of flowers on the stage.

Fully understanding the stark ramifications of his actions, Pastor Pete labored over the letters and emails that never gave him a moment's peace. The most damning of which came from John Rash. It was the last correspondence John would send, before they found his broken body at the base of the grain elevator. Somewhat cryptically, John seemed to blame Pete's sermon for his fateful decision to take his own life.

From that time on, Pete erroneously surmised that if God allowed 9/11 to occur because he was judging the United States for its actions, then just maybe he could achieve God's favor and salvation by his works. So the good pastor filled his day with tasks and avoided deep theological questions for which there were no definitive answers. Instead, he spent the majority of his time doing menial tasks like vacuuming the sanctuary, washing the communion glasses, organizing food drives, planting flowers under the marquee, or registering voters. He kept very busy doing task after task trying to accrue more credits than debits to his ledger. But, there was one horrible debt that he doubted that he could ever pay back. It was something he did as a boy, and it was far too horrible to ever be forgiven.

Finally, Pastor Pete heard the deep resolute banging on the front door of the parish, rousing him from his stupor. By the time he reached for the handle of the front door and saw who is was, he was already defeated.

"What can I do for you, Simon?" Pastor Pete asked, flatly.

"I am so glad that you are here, Pastor!" Simon said with a pained expression. "I have so many questions that I was hoping you could…"

"I don't think that now is great time," Pete said as he started to shut the door. "Perhaps you could come back tomorrow…"

"But, wait," Simon said, instinctively putting out his hand to stop the door from closing. "I, uh, I was wondering if I could at least borrow a Bible from you."

"Sure, hold on," Pete said as he closed the door behind him.

Simon chided himself for his hesitation. In a couple of minutes, Pete opened the door just wide enough to pass the Bible through the slight aperture.

"Here you go," Pete said as started to close the door again.

"Wait!" Simon said this time with great conviction, "I am desperate pastor. I need to know something. I need to know if God has a specific purpose for each person." The pastor momentarily stopped leaning on the door. "I mean…like…is each man's destiny predetermined or is it up to us to decide?"

The Pastor was silent.

"Because," Simon continued," I need to know if this feeling of obligation that I have inside of me to do this certain thing is coming from me or from God. Because if it's just coming from me, my own conscience, or whatever, then I can ignore it and choose another purpose or fate or destiny. But if it's from God…"

The pastor could see that the young man was not going to leave without some sort of answer, so he did what he always did. Refusing to take a definitive position, he instead spoke in ambiguous terms like a fortune cookie or palm reader.

"I don't know what kind of purpose you have in mind, but God knows the future and you don't," Pete said dully. "So, our ultimate fate is not our own choice. It is His. But because you don't know it is also your choice," Pastor Pete said with a forced smile as he started once again to shut the door. "I hope that helps. Now I really must go."

"But wait!" Simon pleaded. "What does that mean? How will I know what to do or not to do?"

"Is there something specific that you feel like you are supposed to do?" Pastor Pete asked, drawing upon a set of predetermined questions that usually did the trick.

"Yes," Simon replied, timidly, "I feel like I…I mean that I had this idea that I should renovate the entrance to the school."

"But, didn't you already do that?" Pastor Pete asked with a raised eyebrow.

"Yes, but, you see, it didn't make any difference," Simon answered. "The farmers are still going to vote down the land tax." He sighed deeply. "I just feel like I…that we…didn't do it the right way or something. Otherwise, it would have changed things, right? God doesn't compel us to do things for no apparent reason, does He? There's got to be a reason, right?"

The Pastor considered his answer carefully. Then he glanced back at the office where the computer screen still displayed the letter from John. "Simon, all I can tell you is that we must all work out our own salvation," Pastor Pete offered through a crack in the door.

Out of desperation, Simon stuck his foot in the door. "Whoa, Pastor, I am sorry, but I need more than that," he said. "Are you saying that there is something that I need to do to be saved?"

Pastor Pete rested his head on the edge of the door for a moment and then opened it up again. "No, I am saying that there is something that you will do because you are saved," Pastor Pete replied, conceding a bit of advice. Simon was baiting him into some deep theological discussion where Pete feared to tread.

"Then what does it matter what I choose if it was already determined anyway?" Simon asked as if in pain.

"As I said, you don't know what you will choose until you choose it, even though God already knew what you were going to choose beforehand," Pastor Pete said. "After all He is the Alpha and Omega. So, it's very, very important that you carefully consider your actions before you carry them out because they can have far reaching consequences. God already knows if you chose poorly or wisely, but you don't. So, there you go."

A terrible thought suddenly occurred to Simon. What had started as a series of questions about why he was in Bethel suddenly turned to questions about Hope.

"But, what if you did something wrong before you ever even knew it was a choice between two different things?" Simon asked thinking of his night with Jez.

Pastor Pete jerked up his head and met Simon's eyes. The color had left his face.

"Simon," Pastor Pete said asked great import, "are we still talking about the school?"

"No," Simon admitted.

The Pastor, misconstruing Simon's reply, regretfully muttered his answer while wrestling his own demons. "Ignorance is not a viable excuse for making a bad choice. I, more than anyone, should know that. It was still a choice, even though you didn't know that it was at the time you made it."

"That doesn't hardly seem fair!" Simon complained.

"Fair?" the pastor said with a laugh. "Where do you even get a notion of 'fairness' if not from God? I think He probably knows what is and is not fair. You are not entitled to making only the easy choices or always being aware of the choices you are making. You are entitled to the consequences of those choices whether you were completely aware or totally oblivious to them at the time you made them."

"But, there's something that I can do, right, to change it?" Simon said, frantic.

"No," Pete answered dully, "there's nothing you can do. What's done is done."

"Well, maybe not change it, but at least make up for it?" Simon countered.

"I don't know," Pete admitted.

"But, you said something about working out our own salvation," Simon exclaimed. "That's what you said. We can right our wrongs!"

"I don't know," the pastor repeated, unable himself to fathom the concept of grace.

"God gives us second chances, right?" Simon pleaded again.

"I honestly don't know," the pastor murmured softly as he started to close the door, "but I pray every day that He does. Good day, Simon." He leaned against the door, put his face into his hands, and wept bitterly.

* * *

Simon had not been himself the rest of the day after his brief conversation with Pastor Pete. Somehow he couldn't get past his overwhelming sense of duty. And yet, he was tormented by the question that cast a shadow of doubt. How could he know if the voice inside of him was from God or from himself? Even though he would be simply going through the motions, Simon put on his umpiring gear and headed to the ballpark. He wasn't about to let Rich down again. And besides, he needed the cash.

In all of the chaos that had transpired over the past couple of days, Simon had completely lost track of time. He couldn't believe that he had actually gone to work on the Fourth of July! But, because it was a weekday and because Andy was at work, Simon hadn't given it a second thought until he saw the stars and stripes bunting adorning the fences for the special occasion.

Once again, Rich had outdone himself. He had gone to great lengths to top the previous year's celebration. Consequently, this year's event promised to provide all of the fanfare and pageantry that the community had come to expect for their children's sports.

Now standing behind home plate beside Joey Campbell and George Lukas with his hand over his heart, Simon stared up at the stars and stripes just as he had done a million times before, but this time something was different. Something was changing inside of him.

As he watched the pained expression of the members of a local barber shop quartet singing the National Anthem, Simon couldn't help but think of the book "Slaughterhouse Five". It was a fictional novel by Kurt Vonnegut about the bombing of Dresden during World War II. Simon recalled how his professor at TCU claimed that the act made us no better than the Nazis.

As Simon considered the absurdity of such a statement, his eyes scanned the massive crowd that had turned out for the all important little league baseball game between the Devil Rays and the Angels. He dropped his chin to his chest and thought of the meager turnout at Pastor Pete's church on Sunday mornings, and he wondered if there were self-professing Christians in Germany before the rise of the Nazi party.

It now being the summer of 2007, he had a hard time imagining what it must have been like to be alive in 1935 with a ruthless dictator rising to power and the whole world on the precipice of warfare. It had always baffled him how no one was able to stop Hitler in his tracks before he hit the world stage.

With the quartet nearing the crescendo, "...the rockets red glare, the bombs bursting in air, gave proof through the night that our flag was still there,..." he wondered if anyone else was thinking about the blood red stripes and the sacrifice so many soldiers had made to protect our freedoms.

Without provocation, a passage from one of the history books that he had read in the chorus room of the school came to mind. The brief chapter was on WWII. Even though Simon didn't think anything of it at the time, the author had clearly condemned the United States for dropping the Atomic Bomb on Japan. In fact, he described it as "...yet *another* shameful chapter in America's history."

It occurred to Simon that the mainstream media was depicting the war in Iraq and Afghanistan following the attacks on 9/11 in much the same way. Often the indignant reporters and haughty commentators slanted their stories in a way that made the Americans out to be the villains of the conflict. By reading the tidbits of information in a lede or watching the edited images on the television, one would think that our brave men and women in the armed services were an unprovoked aggressor. The faulty reporting imbued the exact same tone as the misguided excerpt from the history book.

"What are we teaching this generation?" Simon asked himself. He became enraged when he noticed children sitting in the bleachers, teenagers refusing to remove their hats, and even adults disrespectfully whispering during the singing of The Star Spangled Banner. It was shameful to say the least.

Just as the choir hit the crescendo, "...Oh say does the star spangled banner yet wave, o'er the land of the free...", fireworks exploded behind the home run fence in centerfield. From out of the blue, the thunderous noise brought to Simon's mind his old friend, Shane Gentry, who was at an undisclosed location in the Middle East fighting for his country.

For all Simon knew, his old, little league teammate might be in some firefight at that very moment on the other side of the world, so that kids in the states could play a game without worrying about things like IED's, RPG's, or suicide bombers.

Suddenly, a wave of gratitude swept over him. He was humbled by the notion. By comparison, his problems were insignificant. Thinking of his friend's noble sacrifice, a smile swept across his face. As the smoke dispersed over the ball field, Simon slid his hat back on top of his head and got ready to do his job with a whole new perspective.

Meanwhile, Joey already had his tiny, tattered rulebook out and was checking on the answer to an ominous question that Lexus Helrigle had posed to him before the game. The shrewd coach of the Yankees wanted to know about the penalty for a player ejection.

On page 76, article 5, section 6, Joey had hoped to find the answer to Lexus's bizarre question. The head umpire read aloud to no one in particular, "If a player gets ejected from a game, he is to miss the next two games." They already knew that, but what Lexus wanted to know was what kind of games they had to be. More specifically, he wanted to know if the games had to be scheduled before the season began. To that question there was no answer. Therefore, it could be debated that, hypothetically, a team could schedule a couple of meaningless, ad hoc games in which the player in question could sit out.

"Why would he want to know that?" George asked, almost yelling to be heard above the noise of the raucous crowd.

"I don't know!" Joey replied, loudly, "it does make you wonder. But there's nothing written here that indicates what kind of games the player has to sit out."

"I thought you had that thing memorized by now," George scoffed, having some fun at his mentor's expense. "I can't believe you actually had to look it up. I mean, come on, what's the matter with you?"

"No, no, no" Joey objected, as he placed the rule book back into his shirt pocket. "I don't know *everything*. Even I have to look things up every now and then," he said, altogether missing George's impropriety.

"Oh, brother," Simon muttered as he rolled his eyes.

Completely oblivious, Joey continued preaching on the virtues of umpiring to George and Simon. "Remember, the integrity of the game hinges on the proper enforcement of the rules," he said condescendingly, "so when in doubt, call 'time out'.

"If none of us knows the answer, then we'll look it up. Agreed?" he asked, pulling his face mask over the top of his head.

George and Simon shared a knowing glance as they dutifully nodded in agreement.

"This is a big game!" Joey continued. "It's the 4th. The coaches and players and parents are all amped up. One bad call could set off this powder keg.

"I don't know what Lexus has in mind, but it doesn't sound good to me. So, keep an eye out for anything out of the ordinary.

"Listen, make every call with confidence. And do *not* hesitate; otherwise, we're going to have total chaos. Nobody wants that! Trust me."

Normally, Simon might have been a little nervous before such an important game. But, in light of his realization during the National Anthem, he had a healthy outlook on the situation. Of course, he was going to do his best to make all of the right calls, but he was also going to take time to enjoy being on a baseball field, on the Fourth of July, in his hometown rather than being on some forsaken battlefield in Iraq.

* * *

Just as the first batter made his way to home plate, Shannon Zeal snuck up behind Sharon Fields who was sitting in a lawn chair next to Hannah Grace and Mara Rash. It was so loud that neither of them noticed the unwanted visitor.

"Pssst," Shannon sputtered, tapping Sharon on the shoulder as she squatted down beside her. She was just out of the periphery of both of the elderly Rash women. From across the field in the concession stand, Sharon's brother Rich did notice, however, and he did not approve. He glanced down at his bruised knuckles from the roundhouse that he delivered to the scumbag whom he had caught parking with his little sister.

"Hey, in a couple of minutes tell your aunt you've gotta go to the restroom, and I'll meet you on the other side of the concession stand," Shannon whispered excitedly before sneaking off through the crowd.

Sharon nodded affirmatively with a devious smile, before glancing back to see if her friend had been detected by either Mara or Hannah Grace. It didn't appear as though she had. Since the incident in the woods, Sharon had not only been grounded, but she had also been cut off from all contact with her friends that she had been spending "…too much time with lately." And that included her cell phone. It was worse than prison, or so she thought.

After a very short first inning, Sharon informed Hannah Grace that she had to use the restroom. Hannah Grace didn't change expression but simply nodded reflexively. That same old melancholy feeling had unexpectedly swept over her as she watched parents cheering on their boys. In a flash, she was back in the doctor's office sobbing uncontrollably over her miscarriage while John tried unsuccessfully to console her.

Anytime Hannah Grace drifted, Mara knew where she went. No one had to tell her it. It was written all over her daughter-in-law's face. Inevitably, Mara followed her there. Only she opted for the bitter opium of anger over dark, debilitating despair.

"You aren't the only who's ever lost a son, ya know," Mara snarled between her teeth.

Meanwhile, Sharon looked both ways making sure that the coast was clear before darting into the shadows of the concession stand to talk in secret with her best friend, Shannon Payne. They clasped each other's hands as they wildly whispered.

"Hey, I don't have very long," Sharon said. "They'll be coming looking for me in a minute or two. So, what's up?"

"Okay, so here's the deal, I'm going to get the boys to meet us in the alley behind your house around midnight," Shannon said excitedly. "They can't keep us from seeing them. Who do they think they are anyways? We're not a couple of kids or something."

"I know, right?" Sharon replied. "They just don't get it. They have no idea how Mike and I feel about each other. Sometimes I think that Aunt Grace is the only one who understands. Remember how I told you that she married my Uncle John when she was just fifteen."

"I know!" Shannon said excitedly. "It's like Romeo and Juliet!"

"I *know*," Sharon said. "So, you've talked to Mike and Sean, and they're actually going to pick us up at midnight?"

"Well, not exactly," Shannon said, looking sadly down at her cell phone. "I mean, I've texted Sean several times, but he still hasn't answered me back."

Suddenly, Sharon's expression changed. "You mean tonight, right? He hasn't answered your texts tonight?" Sharon asked, sensing something amiss.

"No, I mean, he hasn't answered me in a couple of days," Shannon said, with tears welling up in her eyes. "Ever since we had that stupid argument!"

"Ahh," Sharon replied as she reached out to console her best friend. "I'm sure it's nothing. He's probably just been busy or something, you know?"

"I don't know," Shannon answered, distraught. "He was pretty mad at me. He called me all kinds of terrible things. It was horrible. Now, I think he might be going out with Becky Hughes!"

Sharon wasn't following her. "What are you talking about?" she asked with grave concern. "Why would he do something like that? You guys have been together all summer."

"She's not as pretty as me is she?" Shannon asked with a look of desperation on her face.

"No, of course not," Sharon answered, reflexively.

"I mean, I'd just die if Sean was going out with her," Shannon said, bitterly followed by a flurry of expletives. "He might be with that little tramp right now for all I know."

"But, I don't get it," Sharon said. "You guys are such a cute couple. He'll come around. At least, your big brother didn't punch him in the face. I wouldn't blame Mike if he never wanted to see me again.

"I'm not talking to that big jerk ever again. Who does *he* think he is? Like he never parked with Rachel when they were in high school."

"Do you really think so?" Shannon asked, brightening up.

"Well, yeah, have you seen Mike's eye?" Sharon asked.

"No," Shannon replied. "I mean do you really think that we make a cute couple?"

"Duh, yes," Sharon answered. "The cutest. He'll get over it and come running back to you."

"Yeah," Shannon said, after an erratic swing of emotion. "That's right. He'll be beggin' for forgiveness. I guess I'll take him back.

"And Mike will get over gettin' his lights knocked out."

"Oh, nice," Sharon said, slapping Shannon on the shoulder. Then she glanced over her shoulder suddenly paranoid about being found out. "I should probably be getting back. Aunt Gracee will be wondering what happened to me."

"Okay," Shannon said, "but tonight, at midnight in the alley behind your house, okay?"

"I'll be there!" Sharon said through a wide grin with her hands clasped under her chin. "Hey, what did you guys fight about anyway?" She casually asked, taking a few steps away from her best friend.

"Oh, it was so dumb," Sharon said rolling her eyes. "I wanted him to come to the clinic with me, and he didn't want to go."

Sharon stopped backpedaling. "Clinic?" she asked. "Sean didn't want to go with you to what clinic?" Just as she said the last words, she felt her face go flush. Somehow she feared that she already knew the answer.

"I know, I was being stupid," Shannon admitted. "He was right. It wasn't a big deal or anything. I mean, I was a little sore afterwards, but nothing like runnin' the mile in gym or something."

Sharon could barely speak. "You-you had an abortion?" Sharon heard herself ask.

"Well, yeah, who wouldn't?" Shannon asked, nonchalantly. "I mean Homecoming is in three months. I'd probably be beginning to show by then. It would be nearly impossible to find a dress that would look good. And prom is in like nine months, so no way..."

Sharon didn't hear anything after that. Her head was spinning, and she felt like she was going to be sick. As she stood reeling in shock from what her friend just shared with her, a giant hand clamped down hard on her shoulder.

"What do you think you're doing?" Rich growled angrily. "I think it'd be best if you went on home, Shannon."

"Yeah, right, Rich," Shannon said. "You're such a big jerk. You can't tell me what to do."

"Yeah, yeah, whatever," Rich said as he grabbed his sister by the shoulders and steered her back towards Hannah Grace and Mara. "I don't want you hanging around my sister anymore!"

"I'll call you later, Sharon," Shannon yelled defiantly as she slowly made her way off in the opposite direction.

But Sharon said nothing. Nor did she fight Rich who guided her back to the lawn chair with his huge arm draped over her shoulder. Almost in a catatonic state, she slumped back into her chair and sat in silence with her hands clasped between her knees. She stared blankly into space while the crowd around her cheered wildly for a stand up double. Meanwhile, Rich filled Hannah Grace and Mara in on what he had overheard the girls discussing behind the concession stand. After shooting a disappointing glance down at his beleaguered sister, he made his way back to resume his duties at the concession stand.

22

FINDING THE BOOK OF THE LAW

For a few innings, Hannah Grace said nothing to her despondent, great niece. Then, thanks in large part to Mara's incessant prodding, Hannah Grace felt obligated to take that particular moment to share something with Sharon that she had only shared with few other people in her entire life. The two older ladies had discussed for some time as to whether or not it would be beneficial to confide in young Sharon or whether or not it would be more prudent to wait until she was a little older. Given the circumstances, however, it was decided that that bit of information might be best if shared sooner rather than later before it was too late.

"Sharon, honey," Hannah Grace started to say as she leaned in closer to her niece's daughter. But, Sharon did not hear her. She was still in shock. While Hannah Grace's lips moved, no one else could hear what she said over the chaotic baseball chatter that enveloped them.

* * *

The intensity of the game had escalated to the point where the parents had breached that inexplicable out of body experience of living vicariously through their children. It was as if they were no longer themselves. The frenzied nature of the heated contest stymied any sense of human decency or decorum. Fathers and mothers who were otherwise cordial and reserved in any other setting now frothed at the mouth due to a sports induced psychosis, an all too common modern day malady.

To everyone's surprise, the game didn't start out that way, though. Lexus Helrigle's Devil Rays jumped on Wilson B Livingood's Angels from the first pitch. After the second inning, the game had become so lopsided that the mercy rule loomed large over the Angels. Jackson Helrigle was pitching possibly the best game of his life after his dad gave him a pep talk or what could better be described as a ultimatum. Lexus's ploy must have worked for the left-handed fireballer was painting the corner's of Joey Campbell's liberal strike zone, and the Angels were dropping like flies.

Conversely, in the opposite dugout, Ralph Livingood had butterflies from the outset of the big game. He was struggling to find the strike zone. As a result, he started to try placing his pitches. His pattern was to get behind early in the count before taking a little off of his fastball just to get it over the plate. The result was a meaty pitch in the upper middle part of the zone, and the Devil Rays weren't missing it.

But Ralph Livingood is a gamer and made of better stuff than that. After the disastrous second inning he began to settle in. Even though his dad didn't allow him to throw curve balls like Jackson's, he still had his patented fastball and a mean circle change. After a rocky start, he began to mow down the Devil Rays lineup in similar fashion to what Jackson was doing on the other side.

By the bottom of the fourth, Jackson was still working on a no-hitter. He wiped the sweat off his brow before placing his cap back on his head and returning his glove to his right hand. In short order, Jackson struck out the first two batters. He looked to his father sitting on the bench. Lexus scowled at his son, clapped hard twice, and spit out some chaw. Mirroring his father, Jackson returned the angry expression and nodded.

Despite Jackson's overpowering performance, there was something in his father's expression that gave rise to a smidgeon of self-doubt. When he saw the intensity of his father's demeanor, he didn't feel support. He only felt intimidated.

And as he dug his foot into the dirt in front of the rubber, he tried his best to quell the rebellion in his consciousness by remembering all of his father's axioms: "Who you are is defined by what you do"; "There are winners and then there is everyone else"; "Do what others are unwilling to do to win". The ploy seemed to work at first. He fired his first two screaming fastballs for strikes.

As Jackson started his windup, he was suddenly overcome by an overwhelming sense of insecurity. And that's when it happened. It's funny how the smallest, seemingly insignificant thing can completely change the complexion of a situation. When Jackson fired the next pitch, the futile batter swung wildly and missed by a mile. Joey jumped out from behind the plate and punched out the batter with great fanfare yelling, "*Strike three!*" Lexus slammed the fence with the palms of his hands and gave out a warlike cry. The Devil Ray's faithful cheered as their beloved boys ran off of the field. The game was over by the mercy rule. Then something quite unexpected happened.

Simon calmly, yet assertively came running in from the first base line waving his arms. He didn't get caught up in the moment or excitement, but instead he had kept a cool head and watched vigilantly. Consequently, he had seen it all clearly and had no doubt.

Automatically, Joey raised his arms high in the air to signal that something was amiss, even though he couldn't imagine what on earth Simon was doing. He walked out to meet the first base umpire just as both teams lined up to shake hands. George also made his way over from third base to join the conference.

"What are you doing?" Joey asked Simon.

"The ball hit the batter's sleeve," Simon said flatly.

"What?" George said as he turned to look at Lexus, standing in front of the dugout with his arms folded.

"Are you sure?" Joey asked.

"Positive," Simon replied. "The end of the bat caught the bottom of his sleeve. You have to give him first base automatically."

"Come on, do you really want to do that?" Joey asked, a bit embarrassed. "I mean the games not even close. These people are going to go ballistic. Besides, I've gotta overturn my call. And Lexus..."

"What are you talking about?" Simon asked. He was getting the sense that Joey was more about Joey missing the call than doing the right thing.

George looked at his mentor Joey as though seeing him for the first time. "Aren't you the one whose always going on and on about following the rules?" he asked Joey. "'When in doubt, call time out', 'What are we without the rules'... 'Always consult the rule book'...all that garbage."

"Yeah, yeah, yeah, I get the point," Joey said, resigned. "All right, as long as you're sure."

Simon nodded. Reluctantly, Joey called the coaches to home plate while the crowd stood in silence. Some of them by now were holding their lawn chairs and coolers in their hands. There was an exchange of words between Joey and Lexus before they both turned to Simon who made a gesture with his hand to his sleeve. Lexus spun out of the pow wow, grabbing his cap off of the top of his head and yelling angrily while Wilson B. jogged back towards the Angels dugout clapping fervently. There was a great deal of murmuring in the stands before Joey turned to the crowd and gave the explanation.

"The ball hit the batter's sleeve," Joey said loudly, "therefore, the batter is awarded first base." He pointed towards first. "There are still two outs!"

Predictably, the Devil Rays' parents went ballistic while the Angels' fans cheered approvingly. Several parents yelled threats to the umpires, forcing Joey to give a verbal warning to the Devil Rays' bench. The players retook the field, the batter made his way to first, and Wilson B. resumed his position as first base coach.

"That was a gutsy call," Wilson B. said to Simon down the first base line. "You realize that Lexus has the final call on hiring anyone at the bank."

Simon didn't bother replying.

Joey yelled out, "*Play ball!*"

From that moment on, Jackson wasn't the same. The worm had turned and now he couldn't find the strike zone. With each ball and each walk, his father fell further and further into a rage which in turn destroyed Jackson's confidence. Suddenly, the bases were loaded with Ralph Livingood coming to the plate. Jackson looked to the dugout for instruction from his father. With the score still 11-0, Lexus gave Jackson the signal to intentionally walk Ralph. The gesture flew all over Jackson. He had a no-hitter going. And now he was going to give up the perfect game with an intentional walk? It was more than his pride could stand. Any shred of support that Jackson felt from his father had been completely vanquished.

And so, Jackson took to the mound. The Devil Rays faithful were getting a little nervous while the Angels' fans were beginning to see a slight glimmer of hope.

* * *

Still, neither Sharon nor Hannah Grace had seen or heard any of the commotion on the field. They were far too engrossed in their own conversation to notice.

"So, what? You're saying that you didn't actually love uncle John?" Sharon asked, confused.

"No, I'm saying the opposite," Hannah Grace said reaching over and placing her aged, wrinkly hands on her nieces young, smooth skin. Mara leaned forward to make sure that Hannah Grace was saying what she thought she ought to be saying and not what she thought she *was* saying.

"I was madly in love with John…just like you're madly in love with Mike," Hannah Grace said.

"Hmm," Sharon responded, still unconvinced. She knew that she couldn't actually say it to her beloved Aunt Gracee, "But with all due respect there is no way that anyone, let alone an old lady, could even begin to comprehend the kind of love that Sharon and Mike had. Normally, she would have dismissed her aunt's assertion immediately. Given what she had just found out about her best friend, she was willing to bask in the comfort of Hannah's warm voice and sympathetic eyes.

Hannah Grace recognized the doubt in Sharon's face and knew that she had to take a more forceful tact if she had any chance of reaching her beautiful, young niece. "My heart skipped a beat whenever I even saw him or heard his voice," Hannah Grace continued, as Mara rolled her eyes and sat back in her chair. "We could look into each other's eyes for hours without saying a word." She recognized that she was still having no effect on her listener. "And when we could we would sneak off somewhere to be by ourselves. John was so handsome and mature for his age. I hung on his every word and treated it like it was gospel." Mara rolled her eyes a second time, gave a deep sigh, as she pressed her cheek against her hand with her elbow leaning on the arm of the lawn chair. "He was four years older and much more worldly, not like the 14 or 15-year-old boys in my class. Most of them were just that. They were boys. John was more like a *man*. He had muscular, tan arms from working all day in the fields." Up to this point, Hannah Grace could tell that Sharon was only mildly interested. Then she thought of it…. "We were like Romeo and Juliet!"

With that Sharon turned and cast a challenging frown of suspicion at her great aunt.

* * *

No one else could hear the intimate conversation. With the bases loaded and Ralph at the plate, anticipation had grown to a near frenzy. Instead of intentionally walking his cousin, Jackson willfully disobeyed his father and hummed a fastball high and tight. To everyone's surprise, Ralph stepped out towards the third base line and brought the meat of the bat around with great speed. It caught the leather sphere in the sweet spot. Both Ralph and Jackson knew it immediately, and in a moment it became clear to everyone else as well. The towering grand slam cleared the fence, landing almost ten rows back in the shoulder high cornfield. The Angel faithful went crazy!

* * *

Sharon and Hannah Grace barely took notice. Gazing into her aunt's hazy blue eyes, Sharon could hear the conviction in her voice.

"Oh, don't be so surprised, dear," Hannah Grace said with a smile, tightly squeezing Sharon's hand. At times she had to raise her voice to be heard over the explosion of cheers. "I may not be able to text or send an email or heavens only knows what else you kids do these days.

"God forbid technology surpasses your generation by so quickly that it renders you dimwitted to your grandchildren. Because when that happens, you'll find yourself trying to convince a young lady that there are some things that are timeless like love, and happiness, and heartache, and even regret."

Now she had Sharon's full attention.

* * *

By the time Ralph stomped on home plate, Lexus was already at the pitcher's mound reading Jackson the riot act. Standing over the top of his boy, Lexus stuck his index finger squarely into Jackson's chest.

"I hope you're happy, son!" Lexus snarled, shaking his head. "I said to not give him *anything*! There goes the mercy rule and the no-hitter. Now, you've given them hope," he said pointing to the celebrating Angels. "I swear. Let this be a lesson to you! There's nothing more dangerous than giving the opposition hope when you had them down for the count. Maybe that was wake up call. Now get this last out and let's get out of this game!"

Jackson said nothing. He knew better. Instead, he gritted his teeth and threw with reckless abandon, fueled only by rage.

* * *

"It was an ice cream social at one of the local farms," Hannah Grace said recalling the details as though it happened yesterday. "We managed to sneak off to the loft of one of the barns, and for a few precious minutes we were completely alone. We knew it wouldn't be long before our parents realized we were missing. John professed his love for me and caressed my hair and reassured me. He had the deepest, most intense blue eyes you had ever seen. I could get lost in those eyes. After a split-second decision in the heat of passion, I did what I said I would never do."

Sharon looked down and bit her lip as her face turned flush with embarrassment.

"But, what difference did it make?" Hannah Grace asked. "I already knew that we were soulmates and that we'd be together forever. It would be just like in the movies."

Mara grumbled something under her breath.

"Well, at least I got a couple of things right," Hannah Grace said, whimsically. "He would be my first and last, and we would be married. It happened three months later in the Ford County Courthouse. Oh, we couldn't be married here in Bethel. It was far too scandalous- as if everyone didn't know anyway. So much for Romeo and Juliet."

* * *

In no more than three pitches, Jackson made short work of the next batter, sending the game into the top of the fifth inning. Simon walked over to Joey and George who were getting a drink from their bottles of water next to the backstop. The Devil Rays crowd was still grumbling over the controversial call, and they were making their displeasure known to the three young umpires who dutifully ignored the stinging barbs. Lexus was particularly sharp with his criticism. The accusing litany bordered on getting personal, but Simon wisely let it roll right off of his back.

"Well, I guess that call turned out to be pretty important after all," George said to his two comrades.

"Every call is an important call," Joey said without even an ounce of humility, "that's why I took control as soon as I saw Simon give his signal."

Simon looked at George out of the corner of his eye, but didn't see a point in trying to argue with the guy. At that moment, they heard a violent thrashing of the chain link fence in the Devil Rays' dugout and turned just in time to see Lexus railing on Jackson who was sitting at the far end of the bench.

"Dude, that's so uncool," George said.

"He's even more amped up than usual," Joey said, nonchalantly.

"Do you think one of us should say something?" Simon asked the other two umpires. His disgust was evident in the tone of his voice.

Nobody answered him for a second. "Na, the kid's an arrogant little punk anyway," Joey replied sardonically, "anything he's got coming to him, he's earned in spades. Karma man, karma!"

Simon leaned back to get a better look into the dugout only to see Lexus striding away from his demoralized son. His respect for Lexus Helrigle was rapidly diminishing by the second.

"Hey, he might be the right one," George said, jokingly.

"Maybe," Joey said with a slight smirk.

"The 'right one' for what?" Simon asked, welcoming the distraction.

"The perfect victim for the perfect crime," George happily replied.

"What?" Simon asked with great concern. "That again?"

"Oh, it's just a game we play," George said. "We think we've pretty much got the perfect crime. We just can't decide who the victim would be."

"That's disturbing," Simon said as Ralph took the mound to warmup.

"Relax," George said. "It's just something to talk about while we're driving around bored out of our minds in this podunk, little town."

"Na," Joey said as though snapping out of trance. "Jackson wouldn't do at all. Yeah, he's a complete jerk, but his dad has some serious clout around here. I think you're right though. A kid would be best, and I agree that it would have to be someone who was practically asking for it. A girl would tug at people's heart strings, no matter how horrible she was. So, it would have to be some terrible little boy who nobody cared about.

"George thinks that it would be better for the kid to be of some notoriety or from a family with some clout who might already have a bunch of enemies or something, but I think it should be somebody that no one would miss. Somebody like…" his eyes scanned the crowd before pointing at an odd little boy walking around by himself far down the first base line. The boy was no more than 6 or 7 years-old, wearing dirty, ripped jeans, a worn out t-shirt, and no shoes. Simon recognized him immediately as a cold chill ran down his spine.

"You can't be serious!" Simon said emphatically.

"Whoa, dude, there she is!" Joey said to George completely changing the subject while pointing at a striking young girl in a short miniskirt.

"Where?" George asked, straining to get a glimpse of the girl in question.

"There," Joey said as he pointed towards the concession stand. "She's hot!"

"Dude, that's Shannon Zeal!" George said with a laugh.

"So?" Joey said.

"She might be hot," George said indignantly, "but she's also only about thirteen. I know you can't tell anymore these days. It's ridiculous. Steroids in the food or something."

Simon was speechless. He was still trying to ascertain the veracity of Joey and George's comments surrounding the last topic.

"And your point?" Joey asked. "We're only six years apart."

"Yeah, but she's…," George argued. "I mean I get your point. If you guys were twenty-eight and twenty-two and married or something, no one would think anything about it."

"I wasn't planning on marrying her," Joey said coldly.

Correctly perceiving the blatant innuendo, Simon stared at Joey in disbelief. "Dude!...He just said she was 13 years-old!" he said, completely disgusted.

"So?" Joey retorted dismissively.

Lexus yelled down to the three umpires with his hands cupped around his mouth, "Hey, blue, let's get this thing going, huh?"

Joey jerked his head around obediently, swirled his index finger in the air, and cried out, "Yes sir. Come'n down!"

* * *

Sharon's face went flush as she turned to look back in direction of her best friend, Shannon. "So, you only did it *once* before you got pregnant?" she asked in utter disbelief.

"How many times do you think it takes?" Hannah Grace asked with a sympathetic smile.

"I, uh, I don't..." Sharon stammered.

* * *

Ralph mowed down the Devil Rays lineup. It was three up, three down. The momentum had clearly shifted in the Angels' favor, and Lexus was fit to be tied. He angrily barked orders at his infield, while Wilson B. exhorted his players on. It became readily apparent to Simon and everyone else in attendance that there were two starkly contrasting styles of coaching on display.

When the Rays were on top, Lexus gloated and strut around the dugout like the blue ribbon rooster at the county fair. He acted as though the players should be grateful merely to be in his presence. In the opposite dugout through the first five miserable innings, Wilson B. clearly felt worse for his players than he did himself.

As soon as the situation was reversed, Lexus quickly turned on his team, and they were not responding. Conversely, with the Angels making their move, Wilson B. lavished accolades and encouragement on the boys who were thriving under his leadership.

It was human nature for Simon to pick sides, especially considering how Lexus had been riding him the entire game. Deep down, he wanted Wilson B. and the Angels to win in the worst way. Nonetheless, Simon also knew that it would have to happen apart from his bias. To maintain the integrity of the game, he would have to make the calls as he saw them.

With the Devil Rays heading into the last inning with a tenuous three run lead, Lexus continued to admonish the Yankees while Wilson B. continued to cheer on the Angels. The game was still very much in doubt as the first Angel stepped into the batter's box.

* * *

"Oh, I didn't mind so much that I was pregnant or that we were the talk of the town," Hannah Grace admitted. "I had always romanticized about having a baby. I thought it would all be so perfect. I imaged that it would be just like playing with my dolls. I didn't care about anything anybody else said. It was just like a fairy tale as far as I was concerned. My prince charming had come, and we were going to ride off into the sunset and live happily ever after just like Sleeping Beauty or Cinderella."

"But, Aunt Hannah Grace," Sharon said thoughtfully. "You told me you never had any children."

Hannah Grace didn't say anything for what seemed like an eternity. She simply just blankly stared back into Sharon's innocent face.

* * *

The pitch tailed off just outside of the strike zone for ball four. Jackson was still having a hard time finding the plate. As the batter jogged down to first base, the Angel players stood shaking the fence of the dugout, screaming wildly. There was more than just a glimmer of hope now, and Simon found it hard to suppress his delight.

By the time Jackson ran the count to 3-0, Lexus threw his water bottle down in disgust. He had had enough. Lexus called time out and made his way to the mound. It was paramount that Jackson come back and get the batter out. If he walked the second batter, then the tying run would be coming to the plate with no outs. After a scathing tongue-lashing from his father, Jackson threw the next pitch into the backstop. Now there were two on with no one out and everything was on the line.

Jackson dug in, determined to prove himself to his father. Even though his arm felt like Jello, the fiery red-head struck out the next two batters. That was the good news. The bad news was Ralph Livingood was making his way to the plate with runners on first and second, and his team was only down by three runs.

* * *

"That's not entirely true," Hannah Grace said to Sharon with tears streaming down her face. "My little boy, Samuel Rash, died at birth."

Sharon began to cry as she thought about what she had almost done with Mike. "So, what happened?" she managed to ask.

"Hmmph," Mara grunted.

"We don't know what happened to the baby, or why it happened," Hannah Grace answered. "I only know that John and I had been married for five months at the time, with no baby. We had both already dropped out of school, and he had gotten a job down at the mill. Folks just didn't get divorced back then like they do now."

"But you loved each other, right?" Sharon asked naively.

"I loved John as much as any 15-year-old has ever loved any 18-year-old," Hannah Grace answered dully.

* * *

Jackson looked towards the dugout to get the signal from his father before taking the mound. And even though Lexus had clearly given the signal to intentionally walk Ralph, Jackson was determined to win his father's love by doing something big like striking out his fair-haired cousin. Jackson nodded at his father, started his windup, and grooved a fastball. With great anticipation, Ralph swung too soon and pulled the meaty pitch. It rose high above the lights into the muggy, summer air. Silence was followed by a few random groans as the onlookers rose from their seats to see where the moonshot would land. Tailing away from the ball field towards the foul pole, the fly ball landed foul by no more than two feet.

Lexus was halfway to the mound barking instructions at his defiant son while mothers wrung their hands and dads paced like caged lions. Towering over his son Jackson, the angry parent leaned down and unmercifully blistered his son in front of God and everyone. They were nose to nose and Lexus' face was turning tomato red. Flecks of spit showered the 10-year-old's face. By the time Lexus made his way back to the dugout, Jackson had clearly received the message. In no uncertain terms was he to pitch to Ralph. Instead, he was instructed to put Ralph on first, load the bases, and pitch to the next kid on deck. But, Lexus was not going to leave it to chance this time. The possessed, little league skipper could have just told the umpire to put his nephew on first base, but instead chose a more vindictive course of action.

* * *

"That's just it," Hannah Grace said squeezing Sharon's hand tightly. "I had no idea what 'love' was. There wasn't any doubt that I had very intense feelings for John, but what were those feelings? Where did they come from? Do you see what I'm saying? I don't know if I loved him as much as I loved the idea of falling in love- if that makes any sense." Hannah Grace sat back and frowned before trying another approach. "Don't you understand? What did we really know about each other? Nothing. We were attracted to each other, but we had no idea if we were compatible. And as it turns out, we weren't."

"But, why not?" Sharon asked. By now she was completely engrossed in the conversation, oblivious to the storm brewing all around them.

"He had a deep, dark secret that we couldn't overcome," Hannah Grace answered.

"Well, that was you, and I'm me," Sharon defensively sputtered. "What may have been bad for you may be good for me. There's just no way of knowing for sure. Maybe Mike and I are compatible."

Hannah Grace smiled delicately and patted Sharon's hair with her hand. "What I went through would have been horrible for anyone, darling," she intimated. "You're right. We are two different people and times have changed, but people are people and God is still God. You and I aren't much different. You could learn from my mistakes. You don't have to repeat them.

"Do you have to get pregnant before you understand the gravity of what I'm telling you now? Do you know what's at stake? If you can just learn from my mistakes, you could avoid that kind of pain and suffering.

"Sharon, what kind of person would I be if I know the danger of the road that you are heading down and choose to remain silent?

"If Mike is 'Mr. Right', he will be 'Mr. Right' today, tomorrow, or ten years from now. Why rush it? Because if he's not 'Mr. Right', you could be giving away the gift that was intended for the real 'Mr. Right' to some boy just because he was the first one to ever pay any attention to you."

* * *

Jackson dug in one more time as he scowled at his father standing in the dugout. Lexus only gave him a resolute nod. Wilson B., standing in the coach's box down the first base line, observed the exchange and contemplated its meaning. Then Jackson reached back and hurled the ball with everything he had left in the tank. The ball was up and in before Ralph ever knew what happened. He had been sitting on a curve ball that never came. When the fastball hit the earhole of the Rawlings helmet, it sounded like a shotgun going off. Ralph folded like a house of cards and there was a collective gasp from the stands. Wilson B. sprinted down the first base line to his son who was lying motionless in a cloud of dust. Simon was the second person to reach Ralph at home plate. Dr. Al-Banna, who happened to be in attendance, was already making his way down from the bleachers to attend to the injured player.

An eerie silence had engulfed the ballpark. The spectators stood motionless watching the hustle and bustle surrounding the downed Angel. The Devil Rays players respectfully took a knee, while parents from both teams crowded in closer, clutching the chain link fence. Even Sharon and Hannah Grace took time out from their intense conversation to make sure that the boy would be all right.

Within only a few minutes, Dr. Al-Banna had Ralph sitting up and going through a few simple concussion tests. As Simon consciously muttered a prayer, he happened to catch a glimpse of none other than Jack Lawless sitting on the far corner of the Yankee bleachers. He took a long drag on his cigarette with a very pleased expression on his face. Suddenly, a sinister thought crossed Simon's mind. He looked over at Lexus who was standing in front of the dugout with his arms folded. Simon grabbed Joey's arm and dragged the head umpire away from the fallen player.

"Hey, what are you doing?" Joey snapped.

"He hit him on purpose, Joey," Simon said. "You have to eject Jackson from the game."

"What? No way," Joey replied. "That's just how he pitches. He's like Bob Gibson, ya know. He was just throwing high and tight, and it got away from him."

Simon was shaking his head even before Joey could finish his sentence. "Lexus gave him the signal," he said. "Think about it. Has Jackson ever let one get away from him like that? The kid's pretty automatic. Don't you remember what Lexus asked you before the game?"

By now George had made his way over to the other two umpires, garnering the attention of the fans. The three of them spoke in hushed tones with their hands covering their mouths.

"What do you think, George?" Simon asked turning to the third base ump. "You got a good look at it."

"I think he could have been throwing at him," George responded almost apologetically.

"Well, I disagree and my decision is the one that counts," Joey said, digging his heels in.

Dr. Al-Banna dragged Ralph to his feet. The Angel parents clapped wildly in relief at first, but it wasn't long before they let loose a barrage of accusations aimed at the Devil Rays hurler. In response, the Rays' parents let fly a volley of derogatory remarks, doing their best to defend their ace. Like wildfire, emotions on both sides raged out of control.

Joey, underestimating the charged atmosphere, waltzed over to Dr. Al-Banna, Ralph, and Wilson B. in order to find out if he could stay in the game. Simon watched intently. He saw Dr. Al-Banna's lips moving, even though he couldn't hear his words above the deafening noise. With a pained expression on his face, Ralph nodded and slowly rose to his feet. Wilson B. helped his son off of the ground while Mrs. Livingood watched with bated breath from the stands. Her hands were cupped over her mouth and her face was flush. Slowly, Ralph made his way down to first base.

Theatrically, Joey raised his arms and moved towards the backstop. As the crowd waited for an explanation, he called out, "The batter was inadvertently hit by the pitch. He's awarded first base. There are still two outs." After which, he pulled his face mask over his face, dramatically clicked his counter, pointed towards the batter's box and hollered, "Batter UP!"

It was if he had tossed a match onto an oil slick. Chaos did ensue. The Angels' parents screamed injustice while the Devil Rays whistled their approval of the call. Immediately, Wilson B. called timeout and accosted Joey behind home plate. Down the third base line, Lexus wheeled, turned, and walked back towards the dugout clapping fervently. Only Simon from his vantage point could see the smirk and his face. At that moment, Simon lost all respect for the banker and wanted more than ever for the Angels to pull out the victory. Joey pulled his mask back off, indicated that time was called, and began his heated discussion with the incensed Angels coach.

* * *

Hannah Grace surveyed the expressions on the faces of the incensed fans lining the ball field. They were pained. They were distraught. They were gripped with emotion. And then she had a thought. Subtly, she leaned in closer to Sharon who was completely taken aback by the surreal scene that was unfolding. The young teenager was appalled by the despicable behavior of the adults.

"Sharon, darling," Hannah Grace said over the din. "You feel pretty strongly about Mike don't you?"

"Yes, I do," Sharon answered resolutely.

"I thought as much," Hannah Grace said. "And you're quite certain that your feelings are so intense that it must be love, right?"

"What else could it be?" Sharon replied not skipping a beat.

"Well, it might just be a delusion," Hannah Grace replied.

"Huh?" Sharon uttered, confused.

Pointing to the rabid parents who were mindlessly screaming insults at one another, Hannah Grace said, "It could be like these parents. They are so caught up in the moment that they're acting like it's the seventh game of the World Series. Do you think this game is *that* important?"

"Huh, no!" Sharon scoffed. "They're 10 years-old. It's a little league baseball game! I think they may have their priorities a little out of whack."

"And do you think that you could tell any of them that right now?" Hannah Grace asked, scanning the angry mob. "Or do you think that they've been so swept away by their emotions that they've become completely irrational?"

"And yet, looking at it from the outside, we can easily recognize their delusion because we are emotionally detached from the situation."

Sharon was dumbstruck at the wisdom of her aunt's most befitting observation. She could see the veins popping out of the neck of a middle-aged woman who was standing directly in front of her at the fence. The woman's eyes were like daggers, and her vile words dripped with hatred. An otherwise, mild-mannered mother had been emotionally hijacked by her circumstances. Then Sharon finally understood what her aunt was trying to tell her.

"Don't feel ashamed," Hannah Grace said, relieved. "Women, well, girls really, have fallen for it since the beginning of time. I was no different. We make these knee-jerk, life-changing decisions based on our emotions or hormones really.

"There *will be* other boys. And finally, one day, if you hold out, your 'Mr. Right' will come along., and you will be so glad that you…didn't."

After a long pause, Sharon asked, "What was the dark secret? The thing you didn't know about Uncle John when you first met him?"

"He had been scarred by a traumatic experience as a child," Hannah Grace said with emptiness in her voice. "After many years, I finally figured out that he was incapable of ever loving me because he could not love himself."

"Oh Aunt Gracee," Sharon said, grasping her aunt's shriveled hand.

"But, that's not the worst part," Hannah Grace managed to say.

"It's not?" Sharon asked.

"No," Hannah Grace said. "It's the thought that maybe there was a man that I was supposed to meet. That he was somewhere out there waiting for me, and I'll never have the chance to meet him. All because I was so sure that what I was feeling at the time was love and not lust."

Just as the words resounded in Sharon's head, she turned to see a psychotic dad climbing onto the top of the Angels dugout in protest. The man clutched the fence with both hands and shook it violently.

"What on earth?" Hannah Grace said, astounded at the absurd behavior. She hadn't even noticed that Mara had already picked up her lawn chair and was heading to the car.

By the time the authorities pried the man off of the fence and escorted him from the premises, Joey had regained enough control to resume the game. The situation was critical. The Yankees were winning ten to seven with two outs and the bases loaded in the bottom of the last inning. Other than Mara and the father in handcuffs, no one was about to leave the ballpark just yet. The Angels still had a chance.

Jackson reached back one more time and let loose one of his patented curve balls. The feeble Angel batter swung awkwardly at the breaking ball and hit it off of the end of the bat. For a moment, everyone froze. The ball hit the dirt just in front of home plate with some kind of crazy spin. What looked like a routine play for the catcher quickly became an adventure. When he bent down to bare hand the ball, it squirted away. The gaff must have sent him into panic mode. Instead of casually picking up the ball and stepping on home, the 10-year-old wildly lunged at it, raised up, and threw it ten feet over the first baseman's head into right field. With one run across the plate and another on the way, the crowd whipped into a frenzy. The Devil Rays' parents were screaming for their boys to get the ball back in, while the Angels' fans beckoned the base runners to come home.

Unfortunately for the Yankee faithful, the right fielder misjudged the speed of the ball. It squirted past him, down the line and rolled all the way to the fence. By the time he picked it up, the batter was rounding second as Ralph crossed home plate to tie the game. The right fielder was able to collect himself enough to hit his cutoff at the edge of the dirt. The third base coach wildly waved for the runner to head home. Lexus stepped out of the dugout as Joey kicked away the bat so as to not interfere with the inevitable play at the plate. The runner started to slide just as the ball reached the catcher's mitt. Through the dust that rose as a result of the violent collision, Joey flung his hands out to his side indicating that the runner was safe! Devil Rays moaned and Angels screamed.

Even before the players could pour out of the dugout and onto the field, Simon came running down the first base line flailing his arms once again. He got halfway to home before pointing at the winning runner and signaling that the batter was out.

Pandemonium befell the baseball park as Joey jogged out to confer with the brazen first base umpire.

"Unbelievable, what now?" Joey asked emphatically, as he approached Simon.

Simon leaned over and whispered in his ear.

"Are you sure?" Joey asked, uncertain.

"Look it up," Simon said, sure of himself.

Joey thumbed through the official rulebook, found the article in question, and read the fine print. Finally, he nodded, turned, and confirmed the ruling. Joey addressed the entire body of silent observers, "The batter did not run inside of the designated box on the way to first base. In so doing, he obstructed the throw from the catcher. Therefore, he is automatically ruled "Out". Game over!"

Simon turned to the bewildered Angels' coach and mouthed the words, "I'm sorry."

The rabid parents were so amped up that Simon wondered if he would need a police escort to get out of the park. One crazy parent emblazoned by the moment, was working his way through the throng of people in search of his son's coach, Rich Land. The big bear of a man had already made his way down the first base line with his arm draped over his buddy's shoulder.

"Man, those were the gutsiest calls that I have ever seen in my life!" Rich proudly said.

"I don't know about that," Simon answered flatly. "I didn't want to make that last one. Believe me. It would have been easier. I really didn't want the Rays to win after seeing Lexus act like that."

"Yeah, but, it was the right call," Rich replied. "I don't know too many guys who would have made it given the circumstances, with everything on the line. You knew it was going to start WWIII, didn't you?"

"What choice did I have?" Simon answered. "What kind of a game would it be if we could just arbitrarily pick and choose which rules to enforce? No win would have any meaning if that were the case. They'd all be hollow victories."

"All the same," Rich replied still beaming with pride. Then he reached out and slapped his old friend on the shoulder. "I saw the same thing you did the second it happened, and I don't think I would have had the guts to make the call." They awkwardly stood in silence before Rich spoke again. "You feel all right? You look a little flush."

"I think I'm just a little dehydrated," Simon answered, wiping the sweat from his forehead.

"Let me get you something from the concession stand," Rich replied.

Just then, the emblazoned parent, confronted his son's coach.

"Hey, Fields, I need a word with you!" the incensed, little man squawked.

"Oh brother, what now?" Rich lamented, even though he knew exactly what it was regarding. It was one of the most common maladies that plague little league coaches all across the country. There was a deep chasm between what the parent thought his son's abilities were and reality.

"Who's this guy?" Simon asked, under his breath.

"Don't worry about it," Rich said calmly. "I got this. Here's a key to the concession stand. Go over and grab a bottle of water out of the fridge. I'll be over there in a few minutes."

As Simon walked away, he could hear the dad tear into his son's coach with both barrels about how much he paid for his son to play baseball. Simon kept one eye on the altercation as he made his way to the concession stand. He was a little worried that he'd have to pull his fiery friend off of the disgruntled parent, but to his surprise, Rich seemed to be taking the tongue lashing in stride. He simply defiantly stood with his arms folded looking down his nose at the disillusioned dad who raged on about his son's lack of playing time.

Impressed by Rich's self-control, Simon unlocked the door and jarred it open.

"Oh brother," Simon said aloud, "these people have lost their minds."

Satisfied with Rich's calm demeanor, Simon felt his hand along the wall for the switch. Just as the lights came on, his elbow jarred something loose from the counter. A plastic jar fell to the floor with a thud, spilling all of its contents. Begrudgingly, Simon bent down to pick up the jawbreakers that had scattered all over the ground. Raking his hand along the floor beneath the cabinets, his fingers felt something peculiar. Curiously, he reached for the rectangular object and dragged it out from under the ledge.

It was a black, leather bound book coated in a thick layer of dust. As soon as he opened the cover, he was staggered to read the inscription: "Presented to Jeremiah Warner by Island Baptist Church on December 24, 2001". Suddenly, Simon remembered the two separate occasions he had seen Jeremy emerge from the concession stand with one of his players.

Thumbing through the worn out pages, it became clear that it had been Jeremy's own personal Bible. In the margins, Jeremy had written his notes, commentaries, and insights. It was an incredible find like gold or hidden treasure. There had been so many times since Jeremy's untimely departure that Simon had wanted to speak with his friend. He had so many questions that he wanted to ask him. And now he held the next best thing in his hands. As he scanned the contents, Simon couldn't help but remember Jeremy's assertion that there were no accidents.

23

THE GRACIOUS HAND OF GOD

It was nearly dawn. Simon's eyes were heavy, but his spirit had been awakened by Jeremy's systematic breakdown of Christian doctrine. Leaving Rich to deal with the disillusioned parent, Simon had snuck off to a quiet undisturbed place where he could fully digest the wisdom of Jeremy's words.

Wrongly assuming that his friend had gotten tired of waiting for him, Rich made his way back to the tavern expecting to find Simon sitting at the bar. Instead, he was nowhere to be found. Rich's series of texts went unanswered.

Initially, Simon had returned to his humble apartment, but when he found his belongings sitting on the porch and read the pink eviction notice taped to the front door, he was forced to go elsewhere. Taking the cash from his umpiring duties out of his pocket, Simon counted out what he owed Jack in back rent and slid it under the door. He smiled with great satisfaction knowing that he was no longer in debt to Jack Lawless. It was as if a great weight had been lifted off of his shoulders.

Then remembering the unlatched doors to the cellar at Bethel elementary, Simon drove back to the school and navigated the darkened tunnel. As he passed the small recess in the wall, he turned to his right, half expecting to see a little boy sitting in the darkness. His heart skipped a beat even though there was no one there.

Minutes later, he found himself sitting in the familiar teacher's chair in the chorus room above the gym. He stayed there throughout the night, completely enraptured by the Good Book and his late friend's notes in the margins. It was a large compilation of works, and a great deal of information to absorb at one time. Of course, he was tired, but what he read seemed to fill the void deep inside of him like nothing else he had ever known. As a result, he hungered and thirsted for the message all the more. With each new chapter and verse, Simon became more fully aware of his present condition. It was dark thirty when Simon came to grips with the depths of his depravity. He had been living a life filled with wickedness. Up to this point, he had been living for himself and residually, Jack, of course. His pursuit of money, position, power, and pleasure was meaningless. Simon was ashamed of himself after coming to the terrible realization.

Just as the first glimmer of dawn began to cast a soft bluish hue behind the giant grain elevators to the East, Simon read the words that brought him low. Jeremy was just beginning to expound his understanding of reconciliation when the words jumped off the page and clamped down onto Simon's chest. Jeremy had written, "Since then, we know what it is to fear the Lord, we try to persuade men..."

"...'We know what it is to *fear* the Lord'," Simon read aloud a second time as he sat up on the edge of his seat and leaned down over the text.

There were plenty of things to fear in this world, but why should anyone fear a loving God? It was a disturbing question. Simon furrowed his brow and turned the page towards the light to read Jeremy's notes in the margin of the text, "I will fear the justice of God's punishment when I break my covenant with Him. I am accountable for my thoughts, words, and actions."

Simon leaned back in his chair and tried to formulate a logical line of reasoning to refute Jeremy's axiom. But, any argument Simon could put together only disintegrated into a series of poor excuses for trying to justify his own rebellious heart. Finally, he was forced to examine the distinct possibility that Jeremy was right.

"If there is a God, then..." Simon said in a barely audible voice. "If there is a God...? How do I *know* that there is a God at all?" Simon shook his head as though clearing his mind. "Now I sound like Joey. How do I know there's a God? Duh, because I exist. Because the universe and everything in it attests to the fact. Because the Bible tells me so. Because I've always known it to be true intuitively in my heart. And Because *He* spoke to me while I was leaning against a fire hydrant standing in front of Pastor Pete's church in the middle of the night."

Simon realized that he had never been more certain of anything before in his entire life. God was there that night. He had made His presence known and spoke to Simon through the words on the marquee, "Come, Follow Me," just as God was speaking to Simon now.

"Of course, there is a God!" Simon dared to say out loud. "And He is my God because He is everyone's one true God." Even though he had already believed that to be true, he had never fully grasped the ramifications that such a declaration should have made on his life. It had never really sunk in, until now. Once he made the slight paradigm shift, everything else fell into place and became perfectly clear to him. It was like staring at one of those funky, Magic Eye Pictures where clarity only springs to life from seeming chaos, but only after the eyes are properly aligned. The image had always been there. It just took a different set of lenses for it come into focus.

Once he came to that rightful conclusion, the remaining pillars of the Christian doctrine fell like dominoes. It was more than just Jeremy's inspired words. The Holy Spirit was moving within Simon, bringing clarity to what he read. There is a God. He is love. He is right and just and fair. He created the universe and everything in it, including man. God gave man free will. As a result, men chose to sin. Since the price of sin is death, God had to send a redeemer to pay for those sins. God sent his only begotten son to earth to fulfill the commands and the scriptures. Jesus Christ is God incarnate. He was born sinless because he was not born of an earthly father. The virgin Mary was found to be with child through the Holy Spirit. Jesus chose to live a sinless life even though he was exposed to the same temptations as any other man. He qualified himself to be the perfect sacrifice to pay for our sins because he was righteous. Jesus paid the penalty of our sins by allowing himself to be sacrificed on the cross in our place. And through the life, death, burial, and resurrection He overcame sin and death. As a result, He offers the gift of eternal life to anyone who chooses to believe in Him by grace through faith. Just as all have sinned through Adam's original sin, all are offered eternal life through Christ's reconciliation.

For a moment, he considered the word "reconcile". It was an exchange of our sin for his perfection. The words of an old hymn came to mind, "...Jesus paid it all, all to him I owe, death had left a crimson stain. He washed it white as snow." All anyone has to do to receive eternal life is confess their sins, ask for forgiveness, repent, and make Jesus Christ their Lord and Savior. Salvation is a gift that is offered to everyone!

Simon paused to absorb everything that had been revealed to him. What struck him the most was that even after all of that- the Bible, the prophecies, the coming of the Messiah, the cross, the apostles, the testimony of believers, the historical records- He still left us with free will.

"We either choose to believe or not believe in the Good News of the Gospel," Simon uttered, mystified by the simplicity of it all. "Surely, there's more to it," his intellect objected. "There has to be something that we have to do in order to earn salvation."

Jeremy dispelled that myth only a few pages later by providing a concise explanation. The youth pastor stated that if salvation were the result of something that we did, then it would completely nullify what Jesus did on the cross and the need for a Savior. To support his claim, Jeremy cited Ephesians 2:9. Simon flipped through the pages of the Bible and read "...not of works, lest any man should boast."

In the margin next to the verse, Jeremy had written a note. It was a quote from C.S. Lewis, "Either Jesus was a liar, a lunatic, or the Messiah. He leaves us no other options." Just beneath those words Jeremy had jotted down his own thoughts, "People should either believe everything Jesus said, or they shouldn't believe any of it. The scriptures are not a buffet to be picked through. Rather it is a sixty-six course meal to be consumed and digested in its entirety."

Simon agreed. If he truly believed in the word of God, then he would have to accept all of it and not just the parts that he agreed with or the ones that were easy to accept. That included the scripture pertaining to "Fearing the Lord." Believers should fear His just wrath for the times we choose to break his law. Fear His judgment. And fear the punishment that we deserve.

An image came to Simon's mind. It was the swift hand of a loving father on the backside of a rebellious child. After a cursory search, Simon found a verse that crystallized the concept. Proverbs 3:12 read, "…because the Lord disciplines those He loves, as a father disciplines the son he delights in," Without provocation, he suddenly remembered an incident from his own childhood. He couldn't have been more than four or five years old when his father gave him explicit rules to stay in the front yard. But, an errant kick had sent his ball sailing into the street. Without thinking, Simon raced after it into the street. When his father saw him defying his instructions, he had no other choice but to discipline his son. Not long after that, Simon found himself pleading for mercy while draped over his father's lap. And the words of his father came to him as if it were yesterday, "This is going to hurt me more than it hurts you, but it's for your own good. You have to learn a lesson. Do you want to get run over?"

Simon didn't have to wonder about what would be the greater injustice, spanking a child for breaking a rule that was meant for his own good or allowing potentially harmful behavior to go unchecked. The vivid recollection brought even more clarity to the phrase, "Fearing the Lord."

"The fear is respect for His perfection, His authority, His rules, and His justice," Simon rightfully concluded. "God only wants what is best for us, because He loves us and doesn't want to see us make bad decisions that would invariably end in our destruction."

The revelation was a defining moment in Simon's life.

"If I know there is a God who created me, then I should be trying to figure out who He is, what His expectations are, and what He wants me to do with my life!" Simon logically concluded.

That was the dagger. Simon hadn't been doing that. Not in the least. In fact, he was embarrassed to admit that he had never even considered it before. Now he was without any excuses. He wondered how he could have been so blind? But, wasn't it obvious? He did not pray on a regular basis. Or read from God's word. He didn't even regularly attend church, let alone commune with other Christians. In fact, his life didn't look much different from that of an unbeliever!

It wasn't an excuse but an admission. Even if he didn't know God's word, he was still without excuse, because his conscience had always testified to the truth. Simon knew the difference between right and wrong. Until now, he had simply chosen to not always abide by it. Anytime he had to make a decision, there had always been conflicting voices that he heard debating in his head. One that encouraged him to do the right thing, and another that implored him to do the wrong thing. But there was also a third discernible voice that exhorted him to choose the right thing even when it was inconvenient or even harmful for him to do so. Jeremy confirmed as much in a note in the margin of the next page, citing the Law of Human Nature from C.S. Lewis' "Mere Christianity" who said: "Another way of seeing that the Moral Law is not simply one of our instinct is this: If two instincts are in conflict, and there is nothing in a creature's mind except those two instincts, obviously the stronger of the two must win. But at those moments when we are most conscious of the Moral Law, it usually seems to be telling us to side with the weaker of the two." Jeremy concluded in the margin that the Law of Human Nature directs the two instincts for us to choose what is right, and just, and fair.

After reading the words of the great apologist, the words that Parker spoke at Jeremy's vigil overwhelmed him. If Simon was correct then the assertions of a 10-year-old child had concisely summarized the purpose of life. Parker had said that the ultimate goal of our lives should be to use our talents to do God's perfect will for His glory, so that one day we may stand face to face with Him in heaven and hear the words, "Well done, good and faithful servant."

"I've been looking at the wrong scoreboard to determine if I have been winning or losing!" Simon thought. The morning rays of light now shone brightly just beyond the heights of grain elevators casting three long, skinny shadows over the fresh dew of the playground grass. "That's why Jack was never able to get to Jeremy. He wasn't about money, or things, or status, or even his own safety. His 'one thing' was to serve God by using his talents to serve others. That's how he filled the void inside of him."

Quickly, Simon thumbed through the pages of Jeremy's book trying to find further evidence to corroborate such a notion. He hoped to find something to substantiate what he already suspected to be true. Then he discovered it in Romans. At the bottom of the page, he found the answer. There was more to the Christian life than just being saved. For the first time, Simon read about sanctification. Jeremy referred to it in a note at the top of the page as the process of becoming Holy by setting oneself apart for special use by God.

"So that's what he meant by 'working out my own salvation'," Simon thought. "I've been created for a purpose. I have a specific task that God has set aside for me to do. In order to achieve the task, I will have to become more and more like Jesus everyday. The evidence of my genuine transformation will be in the fruit of my labor. Not that I have to do works to be saved, but as a natural byproduct of truly being saved.

It was an exciting, and at the same time, terrifying thought. What if he failed to achieve his purpose? What if he had already missed his opportunity with the referendum or with Rocky? It was a thought that made him genuinely afraid. Suddenly, he thought of the conversation that he had with Jack while sitting in the lawn chairs behind his apartment building.

"That's it!" Simon said, jumping out of his chair. "Jack was right. My thing is *fear*! But, it wasn't what I *was* afraid of. It was what I *wasn't* afraid of! I didn't fear the Lord."

At least, Jack almost had it right. That was the genius of his deception. It was couched in truth. He was barely off the mark when he said that the key to happiness was finding the one thing that makes a person happy and then doing it. Simon nearly laughed out loud at the absurdity of such a faulty assertion.

"What if what made you happy was doing nothing, or stealing, or...what if it was raping women, or murdering children? Or marrying your dog," he thought.

How ridiculous! And yet, somehow, he had almost fallen for it. "The key to happiness is not finding out what makes *me* happy," Simon realized, "it's finding out what makes *God* happy and then doing it. More than likely, doing what makes God happy will make us happy. It's the only thing that can truly fill the void in our lives! Wow."

If all of that were true, the implications were far reaching. All of his life he never had money or possessions or status. The majority of his thoughts, plans, and actions surrounded acquiring those things, so he could finally be somebody and be content. His greatest fear was to fail at that endeavor. Everything he had ever known in the secular world had only supported that notion, and he had fallen for the lies hook, line, and sinker. All of this time he had been a slave to the things of this world, wanting everything and being satisfied with nothing. Now he was finally ready to be a slave to righteousness.

Simon set Jeremy's book on the desk in front of him, got down on his knees, clasped his hands, bowed his head, and prayed, "Lord, please show me your will for my life to glorify you!"

As he prayed, the long, skinny shadows in the schoolyard slowly retreated towards the base of the grain elevators as the sun ascended in the East. Finally, Simon lifted his misty eyes.

There was no bolt of lightening, no thunderous earthquake, and no burning bushes. There was only a soft breeze as Simon took notice of an edition of *The Bethel Chronicle* sitting on the desk beneath Jeremy's Bible. Out of curiosity, Simon slid the book off to the side, lifted the newspaper, and read the headline. It was the article about repainting of the entryway to the school and the unsuccessful attempt to sway the referendum in favor of the new school.

Simon sighed as he shook out the paper and held it out in front of his face. Carefully, he examined the before and after photos of the entryway one more time. As his eyes surveyed the grainy, black and white photograph taken in 1935, his attention was once again drawn to the corner of a picture frame or plaque hanging on the wall next to the staircase. The two photographs taken from almost identical angles only served to highlight their dissimilarities. Simon bit down on his bottom lip as though he were ruminating on the implications of the seemingly inconsequential differences. Finally, his eyes were drawn to the top of each photo. Somehow he had never given much thought to the chandelier that was hovering over the heads of the students in the old picture. It was conspicuously absent from the newer photo taken just a few weeks ago.

Instantly, Simon was reminded of his own disappointment at how the mere cosmetic improvements failed to recapture the grandeur of the once proud building.

Quickly, he rose up and hurried down to the entryway. Looking at the entryway from the same vantage point that both pictures had been taken, he held the old photograph out at arms length and compared it to the present reality. In the full brilliance of the morning light, all of the imperfections became glaringly obvious. The building was only a shadow of its former self.

It was a fact that saddened him. He was overcome with guilt and shame as he thought of how he had become so full of himself as a result of all the accolades and attention he had received. His stomach turned as he thought about the smugness with which he answered the reporter's questions in the article. Then he remembered his drunken behavior at the tavern the day Rocky slammed his necklace onto the bar. He couldn't get his friend's look of disgust and disappointment out of his mind.

"What was I thinking?" Simon muttered. Solemnly, he bowed his head and closed his eyes for a moment. When he opened them again, he held the old newspaper photo out and compared it one last time to the genuine article. Now, looking at it with an honest eye, it was obvious that he had come up woefully short of his goal.

Dismayed, he looked skyward to where the chandelier had once divinely presided over the entryway. Then he made his way to the stairwell and rubbed his hand over the warped wall where the mysterious fixture had hung in the picture taken in 1935.

"What was it that was so prominently displayed here in the entryway?" Simon thought.

For some time, he tried to imagine what could have possibly been on that wall before he was struck with an epiphany. If God had brought him back to Bethel for a purpose, and that purpose was to restore the school in order to sway the vote in favor of the referendum, then that was what he needed to do. However, it was not going to be with scrapers and paintbrushes but with a sledgehammer and a circular saw. Instead of trying to make the exterior appear transformed, he would actually have to transform it. The conclusion resonated deep down inside of him, and he was left with only one thought, "But, how in the world am I going to do that?"

Little did he know it, but the answer to that one simple question would officially qualify him as certifiable to the rest of the secular world.

* * *

Once again, he bowed his head, said a prayer, and consulted Jeremy's Bible. There he found the words, "Does a builder start a project without counting the cost?" Immediately, he knew what he needed to do. It wasn't long before Simon was standing in front of Andy Cross in the basement next to the boiler at Philo Grade School.

Andy was on his back beneath the ancient furnace grunting and groaning as he strained to work loose a rusty, old bolt. He paused for a moment and then turned his head to look at Simon.

"Oh, I'd say it'd cost a good thirty to forty grand if ya was to do it right," Mr. Cross replied indifferently.

"Wow, that's considerably more than I was hoping you would say," Simon admitted after making a few of his own calculations in his head. "Where would you start?"

"Well, the first thing that'd have to be done…" Mr. Cross began to say before something unsettling occurred to him. "…What do you want to know for?"

"Because I need to know how much money to ask for, or raise, or…," Simon plainly replied.

"For what?" Mr. Cross asked, not allowing his mind to go there.

"To renovate the interior school of course," Simon answered, almost exasperated.

"I thought we done that already!" Mr. Cross said, climbing to his feet. "You got a bunch of people to help out. You even said so yourself that we done all we could do." He was now absentmindedly wiping his greasy hands on a rag.

"But, it wasn't enough," Simon argued while holding up the article in his right hand. "They're still going to vote down the referendum. And I *did* think that we had done all that we could do, but I was wrong. Don't you see? We have to make it look *exactly* like it did originally. Then people will get nostalgic, you know? It will make them remember how things used to be. It will make them care again."

Mr. Cross fidgeted nervously. "I-I don't know I…" he sputtered.

"Come on, Mr. Cross, we can do this," Simon said enthusiastically, taking a few steps towards him. "We can make a difference here for future generations. This could be our moment."

Mr. Cross spun away from Simon, flung himself on the ground, and slid back under the old boiler that only he could fix. "No sir, I don't want no part of it," he muttered angrily. "I got too many things to do to get ready for the school year. Who else is gonna do all this work, huh? Me! That's who. Just me. Now go on, get!"

Simon stood for a moment, dumbstruck at the unexpected hostility from the old, public servant. "Well, if it's all the same to you, I'm going to move forward with it," Simon said, unapologetically.

"Do what you gotta do," Mr. Cross gruffly answered as he returned to working on the rusted bolt.

Simon stood there for a few more seconds watching the stubborn custodian strain against the unyielding bolt before heading back to Bethel to pay Thelma another visit at her trophy shop.

* * *

Having his enthusiasm slightly diminished by Mr. Cross's unexpected rejection of the venture, Simon waited with bated breath for the aged principal's response.

For some time, Miss Harold sat hunched over a blue ribbon. She was once again wearing a magnifying glass that looked more like a small, black telescope attached to her forehead like a coal miner. Completely engrossed in the meticulous nature of her work, the old curmudgeon didn't even bother looking up when Simon first entered the shop. Nor did she so much as shoot Simon a sideways glance during his prepared speech about the virtues of his proposed project. Again, he closed his eyes and asked God for the right words.

While he spoke, Miss Harold carefully attended to the embroidery of the ribbons. After he had finished, Simon happened to notice that all of the ribbons in the box next to her desk were blue. Finally, she answered him.

"And do you have any idea how much it would cost to complete a project of that scale?" she snarled.

"No, not exactly, but Mr. Cross estimated somewhere in the neighborhood of thirty to forty-thousand dollars," Simon answered.

"Cross?" she snapped, peaking at him over the top of her magnifying glass. "Is he in on this too?"

"No, ma'am," Simon regretfully replied. "In fact, he seemed completely put off by the idea."

"Figures," Miss Harold grunted.

"How so?" Simon asked, more than a little surprised by her response.

"Well, it's two fold really," Miss Harold answered. "For one thing, he's overwhelmed as it is, trying to get two old buildings ready for another school year. And second, it's about job security."

"Ma'am?" Simon asked.

"Think about it," Miss Harold continued, "would we really need a janitor of his expertise if we had a brand new school to take care of? No sir. We'd only need one custodian with a base level pay who could handle a broom and a dustpan. Mr. Cross has been keeping Philo and Bethel Elementary schools up and running for over forty years now. It's what he does. It's what he knows. It's who he is. And you come in and ask him to help you change all of that? To make him obsolete."

Simon had never considered that possibility before, but somehow it made sense. Mr. Cross did take a great deal of pride in doing his job. He loved regaling the tales of when he had to get up in the middle of the night, walk over to the school, and load the boiler with coal in the dead of winter. The more Simon thought about it, the more her assessment seemed to have some merit. A new school with nothing to fix or maintain might be his biggest fear because his services would no longer be needed.

Miss Harold snapped him out of his musings, "So, how do you propose we pay for this little…little…"

"Reclamation project?" Simon interjected.

Miss Harold paused and sat back in her seat for a moment, struck by the words

Simon had chosen. "...Okay...reclamation project," she continued. "I mean if we had that kind of money, we could practically build the new school."

"I'll come up with money," Simon boldly insisted.

"You're just going to dig up forty grand somewhere," Miss Harold said with a chuckle.

"No, of course not, but I have a feeling that we'll get what we need to do the job," Simon challenged.

"But, how do you know?" Miss Harold asked brusquely.

"I just know," Simon replied coyly.

"But, how?" she snipped. "How could you just *know* something like that?"

"Because, I..." he stammered with his eyes searching the room.

"Yes? Well, what is it?" she said, trying her best to intimidate him.

"Because I have faith!" he admitted after being provoked.

"*Faith?*" she said with a laugh. "Faith in what, yourself?"

"Faith in God, okay?" he intimated. "I have faith that God will provide the resources for us."

"Which God?" Thelma asked, still unconvinced.

"What?" Simon asked, caught off guard.

"Which God do you have faith in?" she pointedly asked.

Overcoming his inhibitions, he finally blurted out, "The Christian God of the Trinity!" There he said it. And now she would know.

Thelma covered her mouth with her fist and looked him over through the magnifying glass as if trying to peer into his very soul.

"I believe that God will give us the money because I believe He is calling me to do this thing," Simon said with great conviction.

Finally, she had heard what she had been waiting to hear. For the first time in many, many years, she heard something that used to be commonplace in Bethel. It was something that she used to even see in her own reflection many years ago. That same something had sadly faded over the years. In fact, it had been so long ago that she had nearly forgotten what it looked like. She reached up, pulled her glasses off of her face, and chewed on the frames.

"Faith, huh?" she squawked.

"Faith," Simon repeated.

"That's all ya got just Faith and nothin' else?" she asked.

"Just Faith," he replied, unapologetically.

"Even if you could raise that kind of cash, you have other duties..." she began to say.

"I'd get them done each day before working on the entryway," Simon replied. He was empowered by what appeared to be a conciliatory statement on her behalf.

"You don't have much time," she said.

"I'll get it done," Simon said.

"This isn't about Hope Wiseman is it?" she said squinting through one eye and pointing the glasses accusingly at him.

"What? Hope?" Simon scoffed.

He hadn't thought about the obvious impropriety before even being asked the question. After he examined his own heart to see if the charge had any merit, he answered, "No ma'am. This is about something much bigger. It's about…" He had to stop short for a moment and think about just how much he could divulge to her about his recent revelation. "It's about stepping up to the plate and answering the call. It's about…"

Thelma put up a hand as if she had heard enough. "I guess you need to get to work then," she said, "but before you get started, you're going to need a contractor. Tell you what. On the left hand side of my desk under a stack of manilla folders and forms from the state you'll find a list of phone numbers. On that list, is the name of a contractor who'll give you a fair estimate. Cross said forty-thousand, huh? He was just trying to scare you off. Mention my name to this guy, and he'll give you a reasonable price for coming out. He owes me one anyway, and if he tells you that he doesn't owe me one, tell him that he soon will owe me one, so knock it off."

"So, that's a yes?" Simon asked, nearly overcome with excitement.

"Under a couple of conditions," Miss Harold said. "One, you have money in hand before you spend it."

"Okay," Simon replied, "and what's the second condition?"

"Don't tell *anybody* about what you're doing," Miss Harold snapped. "I mean no one. There are people out there who will only serve to undermine anything good you try to do in this town and that includes half of the people serving on the school board."

"Okay! Deal! Thank you, Miss Harold, you won't regret it!" Simon said, backing away towards the front door of the shop.

She considered for a brief moment if she should say anything else before deciding that Simon would need his youthful, unbridled enthusiasm. "What are they going to do, fire me?" Miss Harold snarled, as she put her glasses back on. Carefully she loaded another blue ribbon into the press. "Once you got the thing tore apart, they'll have no other choice but to have us put it back together again, anyways." The jingle of the bell above the door announced Simon's exit from the building.

Miss Harold looked up for a moment and thought about the implications of what she had just agreed to. "God help us," she muttered as she raised the lever to get a peak at the golden words inscribed on the blue ribbon that read, "Participant."

"Hmmph," she grunted as she laid it down, grabbed another blue ribbon from the box, and then another, and another, until finally there were more than enough to go around.

* * *

Fueled by the surprising support of Miss Harold, Simon hurried to the old principal's office in order to find the phone number of the contractor who owed her a favor. For the first time in his life, Simon stood behind the large, imposing walnut desk. He looked over the cluttered mess in disbelief.

"Stack of manilla folders, huh?" he said in wonder. "The whole thing is covered in manilla folders!"

Then he remembered that she had said to look on the lefthand side of the desk. But, from which side of the desk? Randomly, he picked a side and started his search. His left hand held the stack in place, while he walked his fingers down to the bottom of the stack with his right. It was slow going, because he didn't know exactly what he was looking for. Before him lay the proverbial needle in a haystack. Only the needle was a single sheet of paper hiding in a morass of state and federal documents.

After ten minutes of searching, he muttered to himself, "What is all of this stuff anyway?"

Partially out of curiosity, but mostly out of consternation, he began reading some the documents that had been tucked away in the folders. There were state IEP folders, discipline logs, inclusion documentation. In another pile, there were a series of IGAP test prep booklets, and IGAP test results. In yet another stack, there were state standards, school district budget records, and a guide to federal rules and restrictions.

Simon shook his head in dismay as he moved from stack to stack across the desk. At the bottom of the very last stack buried beneath an avalanche of bureaucratic red tape, his fingers ran across something that felt different from the regular folders that he had been shuffling through. It had a hard, leather cover and was rectangular in shape. Simon leaned out over the stack and careened his neck to get a good look at the unidentifiable object. Finally, his hands found the edges of the hardcover book, and he dragged it out from under the weighty folders. To his surprise, it was an old, almost antique copy of the Constitution. Simon blew the dust off of the ragged book and set it down next to him on top of a separate pile of folders. Then he reached his hand back down into the stack and pulled out another large, musty book.

He hadn't anticipated what he had found there. It was the Bible. Carefully, Simon set down the stack of folders that he had been searching through so that he could more closely examine the worn out pages of the old book.

"I guess that explains Miss Harold's unexpected reaction to my declaration of Faith," Simon mused.

After a few more minutes, Simon set aside the Good Book and the Constitution and resumed his original task. Digging to the very bottom of the pile, he pulled out an unidentified, wooden object and a single piece of paper. Simon held the wooden object out in front of him. It was a paddle. In fact, it was *the paddle* that all of the kids had feared when he was a student at Bethel Elementary. Before anyone even considered breaking the rules, they thought of the paddle. It represented power, authority, and justice. And it was very effective for maintaining order and discipline.

"That's strange," Simon thought as he turned the paddle over in his hand. He had only known one or two classmates who had ever claimed to have gotten paddled, and until now, he had never even laid eyes on it. "Funny," he mused. The mere threat of the paddle held such power over him to follow the rules. And it worked. "But how?" he contemplated. "Surely, somebody, at some point, had actually been paddled, and somehow that lore was enough to keep the rest of the kids in check. What a strange phenomenon." Simon wondered if it still had the same affect on the students in the school now. He thought of Little Simon Adamson and the story that Mr. Cross told about the unruly child biting a little girl. "Surely, if that story were true, it would have warranted strong disciplinary measures."

Simon set the paddle down on top of the Bible before remembering that he was holding a piece of paper in his other hand. Finally, he had found what he had been looking for. Written on a yellow piece of notebook paper was the list of phone numbers that Miss Harold had referenced, including the number of the contractor. Simon took the phone list, the paddle, the Constitution, and the Bible and he made his way back up the stairs to his favorite chair in the chorus room.

* * *

With the official estimate in hand, Simon waited impatiently in the lobby of the bank. After a few minutes, Will poked his head around the corner and called out to Simon.

"Pssst, Simon," Will said, motioning for his friend to follow him down the long hallway to the conference room, "Lexus is just rapping up a meeting and will be with you in a minute. You can hang out in here and wait for him."

"Thanks, man," Simon said as he took a seat in one of the green leather chairs at the large, boardroom table.

"So, are you going to take it?"

"Take what?" Simon asked, confused.

"The job, idiot," Will replied, smattered with a few colorful expletives. "Are you going to take the job?"

"Oh," Simon said looking around at the impressive boardroom. He had all but forgotten about the offer. "Oh, no, I don't think so."

He was somewhat distracted as he looked at all of the degrees, plaques, awards, and clippings of Lexus Helrigle. There on a shelf proudly displayed above Lexus's diploma from Harvard were three Golden Cow championship baseball trophies form the Dairy League.

"What?" Will said stepping fully into the conference room. "Are you crazy? You…" Then he heard the sound of a door opening at the end of the hall.

"I wish we could help, Mr. Cain, but we already sold off your mortgage to another company," Lexus said, feigning expression of regret.

"Well, thanks for your time anyway Mr. Helrigle," Danny said, dejected.

"No problem, and best of luck to you and your wife and that little one," Lexus said as he showed Danny the door. "I hope she gets better soon, real soon. We're all sending positive thoughts your way."

"Oh, uh, thanks," Danny said without any inflection in his voice.

Simon and Will looked on as the distraught father slumped his shoulders and walked off down the hallway towards the lobby. He looked haggard and worn. His face bore dark bags under his eyes and a grizzled beard. Suddenly, Simon remembered the conversation he had overheard between the young man and the owners of the hardware store.

Lexus stood in the doorway to the conference room for a second with his hands in his suit pockets looking down the hallway. He smiled, shook his head, and clicked his teeth. Then he let out a deep, audible sigh, and turned towards Simon sitting in the conference room.

"Simon!" Lexus said enthusiastically through his hoarse, raspy voice.

Will stepped back against the conference room door pressing his chin into his chest in an effort to get out of the way of his superior. Simon stood up and stuck out his hand.

"Ha, good to see you, my boy," Lexus said, grinning from ear to ear. "As you can see, my voice still hasn't recovered from the game last night." He pulled out a chair at the head of the giant table and took a seat. As he did so, he motioned for Simon to have a seat. Slumping back in his high backed, swivel chair, Lexus crossed his legs, leaned his elbow on the polished table, and propped his head against his thumb and forefinger. "What a game, huh, crazy?"

"Yes, it was," Simon replied, nervously biting his bottom lip.

"And what a great call, man!" Lexus said, reaching out and slapping Simon's knee before resuming his relaxed position. "Man, saved our bacon. That was something. Will, did you hear about the game?" Lexus asked, turning towards his understudy.

"Yes, yes I did," Will replied, disingenuously. "Wow." He was clearly uncertain as to whether Lexus wanted him in the room or not.

"I tell you what," Lexus continued, looking back to Simon, "I had never heard of that rule in my life. Boy, oh boy, you really showed me something last night."

"Yeah, it helps to know the rules if you're going to call the game," Simon replied.

"Well, it's one thing to know them, and it's another to be able to take control and enforce them in the heat of the moment," Lexus said, beaming. "Took some guts. Jackson sure was lucky that you made the right call." Then he lifted his eyebrows, glanced at Will, and burst out in laughter. "I mean, I actually let him sleep in the house. Ha!"

Will, picking up on the signal, burst out laughing as well. Simon, however, remained stoic.

After an awkward pause, Lexus asked, "Well, what can I do you for today? Have you come to accept my job offer?"

Will finally dared to speak. "Do you want me to leave?" he asked submissively, pointing towards the door.

Lexus, never taking his eyes off of Simon, gestured for Will to stay and sit.

Will took out a pen and notepad and waited for Simon's response. Suddenly, the reality of the situation began to take hold, and his heart began to race. He said a short prayer to himself, and answered, "Well, sir, that's actually not the reason I came here today…" Simon began to say as he folded his hands and set them on the surface of the shimmery table in front of him.

Then he proceeded to tell Lexus and Will all about everything that God was telling him to do at the school. During the long monologue, Lexus never uttered a word or changed his blank expression. With dull, steely eyes he continued to stare at Simon, tactically absorbing the information.

Meanwhile, Will was frantically writing as he did his best to capture the meeting minutes. From time to time, he would shoot a glance at Lexus during the most outlandish parts of Simon's incredible story. When Simon was finished, he took a deep breath, sat back in his chair, and waited for Lexus's answer to his most unusual request. The banker sat back in his chair, put his hands behind his head, and stared at the ceiling in silence. In an effort to break the awkward silence, Will began to speak before Lexus raised his hand.

"Well, Simon, that was a very interesting story, but…" Lexus started to say.

Just then Wilson B. happened to be walking down the hallway past the conference room. His head was down as he poured over a financial report. Lexus caught a glimpse of him out of the corner of his eye and called out to the vice president of the First National Bank of Bethel.

"Livingood," Lexus said, "come in here a minute. You gotta hear this."

Wilson B. stopped, retraced his steps, and stuck his head in the doorway to the conference room. "Yes?" Wilson B. asked with his eyebrows raised. "Oh, hey Simon, how are you?"

Simon rose out of his seat to shake hands.

"Thought I might have to step in between you two," Lexus said with a chuckle.

Wilson B. clearly understood the inference. "No, no hard feelings," he said. "Just calling 'em like you saw 'em, right Simon?"

"Yes, sir," Simon said, sitting back down.

Lexus gestured for Wilson B. to have a seat. "I don't know if you knew it or not, but Wilson B. here actually oversees all of our loans," the shrewd banker said to Simon. Then he turned to Wilson B. and said, "I'd like for you to hear this. Simon has a very unusual request for a loan. Please, sit."

"I'd love to, but my wife is in my office waiting to go have lunch," Wilson B. replied.

"This is really fascinating," Lexus said. "Hey, she's the head of the PTO at the school, right?"

"Yeah, that's right," Wilson B. answered, thrown off a little by the seemingly irrelevant question.

"Bring her in here, she'd be interested in hearing this too," Lexus said. He pointed at Simon. "You don't mind, do you?"

Simon shook his head dismissively, but on the inside he was beginning to feel a little sick to his stomach. All of a sudden, he remembered Miss Harold's stipulation of keeping the project under the radar, and his palms began to sweat.

Wilson B. could always tell when Lexus had already set his mind on something. There was no point in trying to change it. Obediently, Wilson B. walked down to his office and returned a minute later with his wife in tow.

"You remember Angie, don't you?" Wilson B. asked Simon.

"Yes, it's good to see you again, ma'am," Simon said, rising to his feet.

"Oh, please, sit back down," she said, still confused as to why she was there.

Wilson B. and Angie made their way around to the opposite side of the boardroom table and sat down.

"Simon here was telling me about a little...what did you call it?" Lexus asked, pointing at Simon.

Nervously, Simon covered his mouth as he cleared his throat. "A reclamation..." he started to say before quickly correcting himself, "...a renovation project."

"Oh really?" Angie said, genuinely interested.

"Would it be similar to the one at the school?" Wilson B. asked.

"Well, actually it would be at the school," Simon sheepishly replied, recalling the amount of work the Livingoods had put into the painting of the entryway.

"So, are you wanting to repaint the classrooms or something?" Mrs. Livingood said with a bright smile. "Because I was thinking the same thing while we were painting the entryway. It would be so nice for the kids to start the new school year with freshly painted classrooms..."

"No," Lexus said flatly, "he wants to renovate the entryway.
Simon blushed.

"The entryway?" Wilson B. repeated.

"It's not that I want to, I...I..." Simon stammered.

"Oh yeah, that's right, God told him to renovate the entryway," Lexus said.

The Livingoods shot Lexus a perplexing look before returning their gaze to Simon for confirmation.

Backpedaling a little, Simon made a feeble attempt to explain himself. "Well, you see... it's really... it's about the referendum," he said taking a different approach. "You see, I was reading the article in *The Chronicle*. Well, I was actually praying at the time, and then I saw the article. I don't know if you read it, but the article indicated that merely painting the entryway was not going to change the results of the referendum."

Simon looked around the table at the blank stares.

"And I don't want all of our work to go for naught," Simon added, embarrassed. His mind scrambled for the words to explain. What had seemed so clear to him earlier in the morning now seemed crazy. Had he become some kind of religious freak or something?

Simon tried to dismiss the persistent thought from his mind. As a result, he started by giving a somewhat benign, secular answer. "I mean, the whole idea of painting the entrance was to get the referendum passed," he continued awkwardly. "Now that it appears to have made little to no difference. So, I think we should… what I mean to say is…we ought to…"

"Take it to another level?" Wilson B. offered.

"Yes," Simon replied, thankful for the help. "Exactly, take it to another level."

"Just playing devil's advocate here," Lexus began to say with his hands pressed together in front of his mouth like a church steeple. "What difference would it really make for the kids being in a new building? I'm just trying to look at it from the landowners' perspective, you know. The ones whose taxes will go up and actually have to pay for the thing. After all, it is the same superintendent, school board, principal, teachers, textbooks… So, what difference does it make if they're in a 'new' school?"

The directness of the question slightly awoke Simon from his position of uncertainty. Getting a little defensive, Simon shifted in his seat and sat forward leaning on his forearms.

"Mr. Helrigle, there are many, many pragmatic reasons that more than justify a new building," Simon said with conviction.

"Such as…?" Lexus said, calmly.

"Such as," Simon said, his eyes searching as though the answers were written on the walls of the conference room. "Such as the safety of the children. There's mold, and asbestos, and fire hazards…handicap accessibility…"

Lexus rolled his eyes and smirked. Simon looked around the room to see that the argument was failing to capture the imagination of his audience.

"Okay," Simon said, "what about technology, having the school wired for laptops and wireless high-speed internet?"

"Didn't Jack offer to make some upgrades?" Lexus asked.

Simon closed his eyes for a second and took a deep breath. Then a still soft voice spoke to him. And Simon remembered a quote from Thomas Jefferson that he had read in the New England Primer. Jefferson stated that commerce between master and slave is despotism. He continued that nothing is more clearly written in the book of fate than that these people are to be free, and he concluded that we are to establish the law for educating the common people.

"Yes, but it's so much more than that!" Simon said just as the spirit began to move within him. "It's more about where our priorities lie. What do you think it took to construct that building back at the turn of the century? What kind of capital did the people of Bethel have to generate? What kind of sacrifices did they have to make? Where were their priorities? They valued education, holding it in high enough regard to make the school the most impressive building in the entire county. And that was at a time when they knew good and well that the vast majority of those kids were simply going to go back to working on the farm after they graduated, but they got it! They understood that true freedom comes through wisdom and discipline. They knew that an education was the one thing that could never be taken away from their children.

"A new building would send a message to the next generation that this is important. People would realize that this takes priority. This is fundamentally who we are as a nation. After all, isn't education the cornerstone to life, liberty, and the pursuit of happiness?"

Will couldn't help himself, he started sarcastically humming, "God Bless America".

Incensed by the overt subterfuge of his friend, Simon gritted his teeth and quipped, "That's right. God Bless America! God Bless the America that our Framers created, the one that people have given their lives for, the one that people put their lives on the line for us everyday." Fueled by the mocking and snickering, Simon started to raise his voice before a strange calmness overcame him. "Look, all of us are beneficiaries of the sacrifices of the generations that have come before and that includes the mockers sitting in ivory, air conditioned towers who scoff at a sentiment like patriotism."

"Whoa, settle down there, Simon," Will said, haughtily. "I mean, nobody loves this country more than I do."

"No, I don't think so," Simon replied, shaking his head. "I don't think you love the America that I love. I think that maybe all you see are dollar signs. I think maybe you love the America that hides behind the 1st Amendment to put up an adult, strip club superstore kind of thing next to the interstate instead of a school. What kind of message does that send to the kids? Where are our priorities?"

Stricken by Simon's rant, Will's panicked eyes darted to meet those of his mentor, but Lexus refused to surrender a visible reaction. Instead, he looked on with haughty eyes in eerie silence.

"What are you talking about, Simon?" Mrs. Livingood asked, letting out a nervous laugh.

"I am talking about the land by the interstate where they want to build the new school," Simon replied.

"What about it?" Wilson B. asked, sitting forward in his chair with a look of confusion.

"Jack Lawless wants to put a strip club slash porno outlet on that site instead of the new school," Simon said uncertain as to whether or not Wilson B. was feigning surprise.

Will conveniently stopped taking notes for the moment.

After a brief pause, Wilson B. glanced at his wife and then turned to Lexus. "What about it, Lex'?" Wilson B. asked. "Is there any truth to what the kid's saying?"

Lexus gave a contrived look of bewilderment. "Goodness, I don't know," Lexus said flatly. "I hadn't heard of anything like that."

"Well, the bank holds the deed to the property," Wilson B. said matter-of-factly. "I would have been informed if there were any offers on the table for that particular property, especially given the circumstances."

"Hmm, no, there's no offer on the table, I..." Lexus sat forward and snapped his fingers. "Say, let me get Claire on the phone. She's got the property listed," he said pulling out his iPhone. "I'll give her a quick buzz and see if we can't clear this whole thing up." Lexus dialed the phone, held it to his ear, leaned way back in his leather chair, and tapped his fingers on the polished table.

Everyone waited expectantly in silence. Simon sat back and folded his arms, marveling at the theatrics.

"Hey, hon," Lexus said casually. "What, yeah, we can do that...hey, I got a question for you. You're where?" Lexus stood up with the phone still held to his ear and walked over to the doorway. Sticking his head out, he dropped the phone to his side. "She just so happens to be in the lobby," Lexus said as he ushered his wife into the room. "Hon', you remember Simon."

"Sure do, the famous organizer of the school painting project," she replied. "How are you? Oh, hey, look the gang's all here," she added when she saw the Livingoods sitting across the table.

"Hon', why don't you have a seat with us," Lexus offered. "Simon here was just saying that Jack Lawless had plans to turn the property slated for the new school into some kind of 'dance club'," Lexus said coolly. "Do you know anything about that?"

"What?" Claire replied, coyly. "No, I hadn't heard anything of that nature. In fact, I was just looking over my listings earlier this morning and there are no offers at the present time."

"Huh, well that solves that little mystery," Lexus said. "It seems as though you have been misinformed, Simon."

"I should hope so," Mrs. Livingood said. "People would be irate to have one of those...those... establishments in Bethel. It's bad enough that they've got that one in Neoga."

"Well, not only that, but Bethel's zoning laws would have to be changed before anything like that could happen," Wilson B. said confidently. "It's not as simple as someone purchasing a property, putting up a building, and slapping a sign in the window that says 'Open for Business'."

"True, true," Lexus said, "I nearly forgot all about those pesky zoning laws. Now, Simon, I don't think anyone here minds the idea of you are trying to renovate the old school building. It's admirable. But, as a businessman, I just can't go around giving out loans to every Tom, Dick, and Harry. We need more than just the eye test to do that sort of thing. So, we would need to know how you propose to repay that kind of debt. First off, how much do you currently have in your savings account?"

Will smiled knowingly, as he resumed jotting down the minutes.

"We can't have bad, um, unsecured loans," Lexus said with a laugh. "I mean the last thing I want to do is repo a school building. Ha! So, how much are we talking here?"

"Nothing," Simon answered, more than slightly embarrassed.

"Do you have a full time job lined up with a substantial salary, something with benefits perhaps?" Lexus asked. "You've made it clear that you're not accepting the position at the bank, right?"

"No, I have not procured a permanent position at the present time," Simon regrettably replied.

"Some sort of trust fund perhaps, there uh, Pip'?" Lexus asked incredulously. He looked around the room at the dismayed faces.

"How about a wealthy godfather who is bequeathing you his entire million dollar estate then?" Lexus said sarcastically, provoking laughter from around the room.

Simon shook his head in the negative, before he said, "I was hoping to take out a loan that would cover the cost of the entire reclamation...sorry, I mean renovation project."

Mrs. Helrigle,who was more interested in investments than charity, looked at him coldly with sullen eyes.

"So, how much money are we talking here?" Wilson B. asked.

"I've got the bid from the contractor right here," Simon said, sliding the piece of paper across the table.

Lexus picked up the paper, unfolded it, and read the contents. "Twenty-thousand is a lot of money, Simon," he said.

"That's everything, from the floors to the chandelier," Simon said proudly.

Mrs. Livingood's eyes widened at the dollar amount. "Chandelier?" she repeated.

"And how do you know that you'll be able to repay that kind of debt?" Lexus asked directly.

"I have faith," Simon replied.

"Faith in what?" Wilson B. asked.

There was an awkward pause as Simon searched himself for the answer. It was then that he came to the realization that in order to fulfill God's purpose he was going to have to share it with others. Now he found himself on the precipice of making his first public profession of faith. Suddenly, there was a lump in his throat as though he were about to speak it into existence. And once it was out there, he knew there would be no taking it back. Just as the anxiety reached its crescendo, Simon remembered reading a note in the margins of Jeremy's book, "Do not be afraid of what you will say or how to say it." Then, unashamedly he replied, "I have faith in God."

Will slapped his pencil down at the notepad, rolled his eyes, and said, "Jesus, you can't be serious."

Lexus sat back in his chair and remarked, "I would have felt better about the whole deal if you would have said you had faith in yourself."

"Well, I can't honestly say that," Simon truthfully answered.

The words hung heavy in the air for a moment before Wilson B. said, "Set aside the monetary issue for a moment, do you possess the skills to complete that kind of undertaking?"

"No, not in the least," Simon replied coolly.

"Let me get this straight," Lexus said. "You're willing to gamble away your future with no means of repaying the loan for a project that you don't have the skill set to complete. Does that about sum it up?"

No longer able to contain her objections to the blabbering of such a naïve, impudent boy, Mrs. Helrigle blurted out, "How can you even justify asking the bank to lend you that kind of money?"

"Justify?" Simon asked with a quizzical expression.

"I think what she's trying to ask is by what authority," Mrs. Livingood explained. "In other words, who gives you the right, the permission, to renovate the school?"

Simon gave a befuddled expression and answered, "I am justified through faith in Jesus Christ."

"Here we go with the faith thing again!" Mrs. Helrigle said, rolling her eyes and throwing up her hands.

Again, Mrs. Livingood tried her best to frame Mrs. Helrigle's obvious exasperation into a reasonable question. "I think that what we would all like to know is how can you guarantee that the bank lending you the money is the best thing to do?" she asked.

"I guess I would say that if God..." Simon started to say.

"God, ha," Lexus scoffed. "And tell me, Mr. Freeman, how is it exactly that you *know* that there is a god in the first place?"

By now everyone in the room was sitting forward in their chairs, as all eyes went from Simon to Lexus and back again.

"I know there is a God because I can see, hear, taste, touch, and smell,"

Simon replied with humility. "Everything in the universe is evidence that there is a creator. His eternal power and divine nature can be seen everywhere you look, so that men are without an excuse."

"Now don't get me wrong, I'm a Christian too," Mrs. Livingood said placing her hand on her chest. "After all, we go to church every Sunday. But, I'm curious. How do you know that it all wasn't all by chance? That there wasn't some big bang, and from it came a planet, a cell, a fish, a monkey, and a human."

"Because I *don't* have enough faith," Simon answered.

"Oh, now he doesn't have enough faith!" Will said mockingly as he shook his head while jotting down the statement.

"No, I don't have enough faith to believe in 'out of nothing, from nothing, for nothing'," Simon answered. "That's the second reason that I know there is a God, because in my heart, in my deepest inward being, I know that there is a God. He made me that way."

Lexus rolled his eyes. "I think you're delusional."

"If you're hearing voices in your head, you need to get it checked out," Will said smugly.

But, Mrs. Livingood shushed Lexus' understudy while Wilson B. intently stared into Simon's eyes as though looking for any indication of disingenuousness or sincerity.

"No, I can see that," Mrs. Helrigle surprisingly blurted out. "It's kinda like what Pastor Algood preaches about. It is what I think has made Lexus and myself so successful. It's our little secret to success, I guess you could say. Pastor Algood always says that there is something bigger than ourselves. There is a god. But, it's more like a spirit that you can actually tap into it if you have enough faith. You can harness the power of the spirit to maximize your potential for riches, or power, to enlarge your territory or real estate business or whatever."

"Yes, I've heard him say that many times in his sermons," Wilson B. confirmed.

"No, but that's not what I'm saying," Simon objected. "No, I'm simply saying that God has prewired us to know Him."

"That's it?" Lexus asked sarcastically. "Wow. Such a revelation!"

"Well, no," Simon answered. "I know because the Bible tells me that there is a God." Simon could see that he might be losing the attention of his audience who were talking among themselves.

"And I know because I have met Him, personally," Simon boldly added. Now it was out there now, and he couldn't take it back. Everyone stopped with the sidebar conversations and stared at Simon as though they were looking at an alien. Now that he had their full attention once again, Simon began to give his testimony of how he was lost, and how he realized that he was a sinner, and how he had reached such a low point that he cried out to God. And he told them how God had answered that prayer through the sign on the church, and how he had been saved that night. He also told them all about the curse and his purpose and the article in the paper. In fact, he told them everything leading up to where he sat now at the head of the conference table in the First National Bank of Bethel asking for a loan to fulfill God's purpose. When he had finished, everyone sat in awe.

Finally, Mrs. Livingood said, "Let me get this straight. You thought you could get the referendum to pass by painting the entrance to the school. And you thought that passing the referendum would somehow put an end to the curse of Jessie Joseph. Is that right?"

"I know, it sounds stupid," Simon replied, embarrassed. "I guess I was wrong about that…"

"Aren't you afraid that you might be wrong about everything else, too?" Mrs. Helrigle asked.

"Not nearly as afraid as I would be if God asked me to do something and I didn't do it," Simon replied. "The way I understand it, I cannot serve both God and money, so I am not concerned about my ability to complete the project or repay the loan."

"Ha!" Lexus said, as he sat beneath all of his plaques, diplomas, awards, and of course, the trophies of the Golden Cows from the Dairy League. "Funny how it's always the ones who don't have the money who aren't concerned about the money. And yet, here you are asking me for a loan.

"Why doesn't god just give you the money himself and take out the middle man? I'll tell you why. It's because he doesn't exist! Let me tell you something Simon, it's no different from when you thought you were chasing ghosts around the school. It's just one big hoax."

"Lexus…" Wilson B. started to say before the bank president cut him off with a wave of his hand.

"No, no, no," Lexus said in hoarse voice as he stood up out of his chair. "I've listened to him, now he can listen to me for a second. Let me tell you something that I learned a long time ago that may help you out. You've got to look out for number one, because no one else will. And if you want something in this world you're going to have to go after it and get it yourself, because no one is going to just give it to you. The sooner you stop believing in fairytales, the sooner you can get past them, and start living in the real world. The First National Bank of Bethel does not give out loans based on myths. So, if you want to come back and propose a business plan to make money, then maybe we can talk. Until then, good day, Simon."

When he finished his angry diatribe, Lexus took his wife by the arm, lifted her from the chair, and guided her out of the room with his loyal assistant close in tow.

24

BEING RATIONAL

Simon returned to the school later that afternoon dejected, yet still determined to keep at least one of the promises that he had given Miss Harold. Without much else to do, he returned to the basement of the elementary building and resumed the unenviable task of cleaning out what little remained in the back of the dingy storage room. As Simon listlessly pulled out a few dusty, ancient relics, he replayed the meeting at the bank over and over in his mind. He just couldn't imagine what had gone wrong. Clearly, he had emptied himself, called upon God's will, and followed His direction, so how could have it all turned out so badly? Maybe he was mistaken. Maybe he had been acting once again on his own apart from God's will. He knew full well where that had gotten him the first time as he thought of Rocky and Hope.

As Simon lost himself reflecting on Hope's beautiful face, a familiar pain overwhelmed him, and he was reminded of his own folly. Robotically, Simon bent down and picked up an armful of old board games that someone had stashed away in the cavernous reaches of the storage room. Just as Simon stepped out into the natural light spilling in through the basement windows, the top board game slipped off of the stack and toppled to the ground. It fell with a great crash as pieces went everywhere.

"Oh no!" Simon sputtered.

Looking down at his side, he could see the contents of a game he had long ago forgotten about called Othello. One of the round, black and white game pieces rolled back into the storage room and hit a tarp covering a flat, rectangular object lying on the floor. The small disc bounced back and violently twisted in circles before finally settling on the dusty ground.

Simon set the other board games down on the floor and walked back into the storage room to retrieve the stray piece. When he bent down to grab it, he noticed the tarp. Out of curiosity, he lifted up the skirt of the tarp and peered into the darkness.

"My God," he said under his breath.

* * *

Simon, covered in dust and flakes of debris, peered through his protective goggles over the top of his industrial mask. He was looking at the point on the wall where he had made his mark. His arms ached as he wiped the sweat from his forehead with the back his glove, as he leaned against the wooden handle of the sledgehammer. To say that they didn't make them like they used to, would be a gross understatement for the old building. With great force, Simon had time and again driven the head of the hammer into the wall to no avail. At first, his effort only rendered a great deal of loud banging, but with each blow thereafter, a small crack began to crawl across the wall. With several more sharp blows the small crack began to spread out like a massive spider web. The visible signs of progress began to strengthen his resolve. Suddenly, the crack turned into a chip, and the chip in turn became a hole, exposing the sturdy underbelly of the old building. Finally, an entire section of drywall came tumbling down the stairs with a great crash.

"Well, no wonder!" Simon murmured as he rested a moment trying to catch his breath. His eyes scanned the wall next to the staircase. Something of great significance must have hung for a number of years to have pulled out the support behind the wall, causing it to warp and bow. For the life of him, Simon could not remember exactly what, if anything, hung there when he was a student. All he could be certain of was that *something* once hung there. In the recesses of his mind, a dark shadow mixed with flashes of gold or maybe even bronze occupied the fringes of his memory of the stairwell. But, as he turned his mind's eye to identify it, the picture faded into nothingness and filled him with a sense of longing and frustration.

Whatever it was that had hung there had pulled the plaster away from the framework causing the entire wall to buckle under its weight. After reading about quick fixes to the structural problems on the internet, Simon decided that the wall had to come down before he could make it right again.

With great resolve, Simon let out a gush of air, lifted the sledgehammer one more time off of the floor, and raised it with both of hands over his shoulder. With a grunt, he wildly wielded the hammer downward. It took every bit of strength that he could muster to deliver the final blow, but when he did a much larger section of drywall came crashing down. As the debris fell to the ground, it caught the stair railing and unexpectedly ripped it off of the wall. Residually, the dislodged railing pulled loose another large section of dry wall and plaster that would need to be fixed now as well. Simon jumped out of the way just in time as a plume of fine dust exploded in front of him.

Already a bit jumpy from the loud commotion, Simon was all the more startled to hear a determined rapping on the front doors. His heart racing, he leaned forward and squinted, trying to get a glimpse of his unexpected visitor through the windows of the doors.

"Oh, man," Simon said aloud. He glanced around at the destruction he had wrought to the entrance to the building, the filthy condition of his appearance, and the proverbial smoking gun that he was holding in his hands. Resigning himself to the fact that he had been found out, Simon dutifully moved towards the door.

Slightly embarrassed, Simon drooped his shoulders, took his goggles off, pulled the cupped mask over his head, and dropped the handle of the sledgehammer before allowing gravity to pull him down the remaining steps to the entrance. Fully expecting to the see the police, Simon was more than a little surprised to recognize the faces of Wilson B. Livingood, his wife Angie, and their son Ralph who were all frantically motioning for Simon to come and unlock the door.

Obligingly, Simon pushed on the long, metal handle and swung the door wide open. He was convinced that the jig was up and that his little project was in jeopardy of being shut down before it ever even got off the ground.

"Come on in," Simon said sheepishly, scratching his sweaty forehead with a gloved thumb as the family made their way inside.

As if under some kind of strange trance, they shuffled their way into the lobby of the school. Now standing side by side with pained expressions, they took note of the great destruction that had been wrought. Simon took a step forward and stood next to them. For the first time in almost six hours of swinging a sledgehammer, he was able to assess the damage that he had inflicted.

No one spoke a word. Instead, the four of them stood there with their arms at their side, mouths agape, speechless. Simon was once again reminded of the barbershop quartet at the ball game and Vonnegut's famous book about war, destruction, and annihilation. While his visitors bore the expression of shock and disbelief, Simon's face only revealed determination.

After what seemed like an eternity, Mrs. Livingood asked, "What have you done?"

"Well, I..." Simon started to say.

Before he could find the words, Ralph chimed in, "He wrecked our school; that's what."

"That's obvious," Mrs. Livingood replied, "but did someone give you permission?"

"Or better yet," Wilson B. said, "did you somehow get the money to fix it?"

"No," Simon heard himself quietly say. Suddenly, a stark sense of reality swept over him, temporarily blunting his assuredness. His silence spoke volumes.

"I mean, by what authority did you do this if you haven't even secured the funds to make it right again?" Mrs. Livingood asked.

Then suddenly, Ralph caught a glimpse of the massive chandelier hanging from the ceiling above the landing.

"Wow! Cool! Check it out!" Ralph blurted out, as he charged up the stairs and raced across the plastic drop cloth. Now he stood amongst the rubble on the landing, looking up at the impressive fixture.

Wilson B. and Mrs. Livingood gravitated towards the captivating light and slowly ascended the steps. Simon looked on as the three members of the family stood directly beneath the brilliant light, admiring the magnificent beauty and craftsmanship of the priceless antique. The sparkling crystals that refracted the light into millions of tiny dancing slivers was only made all the more wondrous in direct contrast to the vast wreckage it was presiding over. Simon made his way up the steps to join them under the awesome chandelier.

"Simon, where in the world did you get this?" Wilson B. asked in complete awe.

"Believe it or not it was here the whole time," Simon answered enthusiastically, forgetting for a moment the potential trouble he was in. "It was just buried in the basement and hidden under a withered old, worthless tarp."

"No kidding?" Wilson B. said with a chuckle.

"It's absolutely breathtaking," Mrs. Livingood said, still staring upward. "I have never seen anything more beautiful in my entire life."

"There's no telling how much something like that is worth," Wilson B. said. "You've stumbled upon quite a treasure." As he looked up at the relic, his smile faded away and was eclipsed by a look of grave concern. Slowly, his chin dropped, and he turned towards Simon as the color ran out of his face.

"What is it?" Simon asked.

Wilson B. lifted his arm from his side. He was holding an old yearbook in his hand while his index finger held the place of a specific page. Confounded, Wilson B. motioned for him to take the book. With some trepidation, Simon took the yearbook out of Wilson's trembling hand and flipped it open to the marked page. Looking down at the photograph, the hairs on the back of his neck stood up. It was a colored picture of a fourth grade class from 1979, with the magnificent chandelier hovering high above the students in the background.

"What? Wait! Is this your...? But how did you know that...?" Simon began to say as he looked at Wilson B.

Wilson B's face was pale and his eyes welled up with tears. He was nervously biting at his bottom lip, unable to speak.

"Honey?" Mrs. Livingood said as she moved to her husband's side and slid her hand under his arm. "It's all right," she said before turning to Simon with a slightly pained expression. "You see, he's been wrestling all day with what you said in the meeting at the bank today. It's been pretty much consuming him. In fact, it's all he's been able to talk about is God and faith and purpose; you know, everything that you told us at the bank about your reasons for wanting to do the renovation."

After collecting himself, Wilson B. cleared his throat and said, "You see, I was very troubled by what you told us. I thought to myself, 'How can such an intelligent, well-educated, levelheaded kid with such a great future say such crazy things?' I wondered if *you* actually believed what you were saying. Then I thought maybe you were just psychotic or on meth or something. But, as I tried to totally dismiss your outlandish story, I simply couldn't shake the look of determination on your face and the conviction I heard in your voice. And the more that I tried to ignore it, the more that a small still voice kept nagging at me. After a while the whole thing became quite disturbing to me. I wanted to find something, anything, that would prove you wrong. Some bit of irrefutable evidence. Then it came to me. I grabbed my old yearbooks out of the basement and found this picture of my fourth grade class.

"I brought it down here because I wanted to prove to you that there was no way that you would be able to completely renovate the school," Wilson B. admitted. "I had to prove to you that your claim that some kind of all-powerful God had given you the specific purpose of restoring the lobby was just something you had made up in your head. I told myself that all I had to do to prove to you that this whole thing was nonsense was to provide one bit of concrete evidence. I wanted to give you this picture as evidence that what you were proposing was impossible, so that your spirit would be crushed and you would completely give up on this ridiculous idea. I wanted to show you that there was *no way* God was going to be able to provide a chandelier to replace the one in the picture. And then maybe I could have some peace of mind again."

"I don't understand," Simon replied. "Even if I do believe that God wanted me to do this, why would you care? What difference does it make to you?"

"Don't you see," Wilson B. answered through gritted teeth and watery eyes. "What you claimed challenged my entire system of beliefs that I have built my life upon. If what you're saying is true, that there is a God who made me, who cares about me, and wants to have a relationship with me, and has a purpose for me, then it would change *everything*."

"Simon, I guess what we want to know is how can you be so sure that what you're saying is true?" Mrs. Livingood asked. "What real evidence do you have?"

Simon looked around awkwardly for a moment before he remembered the picture that he was holding in his hands. "Well, I would say just take a look at the picture for starters," he offered, " It's like a sign. I don't believe in coincidences.

"Wilson B. brought a picture of a chandelier, but God provided the actual chandelier. It may have seemed impossible to you and me, but the reality is that nothing is impossible with God. I knew what God was telling me in my heart. Then I compared it to what I have read in the Bible, and now I have all the evidence that I need to validate the authenticity of His promise," Simon said as he pointed at the light.

"Okay, Simon, but it could also just be some kind of freakish coincidence or some kind of self-fulfilling prophecy," Mrs. Livingood skeptically answered. "What we need is some sort of proof that isn't debatable. I mean, it's like you said about how you originally thought all of this was to reverse the curse of Jessie Joseph. How do you know that isn't true? How do you know that the things they say Jessie Joseph did aren't any more or less real than what the Bible says about what Jesus did? How do you know they're not both just a myth?"

"Oh, I'm not sure that I'm qualified to answer that for you," Simon answered. "I mean, I'm no theologian, or Biblical scholar. It's not like I'm trained to answer these kinds of questions."

There was silence for a moment as Mr. and Mrs. Livingood stared longingly at him as though inaudibly pleading for some kind of response. Simon could tell by their expression that the answers that he had at his finger tips weren't going to be sufficient enough to give them the answers they were looking for. As his mind raced, he felt the weight of this pivotal moment for the Livingood's passing him by. Not knowing what to do, Simon closed his eyes and asked for help from above.

Out of the blue Ralph innocently asked, "Like, how do you know that God or anything else exists if you can't see it, or feel it, or hear it, or whatever?"

Up to that point, Simon wasn't even sure the young man had been listening at all. During the conversation, Ralph seemed to have gotten bored and wandered off to explore the disaster area before being naturally attracted to the sledgehammer that was now draped over his shoulder like a baseball bat.

When Simon saw the sledgehammer an idea came to him. "Well, Ralph, let me ask you a question," Simon said, suddenly inspired. "If you drop that sledgehammer what is going to happen to it?"

Ralph sheepishly smirked and then glanced at his mom and dad. "Uh, it'd fall?" he answered, unsure of the simplicity of his answer.

"What if you dropped it a hundred times?" Simon purposefully asked.

"Same thing," Ralph replied.

"What if you never *actually* dropped it?" Simon asked. "Would you still believe that it would fall? There's no doubt in your mind that it would fall and not fly around the room or something?"

"Well, yeah, duh," Ralph answered.

"Why?" Simon asked.

"Why what?" Ralph asked, confused.

"Why would it fall?" Simon continued.

"Because I just know," Ralph answered.

"That's right," Simon said. "You just know, because when you drop things they fall to the ground. You have experience. You have evidence. So, you have faith that objects fall even if you don't actually drop them. And what makes it fall, smart guy?"

"Gravity," Ralph answered more sure of himself this time.

"Yes, exactly, gravity," Simon said. "But, how do you know that gravity exists if you can't see it or smell it or touch it? You know because you see the results of gravity. Do you think there are people out there who would argue that gravity doesn't exist if you can't see it, feel it, or hear it?"

"I don't know, maybe," Ralph answered, "they'd be pretty dumb. But, I bet if you dropped the sledgehammer on their toe they'd know it exists."

"They just might," Simon said with a laugh. "You could say that it takes faith to believe that gravity exists, but it is almost common sense because of the overwhelming amount of evidence. Scientists can measure gravity, but they still can't fully explain how it works. And yet the Bible tells us that in Him all things are held together. You see it is not a faith without evidence that we believe in God. It is believing in the evidence that He gives us. When we look at creation it becomes common sense that there is a Creator just like it's common sense that the sledgehammer will fall to the ground when you drop it."

"But, why do we have to rely on faith?" Mrs. Livingood asked, exasperated. "Why can't He just make it clear to us?"

"Oh, well now, I might just be able to give you an answer for that one," Simon answered excitedly. "I was just reading about that earlier today in Jeremy's notes."

"Jeremy?" Wilson B. asked.

"Yeah, you know, Jeremy Warner," Simon answered looking for the book under the drop cloth and debris. He found it sitting by a computer that he had dragged out into the hallway in order to look up remodeling tips on the internet. "Yeah, here it is," Simon said as he enthusiastically rifled through the thin, worn out pages of the book. Wilson B., Angie, and Ralph moved in closer to get a better look.

"Where did you get this?" Wilson B. asked.

"I found it in the concession stand," Simon replied as he thumbed through the pages. "It has all kinds of notes written in the margins. And there was something that I read in Romans that might answer your question." His eyes followed along as his finger scanned the text for the right verse. "Here it is!" Simon nearly shouted. "Listen to this."

The Livingoods huddled closer together so they could follow along as Simon read the text aloud.

"Romans 1:16, 'we are justified through faith, first to the Jew and then the Gentile,'" Simon read proudly. After reading the sentence, he looked up to gauge the reaction of his listeners.

The Livingoods looked curiously at Simon.

"Don't you see?" Simon asked. "The Bible says that it is by faith that we are justified."

"By faith?" Mrs. Livingood repeated with a dissatisfied expression on her face as Wilson B. continued reading the context surrounding the verse.

"Yeah, what's wrong with faith?" Simon asked, disappointed.

"It's just that it seems like faith is such a cop out," Mrs. Livingood answered. "I mean you could believe anything by just having enough faith. Like Santa Claus, or the Easter Bunny, or evolution. We even have to have faith that what the Bible says is true. I mean how do we really even know that the Bible wasn't corrupted either by somebody copying something wrong or even worse by manipulation?"

"Ha, Santa Claus…" Ralph said knowingly under his breath, having just discovered the truth himself the previous year.

"I had some of the exact same questions, believe me," Simon said with a smile. His eyes danced around the room. "There was this book that Jeremy had recommended to me during one of our conversations before he died. Let's see,…" Simon handed over the Bible to Wilson B. who was still enraptured by the letter to the Romans, "it's called, uh, man, where is it? I was just reading a little bit of it yesterday. I haven't finished it, but it's really good. Oh, here it is! 'A Case for Christ' by Lee Stroebel," Simon said holding up the cover of the book to show Mrs. Livingood. "In this one chapter he interviewed this Metzger guy from Princeton who said that the sheer number of copies from all different regions of the world confirm the validity of its contents. All of these other widely accepted historical documents have much few copies, while they have found something like twenty-five thousand ancient copies of the Bible, each with almost identical content. So, even though God used like forty some authors over some seven hundred years to write sixty-six books, it tells one story that has yet to have been disproven by historical or archeological discoveries. It's not faith without evidence, it is faith in the evidence."

Mrs. Livingood walked over, took the book from his hands, and started to read its contents.

"It's pretty amazing when you think about it," Simon said. "Look, I'm no expert. So, I defer to the experts. This Metzger guy says the Bible is like 99.5% pure. Besides, if there was even one shred of historical or archeological proof to deny even one sentence in the Bible, don't you think that it would be splattered all over CNN and the New York times?"

Mrs. Livingood had obviously done some research of her own and fired back some very thoughtful objections. In a very articulate fashion, she postulated each of them for Simon.

Simon finally said to her, "I don't know. Those are very good questions. Hey, why don't we just look it up and find out together? I'm still learning myself. I don't have all of the answers."

Pulling up a search engine on the internet, Simon found excerpts from a book entitled, "I Don't Have Enough Faith to Be an Atheist," and some great articles from a pastor named R.C. Sproul and an apologist named Ravi Zacharias.

The search for information broadened in its scope and continued late into the night. It was unlike anything Simon had ever been a part of before. It was an open, respectfully candid, discussion about religion. No, even more than that. It was a discussion about God. The four of them sat there on some old newspapers that Simon had laid down on the floor of the landing to protect the hardwood. They talked late into the night, rummaging through the pages of the books from the public library and looking up even more information on the internet.

While the Livingood's listened intently to what Simon had to say, he became keenly aware of the irony, and he was deeply humbled. Only a few weeks before, he had been firing the same difficult questions at Jeremy, and now he found himself offering up his old friend's answers to others who were also in search of the truth.

As time wore on, he could tell that some of the answers he provided might have even helped the Livingoods with their struggle to understand. He closed his eyes and offered up a prayer of gratitude. For a short time, each of them separately read excerpts from some of the world's greatest philosophers, theologians, and historians thanks to the miracle of the internet. Eventually, Ralph's heavy eyes blinked slower and slower until the boy was fast asleep, curled up on the drop cloth under the warm golden glow of the chandelier. Just when Simon had assumed that the evening was coming to an end, Mrs. Livingood leveled the most pointed question yet.

"Okay Simon, you have helped explain a great deal to us about the issues that for years have kept us from fully believing in God, and I am definitely willing to open my mind and try to learn some more," she began, carefully choosing her words, "but when I asked you earlier how you know that the story of Jesus was real and the legend of Jessie Joseph wasn't, you said it had to do with having belief in the evidence. And that's why you believe that everything written in the Bible is true, right?"

"Yes, that's right," Simon answered.

"But, why don't you believe in the evidence that speaks to the authenticity of Bethel's curse?" she asked frankly.

"I don't understand," Simon sputtered, taken aback by the question, "What evidence are you referring to?"

"You said that you saw the little boy twice, once in the doorway to the classroom, and once in the well, right?" she asked.

"Yes, but I later discovered that the little boy was actually Simon Adamson, who lives just down the street," Simon replied. "I would say that's an example where at first what appeared to be evidence of an actual curse actually ended up disproving the legend upon closer examination."

"Okay, but what about the hidden graveyard and Jessie and Adam's tombstones?" Mrs. Livingood pressed.

"Well," Simon answered, pondering the question for a moment. "I would say that evidence would definitely suggest that they were real people who once lived in Bethel and have since passed away."

"And that's it, nothing more?" Mrs. Livingood asked. "Even though it supports the old legend?"

"I think that people often start with some kind of predetermined conclusion or answer in mind and discriminately use factual things as evidence to support it," Simon answered as best he could. "I mean what came first? The legend or the graveyard? I mean some kids hypothetically could have stumbled upon the graveyard and then made up the whole story completely from their imagination. I think it would be better to look at all of the evidence in its entirety and then come to a conclusion.

"Yes, there were other little coincidences that supported the legend, but once you look at it in detail you realize that it is all so loosely connected that it could support any number of contrived stories."

"But, didn't you tell us that when you did some research at the library you actually found several tragic accidents in which the dates coincided with the curse?" Mrs. Livingood asked.

"Yes, I found three tragic accidents in the past eighteen years," Simon said, shrugging off the question. "But again, how many towns in America have had similar tragedies? And while they were spaced out at exactly six years apart does that really mean it's a pattern?"

"You only found three?" Mrs. Livingood asked.

"Yes, well, actually I couldn't go back any further than that because I was having some…uh… issues with the microfiche," Simon replied.

"So, you didn't find anything about a trial in any of your research?" Mrs. Livingood asked spinning a tattered, yellow section of newspaper around for Simon to read.

Wilson B. stopped reading for a moment and looked up from the notes in Jeremy's Bible.

Simon felt his face go flush as he moved in closer to read the fine print. The article told of a young teacher named Jessie Joseph who was sentenced twenty to life in prison for the death of one Adam Potter and a number of other heinous crimes. Simon desperately grabbed the paper and flipped it over, but there was nothing else there regarding the trial.

"Where did you find this?" Simon asked, rising to his feet as he wildly looked around the room.

"It was laying on the floor right in front of my face," Mrs. Livingood answered. "Where did you get these old papers from?"

"I found them in the storage room in the basement!" Simon replied, completely blown away by the discovery. "There was a large stack of them lying in a crate!"

Pretty soon all three of them were eagerly riffling through the old newspapers, trying to find more evidence to corroborate the legend. After an exhaustive search, they did not find anything more regarding the trial, so Mrs. Livingood suggested that they look for any other tragedies that might prove that there was a pattern. Much to their dismay they did find plenty of tragedies, but they were run of the mill accidents and disasters that did not fit the legend's profile or cyclical nature. Frustrated, Wilson B. leaned against the wall and stared at the chandelier while Simon and Mrs. Livingood continued to sift through the dusty papers.

"What's the matter, honey?" Mrs. Livingood asked, noticing her husband's pensive demeanor.

"I don't know," Wilson B. said, trying to formulate his thoughts. "It's just that Simon made some great points. You know, about the evidence to support the veracity of the Bible and the existence of God. It just seems a like a contradiction to say that this evidence doesn't support the legend even though we now have proof that all of these incidents really did happen. I mean, you even found evidence of a trial and sentencing of that wacko, Jessie."

"Now don't get me wrong," Simon answered. "I know that we found some historical evidence, but it's not connected. All of these articles are just more random pieces of evidence."

"Oh come on," Mrs. Livingood said, "it seems more than coincidental. It's downright creepy, 'murder' and 'heinous crimes'. If that doesn't support some kind of validity that something terrible happened here."

"Angie's right, it seems like there might be something to this after all," Wilson B. said without looking up. "I just think that with some more digging..."

Simon shivered at the memory of the bodies he had exhumed. Not daring to divulge his secret, Simon said, "Maybe, but, I just think there's more to knowing something to be true than just what you read in the papers. That's all that I am saying. Even if Jessie actually murdered Adam, that would only prove there was a tragedy. It doesn't prove there is any kind of curse associated with it."

"All I'm saying is that, 'isn't it possible that they could be connected?" Wilson B. suggested. "Is it impossible that Bethel is under a curse as a result of a tragic event like a murder or something even worse than that. I mean, why do the two things have to be mutually exclusive? Look at all of these articles about terrible things that have happened to the people in this community over the years!"

"It's true," Angie said, looking down at the collection of articles they had amassed. "Maybe, it all comes down to how you define a curse."

Wanting to dismiss the myth altogether, Simon shook his head and waved his hands as though he were trying to waft the statement out of the room. "That's the problem with merely relying on what is seen," Simon said. "Yes, now we definitely know there was a murder, we know there are twelve grave stones, we know there are tragedies. But, the problem is that we have to fill in the gaps between what we know and what we don't. That is very dangerous.

"If that is all that we have to go by, then we can't come to any reckless conclusions, until we find...we find..." He paused for a moment trying to convince himself, as he struggled to articulate his next point. "Look, we might find other evidence later about the heinous crimes. Or we may discover something that completely refutes the curse, but we need to be very careful because we don't want to be fooled by misleading evidence, like when I found out the little boy hiding in the well is actually a real boy."

"True," Angie replied. "But, all I am saying is that I can't imagine a community being any more cursed than one whose children have to go and hide in a well or the basement of a school because they are so scared."

There was a long, awkward silence before Wilson B. finally spoke. "Look, Simon, here's the thing that I can't get past," he said. "You said that you believed that there was a God because of the evidence, but you don't believe there is a curse despite the evidence."

"For instance, you said that creation itself testifies to a creator," Wilson B. continued, "but you don't believe that the coffin, or the gravestones, or Jeremy's death provide any legitimacy to a curse. Then you say that the story in the Bible is real but that the newspaper article in your hand isn't?

"You also suggested that my bringing the picture of chandelier to the school tonight was by divine intervention, but you're acting like Angie finding the newspaper clipping about the trial of Jessie Joseph was a mere coincidence. I thought you said there were no accidents."

"What are you getting at?" Mrs. Livingood asked.

"What I'm getting at is there seems to be a double standard," Wilson B. said, exasperated. "How do you know when a story is fictional or nonfiction, myth or historical, real or make-believe? Because it seems to me that the legend meets all of the same criteria for authenticating the existence of God. It's maddening! You know that this is why most people don't even like thinking about this kind of stuff let alone talking about it. There doesn't seem to be any definitive answers. Everybody just goes around believing what they want to believe. So, I really would like to know, Simon, how do you know that God is real?"

Simon could hear the sincerity in Wilson B's voice. He looked around the room in quiet desperation as he tried to find some definitive proof of the existence of God. Confounded, he lifted his chin to the ceiling, let out a deep sigh, closed his eyes once more, and asked for help once more. When he opened his eyes, he was staring directly into the brilliant chandelier, and the answer came to him.

Excitedly, Simon asked, "Wilson, what was the small, still voice inside of you that kept nagging you about my testimony?"

"I don't know," Wilson B. said glumly, "my own conscience, I guess."

"I would argue that it was more than just your conscience," Simon said hurrying over to find some more of Jeremy's notes. He picked up the Bible and thumbed through the pages to find the passage. "Jeremy called it 'General revelation'. Let me read this Bible verse to you. In Romans 1:18, it says that the wrath of God is being revealed from heaven against all the godlessness and wickedness of men who suppress the truth.' All men and women know in their heart of hearts that there is a God. His existence is so evident to our souls that we actually have to work to suppress it."

"But why would we do that?" Wilson B. asked desperately.

"I don't know, maybe it's our sinful nature," Simon offered. " Maybe we don't want a God ruling our lives, telling us what to do. Maybe we want to be in control. Maybe, we want to be our own god.

"It is quite possible that the small still voice inside of you was from the Holy Spirit. And the reason that you couldn't shake it was because a part of you recognized it as the voice of God speaking to your soul."

And there it was. Simon's words rocked Wilson B. like a heavy weight fighter who took a devastating uppercut. He was reeling from the sudden revelation. He couldn't deny the existence of God anymore than he could deny his own existence.

"You see, we know that God is real because there is something inside of us that recognizes Him," Simon asserted. "You hear it. I hear it. But we try to ignore it because we want everything to be about us, when it's not. It's all about Him!" Inadvertently, he pointed up at the giant chandelier. "Sure, we can intellectually conclude that there is a God. But, God can be proven by using more than our intellects. He gave us another way of discerning truth in our hearts. That is how we are able to discern a myth like Jessie Joseph from the historical account of Jesus Christ.

"He's seeking you, Wilson! And He wants to have a personal relationship with you!"

Simon paused almost out of breath from trying to get the words out fast enough. Wilson B's eyes were glossy and his face was waxen as he nervously bit into his bottom lip again. Simon looked over at Mrs. Livingood who was wiping away the tears rolling down her cheeks.

"Simon, I want to know God, can you help me do that?" Wilson B. humbly asked.

"Sure, I would be honored to," Simon answered, overcome with emotion at the awesome privilege.

The three of them bowed their heads and huddled together while Ralph lay peacefully slumbering in the warm glow of the light. Simon guided the Livingoods as they proclaimed Jesus as their Lord and Savior, asked for His forgiveness, and repented of their sins.

When they had finished hugging one another, Wilson B. pulled out his check book from his back pocket and scanned the ledger. "Now, Simon, we obviously can't cover the entire amount of the renovation, but how much do you think you need to get started?" he asked.

"I-I have no idea," Simon sputtered.

"Here's the thing," Wilson B. continued. "I can't just up and quit my job. I don't think that would be the prudent thing to do at this point…"

"What? Why would you quit your…?" Angie began to ask.

"Because…," Wilson B. started to say. "Look, one thing that has become abundantly clear is that the way we have…the way I have been conducting business over the years has been completely self-serving. Lexus and I have always abided by the mantra, 'Business is business.'

"In other words, we were our own gods deciding what was right from wrong based on profit. We decided what was ethical and unethical at the bank to suit our own interests. And now I am so ashamed of myself!"

"What do you mean, Wilson?" Angie asked. Simon could hear the concern in her voice.

"Lexus, Jack Lawless, and bank's board of directors have basically done everything from creating a bubble in the local real estate market to running our own little Ponzi scheme," Wilson B. admitted. "It's complicated, but let me try to break it down for you." The more he talked the more he came clean with the bank's unethical business dealings and faulty loans.

Simon listened in utter disbelief at the depths to which Lexus went to in order to swindle money and hoard power. It became apparent that Jack had his clutches on every aspect of life in Bethel from the bank, to the school, to agriculture... And Wilson B. had been smack dab in the middle of it all.

"Oh, Wilson B., how could you?" Mrs. Livingood asked, genuinely shocked and disappointed with her husband's shady business dealings. "I feel nauseous."

"I guess I have been lying to everyone, including myself," he admitted. Then he turned and placed one hand on his wife's shoulder and looked directly into her eyes. "But no more. I am going to make good on this. You'll see. Maybe I can keep at least a few people from getting hurt and losing everything before it is too late. But, you would not believe how complicated it is and how deep it runs both inside and outside of the community. There are some very important people who are going to be exposed, and they're not going to be too happy about it. It's going to take time for me to maneuver without Lexus or Jack getting wise to me, so I will have to act like everything's normal for a while.

"In the meantime, I'm going to have to figure out how to float the necessary funds to you to get this renovation started. Maybe, I can use the school account somehow to wash the money. I also have some favors that I can call in. I don't know. I'll figure it out. Until then, I need you to keep our little secret."

Simon nodded affirmatively. He was at a total loss for words after getting insight into the dirty dealings of the bank. And he marveled at how the power of the Holy Spirit was already at work in Wilson B's life. It was a lot to take in for one night, as the soft, orange glow slowly filled the Eastern sky.

"Well then, I guess we had better go before we get found out," Mrs. Livingood said, wiping away her tears with a kleenex.

The three of them agreed to work in secrecy as long as possible. Simon would continue with renovating the entryway, while Wilson B. would work behind the scenes at the bank to subsidize the operation. As Simon watched form the landing, the Livingoods dragged their groggy son out to the SUV, loaded up their things, and drove off in the wee hours of the morning.

Simon was overcome with the knowledge that he had just seen God's work first hand. Just as he turned to ascend the stairs, he caught a glimpse of the article about Jessie Joseph laying next to Jeremy's Bible on the bottom step. He picked up the old, discolored newspaper and read the blurb about the sentencing of Jessie Joseph one more time.

"Wait a minute!" he said aloud, after he remembered something that had caught his eye while searching through the stack of manilla folders on Miss Harold's desk in the principal's office.

* * *

Simon lifted the heaping mound of folders off of the top of the desk to uncover a stack of old newspapers clippings. After riffling through several soiled clippings, he realized that what lay before him were the missing articles from the microfiche machine at the public library. The "someone" who had cutout the issues from the public records was none other than Thelma Harold!

Hurriedly, Simon grabbed the rest of articles from off of the desk. As he turned to walk out of the room, he accidentally knocked the old, wooden paddle and a stack of manilla folders onto the floor. Annoyed, Simon set the clippings down and picked up the infamous paddle. Turning it over in his hand, he could sense the awesome power it yielded.

When Simon went to set it back on the desk, he noticed the cracked, leather bound Bible that had been buried under the avalanche of bureaucracy. Overcome with curiosity, he picked it up and thumbed through the stiff, worn pages only to find that it too was riddled with notes just like Jeremy's. He turned to back the inside sleeve and read the inscription, "Dedicated to Thelma Malone Harold by the Bethel Presbyterian Church on June 14, 1926."

Simon decided to set Thelma's Bible aside for the time being. There were pressing matters at hand. So he gathered the forgotten newspaper articles and headed for a secluded place where he could more closely examine the newly discovered evidence. Once in the comfort of the chorus room, he took to the task of discerning fact from fiction as it pertained to the veracity of the legend.

For several hours, Simon read the accounts of a series of tragic deaths that had taken place in Bethel over the past seventy-two years. In some ways, the evidence did in fact support the notion of a curse. The stories were unbelievably sad, of course, especially when there was no rational explanation for why they had happened.

Simon was particularly moved when he considered all of the friends and family members who were left behind to deal with the unanswerable questions and unbearable despair. After each untimely death, the loved ones were charged with the unenviable task of trying to make some sense of it all. Somehow they had to eventually put their lives back together and move on.

However, other details failed to further substantiate the legend of Jessie Joseph. While it was true that the three most recent events, including Jeremy's untimely death, occurred in increments of every six years, the preceding tragedies revealed no such pattern. What is more, some of the tragedies in the documents that Miss Harold had collected over the years were in no way relegated to minors which also belied the myth.

Simon carefully laid out the articles on the floor in chronological order in an effort to discern some semblance of continuity that might corroborate the legend. They read as follows:

On July 3, 1989- Cody O. Alleghany, age 11 months, was found dead at 3:16 p.m. by his mother, Mary Alleghany, after falling down the grand staircase of their old farmhouse. The article went on to say that the father, Joseph Alleghany, while tending to the animals in the barn, heard the mother's screams after having found the child unconscious. Authorities later had to forcibly remove the lifeless body of the child from clutches of the hysterical mother sitting at bottom of the stairs.

June 4, 1985- Ishmael Jaffree Jr., age 4, drowned in the family's swimming pool at 6:07 p.m. while his twin siblings blew out their candles for a birthday party surrounded by family and friends. His father stated that no one could hear the thrashing or gasping of the child due to all of the chaos and noise from the other children. He stated that there was not even one moment of silence in which the doomed child could be heard.

November 17,1980- Slade Stone and his father, Sydell, drowned at 5:03 p.m. in Shelbyville Lake near the dam after teenagers removed a sign that detailed the park rules and the times that the turbines would be turned on and off. Witnesses said that Slade Stone, age 7, slipped and fell into the water and his father dove in after him to save him. Neither the boy nor the father resurfaced. The state refused to place accountability on the park rangers and were unable to identify the individuals responsible for taking down the warning sign.

June 22, 1973- Melissa McCorvey was pronounced dead at 2:35 a.m. due to respiratory and digestive issues after being born prematurely at twenty-two weeks. Her mother, Norma McCorvey, was later released from Carle Hospital in Champaign, IL with only minor complications. Mrs. McCorvey alleged that her husband, Woody, allegedly gave her a punch to the gut during a domestic dispute.

November 12, 1968- 18 year-old private 1st class, Samuel Epperson of the 101st Airborne Division, was killed by friendly fire during Operation Rolling Thunder in Vietnam. According to his mother, Susan Epperson, he enlisted in the Army after graduating from high school because "he was committed to stopping the spread of such a bankrupt and hopeless ideology as Marxism."

June 25, 1962- William J. Vitale Jr., age 10, died due to internal bleeding after being bitten by a snake while playing in the Embarrass Creek. The venom had coursed through the boy's veins at an alarming rate after being bitten by a black rattler.

May 26, 1952- Lewis A. Wilson, age 1, was pronounced dead at 5:27 p.m. as a result of overexposure to carbon monoxide. A coroner report showed that the chemical poisoning was the result of a faulty furnace. As a result, there was nothing to repress the amount of toxins that the infant inhaled.

March 8, 1948- James McCollum, age 3, was pronounced dead at the scene after his mother, Vashti, had accidentally backed over him in the car. Authorities were conducting an investigation in order to determine whether or not the incident could be ruled a homicide.

December 7, 1941- Robert Apple, F1c, USN, age 18, was presumed to have died aboard the U.S.S. Arizona during the surprise attack on Pearl Harbor by the Japanese Empire. The young man's remains were never recovered.

Simon sat back in his chair and sighed. The accounts were undeniably tragic. In fact, when he tried to put himself in the place of the bereaved families, he couldn't imagine how they could go on after such loss and sorrow.

"Why would God allow such things to happen?" he said under his breath.

Then a profound thought crossed his mind. As horrific as the events were, were they any different from any other town in any other state across the country? Curse or no curse.

Even if he thought that there was something extraordinary about the unfortunate deaths throughout the generations, what did it all really mean? How did it involve him, if at all? And even if it did, what could *he* possibly do to stop it from ever happening again? He was determined to get some answers and was pretty sure he might know where to find them.

25

THE DAUGHTER OF BABYLON

Simon stood at the edge of the workbench holding up one of the newspaper articles as he accusingly asked Thelma, "Do you happen to know how these made their way to your desk?"

Miss Harold didn't bother looking up from her work. Instead, she sat on her stool hunched over the multitude of blue ribbons she was busy embossing. Wearing her conspicuous head gear, she tediously worked the ribbons over in her tired, feeble hands. Finally, she answered in a grizzly voice, "I should hope so, seeing how I'm the one who put them there."

Simon dropped the paper to his side, stood straight up, and blankly stared at Thelma upon her perplexing admission. "Well, then," he stammered, "seeing how you are so well informed, are you also aware that these very same articles are missing from the archives in the Bethel public library?"

Sticking her tongue out of the corner of her mouth, she maneuvered a new piece of cloth into the embossing mechanism. "It's tricky," she said.

"What is?" he desperately asked.

"This machine, ugh, it's about as old as I am, and that is just a little younger than dirt," she mused. After a couple more seconds, she finished. "There. Got it. Now what is it you're blabbering about, Freeman? I ain't got much time. We're all on a deadline you know," she said finally looking up at him through the one-eyed magnifying glass. "What are you implying? I never 'took' nothin' from the library!"

"You didn't?" Simon asked.

"Oh no, I'm the local constable for heaven's sake," she sputtered before picking up a coffee mug and taking a sip. "I never let them *get* put into the periodicals at the library in the first place.

"Why? Who wants to know?"

"But why would you do a thing like that?" Simon asked exasperated.

"What difference does it make to you?" she asked defensively.

"I'm just trying to…," he started to say, choosing his words carefully. "I'm trying to make some sense of…"

"Make sense of what?" she snapped.

Regretfully, he blurted out, "Make sense of the curse!"

Thelma was unable to hold back a tiny smirk before deftly setting her mug back down on the table. Deliberately, she began to toil once again at her work.

"Wait…that probably sounds a little ridiculous," Simon admitted.

"Make some sense so you can what?…Stop it?…Defeat it?…End the vicious cycle?" Thelma surprisingly snarled as she reloaded the machine.

Simon was frozen from shock as if someone had just doused him with a bucket of ice water. "What do you know about the curse?" he begged to know.

"Huh! 'What don't I know about the curse' is a better question!" she barked. Brusquely, she set the magnifying glass on top of her head, turned towards Simon, and leaned on her knees with both hands. "Tell me somethin', you think you're the first person who ever tangled with the likes of Jack Lawless?"

"Jack?" Simon dumbly repeated. "Well, I, uh…."

"Don't just stand there stammerin' and uh, uh, uh, stutterin', answer me boy!" she demanded.

Suddenly, Simon was once again a frightened school boy who had been called to the principal's office. His head was spinning and his mind reeling.

"But, what does Jack have to do with the curse?" Simon asked, lifting his shoulders to his ears.

"Oh, brother," Thelma muttered, looking down at the floor and shaking her head.

"Well, *tell me*," Simon demanded, "what does Jack have to do with Jessie Joseph and Adam Potter?"

"Who said anything about Jessie Joseph or Adam Potter?" Thelma snapped.

"Is that why you pulled out all of those random articles and saved them all of these years?" Simon asked. "To figure out how to end the curse?"

"Random articles!" she said, scowling at him. "I've been at that school for a coon's age. They were like the children I never had. Their protection was my responsibility! And all of them tragedies happened on my watch.

"Do you know what it's like to have to sit back and watch that snake weasel his way into every aspect of our lives…?"

Simon's mind churned as he tried to put it all together. What was he missing here?

"Wait a minute," he said. "If they are all your children, then where are the most recent articles on the tragedies from the past twelve years? Where are the articles on the electrocution in 1995? Or the car crash in 2001? What about the articles on the investigation into Jeremy's death?

Simon's eyes desperately searched the tiny trophy shop as if looking for answers as he waited for her reply. When his gaze fell upon a picture frame commemorating the first dollar Thelma had earned at her establishment in 1992, it came to him.

"You gave up!" he said accusingly. "You-you just stopped trying to solve the curse?"

"Solve *the* curse," she quipped. "Boy, you haven't the slightest... There's no *solving* the curse, at least not for the likes of you or me. There's only learning to deal with the curse.

"I don't know. Maybe I just can't take another one. Besides, knowing what I know, there are always going to be more tragedies, and there isn't a thing that you or I can do to stop them."

"Even so, I'd rather prefer to not think of it as giving up, so much as preparing for my retirement."

"If it's true that no one can end the curse, then what am I doing here?" Simon asked. "Why am I killing myself over there at the school trying to return things to some sort of pre-curse, 'Little House on the Prairie', utopia, if it is all in vain?"

"Now, I can't tell you that," Thelma replied as she collected herself. "That's your deal not mine. That's something you need to look deep inside yourself for the answer. Why are you *here*? Huh?"

Simon slowly shook his head as he blankly stared at the old, worn out hardwood floors. "I am not sure exactly," he admitted. "A big part of me would love to go. Just leave this place, go on my way, and finish what I originally set out to do."

"So why don't you?" Thelma asked, already knowing the answer. "Why are you still hanging around in this forsaken, little town?"

"Because there's something inside me that is compelling me to stay," Simon said, vexed by his condition. "It gnaws at me, driving me to complete this task. In fact, it torments me, not allowing me to rest until it is finished. Do you know what I mean?"

"Yes, I'm afraid I know *exactly* what you mean," Thelma answered empathetically. "Then you need to see it through to the end. Listen, I wasn't up to the task, but maybe you are. Maybe you can beat him."

"Him?" Simon asked with a puzzled look on his face. "You keep saying Him. I'm talking about the curse!"

"Yes, him!" Thelma answered, exasperated. "Jack, of course. Haven't you at least figured that much out yet?"

"You mean Jack Lawless?" Simon asked, before a chill ran down his spine. He remembered the night when in a drunken stupor he thought he saw Jack morph into a dragon and fly off into the night sky. "What are you saying?"

"I'm saying that you'd have to be pretty stupid, or naïve, or both to not even know who your enemy is," Thelma answered gravely. "Could someone please tell me how you can win a war if you can't even acknowledge who it is you're fighting?"

"You can't be serious," Simon said. "You're telling me that Jack's been around since 1935?"

Then and now, one in the same," Thelma answered dryly. "Who knows how it all works exactly. But, yes, he's anywhere we allow him to be at any time."

"You're not making any sense," Simon replied.

"Ain't I?" Thelma answered. "You need me to be able to explain how it works for it to actually work? Ever hear of a cell phone? How does it work? There are a handful of people on the planet who can explain it, but there's not one person in the world who would say it doesn't work. That you can't punch a few numbers and within seconds get ahold of anyone in the world at anytime."

"But, what you're saying is crazy!" Simon said, questioning the old woman's sanity.

"Oh, don't act like you haven't already thought about it," Thelma said, pointing a finger at him.

"So…what?" Simon started to say as he considered the ramifications of her claims. "Jack somehow coerced, or caused, or was accomplice to the original tragedy that took place in Bethel?"

"Yes, yes, and yes," Thelma replied.

"I think your brain might be turning to mush," Simon dared to say.

"I am too old and too tired to be battling with Jack anymore, but my brain is still sharp as a tack," Thelma replied unapologetically while tapping the X-ACTO knife at her temple. "Now it's time for someone else to fight the good fight. My race is almost run."

"Someone else?" Simon replied, realizing the implication. "Oh no, I'd…I don't think…wait a minute." He paused for a moment as it all became abundantly clear. "You *meant* for me to find the stack of newspapers!"

"…and the folders, and the paddle, and the Bible…," Thelma admitted, as she pulled the looking glass down over her eye once more and resumed her task.

"Yes, but what good is any of that going to do me?" Simon asked despondently.

"Boy, you still haven't learned a thing, have you?" she said without looking up. "Maybe I was wrong about you. Tell me, Who is Jesus Christ?"

"What?" Simon sputtered. "Who is Jesus Christ?"

She sat up straight in her chair, folded her arms, and frowned at him, waiting for the question to register.

Finally, Simon confessed, "He is My Lord and Savior."

"So, maybe you don't have a say in the matter after all," she said matter-of-factly. "Maybe this is *your* fight now."

With her words hanging in the air, he once again remembered his conversation with Jeremy about purpose. Thelma stopped for a moment setting aside a freshly printed blue ribbon.

"And listen," she said sternly, pointing an X-ACTO knife at him, "don't lose faith, don't waver in your conviction, and never, and I mean never, give Jack so much as even an inch." After which, she picked up the next ribbon and set it down on the machine.

"But, I didn't say I was going to…" Simon started to say, "but I didn't agree to…I mean, I don't *have* to do anything, you know?"

Without looking up from her tedious work, Thelma replied coolly, "Well, go on, then. Get!"

Simon stared blankly at the top of her gray head with consternation. He took a step towards the front door of the store and then stopped. He muffled something under his breath and bit his lip before letting out a gush of air.

"What, still here?" she asked sarcastically. "All right then, as I was saying, I found out the hard way, once you start giving an inch, Jack takes a mile. First, it was instruction from the Bible, then it was merely reading from it, then it was no prayin' to Jesus, then no pray'n at all, then not even a moment of silence, now it's no 'under God' in the pledge.

"Before I knew it nothing was acceptable and everything was permissible all at the same time. These days everyone's a winner and no one is a winner," she continued as she held up yet another blue ribbon and setting it down onto a large stack. "I mean, if everyone passes the test then how do you know if anyone passed the test? If that's the case, then it wasn't really a test in the first place, now was it?"

"Nowadays, up is down and down is up!" she said as she built up steam. "Heard a kid say to his momma the other day that his ice cream was 'wicked good.'

'Wicked good'?" she snarled, shaking her head. "That's where it all starts, ya know. That's how Jack does it. He sucks the life out of words, until they're meaningless. 'Pro Choice', huh? Like if you ain't for killing babies you're against choices.

'Planned Parenthood', that's another one. Like two teenagers were plannin' anything during the two minutes they was gettin' their jollies. They make it sound like some young married couple goes in there to put together a *plan* for starting a family. Huh! They *should* call it 'Unplanned Parenthood'.

"Ever read Sanger's original mission statements?"

"What are you talking about?" Simon asked, in response to her diatribe.

"What am I talking about?" she snapped, slamming her fists on the table. "I'm giving you rubies and gold. What I'm givin' you is even better than rubies or silver or gold. I am giving you pearls of wisdom."

"If you know so much, then why don't you do whatever it is that needs to be done yourself?" Simon asked, defensively.

"Let's see, how can I put it to you so you can understand?" Thelma answered looking up at the ceiling. "It's like Yoda in Star Wars."

"'Yoda in Star Wars'?" Simon repeated sardonically.

"You've seen Star Wars haven't ya?" she asked, perturbed.

"Of course, I've seen Star Wars," Simon answered.

"Then 'yes' *I am your* Yoda," she said, proudly.

"So, I'm like Luke Skywalker or something and you're my Yoda," Simon said, rolling his eyes, now questioning his own sanity.

"Yoda or Merlin. Like Merlin. You were a Lit major, right?" she asked. "Then I'm your Merlin. I've done all I can do and now it's your turn. All I can do is share my knowledge with you."

"My turn?" Simon asked, regretting the question as soon as it came out of his mouth.

"Yes," she replied, resuming her work. "Your turn."

After an awkward silence, Simon finally asked, "All right. Supposing for a second that you aren't completely off of your rocker, why don't you just tell me things straight out? Tell me what I need to know. Why all this cloak-and-dagger stuff.

"Like, like finding the newspapers and stuff. Why not just bring that stuff to me instead of me having to miraculously, somehow stumble across it? I mean, what if I never found it in the first place?"

"Well, now, that's just it, isn't it?" Thelma lamented. "Wouldn't it be great if everything was just handed to us on a silver platter. I mean how easy would that be? But, no, that's not the way it works. I don't make the rules.

"Others can lead you, guide you, exhort you, even show you the way; but, you have to seek it for yourself. There has to be accountability and ownership. It's what separates the have's from the have not's. It is what this great country of ours was built upon. Those who don't work, don't eat. Ya know? William Bradford. Jamestown. Ever heard of him? His words, not mine. Look it up for yourself if you don't believe me. That *is* the American Dream. It's not winning the lottery, or being awarded some kind of crazy lawsuit, or being granted disability. It's life, liberty, and the pursuit of happiness. 'Pursue' is an action verb I do believe not an 'inaction' verb. Got me? It is having the opportunity, not the guarantee.

"And where does that right come from if not the constitution, and where does the constitution come from, if not from the Bible, and where does the Bible come from, but God himself? Slowly, but surely, we have given ground, and given ground to...to..."

"...To liberalism?" Simon interjected, trying to finish her thought for her.

"No," she said looking around the room.

"...To progressives?" Simon said, trying again.

"No! It's somethin' that undergirds all of that nonsense," she said raising her arms up in the air and spinning around in her stool, looking at all of the trophies, plaques, and ribbons. "No, I'm talking about entitlement- something for nothing. Gettin' what you want without any consequences or obligations. Makin' yourself your own god, with your own rules.

"And there is only one thing that I know of that is offered for nothing in return, and you already got that. Said so, yourself. That's where the confusion lies. We should be extremely grateful to receive the free gift of salvation. But, it don't end there for cry'n out loud!

"That's when we start giving ground; giving in to our own doubt, our own lack of faith, and our willful disobedience to the word of God."

Simon had become enamored by the old woman's sage advise and her strong conviction, so much so that he hadn't even noticed her staring longingly out the window of the small shop to the top of the grain elevator on the other side of Main Street.

When she had finished, she looked over at Simon only to see him completely transfixed. She squinted for a moment and turned to see what his gaze was fixed upon. Knowingly, she looked back again at Simon out of the corner of her eyes.

"We have been deceived by the master of deception," she continued, carefully choosing her words as she took the 2007 Dairy League trophy off of one of the shelves and clutched it in her hands. "We have traded what is good for shiny, gold idols. And we hand out First Place ribbons to every participant regardless of how they finished. Jack has managed to confuse us about what success truly is. We have been conditioned. We have been told to vanquish failure completely, making the very word taboo. So, we do everything in our power to shelter our kids from trials and tribulations and conflict."

"What?" Simon said, as if coming to his senses again. "Isn't that a bit hypocritical, considering you profit from that kind of mentality?"

"Oh, I have had my own failures to be sure," Thelma said, drooping her shoulders. "There was a time when I fought tooth and nail for every inch of ground, on each and every front. But the enemy continues his assault, wave upon wave. Eventually, I grew tired, or lazy, or discouraged, or just plain old. I don't know." She paused, looking forlornly at the floor.

Simon mulled over her words for a moment, before her heart was stirred once more, and she continued, "But you don't have to repeat my failures. You can learn from them. Avoid my pitfalls, and move the ball down the field. *You* might not be able to end the curse, but you *could* make sure that people respond the right way to it!"

"Huh," Simon scoffed at the enormity of what she was suggesting. "By what, making trophies?"

"Mercy, no!" Thelma replied, as she sat up and bit her bottom lip. "There was a time when Jack had me convinced that I could help kids do great things, exclusively by building up their self-esteem.

"Instead, we've done them a great disservice. But, God can take our greatest failures and turn them into His greatest achievements. He can take a curse and turn it into a blessing!

"Like this place for instance, it may not seem like much, but He uses the proceeds to buy ink cartridges for the copy machine, paper, supplies…and even a meager teacher's aid salary," she confided, as she raised her eyebrows.

"Teacher's aid?" Simon repeated with great misgivings.

"Currently, the position is vacant, but we are looking for the right person," she intimated.

"Pay all that money to get a college degree to become a teacher's aid?" Simon asked as if he had just smelt something putrid.

"I know it would be considered a failure to society at large, but you would be surprised how high you can climb by stooping so low," she added.

"Thanks a lot, Yoda," Simon quipped. Suddenly his heart ached as he spontaneously imagined working with Hope. Somehow it always came back around to her. But, then, the title "Teacher's Aid" jarred him out of the daydream. "But what about Jessie Joseph, what does he have to do with any of this?"

"Well, there's nothing you can do to *change* the past," Thelma said, discounting his question. "Don't waste your time chasing ghosts, especially when Jack's plotting and planning the next tragedy right under our noses."

"What do you mean?" Simon asked, taken aback.

"Let me ask you this, if you were a shepherd watching a flock, and even one lamb strayed, would you drop everything and go save him from imminent danger?" Thelma asked, purposefully.

"But, Jessie Joseph…" Simon started to say.

"Oh, for heaven's sake!" Thelma grunted, turning her head and waving her hand at him. "If you want to know about all that, you should go ask someone who was actually there when it happened. Cause I wasn't. Besides, I've already given you everything you need. So, what are you afraid of?"

"Afraid of?" Simon repeated, remembering Jack's assertion and his own revelation.

"Failure? Ridicule? You are so much like your father; so much potential," she mused. Thelma was not above using such a tactic, and the reference to his father staggered Simon. "The real question is, are you going to be a stand-up guy and own up to your obligations? Or are you going to run from them?" Finished with her exhortation, she set her headdress back on and took to her work again. The wily, old gal knew how to push people's buttons. She knew exactly when to press forward and when to pull back. This was more like a full out assault.

Simon's face went flush as he tried to muster the words to express all he had been dealing with inside of him, but when he tried to press the issue regarding his father, Thelma stonewalled him, offering no solace. She needed to start a fire and had over the years become adept at generating a spark. Intense friction was her specialty.

Cut to the quick, Simon wandered back to the school for some serious introspective thinking.

* * *

While sifting through the documents that Thelma had left for him on the desk, a heavy languidness came over him, and he finally succumbed to the mental and physical exhaustion. On the floor next to him lay the soiled old newspapers and the black and white photograph. In his lap, he held the old paddle in one hand and his cell phone in the other, while the state IEP folders sat in the trash can. The Bible lay open to the book of Matthew on the desk in front of him with a highlighter in the fold.

It was there in the quiet of the chorus room that he laid his head down and dreamt of things told and untold, remembered and forgotten, spoken and unspoken. Of fishermen and plentiful fields. And of a lamb who had strayed and the shepherd who sought him.

* * *

Simon stood bent over trying to catch his breath while standing on the concrete slab situated in between the dilapidated farmhouse and the old, defunct barn on Clay Potter's property. With a perplexed expression on his face, he studied the structural design of the well where he had seen Little Simon's dirty face peering up at him.

When Simon tried to imagine himself sitting at the bottom of the well, he suddenly came face to face with his own ghosts. He remembered the fatherless household and the parade of men came and went over the years. Each one of the suitors purporting to be a father figure of some kind, only to later prove themselves a poor substitute. Simon had wanted to run many times. He had wanted to hide. He wanted to find somewhere far away where no one would ever find him. And sometimes he just wanted to crawl into a hole and die. Staring at the bottom of the dried up well, he wondered if he might just see his own face staring back up at him.

After conceding such a telling admission, he was soon down on his hands and knees examining the slight aperture of the hole and trying his best to figure out how the frightened little boy was able to get in and out of it. Still afraid of what he might find, Simon reluctantly lay face down on the ground that was still damp from the early morning dew. Blindly feeling his hand along the brick into the deep, dark recesses of the interior walls, he hoped to find something more than memories of his own past.

Then he found it. It was a ledge. Breathlessly, he reached deeper into the ground as his imagination offered up all of the horrible things that might be lurking there. But, his trembling hand only discovered a second and then a third ledge. It became evident that there were missing bricks, or gaps, forming a recess in the wall about every two feet apart that could potentially provide a makeshift ladder in which a very slight child could climb up and down.

"So that's how he gets down there!" Simon said aloud.

"Who does what?" a voice called out from behind him.

Simon's heart skipped a beat as he jerked his head up to identify the unexpected visitor.

"Rocky, you nearly gave me a heart attack!" Simon said with a sigh of relief. He rolled over on his back for a second before standing to his feet.

"Who were you expecting, the Prince of Darkness?" Rocky asked with a mocking, sinister chuckle.

"What?" Simon asked, unsure.

Rocky turned and pointed down to the abandoned farmhouse at the bottom of the hill, "I figured maybe you were one of the Satan worshipers making sacrifices at your shrine."

For the first time, Simon closely analyzed the bizarre, spray-painted graffiti and the widely recognized symbol for anarchy. Not far from the house lay a black, ashen fire pit complete with smoldering logs, smashed beer cans, and some sort of half melted seed bags.

"Ridiculous, huh?" Rocky commented, shaking his head.

"Yeah," Simon mused. Then he shifted his attention back to Rocky. "So, what are you doing out here at the crack of dawn anyway?"

"I could ask you the same thing," Rocky said in response, "but it looks like you've been doing something stupid like jogging. So, a better question would be, 'why?'."

"I just started back at it actually," Simon said. "You know, try to get back into some semblance of shape."

"Oh, uh-huh," Rocky said, unimpressed.

"What about you?" Simon asked.

"I'm just taking a little break from seeding the next field over the hill," Rocky answered. "I bring the bags over here sometimes to burn em' up."

Simon glanced down at his watch, "At *six o'clock* in the morning? Awfully early to be spraying isn't it?" Simon asked.

"Na', man, it ain't early," Rocky replied. "I've been up for a couple of hours already. Early to rise, early to bed. At least, that's what Jack always says."

"Jack?" Simon asked.

"Yeah, he's the owner of the fertilizer company that I work for," Rocky said indifferently.

"No kidding," Simon replied.

"Yeah, and I'm not spraying anything," Rocky added. "I'm putting down seed."

"Seed?" Simon asked.

"Un-huh, we seed, spay weed killer and anhydrous ammonia, besides all of the other traditional fertilizer stuff," Rocky replied dully.

"Seems like a strange time of year to be planting seeds," Simon said, looking around at the nearly waist-high beans surrounding the abandoned farm.

"Yeah, I don't know how it all works," Rocky admitted. "It's all pretty technical really. I just take what they tell me to take and put it down where they tell me to put it down."

There was an uncomfortable break in the conversation before Simon asked, "Well, I suppose you have lots of fields to get to today…"

COLIN BRISCOE

With the underlying meaning missing the mark with Rocky, he answered, "Na, it doesn't matter. One field or ten fields, I get paid the same. So..." Rocky shrugged, not bothering to finish his thought.

It was then that Simon recalled the ugly exchange between the two of them at the Bethel tavern. The thought of driving Rocky from the faith because of his own stupidity turned his stomach, and he suddenly wanted desperately to try and repair the damage. Changing his demeanor, Simon extended an olive branch.

"Hey, Rocky about last week in the tavern..." Simon began to say.

"No worries, man," Rocky interrupted, as he waved him off and casually looked around.

"No, I was a real jerk," Simon confessed, "and I want to say that I am truly sorry. I guess you could say I was backsliding that day."

"No biggie, let's just forget it, okay?" Rocky said. "To each his own, ya know."

Simon cringed, recognizing a 'Joeyism' when he heard one. "No, it is a biggie," he continued. "I hate that my actions may have turned you away from seeking a relationship with Christ..." he began to say before Rocky cut him off.

"Really, apology accepted, no harm done," Rocky interrupted. "Let's just forget about it and move on."

"Okay," Simon said, ashamed by what he had done. Then he was reminded of what Pastor Pete and Thelma had both said about not being able to change the past. Once again, there was a lull in the conversation as Simon contemplated the potential ramifications for Rocky as a result of his being a hypocrite. Determined, Simon did his best to salvage the conversation.

Desperate to break the silence he asked casually, "So, tell me about all of this," as he made a gesture towards the graffiti on the house. "Kids come out here often?"

"Yeah, I guess so," Rocky said, glancing around. "They come out here to party. You know, get drunk, or high, or just be typical teenagers."

Simon's shoulders slumped forward as he thought of yet another regretful decision he made the night had gotten together with Jez. Placing his hands on his hips, he looked at the ground, bit his lip, and shook his head.

"They do, huh?" Simon asked absentmindedly.

"Uh-huh, pretty harmless stuff really," Rocky said arbitrarily. "Just a bunch of bored kids. I used to come out here all the time myself."

"Is that a fact?" Simon asked, doing his best to feign interested. "You weren't afraid that you'd find yourself on Satan's altar?" Simon asked, pointing at the fire pit next to the boarded up house.

"Nah, I think all that junk just kind of makes the girls freak out, so they're more likely to grab on to ya," Rocky answered. "We used to come out here a lot and light fireworks, stuff like that. This slab of concrete up here on the bluff makes for a really good launching pad."

"I bet it does, high up here on the hill and all," Simon responded. "You could probably see the lights for miles." Simon folded his arms and looked down at the old, cracked cement. "What was this for anyway, any idea? Seems like a pretty random location for a shed, being as far from the house and the barn like it is."

"Oh na' man, it was a threshing floor," Rocky answered.

"A *threshing floor?* What's that?" Simon asked only with mild interest.

"Well, back in the day, some of the 'old school' farmers would use a threshing floor to separate the wheat from the chaff," Rocky answered.

"Really, how would they do that?" Simon asked, finding himself suddenly intrigued.

"The way my dad described it, after they cut down the wheat they'd bring it up here to the high ground where the wind comes whippin' through," Rocky answered. "Then they'd take pitch forks and toss it up into the air." By now, Rocky was pantomiming the process as he described it. "The wind carries off the chaff, while gravity pulls the seeds back down to threshing floor. After that, they'd gather the seed into the barn and burn up the chaff in the fire."

"Huh, that's interesting," Simon said sincerely. "But, I didn't know they had concrete back in the day?"

"What? Na," Rocky said, looking down at the cracks in the pavement. "It's not as old as you'd think. They may have done it during the depression or something when they didn't have enough money for gas. Or they may have just done it for kicks or something. You know, some sort of harvest tradition. It was like a kinda symbolic thing or whatever. Or maybe they were purists like the Mennonites. Who knows?"

"Well, you learn something new every day, I guess," Simon said. "Thanks for the history lesson."

"No problem," Rocky answered, before an inquisitive look came over his face. "Hey, you never said why you were reaching down into the well? Cause if you're thirsty, you're out of luck. This well ran dry a long time ago."

"What? Oh, I no..." Simon stammered as he searched for a plausible explanation. "Actually, I was looking for someone."

"Looking for someone," Rocky said with a laugh. "In an abandoned well."

"Yeah, it sounds crazy, right?" Simon cautiously replied. He decided to take a chance and confide in Rocky. "Do you know a little kid named Simon Adamson?"

"Know him?" Rocky said with a laugh. "Who doesn't? That little kid's a nightmare! He's constantly getting in trouble, tearing stuff up, break'n windows, all kinds of stuff. They even say he bites kids on the playground. Thinks he's a vampire or something, somebody said. Is that who you're looking for?" Rocky asked as he took a step closer to the narrow hole and careened his neck to get a glimpse at the bottom.

"Yes," Simon answered flatly. "Andy Cross told me that the kid once told him that he comes out here sometimes to...uh...'play' in the well."

"No kidding? What a weirdo," Rocky said in disbelief as he looked over the ledge of the well into the abyss. "Crazy. Doesn't surprise me though. Kids' a whack job. He's the kind of kid you read about going into the school and gunning everybody down.

Then he added dryly, "He's lucky those boards down there haven't rotted out yet."

"What do you mean?" Simon asked.

"That's not the bottom," Rocky observed. "Sure it looks like the bottom, because there's a bunch of dirt and junk covering the boards. But, it's just a catch basin. The well goes down another sixty or seventy feet probably."

"So, if the boards rot out…" Simon started to say.

"Then that kid's outta luck," Rocky mused. "If he survived the fall, he'd be stuck for sure."

For a moment, the two of them stared at the bottom of the well as the blazing sun started to rise above the tree line. Instantly, they could feel the intense heat bearing down on them.

Somewhere in the back of Simon's mind, he recollected the conversation he had with Miss Harold. "Tell me something, Rocky," Simon said suddenly overcome with sympathy. "If some little kid from town- other than the Adamson boy- wandered out here and fell down into the well. What would happen?"

"I don't know any normal kids who wouldn't be too afraid to come out here by themselves," Rocky replied.

"Yeah, but supposing they did anyway," Simon said, pressing the issue, "like on a dare or something."

"What would happen?" Rocky repeated, taking off his mesh hat and wiping the sweat from his brow.

"Yeah, what would people do?" Simon asked.

"Everything they could to get em' out, I guess," Rocky supposed.

"That's what I thought you'd say," Simon solemnly replied. "And what about Simon Adamson?"

"I don't know that anyone would ever know he was missing," Rocky said with a shrug.

"So much for No Child Left Behind," Simon muttered.

* * *

Simon lifted his eyes skyward and spoke, "Do you really want me to do this? Because if you don't, then please let me know." He paused for a couple of seconds. "I mean, if not, I can get in my car right now and just drive away." He waited for a reply, but there was none forthcoming.

Nervously, Simon shifted the heavy bag of groceries in his arms as he stood where Jeremy once stood on the front porch of Little Simon Adamson's house. Briefly closing his eyes, Simon's lips moved as he said yet another short prayer. He was trying to muster the courage to knock on the front door. When one of the bags nearly slipped from his grasp. He lifted his knee, repositioned his arms, and secured the bag.

"That's it," he said, gritting his teeth. As he leaned one of the brown bags against the wall, he managed to deftly clench his fist and rap on the door.

After a moment, the young girl whom he had seen before with the tattoo's, colored hair, and piercings answered the door.

"Yeah? What do ya want?" she asked, annoyed.

Up close, Simon was able to see how disturbingly young and surprisingly pretty the girl was behind a cloak of heavy mascara and long, streaky bangs.

"Are you from the agency or somethin'?" she asked coldly.

"What, oh no, well, you see I…my name is…" Simon sputtered while still struggling to hold the sacks of groceries.

After muddling through only a partial explanation, the young girl looked at him quizzically.

"Did you say Jeremy sent you?" she asked. "Cause he died, ya know."

"Yeah, I'm aware…you could kind of say that…no, you could definitely say that Jeremy sent though," Simon replied, visibly flustered.

"I mean, I know he died of course. But, I know he wanted me…would have wanted me to…do this."

Suspiciously, she narrowed her eyes and gave him the once over before finally stepping aside and holding the door open. Simon stood frozen for a second uncertain.

"Well?" she asked impatiently. "Ya, comin' in?"

"Oh, yeah, thank you," he replied meekly as he walked through the front door. Based on the deplorable conditions, it became immediately clear to him how meager an existence the two of them were eking out. Simon had heard before of people living in squalor, but he hadn't actually seen it first hand until now. Clutter filled every room in the house while heaping mounds of laundry, piles of trash, and bits of food covered the filthy furniture and dirty floors. The residual stench was so overpowering that it was almost unbearable. Words couldn't begin to describe the horrid conditions.

Even the very structure of the house was in complete disrepair. There were portions of the ceiling falling in, holes in the floor that exposed the crawl space, and large cracks that canvassed the walls. It was truly a wonder that the building hadn't been condemned a long time ago. To think that anyone in the world, let alone the United States of America, had to live like that was overwhelming.

Simon did his best to keep his emotions in check as he followed the young girl to the kitchen. He didn't know whether to be angry, distraught, or utterly ashamed.

The girl shoved aside some dirty dishes in order to make room for the groceries.

"You can just set those down anywhere," she said flatly. "It don't matter."

Obediently, he set down the brown bags and turned in time to see the girl walking away from him down the hallway towards a back bedroom.

"This way," she said without the least bit of emotion in her voice.

Simon's heart skipped a beat as he recalled the swirling accusations that had been leveled against Jeremy after his demise, regarding his time spent in this house. Suddenly, wild, implausible thoughts filled his mind. The entire experience was so surreal.

"What am I doing?" he thought in a panic. "What have I gotten myself into?"

At the end of the hallway, the young girl stopped, turned around, and leaned against the door.

"In here," she muttered as she took out a lighter and a fresh cigarette.

Timidly, Simon stepped forward and peered around the corner of the doorframe into the small bedroom where he saw a little boy playing a video game on the floor. He was sitting with his back towards them. While the young girl took a long drag off of her cigarette, he got the distinct impression that this had become almost like some sort of routine that had been previously established with Jeremy. The girl said nothing. Disturbed by his own imaginings, Simon couldn't help but think of the times he saw Jeremy coming out of the dugout, alone, with boys from his baseball team. Flustered, Simon's eyes darted back and forth between the boy and his mother.

Without saying a word, she turned her head to the side and blew out a puff of smoke. Once again, she narrowed her eyes as if sizing him up. Finally, she said, "I'm goin' to be just down the hall watching TV." She stepped forward and pointed her index finger in Simon's face. "If you so much as touch him, so help me God…" Then she turned her head to the boy and said, "Simon, this here is Mr…

"…Freeman," Simon interjected.

"…Mr. Freeman," she continued. "He was a friend of Mr. Jeremy's. He's come by to see you." With that, she moved past him and walked back down the hallway to the front room of the house, casting one last, icy stare at him over her shoulder.

Simon let out a gush of air and breathed a huge sigh of relief. Then he turned his attention to little Simon who was evidently so absorbed in his game that he hadn't even bothered to acknowledge his presence.

Not knowing exactly what to say, Simon furtively moved in a little closer to see what had captured the boy's attention. It was a handheld video game.

"Say, uh, is that one of those Game Boy's?" Simon asked, chastising himself for the stupid remark. After getting a little closer, he noticed the dirt behind the boy's ears and on the back of his neck. There was no doubt that it was the same boy who he had mistaken for Adam Potter.

There was no answer.

"That's pretty cool," he said, realizing that he was being lame. "I-um, I just came to meet you. I have heard a lot about you. And, of course, seen you at the school." The boy continued staring down at the flashing images while his fingers and thumbs feverishly worked over the buttons.

"Hey, I bet you didn't know that we have the same first name…Simon," he said, rolling his eyes.

Silence.

Desperately, he looked around the room, hoping that he could use something as a talking point. Clumsily, Simon did his best to connect with the preoccupied child.

"Say, where did you get that cool game anyway?" Simon asked, not expecting a response.

"Ah, I got it for Christmas last year," Little Simon surprisingly replied with a slight speech impediment.

"Really?" Simon asked, wondering if it might have been Jeremy who had given it to him. "That's pretty cool."

"Yeah," Little Simon replied flatly.

For some time, it went like that. Simon did his best to reach the boy on some kind of more meaningful level, but each attempt only resulted in the same short, nondescript answers. The visit was turning out to be some sort of uncomfortable, interrogation. Still, Simon was pleased with himself for being obedient to the small, still voice inside of him, and he was glad to finally have an opportunity to meet the troubled child.

Even during the short time they had been together, the neglected child seemed a little emotionally unstable. Within a relatively short period of time, Simon was witness to wild swings in his temperament. One moment, Little Simon would be sullen and withdrawn, and the next minute he might exhibit a sudden burst of violent temper. While Simon conceded that some of what he had observed could be attributed to the nature of playing video games, it didn't take a child psychologist to understand why there might be something wrong with the little boy.

Simon decided to try and get the child's attention off of the game completely in order to get a better engage him in a conversation. Suddenly, an idea came to him. In an effort to gain some of Little Simon's trust, he lowered himself onto the floor and sat next to the boy. Now they were at almost eye level.

"Hey, I bet you and I know some of the same people," Simon said, nonchalantly. "Do you mind if I sit next to you?"

When he finally took a seat on the floor, Little Simon instinctively slid away from him without even looking up from his video game.

"Yeah, I think you know a friend of mine," he said manufacturing some enthusiasm. "Do you know Ms. Wiseman?"

Little Simon stopped punching the buttons for a brief second, almost smiled, and glanced at Simon out of the corner of his eye.

"You know her?" he asked. "I thought maybe you did."

Outside of mispronouncing his "r's", it was no different from the average 6 or

7-year-old. By the way people had talked, Simon was almost expecting some kind of monster. Given a different environment and some different clothes, he might have been perfectly normal.

"I like her," little Simon said after resuming his game. "She's nice."

"Yes, she is," Simon replied. He was amazed at how well the visit had been going and chastised himself for his preconceived notions.

"Look, I almost made it to level five," little Simon said proudly, lifting up the game to show his visitor.

"Wow, you must be pretty good," Simon said, gaining some confidence. "Hey, you know who else was a friend of mine?"

"No, who? Oh man!" the boy said, as he lifted up the Game Boy and worked over the buttons some more.

"Jeremy Warner," Simon said with a smile. "I know he used to come visit you."

Immediately, the boy dropped the game to his side and stared blankly at Simon who took note of the sudden shift in the boy's demeanor.

"What's wrong?" Simon asked.

"Nothin'," little Simon answered avoiding eye contact and pretending to be distracted. Then he unexpectedly stood up, dropped the game boy to the floor, and walked over to his dresser on the other side of the room.

"Didn't you like Mr. Warner?" Simon asked, picking up on the sudden shift.

The boy nodded with a furrowed brow and said, "I don't want to talk to you anymo'." With that, he turned and began to fidget with some plastic toys on his dresser.

Simon frowned, "Did Mr. Warner say something or do something that you didn't like?"

Without warning, the little boy scowled at Simon, and said through gritted teeth, "I don't have to talk to you, stupid-head."

"But wait, I was just..." Simon started to say as he rose to his feet.

"*No!*" the angry boy suddenly spit on Simon's shirt before running out of the room.

Alarmed, Simon moved deliberately so as not to alarm the young mother. He followed after the boy, but by the time Simon made his way into the hallway, all he saw was the screen door slamming against the frame of the house.

The young girl called out flatly from her usual spot on the couch, "Simon...?"

"Uh, he took off," Simon said as he made his way through all of the junk and the clutter to the living room area. "I guess he was tired of talking to me."

The young mother took another drag on her cigarette and swung her legs up onto the couch, never taking her eyes off of the television. "He's always runnin' off somewhere," she said under her breath.

"Do you even know where he goes?" Simon asked almost accusingly. As soon as the words rolled off his tongue, he knew he had crossed the line. The girl shot him a look of resentment, leaned her head on her hand, and turned back to *The View* without dignifying the remark.

"Sorry, that's not really any of my business," Simon said, apologetically. Now he understood why Jeremy was seen making so many visits. If anyone was going to break through to little Simon Adamson, it was going to take some time. And in order to get that time he had to be welcome in their home.

Simon glanced around the room as the words of Thelma Harold echoed in his mind, "You'd be surprised how high you can reach if you are willing to stoop so low."

"Hey," he said, trying to be more upbeat. "Would you mind if I tidied up a bit in here?"

The young girl looked out of the corner of her eye at him through her long, bleached bangs.

"Knock yourself out," she said finally.

After a few hours, Simon emerged from the house onto the saggy front porch with two large bags of garbage. He was very troubled by his conversation he had had with little Simon and wondered what it was about Jeremy that set him off. While he was glad that Jeremy was obviously not having anything going on with the young girl, he wasn't completely exonerated just yet. The very thought made him spontaneously shiver. Even though Simon had every confidence in Jeremy's character, the reaction of the little boy at the mere mention of his name was striking and undeniable. And Simon was determined to find out why.

Still, as he descended the steps, he couldn't help but allow himself to smile at his willingness to follow Miss Harold's advice. In return, he was given one of the greatest gifts known to man, performing an act of kindness for someone else without getting any credit or expecting anything in return. There was no doubt in his mind that he was now listening to the small, still voice.

Across the street, Pastor Pete widened the blinds of his office window with his thumb and index finger to get a better look at the expression on Simon's face. Contemplatively, he looked down and stared at the floor before walking to the opposite side of the room and picking up the phone. Now peering out the opposite window towards the old school building across the street, he waited for the party on the other end of the line to pick up. After a beep, the voice message said, "*Hello, you have reached Hope Wiseman. I am unable to come to the phone right now, but if you leave your name and number, I will be glad to get back to you as soon as possible. Thank you and have a blessed day.*"

26

FROM THE TOWER TO THE CORNER GATE

Spiritual inertia is the best way to describe what Simon was experiencing over the course of the past three weeks. Ever since he discovered Jeremy's notes in the concession stand, something had been building up inside of him. It was indefinable and yet powerful all at the same time. Simon could only describe it as transforming faith into action. And the result had been life changing. It was the strangest thing. He was dirt poor and felt rich, exhausted but energized, blindly obedient and yet intensely focused.

Ever since the first day he chose to minister to Little Simon Adamson, he had developed a regular routine that he had been had been following religiously. Each morning, he would get up at 5:00 a.m., read the Bible, spend some quiet time in prayer, and then go for a little run. By six o'clock, he was at work, completing the menial tasks necessary for getting the building ready for the upcoming school year or occasionally running a check to the bank for Thelma. When lunchtime came around, he would withdraw to the comfortable chair in the chorus room and study the materials that Thelma Harold had purposely left for him to find. He even pulled the state's IEP manilla folders and state tests out of the garbage can and began trying to make some sense of it all. After lunch, he would continue working on the checklist that Andy Cross had put together for him. Thelma had kept her word by making sure that Andy and Mr. Gettby would be preoccupied with getting the Philo Grade School ready for the coming school year, allowing Simon to work in almost complete autonomy.

After his workday officially ended at 2:30 p.m., Simon would resume the monumental task of restoring the entryway to its original condition. It was an especially daunting task considering his ineptitude for construction and handiwork. While he relied heavily on YouTube and Google as his teaching tools, progress was often slowed by using the methodology of trial and error. Actually, it was mostly error. To make matters worse, the weather had not been cooperating in the least. The heat index flirted with record highs, and it had not rained since the night he had last seen Hope. Humidity hung heavy in the air like a wet blanket, making even the easiest of tasks seem arduous.

If Simon had spent anytime whatsoever at the tavern, he would have heard the bellyaching of the farmers who came there for lunch each day. With the latest forecast, they let out a collective groan and helplessly stood by as their yields exponentially diminish. The hard, dry ground was beginning to crack because there was no rain in the land as the dismayed farmers covered their heads in their hands in anguish.

But Simon hadn't seen or heard much from anyone in recent days. Will was busy preparing for summer school, midterm exams, while Rocky spent a great deal of time at the wheel of his giant contraption, planting seeds and spraying weeds. Rich was in the thick of the Dairy League pennant race, and Rob was preoccupied with pushing whole life insurance when he wasn't helping Jack with plans for the new adult superstore.

Oddly enough, Jack himself was nowhere to be found ever since Simon had become immersed in fulfilling his commitments. Not that Simon had given him much thought. These days the greater part of his attention centered on the curse, his purpose, Little Simon Adamson, and of course, Hope.

As invigorated and committed as he was to the completing the task at hand, there were still times when his lack of skill had culminated in fits of frustration. His exasperation was only further accentuated by the extreme heat and humidity. After all, he was still human. If failure was the great teacher that Thelma claimed it to be, then Simon was no doubt in the doctorate program. Yet, even in those moments, it didn't take much to bring him out of his stupor. Often, it only took a few words from Jeremy or a timely verse or a short prayer to snap him out of it. Then he was back at it again, ready to give it another go.

More than just the mental challenges, the project presented him with physical challenges as well. Trying to use one inanimate, unforgiving object to manipulate another unforgiving inanimate object, often resulted in bloody knuckles, a bruised shin, or a knot on his forehead. Simon couldn't begin to count the number of times his screwdriver slipped, or he raked his hands over a two-by-four, or he smashed a finger after missing the head of a nail. It was all in a days work. Nothing came easy or natural. Everything was a struggle.

Just when he thought he had something put together correctly, he would discover that it was backwards, or inverted, or upside down. Fueled by aggravation, he would have to take it apart once again and start all over. Whether it was the floor, or the walls, or the ceiling, or the doors, the pipes, or the wiring, it made little difference. They each presented him with a unique challenge that was completely foreign to him.

It was in those moments that he would remember what Thelma had told him about society trying to eliminate failure from the curriculum. Consequently, he couldn't help but shake his head and smile at the wisdom in her assertion of the value of failure. Whether it was cutting a board after measuring it wrong or having 220 volts climb up his arm and smack him in his ear, Simon could all but guarantee that he would never forget the lessons learned in those moments. And he would have all but guaranteed that he would never repeat those same mistakes if not for *two* incidents with the industrial sander. Still, he couldn't help but notice that the degree to which he remembered how to do a particular task was often proportional to the amount of struggle or pain or both he often had to invest in order to learn it in the first place. It was like one of those cruel ironies in life.

Fortunately, Simon had the luxury of making mistakes without completely exhausting his resources. Somehow each time he went to the hardware store there was always more money in the school account just as Wilson B. had promised. Simon had been so busy that it was understandable why he hadn't noticed the Livingood's ski boat was no longer sitting in their garage.

Progress had been made even though it didn't feel like it. And so it went day after day for twenty-one days. One step forward and three steps back often only felt like three steps back. And he was about to discover that it was time to retreat one more time.

Simon had a look of confusion on his face as he stood up. He yanked off his ball cap and scratched the top of his sweaty head. Squatting back down, he looked from one side of the framed wall to the other and took out a tape measure.

"What?" Simon sputtered as he measured it a second time. Then he did it a third time. "What the…? How on earth did I do that? Ah, *come on!*" he yelled out after discovering that the frame he had just put together didn't line up with the stairs and ceiling. The realization had set in that he was going to have to tear it all down again and start all over from scratch.

"Hello," a sweet voiced called out from the bottom of stairs. "Knock, knock. Are we interrupting?"

Embarrassed by his outburst, Simon turned to see Mrs. Hannah Grace Rash, Mrs. Mara Rash, and Pastor Pete coming through the front doors of the school.

"What? Oh, no," Simon said, masking his frustration. "I just…I was just. It's no big deal really. I just realized that I'm going to have to reset this wall…again."

"Oh dear, that's too bad," Hannah Grace said loudly, trying to be heard over the Switchfoot song playing on the radio.

"Hello, Simon," Pastor Pete said with a warm smile before surveying the condition of the barren wall. "Oh my…" he muttered as his eye jumped around the dismantled entryway, taking note of the dust, debris, and drop cloths.

"Oh yeah, sorry, just a minute," Simon said as he ran over to the radio and turned it down.

The three visitors stood at the foot of the stairs, dumbstruck. Simon noticed that Hannah Grace and Mara were using hot pads to carry covered dishes, while Pastor Pete held a brown grocery sack in one arm and a covered picnic basket in the other.

"This is really…something," Pastor Pete commented, with a worried look on his face. "You've got quite a…a uh, a thing going on here."

"Yes, it is pretty involved," Simon admitted.

"Uh-huh," Mara grunted with a disapproving expression.

After an awkward pause, Simon asked, "Is there something that I can do for you folks?"

"Actually, we had just taken some food over to the Cain's," Hannah Grace said. "I don't know if you heard but their little daughter, Pearl, is quite ill. Anyway, we heard how hard you had been working over here, and uh…," Hannah Grace said. It took a moment for her to get beyond the wreckage. "…And, on behalf of the congregation at the 1ˢᵗ Church of Bethel, we would like to present you with a token of our appreciation. We made a little something for you as well." She held up a steamy casserole with a broad smile on her face.

Simon suddenly became keenly aware of his unsightly appearance, noting in particular the large sweat circles underneath each of his arms, his torn shirt, pungent odor, and large band aid adorning his forehead. "That is very, very kind of you," he said, wiping his hands off on a handkerchief.

Truth be told, he looked a fright and smelled like a goat, but Mrs. Hannah Grace, being ever the lady, noted his embarrassment and reassured him. "Oh, don't you worry about how you look, you've been working hard," she said.

"Oh, I-I couldn't possibly accept," Simon said as he breathed in the heavenly aroma. "There are people who deserve it more than me. Besides, I've had some dinner."

Hannah Grace glanced down at the half-empty bag of Cheetos and empty Mountain Dew can sitting on a saw horse. "Don't be silly," she quibbled, "besides, we insist. Now is there somewhere that we can set these down?"

Obligingly, Simon acquiesced and decided to accept their generous gift. After all, he was famished and had not had a home cooked meal in ages. "Yes, here, I'll take it and put in on the table in one of the classrooms," Simon answered. "Thank you so much!"

Hannah Grace carefully handed over the scalding hot dish. He took the hot pads into his hands and started up the stairs to the first landing. Looking back over his shoulder, Simon called out, "Come on up. I'll just grab some chairs and we can all…"

When he turned and saw their expressions, he stopped dead in his tracks and followed their gaze up to unlit chandelier. Reaching over with his elbow, he flicked the switch on. Instantaneously, brilliant, white light reflected off of the shiny tin ceiling, illuminating the entire room.

For a minute or two, they stood in silence with their mouths ajar, taking in the magnificent chandelier and ornamented ceiling.

"Oh wow," Hannah Grace muttered, placing a hand on her chest. "It's so beautiful."

Mara and Pastor Pete were speechless.

"Isn't that something?" Hannah Grace said, getting teary-eyed.

Mara merely grunted, "Hmmph, where on earth did he get *that*?"

"Mother," Hannah Grace said in a whisper while frowning at her cynical mother-in-law.

All the while, Pastor Pete had been gripped by something far more intense than admiration or curiosity. His fearful face went ghost white, beads of sweat dampened his forehead, and his shoulders tensed up as if readying for impact. Even if the others had known the outwards signs of PTSD, there wasn't anything they could have done to have stopped it. Deep inside, Pastor Pete's heart raced, his stomach tightened in knots, and his legs were like two numb sacks of concrete mix.

"Pastor Pete?" Hannah Grace asked with great concern after noticing his change in demeanor. "Are you all right?"

"What?" the good pastor sputtered. He impulsively shook his head as if coming out of a trance. "Oh yes, what? I…" he leaned down, placed the grocery bag on the bottom step, and nervously wiped his palms on the sides of his slacks. "Yes."

"Are you sure?" Simon asked, taking a step towards him. "You don't look so good."

"No, no, I'm fine," he said as he slowly retreated towards the front doors. "I suddenly just remembered that I have some other affairs to attend to at the parish." Reaching blindly for the door handle with a wave of his arm, Pastor Pete took another glimpse of the giant chandelier before stumbling out the doorway.

Mara rolled her eyes.

"Okay, well, see you later, and thanks again for the food," Simon called out. He leaned down and peered out the glass of the front doors. "Is he going to be okay? Maybe we should call Dr. Al-Banna."

"I don't know," Hannah Grace answered as she placed her index finger on her cheek. "He seemed just fine before we came in."

"Ahh, phooey," Mara spouted, completely disregarding the dramatic change in the pastor's manner "Probably left the hose on again in the rose garden or something."

"Mother, sometimes you can be so insensitive," Hannah Grace said, scolding her mother-in-law. Then she looked back up at Simon slightly embarrassed. "I don't know what got into him."

"It was kind of strange," Simon admitted.

"It was," Hannah Grace noted. "One minute he was acting fine, and then…it was after you turned on the lights, like he suddenly remembered something." She looked up a second time at the resplendent chandelier. "It really is spectacular, isn't it? Have you ever seen anything like it, mother?"

"Yes," Mara replied dryly.

Simon and Mara turned to the tiny, old woman.

"What?" she snapped. "It only stood up their for fifty years or more."

"It's the *original*?" Hannah Grace asked, turning towards Simon. "Was it under the ceiling tile?"

"No, actually, I found it in the storage room down in the basement," Simon replied.

"But the tin ceiling had been there this whole time?" Hannah Grace asked. Drawn by the incandescent, white light, she slipped off her shoes and slowly ascended the steps towards the landing. Defiantly, Mara folded her arms and stood her ground.

"Yes, it was there all of these years just waiting to be rediscovered," Simon said. "Let me just set this on the table in the classroom. I'll be right back."

When Simon returned, Hannah Grace was digging through her purse. "That reminds me," she said. "I wanted to give you this."

"What is it?" Simon asked, taking it into his hands. Turning the colored photograph over in his hands, he quickly realized that it was yet another class picture taken on the steps of the entryway. "Oh thanks, I actually have one just like it," Simon said, dropping it to his side.

"Oh really?" Hannah Grace said, disappointed. "Oh well, I just thought that it might come in handy for the renovation. You can keep it if you like. I have no need of it anymore. It's old, and..." her voice tailed off as she dropped her head and wiped her nose with the back of her index finger.

"Oh, okay, thanks," Simon replied, glancing down again at the picture.

"You know," Hannah Grace said, looking up again. "When pastor first told us about what you were trying to do, I have to admit that I thought that you were a little misguided. After we repainted the interior and what not, I thought that it all looked good enough, but now seeing this..." she gazed up admiringly, "I have to say I think this just might get people's attention after all."

"Really?" Simon asked, enthusiastically.

"I do," Hannah Grace replied. "Tell me, how in the world did you get such a good idea."

Simon initially balked at answering the question directly. But, then he looked up at the chandelier for a moment before daring to the make the bold assertion. "God gave it to me."

"Ha!" Mara blurted out at the foot of the stairs.

"Mother!" Hannah Grace snapped, completely mortified by mother Rash's crass objection.

"What's the matter, Mrs. Rash, don't you believe in God?" Simon asked.

"Of course, I believe that there *is* a God," Mara snapped.

"Well, then, don't you think that He could give Simon the idea, mother?" Hannah Grace asked, diplomatically.

"I chuckled because you asked him where the 'good' idea came from," Mara mused. "How do you know it is such a 'good' idea?"

"Wait a minute," Simon said, confused. "So, let me get this straight, you're not saying that God didn't give me the idea. You're just saying that God might have given me a bad idea?" He was completely baffled by the assertion.

Mara shrugged her shoulders.

"Why would God give somebody a 'bad' idea, mother?" Hannah Grace asked.

"I don't know, maybe to make him look like some kind of jackass, teach him a lesson or somethin', who knows why He does what He does?" Mara replied. "Certainly, after everything you've been through, you're not so naïve as to think that everything that comes from God is good."

"I would agree that there are things that don't seem good at first, but I think either way it ultimately works for our good," Simon answered meekly, recalling some passages from Jeremy's Bible. He recognized the opportunity and wanted to make sure he didn't make the same mistakes that he had made with Rocky.

"Oh brother," Mara said, rolling her eyes again. "Tell me. What makes you believe such drivel?"

"The Bible tells us that God is Love," Simon replied with confident, humility.

The very words sent Mara into a tizzy. Immediately, her wrinkly face turned bright red, and she shook as she hissed through gritted teeth, "Is that so? Then how is it that He took the only son that I will ever have away from me? Huh, how's that 'good'? God is love, huh."

In a flash, Simon remembered Mara's adamant claims the night he helped the old woman take in the groceries. Mara's words, *They killed him!* echoed in his ears, and he remembered the article from the newspaper clipping.

Hannah Grace fought back the tears and choked out the words, "Mother Rash, please stop. God is not to blame for John's death."

Simon was stunned by the dramatic turn that the conversation had taken.

"Then who is, huh?" Mara growled. "Who else is to blame?"

"Mother, God did not push John off of that grain elevator," Hannah Grace said, squinting as she rubbed her temples. "It was from all those years of torment and drinking. *You know that!*"

"I know no such thing!" Mara said, the bitterness dripping from her words. "Why did he set out to drink'n in the first place? It's the same reason you take that 'medicine' of yours. All them demons."

"I know where your so called spells come from. And I know you put on this front, actin' all high and mighty, goin' round, taken food to folks and doin' charity, but you can't hide your true self from me. Deep down, you're every bit as angry at God as I am, maybe even more. And I got news for you, them pills of yours ain't never gonna take away the pain neither. Trust me on that one, darlin'."

Hannah Grace broke down, crying. Simon reeled, temporarily stunned by the raw emotion. Remembering the details of the article in *The Bethel Chronicle*, Simon gently asked, "Mara, who do you think was responsible for John's death?"

"Everybody!" Mara snapped, waving her arm around in a giant circle.

"Everybody?" Simon repeated. He was trying his best to make sense of what she was saying.

"Yes, everybody," Mara continued. "Everybody in Bethel went around judging him all the time, treating him like he was some sort of criminal when that snake, Jessie Joseph, were the real criminal, do'n God knows what to our babies right under our noses. Right up them stairs!" she boldly declared, turning around on the landing and pointing towards the chorus room..

Simon froze at the mere mention of Jessie's name and his unspeakable crimes while Hannah Grace sobbed uncontrollably.

"Wait," Simon heard himself say out loud, "Jessie Joseph actually did all of those terrible things that people say he did?"

"Of course!" Mara replied angrily.

"Mother, we don't know that," Hannah Grace objected.

"We don't, huh?" Mara snapped, "then how did Adam Potter suddenly turn up dead, huh? Tell me that!"

"So, Jessie Joseph murdered Adam Potter?" Simon asked, completely enraptured by Mara's words.

"In the closet, in that very room right there, yes, he did," Mara answered, pointing towards the 1st grade classroom where Simon had first thought he had seen Adam's apparition.

"The authorities said it was an accident," Hannah Grace insisted.

"Oh, everything's an accident with you!" Mara gasped. "Nobody's to blame. It was just an accident, that's all. Then why did that sicko go and blame it all on my John if it truly were an accident?

"No, Jessie suffocated that poor child and blamed it on them innocent boys." Then she turned towards Simon, with daggers in her eyes. "So, you tell me college boy, how does a God of love allow such terrible tragedies to happen to good people like that? Huh, how? Tell me. How did *that* work for anybody's 'good'!"

The sun was setting in the West casting an orange glow on the lobby which only served to further accentuate the shining chandelier above Simon's head. He stared blankly at the furious, old woman then turned to see the tears running down Hannah Grace's anguished face. Uncertain of what to do, he closed his eyes for a brief moment and mumbled a few words. Inexplicably, a calmness swept over him, and he finally spoke.

"Mrs. Rash, I am so sorry for your loss," he began. "I truly am. And believe me, I don't claim to have all of the answers. But, I know that God is love in the same way I know that He is good. It is because the Bible tells me so. If He is love, then I have to believe that He wants what is best for us even when we don't know what that is. And if we believe in Him and in His son, our Lord and Savior Jesus Christ, then we *know* that it is possible for seemingly tragic events to ultimately work for a greater good."

"For a greater good?" Mara repeated in disbelief. "Tell me. Have you ever lost a child?"

"No, no, I haven't," Simon said, sympathetically. "But, I have experienced loss," he said, thinking of his father, and of Jeremy, and of Hope. "What's more, just because I haven't experienced the exact same kind of loss as you does not disqualify me from sharing the truth with you.

"I have come to believe that if God is love then He cannot deny himself. He is constant. He cannot change. So, out of love God gave us free will. As a result, we either make good choices or bad choices. Either way, I think He either causes or allows the consequences of the choices to mold us in His image if we allow Him to do so.

"Even though God already knows what we will choose, we don't in the moment. In that way, we are able to be active participants in shaping our own destiny. We are responsible for working out our own salvation. It is out of love that he allows us to feel pain and suffering sometimes with the intent of bringing us closer to Him. Can't you see that it is for us to become more like Jesus so that we may have a more intimate relationship. I myself may not have ever lost a child, but I know someone who did."

Hannah Grace looked up at Simon and said, "But, I didn't have any choice in what happened to my husband as a child, or his dark depression, or his death."

"No, of course not, it sounds like a choice he made, and you both are left dealing with the aftermath of his decisions," Simon replied, thinking of the permanent stain on his heart from the night with Jez. Hope was paying for a bad choice that Simon had made with Jez. "We don't live in a vacuum. Our lives are so interconnected with the people around us that they are sometimes very deeply affected by our choices and vice versa," Simon continued, "and sometimes the opposite is true as well, I think. If we make good choices, then it can positively affect the people around us.

"Regardless of the temporal circumstances that we have been dealt, we have a choice on how to respond to them. That's the real test. God is more concerned with our eternal circumstances. He wants us to choose to seek Him in every circumstance. If we are looking for it, we can find the good in any situation. In fact, we may be in even more danger when things seem to be going great, because that's when we think that we don't need Him."

"So, you think that God allowed my John to die in order to bring us closer to Him, to be more like Jesus?" Mara said in a disgusted tone of voice. "So, what, I should be *thankful* or something?

"I don't know exactly," Simon replied, shaking his head and looking down at the ground for a moment. "I obviously don't have all of the answers. There is sin. We are in a fallen world.

"But, I do think that God has the ability to take our poor choices and turn them into something good. And we can find the good that comes from a tragedy if we choose to look for it.

"Look, all I am suggesting here is that when people try to figure out why God would allow bad things to happen, they all too often overlook the most crucial piece of the puzzle. They stop and consider the issue of free will. God loves us so much that He gives us a choice. I mean what kind of God would he be if He forced us to love Him? And if we make a bad choice should we turn around and blame the One who gave us the choice in the first place? We often blame God instead of ourselves for our sins, when it probably hurts Him far greater that it does us!

"It's kind of ridiculous, really, when you think about it. What kind of God would He be if every decision that we ever made only resulted in a good outcome? After all, is that really a choice? No, of course not. For free will to truly exist, there must be equal but opposite choices.

"I think that for God's love to be experienced to its fullest it must be reciprocated not out of duty or obligation but out of choice. We love God because He first loved us. We love Him because we choose to, regardless of our circumstances.

"But, yes! God can absolutely make something good come from tragedy. You have to look no further than the cross to understand that! 'For God so loved the world that He gave His only begotten son, so that whosoever believes in Him shall not perish but have eternal life'."

Mara and Hannah Grace listened intently as they tried to process what Simon was telling them.

"Haven't you ever had to let someone you love choose to love you in return, only to be rejected?" Simon pleaded, thinking again of Hope. Hannah Grace nodded in agreement. "You can't force someone to love you. That's not love! How much more do you think our Creator feels, then, when we choose to reject Him?"

"But, sometimes it all just seems so senseless," Hannah Grace admitted, beginning to weep again. "Why did He have to allow one innocent boy to die and another to be wrongfully accused? What was the point of that senseless tragedy?"

Deeply affected by her grief, Simon felt tears welling up in his own eyes. He hesitated in responding when he realized the potential impact of his words. "What if I'm wrong," he involuntarily thought. Then he lifted his eyes to the chandelier before regaining the courage to respond.

"I know, so much of it is a mystery to us," Simon acknowledged. "If we knew all the answers it would rob us of free will, and we would never be able to receive the greatest gift of all that comes from not knowing all of the answers. We would miss out on the gift of salvation through Faith and Faith alone. We have to remember that God has the ultimate goal in mind for us at all times. He wants to adopt us into the Kingdom of Heaven, so that we may live with Him for all eternity. And He will use any means necessary for us to achieve that goal.

"When we look at it from that perspective, then how do we really and truly know what is a tragedy? Is it so hard to believe that God can use a broken relationship, or a painful experience, or a lost loved one, to win us back to Him or to shape and mold us in His image. If that is the case, then how can they be considered tragic at all? I mean, if that's what it takes, then so be it. There's so much more at stake than what we experience in this life. What would be really tragic is choosing to reject him after he went to such great lengths to save us. John made his own choices, but you have to make your own!"

Up until the last point, he had been steadily winning over his listeners, but the last bold statement was more than Mara could bare.

"I think you're full of it," Mara snarled as she turned to go, "and I don't want anything to do with a God like that."

Simon was mortified. Just as in the case of Rocky and the Helrigles, his words and actions had pushed Mara even further away from God. He dropped his head as the weight of his failure swept over him. But then, Hannah Grace unexpectedly moved toward Simon and took ahold of his elbow.

"Simon," she said, looking at him through red, swollen eyes. "I want to know that God. Tell me how I can know Him. I want that kind of peace and understanding in the midst of pain and tragedy."

With one arm draped over each other's shoulder, the two of them stood under the brilliant chandelier, bowed their heads, and prayed. With Simon's help, Hannah Grace admitted her sins, asked for forgiveness, and prayed for repentance.

* * *

For some time, Simon sat on the top step of the landing with his head resting in his hands. Simon sat in wonder under the warm glow of the giant chandelier. He hadn't moved from that spot since walking Hannah Grace to her car. It had been a great deal for him to take in for one night. First, there was Pastor Pete's abrupt exit. Then there was the revelation that Jessie Joseph had actually murdered Adam Potter in the 1st grade classroom. And that John Rash had been falsely accused of the murder by Jessie himself. Finally, there was Mara's rejection of God and Hannah Grace's prayer of salvation.

Simon considered once again the article that specified the details surrounding John's apparent suicide after plummeting from the grain elevator. Could he have been the eleventh victim in a long line of tragedies in the city of Bethel? If so, what could it all possibly mean? And what good could come from it?

After all, Mara rejected God. On the other hand, Hannah Grace received Jesus Christ as her Lord and Savior as a result of something Simon had said. Did he really and truly believe his own words that he spoke there that night? Was it him speaking or something much greater speaking through him? What was his purpose here? If the cycle of tragedies could never be stopped, then how could he change their adverse affect on the people of Bethel? There were still many questions yet to be answered and holes to be filled in as it pertained to the myth.

The whole thing seemed crazy. Then he remembered something one of his English professors said in a lecture one time at TCU, "Sometimes reality is so bizarre that it cannot even be used in fiction because it defies the reader's suspension of disbelief." What he meant, of course, was that sometimes life was so incredible that even a willing audience wouldn't buy it. One example he gave was a young slight of build Japanese kid eating sixty-three hot dogs in twelve minutes. Another example was a 75-year-old nun who had completed the Hawaii Ironman triathlon twenty years in a row. Then there was a man who taught his border collie to recognize 1,022 different words.

Simon's smile slowly faded as he thought of another example that the professor didn't use. It was of a 500-year-old man building a 450 foot long boat over the course of about seventy-five years. He had looked it up. "Reality *is* crazy," he said to himself. "Just like Noah was crazy. Just like anyone who is called to do anything is crazy."

Simon thought of Hope and her words on that fateful night when he had reluctantly told her about Jez. Impulsively, he took out his cell phone and started to dial her number, but then thought better of it. He slammed it closed, opened it a second time, started a text, and then slammed it down again.

"How could God use someone like me?" Simon thought to himself. "I'm just a big phony and a giant hypocrite." His heart ached, and he was suddenly overcome with an intense feeling of inadequacy.

Like a caged animal, he rose to his feet and paced back and forth on the landing. Without realizing it, he had walked into the classroom where Mara had indicated that Adam Potter had been murdered by Jessie Joseph. Warily, Simon flipped on the light switch and made his way over to the notorious closet.

Simon took a deep breath and reached for the doorknob with his now trembling hand. Taking a deep breath, he turned the handle and opened the door. Not knowing exactly what he might find, Simon peered around the creaky door with bated breath, but there was nothing there other than a bunch of supplies and random junk. He stared at the nondescript closet and tried to comprehend what might have happened there.

"Does God really allow tragedies just to bring us closer to Him?" Simon wondered. It just seemed like there had to be more to it than that. He had to admit that it did seem pretty callous of God. What was Simon missing?

If what Mara had said were true, then a little boy died there tragically seventy-two years ago. Something must have happened. Otherwise, why would two grown women wreath in pain at the loss of a man who killed himself by jumping off of a building in order to put an end to some catastrophic event he had experienced as a child. Simon tried to imagine the depths of pain and suffering that a parent experiences when they lose a child or when one loses a spouse.

Unprompted, he remembered the photograph that Hannah Grace had brought to him. He took the folded up photograph out of his pocket and examined it more closely this time. When he did, the hairs on the back of his neck stood up and his heart skipped a beat as his eyes wildly examined the photo. It was the same first and second grade class picture taken on the stairs of the entryway in the fall of 1935; only this time the names of the teacher and students were listed at the bottom of the picture.

The teacher in the photo was none other than Thelma Malone Harold! Simon nearly fell over from shock. He remembered what Thelma had said to him about her not being there when the tragedy took place. Simon had no sooner absorbed one great shock when he noticed the picture of a striking, young teacher's aid standing next to Miss Harold in the photograph. It was the first time he had ever seen a picture of the Jessie Joseph. Simon peered into the charcoal eyes of the dashing young man as if it could provide him with some further insight into the depths of such deep depravity.

"So, this was the face of evil," he thought. In reality, outside of the dark eyes, there was nothing very striking about the young man's appearance. It could have been anyone, really.

The old, cracked picture had even more to reveal. Holding it up closer to his face, Simon used his index finger to find the name of Adam Potter. When he found him, Simon was surprised to find a little girl sitting next to him named Evelyn Potter. Standing just behind their expressionless young faces was a dapper looking little boy named John Rash. Before he finished reading the names of students, something grabbed his attention that could not be ignored.

On even closer inspection, the grainy photograph revealed one more deep secret. To the far left of the picture on the wall of the staircase was the corner an elegant commemorative plaque. Based on its location, Simon surmised that it was likely to be the cause of the wall bowing. It must have been made out of some kind of heavy material to cause that kind of structural damage. What was it a plaque of? And why did it no longer reside on the wall?

Simon squinted, trying desperately to make out the tiny words of the inscription. Only the very end of a few lines could be seen in the snapshot. They were, reading from top to bottom: "…And for the support of…, …firm reliance on the protection of…, …lly pledge to each other…, and …sacred honor.…"

Unfortunately, many of the words written on the plaque were blocked out by Miss Harold's shoulder. Simon mouthed the words several times, trying his best to decipher them. If he was going to get the entryway back to its original condition, he was going to have to find out exactly what was hanging on that wall all of those years.

"…firm reliance on the protection of…" he said aloud. Somehow that phrase seemed very familiar to him, but he couldn't quite put a finger on it.

Simon took the photograph up to his favorite chair in the chorus room where he laid out the new bit of evidence amongst the newspapers and manilla folders on the floor. For some time, he studied his newly acquired piece of the puzzle in the context of the other information that had been made available to him. He did his best to connect the dots, but he was still missing something important. What was it? For the life of him, he couldn't imagine what it could be.

First thing in the morning, he was going to get some answers. Now, thanks to Hannah Grace, he had the ammunition that he needed to do just that. His eyes grew heavy and his mind fatigued. There was nothing more to be done tonight. Simon decided that the best thing to do at this point was to try and get a few hours of shut-eye before daybreak.

* * *

Sitting on the steps of Pastor Pete's church across the street from the old school, Jack Lawless nervously puffed on a cigarette as he watched the lights go out in the window to the chorus room above the gymnasium.

* * *

The sun rose above the enormous man-made mountains that were once again casting a giant shadow over the small, Midwestern farming community. When the light broke through the window of the chorus room, it penetrated Simon's unconsciousness and roused him from his slumber. Turning his head and squinting, he reflexively lifted his arm to block the intense rays of light. Out of the corner of his eyes, he could see the heights of the grain elevators. At once, he was reminded of John's tragic fall and of all of the events that had taken place the night before.

Newly energized, Simon jumped out of the familiar chair. By now, he was well aware of what time the sun climbed over the top of the elevator, and he also knew that Thelma Harold would soon be opening her shop. In a flash, he grabbed the colored photograph, darted down the staircase, ran across the gym floor, and ascended the steps that led to the entryway. When he reached the landing, he suddenly stopped dead in his tracks.

On the staircase leading to the front doors of the school, there was a stranger. The man was bent down, taking measurements of the crooked, faulty wall that Simon had constructed the day before. At first, he thought it might be Andy or Mr. Gettby. Cautiously, Simon moved in a little closer to get a better look at the intruder.

Simon was certain that he had never laid eyes on the uninvited guest before in his life. Outside of the man's neatly trimmed beard there was nothing particularly beautiful or majestic in his appearance that distinguished him. When the visitor finally stood back up, Simon noticed the tool belt around his waist.

"Excuse me," Simon finally said. "Can I help you?"

When the stranger turned towards Simon, he revealed a warm, familiar grin. "Actually, I have come to help you," he said.

"What?" Simon asked, taken aback. "Really? Did Miss Harold send you?"

"You could kind of say that," the middle-aged man pleasantly replied, "she requested my presence. You didn't think you were going to have to do all of this by yourself, did you?"

"Ohh, right," Simon said with a wink. "Thelma mentioned something about calling in a favor. You must be the, the..."

"…The carpenter," the man said with a smile, pointing to his tool belt.

"Yes!" Simon said, suddenly relieved. "Oh, you don't know how glad I am to see you! I've pretty much been making a mess of things."

"Yes, I can see that," the kindly stranger remarked, putting his hands on his hips and taking notice of all the destruction Simon had wrought.

"Yes, well, I-I'm not exactly what you would call, 'handy' with tools," Simon sheepishly admitted. "I've pretty much been learning on the fly. You know, sorta feeling my way as I go."

"I kind of gathered that," the carpenter said with a chuckle.

"Yeah, I've been watching YouTube videos and stuff," Simon said, pointing to the computer sitting on a desk on the landing.

"Technology," the carpenter said, shaking his head. "It can be your best friend and worst enemy all at the same time."

"Well, I was thankful to have it," Simon humbly admitted, "it can be a good thing."

"Yes," the carpenter agreed, "it can be. It depends on how you use it, like lots of things in life."

Then he paused as if allowing the words to sink in, before he spoke again.

"I *do*, however, love the chandelier," the carpenter said, admiringly.

"It's pretty magnificent isn't it?" Simon replied, gazing heavenward.

"It certainly is," the man replied.

"I found it tucked away under a tarp in the basement," Simon said.

"Hmm, sad," the carpenter said.

"Yes, it is," Simon agreed.

"Now, about this wall…" the carpenter said clapping his hands.

Simon scratched his head and said, "Yeah, about that," he said with a laugh.

Strange, Simon wasn't the least bit offended or defensive about the carpenter's observations. It was as if all of Simon's fears and insecurities had suddenly been defused. He didn't know if it was the stranger's demeanor, or his deep, resonating voice, or His warm smile that put Simon at ease.

He took a few steps down the stairs and stood next to the stranger as they observed the framework. "It probably all needs to come down," Simon said.

"I think so," the carpenter agreed.

"I just can't get the thing lined up correctly," Simon said, exasperated. "I don't know what I'm doing wrong. It's like nothing in this place is at a right angle. Ya know?"

"Yes, that is often the case," the stranger agreed, "but that is okay if the foundation has been set properly. If that is the case, then we can figure it out from there. All that we need to do is get everything else in line with what we already know is 'right'."

"Oh, that makes sense," Simon replied. "Is this foundation sound?"

"Yes, it is," the carpenter said reassuringly.

"Then what do you suppose happened to the wall?" Simon asked.

"Over the course of time, it buckled under the weight and the pressure from whatever was hanging on it," the stranger confidently answered.

"I think you're right," Simon agreed. "Something very heavy evidently hung from it for many years. Look at this picture. You can see some kind of commemorative plaque hanging on the wall in the corner of this photograph."

Simon held up the photo, but the carpenter paid no attention to it.

"I remember," the carpenter said, as he more closely examined the frame that Simon had haphazardly slapped together.

"You do?" Simon exclaimed. He couldn't believe his luck. "What was it?"

"Sure, I do," the carpenter said flatly as he laid the level against the baseboard. "My Father has lived in Bethel his entire life. It was a bronze, commemorative plaque of 'The Declaration of Independence'."

"I knew it!" Simon said, excitedly. "Well, at least I knew it had to be something like that. 'The Declaration of Independence'. Are you sure?" But, the carpenter made no reply. "Wow. How about that?"

Then Simon was saddened because he remembered that he had been convicted to return the entryway to exactly how it looked before the tragedy in 1935.

Somewhat disheartened, Simon said, "Where on earth would I even begin to look for something like that to replace it?"

"Who said anything about needing to replace it?" the carpenter asked while holding out his measuring tape. "Say, can you give me a hand?"

"What? Oh yeah, of course," Simon said as he bent down to take hold of the opposite end of the measuring line. "Well, if I could get my hands on the original, I'd just use that, but..."

"...Yes sir, the measuring tape never lies," the carpenter proclaimed.

"What is it?" Simon asked.

"All of this framework is definitely going to have to come down," the stranger replied.

"Oh, man," Simon said with a contrite spirit.

"Don't beat yourself up too badly," the carpenter said. "Look, you started in line with the foundation, but then, right here...do you see it?" he said pointing at a board that had been laid next to one of the originals. "Somehow you started to get a tiny bit out of kilter. That doesn't seem like much of a mistake, but when you laid down the next piece it got even farther out of line. Then each time you set down a new two-by-four it got further and further out of alignment because you were basing it on an untrue landmark. By the time you got to the end of the wall, the whole thing was way off the mark."

"Wow, so how do you fix it?" Simon asked, innocently.

"Let's take the entire frame back down, and I will show you the way," the carpenter said.

"Ah, man, so we have to start all over again?" Simon moaned.

"No," the stranger replied confidently. "We first find out what is true and then do away with the rest."

"But wait, didn't you say that only the first section was in line?" Simon lamented. "What a waste of time."

"It was not a waste of time if you learned from your mistake so as to not make the same mistake again," the carpenter chastened. "The key is to only take from an experience the things that will help you be more successful in the future, and leave from any given experience the things that would keep you from being successful in the future. For instance, the pain of having to tear it down should be a great motivator next time to make sure that you remember how to do it right. But, having failed shouldn't hurt your confidence to give it another go. That's what you have to leave behind. Just because you had a great failure, doesn't make *you* a great failure. If you learn from the failure, then it was a 'great' failure!"

"But, how do we know that first board was laid correctly?" Simon asked.

"Because it is in line with the opposite wall, and the opposite wall is in line with the foundation," the wise carpenter said.

Simon looked over to the wall on the opposite side of the staircase. "How do you know that?" Simon asked. "I mean, no offense, but if we keep aligning each new wall off of another one that is out of whack then we'll never get the thing right."

"Trust me, the opposite wall is perfectly aligned with the foundation," the craftsman said definitively. "That you can be sure of."

It wasn't what the man said that convinced Simon. It was how he said it. It wasn't like when someone gives their best guess. He said it with authority.

In no time, the two of them had all but dismantled the framework, leaving only the original board that they knew to be true.

"Okay, now what?" Simon asked as he took off one of his work gloves to wipe the sweat from his forehead.

After the carpenter did some more measuring, he took out a lead weight with a string attached to it and said, "We use the same method that was used to set the opposite wall; we use a plumb line."

"Huh, 'a plumb line'?" Simon curiously asked. "How does it work, exactly?"

"I hold one end here at the point that we know to be right and true," the carpenter said while squatting down. "Now you take the opposite end and set it on the mark that I made on the floor over there." Simon took the string between his thumb and index finger and walked over to the spot marked on the floor. "Now, pull the string tight, reach down, and hold it directly over the spot."

Once the string was tight, the carpenter took a section of string between his fingers, lifted it off of the ground, and then let it go. When he did, the chalky string slapped onto the floor leaving a perfectly straight line.

"That's awesome!" Simon exclaimed.

"Yes, it is," the carpenter agreed.

"So, what's next? Do we…" Simon started to say before he heard Thelma Harold's scratchy voice calling out to him from the bottom of the stairs on the opposite side of the landing.

"*Freeman!*" she yelled again.

"Here I am," Simon replied as he stood up to try and get a glimpse of the decrepit, old principal.

Meanwhile, the carpenter stayed silently, squatting down on the floor so as not to be seen.

"I need your help!" she yelled. "Got some boxes that I need you help me take down to the storage room."

"Well, I was just in the middle of…" Simon started to say.

"…Where you at, I don't even see ya!" she said in an exasperated tone of voice. "Come over here where I can see ya. I can't even hear what you're sayin', boy."

Simon looked back down at the carpenter who motioned with his head for Simon to go and see what Miss Harold needed.

He shrugged his shoulders, rolled his eyes, and said, "I'll go and see what she needs. Be right back."

"Remember, she's only as God made her," the carpenter said softly with a warm smile as Simon made his way back up the stairs to the landing.

"Simon!" she snapped impatiently.

"Coming, Miss Harold," Simon replied. When he got to the top of the landing, he glanced back down the stairs toward his mysterious friend, but by the time he had turned around, the stranger was gone. Simon turned in a full circle, trying to see where the carpenter might have disappeared to.

"Oh, there you are," Miss Harold said sharply, "come down here and grab these. They're slippin' outta my hands."

Reluctantly, Simon hopped down the steps and lifted the top two boxes out of her fragile, old hands.

"Whoa, you do have your hands full," Simon said, "let me get those for you."

"Yes, I had taken these records and statements over to our accountant, and now I just need to get them back down to the storage room where they go," Miss Harold said nearly out of breath as they started towards the basement.

"That's why I needed you to get it cleaned out down there," she gasped, reaching the bottom step.

"Oh, about that," Simon said just as she made her way around the corner and saw all of the things that he had pulled out of the storage room laying about on the floor of the basement.

"What in Sam Hill have you been doin'?" she squawked. "I thought I told you to get all this cleaned out!"

"Well, I-I've been working on the entryway and…" Simon said, surprised by how she had somehow conveniently forgotten their conversation about his purpose and the curse, much less about her being his "Yoda".

"Now, look," she said, dropping the heavy box of financial documents onto the dusty, concrete floor. "We agreed that as long as you tended to all of your other duties you could do that other thing," Miss Harold said, clearly agitated, while pointing toward the ceiling. "Paul made rugs while *he* wrote three quarters of the New Testament. And all I'm asking you to do is clean up the basement!"

"Yes, ma'am," Simon replied, nervously. "I have been working on the punch list that Mr. Cross left for me. And the storage room has been completely emptied out. I just didn't know what all you wanted to keep, and what you wanted to incinerated.

"Besides that, I just had a big breakthrough with the entryway thanks to that guy you sent over."

Thelma put her hands on her hips and took a mental inventory of the items that Simon had pulled out of the storage room. "What guy I sent over?" she said absentmindedly. The old principal's words trailed off as her gaze fell upon the still Jesus-less manger. She stared for a moment at it as though pondering its fate.

"You know, the one who owed you a favor..." Simon said, confused.

"Tell you what, Freeman, I'm going to leave all of this up to your discretion," Thelma said, abruptly turning to climb the stairs. "You're gonna have to sort out the trinkets from the treasure."

"But, I..." Simon started to say before Miss Harold stopped, turned her head towards the storage room, and pointed.

"And, by the way, you *still* haven't gotten *everything* out there yet, Heaven's to Betsy, Freeman!" she growled, shaking her head as she slowly made her way back up the stairs.

Inquisitively, Simon stopped short, retreated a few steps, and careened his neck, trying to peer into the darkness of the cavernous storage room.

"What do you mean?" Simon replied. "I don't see anything..."

Then he realized that he was only talking to himself. Miss Harold had already turned the corner and was heading for the exit. Suddenly, he remembered Hannah Grace's crumpled, colored photograph. Retrieving it from his pocket, Simon chased after the old principal, calling out to her, "But, Miss Harold, wait a second!"

When he reached the top of the stairs and turned the corner, Simon caught up to Miss Harold who was waiting impatiently for him.

"What is it now, Freeman?" Miss Harold asked, annoyed.

"I thought you told me that you weren't there the day when the tragedy...the day Jessie Joseph, you know...murdered..." he said, trying to get his breath after racing up the steps.

"Cause, I wasn't," Thelma tartly replied.

"Then what's this?" Simon asked, calling her attention to the photo.

She cocked her head to the side, held it out some distance from her face, and squinted. "Isn't it obvious?" she said. "It's a picture of me, my class, and my teacher's aide." She stuck the picture back in his chest. "Any other questions, Sherlock?"

"Why didn't you tell me you were the teacher who was on a leave of absence?"

Simon asked. "Why didn't you tell me that Jessie was your aid, or that Adam Potter was one of your students?"

"What would have it mattered?" Miss Harold asked. "I told you already, you've got enough to worry about today…in the here and now. Can't change the past."

Simon shot her an exasperated expression.

"…Okay, what do you want to know?" Miss Harold asked, folding her arms.

"Well, for starters, how about what happened the day Adam Potter died?" Simon asked.

"I told you, boy, I wasn't there," she replied. "To this day, I honestly don't know. As they say, there's two sides to every story."

"You mean Jessie accusing John Rash of the murder and then John turning it back on Jessie?" Simon asked. His eyes were wide, and he leaned forward in anticipation of her answer.

"Sounds to me you already got the scoop," she replied.

"Hardly, now start at the beginning and tell me what actually happened that day," he asked, excitedly.

"I can only start at the end," Miss Harold replied. "It was two days before Halloween, on a Friday. I was on leave of absence at the time. Had been out for nearly two or three months."

"Why were you out?" Simon asked.

"Had the 'Dust Pneumonia Blues'," Thelma answered almost whimsically.

"The what?" Simon asked.

"The Dust…it was an airborne illness of the lungs from the dust bowl," she said with a frown. "You heard of the Dust Bowl. Uh-huh. They didn't know if I'd make it. Anyways, the school board decided to hand over my duties to Mr. Joseph. The kids practically idolized him, and he had been doin' a fair to middling job up to that point."

"Was he even a teacher?" Simon asked. "I mean he looks so young in the picture."

"You gotta remember, those were hard times," Thelma said. "People didn't have a lot of money. School board included. They took who they could get at whatever price they could get them. He may have had some training of some kind. I really don't remember. Jessie may have been straight out of boarding school for all I know. In fact, I think he was around 20 years-old in this picture, if memory serves. We didn't need a piece of paper in them days to tell us if somebody was smart. He was bright and more than capable. Jessie had one of those infectious personalities…well, most of the time."

"Most of the time?" Simon asked.

"Yes, most of the time he was very gregarious and outgoing, but other days…," Miss Harold said, looking off into the distance. "Well, he seemed like he was at rock bottom. On those occasions, he would come to school unshaven, disheveled, ya know?"

"So, you do think he was capable of doing the things that they say he did?" Simon asked, mesmerized by what she was telling him.

"Capable, huh," she scoffed. "Who in the world can tell? It's not like they go around with horns sticking out of their heads carrying pitchforks. Haven't you noticed? Most serial killers look like you and me. Well, mostly you. Jessie had his lows to be sure, but as I said, times were hard. A lot of folks went around looking distraught and anxious."

"What did he have to be distraught over, did he ever say?" Simon asked.

"Well, rumor was Jessie was the illegitimate son of Clay Potter," Miss Harold said. As reluctant as she had been up until now, suddenly, she had a change of heart. Her eyes were sullen and empty as though she were going back in time as she spoke. "Mr. Potter was a very prominent man in town. Owned a lot of land. He was a good man, a charitable man. Gave folks a helping hand when they needed it. But, his better half was thought to be barren, and they weren't getting any younger. They was probably in their early to mid-thirties. I know that doesn't seem old today, but ya gotta remember, people in those days didn't live much past sixty. And they wanted to have children in the worst way.

"About that time, they took in a young lady who was a cousin of Mrs. Potter's. It was speculated that either they decided to have the young lady bare Mr. Potter an heir, or he simply had an affair with the young girl. Or maybe someone else got her pregnant. Any rate, folks always said the boy was Mr. Potter's.

"She conceived Jessie, and they both lived with the Potters on the farm until about Jessie's early teens when, to everyone's surprise, Mrs. Potter became pregnant with twins. When Adam and Evelyn Potter were born, Mrs. Potter suddenly had a change of heart about Mary. Up to that point, Mary and Jessie had been living on their farm. We had heard that Mr. Potter did not want to put them out, but simply had to respect the wishes of his better half."

Simon was frozen, hanging on every word.

"Well, no more than six years after that Jessie returned to town by himself," Miss Harold continued. "Although, no one really knew for sure, folks suspected that he came back to reconcile with his father, but Mr. Potter, at Mrs. Potter's urging, publicly didn't want anything to do with him.

Personally, I think that Clay may have pulled some strings behind the scenes to get Jessie his position at the school. Mrs. Potter couldn't make too much of a fuss because it would only incite further suspicion about her husband's relationship with the young man if she made a big stink."

"Do you think that Jessie killed Adam out of revenge?" Simon asked, skipping ahead.

"People had said as much," Thelma replied flatly. "But, the way that it all happened, no one could even be sure who was responsible or even what exactly had happened."

"You mean with John Rash?" Simon asked.

"For one," she answered somberly.

"Well, how exactly did it happen?" Simon wanted to know. "Was Adam suffocated?"

"You would have to ask someone who was there," Miss Harold said. "And even then, depending on who you asked, you would get a bunch of different answers. The official coroners report was that Adam did in fact die of suffocation, but there were no visible marks on the boy's neck. The only thing they found from his physical appearance was that the ends of his fingers showed signs of a struggle."

"The ends of his fingers?" Simon repeated.

"Yes, they were bloodied," she answered. "What we do know is that at some point someone had forced Adam into the closet in the 1st grade classroom, and he never came back out. The official police report said that he had an anxiety induced asthmatic attack, and that he hyperventilated and died. His fingers were evidently bloodied from trying to desperately claw his way out of the closet.

"So, somebody had to have held the door shut because there were no locks on it. But, when the authorities first arrived, Jessie and the students insisted that it was an accident. Then Jessie in confidence later told one of the detectives that John Rash had been the one who held the door shut. A few students came forward and supported Jessie's claims at first. And John didn't deny it. So, the cops took him away to juvenile detention. But, sometime over the course of the next weeks, while the prosecutors were trying to put the case together, the DA was interrogating John. When he realized the trouble that he was in, he began to insist that he wasn't the one who held the door shut. He told em' that it actually was Jessie who was responsible.

"Then came the big bombshell. There were claims of sexual abuse. And crazily enough, the other children began to corroborate John's allegations about Jessie. No one could believe it."

"That seems pretty cut and dried," Simon said plainly. "There was motive and eyewitness testimony. And it makes all the more sense that Jessie would try to implicate one of his students. It's even understandable why the children would be too afraid to come forward at first."

"Yeah, except that there wasn't any physical evidence to substantiate the allegations," Thelma lamented. "Yes, some of the children had bruises and cuts, but what kids don't? Some kids acted kinda weird according to their parents, but there again, what 6 and 7-year-olds don't act weird half of the time? No one knew what to believe. Half of the town sided with Jessie and the other half sided with the kids. Ultimately, the kids stuck to their guns, and it was Jessie who went away to prison."

"Wait!" Simon said. "So, Jessie wasn't hanged in the square?"

"Heaven's no!" Thelma snapped. "No one's been hanged in Bethel since some horse thief around the time of the Civil War. No, Jessie went to Joliet and died six years later of TB."

"And he never swore his revenge on the town or anything like that?" Simon asked.

"No," she said as if smelling something putrid. "That's just what folks say. There was a great deal of bitterness there, I do know that. Jessie went to his grave swearing he was innocent of the charges and spent his all of his time in the penitentiary filing appeals."

"So, where did all of this curse business come from then?" Simon asked.

"Well, not long after Jessie died, one of the, uh, students came forward and said that he had lied to the investigators about the accusations of abuse," Thelma said. "A short time after that one of the young men in town died at Pearl Harbor. From there on, it was another tragic death and another.

"Coincidence is all, if ya ask me, but some people said it was retribution for Jessie's injustice. It just sort of built from there I guess with each time another child died in the community the legend grew."

"There wasn't any sort of pattern to the deaths, like every six years or anything like that," Simon said.

"No," she admitted.

Simon thought for a moment, "But, you must have thought that there was something to it if you kept all of those articles and never allowed them to be archived."

"I said that there was nothing to the curse of Jessie Joseph," Thelma replied. Even as she told the story, her hands began to tremble. "I didn't say there wasn't a curse or a pattern to the tragedies. You gotta understand the impact the whole thing had on the students and their parents; the entire community really. The kids who were witness to Adam's death were particularly traumatized by it all. For years, the entire playground would come to a standstill if anyone let out any kind of scream or yell. Parents telling us that their kids couldn't sleep because of nightmares. The kids even played Bloody Jessie Joseph for a while on the playground…"

Simon's jaw dropped open. "I remember kids playing that game even when I went to school," Simon said, dumbfounded by the realization after having pushed it out of his mind all of these years.

"…They'd avoid the 'evil' areas," Thelma said.

"Evil areas?" Simon asked.

"Yes, where Adam died and the chorus room of course," Miss Harold said. "Psychologists told us that it was all just a way for the kids to cope with the trauma."

"*The chorus room?*" Simon said, glancing towards the gymnasium.

"Yes, it was suspected by the detectives that the seclusion of the chorus room made it a perfect place for Jessie to carry out his heinous crimes. In fact, all of the interrogations with the children started there. They all wanted to know what happened in the chorus room. We finally, had to move the piano to another room. You know how kids are. Pretty soon they believed that it was haunted. People, even adults mind you, claimed they saw ghosts or heard strange noises. Bunch of nonsense."

"You must not have thought that it was all nonsense; otherwise, you wouldn't have kept all of those articles," Simon said.

"There again," she said with a far off look in her eye. "The whole thing was so unbelievable. It sent shock waves throughout the entire community. How did any of it happen, right under our very noses, without anyone suspecting a thing? Up until that point, everyone just trusted authority, just like they trusted one another to do the right thing. When you dropped your kids off at school, you just assumed that they were in good hands; that they were safe. Nobody thought anything of it. But, after the trial it just got worse and worse each time a young person unexpectedly died in the community. It only served to further reinforce how folks were already feel'n."

"So, then, things *did* change after Adam's death?" Simon asked naively, trying to connect the dots.

"Did they change?" Thelma snapped. "Folks became very distrustful of any kind of authority figure, but especially, of teachers and administrators," she said, looking at Simon out of the corner of her eye. "Everyone looked at those in charge with an air of suspicion whether it was teachers, or coaches, or den mothers,...or even preachers. No one was above reproach."

A shiver ran down Simon's spine as he thought of Jeremy and Little Simon.

"Parents became very protective; in fact, overly protective if ya ask me," Thelma continued. "There used to be a day, ya know, when if a student acted up at school, they got twice the licks when they got home. Nowadays, the parents, or uh, most of the time the mother or even grandparent, takes up for their kids straight off even before they have any of the facts. Discipline has all but gone out the window and the kids know it."

Simon looked at her inquisitively, "But, I was always scared to death of the paddle when I went to school here."

"Huh," Thelma scoffed. "That thing hadn't been used in a coon's age. It's all an intimidation ploy with no substance. And don't think the kids don't know it nowadays. We've got to push, pull, plead, beg, or trick most of 'em into doing anything." After reflecting for a moment, she contradicted herself. "Still, I can't say that I entirely blame the parents. That paddle and the chorus room were the only two common threads to every one of the kids stories during the investigation. But, dog gone it! Just because one wacko abuses his authority does that mean there should be no authority or discipline at all? Ya can't keep any order in the classroom if students can't be held accountable for their actions!"

"Miss Harold, do you still have any of the articles on Adam's death that were taken from the public library?" Simon asked.

"No," she said dully. "You don't get it, do you? That was the thing! Like I said, no one knew who or what to believe. People were at a complete loss. They couldn't fix it. They couldn't change the past. Everyone just wanted it all to go away. So, that's what they did. They just swept the whole thing under the rug. And anything related to the incident was incinerated. It became kinda taboo to even bring it up in public. But, you can't keep folks from talking in private. It seems the more we tried to bury it, all the more attention was given to it. Suddenly, there was a certain mystique to it and what people didn't know, they just made up. The juicier the better too. Pretty soon, it was Jessie drowning the entire class in the creek or other nonsense like that."

"And you never tried to correct it?" Simon asked, almost accusingly.

"Don't you think I've tried to set the record straight?" she laughed. "They like their version better. People love horror stories and conspiracy theories, so the more someone argues against their claims only serves to support their theory all the more. They totally disregard any historical or empirical evidence that contradicts their preconceived notions. All of the things that folks don't know or can't understand are terribly inconvenient. Those things torment the soul and exhaust the mind like some sort of riddle. It's hard to figure out. Folks don't want hard. They want easy. So, they pick through the evidence that supports their beliefs, make up what they need to to fill the gaps, and discard the rest.

"Not only that, but I don't know if you've noticed, our society has a slight infatuation with all things scandalous. There's something intoxicatingly alluring about it; something enticing about it. A simple, rationale explanation isn't nearly as appealing."

Simon blankly stared at the old principal as he thought of the night he and his friends rode out to Clay Potter's property to see the grave sight. There was an exhilaration to the experience that was powerfully alluring. He couldn't deny that.

Suddenly, Thelma snapped out of her trance. "But, listen to me very carefully, Freeman," she said, lifting up his chin with her finger. "I told you before, don't get caught up in the past! If you linger on it too long, pretty soon you end up staying there. The point is not to fix the past. That's not why I've told all of this to you. It's not for your entertainment. We ain't sittin' around a campfire, toasting weenies!"

"So, why have you told me all of this then?" Simon asked with a pained expression on his face.

"It is for your edification!" she said with great passion. "Simon, you can't change what has happened in the past, but you can change our understanding of it. You have to sift through the things that are beneficial to take away from the past and leave behind what is harmful. That's a very difficult thing to do for most people. They tend to do the opposite. They hold on to what is destructive and ignore what could be learned from it. I don't know how exactly, but somehow renovating the lobby of the school might help to change the way folks deal with the curse and alter the destructive path that this community is heading down."

Simon stared back in shock. "What are you talking about?" he asked. "You told me there wasn't a curse!"

"I said no such thing," Thelma objected. "Oh there's a curse, to be sure. Don't fool yourself. There's a curse, and the people of Bethel, myself included, have made major mistakes in how we have responded to it. We've given ground, and given ground, and given ground out of convenience in the name of compromise.

"We have to take a stand while there is still time to undo the damage that has been done!"

"I am sorry, but I think you have the wrong guy," Simon intimated. "I'm probably the least qualified guy around to do anything about any of that."

Regaining her composure, Thelma said, "I'm probably talking to the right guy chosen for the job because you are the least qualified. And...."

"And what?" Simon asked with great wonder.

"...And you're still here," Thelma replied as she turned to leave. "You haven't run even though there's nothing keeping you here. You're not like your father at all."

"But, wait, I don't even know what to do…" Simon said. He started to go after her when another voice called to him from the entrance of the school.

"All you can do is what you can do," Thelma said as the door swung closed behind her. "Leave the rest to God."

"Simon?" a voice called out to him.

When he turned and lifted his eyes, he saw Hannah Grace standing at the top of the landing beneath the chandelier with two young girls on either side of her. Simon immediately recognized one of the girls to be Rich's little sister, Sharon. All three of them were wearing ratty clothes with their hair pulled up. Miss Hannah Grace had a warm smile on her face while her two contemporaries seemed less than thrilled to be there judging by the expressions on their faces.

"Uh, what's all this?" Simon asked hesitantly.

"I just thought that you might need some help," Hannah Grace replied.

Simon looked at the unwilling volunteers and asked, "Miss Hannah, may I have a word with you alone, please?"

"Why, of course, be back in a second girls," she said, making her way down the steps to where he was standing. "Stay right there, girls." The disgruntled young women said nothing in return. Instead, they folded their arms and pretended to look around the room in the opposite direction of one another.

"Miss Hannah," Simon said softly.

"Yes?" she said, while keeping one eye on the young girls.

"What was the last thing you and I talked about before you left last night?" Simon asked.

"I know. I know. I know," she answered sheepishly. "You said not to tell anyone."

"So?..." Simon asked as he glanced up at the girls.

"I couldn't help myself," Hannah Grace replied. "I just had to tell them. These two got themselves into a little trouble this summer with their parents. You see they're the best of friends. Or at least they were the best of friends. And, anyways, I won't bore you with the details. But, they're just about as low as you can go right now. And I feel like I am somewhat responsible for what happened between them. So, how could I keep it all to myself knowing what I know now? If anyone needed to hear the message, it was these two, believe me."

Simon folded his arms, let out a sigh, lifted his hat, and scratched his head. "Yes, that's wonderful Miss Hannah, but nobody is supposed to know about this until it's finished."

"Oh, I understand completely, I do," she insisted. "But, you don't have to worry about these two. They've been grounded from just about everything, and they need something to do. Something positive to, you know, focus on, so they can get their minds off of their troubles and remember their blessings."

Simon thought for a moment. "All right, Miss Hannah," he finally conceded. "But, please, tell them that they can't let anyone else know about what we're doing here."

"Okay, no problem," she whispered to him excitedly, clasping her hands. She turned to the displeased young ladies and said, "All right ladies, this is Rich's friend, Simon Freeman, and we are going to help him out in any way we can. So, he's going to give us some instructions, and we can get started."

Simon looked up at the silent girls whose body language revealed their bad attitudes. Then he turned to Hannah Grace and said, "They don't look very happy to be here."

"They're not exactly here under their own recognizance," she whispered.

"How did you get them to come, then?" Simon asked.

"Let's just say I have been mediating talks between the two of them and their parents, and we have struck a little deal," she answered.

"What kind of deal?" Simon asked.

"Well, for the time being I am their only contact with the outside world," she answered with a cunning grin. "If they do well today, there's a chance they will get the doors put back on the hinges of their rooms at home." Then she stood up, clapped her hands, and asked, "So, how can we help you?"

"Can you hang drywall?" Simon asked.

Silence.

"Do you know anything about framing a wall?" Simon asked dully. "Can you handle a hammer? Have you ever seen a hammer before? Do you know about electrical...never mind." Then he had an idea. "If you are willing, maybe you can take care of some of the things on the punch list that Mr. Cross left for me to do. That would free me up to work on renovating the entryway."

The two young girls said nothing. "Sure," Hannah Grace responded for them. "What can we do?"

"Well, let's see," Simon replied. "There are three more classrooms that need to have the floors swept, stripped, polished, and waxed. And all of the desks and chairs from those rooms need to have the gum and junk scraped out from under them. So, what do you say?"

There was still no response, just angry scowls. Simon looked at Hannah Grace who smiled and nodded. "We can do what we can, right girls?" she said, trying her best to manufacture some enthusiasm.

"Great!" Simon said, turning and pointing the way towards the classrooms that were still in need of work, "let's get started."

Shannon and Sharon slinked their way past Simon. Suddenly, he was reminded of the stranger who helped him set the wall. Straining his neck to look around the entryway, he pulled Hannah Grace aside and asked, "You didn't happen to see a kinda middle-aged, bearded dude wearing a tool belt did you?"

"No, why?" Hannah Grace asked curiously.

"No reason," Simon replied, "oh, and by the way, I know what was hanging on that wall!" he said excitedly, pointing to the bare frame next to the staircase.

"What was it?" Hannah Grace asked, excitedly.

"It was a large bronze plaque, commemorating the Declaration of Independence!" Simon answered proudly.

"Hmmm," Hannah Grace said, placing her index finger on her chin and frowning.

"What's the matter?" Simon asked.

"Oh nothing," Hannah Grace replied. "I do remember something like that, now that you mention it. But, for some reason, I thought it was on the opposite wall."

Simon turned and looked inquisitively at the wall on the other side of the staircase.

27

EXAMINING THE WALLS

In the beginning, Shannon and Sharon had little to say to one another. After all, they had completely ruined each other's lives, in so much as the rest of the summer was ruined. And seeing how neither of them could imagine anything much more beyond it, it was sort of true in a teenager's world.

In the interest of her best friend's mental and physical health, Sharon had the audacity to care enough to tell Shannon's mother everything. Then Shannon did the same in kind, although there was very little to say to Sharon's parents after she had already confessed everything. Sadly, the two friends who had been inseparable since preschool found themselves bitter enemies. Each of them had declared their undying hatred for the other. They even said as much…at least by text, until that too was taken away along with everything else. For a time, that's where they sat, each in their own empty, doorless room like some kind of higher order primates at the zoo.

It would have certainly stayed that way until one night when Aunt Gracie came bursting through the front door of Sharon's house with the most wonderful news, or so she said. The Land family was so taken aback by Hannah Grace's exuberance that they thought she had suddenly taken to Nana Mara's home remedy. Aunt Gracie assured them that it was nothing of the kind. After adamantly denying the charges several more times, Hannah Grace shared with them the Good News that she had just heard. There was no denying the outward change to her demeanor, the joy on her countenance, or the conviction in her voice. She spoke so fast that on more than one occasion they had to ask her to slow down.

When she had finished, Miss Hannah Grace made the most unusual proposal, regarding the disciplining of the two wayward teens. Instead of incarceration, she was advocating reform. Even though, Mr. Land, like all good fathers, was leaning towards solitary confinement for the remainder of his daughter's teen years, Mrs. Land was wise enough to know a good idea when she heard one. After all, she told the less reasonable spouse that the longer they try to suffocate their daughter the more likely she would run at the first chance she would get. What is more, she was right.

That is how Sharon and Shannon came to be in the custody of Hannah Grace, being otherwise unwilling participants in some crazy scheme to win votes for a dorky referendum. At least, that's what Aunt Gracie had told them. In truth, Hannah Grace had a different kind of renovation in mind. One that also required a certain degree of demolition before any sort of reconstruction could ever take place.

It had all become abundantly clear to Hannah Grace after observing not only her niece's obstinate insistency of her innocence but also the injustice of her condition. Sharon and Shannon were both wallowing in self-pity while playing the role of martyr. Understanding that plight all too well herself, Hannah Grace decided that something drastic had to be done in order for them to avoid years and years of sorrow and bitterness. Hannah Grace reasoned that putting the girls in a position in which they had to work in close quarters would act as a catalyst for speeding up the healing process. She reasoned that they had to feel the full weight and measure of the liability that they had incurred as a result of their own iniquities before coming to reconciliation with themselves, with each other, and with God.

For the first few days, the girls did the best that they could to work independent of one another even though they were assigned to the same menial tasks. Barely acknowledging one another's existence proved to be difficult. After all, they were purposefully given "two-man" jobs. Icy stares and mumbled slurs comprised the better part of their communication early on. Then, inevitably, they were unable to suppress the deep connection between them. Slowly, irreverence while scrubbing floors gave way to indifference while scraping gum which paved the way for tolerability while pouring wax which eventually succumbed to affability while trying to figure out how to work a floor polisher.

Hannah Grace's diabolical plan of reconciliation began when Sharon turned on the switch to the industrial buffer for the first time. Shannon laughed hysterically and peed her pants while watching her slight friend being whipped around uncontrollably like a rag doll. Once Sharon was finally flung free of the crazy contraption, the two girls fell together laughing until they cried. Bonding over their shared misery, the providential incident laid the necessary underpinning for the next necessary step on the road to recovery. They had to come to the realization that there was something that they needed to be saved from.

By lunchtime on the third day of the makeshift work release program, the girls were once again thick as thieves and ready to reconcile with each other. Unfortunately, they would soon discover that it is sometimes much easier to forgive someone else than it is to forgive oneself.

Gradually, the two young girls were having a change of heart. What originally felt like breaking rocks at Leavenworth now morphed into something indescribable and foreign to them. For the first time in their lives, they were experiencing the intangible, innate gifts that come from manual labor such as a sense of accomplishment and purpose. Neither of them would have ever in their wildest dreams imagined that they could profit such great satisfaction by investing so much of their sweat, tears, time, and sinew. It was counterintuitive to them. Although they were loath to admit it, they were starting to actually look forward to getting up early and coming to the school. It was more than just feeling good about themselves. It was a sense that they were part of something far greater than themselves. They were part of an honorable cause.

As a result their efforts, the three of them had each worked up a healthy appetite. As it approached noon, they listened intently for the familiar sound of the front doors opening. When Hannah Grace finally made her way through the front door carrying her now familiar picnic basket, the girls scrambled down the stairs from the 4th grade classroom, falling all over one another and giggling with great anticipation. Simon took a nail out from between his teeth, set his hammer down, and also made his way down from the scaffolding.

Much to their dismay, Hannah Grace had no sooner made her way into the lobby when she suddenly realized she had left the silverware back at the house. Apologetically excusing herself, she quickly hurried back to the house to retrieve them, leaving Shannon, Sharon, and Simon standing dejected and hungry on the landing in awkward silence.

Realizing that he had a few minutes, Simon quietly retrieved a book sitting next to the laptop, took a seat at the top of the stairs, and began to read. The girls observed the curious, young man for a moment. Shannon caught the eye of Sharon and frowned, which in turn prompted a stifled giggle, and then a snort that caused a bit of a scene. In an effort to play it off, Sharon did her best to divert Simon's attention.

"You finished the wall!" Sharon said before trying to contain her laughter by cupping her lips. Meanwhile, Shannon was bent over looking in the opposite direction in an effort to regain her composure.

Simon glanced up from his reading, "Oh yeah, well, sort of," he responded. "That's all of the lath work. There's still a lot to be done before its finished-finished."

"Like what?" Shannon asked after getting ahold of herself.

"I don't know exactly," Simon replied.

"You don't know?" Shannon sputtered.

"No, I've got to look it up," he answered, glancing at her over the top of his book.

"You mean to tell me that you've torn down something down that you don't know how to put back together?" Shannon asked, doing her best to give him a hard time.

"Well, I'm not a carpenter or anything," he replied. "I'm just learning as I go, so it takes time."

"Why don't you just pay somebody who knows what they're doing to do it for you?" Shannon asked as though she was somehow exasperated by his incompetence.

"Because we don't have the..." Simon started to say.

"...Yeah," Sharon asked thoughtfully. "Why would you try to do all of this if you're not like some kind of expert or something?"

Simon laid the book down on his lap and pondered the question for a moment, debating the degree of honesty with which he needed to answer. Then he said plainly, "Because I felt called to do it."

"Called?" Shannon repeated with a crinkled up nose. She used her thumb and pinky finger to act like she was on the phone. "Oh I get it, like God called you up and said, 'hey, uh, Simon, would you go wreck a school for me?' "

Simon shifted in his seat a little. "God doesn't need a phone," he replied.

"You do know that the whole town is talking about you, right?" Shannon asked.

"Oh yeah, what are they saying?" Simon indifferently asked.

"Did you really think anybody could keep a secret around here?" Shannon asked mockingly.

"Some of them think you're doing something very admirable," Sharon offered, in an attempt to gloss over Shannon's brutal honesty.

"Yeah, but most of them think you're some kind of religious freak!" Shannon added with a forced laugh.

"Is that so?" Simon asked as if he hadn't considered himself the object of idle gossip before.

"I'm afraid she's right," Sharon added, embarrassed by Shannon's lack of tact. "It's funny, people get really worked up about all of this stuff," she said while pointing at the work he was doing in the lobby.

"Really?" Simon asked.

"Well, kinda," Sharon admitted, with an apologetic expression. "Some of the people who helped you paint the school a few weeks ago are a little upset because all of their work was kinda for nothing, you know?"

"Oh yeah!" Shannon commented. "And the farmers are really ticked at you."

Simon considered the implication of Shannon's comment. It had been a while since he had been the object of scorn and hostility, and even then it was only by being heckled by opposing fans in the heat of an intense baseball game.

Again, Sharon made an attempt to soften Shannon's accusations, "Well, it's like they don't think it's fair or something because they assume that they're the ones who are going to have to pay for all of this. That it isn't fair or something when some of them don't even have kids in school and stuff. And that other people who do have kids in school won't have to pay anything."

All Simon could say in response was, "Well, *somebody* has to pay for a new school."

Simon reflected on the observation for a moment as though he hadn't closely considered the issue before. After all, he fell into the latter category if anything. Troubled by the legitimacy of such an objection, Simon remembered Lexus's outburst in the conference room about the have's and have not's.

"Why would 'God' want *you* to fix up some dumb old building anyways?" Shannon asked in a disgusted tone that regained Simon's attention. "I mean, it sounds so stupid."

"Shannon!" Sharon yelled, mortified by her friends comment.

"To be honest, I don't know exactly," Simon replied.

"See! He doesn't even know!" Shannon said. "You don't know how to do it, and you don't know why you're doing it?

"Well, no," Simon said, getting a little defensive. "I just feel like that's what God wants me to do. So, I just put my trust in Him. And now I am kind of waiting for Him to show up. Ya know?"

The two girls looked at one another and let out a burst of laughter. Even Sharon couldn't defend that statement.

"What?" Simon said with a frown. "Don't you believe in God?"

"Well, yeah, I guess," Shannon answered. "But, I don't think He's going to like, show up here in some long beard and flowing white robe any time soon and say, 'Simon Freeman, let me build this wall for you'. Like he really cares!"

"Don't be ridiculous," Simon sneered. "I'm not expecting anything like that. I'm hoping that He'll just let me know why He wants me to do this or at least let me know what He wants me to do next. There's nothing crazy about that. We should expect God to show up."

"Maybe he'll send you a text," Shannon said with a laugh. "He's very busy with all the wars, and hurricanes, and murders, and stuff."

"Maybe," Simon replied sardonically.

"Do you really expect him to do that?" Sharon asked thoughtfully. "Do you expect him to actually communicate with *you* in some way?"

"Yes, as a matter of fact I do," Simon replied. "Because He already did," he added, referring to the message on the marquee at the church.

"Oh, come off it," Shannon jeered.

"Why not?" Simon said with a frown. "You said that you believe in God, right?"

"Well, yeah, but I think he's got more important things to do than worry about Bethel Grade School," Shannon replied with a hint of indecision in her voice. "He doesn't have time for something so trivial. I mean, really, how can he know everything, or be everywhere. Or-or, like how can he hear millions of people's prayers all around the world at the same time, like he's Santa Claus or something?" She said as she glanced over at Sharon and forced an unreciprocated laugh.

But, Sharon was much more interested in Simon's answer. It was something about the expression on her face that told Simon she was genuinely interested. She desperately wanted to know. She wanted answers. And suddenly, Simon realized the opportunity that was at hand for the Holy Spirit to move.

He closed his eyes and said a little prayer in a fraction of a second before continuing, "What does it mean to be 'God' by definition?" Simon asked rhetorically. "Doesn't it mean He made the universe? And if so, wouldn't that make Him extremely powerful and knowledgeable? We are so limited by our own weakness and our own ignorance. In fact, we are so blinded by our limited perspective that we have a hard time even comprehending or even imagining something like that. You know. Look around you. Is it really a stretch to think that He could be all-powerful, all-knowing, and everywhere all at the same time if He made the universe, the whole earth, and everything in it?"

Shannon stared at him blankly.

"It's like, it's like…" Simon stuttered, trying his best to think of something they could relate to.

Beginning to lose interest, Shannon looked down at her cell phone to see if she had any messages.

"Well, it's kind of like your cell phone in a way," Simon said, remembering Thelma's analogy.

"Huh?" Sharon uttered.

"I mean," Simon continued to say, "you can send or receive messages from anywhere as long as you have a signal. Well, what if you had a much larger tower or many more satellites in the sky, so that anywhere in the world you could receive a message at any time? You can imagine that, right, because you have some evidence of it now. You can text or call anyone in the United States, and they can instantly pick up their phone and hear you. Not only that but how many people can use the same microwaves and satellites at the same time? You can even do conference calls with hundreds or even thousands of people at the same time from all over the place. We don't need to know how it works to know that it works, right? And yet that system was man-made."

He could tell that he had their attention now. "How much more possible then, would it be with a system made by the God, who made the man, who made things like cell phones, microwave towers, and satellites?" Simon continued. "We just need to dial in to His number. I thank God that I don't have to know how He hears me when I talk to Him, to know that He does hear me. Because honestly, I am not ever going to be capable of understanding how that works. It is a complete mystery. It's not a contradiction. It doesn't mean that it doesn't happen. It means that you and I don't understand how it happens. Are you going to wait until you know as much as God before you believe in God? If so, then He would be no better than anybody else, and He would no longer be God."

"You said that God created the world," Shannon challenged, "but what about Darwin and evolution, and the Big Bang theory, and all that junk? I'm not a complete idiot ya know. You don't have to talk to me like I'm a child."

"I am sorry, I'm not trying to be condescending," Simon replied carefully. "All right, if you want to talk about this intellectually. Let's talk about Charles Darwin. His theory states that we come from simple single cell organisms. With the technology that he had at his disposal that's *exactly* what a single cell organism looked like. But now, because of all the advancements in technology, we know that a 'simple' single cell organism has as many components as all of New York City. It's extremely complex. It seems the more we discover in the field of science the more absurd evolution becomes. Have you ever heard of the missing link?

"Yeah, hasn't everybody, duh," Shannon said. "It's like an apeman or somethin', right?" She said turning to Sharon who shrugged her shoulders. "Yeah, like Big Foot or something."

"That's pretty close," Simon answered. "So, if humans evolved from four-footed animals to two footed animals wouldn't there be fossils that are irrefutable evidence showing what happened in between? What is the link, right? Did you know that that is only the last link in the chain? There are actually no links between any of the higher order to lower order creatures or any of them in between for that matter. No fossils, no records, no evidence."

"Okay, well what about how old the fossils are, like, carbon dating and stuff?" Sharon asked. "Wouldn't that prove the big bang theory over creation? I mean, I believe in God and creation and all, but I'm just asking."

"Now you're starting to think!" Simon replied. "We need to think about this stuff. Ask questions. Learn about it. And talk about it. Because God tells us those who seek, find. The more we debate these topics, then the faster we will unlock the truth. And the truth will set us free. I don't have enough faith to believe in the big bang theory.

Shannon rolled her eyes.

"No, I'm serious," Simon replied. "That theory states that everything in the universe was compressed into an inconceivably, tiny space. All matter, everything. You, me, this book, this school, the grain elevator, the state of Illinois, the United States, North America, the earth, the sun, and the billions of other stars in the galaxy. I can't even see how this book, " Simon said holding up Jeremy's Bible, "could be compressed into a tiny space like the tip of a pencil."

"Oh yeah, but, '*Do you really have to understand it all before it is real?*'," Shannon mockingly replied in a dumb voice. "Or whatever you said."

"Yes!" Simon excitedly answered. "Now we're starting to get somewhere! Now you are using higher order thinking and reasoning, which separates us from other primates, by the way. When you do that, you will arrive at the truth.

"Both theories have gaps or leaps of faith. So, how do we discern which one to believe and not believe. You just did something that many of the intellectual elites don't want you to do. You used your brain. By talking about it for even two minutes, you figured out that the Theory of Evolution isn't a law and Creationism isn't just some fairy tale. Now you're giving them equal consideration and putting both theories under the microscope.

"When I did that, this is the conclusion that I came to. Even if you put this Bible into a giant blender, mix it, and then let it splatter all over the room," Simon said, "would it ever splatter into a rock, a tree, an ape, and a person? And even if it could, why would it spontaneously explode in the first place? What caused it? So, I guess the blender turned on by itself, exploded, and resulted in a universe that is in perfect order?" Simon walked over to the ladder and lifted up a box of nails. "I've been thinking about this a lot actually, and I have been doing a great deal of research as you can probably tell.

"Look, if I dropped this box of one hundred nails to the floor a million times, would they ever all land in perfectly straight rows? Or build a bridge? No! Chaos never results in order. Not only that, but what caused the box to dump over in the first place?

"No," Simon said, putting the nails back down. "Both theories are demanding a leap of faith. But, which one is more logical? Which one makes sense? That's why I say that I don't have enough faith to believe that I am accidentally here or that I am accidentally breathing, and talking, and thinking."

"But, that's what they teach us in school," Sharon protested in a perturbed tone of voice. "You're wrong. I mean I just took a final on all that stuff last month and got an A'. It was even on the state test as a part of the Common Core standards. My teacher crammed it into our heads all year long!"

Suddenly, Simon thought of Thelma's warning about giving ground.

"Let me put it another way," Simon said, calmly, "if I could get a million monkeys to bang on a keyboard for a million straight years, just banging away twenty-four seven, day after day after day, do *you* think that any of them would ever accidentally write Shakespeare?"

There was silence. Sharon blinked a couple of times unable to muster an objection.

"Well, whatever," Shannon said, dismissing the whole conversation. Unable to respond logically, she ignored the question altogether and changed the topic. "I mean, it's just so dumb anyway. Let's just say for a minute that God does talk to people..."

"Communicates," Simon replied. "I didn't necessarily mean that he audibly talks to us."

"Whatever, 'communicate'," Shannon sputtered, starting to get irritated. "Then why wouldn't He communicate to you how to cure cancer, or save the ozone layer, or something important like that? Huh? Why would He waste His time telling you to fix up an old grade school? Talk about not being logical."

"That's exactly what I have been asking Him; *why?*" Simon humbly answered. "Sometimes I think that it may be to test me just to see if I would really do it. That I would really be obedient to His word."

"So, God's just mess'n with you?" Shannon said sarcastically.

"No, definitely not!" Simon objected. "I believe that God wants the best for me. Don't you believe that?"

"Yes," Sharon answered softly.

"No," Shannon replied.

"You don't?" Simon asked pointedly. "In your heart of hearts, you don't believe that God wants what is best for us?"

Shannon rolled her eyes and said sharply, "If you want to know the truth, if there is a God, I don't think he really cares one way or the other."

Just then Hannah Grace slipped back in the doorway carrying the plastic utensils. "All right," she said looking down at the floor as she made her way inside. "Sorry to keep you wait…" When she saw their faces, she could tell that she had just walked in on something, and she was hoping that she knew what it was. Simon never turned his head to acknowledge her presence. Instead, he stared intently at Shannon. His heart was breaking as her words reverberated in his head.

"Of course, He cares, Shannon," Simon said with a pained expression on his face.

Hannah Grace carefully tiptoed in the doorway and gently allowed the door to close behind her. She stepped off to the side, standing in the shadows. She was holding her picnic basket with both hands in front of her with her head bowed for a moment.

Simon paused to allow his words to sink in. Then he added, "Think of what you are saying. Either way, whether you are an accident or made from some God who doesn't care about you, what kind of world would this be. Nothing would matter. There would be no order, no justice. Anybody could do anything to anyone else and it wouldn't matter. There would be no consequences. It would be total anarchy."

Shannon and Sharon froze with ashen faces.

With great compassion in his voice, Simon added, "Believe me. It wasn't very long ago that I felt the same way that you feel about God. That He's out there, maybe, but that He just doesn't care about me, so why should I care about Him? But then, I was forced to face up to the fact that maybe I wasn't hearing from God because He wasn't hearing from me. Maybe I left Him first. I made that choice before I even knew I was making that choice. In a way, we are all like the prodigal son.

"But, then something very strange happened. When I started talking to Him, He began to speak to me."

"That's a laugh!" Shannon snapped angrily. "Maybe I'm not like you. You don't know me. You don't know what it has been like for me! I never knew my dad. My mom's a loser. Nothin' created me other than two horny teenagers in the back seat of a Chevy with a bottle of Boone's Farm. And somehow I'm supposed to believe that I'm special? That I'm not an accident? And you're going to sit here and tell me that I walked away from Him? Ha!"

The words stung Simon as he suddenly was forced to think of his night with Jez in a whole new light. What if she had been…able? He certainly wouldn't have stopped it from happening. What if he had gotten Jez pregnant, and they had a daughter together, and…Simon tried as best as he could to push the thoughts out of his mind and focus on what God wanted him to tell Shannon.

Without Simon realizing it, streams of tears were now pouring down Sharon's face as she thought about the night her brother pulled her from Mike's car in the woods, and how close she had come to making a huge mistake.

Simon was somehow able to regain some composure before waiting for the just the right words to come to him. "You may have been an accident to your parents," Simon said, remembering what Thelma had told him about God taking something bad and making something good out of it. "But, you were no accident to God. You were intentional. You aren't worthless. That's what Satan wants you to believe. No, no, no! To God, you are priceless."

Simon gently continued, "There is a God, He is good, and He created the universe and everything in it- including you. There is order. There is justice. There are choices, and there are consequences. And through it all, God *does* love you and wants what is best for you." Simon groped for the words to get her to understand. "Shannon, he cares about you so much. He knows the very number of hairs on your head. He knew about you before you were even born. He even knitted you in your mother's womb."

Shannon was now crying uncontrollably, "No," she said. "That can't be. If that's true, then he can't love me."

There was silence. Simon was baffled. His words did not seem to be having the comforting effect on Shannon that he had hoped for. He thought for sure that it would be reassuring for anyone to know that God already knew them in their mother's womb. Instead, Shannon's face was beat red, and she was visibly shaken. Confused, Simon glanced over at Sharon who held her face in her hands, completely broken and weeping. Next, he turned to Hannah Grace who was biting her bottom lip and wiping away tears with a handkerchief.

It never dawned on him that such an epiphany about God could have such a diametrically opposite effect on a person. "Shannon," he said with a great deal of compassion and tenderness. "Why are you here today? What did you do? Why are you being punished?"

"Because!" Shannon could barely say through gritted teeth. "Because I had an abortion! Okay? And Sharon told on me! And Sean hates me. And now I just want everyone to leave me alone! To stop talking about me. To stop judging me!"

"Oh, I am so sorry," Simon said sincerely.

"I'm sorry too!" Shannon said trying to hold back her tears. "I'm sorry I ever told anybody about it! I didn't do anything wrong. Besides, it's my body, it's my life, and it's my choice! People have them all the time. Like they said, it wasn't like it was a baby yet. You're wrong about that. It was just some blob of tissue like the lady said at the clinic."

Simon felt like someone had reached inside of him and pulled out his intestines. His heart was in his throat, and he wished more than anything else that he didn't have to tell her what he suddenly felt compelled to tell her. "Shannon," he said with the demeanor of a fellow violator of the law. He knew she would have to face the truth before she could admit guilt, repent, and be forgiven. "I know this is going to be very hard for you to hear. But, that was a person inside of you. That was your baby."

"No!" she replied, shaking her head adamantly. "It was just a blob of tissue. You're just some loser working as a glorified janitor. What do you know?" Shannon snapped, going on the attack.

Simon realized that the only difference between his night of indiscretion with Jez and this young girl's plight was their circumstances. It was not because he had done the right thing or because he had even wanted to do the right thing. "It's not what I know that bothers me, it's what I don't know," Simon answered as he moved toward her and put his hand on her shoulder. "What I know is that a baby's heart starts beating at about eighteen days. But, even more than that, I don't know how a baby's heart starts to beat for the first time. And more importantly, I don't know when the soul enters a baby's tiny body. No one does. But I believe it is at conception."

"Stop it!" she yelled at him pushing his arm away.

"Shannon, I am not telling you this to hurt you," Simon said with great import. "I am telling you this to help you, so that you can start the process of healing."

"Healing from what?" Shannon snapped. "I'm fine. I don't know what you're talking about. It was my choice!"

"I also believe in choices," Simon admitted.

"You-you do?" Sharon asked, choking back her tears.

"Yes, I am against abortions, and yes, I am 'pro choice'," Simon said plainly. "I think God feels the same way, because He gave us life, and He gave us free will. I have come to believe that our first choice is whether or not to have sex in the first place.

"But, we don't have the luxury of choosing the consequences of our choices. Sometimes there doesn't appear to be any repercussions for our bad decisions. And then other times, the consequence of a bad decision is that a child is conceived. That consequence is chosen by God, not us. Do you understand? Sometimes we make choices without even realizing what we are really choosing between," Simon said, remembering what telling Hope about Jez did to their relationship.

Suddenly, he could speak with great empathy, "You and I are not much different, you know? I have made my share of bad decisions. But, here's the deal, on the night your baby was conceived, you probably thought you were choosing between having sex and not having sex. When as it turns out, you were choosing between having a baby and not having a baby. Just because you weren't thinking about it that way does not mean that it wasn't that way."

"But, that's not even fair!" Shannon protested, stomping her foot like a toddler.

"I know it is hard to hear the truth," Simon admitted. "But, where does our sense of fairness even come from if not from God himself? Fairness can only happen if there is order. That is why I say, 'I believe in choices, and I believe in consequences, and accountability, and justice. God does gives us a choice, but he doesn't allow us to choose the consequence.

"But listen, in response to the consequence of your first choice to have sex, you were given a second choice. Every pregnant woman has a second choice whether it is legal or illegal.

"Really that is secondary to the ultimate issue. The abortion business is about supply and demand. If no one demanded it, then it wouldn't exist. No, I am talking about answering to a higher law. I am talking about God's law. I am talking about justice and retribution that comes from God."

"But, if it is legal then there is no punishment," Shannon argued. "It's not a crime! There aren't any consequences."

Simon mourned for her and her deceased child upon hearing the reply. "There's always a consequence," Simon said sympathetically. "I said that I am pro-life. Many times, I think what gets lost is that we often think we are making a choice between there two equally acceptable options when in most cases there is one right answer and one wrong answer. Abortion is not a wrong choice because I say it is. And it's not right because you say that it is. It is the wrong choice because God says that it is.

"Besides, there was a third option that you could have considered. You could have put the baby up for adoption. There are plenty of people who can't have children of their own."

"Honey, what he is saying is for your own good," Hannah Grace said, softly as she walked out of the shadows. "You can't just bury this inside of you. Your own conscience will never let you be. It will continue to fester inside of you and torment you, leaving you no peace. Believe me. The faster you deal with it, the better you can come to terms with it."

"There's nothing to come to terms with!" Shannon yelled, with a flurry of profanity as she backed her way towards the staircase. "Who do you think you are anyway?" she asked angrily. "Who are you to judge me? You think have all the answers or something? You're sitting here work'n on this stupid building. And you don't even know why. What a joke! You don't know what it's like to be me. How can you say what is right or wrong? You're not me. And you're not god!"

"You're right," Simon answered tenderly, "about a lot of things actually." Shannon stopped in her her tracks at the bottom of the stairs. "I am not you," he continued. "And, you're right, it is not my place to judge you. I am just a person like everybody else. None of us are God. We didn't come up with the rules. God did. We don't get to make our own rules just because we don't like his.

"And Heaven knows, I haven't always been able to always follow His rules. I am just trying help you understand what the Bible says the rules are.

"My intent is to not sound holier-than-though or anything. I don't get to judge. I don't get to decide who goes to Heaven or Hades, but I have to discern truth from deceit and right from wrong. It is not being judgmental to tell someone else what the Bible actually says!"

Simon searched his own heart for a moment. Shannon did have a point. How could he possibly really know how it feels to have to make that decision?

Suddenly, Hannah Grace spoke up. "Shannon, honey," she said moving towards the young, angry girl. "I have been there. I have made the same first poor choice to have premarital sex. And God gave me the same consequence as you. I became pregnant at about your age. So, I *do* understand. I really do.

"What Simon is telling you about God's word is right. The sooner you can come to terms with that the sooner we can tell you the Good News about God's grace and forgiveness. But, there is no Good News if you don't first understand the bad news. You broke God's law, and you deserve justice; just like we all deserve justice. We all deserve to be punishment for breaking the law. But, luckily we don't have to receive that punishment. None of us do. Jesus did it for us on the cross," Hannah Grace was momentarily at a loss for words, trying to find a way for Shannon to comprehend God's grace. "It's like the hymn says, 'Jesus paid it all, all to him I owe, death had left a crimson stain. He washed it white as snow'. Remember the one we sing in church? That's what it means."

The statement jolted Shannon. She began to soften a bit. Until Hannah Grace repeated those lyrics, she was able to easily dismiss Simon's claims because there was no way for him to truly understand her circumstances. But, Hannah Grace, on the other hand was able to empathize with her plight. She had been down the same path as Shannon but had somehow come to the same conclusion as Simon.

Because of her past, Hannah Grace was qualified by God to counsel the young girl that would have been impossible for Simon to achieve.

"But, honey," Hannah Grace said, furtively moving towards Shannon, "you have to take that first step. You have to take a good, hard look at yourself. You have to admit your sin. This is the hard part. This is where you must see the truth for what it is and face the ugly reality of what you have done.

"If you're like me, your ego has tried to justify your actions a million different ways, so that you don't have to feel the pain. You are trying desperately to disquiet your nagging conscience. But, I can tell you first hand that it's fools gold. It's temporary. It's an insufficient band aid. Ignoring the reality of what you did, will only suspend you in a state of bitterness and discontent. It will fester inside of you from now until the end of time, allowing you not a moment's peace. I know it is painful. But, let me tell you what you can expect if you simply confess. You're going to feel intense guilt, pain, and regret at first. This is the brokenness that He requires before forgiveness can take place."

The four of them stood in silence for a moment before Hannah Grace added, "And let me tell you about your baby in heaven..."

Unexpectedly, Shannon's face turned to rage, and she lashed out defensively at Simon, Hannah Grace, and even Sharon with profane, hateful words. Then she quickly turned towards the front doors.

"Wait, Shannon!" Simon called out, "You need to hear the Good News in all of this."

She stopped for a moment with her hands on the door and stared at him with daggers.

"Wait," Simon said, desperately racing down the steps to where she stood. He recognized that they were losing their opportunity. "I-I am not a professional counselor or anything. But, I want you to know something. I do not see myself as being any better than you. I have made the same bad choices. The only difference between you and me is that God did not choose for any of the girls that I have been with in my life to become pregnant. And I am so ashamed now that I understand what was really at stake. I understand how wrong I was.

"And I can't say for sure that if I were in your shoes I would have made the right, 'second' choice in response to the first bad one. But, I know this, it's like Hannah Grace said, Jesus' grace and mercy are sufficient for both of us. When we give ourselves over to Him, He forgives our sins. You can be at peace with yourself.

"Will you do that? Will you please at least listen to what God has to offer you? I am begging you to hear us out.

"We're not trying to hurt you, but you need to understand that this is a big deal," Hannah Grace added.

Shannon said nothing at first. Simon's desperate attempt to reach the confused, young girl backfired miserably.

Shannon turned to go, but then stopped. Unexpectedly, she spun around and spit in Simon's face. "You're right, everybody *does know* about you going out to Jack's strip club, and you being best friends with Jeremy Warner, and you taking groceries over to Little Miss Candy Cain!" she yelled as the doors swung behind her. "You're just a big hypocrite!"

Incredibly, Simon barely noticed himself wiping the spit from his face. He was too overwhelmed by the revelation regarding the conviction he felt from his own guilt and shame. Desperately, he called out, "You need to understand! What you're trying to dismiss as no big deal is a *huge* deal to God!"

He finally understood why Hope had been so angry the night he had told her about Jez. It was as much as about him trying to deceive God as it was about deceiving her. In God's eyes, wanting to be with Jez was as bad as being with Jez. If Hope had been the girl God meant for him then he had betrayed her before he had even met her. And what's worse, he had also betrayed God before he knew Him. It was about trust. It was about a covenant. It was about betrayal. It was about giving in to the depravity of his heart. It was about his ego's justifying his actions and his unwillingness to understand, let alone admit, that what he did was horribly wrong.

He wasn't truly sorry about his actions. He was only sorry that Hope found out. Or sorry that she was that upset when she found out. Now he understood.

He knew why she was so hurt. It was about unfaithfulness. And now, he truly was remorseful.

No longer defensive in his defiance, Simon was now apologetic in his humility. Somewhat dazed by the sudden turn of events, he turned to see Hannah Grace cradling her sobbing niece in her arms.

Even if Shannon hadn't received the message, Sharon had heard it loud and clear. Evidently, she felt convicted of the exact same indictment that Simon was feeling in the pit of his stomach. Now she understood the seriousness of her actions. She understood what could have happened. And why she knew that she needed to be forgiven for her lustful heart. For a moment, he stood there looking up at the two of them standing under the giant chandelier. It was the ultimate picture of brokenness. Then Hannah Grace lifted her glossy eyes towards Simon and motioned for him to come up to the top of the stairs and join them.

Obediently, he climbed the steps and stood awkwardly next to them not knowing what to do.

Hannah Grace asked, "Simon, can you please lead of us in prayer? Sharon wants to be forgiven and receive the gift of salvation."

* * *

After Simon had finished helping Sharon with the prayer of salvation, he made his way down to the basement. He needed a moment. Indecisively, he took out his phone, took a deep sigh and called her number.

"Hope, hey, this is Simon," he said awkwardly as he began to nervously pace around the basement. "Freeman, uh, this is Simon Freeman. And I just wanted to say that I get it now. For what it's worth. I understand why you were so hurt. You had every right to be, and I am very, very sorry. I may have ruined everything between us. Not that there was anything…but, if you were feeling the same way I was feeling…" he rolled his eyes and pulled the phone away from his ear for a second. "Anyway, whatever, I know I'm rambling on here. What I am trying to say is that I miss you, and I want you back in my life. Whatever that looks like. Even if that means just being friends. Please call me back when you get this message, I…" the time expired before he could finish.

He dropped the phone from his ear and stared at it with a look of resignation. What was done was done. Now he would have to wait.

Putting his cell back into his pocket, Simon realized that he had unconsciously wandered to the doorway of the storage room of the basement. Now looking into the cavernous, darkened room, he remembered Thelma's charge that it wasn't completely empty. He scrunched his face and gave a dismissive grunt.

"What is that old geezer talkin' about?" he said under his breath as he took a few steps into the storage room. "Looks empty enough to me." With his next step, he accidentally kicked a paperback book that had been lying undetected on the floor. Simon reached down and picked it up. He lifted the brittle book up to the bare bulb and read the title, "Of Plymouth Plantation". Inquisitively, his eyes fell upon a random passage that read:

> "Upon which," said Bradford, "they set apart a solemn day of humiliation, to seek the Lord by humble and fervent prayer, in this great distress."

The words reminded Simon of Linus' prayer referencing Elder William Brewster from the infamous Thanksgiving Special. He realized that there could be no mistaking what Linus or Charles Schultz, for that matter, meant as Simon's gaze arbitrarily fell upon the back wall of the storage room. However, he was greatly surprised to find upon further inspection there was something about the back wall of the room that seemed quite peculiar.

Dropping the book to his side, he took another step towards the darkened wall. He soon realized that it wasn't made of brick like the rest of the foundation surrounding the parameter of the poorly lit basement. It was smooth and almost completely black. While it took up nearly the entire width of the room, the top of the rectangular object did not quite reach the ceiling.

Simon's heart skipped a beat as he realized what it was he might be looking at. Excitedly, he set the book on a ledge and moved quickly towards the unidentified object before tripping on the lip of something laying of the floor. He barely caught himself on the cool, metallic surface of the rectangular object leaning against the back wall. Gripping his right hand around the side of the large frame, he became filled with excitement. It was just as he had suspected! The bronze plaque was leaning heavily at a slight angle against the brick of the foundation.

Quickly, Simon turned to run out of the room, tripping again the a slight drop off from the uneven surface. He raced down the long corridor to Little Simon's hideout and snagged the large flashlight that he reasoned was still left there unattended. In a flash, he hurried back to the closet, clicked the switch, and banged the side of it until the bulb came to life.

Careful this time to avoid the lip of the slightly raised floor, Simon moved towards the back of the closet and grabbed the edge of the enormous plaque. With all of his nerve and sinew, he wrenched it away from the wall leaving a wide enough aperture to shed light onto the raised, bronze lettering. There was no doubt about it now. It was the unidentified object that had hung from the sagging wall of the stairwell all of those years. It was the commemorative plaque of the Declaration of Independence.

"Hey," an unidentified man called out from behind Simon. The unannounced visitor was standing in the doorway to the closet.

Simon nearly jumped out of his skin as he wielded around and cast the flashlight in the direction of stranger's voice.

"Oh, sorry, didn't mean to startle ya," the man said between bits of chew. "You, Simon Freeman?"

"Yes," Simon answered, suspiciously. "And who are you?"

"Name's Tony, Miss Harold sent me over here," he said indifferently, as he turned to spit on the floor. "Said you needed some help with some woodwork or somethin'."

"Oh, okay, yeah, right," Simon said, trying to regain his composure. "You are a…"

"…Handyman," Tony proudly replied, lifting up the tool belt that was draped over his shoulder.

"Another one?" Simon asked. "What happened to the other guy?"

"Sir?" Tony replied with a confused expression on his face.

"The other carpenter," Simon answered.

"Don't know nothin' about that," Tony said, shifting the large wad of chew from one cheek to the other. "I wouldn't call myself a carpenter exactly, more of a handyman. Like I said. Thelma just said if I did this for her, we'd be even-steven."

"Oh, right," Simon said with a wink.

"I'm just here to do whatever it is you need me to do, so I can settle up the score," Tony said wiping his lips with the back of his hands.

"Is that right?" Simon said. "Okay, well, do you mind giving me a hand then? The first thing we need to do is get this plaque upstairs to the stairwell of the main entryway that I am renovating."

"Uh, yeah, I gathered that," the stout man said with a chuckle. "Lord have mercy, that's a mess up there!"

With no little effort, Simon and Tony wrestled the large monument to the landing and propped it up against the wall.

Hearing the commotion, Hannah Grace and Sharon emerged from the classroom where they had been working on finishing the floor.

"Oh, my word," Hannah Grace said, putting both hands to either side of her face.

"What is it?" Sharon asked.

"It's the plaque that used to hang on the wall of the stairwell," Hannah Grace answered. "I had completely forgotten all about it. Where in the world did you find it?"

Bent over, trying to catch his breath, Simon motioned towards the basement. "It was in the back of the storage room, propped up against the back wall," he gasped.

"My heavens!" Hannah Grace said with a laugh, bringing both hands down to slap her thighs. "It must weigh a ton."

"Yeah," Simon acknowledged, "now I know why that wall had bowed out so badly."

"So," Tony said, wiping the sweat from his brow, "you was the one who reset that wall, huh? I was meanin' to ask ya who done that."

"Oh, no, it was the other guy," Simon started to say before catching himself. Hannah Grace, Sharon, and Tony stared at him with blank expressions.

"I, uh, can't tell a lie," he said trying to recover from his near admission of co-conspirators.

"Man, you done an amazing job, I'm here to tell ya," Tony said admiring the craftsmanship. "I don't have any earthly idea how you got that thing so perfectly lined up."

"Well, I…uh…thanks," Simon stammered. "Now it just needs framed, drywalled, and a couple coats of paint, so we can hang this bad boy back up on the wall." He was starting to see the light at the end of the tunnel.

"Mmmm," Tony mumbled with his hands on his hips. "I don't know what all you was plannin' on doin', but usually you save all that till ya got everything else done. I mean, you're obviously 'the man' and all, but that's just my two cents. It's your call, course."

"I think we are close to being done," Simon said, optimistically.

"You jus' wanted to reset the wall?" Tony asked.

"And we did the ceiling and the chandelier," Simon answered, trying halfheartedly to conceal his pride.

"Uh-huh, oh yeah, I seen that," Tony said, glancing up at the ceiling. "Nice. And that's all you was want'n to do?"

"Well, no, here," Simon said, walking over to the picture of the entryway that Hannah Grace had brought to him, "we were trying to renovate the entryway so that it looked exactly like it did in this photograph."

He handed the photograph over to the handyman.

Tony looked down at the picture, gnawing on some chaw. Then he glanced around the room. "You want it *exactly* like this?" the handyman asked.

"Yes, 'exactly'," Simon replied, looking around the room and admiring the work that had been completed up to that point. Then he turned back to the unshaven handyman who was still carefully analyzing the photo. "What's the matter?"

"Well, son, I'm afraid I've got some bad new for ya if your want'n it to look *exactly* like this here," Tony said, wagging the picture in front of his face. "Tarnation, it's hot in here."

"We could use some rain," Hannah Grace said pleasantly.

"Yes, ma'am," Tony answered.

"What do you mean, 'bad news'?" Simon asked, taking the photograph from Tony's thick fingers.

"Well, hombre," Tony said, "for instance," he said, saddling up next to Simon and pointing at the photo, "see here? For starters you got to replace all of this oak panel'n. That's painstakin' work. See all them angles. Tough cuttin'. Ah, well, you already know that. And the radiators; see 'em here and here. They need to be re-dipped. I mean if ya want it 'xactly. Not to mention the electrical. All them brass outlets, light switches and what not."

Simon's heart sunk as he heard the beady-eyed handyman continue his bleak assessment.

"And that's not the worst of it my friend," Tony said, apologetically.

"No?" Sharon asked.

"No ma'am," Tony replied. "Take a looky here."

"Where?" Sharon asked.

"Here," Tony said taking the picture back out of Simon's hands. "These stairs are not the original. Na, somewhere along the line, they probably started to sag, or weather, or somethin', and the doggone gov'ment- pardon my French- probably made em' replace them with these refabbed jobbies.

"Man, it's hot in here. No air mov'n at all!" Tony muttered.

Simon's face was peaked and his shoulders sagged.

"And with school startin' in a couple weeks, you'd need an entire army to get it done in time," Tony said.

"Like 'Extreme Home Makeover'?" Sharon asked with a smile.

"Yeah, uh-huh," Tony said handing the picture back to Simon, "love that show. Did ya see the one where..."

Simon bent over and leaned on his knees.

"What's the matter?" Sharon asked

"We don't have the man-power, or time, or resources," Simon replied, standing up straight again and putting his hands on his hips.

"Say, what are ya doin' all this for anyways?" Tony asked, as though the question had just struck him.

Before Simon could answer, he noticed Hannah Grace standing under the giant chandelier with a wry smile. "What is it?" he asked her.

"Did you hear his question?" Hannah Grace asked.

"Yes," Simon replied.

"What did I say?" Tony asked.

"Well, are you going to answer him?" she asked Simon, purposely trying to lead him.

Simon thought for a moment before answering. "Do I have a choice?" he asked.

"Not really," Hannah Grace answered.

"What are you guys talking about?" Sharon asked, confused.

"Did you ever think that maybe this isn't just about the referendum," Hannah Grace wisely suggested. Maybe God is merely using this little project of yours as a kind of forum or lightening rod?"

"What do you mean?" Sharon asked.

"People in a small town can't stay out of everyone else's business," Hannah Grace replied. "You couldn't keep a secret in Bethel if you tried. Little-by-little word will get out, and they will begin to trickle in. In fact, the less you say about what you are doing in here, the more they will want to know what is going on within these four walls."

Simon said nothing as he pondered the veracity of Hannah Grace's supposition. He couldn't help but think of Thelma's ingenious demand for complete secrecy.

"People will first come out of curiosity," she continued. "But once they are here they will all want to know why you are doing this. When they ask that question it will give you the opportunity to share with each and every one of them your testimony. Then they will find themselves drawn by an incessant craving to fill an enormous void in their lives to be a part of something bigger than themselves. They will come. People will come."

"Oh, like 'Field of Dreams'!" Sharon said excitedly.

The other three looked over at her quizzically.

"What?" Sharon replied.

"How'd you know that?" Simon asked.

"I've only seen it like a thousand times," Sharon answered. "It's Rich's favorite movie."

"Don't you see?" Hannah Grace said turning back to Simon. "You said yourself. We don't have the manpower, time, or resources."

"That's exactly my point," Simon replied. "How can we possibly get everything done in time?"

"Exactly, the conditions are *perfect*!" Hannah Grace said joyfully.

"For what?" Simon asked, still confused.

"For what we need, silly," Hannah Grace said.

"What we need is a miracle!" Simon retorted sardonically.

"Na,…" Tony objected, taking his hat from off of his head and wiping his forehead with the back of his hand, "…just a cool breeze."

28

THE DEDICATION

Hannah Grace's words proved to be most prophetic. People did come. Word spread through the most ingenious of marketing devices. Hannah Grace simply asked anyone who visited the school to keep what they heard and saw a secret. Suddenly, word spread like wildfire, the message ripped through Bethel and the outer-lying communities. Pretty soon people from all different walks of life descended on the school to see for themselves what all the fuss was about. Typically, once they came and looked around, they stayed. They offered their services for what they considered a noble cause. The differing degrees of diverse knowledge and expertise never ceased to amaze Simon. Just within the tiny community of Bethel, experts in antiquity, masonry, carpentry, electricity, as well as heating and air applied their skills. And there was even one very skilled physician. Most people were not surprised to discover that Dr. Al-Banna had once again joined the cause.

It was all unfolding exactly as Hannah Grace had envisioned. The thrifty project patriarch also happened to set a basket with a note by the front entrance just in case anyone might want to make a contribution to the worthy cause.

What started as a cool breeze was now reaching hurricane wind sheers. No sooner would the project hit a snag before someone new would come forward from out of the blue with the exact set of skills needed to provide the solution. To Simon it became more and more clear that it wasn't just coincidental. It was Providential. God was providing. How else could one explain it? Each of them had been called to be there at a specific point in time for a specific purpose.

Even those who did not have the gift of working with their hands filled a very specific and necessary role which allowed them to contribute in other ways. Working in concert, they set aside their differences, personal agendas, and egos. If they could cook, they cooked. If they could clean, they cleaned. If all they could do was hold a ladder, then by God's grace they held a ladder. It may not have been glamorous, but to the person working on the tapestry thirty feet off the floor of the entryway, holding the ladder was very much appreciated.

Amazingly, there was no end to number of ways in which God made use of each individual's talents. Nowhere was that more evident than in the young man who brought a guitar and provided a spark of energy with uplifting music, or the business woman who decided to put together a gorilla marketing campaign in an effort to generate votes for the referendum. Volunteers copied flyers, drew posters, made cold calls, and went door to door.

Many gave financially, but even those who were in no position gave what they could. When they couldn't give anymore, they offered up their prayers. Support grew and before anyone had even realized it, a grassroots movement had begun. With each new visible change that had taken place in the appearance of the entryway a wave of momentum swept over the town, deeply affecting all who had invested their time and talents. The wave of momentum was palpable, it was real, and people wanted to be a part of it.

Thirty-eight days had passed since Simon first tore down the false ceiling, and thirty-eight days had passed since a single drop of rain had fallen, even though the air hung heavy with humidity like a wet blanket. The cool breeze Tony had prefaced was obviously more metaphorical than literal for the archaic school was never fitted for central air. Even though fans were strategically placed about the room, a body at rest would be drenched in sweat within minutes of entering the sultry, old school building.

Nonetheless, it did little to impede the progress of the workers. They pressed on despite the oppressive drought and residual heat wave. In fact, it was far more commonplace that Dr. Al-Banna would have to force volunteers to take breaks, drink plenty of fluids, and treat symptoms of heat exhaustion. Even in the face of adversity, they enthusiastically continued their work.

Conversely, that same sentiment was not shared by a small contingency of disgruntled farmers, who given the damning forecast, had nothing better to do than to sit on a bar stool bemoaning their dissipating margins and criticizing the crazy zealots down at the school. With each dry stalk that wilted in the intense heat, they saw their yields crumble like the cracks in the dirt from which they were unable to take root. As bad as the weather was, it paled in comparison to the rumors that were circulating about a growing number of residents who had had a sudden change of heart regarding the referendum. It was disconcerting to say the least, for they knew well and good who would be footing the bill for a new school.

As tension rose in step with the thermometer, they agreed that something had to be done, to be sure. But what? They were tired of being told to be patient and wait. Fuming over their frosty mugs, no one had a clue how to turn the tide of public opinion. With an impending dedication ceremony for the restored lobby looming in two days there were only two certainties. First, emotions were at a fever pitch. Second, Jack was undoubtedly plotting and scheming behind the scenes to defeat the referendum, so that he could begin construction on the new Bethel Adult Superstore.

Even as the drama unfolded locally, word of the powder keg like conditions in Bethel made its way down to the all girl's Christian summer camp in southern

Illinois. Through the miracle of technology, Hope had been receiving texts, Facebook, and Twitter in order to track the surprising ground swell of support for the new school. Not only had she taken a keen interest in the turn of events due to her position as a second grade teacher at the school, but she was also very much captivated by the stories surrounding the movement's ring leader, an unlikely hero of sorts named Simon Freeman.

Ever since Hope received Simon's garbled voicemail, she had thought about him more and more. After listening to the message several times over, she came to believe that the apology was sincere. There was a conviction in his voice, and there was a brokenness in his spirit that spoke of pain, regret, and repentance. While it did make a difference that he wanted her in his life regardless of what that relationship might look like, that was ultimately not the reason she decided to eventually return his call. Had that been the case she would have gotten back to him the same night that he left the message. Instead, she exhibited amazing restraint by keeping her emotions in check and wisely waiting for the seeds of his words to take root and bear fruit.

There was no question that she still felt the pain inflicted as a result of his being less than forthright with her about his indiscretion. But now, with each new bit of information that she received, she was starting to become convinced that real change had taken place in Simon's life. It was the kind of change that produced a certain degree of admiration and affection.

Hope could see the dramatic changes that had been made to the school and how it was impacting the community. As a result, it became evident to her that God had to be in it. And if God were in it, then He must have forgiven Simon.

She reasoned that if Simon's indiscretion had been so reprehensible to her then how much more reprehensible had his unfaithfulness been to God? If God could forgive Simon, then… It was there in the stillness of the counselor's cabin at the break of dawn that Hope deliberated these mysteries during her quiet time with the Lord.

Had it been exclusively up to her emotions, she would have already driven back to Bethel by now. In her heart, she was ready to give Simon a second chance, but in her head there was one thing that she was having a very difficult time processing. It was the message that Pastor Pete had left for her that she found particularly troubling. Hope kept hearing the pastor's words echo in her ears, "… It appears that your friend Simon might be heading down the same path as Jeremy Warner." She prayed that she didn't know what that meant.

Not taking the words at face value, she decided to call the pastor. When she finally got ahold of Pastor Pete, he downplayed the implications, admitting that he was merely being speculative based on some casual observations. On multiple occasions, Pete had seen Simon carrying an armful of groceries up the Adamson's porch steps. There was no hard evidence of impropriety or wrongdoing. After an awkward pause, the Pastor was quick to add that Simon had been faithfully attending church for the past four Sundays, sitting in the front row and dutifully taking notes.

Nonetheless, the insinuations plagued her just as it had with the circumstances surrounding Jeremy's untimely death. Up to this point, her head had been able to keep her heart in check. But now, with camp nearly over, she had to decide if she would try to see Simon before he left for the East coast.

What Hope couldn't possibly have known from hundreds of miles away was that Simon's intentions were pure, and that his weekly Sunday trips to the Adamson house were as purposeful as the renovation to the school. Simon had taken up the mantle of his late friend Jeremy. He was in fact heading down the same road.

After church, he would take a handful of groceries over to the house, set them on the kitchen table, and then make his way back to Little Simon's room. While the wayward child practiced shooting people, Simon would do his best to make a connection, forge a relationship, and share the Gospel.

For all of his trouble, Simon had been spit on, yelled out, cursed, and bitten. The disturbed child's reactions were even more stark when Simon would track him down at one of his favorite hideouts. In those moments, when the little boy was backed into a corner, he *was* a vampire. He was full of hate, venom, and malevolence.

At face value, it defied all reason that a 6-year-old boy would find comfort and refuge in lonely, deep, dark places. But if anyone up to that point had ever bothered to delve into the matter, it would have made complete sense to them. For the odd behavior all began when his mother first starting bringing her work home with her in order to subsidize her nasty habit. And when the strange noises coming from her bedroom could no longer be drowned out by CSI, or Smallville, or even Scooby-Doo, Little Simon would escape into darkness and wait until the intruder had gone.

Even without being privy to that information, Simon quickly concluded that Little Simon was easiest to approach while playing video games in his room on Sunday afternoons. Only when the boy was completely immersed in his games could Simon get close enough to carry on any semblance of a conversation or gain a foothold on which to build some trust. There were times when he felt as though he was beginning to make some progress like when Little Simon would show him a certain level he reached or a new high score that he achieved. More often than not, though, Simon felt like he was getting nowhere fast. In those moments, the little punk would violently kick or punch at him in a fit of rage. And Simon often wondered why he even bothered to try.

But he was determined to reach the distant child and would not be easily deterred. He was on a mission. Even though it was insanely frustrating at times, he was going to get through to the boy, even if it killed him.

Then one day, he had a breakthrough. Little Simon had been playing his handheld game in his room when Simon settled down on the floor next to him.

As per usual, the boy failed to acknowledge his presence and completely ignored Simon's attempts to initiate a conversation. Dejected, Simon was just about to give up and head back to the school before Little Simon, without so much as glancing up from his game, leaned into Simon and cuddled up next to him while he pecked away at the controller. For almost an hour, Simon sat there, teary-eyed, looking down at the top of the boy's dirty, matted hair.

After some small talk, Simon decided to seize the opportunity and ask the question that had been plaguing him. "Simon," he said to the boy.

"Yeah," the distracted child answered, while staring down at his game.

"How is it you're not afraid to leave the house at night and wander around town all by yourself?" Simon asked.

There was silence while the boy continued to peck away at the controls. He merely shrugged his shoulders.

"I think you're a very brave little kid," Simon replied, trying to win him over. "I know I wouldn't have had the courage to do that when I was your age."

Silence.

"Aren't you afraid?" Simon furtively asked.

"Na," Little Simon answered, shifting a little in his seat.

"Ya know there's nothing wrong with being afraid sometimes," Simon said.

"What are you afraid of?" the boy asked while continuing to play his game.

The question hit him like a ton of bricks as if he'd somehow been purposely suppressing the answer to that very question. After some thought, he decided that he definitely wasn't afraid of Jack. Reflexively, the first thing that came to mind was a fear of failure. Like some sort of mental ink blot test. There was the fear of not having money. Not having a nice house. A nice car. Or a beautiful wife. Not being considered successful by society at large.

But now, he was convinced that wasn't it anymore. He now knew what he was afraid of.

"Well, lots of things, I guess," Simon said, shooing a legion of demons from his past and out of his consciousness. Then he looked down at the troubled child whom he supposed had a whole different set of fears of his own.

"Well, I ain't afraid of nothin'," the boy said smugly.

"Really?" Simon asked, surprised by the assertion. "How come?"

The boy stopped and looked up at Simon with an icy stare. "Don't you know?" he asked.

"Know what?" Simon asked.

"I'm a vampire," Little Simon answered.

Simon smiled at first, before realizing that Little Simon was dead serious. Remembering what Andy Cross had told him about the little boy biting a girl out on the playground, he no longer was amused by the notion. As he pondered the seriousness of the boy's mental condition, Little Simon returned his attention to the violent video game.

Suddenly, Simon came to a scary realization. "So, if you're the vampire, then..."

"...I don't need to be afraid of the dark," the boy said, his fingers more rapidly tapping on the buttons of the game. His face was stern, and he was visibly getting agitated by the inquisition.

"Still, aren't you at least a little bit afraid of what else might be lurking out there in the darkness?" Simon asked with slight trepidation.

The boy's answer sent chills down Simon's spine. Little Simon momentarily set the game down on his lap and looked up at Simon and coldly said, "How can I be afraid of what I am? I am the darkness. Everyone else should be afraid of *me*."

Through pursed lips Simon asked, "Are you scary?"

"Yes," he said plainly. "So scary that nobody 'll ever mess with me."

"Are you...the *devil?*" Simon ventured to ask.

"No, stupid-head," the boy answered angrily. "I already told you, I'm a *vampire!*"

Almost relieved, Simon turned his head and let out a sigh.

"But, I know'd where the devil lives," Little Simon said, eerily through gritted teeth.

Thinking he might already know the answer, Simon's voice quivered as he asked the question, "Where Simon? Where does the devil live?"

"In the old, abandoned house by the well."

"Where you hide?"

"Uh-huh."

"Aren't you afraid of him?"

"No."

"Why not?"

"Because he and me, we got a deal. He said he won't hurt me if I don't tell..."

* * *

Simon stared at Jack who was standing off by himself just outside the double doors to the front of the school smoking a cigar. When their eyes met, the shrewd businessman grinned widely and tipped his hat. Simon had been so immersed in his work that he had all but forgotten about the wily, silver fox until his unsettling conversation with Little Simon Adamson.

Jack's conspicuous absence had allowed Simon to see what life would be like without him in Bethel altogether. Because Simon hadn't seen or heard from him, it was as though he didn't even exist. Something had been keeping Jack at bay for the past forty days.

During that time, Simon could pretend that the man stirring up dissension in the community didn't have his clutches in almost every aspect of life in Bethel from the school board, to the fertilizer dealership, to the real estate market, to the boardroom of the bank, to the strip club, to unsecured loans, to government contracting. The list went on and on. Until now, Simon had supposed that Jack had lost interest in his little project or that somehow Wilson B. had somehow been keeping him preoccupied by fighting a zoning restriction battle.

But now as the large crowd pushed their way into the entryway of the school for the unveiling of the Declaration of Independence on the new wall next to the stairwell, an uneasy feeling came over Simon. Suddenly, with his presence, a dark cloud now hung over what had become the proudest day of Simon's life. He had overcome his misguided fear of failure. Against the odds, he had given up his "one thing" in order to seek God's will for his life.

Had Simon finally defeated Jack? Had he ended the curse? Could it really have been that easy? Simon smiled at the notion. Like the game of Othello, Jack had been flipping the allegiance of the people of Bethel by subjecting them to a series of bookend tragedies.

"So, why hadn't there been more resistance from Jack?" Simon thought as the smile faded away from his face. "Why hadn't there been more opposition if Jack had actually loosened his grip on Bethel?"

The word on the street was that the wealthy landowners were furious with him and the project. And yet, outward hostility was eerily almost nonexistent. Outside of a few malcontents who had protested to hanging the Declaration of Independence back up on the wall, there had not been any confrontations.

Simon was well aware of Jack's plans for the property where the new school was to be built. And now, due to the excitement surrounding the refurbished building, enough support had been generated to make the outcome almost a foregone conclusion. Hannah Grace had been right, people did come, and Simon was able to share his testimony with each and every one of them. Like a white chip on an Othello board, the project connected the people to a more innocent time and place. Long before the first debilitating tragedy, a white corner piece had been set that could never be converted into a dark one.

And now it was reconnected to the refurbished entryway. The world had been turned upside down or arguably, right side up for everyone caught in between the two bookend landmarks in history. Almost the entire board had been converted to white. Only this time it had nothing to do with something as trivial as color but with the content of one's character. People were going to show up to the voting booth in droves. So, why wasn't Jack fighting back? And why was he here now?

It didn't make any sense. Not only had they received little to no resistance from Jack, but there wasn't so much as a peep heard from the wealthy landowners who would suffer the most financially from the referendum. Had they been won over too?

Even more peculiar was the strong support given to him by the man whom Simon suspected would have been one of the biggest detractors, Dr. Al-Banna. Much to Simon's surprise, the good doctor had actually been one of the biggest advocates and financial supporters of the renovation project. In fact, Dr. Al-Banna had been such an ardent supporter that he told Simon that he would be honored for him to provide the opening remarks at the ribbon-cutting ceremony.

Now, as Simon watched Dr. Al-Banna wind his way through the throng of voters, he was once again struck by the notion that a Muslim of Egyptian descent would have such personal affinity for the Declaration of Independence. The only way Simon could make any sense of it all was to chalk it all up to divine intervention. Because if it wasn't from God, then…

When Simon looked up again, he realized that Jack had abandoned his post in front of the school. Disturbed, Simon careened his neck and scanned the crowd to find the dissenter. From behind the podium at the top of the landing, Simon surveyed all of the bright, shining faces that were beaming back at him. With the heat index well over one hundred degrees, most of them were fanning themselves with "Yes We Can" fliers that had been printed specifically for the occasion.

Simon suddenly lost his train of thought. Caught up in the moment, he was overcome by the sheer number of individuals who had sacrificed so much of their time, energy, and money to make his vision come true. When their eyes met his own, the people would often smile, nod, whistle, or pump their fist in the air. There were the Livingoods, Hannah Grace and Sharon, Pastor Pete, Andy, Miss Harold, time, and many, many others. He even spotted Joey and George standing in the very back of the crowd. Finally, his eyes fell upon the young man who gave the eulogy at Jeremy's vigil.

Parker's words came to him, *"The ultimate goal for every one of us should be to one day stand before our Lord and Savior Jesus Christ and hear the words 'Well done, good and faithful servant'."* That statement had had such a profound effect on Simon. It had completely altered his world view.

Suddenly Simon realized that he had actually done it. He had followed God's good and perfect will. He had completed the mission. The curse of Bethel had been put to rest. Now he could continue on his journey to New Jersey with a clear conscience. He had done it.

Just then, Jack snuffed out his cigar with his foot, stepped over the threshold, and made his way into the building.

Almost no one noticed as Dr. Al-Banna deftly moved behind the podium and raised his hands in the air to silence the exuberant crowd. Simon was somewhat troubled by the good doctor's opening remarks even though no one else seemed to give them a second thought.

Dr. Al-Banna bowed his head and began the invocation, "God is Most Great…."

Obediently, the people of Bethel bowed there heads and closed their eyes. As Simon followed suit, his heart grew troubled. Where had he heard those words before? Something nagged at his conscience. Just as he was about to remember where he had heard the phrase, Dr. Al-Banna concluded his prayer.

"Amen," the well-respected physician said. "It is with great pleasure that I stand here before you today." Suddenly, his cell phone buzzed. He lifted it from his belt to read the message. "Excuse me," he said to the crowd. Then set the cell phone down on the podium and said, "Sorry for the interruption. This message actually is regarding the Cain's baby girl who has taken quite ill."

There was silence.

"She has just been admitted to a children's hospital in Indianapolis for further tests," Dr. Al-Banna continued. "The family has asked me to keep everyone abreast of the situation as it unfolds."

A murmur swept through the crowd.

"Until then, they would kindly appreciate your support and prayers," the doctor added. "Now, I know that the air is quite stifling, so I will try to be brief. Be that as it may, I wanted to make one or two points before I turn things over to my good friend, Simon Freeman.

"This project has meant a great deal to me and my family," he continued. "As many of you know, the city of Bethel has been kind enough to allow the people of my faith to use this building as a place of worship until such a time as we can find a suitable site for a new mosque. And I believe it is in the spirit of religious freedom that the forefathers of this great country framed the constitution. As an aside, it would probably not surprise many of you that Thomas Jefferson himself actually had a copy of the Quran in his library.

A resounding round of applause and whistles echoed through the entryway. Simon's face soured as he tried to interpret the meaning of the unbridled enthusiasm. As the clapping finally subsided, Dr. Al-Banna continued.

"I know, I know," Dr. Al-Banna said, raising his hand to quiet the crowd," that there was some concern about the permissibility of displaying the Declaration of Independence in a public institution. I also am aware that there were a handful of dissenters who expressed their, uh, misgivings about exposing our school district to legal action. But, I am happy to say that the school board's attorney has looked into the matter and has found no precedent for any recourse for the public display of this historic document."

Jack made a mental note of it.

"Furthermore, we have made every effort to ensure that we are not offending anyone or infringing upon anyone's rights. So, once again, our attorney reached out to the NEA, the Civil Liberties Union, the Freedom from Religion Foundation, and the ACLU. And according to him, we have received their blessings, only this morning," Dr. Al-Banna exclaimed as a broad smile swept across his face.

The crowd again exploded with resounding applause.

"Which leads me as to why we are standing here today," Dr. Al-Banna continued. "Really, it is because of one young man's vision for progress, for a more sophisticated and more tolerant society. To borrow a phrase from Presidential candidate, Barrack Hussein Obama, we have hope that we can make real change in our community for future generations. Senator Obama's improbable run at the

White House, and Simon Freeman's renovation of this building have both shown us that against all odds, anything is possible."

Jack raised his hands high above his head and clapped vigorously as he looked around the room sharing smiles with the other spectators.

Simon bowed his head and blushed at the thunderous applause from the crowd as a photographer from the local paper snapped a picture. It was easy to see why the young Egyptian doctor was so well liked in Bethel. He had an unassuming, congenial way about him that made him very approachable. And yet, his clinical knowledge and expertise garnered the respect that he so richly deserved. Over the years, it had also become obvious to everyone how much the doctor cared for his patients as evidenced by his genuine concern for the Cain's sickly child.

Simon too had grown quite fond of Dr. Al-Banna, not merely because of his most generous contributions to the project, but because he had worked so tirelessly to see it through to its end. During those late nights, he and Simon had developed a mutual respect for one another. Because of that respect, they dared not broach the subject of religion. Each man was deeply committed to his beliefs. Each one was deeply spiritual in his own way. They allowed the integrity or their actions and the manner of their speech to bear witness to their strong convictions.

Whether it was their suffering for a common cause or merely the sheer length of time that they had spent in one another's company, each one only took part in discussions that touched the fringes of their beliefs. They consciously did their best to only focus on areas of common ground between the two great world religions.

As Simon listened to his friend giving the introduction, he wondered why it couldn't be like that with everyone. Proudly, Simon considered the maturity of such a relationship as a beacon of hope for the rest of society. They had been the epitome of coexisting peacefully.

Jack recognized the good doctor's efforts to choose his words carefully so as to not offend anyone, and he smiled approvingly.

"Yes," Dr. Al-Banna said to resounding cheers. "One young man's vision inspired others to action, and in the process, not only changed a building but forever changed a community."

Simon looked about the room at all of the bright, shining faces who returned expressions of admiration and approval. Those whom he had counseled such as Sharon and Hannah Grace. Those whom he had received counseling from such as Pastor Pete and Miss Malone. Those who gave of their time and offered their skills such as time. And those who worked silently behind the scenes such as the Livingoods. And dozens and dozens of others who gave sacrificially of themselves. All because of the work he had begun.

"He alone, in the face of stern opposition, knew that education would be vital to shaping and molding the next generation to come. As a result, he has given the young people of Bethel an opportunity to gain greater knowledge in order that they may open their minds and more freely accept those who might look different or sound different from themselves. From the time I started working on this project, Simon has been the model of acceptance and great compromise.

"We know that peace will not come about without tolerance and tolerance will not come about apart from education. So, tomorrow is not just a referendum on a new building, it is also a referendum on a new society, one befitting of a new America. We are talking about a *New World Order* here. By voting in favor of the new school, you will be all but guaranteeing that this document of antiquity hanging behind this curtain will be the lever by which future generations can transform this country into what we would want it to be. Thereby, opening the door for a stronger, bolder, more progressive generation to enter into. Just as Presidential hopeful Barrack Obama has said, it is the 'Change We Need.'

Just as the crowd broke into a frenzy, Simon couldn't help but feel his chest swell with pride. Too caught up in the moment for Dr. Al-Banna's words to fully sink in, Simon basked in the glow of the flattering accolades. As he basked in the adulation, Jack moved in closer, completely undetected.

"Simon, my friend, will you be so kind, uh, to say a few words," Dr. Al-Banna said, leaning into the microphone as he wildly clapped. "Please, please…" he said gesturing for the crowd to quiet down again.

Simon broadly grinned, and with quasi-reluctance, slid behind the podium. Taking the microphone awkwardly in his hands, he leaned forward, cleared his throat, and began to speak. The flowery words poured out of his mouth and dripped like honey off of his tongue. Like some strange out of body experience, they echoed through the chambers of his mind before falling on a numbed conscience.

Even if Simon hadn't heard his own words, there were others in the audience who had taken great interest. Jack for one found immense pleasure listening to the long monologue that was mired in a deluge of "I's", "My's", and "Me's." Finally, drawing his ingratiating speech to a close, Simon pulled the rope that drew open the curtain revealing the shiny, bronze monument of the Declaration of Independence.

Simon raised his arms high above his head and dramatically pumped his fists in the air. Never having considered it before, Jack began to entertain the notion of a future in politics for the young Freeman and made a mental note of that too.

The rest of the ceremony was a blur, as a parade of well-wishers made their way down the long procession to express their gratitude to Simon. He was more than happy to accommodate each and every one of them. Jack also took note of how Simon had a knack for making each person feel like they were the only person in the room. Time and again Simon would grab the back of the person's elbow and pull them in closer to say something in their ear. Then they would pull back and share a laugh.

Jack couldn't resist comparisons to one of his other protégé's from Arkansas who had made a considerable career for himself in politics. Often the exchange was wrought with hyperbole along the lines of, "Thank you for bringing us all together," or "You have saved the day". One individual had the audacity to suggest that Simon had, "...Breathed life back into the community."

As Simon would soon find out, they were all too kind. Through the throng of supporters, Simon did catch a quick glimpse of Jack standing on the staircase. He was leaning against the blank wall opposite the shiny plaque with his arms folded. His countenance bore a very proud expression.

Just then, Wilson B, Angie, and Ralph Livingood happened to make their way to where Simon was standing at the podium. Forgetting himself, Simon spontaneously took Wilson B's right hand into both of his own and wildly shook it. Without thinking, Simon profusely thanked him for his generous support. Wilson B. nervously looked about the room as he quickly withdrew his hand, but it was too late. Jack had seen it all and understood the implication.

Simon had only taken his eye off of Jack for a second, and he was gone again. In all of the commotion, he had lost sight of the shadowy figure. Desperately, Simon scanned the room, searching the crowd. From out of nowhere, the shrewd, old codger saddled up next to Simon and whispered in his ear.

"Oh, hey, there you are, Jack," Simon awkwardly sputtered.

"Ha!" Jack said putting his arm around Simon's shoulder. "You did it my boy. You did it. Ha! Wilson, did you ever think you'd see the day when a land tax would pass in Bethel of all places?"

"No, no, I didn't Jack," Wilson B. said, as he placed his hands on his son's shoulders in an effort to start guiding him through the crowd towards the exit.

"Miraculous!" Jack said to Wilson B. over the noisy crowd.

"How's that?" Wilson B. asked, leaning towards Jack.

"I say, it's miraculous how Simon, here, was somehow able to fund this little endeavor," Jack said loudly with a great number of people within earshot. "It must have cost a small fortune."

"Oh, yes," Wilson B. said. "I'm really sorry, but we should really be going. I've got a...I've got this...anyway, we'll see you later."

"All right, you folks have a nice evening," Jack said. Then he turned back to Simon. "Well done, my boy! Well done! There's nothing I like better than seeing people put aside their differences and rallying for a cause. Ha!" Jack said, pointing at the shiny monument on the wall. "And it takes a special person to ignite the flames of passion by scratching the pride of the common man. I knew there was something special about you, my dear boy.

"I don't know what 'it' is, but whatever 'it' is, you have 'it'. You have that kind of cult of personality that brings people together. It's that kinda mindless, unbridled fervor for conformity that will one day bring about world peace- or how did doc put it? Somethin' about new global...or globalism; oh yeah, it was a New World Order. The sky's the limit. Gives me goose-bumps just thinkin' about it. Ya know, I've got a soft spot in my heart for community organizers!"

Then Jack suddenly changed to a grave expression. He grabbed Simon by the forearm and patted him on the back. "Shame," Jack intimated, whispering into Simon's ear. "Another time, another place. Maybe under different circumstances. Who knows, we could have done great things together. Right now, they all believe in *you*."

Simon relinquished an awkward grin as he tried to figure out what Jack was trying to tell him.

"Ha! Well, any hoo," the old man said aloud, "I best be on my way. Enjoy tonight, Simon, because you never know what tomorrow may bring."

Before Simon could respond, another wave of people completely enveloped him. Distracted, he looked on as Jack made his way around the outskirts of the crowd to the opposite side of the landing where Tony stood leaning against the wall. Simon could see the two of them talking but couldn't make out what they were saying. Jack handed something to Tony, shook his hand, and descended the steps towards the basement.

A few hours later, it was all over. Simon was finally left standing alone behind the podium at the top of the stairs guzzling a bottle of water, as the last of the multitude made their way out the front door into the steamy, dusk air. Misty-eyed, Simon was overwhelmed by all that had taken place. For the first time, he was able to take in the finished product in its entirety. The renovation was finally finished, and it was utterly beautiful.

"Purdy, ain't it?" Tony said, from the base of the stairs behind Simon.

"Oh, hey, Tony, yeah, it turned out all right," Simon replied, turning away for a moment and inadvertently wiping the moisture from his eyes. "Big night, huh? The heat certainly didn't keep the crowd away."

"No sir," time agreed, wiping the sweat off of his forehead with a do-rag as he made his way up the stairs to meet Simon on the landing.

"There were times when I didn't think there was any way we were going to get it done before the referendum," Simon said proudly. "But, we did it"

"Well, sir, as my daddy used to always say, 'folks 'll work for a goal, but they'll die for a cause'," time casually replied.

"'A cause'...?" Simon repeated with a puzzled expression as he recalled Jack's comments.

"Ya know, a cause, a project, somethin' to get behind, make em' feel good about themselves," time said, struggling to clearly define it. "And now this un's done, folks'll go on to the next thing like cleaning up Hazel park or the annual bike-a-thon for multiple sclerosis...or like raisin' money for the Cain family with the little street fair they got set up for tomorrow here in front of the school."

"Yeah, those are all great causes," Simon said, looking around the room. "But, this isn't the same thing."

"How do ya mean?" Tony asked, leaning back, lifting his chins, and narrowing his eyes.

"I mean, yes, the project is done, but its impact on the community will have a lasting effect," Simon said, starting once again to doubt himself. "I mean, the new building will make a difference, right?"

Tony stared back and said, "Fraid I ain't follow'n ya."

"Well, maybe it won't exactly change *everything*, but you heard Dr. Al-Banna tonight," Simon replied. "It's the start of something, not the end of it. You heard the applause. This wasn't just some kind of 'feel-good' moment. This was real change, right? I think people now are going to get more involved with-with-with their church, with the community, with politics…with education."

"Uh-huh," Tony said skeptically.

"…With church…" Simon said emphatically.

"Ya already said that one," Tony snorted.

"Well, don't you think so?" Simon asked, almost pleading for some kind of affirmation. But, none was forthcoming.

Tony was distracted as he looked out of the corner of his eyes towards the front door. Then he twitched his head several times in that direction.

"Huh? What? What are you?…" Simon said, before picking up on time's intentional signal. When Simon finally looked in the direction of the front doors, he saw the most beautiful thing he had ever laid eyes on. He saw Hope. "Oh," he said under his breath.

"Hi there," she said, holding her purse with both hands in front of her and nervously twisting from side to side. Then she reached up delicately and swiped her silky, blond bangs out of her eyes.

"Hey there," Simon replied dumbly with a ridiculous wave.

"Am I interrupting something?" she asked sweetly, "because, I could come back later," she added pointing over her shoulder to the front door.

"No, no," Simon said mindlessly, distracted by Hope's summer dress and glistening, tan skin. "I-I didn't know you were…I mean, I didn't see you…"

"I think it's even more spectacular than they had said," Hope uttered in amazement, looking around the room. "The pictures on Facebook don't do it justice. It's more beautiful than I even imagined."

Without taking his eyes off of her, Simon replied, "Yes, it is."

He stood still for a moment in silence under the giant chandelier watching Hope gracefully move towards the bronze monument and run her delicate fingers over the smooth surface. If there were any question as to whether he had completely gotten her out of his system, they were undeniably refuted.

After an awkward pause, Tony looked at Hope and then back at Simon who was standing there with a stupid grin on his face. The handyman stopped working his chaw for a moment and said, "Boy, would ya look at that, nine o'clock. It's gettin' late."

Still, neither Simon nor Hope acknowledged the bystander's observation. Then Simon turned towards Tony and stared purposeful daggers.

"What? Oh, yeah, well, anyways," Tony said through a mouth full of chaw.

"Everything's a go for tammarra'. 'Member, Ray from the city's bring'n them votin' booths over first thing in the morn'n. I'll meet ya here round six," he said as he started to lumber his way down the stairs.

"What? Yeah-yeah, okay, got it," Simon said distractedly, turning his attention back to Hope.

"Oh, hey, nearly forgot to give you this," Tony said, snapping his fat fingers. He reached into his front pocket, pulled out an envelope, and handed it to Simon who mindlessly took it from him and shoved it into the front pocket of his tan cargo shorts

"Ma'am," Tony said, donning his mesh John Deer hat as he passed by Hope who was making her way up the stairs in the opposite direction,

"Hello," Hope said with a warm smile.

"Well, I'm go'n now," the stout handyman called out to the couple who now stood in scandalously close proximity to one another under the chandelier. He stopped with one hand on the door. "Okay then, I'm gone," he said turning back one more time.

Still, no response.

"Ahh, forget it," he muttered with a wave of his hand before heading outside.

29

A LIFE NOT OUR OWN

Simon and Hope stood facing one another in uncomfortable silence before Simon asked, "Were you here for the ceremony? I didn't see you in the crowd."

"No," Hope answered, the light sparkling in her soft, blue eyes, "I tried to get here on time. I really wanted to be here for it."

"You did?" Simon asked.

"Well, yeah, of course," Hope replied coyly before nervously looking down at the expanse between them. "You know, between getting the girls off with their parents, and packing, and fighting traffic...not to mention I dropped my cell phone and smashed it to smithereens at a truck stop," she added, failing to mention how long it took to pick out the right outfit and fix her hair.

"Good, I'm glad," Simon started to say. "I mean, I'm not glad it took so long... or that you smashed your cell phone. I mean, I'm glad that you wanted to be here." His heart was pounding in his chest. Once again, he could sense that intense, undeniable chemistry between them. It was just as strong as before. And even though they had been texting more and more frequently as of late, he knew that eventually they would have to deal with what had happened in the past before they could ever move on to the future. For the time being, Simon simply wanted to bask in her presence. Desperate to linger a little longer in the moment, he opted for small talk instead.

"Well, what do you think?" Simon asked.

"About the school?" Hope replied.

"Yeah," Simon said, pretending not to notice the inference.

"I thought you may have been asking about...," Hope said clumsily, "...it's nice."

"Just nice?" Simon said with a grin.

"Well, you know; nice and old," she said, playfully teasing him.

"'Nice and old'," Simon repeated, recognizing her dry sense of humor. "Oh, I see, having a little fun at my expense."

Hope's beaming face and playful disposition infused a boost of confidence that

545

at once put him at ease and diffused any tension that may have existed between them.

"Well, that was kind of the idea, right?" Simon said, energized by Hope's flirtatious banter. "We wanted to let people see that this *old* building at one time was pretty *nice* I think it may have actually worked. You should see the look on peoples' faces when they walk through the front doors for the first time. It's almost like they are stepping back in time. We wanted the younger generation to have an appreciation for what things were like in the old days, and the older generation to remember how things used to be. Judging by their reactions, I think we accomplished our goal. Some of the old-timers actually breakdown and weep when they see it because for the first time they really begin to realize how far things have slipped into decay."

"Really?" Hope asked, moved by the notion.

"Yeah," Simon replied, "I know it sounds strange, but they say they are just so overcome by memories of a simpler time and place. I mean the entryway looks *identical* to how it was in 1935," Simon said, unable to contain his excitement. "People brought in tons of old pictures for us to use as references to make sure we were getting it exactly right. Would you like to see some of them?"

Simon grabbed a few tattered photos off of a shelf beneath the podium and handed them over to her. When he did so, he noticed Dr. Al-Banna's pager.

"Huh, Doc will be looking for this," Simon said, lifting up the pager to show Hope.

"Oh, yeah, I would think so," Hope replied, as she took the pictures out of Simon's hands.

"I'll make sure that I get it back to him first thing in the morning," Simon said putting the pager in the front pocket of his shorts.

Suddenly, a bolt of lightening flashed all about the room followed by a low rumble.

"Whoa, that was close!" Simon said, leaning down to look out the windows of the front doors to the school. "Don't tell me it is finally going to rain. I didn't see anything about it in the forecast."

"I think it's heat lightening, actually," Hope replied, stepping closer. "The wind seems to be coming out of the East, so it doesn't look as though the farmers will get the rain that they desperately need tonight."

"Unbelievable, isn't it?" Simon said. "It has been one hot, dry summer."

"It certainly is hot in here that's for sure; like a sauna," Hope said, thumbing through the pictures and blowing her bangs out of her eyes. "Sticky, you know, almost like there's no air moving at all."

"Yeah, I can't believe the school district never installed air conditioning," Simon replied. Nervously, he quickly added, "I'm sure you've heard by now, but it's been forty days since the last drop of rain fell." He was still doing his best to keep the conversation light. "I, uh, listen to a lot of talk radio while I'm working...so, I hear the weather report about every fifteen minutes in between Ravi Zacharias, Bryan

Fischer, Robert Jeffress, Sandy Rios, Crane Durham, Tony Evans, Chuck Swindoll, David Jeremiah, Jay Sekulow, Jack Graham, Tim Wildmon, Alex McFarland, Bert Harper, Tony Perkins, R.C. Sproul, Mark Levin, Michael Savage, um, you know,… people like that." He secretly chastised himself for sounding like a total moron.

"Hmm," Hope replied as she held up a picture and compared it to the room.

Simon nervously put his hands in his pockets and breathlessly watched her for a moment. She was so beautiful standing in the light of the chandelier that everything else seemed utterly meaningless.

"I thought you said that you weren't very handy with tools," Hope said, impressed by the craftsmanship.

"Believe it or not, only a month ago I barely knew what end of the hammer to hold," Simon said humbly, "but I've learned a lot working with all of the volunteers and looking up things on the internet. We just trying things out, you know. There's a lot of trial and error. Put it together. Get it all wrong. Tear it apart. Do it over again the right way."

"Well, I would say you had a natural gift for it," Hope said, admiringly.

"Thanks," Simon replied, "hey, I have an idea," he said, clapping his hands together with great exuberance and slowly backing away. "Why don't you use those pictures as a point of reference, and I will give you a virtual grand tour of what all we have done."

Hope nodded in agreement with a warm smile.

"Yeah?" Simon asked. "Okay. Let's start over here," he said pointing towards the nearest wall. "Take these paintings of Washington and Lincoln for instance," he said excitedly moving up the stairs towards the landing, "one of those old photographs revealed these paintings; which everyone had somehow managed to forget about. You can see them in the background of…yeah, that one. We looked and looked all over the internet, but couldn't find anything, anywhere like them. So, M.J. Meneley… Do you know M.J.? …Of course you do, it's Bethel right, everybody knows everybody. What was I thinking? Silly question. So anyway, the guy's an amazing artist. He created these replicas. Nice, huh?"

Hope nodded, mirroring his enthusiasm.

"Oh, and the tin ceiling, it was here the whole time, hidden underneath the nasty nineteen-seventies drop ceiling panels," he continued. "You can barely see it in each of the photographs. Like here and here…

"It's beautiful," Hope said lifting her eyes upward.

"… And, oh yeah, the staircase," Simon continued. "We had to start over from scratch on these puppies. Tony and I completely ripped out the fabricated, industrial stuff and actually made brand new stairs of solid oak. That was a very involved process, to say the least. And you saw the bronze monument, of course."

"Of course," Hope replied still smiling.

"Let's see," Simon said, looking around. "What else? Oh yeah, how could I forget? The best, the best of all was the…"

"...The chandelier," Hope said standing now directly beneath it and gazing up towards the light.

Simon stood watching her while she basked in the warm glow of the light, and his heart skipped a beat. "Listen to me," he said, embarrassed, "I'm rambling on like a complete idiot."

"No, I think it's cute," Hope started to say as her expression became somber. "But,..."

"But, what?" Simon asked, suddenly preoccupied by the word "cute" as it reverberated in his ear.

"No, it's nothing," Hope said handing back the pictures. "This is great. It's amazing, really. It's beautiful, just beautiful. You've done an amazing job."

"...But..., you said but," Simon said, still smiling. "What is it? Did we forget something?"

"No, no," Hope said. "It's nothing like that."

"Then what is it?" Simon asked.

"Well, there's no question that you completely changed all of the external appearances," Hope said, "but what lies beneath the surface? Did you actually make any structural or foundational changes as well?"

Simon stared at her blankly. "Not really, I mean, the foundation and framework are still strong for the most part. Except, of course, for this sagging wall. A carpenter had to show me how to fix it."

"A carpenter? Really?" Hope replied. "What was his name? Maybe I know him."

"I am...I am...I am not sure," Simon answered.

"Huh, well, I guess what I am asking is," Hope said, still circling the real issue at hand, "aside from all of these improvements that can be seen on the surface, is there more to it? Did you accomplish whatever it was you had set out to accomplish'?"

"Oh," Simon said, still doing his best to avoid the heart of the issue, "well, I guess so, to answer your question. Like I said, it looks like the renovation achieved its ultimate purpose. When people see how beautiful the building once was, they realize how important the school used to be to the community, how much of a priority people used to place on education. Then we ask them to consider voting in favor of the new school.

"And, well, I don't want to be premature, but based on a little straw poll we conducted, it appears as though the referendum is going to pass tomorrow. So, it looks like sometime in the not-so-distant future you will be starting the school year in a brand new, state of the art facility *with* central air."

This time Simon's enthusiasm was not met with the same degree of excitement. "I did hear that, and that's great," Hope said carefully choosing her words. "I don't mean to take anything away from what you have accomplished here. It is very impressive, it really is. But..." Suddenly, she stopped short.

"...There's that 'but' again..." Simon said.

"No," she said reluctantly, looking down and nervously fidgeting with her fingers. "This is your night. Maybe I should just keep my big mouth shut for once. I really didn't *want* to get into all of this tonight."

Simon walked over, leaned down, and turned his head to the side in an effort to make eye contact. "No, really, I want to hear what you have to say," he said with great sincerity. "I value your opinion. I want to know what you really think. Now what were you were about to say?"

Hope looked up at him with her soft, blue eyes, contemplating. She took note of his broad shoulders and sinewy arms, a testament to the hard labor he had undertaken. Simon had definitely changed since she had last seen him. Now it was time to find out to what degree. "Okay," she said after a moment of deliberation. "One of the questions that I keep asking myself is whether fixing up the old school or building a new one will make any difference either way? Are all of these changes you've made just superficial or is there any real substance to them?"

"Wow, you don't pull any punches do you?" Simon asked, desperately to keep the conversation topical.

"I'm sorry, but I don't think there is time for 'pulling any punches'," Hope said soberly. "In a couple of days, I will be starting a new school year- and you- you will be heading off to start a new life in New Jersey. The urgency of the situation doesn't leave us much time for the usual niceties."

She paused for a moment as if gauging the expression on his face. Simon had been so caught up in renovating the school that he had all but forgotten about his uncle, the promise of a lucrative sales position, and the fact that the summer was coming to an end. A knot began to tighten in his stomach because he knew what she was saying was true. Soon he would have to make some serious decisions about his future.

"I just want to be completely open and honest with you," Hope continued to say. "I want *us* to be able to be completely honest with each other about… everything. No regrets. You know?"

"I would like that," Simon replied, hanging on her every word.

"That's good, I'm glad," she answered. "So, back to my original question. What is it that has really changed here? Do you still feel like you were *called* to complete the renovation?"

There was the topic he had been hoping to avoid. With only slight hesitation Simon answered, "There's no doubt in my mind." All of a sudden, he was painfully aware of the direction that the conversation was heading. Even though it was necessary, he knew that it wasn't going to be pleasant.

"How do you know?" Hope asked.

"It's kind of hard to explain," Simon replied, failing to mention anything about the curse for fear of sounding like a kook again. "It's just a feeling I get. I just *know*. You know? I mean have you ever felt so compelled to do something that defied logic, and yet, at the same time couldn't explain why?"

For the time being, Hope chose to avoid the parallels between Simon's question and the reason for her being there. Instead, she zeroed in on the true motives of his heart, "So, you *know* that you were called to do it, but do you still think you know the reason *why* God called you to do it?" Hope asked.

"I guess that it was to get people interested in education for future generations or something along those lines, maybe," Simon answered, guardedly.

"So, it's no longer about ending a curse then?" Hope asked, being brutally direct.

Simon cringed. "Yeah, I mean, I guess so," he admitted, overcome with embarrassment by the wild assertions he had made to her while sitting on the dock more than a month ago. "I mean, of course, I now know that I wasn't seeing ghosts or anything crazy like that. Pretty much anything that I thought confirmed the legend of Jessie Joseph actually had a rational explanation," he finished with a forced laugh.

"But, that night you came to see me, you were so sure about…everything," Hope said with a pained expression. "What made you change your mind?"

Simon thought about his darkest hour, the night at the cemetery when he had dug up Jessie Joseph's coffin only to find his old, decayed remains still inside. He started to tell her about the night he hit rock bottom before being overcome with foolish pride. "It was…It was probably when I realized that what I had thought was Adam Potter's ghost actually turned out to be a strange little boy who was just too scared to go home."

Hope frowned and stared at him with a look of deep concern. Simon could sense her deep dissatisfaction with his answer, and he could see the wheels turning in her head. Clumsily, he made a halfhearted attempt to salvage some dignity.

"I *am* still convinced that I was supposed to complete the renovation," he admitted. "There's no doubt in my mind about that, and anyone can see the results for themselves." After looking around the room, he continued, "It may not have been what I thought it was, you know, some kind of supernatural phenomenon or something. I mean something 'real' happened here; something tangible.

"I wish you could have seen how the people responded. The volunteers were so excited to be a part of something positive after Jeremy's murder and the lingering investigation. There was such a great…energy, you know? You could feel it in the air. It was almost palpable.

"I don't know. Maybe the whole idea wasn't about a curse. Maybe it was about unifying the people or something. Maybe it was giving them a cause to rally around. And maybe that is why God put it on my heart to do it," Simon finished, in an effort to make everything sound more palatable.

Hope pensively chewed on her bottom lip as she tried to process his words.

Wrongly surmising that his previous, extraordinary claims had lessoned her opinion of him, Simon attempted to reassure her. "As far as Jessie Joseph and all that other stuff, I'll just have to plead temporary insanity I guess. I made the fatal mistake of analyzing the evidence with a preconceived conclusion in mind. When I came to see you that night at camp after pouring through the archives at the library, I hadn't had much sleep. I hadn't eaten. It wasn't that long after Jeremy's funeral, and all of those articles about all of the tragedies just seemed to confirm everything that I had suspected.

By now, Simon felt foolish. Any false bravado generated by Dr. Al-Banna's speech was now being dissolved in a boiling cauldron of humility. Completely vanquished, he paused as if waiting for Hope to show him a little mercy.

After a moment, Hope did speak, but her response surprised him to say the least. "You can be so frustrating!" she insisted. "Do you know that? I thought you said you wanted us to be perfectly honest? Don't just tell me what you think I want to hear!

"It wasn't the presence of the supernatural that I found so troubling when you first told me about all of this, as much as it is the absence of it now," Hope replied. "When you told me how you felt that night, I could hear the conviction in your voice, and I could see the sincerity written all over your face. I believed you, because I believe the Holy Spirit does compel us to do God's will. But, if you are now telling me that this project is all about some sort of warm and fuzzy, feel-good thing to bring the community together for a little while, then I think it is safe to say that God wasn't in it at all," Hope said unapologetically.

"So, let me get this straight," Simon replied, completely caught off guard by her observation. "You are willing to accept that I was called to do all of this to end a curse, but you are not willing to accept that I might have been called to do it in order to bring the community together? Is bringing the community together such a bad thing?"

"It all depends, I guess," Hope answered.

"On what?" Simon asked, starting to get a little defensive.

"On *why* they are coming together," Hope answered thoughtfully. She could tell by the look on Simon's face that they weren't quite seeing eye to eye. "Let me explain," she continued, "I think that the motivation and intent for doing a particular task is just as important as the task itself. Even more so, actually, because it reveals a person's heart. If this were all about self-promotion, or proving something, or feeling good, or a power grab, or...winning over a girl, then it has nothing to do with God. It's pretty much all about you at that point. And if that's the case, then maybe it's just a convenient cover to say something like 'God made me do it'."

At that moment, Simon remembered his revelation about why Hope had gotten so angry with him when he admitted to having a desire to be with Jez on that fateful night on Potter's property. The act would have only been an expression of the true desires of his heart. Just because he wasn't able to carry out the act doesn't mean he wasn't guilty.

Simon could see that it didn't matter if the act of renovating the school was considered a worthy cause. To Hope it was a matter of the heart. The fact that the task was a good thing only made it all the more difficult for Hope to decipher his true intentions. Was it about pride or servanthood? Self-indulgence or obedience?

Hope could see the light in Simon's eyes. "I can't read your heart," she said, "but if God isn't the source of your motivation for doing all of this, then you would be no more than some sort of community organizer with a gift for rallying people and inciting them to action. The history books are full of megalomaniacs with that kind of a gift who in the end only brought about pain and suffering to the world because deep down they only wanted power, wealth, fame, and pleasure. So, 'yes', knowing why you did this makes all the difference in the world to me."

Simon didn't know how to respond. Clearly, he understood what she was saying. The realization left him feeling bewildered and utterly deflated, because it left him second guessing whether it was all about himself after all.

"On the other hand," Hope said, softening a little when she realized that she finally might be getting past Simon's politically correct answers to the real heart of issue, "if God is truly in this, and I would believe you if told me that He is, then He is doing something far greater than running a self-help seminar or feel-good rally.

"That's why I came here tonight. I wanted to find out for myself if your intentions were pure because I need to know. Which is it, Simon? When you say that God is calling you to do this, is it God's voice or is it your own?"

The question hung heavy in the humid air.

"How would I know for sure?" Simon asked with anguish when faced with a question that he had struggled with for so long. Only now was he beginning to understand the significance of his answer. Hope wasn't merely referring to the changes that had taken place in the school. She wanted to know about the changes that may have taken place in him. Was his repentance genuine? Had he really been seeking God?

"Well, I think it is safe to say that we will eventually know by the fruit it produces," Hope said, encouragingly. "We know that all things work for the good of the believer. We'll know in time, because a good tree can only produce good fruit. A bad tree can only produce bad fruit. We'll know because in the end if it truly is the Holy Spirit at work then the renovation will further God's Kingdom in some way."

Simon recognized the reference to Jesus' Sermon on the Mount and smiled, but then he became sullen and asked, "And what if it doesn't produce 'good fruit'?"

"Then it'll just be a nice building, and everybody will go on with their lives just as they had before in search of the next thing to try and fill that empty void in their lives," Hope answered, glumly. "There will be no real change. Because that's how the devil works. He's always keeping people temporarily satisfied, and eternally dissatisfied, searching for that next short-lived feeling of self-worth and wholeness."

Simon recalled what time had said earlier about people going on to the next cause, and he shuddered. His mind raced. Try as he might, he still could not come up with of a single solitary reason for how fixing up an old school would further God's Kingdom. Desperately, he asked, "Okay, but what about in the short term. Is there any more immediate way to tell whether or not it was truly God's will?"

"Possibly," Hope said. "I would expect if the project were truly from God then there would be opposition of some kind. Nothing causes more objection from unbelievers than doing something in the name of Jesus Christ. Was anyone upset or offended by what you were doing?"

"Yes," he answered, prematurely. Then he quickly recanted, "Well…at first there was some opposition, but then it…" His countenance fell as he reflected back for the first time on the series of events that had transpired since committing to the project.

"Then it what?" Hope asked.

"It just kind of died off," Simon answered, unable to identify the reason.

"Really?" Hope asked. "When?"

Simon didn't know if he could accept that he had once again drifted away from God's perfect will. Now he was forced to more closely examine what had taken place over the past month. And he did not like what became immediately apparent to him. When Simon spoke of the early, mild opposition, he was primarily thinking of people like Rich, Andy, Pete, some of the farmers, and Jack, of course, who either dismissed his personal experience, or the project, or both.

In the beginning, Simon had set aside time every day to be in the word. To study it. To know it. That was how he was able to recognize Hope's reference to the Sermon on the Mount. Moreover, he had spent a great deal of time in prayer, communing with God. He had even been able to share his testimony with others.

Then something happened after that without Simon even realizing. It was such a slow, incremental shift. The more he had become preoccupied with the project itself, the less time he had spent in the word, the less time he had to commune with God in prayer, and the less he had to share his testimony with others. Now, in retrospect, it seemed that the more he busied himself with the task at hand the less he had relied on God, and the more he had relied on himself and the charity of others like Dr. Al-Banna.

Under the guise of respect for the good doctor and his family, Simon had purposely stopped vocalizing his beliefs and had even turned off the programs from American Family Radio. Now Simon had to consider the question, "Was it merely a coincidence that opposition faded as his focus on Jesus faded?". Simon was awestruck. He blinked a couple of times, and then looked at Hope as if she was only now coming into focus.

Hope recognized the moment of awakening for what it was and said, "I don't blame some of the farmers for being up in arms over it. After all, they're the ones who'd have to pay the discretionary tax."

"True," Simon mumbled, never having considered it from their point of view. He had been so busy trying to fight for what he believed in that he hadn't ever bothered to consider if the increase in taxes for a select few might be unfair. He could hardly believe it, but sometime during the last couple of weeks, the project had grotesquely morphed from fulfilling God's will into simply winning a vote. Simon had somehow allowed himself to be duped. He had gotten completely off track from his original, pure intentions.

Winning the referendum had become his "one thing" rather than doing what was right in God's eyes. Jack must have been so happy with him. In the process, the shrewd businessman managed to divide the entire town by their socioeconomic status rather than by their spiritual beliefs as it pertained to the importance of education, wisdom, and understanding.

"Some of the farmers objected, but I would hardly call it a protest," he admitted.

"What about Dr. Al-Banna?" Hope asked. "Did he offer any objections to what you were doing?"

"No, in fact, he became one of the biggest supporters," Simon confessed.

"And nothing from Jack Lawless?" Hope asked, finally getting through to the man she had spoken with on the dock at the lake.

"Not a word," Simon answered with a grave expression as he began to realize the implication. His bubble had burst. How could he have been so blind and foolish? What had he really accomplished if he had failed to complete the work that God had begun in him?

Hope could see that the wind had been completely taken out of his sails. She had come with the intention of leaning on him, testing his metal, trying to find out what he was made of. With the clock ticking, she felt that she had no other choice. There were some things that had to be said. Now, looking into his sullen eyes, she saw a genuine humility befitting the circumstances. That look, as much as anything, told her what she needed to know.

Feeling like Simon was now able to hear what she had come to say, Hope sought to comfort him by extending an olive branch. Intently, she took him by the hand. When she did, she noted the fresh blisters and rough calluses of his palms from hours and hours of manual labor. "I didn't come here to pass judgment on you," she said, "and I did not come here to simply throw stones. God knows, I am not perfect either. It is very easy to get off track and forget why it is you are doing what you are doing. It's like we somehow get lulled to sleep. Believe me, I know."

"Yeah right," Simon said. "I don't see any holes in your swing."

"Any what?" Hope said with an encouraging smile.

"It's a baseball term," Simon said. "Having 'no holes' is analogous to having a perfect swing."

"No, no, no," Hope said, dropping her head and withdrawing her hand. "I'm afraid I have as many 'holes in my swing' as the next person; maybe more."

"Oh, really?" Simon asked. "Somehow I find that hard to believe."

She took a deep sigh before continuing, "Well, do you remember when I told you about a meeting the teachers had just before school dismissed for the summer?

I never told you what it was about. The teachers were actually taking a vote to determine which students would be moving on to the next grade level."

"You mean like choosing which kids pass and which kids fail kinda' thing?" Simon asked, genuinely surprised.

"Yes, that's exactly what I mean," Hope admitted. "Evidently our failure rate was too high, and if we didn't get it under a certain percentage then we could lose our federal funding. So, some of the teachers suggested that we take a vote to decide which kids got held back and which ones moved on in order to lower the percentage of failures. We arbitrarily picked winners and losers."

"But let me take a wild guess, *you* didn't vote, did you?" Simon asked, presumptuously.

"No, I chose not to," Hope replied with tears unexpectedly welling up in her eyes.

"I didn't think so," Simon said, as though his point had been made for him.

"But, that's just it," Hope adamantly replied. "I didn't *do* anything. I passively sat by and let it all happen. In doing so, I became complicit to the act. There's no honor in that. I was afraid to actually stand up for what I believed in because I was afraid of recourse. I ran away for the summer and hid, like Peter, hoping no one would find out what we had done. But, you can't run from God."

Simon tried to downplay the incident. "From what I heard, it sounded like it wouldn't have made any difference anyway," he said.

Hope frowned and bristled, recognizing the danger of his offering up an excuse. "That may be true," she replied sternly, "but sometimes you have to stand up for what you believe in regardless of the outcome, and that should have been one of those times for me. It was too important. Don't you see the damage that was done by abstaining? Now no one knows where I stand on the issue."

"In a couple of days, when the students come to school for the first time and look around the room, they will realize that the homework, the tests, the projects, and the grades from the previous year didn't really matter, regardless of what they may have been told. I can tell you this much, the kids may not have learned the material, but they will have *learned* something when all is said and done. They will have learned that there is no direct relationship between doing the work, mastering the material, or behaving in class, and moving on to the next grade level. That there's no correlation between choices and consequences. They will have learned that there is no accountability. And you know what, they will be right. The vote was arbitrary. It was not founded on any rules, or regulations, or precedents.

"The only certainty was that if they just behave badly enough like the Simon Adamsons of this world, then they are guaranteed to be passed on to the next grade level!"

Simon immediately recalled his own experiences with the horribly behaved child. He glanced down at the bite mark on his arm before he asked, "But, why would the worst behaved kids be the first to get a free pass?"

"Because the teachers simply cannot take another year of having that kid in their classroom," Hope replied.

"Forgive me for asking, but why don't the teachers just *make* the kids behave?" Simon naively asked.

"You haven't taught in the classroom before, have you?" Hope asked. "It's not that the teachers don't try to make them follow the rules. In fact, we spend an inordinate amount of time just trying to figure out new ways to get the students to follow the rules and do their homework."

"Then what's the problem?" Simon asked.

"Well, one of the biggest problems is that there is no real authority behind the rules," Hope said, looking forlornly at the newly hung monument on the wall.

"Really?" Simon asked, "man, I remember when I went to school here everybody was scared to death of getting paddled by old Miss Harold. Anytime I even thought about breaking the rules, the mere threat of getting whacked by that thing kept me in line."

"That's just it," Hope lamented, "these days, that's all that it is. It's just an idle threat. And the students know it. Sure, teachers try to put on a good front by writing names on the board, or pulling sticks, or sending notes home to the parents, or keeping a discipline log. But, it's all theater at the end of the day. There's no real teeth to any of the rules."

"Why not?" Simon replied. "What happened? Didn't there used to be?"

"I think it comes down to the teachers and administrators being afraid of being dragged into some kind of frivolous lawsuit," Hope honestly answered. "You know, it wasn't long ago that teachers were in control of the classroom because they had the full support of the administration and the parents. If a student got in trouble, they got it twice as bad once they got home, but something happened along the way. Nowadays, it is much more likely that the parent comes to the defense of the child first and questions the authority.

"I have no idea when it all changed, but what ends up happening is that the teachers just kick the can down the road and pass students who don't deserve it."

"So, is that pretty much true of all the students?" Simon asked.

"No, no," Hope replied, "of course not. There are always going to be the achievers who do the work and obey the rules. And the vast majority of teachers still do their best to provide a good education to the students despite all of the nonsensical state and federal mandates that are handed down to them.

"But now the balance is changing. There seem to be as many students and parents who don't care as those who do. And the ones who don't care take eighty percent of the teacher's time and energy. They create a ton more paperwork and meetings; not to even mention how physically and mentally draining those kids are to deal with."

"I know that I have only been in the classroom for one entire school year, but I can already tell you this much. Regardless of how hard a teacher works to motivate the students, or how much effort they put into a lesson to make it interesting, it all comes down to one thing. Kids cannot learn if they don't *care*.

"Meanwhile, the politicians, the bureaucrats, and the media try to put *all* of the blame on the teachers and the schools. Their answer is to throw more money at technology, and training, and standardized testing to hold the teachers and schools accountable. That's all well and good, but that is only half of the equation. What responsibility do the parents and student have? If they are not held accountable, then how can the teacher be expected to shoulder all of the burden? From what I have observed, out of desperation teachers end up teaching to the test and the lowest common denominator.

So, the states and federal government continue to 'raise' the standards to give the appearance of improving education, and residually the teachers have to water everything down so they don't have poor test scores that would qualify them as a failed school by the very people who set the unrealistic expectations in the first place. As a result, teachers use memorizing gimmicks and tricks, smoke and mirrors, and short cuts just to get as many students to crawl over the bar as possible.

For instance, they will tell a second grader to learn that they need to learn how to multiply and then hand them a calculator. Pretty soon they will be introducing Algebra to 1st graders. In the name of No Child Left Behind, the rest of the world is leaving America in the dust because our children can't add, subtract, or multiply. And forget about trying to get them to write a complete sentence.

"About half of the students in any given classroom in America are coming away with no problem solving skills, no communication skills, no work ethic, and now no sense of right and wrong. And yet, they come to expect the same rewards and benefits of those who actually do the work and obey the rules. And don't even get me started on physical education..."

"Wait," Simon said. "I don't get it. Why would the bad students expect to get rewarded?"

"Well," Hope said, taking a deep breath. "If there is no negative reinforcement for breaking rules or not turning in work, then teachers overcompensate with a ton of positive reinforcement. Which would be fine if done in moderation, but when done in excess it becomes borderline bribery. We teachers stay up half the night trying to come up with gimmicks to get them to do what they should already be doing in the first place. So, like some kind of glorified dog trainer, we toss them a treat for doing what should be expected of them anyway. After a while students begin to expect greater and greater rewards even if they really didn't do anything to earn it.

"That's not the worst of it," she continued. "Sadly, when the students become over inundated with pizza parties, candy, and extra credit, they become inoculated to the rewards. Either the teachers have to continuously up the reward, or they no longer motivate the student to perform.

"Many teachers and administrators resort to unnecessarily labeling the worst behaved kids with some kind of this or that, just to have a documented excuse for poor test results. We slap a label on them, a modification plan, and a prescription and off they go."

"It is especially true of those students whose only disability is their home life, poor parenting, and a lack of discipline. How insulting is that to kids who have legitimate disabilities!"

"And the parents don't object to any of that?" Simon asked.

"What?" Hope said. "No way! In fact, I have seen parents, on hearing that their child has been diagnosed with this or that, act like they just won the golden ticket to Willy Wonka's Chocolate Factory. It's like they're off the hook or something. Again, I am *not* talking about legitimately disabled students. Please don't misunderstand me.

"Here's the problem that I see. Once these posers have a label, they become exempt from expectations. Without holding students to expectations, they cannot accomplish anything. We are doing them a great disservice because *we* are disabling *them*! They become convinced that they cannot control their impulses, that they need to be medicated, and they very well could end up wearing it like a badge of honor for the rest of their lives. The kids who are following the rules and doing the work see the ones who aren't get equal rewards. It's the whole 'everybody gets a blue ribbon' mentality. Frankly, it disincentives them too. Pretty soon nobody is working to the best of their ability."

"I mean, I get what you're saying," Simon replied, playing devil's advocate, "but I still think you're making a bigger deal of it all, than it really is. So, a few kids moved up a grade who really shouldn't have. In the big scheme of things, what does it really matter?"

"Don't you get it?" Hope asked. "That sense of entitlement has crept into every aspect of our society. We have raised an entire generation in a school system that failed to teach them that there are consequences for their actions. That there is absolute truth. That there is right and wrong.

"And we wonder why there is no sense of accountability. The same kids who did nothing in school and still graduate, do nothing in society and still expect to be taken care of by the same government that 'educated' them. They sincerely think that they deserve everything from housing, to health care, to food, to wireless, to cell phones, to cable TV. And why wouldn't they? We are conditioning them to think that way. It is a self-fulfilling prophecy. We are turning contrived 'disabilities' into a real ones.

"To make matters worse, there are those in politics who use the promise of allowing them just enough entitlements to eek out an unfulfilling existence as a platform to get elected into office. And the sad thing is that the takers are so ignorant that they demand free crumbs from the floor when they could maximize their abilities and opportunities to feast at the table. Unknowingly, they willingly trade in the possibility of abundance for the guarantee of poverty.

So, they continue to elect the politicians who provide those entitlements, and it becomes a vicious downward cycle.

Simon couldn't help but thinking of Rocky who was still living in his parent's basement.

"And I am sitting there thinking, 'the whole thing is completely upside down from how it used to be or from how it should be'. We're teaching to the bottom. We're accepting apathy and ignorance, while rewarding failure, celebrating mediocrity, and punishing the achievers who will someday have to work to provide for the very kids who make the classroom environment miserable for them every single day.

"Meanwhile, the state shrugs off its responsibilities by saying, 'It's not our fault, we're demanding more and more every year...' When they are missing the most crucial piece to the puzzle. The majority of people don't value education. They take it for granted. They don't see it as a pathway to freedom or achieving the American Dream. They don't see it as a tremendous privilege that we have in this country."

"So, are you suggesting that education should not be a basic right or something?" Simon asked.

"What?" Hope asked. "No, of course not. What I am suggesting is that people can choose to forfeit their rights by the decisions that they make. Yes, everyone should have the right to a public education at least through high school. What I'm saying is that if someone is not doing the work, or constantly keeping other students from learning, they could be choosing to give up that right. They could be sent to a trade school or military school or reform school which might be perfect for some of them. There is no shame in mastering a trade or protecting our country. Or they might just gain a new appreciation for the education that they are already being offered.

"It is just so sad," Hope lamented. "How did we let it get so out of hand? When did all of this start? When did we go from being the land of opportunity to the land of entitlement? How did we go from being self-reliant to being so dependent on handouts and freebee's?"

Simon looked down and thought about it for a moment, then said, "What's the other problem?"

"What?" Hope asked.

"You said there were two major problems," Simon said, "Apathy and...?"

"Oh right,...greed," Hope answered. "There are those who prefer for the masses to be undisciplined and without knowledge so that they are easier to control and manipulate. Some people actually profit from the ignorance of others."

"Huh, it sounds like a much bigger problem than something that's just happening at Bethel Grade School," Simon said, accidentally tempting her again with another excuse. "I really don't think anyone would blame you for not speaking up given the situation."

"Yeah, but isn't that everyone's excuse for not taking action?" Hope replied.

"Isn't that a sad commentary? Don't you see that by failing to stand up for what is right, I became a part of the problem. There are consequences to my actions too.

"So, why didn't you say anything, then?" Simon asked, almost exasperated by her insistence on holding herself to such high ethical standards.

"Like I said before, I was afraid," Hope admitted, looking down and fidgeting with her fingernails.

"You? Afraid?" Simon said.

"Yes," Hope admitted. "I was afraid of what the other teachers would say. I was afraid of what people might think of me. I was afraid of being in the newspaper and of lawsuits and of all sorts of crazy things that were running through my head at the time. I just wanted to shrink back in the shadows until the whole thing blew over, but afterward I was so ashamed of myself."

"I wouldn't be so hard on yourself," Simon ignorantly offered, "everybody gets scared now and then."

"But, that's not it," Hope replied, looking up at him. "After agonizing over it for sometime, I realized something. I realized that I wasn't ashamed because I was afraid. I was ashamed because I was afraid of the wrong things. I should have been more afraid of sending the wrong message to the students and their parents. I should have been more of afraid of a society that doesn't believe in consequences, or accountability, or achievement, or absolutes. I should have been afraid of my own consequences for not doing what I knew God would have wanted me to do!"

The last statement rattled Simon. Up until this point, the conversation had somehow seemed distant to him, as though he were a distant spectator. Hope's last comment brought it uncomfortably close to home for him. It was like he had been casually observing a ravenous, pacing lion behind bars before realizing that he was actually standing in the den with it.

"You seem to be a little uncomfortable by what I am saying," Hope said while she studied his pained expression.

As Simon remembered some of his other conversations about God and what He wanted, he suddenly became keenly aware of how pious Christians can sound.

"It's not an easy thing to talk about," Simon admitted.

"What's not easy to talk about?" Hope asked.

"To talk about God, and what He wants from us," Simon said. "It's just so hard to know for sure. And most people *don't* want to talk about it either. Trust me. It's just so…so…unnatural."

Simon struck a nerve.

"Did it ever occur to you that it *should be* natural?" Hope countered. "I would say that is getting down to the heart of our problem. The very fact that you, a Christian living in the United States of America, feel uncomfortable talking openly about your religious beliefs speaks volumes about the enemy's full frontal assault to completely eradicate God and Christianity from every aspect of our culture. And in the process, we have drastically changed what it means to be an American."

"...'Drastically changed what it means to be an American'?" Simon repeated. "That seems a bit dramatic, don't you think?"

"Is it?" Hope asked. "Let me ask you, what is it to be an 'American'? Is it about earning or entitlement? Does the government serve the people, or do the people serve the government? Are our laws meant to protect us or oppress us? Is saying what you believe, freedom of speech, or is it a hate crime?

"You see, I believe that we have become tolerant to everything in this country except for intolerance. We have confused absolute truth and the pursuit of happiness with absolute happiness and the pursuit of truth. We have bought into the notion that doing nothing and having something is better than doing something and earning everything. That receiving an income is respectable while earning a wage is somehow for chumps who haven't learned how to work the system.

"I mean it's gotten to the point that many Americans would consider winning the lottery, or being awarded a large settlement, or getting a monthly disability check the 'American Dream'. You would be amazed at the number of students who think that sitting around on their duffs, sucking air conditioning, feeding their faces full of junk food, staying up to all hours of the morning watching cable TV, or playing Xbox is heaven on earth. In the meantime, they all think they're going to play in the NBA or win American Idol. And yet they wonder why they are so anxious and depressed.

"For the vast majority of them, it's all a big, fat lie," she continued, "it's fools gold. It is sucking the life out of this once great nation, because freedom is inherent to personal achievement, and personal achievement is inherent to self-worth, and self-worth is inherent to real, genuine happiness."

"Doesn't that philosophy seem kind of cold and calloused?" Simon asked, feeling overwhelmed by the enormity of it all. "I mean, if it's all about personal achievement then that leaves no room for charity. That hardly seems Godly, especially to unbelievers."

"I never said that it was *only* about personal achievement for everybody," Hope replied. "I believe in charity. In fact, we are commanded to take care of the widow and the orphan; we are told to take care of those who can't take care of themselves. The whole social security system was originally implemented under that premise, but we aren't merely taking care of those who cannot take care of themselves. We are *creating* an entire generation of people who refuse to take care of themselves.

"When we embrace that mentality we are no longer the land of opportunity. We are the land of handouts. When handouts are given to someone who is not vested then it is taken for granted and abused. It doesn't matter whether it's housing, education, food stamps, cell phones, or health care.

"And yet, they're still miserable. They think the cure to their misery is more free stuff. What they don't realize is that it will never be enough to fill the void inside of them that will provide them the hope, self-worth, and happiness that they are seeking.

"Sometimes the greatest gift is self-sufficiency. Our whole political system was originally designed to allow people to reach their full potential. The primary purpose of the government was to protect the rights of the people and create an environment in which free enterprise and competition can thrive. The rules and laws were put in place to do just that, but when there are no consequences to breaking rules or when the interpretation of rules changes the initial intent of the law, then our basic freedoms are slowly and systematically eroded. At that point, the people are no longer protected under the law. Instead, they are held hostage by those who use the law for their own self-interests through warped interpretations and arbitrary enforcement.

"Without ever counting the cost, we have built a morbidly obese government that employs more and more people on the one hand, while simultaneously creating more and more people who are dependent upon it. So, at the top there is power and greed, and at the bottom there is apathy and freeloading. What do you think all of those people on the payroll are going to vote for, but more government and more services? And they do it all now on the backs of the average American worker.

"But, one day it will all come to a head, because the reality is *someone* has to pay for it. Right now, we are internally hemorrhaging as a nation.

"In our lifetime, what was once a beacon of hope and freedom for the rest of the world has morphed into just another socialist, Nanny State where the vast majority of people are in one way or another dependent on the government to survive.

"Cleverly, those in power use the system as a political lever to get re-elected while silencing opposition through political correctness and intimidation. They more than insinuate that any objectors must be either heartless or racist, or both.

"The poorest among us continue to suffer because they think that the government will take care of them! If that's the case, then why do you think drugs and alcohol are so high in demand? It's an escape from the hopelessness and despair that this type of political system breeds. Have you ever been to Russia, or Cuba, or China, or Venezuela?

"People cannot be content in having no purpose or in being given barely enough to survive, but it's like a narcotic. People get hooked on it, expect it, demand it. There comes a point where it becomes their identity. They know nothing else and become afraid to take the risk of trying to make it on their own. Sadly, they will never know the reward of sacrifice, hard labor, self-sufficiency, and sense of accomplishment that was the American Dream. We are raising an entire generation of willing victims who aren't going to be able to handle, well, *anything* in life. Over time, the people themselves have become complicit with their own oppression simply by inaction and complacency.

"And I am no better," Hope said. "In fact, I am much worse because *I* should know better. That was what was at stake in that meeting. That was why it was so important for me to speak out. It wasn't just about passing along a few students to meet a contrived standard. It was about being on the front line in the fight against tyranny versus cowering in a bunker and waving a white flag."

Simon was at a loss for words. There was no denying the truth when he heard it. "But, you're just one person," he said almost pleading. "What can you really do about it? The problem is so enormous!"

"Well, I can't change the world," Hope simply replied. "I can only do what God has called me to do in the position that he has put me in. As a second grade teacher, I can empower students by giving them knowledge, by instilling a strong work ethic, and by providing them with a sense of right and wrong. I can teach them that our actions, words, and ideas have consequences and that they will be held accountable for the work that is required of them. I can teach them that they aren't the result of some cataclysmic mistake. That they were purposely and wondrously made." She paused and then turned and pointed at the new monument hanging on the wall before adding, "I can teach them what it means to have inalienable rights. I can teach them what life, liberty, and the pursuit of happiness are really all about."

"We have to do what we can because it is too important! There is so much at stake! We need to change the course this country is on before it is too late!"

Suddenly it occurred to Simon that he had very recently heard the same kind of rhetoric. "Huh, that's funny," Simon said, "Dr. Al-Banna said something very similar at the commencement ceremony."

"Oh, really?" Hope asked, skeptically.

* * *

"Yes, he also talked about the American Dream," Simon said. "He was also passionately advocating personal responsibility and moral obligations. He was talking about the importance of speaking truth to the next generation and for fighting for what you believe in; all of that stuff."

"Is that so?" Hope asked with a grave expression.

"Yes, he was," Simon said. "Dr. Al-Banna was also calling for change. In fact, during his speech, he quoted that Obama guy's campaign slogan. What was it? It was something about needing to make a fundamental change in this country. Oh, it was 'Change We Need', or no!...'Hope and Change'. I don't know. Anyway, it was the same sentiment. He called it a 'brotherhood' I think."

"Hmm," Hope said, now fixing her eyes on the opening lines to the historic document on the wall. "To tell you the truth, I find all of that to be very disturbing, actually."

"What? But, why?" Simon asked, surprised. "Isn't that the same thing you were just talking about a minute ago. Weren't you just talking about changing the course of our country?"

"Yes, I was talking about a change, but I highly doubt that it's the same kind of change that Dr. Al-Banna or that Obama character was talking about," she quipped. "That's what I was saying earlier. Things aren't always what they appear to be on the surface. You see, a word like 'change' is so vague." She was now beginning to allow her passion to bubble to the surface once again. "Unless you clearly define it, 'change' can be anything it currently isn't. So, by intentionally leaving the term open-ended, people can insert whatever meaning they like to the word. Naturally, the listener assumes it to be the same sort of change that they would like to see take place. More than that, people always seem to assume it is going to be a change for the better.

"I would actually be very interested in hearing Dr. Al-Banna, or even Senator Obama for that matter, actually define exactly what kind of fundamental change each of them are proposing. That's the only way we can be sure whether we agree or disagree with the change they are calling for."

"I don't know about Obama, but I can't imagine Dr. Al-Banna's having anything but the best of intentions for Bethel," Simon objected, defending his friend. "After all, he's a very well respected member of the community. Nearly everyone that I talk to thinks very highly of him. I myself have found him to be a very kind, caring, intelligent person. I mean, I know that he is *very* religious, but so are you. That hardly makes him a bad guy. In fact, he actually contributes a great deal of his time and money for things that ultimately benefit the community like the parks and this project."

"But, *why* do you think Dr. Al-Banna would do all of that?" Hope asked. "Why do you have to guess at what his intentions are?"

"Well, I can't say for sure, but I would say it's because he really cares about the people of Bethel," Simon said, trying to reassure Hope. "Earlier you were talking about judging people's hearts by the fruit of their works. All I am saying is that based on all of the things he has done for Bethel, I think it is reasonable to conclude that his intentions are good."

"I have no doubt that he is sincere," Hope answered, "but that's the very point that I have been trying to make. You are making an assumption, but you have never actually asked him what he thinks. You are assuming that you and Dr. Al-Banna would agree about what is a 'positive' change of direction for the community."

"Judging him strictly by the fruit of his labor is good, but it is not enough. You also need to know his motivation for donating his time and money. You have to match his words with his actions. Look, some things can be taken at face value. For instance, when the school building was rundown and falling apart, it was merely symptomatic of the way people in this community really felt about school and education and learning. Just like that amazing new ball park that Rich and those guys built is symptomatic about how people around here really feel about youth sports."

"Or like the Bethel Tavern," Simon said, beginning to follow along, "like what you see is what you get. The fact that people have poured a lot of their time and money into a particular thing says something about their priorities."

"Yes!" Hope exclaimed, relieved that they were finally on the same page. "You can get some sense of what a particular community is all about just by driving through town and making some casual observations."

"Well, then maybe his involvement in rebuilding the school is a good sign," Simon suggested. "Isn't this just as impressive as the baseball field or the Bethel Tavern?" he asked, pointing at the remarkable renovation.

"Maybe even more so," Hope said with a sigh, looking around the room before turning back towards Simon, "but other things are not what they seem on the surface. That's why we owe it to ourselves to examine them more closely. To ask questions. To investigate. Each person has to come to their own conclusion regarding four critical questions: 'Where did we come from?', 'Why are we here?', 'What happens to us when we die?', and 'How does that relate to what we do while we are alive?'.

"I'm only articulating what everyone has to think through and decide for themselves anyway. So, if the answers to those questions are that important, then shouldn't we spend a great deal of time discussing them? The only people who don't want to do that are those who are not interested in the facts. They are unwilling or afraid to apply reason and logic. Any religion that is opposed to open debate is analogous to a cult! I mean, if they are so certain that what they believe is the truth, then why are they so afraid to openly discuss it and share it with everyone else? What would be the motivation for anyone in an authoritative position to keep individuals from thinking for themselves other than power and control?

"Look, all I am saying is that we are called to be as shrewd as snakes and as innocent as doves. We need to be able to have open and candid debate about these things. It is undeniable that there are Muslim and Communist countries out there that discourage freedom of religion and freedom of speech. Why is that? And is that who we want to be as a nation?

"So, when you say that you think Dr. Al-Banna wants this community to progress in the right direction, it reminds me of something C.S. Lewis once wrote. He said that the key is defining what the right direction is. If his definition of the right direction is polar opposite from mine then what he considers progress is actually moving even farther away from where I think this community should be heading. Like Lewis said, in that case, the fellow who stops, retraces his steps, and returns to the junction in the road where they took the wrong turn is actually the one making the most progress.

"For that reason, we need to know what the *right* direction means to Dr. Al-Banna or even Obama for that matter. We need to ask that question. We need to see if his words align with the fruit he is producing. And if he isn't willing to directly tell us his intentions, then that too speaks volumes. The question is will it be too late by then to turn around and return to the place where we got lost?

"That's all that I am saying about Dr. Al-Banna. He is a really nice guy. And I really like his family too, but we owe it to ourselves to know why he is contributing his time and money to all of these things. What is his motivation? On the surface, all of that seems wonderful...."

"There's that 'but' again..." Simon said.

"And...," Hope said emphatically, "...he's also a devout Muslim."

"Well, isn't religious freedom one of the things that makes our nation exceptional?" Simon asked, feeling himself bristle at Hope's seemingly prejudice comment. He couldn't deny that he was beginning to feel a little uncomfortable talking about this particular subject. Nervously, he found himself suddenly looking over his shoulder to make sure that no one else had stumbled upon their conversation. The last thing that he wanted to do was accidentally offend anyone, especially Dr. Al-Banna.

"Yes, we can thank God that we have freedom of religion, and I would be the first to fight for that right," Hope said.

"Well, then, wouldn't you agree, that is one of the rights protected by the very document that Dr. Al-Banna paid to have re-dipped and hung on the wall of our school?" Simon replied.

"Of course, but at the same time, I would also argue that the framers of that document would say that those rights don't come from the document itself but from the Judeo-Christian teachings in the Bible," Hope boldly replied. "It doesn't come from the Quran. And it only takes a cursory glance at Islamic countries and Christian countries to realize that they are in direct opposition. I mean how many Christian churches are in Afghanistan or Iran or Saudi Arabia or Syria or Turkey?

"I am not just making this stuff up. Think about it. What would happen if a Muslim spoke freely about his religious beliefs on any street corner in America? And what would happen if a Christian did the same in Iran or Saudi Arabia? We don't have to wonder, we can see the differences in the world today and the contrast is stark. It is not hypothetical. Our Founding Fathers, the vast majority of whom were God-fearing Christians, wrote our founding documents that allow Muslims, or any other religious group for that matter, to publicly practice their religion as much as it allows me to practice mine."

"But, isn't that a good thing?" Simon asked.

"Absolutely!" Hope agreed.

"Then I'm not following you," Simon said, struggling to understand her objection, "because what you are saying sounds contradictory. It sounds like you are saying that everyone should have a right to believe whatever you want to believe as long it is exactly what Christians believe."

"If you take the time to hear me out, you will find that there is nothing contradictory about what I am saying," Hope said. "Look, it is about what we have been, compared to what we are, compared to what we are becoming as a nation. It is not all the same. The United States has historically been regarded around the world as a Christian nation because our laws that have governed this land since our country's inception are predominately based on the laws that are taught in the Bible. For goodness sake, Leviticus is quoted more times than any other reference for shaping our entire judicial system. You don't have to believe me, go to the Library of Congress and read the documents for yourself. Read the Federalist Papers. Read Common Sense. Read letters from people like John Adams and George Washington and even Thomas Jefferson.

"So, here's the thing. Christianity is a religion of free will. We are a Christian nation that allows the practice of other religions, but this is the key...*please, listen to what I am saying!* No one is arguing that Muslims cannot live and practice their religion in the United States. Our forefathers instituted the Free Exercise Clause so that the *citizens* of this great nation could have the freedom to believe, express, and practice one's own faith according to one's own conscience. It's a guaranteed right in the First Amendment."

"Exactly!" Simon replied.

"*But!...*" Hope said forcefully, "this is what people don't understand today. Those liberties are *not* absolute. They must operate within the bounds of *our* laws. No one can use the freedoms protected in our laws as a means to institute their own laws, thereby creating their own enclaves within our country. We have freedom of religion, even for religions that don't believe in freedom of religion, as long as they do not turn around and undermine our liberties and use them to implement their own rule of law."

"What exactly are you saying about Dr. Al-Banna then?" Simon asked. "Because it sounds like you are making wild accusations about the intentions of a well-respected man that could seriously tarnish his image without having any real evidence to support it."

"Why are we Christians held hostage by our own compassion?" Hope replied. "We still have to be discerning. I have not accused Dr. Al-Banna of anything! I am, however, raising a question that we all deserve to hear the answer to. What is his motivation for what he does? What is his ultimate goal? I want to know where his allegiance lies. I suspect that he is a peaceful Muslim who has come here to be a proud citizen of the United States, but I don't know his heart. Is he trying to assimilate to American culture or does he have an agenda to completely change our culture? Does he consider himself to be privileged to be a Muslim who can freely practice his religion because our Constitution gives him the right, or does he simply look at our Constitution as a vehicle by which he can achieve his ultimate purpose of establishing a different set of laws? Why shouldn't we have a right to know the answers to those questions?"

"It's not as if we don't have evidence of him already changing Bethel since his arrival," Hope continued. "Dr. Al-Banna has started a Mosque that uses our public school as their meeting place, students no longer have to stand for the pledge of allegiance, and they no longer serve hot dogs in the cafeteria. That's one freedom that has already been taken away from the vast majority of students to capitulate to the minority due to one family's beliefs. I would say that is 'real' evidence."

"I have to say that you sound a little paranoid," Simon scoffed. "Come on, hot dogs? You really think that someone would be zealous enough to change the menu in the cafeteria?"

"Laugh if you'd like," Hope said. "If our very way of life is at stake, then we should be vigilant. Look at what is taking place in France, England, Austria, Hungary, and Germany. Are the Muslims in those countries trying to assimilate and living by the laws of those democracies, or are they trying to abide by a law that they feel supersedes the laws of the countries they migrated to? And have those governments naively, out of blind tolerance and compassion, been allowing them to live according to their own laws instead of capitulating to the old laws? If so, how's operating a single country under two different sets of laws working out for them?

"If these things are not a threat, then great, but what if we are ignoring the handwriting on the wall? Only time will tell if people like me are a bunch of Chicken Little's or Paul Revere's. Because the way I see it, if *I* were to invade an enemy's country, I would start with an aerial attack and then follow it up with a ground assault. Once I felt as though I had won the battle, I would erect a monument like a mosque to commemorate the battleground where I had conquered my enemies. They don't have to land in assault vehicles like 'Saving Private Ryan' when our loose immigration laws allow them to stroll across our borders undeterred and undetected. Do we really know who are the people who are living amongst us and what their true intentions are?"

"Honestly, I have to say that you kind of sound like one of those wacko extremists," Simon replied, in a poor attempt to lighten the conversation while still making his point. Realizing that his remark was not well-received, he continued, "But seriously, I think sometimes it is that kind of talk that discredits Christians and keeps us from being taken seriously in the marketplace of ideas.

"What you're saying is just so out of the blue…"

"It's hardly out of the blue," Hope responded. "This conflict has been going on for hundreds if not thousand of years. You're eyes are just now being opened to it. Now it has finally creeped into your little insulated world. That's all."

"And if what I am saying is so ridiculous, then let me ask you something," Hope said in her defense. "Did Dr. Al-Banna ever mention to you his plans to build a new, much larger Mosque, or Islamic center as he calls it? Right now he is working with the city council to get approval to lay claim over Clay Potter's property."

"So, they have the right to," Simon replied, somewhat taken aback. "It's a free country, isn't it?"

"Yes, I agree, but we have a right to know why," Hope stated. "A large mosque in the middle of nowhere would indicate that he has the intention of spreading his beliefs and drawing converts. Or maybe he plans on bringing in more people from other countries who think more like he does. All of that leads to some very interesting questions. What is his ultimate goal? Where is he getting the funding to build it? After all, a family practice doctor in Bethel, IL is not loaded with cash. It goes back to what I said earlier about the buildings in town reflecting what is important to the people of Bethel. If the people really wanted an Islamic center, they would provide the funding themselves. If that is the case, then there is no need for secrecy as to where the money is coming from. Why are we so afraid to ask the tough questions? Have you ever bothered doing some research on what purpose a Mosque serves according to Islamic tradition?"

Simon laughed out loud and said, "Hope, I have to tell you that all of this sounds a little crazy. You act like Dr. Al-Banna is some kind of terrorist or jihadist or whatever they call them. I think I know this guy pretty well. He's not some extremist. Personally, I would be embarrassed for him and his family if anyone posed those kind of insulting questions."

"But, that's how our enemies completely neutralize us," Hope replied. "They silence the opposition. They have convinced us, along with the more peaceful Muslims, that by merely trying to decipher who the enemy is we are 'insulting' them or violating their rights. They portray us as a bunch of racists or something.

"The zealous Islamic groups capitalize on the American ideals regarding religious accommodation to implement their own religious, slash, political ideals. I say 'slash' because for the Muslim, religion and politics are one and the same. It is a theocratic religion.

"What if their ultimate goal is to subjugate everyone under their religion, their belief system, and their laws as taught in the Quran? The result would be a theocracy in which there would be no religious freedom. Look at Egypt, look at Pakistan, look at Syria, look at Jordan, Turkey, Saudi Arabia... The whole concept is completely un-American. The government cannot force people to believe or worship a certain way.

"To be a jihadist does not necessarily mean a Muslim has to be violent. There is also a 'civilized jihad' or political jihad with the same ultimate goal of instituting a Muslim theocracy. Is it really some kind of violation of their civil rights if all we are trying to figure out is if they have the intention of changing who we are fundamentally as a nation? If all Dr. Al-Banna is doing is trying to peacefully practice his religion, then I applaud him. We're a free society. By all means, let the people hear his message, find out what Islam is all about, and choose whether they agree or disagree. At the end of the day, if there is a great demand for the Islamic center, then it should be built. If people do not receive Mohammad's message in the Quran, then in a few years the building might be converted into a YMCA or something. It is the American concept of free will that allows supply and demand to determine whether a product, or in this case a religious view, is really wanted by the people.

"I believe that Dr. Al-Banna has just as much of a right to peaceably promote his religion, as I do mine. But, time will tell if the people 'buy' what he is selling, because in America, people still have a choice; at least for the time being."

"Then what's the big deal," Simon asked, "if you are supporting his right to free speech and his congregation the right to assemble?"

"My problem has to do with people having all of the information at their disposal to make an educated decision," Hope replied. "Do the people even know what they are choosing between? For instance, do people even know that there are passages in the Quran that promote violence and deception as a legitimate means for spreading Islam? Because that is in direct opposition to the Bible that identifies murder and deceit as sins. I have a hard time believing that a religion that approves of those kinds of tactics would be content with waiting until they have won the popular vote before implementing their ideology in society. And once in power, they have not proven to be open to debate over doctrine in other parts of the world.

"It is well documented that Islamic extremists have already been attempting to use our own laws to implement Sharia law without the consent of the majority. And some of our own intellectual elite with the help of radical judges are actually helping them do it. That is subversion and high treason. Our enemy is holding us hostage by wielding the weapon of political correctness to paralyze us with fear. We have become so 'sophisticated' at our institutions of higher learning that we have almost completely eradicated logic and common sense."

The word 'fear' once agin struck Simon. "But, what are they afraid of, exactly?" he asked, recalling his 'one thing'.

"They are afraid of being demonized," she replied. "In fact, I read an article by a guy named Dr. Tawfik Hamid. In the article he said that Western academicians and politicians want to appear tolerant at all costs even to the point of tolerating an illiberal, or intolerant ideology because to appear intolerant is to appear unenlightened, even unintelligent. Peer pressure and political correctness and large, anonymous grants, weigh heavily, as do opportunities for promotion or election. To those from the West, intolerance is an intellectual 'mark of shame'.

"What he is really saying, is that we have become so open-minded that our brains have fallen out," Hope said sarcastically. "There's a giant hole in New York that makes it pretty obvious that we *do* have an enemy who wants to wipe us off of the face of the earth.

"Who in their right mind would argue that we have no right to identify our enemies? Why can't we drag them out of the darkness and into the light? Why can't we find out what is being preached and taught in the Mosques? It is more than our right; it is our responsibility to do so. People have to recognize that even in a free society there are going to be some limitations to certain rights for certain citizens when it is necessary for our survival.

"It is our duty to ask questions, gather information, to investigate. And yes, some of those questions are going to be a little uncomfortable. But, we have to find out who we are up against. In a time of war, I would much rather a hundred-thousand innocent people come under a little scrutiny than have even one extremist go undetected because the potential consequences of the latter are so dire. There's no question that we need to racially profile individuals because it is a certain demographic who are strapping bombs to themselves and hijacking airplanes and beheading people. Anyone who has an ounce of common sense would have to say, duh."

"But, is that fair to those Muslims who have no intention of harming anyone?" Simon objected.

"Of course it is not fair! I agree," Hope said, "but it's not fair to the victims of these extremists' attacks either. The safety of our people trumps the myth of fairness on this particular point. The ideologues declared war on *us* when they rammed two planes into the Twin Towers. Go look at the hole, go online and watch the execution of Christian prisoners in foreign countries, look up Army Major Hasan's own writings. How real does it have to get before we come to our senses?

"It just so happens that these particular ideologues are citing the Quran as their source of motivation and inspiration for carrying out these heinous crimes. I know there are people who think we are randomly picking on Islam, but I have news for you. It wouldn't matter if some other extremist groups were using the Tora, or the Gita, or the Book of Mormon, or even the Bible as their source of motivation for carrying out unprovoked attacks on innocent people, we would be forced to react in the same way. We would have no other choice but to racially profile that particular group until the problem was eradicated."

"You're probably right," Simon reluctantly agreed.

"Probably?" Hope snapped. "Think about it. Let's say a group of extremists posing as Christians rammed an airplane into the Mecca during Ramadan and killed a bunch of civilians. How would real Christ followers react around the world? Christians would be outraged that these imposters would defile the Bible and Jesus's teachings in such a way. There would be a public outcry to join the Islamic community in seeking out those cold-blooded killers and bringing them to justice."

"But, you can see why Muslims get defensive for feeling like they are being wrongfully accused when it is just a small number of extremists misrepresenting their faith," Simon said.

"Definitely, I sympathize with their situation, but they need to be equally sympathetic with our situation as well," Hope replied. "While they're busy getting their feelings hurt, we are worried about standing on the corner in Times Square while one of these so called Lone Wolves set off an SUV full of explosives, or sit in an airplane while one of these degenerates sets his underwear on fire, or get gunned down at an office Christmas party.

"And, by the way, let's consider for a moment what a small number of extremists means. If there are two billion Muslims in the world, even a tiny fraction could be somewhere in the millions. I mean, why has it taken over ten years for the greatest army in the history of the world to win the wars in Iraq and Afghanistan? For all of George W. Bush's waterboarding, or interrogation tactics, we still haven't even been able to find Obama...I mean Osama."

"I don't know that everyone would agree with you on that particular point," Simon countered. "I heard that Obama guy say in a speech while campaigning in the Iowa primary that he opposed the war in Iraq from the beginning because Bush had no justification for caring out the invasion. He must feel like the threat is minimal or that we're just dealing with a small number of extremists because he said that we should have never gone to war in the first place."

"Well, I would bet that the people who were in lower Manhattan on September 11th wouldn't have called the twelve terrorists a minimal threat," Hope replied. "Look, I don't agree with everything President Bush does. In fact, there are a ton of things that I don't agree with him about.

"But, I would say that it's easy for anyone to say what they *would have done* had they been in President Bush's shoes after the biggest attack on U.S. soil in the history of our country. It's easy to play armchair quarterback especially when it is politically expedient to do so.

"I guess Obama would have handled the situation perfectly. He probably would have heard all of the conflicting intelligence reports about whether or not Saddam had dirty bombs or nuclear capability and chosen to not act. Even though this evil dictator in the Middle East had already killed thousands of his own people. Mind you, it was only a few months after three thousand American citizens were murdered at the hands of Al-Queda. Now that would have been a gutsy call.

"I mean if Bush really did go to war in Iraq for personal gain, then there is a special place for him.

"But, I wish people would think about the implications if President Bush decided not to invade Iraq, and Saddam actually had been developing that kind weaponry. I suppose there are people who would hear all of the conflicting intelligence reports, study his past history of using chemical weapons used in the Iraq civil war, and watch UN inspectors being denied access to Iraqi military installations and not act.

"Who in their right mind would sit back and wait for a country like Iraq to develop long-range missiles or nuclear capability without trying to stop it? I suppose Obama would have just signed some sort of pact or peace treaty with that maniac.

"But, isn't it funny how there have not been any major attacks on U.S. soil since we decided to take the fight to them? The extremists haven't had the luxury of sitting back and plotting their next horrific assault They're too busy running and hiding. Is that a mere coincidence?

"So, I am sorry that it is a hassle for a person to be profiled because they are Muslim or they are of Middle Eastern decent, but their anger and frustration should not be directed at the American people. It should be directed at the extremists who are doing all of these atrocities in the name of their religion.

"The Muslims should be even more angry than we are with the terrorists because those people are carrying out these unholy attacks and misrepresenting the teachings of their prophet, Mohammed; that is if they truly believe Islam is a religion of peace.

"The nonviolent Muslims who are citizens of this country have a choice *because* this is America. They can either choose to be offended by the temporary scrutiny and limitations of their rights and direct all of their time, energy, and efforts towards fighting for their civil liberties in the courts, or they could choose like some of them have done to direct their efforts towards helping us speak out against, identify, fight, and eliminate the rebellious extremists.

"If they really wanted to protect the American way of life, they could choose to be completely transparent and cooperative. If they look at this objectively, then they will realize that no one wanted to profile them before nineteen people of Arab decent murdered three thousand of our men, women, and children in the name of Allah. No one will want to profile them when we are at peace again.

"Look, there are thousands of our U.S. troops in the Middle East putting their lives on the line every day. Didn't you say that your friend Shane was over there now? Why? What are they fighting for if it is not to protect the American way of life?"

Simon looked up at the constitution and let Hope's words sink in before he said, "I still feel confident that Dr. Al-Banna would not have any objection to letting anyone know his true intentions, or about building a new Mosque, or even where the funding is coming from. After all, I think he is a man who loves this country as much as we do. Like I said earlier, 'why else would he pay for the Declaration of Independence monument to be re-dipped?'. Look at it. That thing will last forever now. You could throw it into a blazing furnace and it would come out completely intact. I mean, the man spoke expertly on the Constitution as though he had been studying it for a number of years. Why would someone take the time to do that if they didn't truly believe in it?

"Well, if that someone happened to be a member of the Muslim Brotherhood," Hope replied, "I would say the intention of becoming an expert in our laws would be to use them against us or to find loop holes in them to eliminate and destroy our civilization from within. It would be to sabotage it like a judicial Trojan horse. That is what I meant be using the Constitution as a medium to institute their own law. It is the divine law taught in the Quran, which they believe trumps all other laws. Muslims call it Sharia."

"See, that's what I am saying," Simon responded, "you wouldn't have those same concerns about Dr. Al-Banna if you could have heard him speak tonight about our founding documents. He was so eloquent, so...sincere about our things like inalienable rights and the laws that protect them."

"That's it!" Hope replied, excitedly. "You just hit the nail on the head. The real underlying issue here is not 'do we have inalienable rights'. It's not even a bone of contention that inalienable rights come from a higher power. Most people would agree with that assertion. The real issue here is 'where do inalienable rights come from?'. Who is that higher power? What is the source from which we derive our laws that protect those rights? I would think that a true Muslim would say that life comes from Allah, that liberty is only for Muslims under Sharia Law, and that the pursuit of happiness is fulfilling the will of Allah by doing enough good works to gain entry into paradise.

"We need to know who is the God in 'One Nation under God'? Dr. Al-Banna would say it is Allah, while I would say it is God the Father, the Son, and the Holy Spirit. We also need to clearly define what laws we are going to follow. Dr. Al-Banna would probably say Sharia Law, while I would say the Ten Commandments. And we need to decide which resource we are going to reference. Dr. Al-Banna would say it is the Quran while I would say The Bible. Clearly, there is an infinite difference between those two completely divergent systems of belief. On the surface they may appear to be very similar, but when anyone expresses their thoughts on the Declaration of Independence without divulging their foundational religious beliefs, then they are failing to get down to the heart of the issue. We have to decide what we believe as a nation.

"That is why I contend that hatred for our country is not hatred for our laws. It is not a hatred for the Declaration of Independence or the Constitution. It is not even hatred directed at an ambiguous, ill-defined God. The real hatred for our country stems from a hatred for Jesus Christ, and our history as a Nation who believes in the authenticity of the Bible in its entirety as the source of all truth.

"That is why Islamic extremists are not the only enemy of this great country of ours. It is *anyone* who wishes to divorce the United States of America from the Gospel and from Jesus Christ. Even though there are many battles being fought on many different fronts, we know there is ultimately only one enemy.

"And Satan is fully aware of what the result will be once he is able to convince us that Jesus was not God incarnate, and did not fulfill the law in his death, burial, and resurrection. He knows that truth would become relative at that point. And once truth becomes relative, the entire foundation that gives our Constitution its authority crumbles into a shifting sand of cultural relativism.

"God help us when that day comes, because on that day the documents will be worth little more than the paper that they are written on. The very meaning of words will be susceptible to being twisted, edited, interpreted, and manipulated by those who merely wish to use them for their own devices."

A part of Simon recoiled, as Hope spoke. His face winced at her assertions, and yet, he heard truth in it as well. A part of him was deeply offended, while another part was equally ashamed for not having as strong of faith.

"But, can't you see that what you are saying would be so incredibly offensive to so many people?" Simon said with his ego lashing out. "What gives one person the right to define absolute truth for everyone else? You said yourself that free will is one of the hallmarks of our society."

"First of all, I said that I believe that free will is the hallmark of a *Christian* society, but not free will apart from consequences for making bad choices," Hope replied. "Second, in a constitutional republic the people determine what should be taught as absolute truth.

"Besides, I never claimed to be dictating absolute truth to anyone. Absolute truth is dictated to me just like it is for everybody else. I mean, no one determined that one plus one equals two," Hope said. "It's like this; I could teach my second graders math facts, or I could let them how to figure it out for themselves by trial and error. One plus one will always be two whether my students learn it from me or figure it out on their own. In the end, there is only one right answer and an infinite number of wrong answers, whether my students choose to accept it as fact or not. They have free will to answer incorrectly. The same is true with Natural Law.

"But, it's not being tolerant to let the students answer six when the answer is two. In fact, it's unconscionable. Even if the student truly believes that the answer is six, he is still wrong, no matter how 'offended' the student is that you marked his answer wrong.

"You can't compromise, either, and say that the answer is four, because obviously that is also a wrong answer. We can't find an answer that we both agree upon and just make up the right answer in the name of compromise. Sure, it is intolerant to say that the answer has to be two, because there *is* no other right answer. That's why we call them math facts, and that is why I can be confident that the answer is two. It may come across as arrogant to say the right answer, but if my confidence offends someone, it is probably because they arrived at a different, incorrect answer. The wrong answer that is closest to being right is the one that is the most deceiving.

"The way I see it, Christians and Muslims might both be wrong, but they can't both be right, because they are arriving at completely different answers to truth. Their facts directly contradict one another. You can either believe what I am telling you or you can figure it out for yourself. The next time you talk to Dr. Al-Banna ask him about Islam and what he truly believes, and you will see what I mean. We don't just all believe in the same God with different paths to reaching him."

"But, don't you see that when people of other faiths hear Christians say things like that, they think we're a bunch of know-it-alls?" Simon asked. "Can't you see how it could completely turn someone off and turn them away? That's why I tried to avoid those conversations with Dr. Al-Banna. It was out of respect for him and his beliefs."

Sensing a wavering in Simon's faith and defense of tolerance, Hope replied flatly, "Honestly, I think that's just a cop out."

"What?" Simon asked, getting more than a little defensive.

"Either you were trying to avoid what might be an uncomfortable conversation, or you don't really believe what you say you believe, or you really don't care about your friend," Hope said, flatly. Simon stood speechless, as he tried to pinpoint the real reason for failing to share his faith with Dr. Al-Banna.

Hope took the opportunity to make another point. "I have heard that it has been said that those who are unwilling to believe in something will fall for anything," Hope said. "That is why I said that we need to decide what we believe."

"What's that supposed to mean?" Simon asked, gruffly.

"I guess it means that if you don't truly, deep down in your heart, believe in your convictions then you leave yourself wide open to believe in someone else's," Hope said almost sorrowfully. "All that it takes for evil to persist is for good men to do nothing. Nature hates a vacuum. A country that believes everyone is right or that no one is wrong cannot stand, according to Edmund Burke. If you are not sure enough in what you believe, then the next person will be. If that happens to be the Muslims, the socialists, the secular humanists, the atheists, the liberals, or whomever, then that's who will impose their beliefs on the rest of us.

"There is only one truth for the Christian, and it is found in the inerrant word of God that reveals his true character. To make a conscious decision to overlook a blatant falsification under the guise of civility is to choose to live on the opposite side of truth outside of the perfect will of God. Even though there are an infinite number of alternate paths to truth, there is only one enemy, wielding only one weapon, to get people sidetracked. That weapon is deceit. And the greatest deceits are always cleverly couched in bits of truth.

"But what you are saying is so offensive, so exclusionary," Simon said.

"To whom," Hope asked, pressing, "to you?"

"No, of course not, but..." Simon said, hedging a bit.

"Let me ask you, which is more offensive,..." she asked, trying to determine if they were equally yoked, "...To know that we have the answer to who we are, why we are here, and what happens after we die and tell others about it; or to know that and *keep it to ourselves*?" she asked, passionately. "How much must I have to hate someone to know how to gain eternal life and not share it with them? If you were diagnosed with cancer, would you really be 'offended' if I told you that I knew a cure? Heavens, no!

"So, why are people so against having anyone tell them about being saved through the work of Jesus Christ? Could their being so greatly offended really be due to the fact that some small part of them knows it to be true? So much so that their rebellious nature has to actively suppress that truth? Who doesn't want to have things their own way? No one likes to have someone else tell them what they can and cannot do. Our sinful nature wants to make our own standard for right and wrong so that we may silence our conscience and participate in the moral filth and fleshly desires of our hearts. We want nothing more than for our choices to have no consequences, because we want to rule our own lives. We want to be our own god.

"But, nothing could be farther from the truth. Our ideas, words, and actions all have consequences. God blesses those who live according to His will and punishes those who don't. The Bible can't be any clearer on that point. Christians don't have the luxury of picking and choosing which verses from the Bible they agree with.

"That is why it is so important that we seek truth in the Word, so that we can be sure that we are standing on the right side of it," Hope said. "Once we discover the truth, we have an obligation to share it. That is why I was so ashamed of myself for not standing up for what was right. Truth does matter.

"And that is why I am renewing my personal covenant with God," Hope continued. "Given the same opportunity again, I *will not* back down. I will not run away and hide. I will stand up for what I believe in whether it be in a private meeting, or a public forum, or in the classroom, or even on the chopping block."

* * *

"Wow, I don't know how we got so far off track in this conversation," Simon said, trying to lighten things up. "Weren't we talking just about the school?"

"That's what I have been trying to tell you," Hope said. "I think those two things could be one and the same. George Orwell said that those who control the past control the future and that those who control the present control the past. We have to make a stand for what we are teaching our children in the classroom.

"Do you know what Jack Lawless's stipulation was when he offered to pay for the upgrades to the old school building?" Hope asked.

"No," Simon admitted, recalling the town hall meeting when Rob spoke on behalf of Jack.

"Jack only wanted two minor concessions for his grant," Hope said. "He wanted to choose the director of Human Resources for the district, and he wanted exclusive rights to picking out the textbooks.

"Why should one man be able to decide for everyone else what is taught in the classroom? I don't even think it should be left in the hands of a small committee. I think it should be the people's choice within each community. Let the majority decide what they want taught in the schools to our children. If that's Christianity, then so be it. If those in the minority don't like it, they can either opt their children out or move to a community that agrees with *their* system of beliefs."

"How can you be so sure that the Christians are the majority?" Simon asked.

"I can't," Hope said, regretfully. "Here's the thing, only about half of self-professing Christians actually voted in the last general election for the President of the United States. All we need is for Christians to vote according to their faith and their beliefs!"

Simon again recoiled at the notion of teaching about faith in a public classroom. Before he realized it, he heard himself mechanically respond, "But, what about the separation of church and state?"

The expression on Hope's face revealed her disappointment. "Simon, the Christians *are* the church," she replied. "The church is not a building.

"Don't you see? The Holy Spirit resides in you and me. In order to take Christianity out of the public schools, they would have to take the Christians out of the school, because we are charged with living out our faith. I am salt and light whether I have a cross hanging on the wall in my room, or a Bible on my desk, or say a prayer before I eat my lunch or not.

"Being a Christian guides me to think how I think, to say what I say, and to do what I do. It is who I am just like Dr. Al-Banna's beliefs define who he is, just like a liberal's beliefs define who they are. Everything they do, and say, and think reflects their own deep seeded beliefs too."

"But you said yourself that you aren't perfect," Simon said, now exposing his lack of fear of God. "Aren't you afraid of doing or saying something that unintentionally drives people away from the Gospel? I mean, Christians, whether it be politicians or musicians or actors or preachers or even teachers, go around spouting off about all of these grandiose ideals of laws and standards that even they themselves cannot live up to. When they trip up and break the very rules they are espousing, it is devastating. It is that kind of blatant hypocrisy that drives people away. So what gives you, or anybody else, the right to tell other people what they should or should not believe if you can't live up to the very standards you are promoting?"

"If not me, then who?" she asked. "If not now, then when? If we wait until we are perfect before we share the Good News of the Gospel, then no one will ever be able to share it. For whatever reason, God chose imperfect people to carry out the Great Commission. Can a baseball player describe what a perfect swing looks like, even if he himself strikes from time to time? To use your analogy from earlier truth, we will never bat a thousand in this life. But, I can go from batting .250 one year to .300 the next to .350 the year after that. We can make progress in the right direction.

"While it is true that a believer becomes perfect in Christ when they are saved, they are still woeful sinners while in the flesh. Just because we are saved and devote our lives to Christ, does not mean that we instantly become perfect. That is why the spiritual walk and fruit of the spirit are so important, because they validate the authenticity of the conversion of the believer. When someone who calls themselves a Christian sins, do they have remorse, do they confess, do they accept the consequences, do they ask for forgiveness, and do they repent? Are there clear changes in their lifestyle and in the things they say and in the things they do? Do they strive for perfection each and every day even though they can never fully achieve it in this life? The very fact that we are *not perfect,* that we are hypocrites, is why we needed Christ to die on the cross for us in the first place."

"And that is why I came here tonight," Hope said, solemnly. "I needed to know if the changes were substantive. I need to know if the change in *you* is authentic. I need to know if all of these changes that I see on the surface are superficial. Is all of this the fruit produced by the Spirit at work in your life?"

Simon was staggered by the admission.

"You see, I *do* believe that God has given you a specific job that only you can complete, because I believe that he has given each and every one of us a task that we were uniquely and wonderfully made for," Hope said, allowing herself to be vulnerable.

"And I do believe that God spoke to you that night in front of the church. Not in words audible for the ears to hear, but I believe you heard him in your heart because I could hear it in your voice, and I now I recognize it by your willingness to be obedient to His voice. You see, I know about deep, still voices because I have heard those voices too."

"You have?" Simon asked, suddenly transfixed by Hope's transparency.

"Yes," Hope replied, "on several occasions."

"Like when?" Simon asked, now engrossed by what Hope was divulging to him.

"When making some of the biggest decisions in my life," Hope admitted, "like choosing what college to attend, or becoming a teacher, or accepting the job at Bethel Grade School. I believe that God called me to do all of those things, and I believe that he has called me into this mission field."

"But people would be outraged if they found out that you were purposely using your position of influence to convert your students to Christianity," Simon said, almost exasperated.

It now became clear that Simon still had a ways to go in his walk after comparing his faith to Hope's. Simon felt the difference as well. There was a fierce struggle raging within him to either reject or accept what she was telling him.

After contemplating his objection, Hope looked into Simon's eyes and sighed. "That is what I have been trying to tell you," she said, unapologetically. "There are more important facts to teach kids than just one plus one plus one makes three. For example, it is far more important that they know how three can be one like God and one can be two like Jesus.

"God has blessed me with certain talents for working out my own salvation. This is the cross that I am supposed to bear."

Simon frowned, still not altogether sure about what it meant to lift his own cross and work out his own salvation. Putting all of that aside for the moment, he considered the degree of liability that Hope would be exposing herself to by living out her faith. In a feeble effort for his rebellious nature to dissuade her, he said, "What you're proposing will be extremely offensive and controversial to a lot of people."

Hope was now becoming troubled by Simon's countenance and the sound of his voice. "Let me ask you, 'What is more offensive than allowing someone to go on thinking that something is right when it is wrong?'," Hope asked. "That someone passed when they really failed? Life is not like that, and death is certainly not like that. Salvation is not graded on a curve and there are no retakes. Truth matters. And if we don't choose to stand up for what is right as a people, then we will soon be undone as a nation."

"All that I am saying is that it is just so... *radical*," Simon objected.

Undaunted by the charge, Hope replied, "That may be, but it is a sad day when trying to return our country to its spiritual foundation is considered radical. If that is how you define 'radical change', then I guess that makes me a radical, because just like Obama, I want to change this country. Only, I want to change it back to how it once was. I want to pray at the beginning of the school day, to memorize Bible verses in the curriculum, and to teach the Ten Commandments in the classroom like they used to. I think that each individual community has the right to make that choice."

Once again, Simon's ego bristled at her resolve and said, "You do realize that if you say that your goal is to return this country to our roots, you are probably just going to be dismissed as an ignorant racist who wants to return to the days of slavery."

"Racist?" Hope scoffed.

"Sure," Simon said, "it's impossible to separate a return to our roots as a country from the subject of slavery. Most of these founding fathers that you're talking about were slave owners themselves."

Hope unexpectedly burst out in laughter.

"Why are you laughing?" Simon asked, caught off guard by her reaction.

"Because it is such a ridiculous accusation for a true Christian," Hope said. "For one thing, we just talked about the hypocrisy of Christians. Those who do not know the past are condemned to repeat it. I will continue to learn from history the lessons it has provided. But, I have no desire to commit the same sins as our ancestors. That's idiotic! Second, when a person makes racist remarks or exhibits racist behavior that more or less acts as a litmus to the authenticity of the believer. Nothing in the Bible advocates judging others on the basis of their *skin* color. It's antithetical. And isn't it just like Satan to divide us by something as inconsequential as race. It's a great distraction to keep us from focusing on what really matters, like the content of our character.

"The one other thing at play here. In a very real sense we are *all* slaves. Either we are a slave to sin or a slave to righteousness. Color has absolutely nothing to do with it. It all comes down to a person's heart.

"We all have a master," Hope stated. "Either our master is God or Satan. And what she said next staggered him. "Which begs the question that everyone must deal with at some point. This is what I really want to know. Simon, who is Jesus Christ to *you*?"

Without hesitation, Simon replied, "He is my Lord and Savior."

The words of affirmation hung in the air for a moment before Hope let her guard down and smiled. "Good," she said, "and that is why I think that your mission and my mission might ultimately be one-in-the-same." The weight of the assertion pressed down on him like the sultry night air.

"You think you might know why God called me to renovate the school?" Simon asked, dumfounded.

"Yes, I do," Hope replied, stepping closer and taking him by the hands, "you see, I *do* believe that you were called to end a curse."

Shocked by the revelation, Simon's eyes widened as he tried to fully comprehend what she was telling him. "You think I was called to end the curse of Jessie Joseph?"

"In a way...yes," she said. "I think that Bethel is under a curse, but I don't believe that the curse is the result of Jessie Joseph's vengeance. I think that it is the result of God's vengeance."

"What are you talking about?" Simon asked.

"I think that God is angry at the people of Bethel for the same reason he is angry with our country, because we have turned our backs on Him," Hope replied. "Just take a good look around. God cannot be happy with the things that have been going on in this community, from the predatory, high risk loans, to the adult superstore, to the meth labs, to the building of a Mosque, to the murder of a youth pastor.

"No, you didn't see the ghost of Adam Potter, you saw something far worse. You saw a 6-year-old boy who sneaks out his house in the middle of the night because he is more afraid of what is in his own home than what might be waiting for him in the dark. So, he make believes that he is a vampire and hides in a dried up well on Clay Potter's property. Meanwhile, everybody in the whole town knows about his situation, and no one ever comes to his rescue. Suppose for a moment that Little Simon was physically trapped in that well. The entire community wouldn't mind rallying around a cause like that and doing everything in their power to get him out. The fact is that he is trapped in something far more dangerous than a well, and yet no one bothers to lift a finger. That is, no one cared until Jeremy...and now *you*.

"Is it any wonder that we are under God's judgment? I think that those tragedies are the result of His wrath!"

"But, if God is a loving God," Simon said, daring to explore Hope's hypothesis, "how could he possibly do such a thing? How can He *allow* so many tragedies, much less bring them about?"

"God *is* love," Hope said, "but, at the same time, He cannot deny Himself. To be love He must hate evil behavior and perverse speech. That's what I think of when I see depravity in our own little community on the same level as Sodom and Gomorrah, or I see unfaithfulness to the same degree as Israel and Judah just before the exile to Babylon.

"Have you ever read Jeremiah, or Ezekiel, or Lamentations, or Daniel, or Hosea?" Hope asked, lovingly. "Which of those transgressions for which God brought judgment on the his people cannot be found in Bethel today?

"There was a time when we were a prosperous, peaceful society, but I would argue that it was not in and of itself the result of adhering to traditionally held ideals of the American Dream like hard work and perseverance.

"We were prosperous because we were blessed. We were blessed because our Lord and Savior, Jesus Christ was a part of every aspect of the community. We were blessed because we followed his commands and abided by his laws."

"Suppose for a moment that that were true, what does any of it have to do with Jessie Joseph, or Adam Potter, or rebuilding the school, or even me for that matter?" Simon asked, his mind racing.

"I don't know exactly," Hope said, "but it makes me wonder. Something in the past had to have happened that changed Bethel. Something in the past triggered a series of events that led to a systematic removal of Jesus Christ from the public arena. It may have been a small, subtle change at first, but something happened that started us down the wrong path in the wrong direction. We're not progressing, but digressing. And now, all these years later, we are way off of the mark.

"All I know is that there was a time when we were a Christian community in a Christian nation. We more closely adhered to the teachings of Jesus, but over the past seventy-two years we have drifted further and further from Him and His teachings. There must have been a watershed moment in which Christians compromised their beliefs and began to give ground, and we have been retreating ever since."

"I still don't see what it has to do with me and my, uh, calling," Simon replied.

"Think about it," Hope said. "Is it merely a coincidence that you felt called to restore the school back to its original condition at the same time I felt called to take my stand? I don't know how it all fits together or if it does at all, but what if you were right? What if the purpose of your project is to remind people of something. Not necessarily just to remind us of the value of education, but to remind us of the value of wisdom and discretion as taught in the Bible. Maybe it was about our priorities. Maybe tonight wasn't just about the end of a renovation or a vote on a referendum."

Simon's face fell. He dropped her hands for a moment and stepped away, "Wait a minute. What?" Simon asked.

"Listen, what if the American Dream isn't as much about achievement as it is about showing our love for God through obedience?" Hope proposed. "After all, it is God who gives us life. The Ten Commandments give us liberty. What if the pursuit of happiness really isn't about having lots of money, or having the biggest house on the block, or the nicest cars, or a vacation home in the Bahamas? What if genuine happiness is discovering your God given talents and using them to fulfill His will for your life for His glory. Maybe that is the only way to truly fill the void in people's lives. Maybe Parker was right. Maybe that should be everybody's 'one thing'."

Simon stood, speechless beneath the inescapable glow of the giant chandelier.

"Is it possible that God doesn't want you to take that job in New Jersey?" she said, now shyly looking to the ground and wiping her bangs out of her eyes before taking another step towards him. "Maybe he wants you to stay here with me. Maybe he wants us to work together. Maybe He even wants us *to be* together. Maybe you're calling and my calling are intertwined in some way."

Simon's heart skipped a beat.

Hope took a deep breath before revealing her true feelings and making herself completely vulnerable to him. "You see, from the time we first met, I have heard that same audible voice that had compelled me to act at all of those other critical times in my life," she confessed. "But I was trying to suppress it, because I wanted to make sure that I wasn't being misled by the flesh. I was trying to figure out if the voice inside of me was from me or from God. So, I decided to pray, and be patient, and wait.

"Then, out of the blue, you showed up that night at camp. There was something different about you. There was a light in your eye that I hadn't seen previously, and the more we talked, and the more you shared with me your innermost thoughts, the more certain I was that the voice was from God."

She paused for a moment and looked down at the shimmering, hardwood floor between them, and said, "But no sooner had I allowed myself to believe that, than you decided to tell me about Jez. I was... I was devastated because I had just come to the conclusion that I was in love with you. I thought, 'how can the man I am supposed to be with want to be with anyone else, let alone someone who does *that* sort of thing for a living?'."

Hope looked away and involuntarily shuddered as the words rolled off of her tongue. Simon scrunched his face together as he tried to analyze what she meant by 'that.'

"I always thought that when I finally did find the guy that God had chosen for me to marry," Hope continued, "that he would have saved himself for me just like I had saved myself for him. When you admitted that you even *wanted* to be with Jez, I got scared, because you had been so willing to frivolously give yourself away to anybody. I didn't think I could ever trust that you could be faithful to me if that were the case."

Simon's shoulders drooped on hearing her words, and he could not bring himself to look her in the eyes. Hope leaned down to one side and re-established eye contact.

"I have to admit that when you left those messages about your conversion," she said, "I was a little skeptical. But mostly I was angry. I was angry at God for forgiving you, for showing you mercy. You had broken my heart. When I went over and over the whole thing in my mind, I thought, 'why should God forgive you. Why should he give you comfort and peace'? You didn't deserve that. I was the one who had been faithful. I was the one who kept myself pure. I was the one who was hurt by your careless decisions. Then I was the one left to wrestle with my own pain, hate, and vengeful heart.

"Desperately, I tried to forget that the whole thing had ever happened. I tried to completely block you out of my mind and pretend you never meant anything to me. That would have been a whole lot easier, you know. As much as I tried, I couldn't deny my feelings. I was so angry with you because I had an unconditional love for you. Had I not been in love with you, I don't think I would have been angry at all. I may have been disappointed in you as a friend, but not seething with anger. That told me just how much I loved you.

"I soon realized that my anger stemmed primarily from my jealousy. I was jealous, but not in the traditional sense. It was like jealous for guarding what was rightfully mine. Honestly, I wanted justice to be served. I wanted you to pay for what you had done to me, maybe even more so because I love you.

"Really, I wanted to be the sole object of your desire and devotion. I didn't want to share that with anyone else. And that's when it hit me. That is how God must feel about me when I desire anything other than him. How many times must that occur each and every day? I mean, I can't even keep the first command, 'Love the Lord, your God, with all of your heart, soul, mind, and strength' for more than a minute, and yet that is what is required of me.

"All of a sudden, I felt like Jonah after God grew a plant to shade him from the sun. I was being a total hypocrite. Who was I to judge you? As much as I hate to admit it, there have been times when I had *wanted* to be with some guy whom I was attracted to. Maybe just as badly as you desired Jez that night. Of course, there is a huge difference between entertaining those thoughts and acting on them...from our limited, worldly perspective. To God, the only real difference between your desirous heart and mine was that I never put myself in as vulnerable of a position as you had put yourself in that night.

"It was then that God showed me something that truly humbled me. In those moments of weakness, the times when I lusted in my heart to be with some random guy on the street or on TV, I was not only being unfaithful to whomever my future husband might be, but more importantly, I was being unfaithful to a jealous God who deserved my full devotion. In a very real way, your infraction was worse because you took it to another level, but by God's standards we are both outside the bounds of the law anytime we linger in those kinds of thoughts. We each become equally guilty, and equally deserving of the same consequences.

"And for the first time, in the midst of my pain, I could sympathize a little with how heartbroken God must have been at the times I had been unfaithful. That includes things like jealousy, gossip, foolish pride, and even lust. Through this experience, I realized just how desperately I needed God's mercy and grace.

"I came to the conclusion that I could not expect God to forgive me for my sins until I was willing to forgive you for your sins, so I did. Now, after admitting my sins, He has forgiven me because I have forgiven you. Simon, I do forgive you."

Tears were welling up in Simon's eyes.

"However..." she said, with a grave expression, "... there are actually two separate issues at work here. It would be one thing if I were to offer that to you with the knowledge that I would never have to see you, or interact with you again. That's quite a bit different from offering a second chance."

Simon couldn't contain the spontaneous smile from emerging out of the corner of his mouth.

"If I were to give us a second chance, I would have to know something," Hope said. "I would have to know that you do understand the seriousness of your actions, that you truly are sorry for what you have done, and that you will never do something like that ever again; not that you won't ever have a fleeting temptation to lust, but that you will never give in to those temptations. I need to know that you're not the same guy who came to Bethel a couple of months ago. I need to know that you have truly changed and that from here on out you're going to make better decisions.

"Before you answer, I will tell you that it might not be easy for me to fully trust you for a while. God knows your heart. I don't. All I can see is your actions. And it may take some time. time that we don't have unless you decide to stay in Bethel."

There was a deafening silence. Even though Simon understood that his previous desire for Jez was wrong, he still was having a difficult time grasping the magnitude. Of course, it stung a little when Hope said that she had wanted other guys at different times in her life, but those feelings provided some empathy for what she felt.

Still, he wasn't able to fully appreciate what it took for Hope to forgive him. Inside, a war raged back and forth between elation on hearing of her affection for him and condescension for being above reproach for his indiscretion.

Still searching his eyes, Hope patiently waited for a response.

His silence was both equally alarming to his state of indecision as it was hopeful due to a lack of objection. Going out on a limb, she decided to say what she had come to say, "Simon, I am willing to start over and see what God might have in store for us if you are. Maybe the plan he has for your life and the plan he has for mine are the same plan."

He was at a loss for words and didn't know what to say. It was a great deal for him to take in all at once. Through all of the emotional clutter, there were two things he was certain of. First, it was readily apparent just how deeply and sincerely Hope was convicted in her beliefs. Second, if she were right, then he knew that he still had a very long way to go as a believer.

Even so, he still wasn't sure that she was right. Was Hope just some religious nut, or was she simply that much closer to understanding God than anyone else he had ever known? The question raged inside of him because of the potential ramifications. If she was just an overzealous wacko, then he knew exactly what to do. He would finish cleaning up the basement, pack his things, and head for the coast. The alternative was much more complicated.

What if she was right? What is that truly was God's plan? Only a few hours earlier Simon thought that he had all of the answers. He had put his life on hold, completed a monumental project, and received the accolades for a job well done. Now having taken time out of his life to do what God had asked him to do, he was ready to get back to doing what he had set out to do. The very suggestion that the renovation might only be the beginning of the task, and not the end, was almost incomprehensible. Something inside of him violently objected, nearly crying out in opposition.

Still, another side of him wondered if there was any merit to what she was saying. Was it fate or a coincidence that brought them to this point? After wrestling with the issue for a moment, he knew that he couldn't explain what brought him back to Bethel or why he stayed. He couldn't say why he wanted to do the school renovation, and he had no idea what he would do next. There was something else that became abundantly clear that complicated matters greatly. He knew that he was madly in love with Hope.

The moment he came to that realization, she seemed to know it too. A warm smile ran across her angelic face.

"I think I know what I want to do," Simon replied, conceding a smile.

"Wait, before you make your decision, you should have all of the facts," Hope said. "I want you to carefully consider what I am about to say.

"If the Holy Spirit were truly moving within in you to complete this project, then I think there is a very good chance that there is more work to be done here based on how little opposition that you faced. I have heard it said that during the course of our lives we are either in a storm, coming out of a storm, or getting ready to head into a storm. I mean, Jesus himself warned us that we would be persecuted for following Him. If that is the case, then you better get ready."

"Hope, I..." Simon started to say with a pained expression.

Suddenly, they were startled by a booming voice that called out from the back entrance to the gym, "*Simon!*"

Immediately, Simon recognized it as Rich's old, familiar voice.

"That's okay, we can talk more in the morning," Hope said, taking that as her cue and backing away towards the doors. "I don't want you to answer tonight anyway. I want you to sleep on it and to pray about it. Then give me your answer."

"Wait, don't go," Simon pleaded.

Rich's voice boomed again, "*Simon! Are you in here somewhere?*"

Simon looked over his shoulder in the direction that the voice was coming from, but chose to ignore it.

"Hang on a second," Simon said to Hope. "I'll just get rid of him."

"No, that's okay," Hope said. "It's late, and I really should go, but there is just one more thing I need to know before I go."

"What is it?" he asked, almost in a panic.

"I need to know if there is anything else you would like to tell me about," she asked with grave concern. She was still holding his hands but starting to pull away towards the door. "You know, like the thing with Jez. If you tell me now, I think I can deal with it. We just need to get it all out in the open, but I just can't handle any more surprises. I need to know that I can trust you."

"...*Simon*, where are you at, dude?" Rich called out.

Simon turned his head and called out, "Up here!" Then he turned back to Hope. "No, there's nothing, I promise, nothing like that," Simon said with his mind racing.

"Please, don't make any promises," Hope said, pulling away so their finger tips were barely touching. "Simply let your 'yes' be 'yes', and your 'no', 'no.'"

"Then...no," Simon replied.

With that, Hope rushed back into Simon's arms and kissed him tenderly on the lips. She pulled back and looked into his eyes. Then she hurried down the steps and ran out the front door, leaving Simon standing alone under the magnificent chandelier.

30

THE DESOLATION OF THE OBAMANATION

"There you are," Rich said, looking up at his friend standing on the landing. "Wilson B. said, I'd find you here."

Simon was still facing the front doors, trying to fully grasp the enormity of all that Hope had told him. Reluctantly, he turned to see Rich at the foot of the steps adorned in full managerial garb, from cap to cleats. He was standing with his arms folded, and he was seething mad.

"What?" Simon asked, somewhat dazed.

"Dude," Rich said, exasperated, "we have got to have you back out there umpiring. Joey has brought in some guys to fill your spot, and every one of em's been terrible."

"Really?" Simon asked, obviously distracted.

"The first guy," Rich said, "he didn't have a clue. I don't think he has ever even laid eyes on a rule book. And, and, and, the second guy was even worse. You wouldn't believe this guy. Oh man, I don't think he'd ever even seen a baseball game before much less played in one. And this moron, Joey brought with him tonight," Rich said shaking his head in disgust, " he was out of position all night. I couldn't take it. I had to say something. The guy almost cost us the game on a bang-bang play at first."

"What?" Simon asked, as if he were only just now entering the conversation.

"Haven't you been listening to a word I've said?" Rich asked, getting testy. "Joey and George can't find anyone decent to ump first base."

"So?" Simon replied, incredulously.

"So?" Rich repeated. "So, the playoffs are next week. I need you out there."

"'Need me out there'?" Simon repeated as he started to clean up from the dedication ceremony. "Just have Joey and George do it. You don't need three guys anyway. It's little league baseball."

Rich frowned as he followed Simon around the landing passionately pleading his case. "No, no, no," he said, "you don't get it. Those two are on some kind of power trip, making the whole thing about *them* instead of the kids."

"I can see Joey doing that, but George was acting like that too?" Simon asked, as he picked up a broom and began to sweep the floor.

"Well, not George so much," Rich conceded, instinctively picking up the dust pan, "but Joey was a nightmare, man."

"Joey knows the rules," Simon said as he swept up some dust bunnies.

"Of course, he knows them," Rich growled, bending down to hold the dust pan on the floor. "That's not the problem."

"Then what is the problem?" Simon asked, still preoccupied by the weighty decision that he had to make.

"The problem is…," Rich replied, motioning with the dust pan for Simon to sweep up the pile he had made, "…the guy thinks he's God's gift to umpiring. That's the problem. All the power's going to his head or something. I don't know. He's Hitler with a balls and strikes counter.

"It's hard to explain exactly what it is he's doing. I don't know. It's like he's not interpreting the rules to make sure that the game is an even playing field, ya know? It's like he's abusing his authority to interpret the rules in his own way. The result is that he basically ignores the real rules and sets a new precedent. In the process, he makes up his own new set of rules and then uses them as a hammer to control the game and determine the outcome. It's almost like he's choosing winners and losers based on how he calls it. I don't know. It's weird. And I don't think it's arbitrary, if you know what I mean. I think he's got some kind of agenda."

"Sounds a little conspiratorial, don't you think, even for Joey?" Simon asked, shuffling the broom along the shimmering wood floor.

"Well, at the very least, he's power trippin'," Rich replied. "I mean, the guy punched out some poor kid on a backwards K' like he was in the seventh game of the World Series. So, I said, 'that's kind of 'Naked Gunnish' don't ya think?' And he gave me a warning. A warning! I mean, how ridiculous is that?"

"So, fire him," Simon said, taking the dust pan out of Rich's hands and dumping it into the garbage can..

Rich frowned as he took the broom from Simon and put it back in the closet. "Fire him, I can't just…what in the world is this?" Rich asked, looking up and noticing the monument for the first time.

"It's the Declaration of Independence," Simon said as he began to gather the curtain up into his arms and fold it.

"I know that!" Rich adamantly replied, taking two corners out of the curtain out of Simon's hands and backing up away from him.

Simon looked up at his burly friend who was still covered in a thin layer of dust from the ball park, as they folded the curtain one time over.

"Really? You do?" Simon asked, raising on eyebrow.

"Okay, I probably knew it at one time…anyway I can't just fire Joey," Rich complained, as he turned the curtain over. "No, the other way,…here like this."

They walked towards one another and held the corners together. "It's much more complicated than just firing the guy. Lexus is the head of parks and recreation, and he hand picked Joey himself. I think Lexus wants to offer Joey a job when he gets out of school. So, basically, Lexus has Joey in his back pocket. He's like untouchable until someone else is in charge of the parks."

Simon grabbed the perfectly folded up curtain out of Rich's arms and blankly stared at his friend. "Are you serious?" Simon said. "Are you really suggesting that Lexus is somehow fixing Little League baseball games by bribing Joey?"

Rich dropped his hands to his side and said, "Look, Joey's uncle owns the rights to the group of umpires that we contract with. Lexus pays his uncle. His uncle pays Joey. Joey calls the game. And around and around we go. So, what do you think is going on?"

"I guess anything's possible," Simon said, conceding the point. As ridiculous of a notion as it was, Simon had a hard time caring at the moment. There were far too more urgent matters for him to sort through at this point. He didn't have time for things that were completely out of his control.

"I'm telling you," Rich said, grabbing the folded curtain back from Simon before smoothing out the wrinkles with his enormous hands. "That trophy has been sitting in the tavern for almost a year now, and it's eating Lexus up. He wants it back in the bank, and he's willing to do whatever it takes to get it. I am telling you, I know the guy." Then he looked down at the blanket he had been smoothing out. "What is this thing anyway?"

"One of the wise men's robes," Simon said with a goofy smile before taking it out of Rich's large hands.

"Huh? '…wise men's robe'?" Rich repeated with a confused expression.

"From the nativity scene…never mind, I'll take it," Simon said. "So, what does this have to do with me?" he asked as he placed the folded up purple robe into a cardboard box.

Rich had a bewildered expression on his face. He was still trying to figure out who the wise men were. "What's this got to do with you?" Rich asked. "Everything! You're the great equalizer. You can balance Joey out. You can keep him in check. You know the rules just as well as he does, and I know I can count on you to do the right thing. This is right up your alley. Dude, it's this whole do-gooder kick you've been on lately. Now, do the right thing!"

Suddenly, Rich could see he was losing traction. He thought for a moment in desperation, before he formulated his best argument yet. "Think about the kids, man," Rich pleaded. "Is it really fair to the kids? It should be all about the kids like Parker and, uh, Randy."

Simon stopped and stared at Rich. "What about George?" he asked. He bent down to pick up the oversized box that he had just dropped the robe into. When he did, the envelope that Jack Lawless had left for him fell out of his pocket onto the newly waxed floor.

"George?" Rich asked. "Let me tell you something about George. He's a brilliant kid and all, but he's a follower…"

While Rich decried George's shortcomings, Simon deftly picked up the envelope and turned it over in his hands as if seeing it for the first time. With a perplexed expression on his face, he carefully opened it and extracted an old, yellowed photograph. It was a black and white class picture from 1935, not unlike the many others that he had used to recreate the look and feel of the old entryway. Only this particular photo did not appear to have been taken from a yearbook, instead it had been cutout of an old newspaper. It even included a caption, "*Mr. Jessie Joseph pictured with the first and second grade classes*". Upon closer examination, the picture seemed to reference a heretofore unknown accompanying article that made special mention of Jessie and four of his students: Adam Potter, John Rash, Andrew Cross, and Peter Cross.

Simon was floored by the revelation and his expression gave him away. "Peter Cross, Peter, Pete, Pete Cross…Pastor Pete Cross?" Simon blurted out.

"…Bottom line George is more or less Joey's disciple," Rich said, before Simon's words registered. "What's wrong?"

"Check this out," Simon said, turning the tattered piece of newspaper around. "Mr. Cross and Pastor Cross were both in Jessie Joseph's class!"

"What?" Rich said. "Let me see at that." Rich took the frayed picture into his thick hands and examined it closely. Then he shrugged and handed back the picture. "Yeah, that's pretty wild I guess. So what?"

"So what?" Simon scoffed, taking the photo back. "So, I never knew that before. I mean, neither one of them ever said anything. It never occurred to me that I might actually know somebody who was in that class on the day…" His mind began to race as he considered all of the things that he and Hope had discussed regarding the purpose for the renovation and what might still be in store for them. "Oh man, this is huge!" Simon said while taking another look at the photo.

"I know!" Rich said, thinking that he was finally getting through to Simon. "There's a lot riding on this tournament."

"Yeah…wait…what?" Simon said, temporarily confused. "No, no, no, I'm talking about the renovation. I'm talking about the purpose for…wait, what are you talking about?"

"Oh, man!" Rich said, rolling his eyes. "Haven't you heard a word that I've said? I'm talking about the tournament next week. I need *you* to umpire."

Simon, still preoccupied by his recent discovery, folded the picture back up and stuffed it into his shirt pocket. Absentmindedly, he bent down, picked up the large box, and began carrying it towards the staircase.

"You got that?" Rich asked, noting the size of the box. "Can I help you with it?"

"No, I'm good, thanks," Simon said. "Oh, hey, you can grab that belt over there, though."

"The bottom line is that you can even the playing field, if you're umping first base," Rich said, as he searched the floor all around him. "What do you need?"

"The draw string for the curtain, the golden rope thingy," Simon said.

"Where is it?" Rich asked.

"It's over there on the podium," Simon replied as he motioned with his chin.

"What?" Rich said. He looked all around the podium. "I don't see it."

"It might be inside of it," Simon said, looking over the top of the box that was cradled in his arms.

"Oh, here it is," Rich said, holding it up. "The thing is, George respects you for whatever reason. He looks up to you."

The remark once again captured Simon's attention. "Really?" he asked, perplexed. "I thought he considered me a total hypocrite after that stunt I pulled at the bar."

"Yeah, well, maybe," Rich said, trying to play on Simon's ego. "I don't know. Something about this project you've been doing changed his mind. I think he's impressed with it. He said something about it the other day."

Rich paused and looked around the room as if seeing it for the first time.

"Really?" Simon mused. He couldn't help but think about what Hope had said about the fruit of the project, and how God might use it. For the second time that night, he considered how the project had given him credibility and a platform.

"I guess," Rich said, looking around the room with a disapproving expression. "So, this is what you've been spending all of your time doing?" Rich asked while leaning in to get a better look at the painting of George Washington crossing the Delaware.

"Yeah," Simon said, as he held the box up with one knee, opened it, and stuffed the cord inside.

"I don't get it, man," Rich said. He scrunched up his face as if he were getting a fresh whiff of a pungent odor. "Why'd you do it? I mean, don't get me wrong, to each his own. But why in the world would you waste all your time doing all of this?"

"You're not serious," Simon answered in disbelief. "I sat there in that storage room at the tavern and poured my heart out to you about all of this, and you totally blew me off. Are you really asking me 'why I did this?'." He repositioned the large box and headed down the stairs towards the basement.

"What? That?" Rich said. "You were talking crazy talk; all about ghosts and goblins and what not."

Simon stopped on one of the steps and looked back up over his shoulder. "Seriously? Goblins?" Simon repeated.

"I'm just sayin'," Rich continued, "you weren't making any sense. Honestly, I thought you might be making some visits to one of the local meth labs or something. I...wait a minute...where are we going?"

"I have to take this down to the basement," Simon replied.

"The basement?" Rich asked with slight trepidation.

"What? Oh, come on, all of a sudden you believe in ghosts," Simon chided.

"Big tough guy like you. I've been working here nonstop around the clock for a month straight, and I haven't seen any signs of Jessie Joseph. "

Simon stopped on the last step leading down to the basement before realizing that he only was hearing his own set of footsteps. Quizzically, he turned around to see Rich still standing at the top of the stairs, jut his neck out to get a long hard look at the dank, dark basement.

"You can't be serious," Simon said. "You were just giving me a hard time about believing the legend and...wait a minute...that's why you didn't go with us to Potter's that night isn't it? It's not because you don't believe in the legend. It's because you *do*."

"What? That's ridiculous," Rich said, finally coming out from behind the wall. Slowly, he eased his way down the steps. "My allergies have been acting up, and with all of this moisture and mold down here...Oh, shut up. If you must know, I'm also not real excited about bumping into your little vampire-boy down here either. That kid freaks me out! And you said something about an infestation, didn't you?"

"You're scared, admit it," Simon said, a little amused by it all.

"If you can't be scared about a 6-year-old who calls himself a vampire, sneaks out of his house at night to hide in a creepy old basement, and bites people, then what can you be afraid of?" Rich asked, staying close to Simon as he made his way to the storage room.

Simon held the box precariously on one knee as he reached up with his right hand and groped for the light switch dangling from a bare bulb in the closet.

"Yes, Simon Adamson has some serious problems, but he is just a scared little kid," Simon said, as the light came on in the room. "Now, you on the other hand,... look at you. You're genuinely afraid right now, and that's the reason you didn't go with us to find the graveyard that night."

"Who goes looking for a graveyard?" Rich snapped with his anger beginning to overcome his fear.

"So, it is true," Simon said, "I knew it. Well, I wish you would have been there that night. You might have saved me from making one of the biggest mistakes of my life."

"Biggest mistakes of your life?" Rich squawked. "What are you talking about?"

"With Jez," Simon admitted.

"I should hope that wasn't a 'big mistake'," Rich snapped, his temper beginning to surface.

"What are you getting so bent out of shape about?" Simon asked. "I was the one who nearly wrecked everything with Hope for some stupid one night fling."

"Well, I was the one who was out a hundred bucks!" Rich said before he could take it back.

"What?" Simon asked as he dropped the box onto the basement floor. "Wait a minute. You *paid* Jez to do that?"

"Well, yeah, what are best friends for?" Rich asked. "Anyway, what are you getting so upset about? I wanted you to have a good time." Rich could tell by Simon's expression that he was angry. "Look. We're just guys. We have needs. Hope can't blame you for being a guy, can she?"

Simon's face went flush. So, that was what Hope was talking about. Suddenly, he knew what she meant by '...doing, *that* for a living.' It would have been bad enough if Jez would have just been any other girl. Now it made even more sense as to why Hope had been so upset by his carefree attitude about the situation and why she had had such a hard time forgiving him.

An enormous sense of shame and guilt overwhelmed him, as he ran his tongue over the sore on his lip. For the first time, he became keenly aware of how people could be unfaithful to a future spouse that they had yet to meet. He contemplated the potential venereal diseases that he might have exposed himself to. All at once he felt sick to his stomach.

"I-I just wanted you to stay," Rich stammered, seeing the hurt look on Simon's face. "I just paid her to flirt with you a little, ya know. I wanted her to show you a good time. And it worked. You stayed. So, that's good, right? It kind of all worked out. It's not like you caught anything from her or got her pregnant...right?"

Simon didn't say a word, as he thought about what nearly had happened. Suddenly, he felt nauseous. "Nothing happened," Simon said flatly.

"What?" Rich said, taken aback. "That little skank." For a brief moment, he fixated on being taken in the business transaction. Quickly, he shrugged it off and said, "So, nothing happened. No harm, no foul. Hope has nothing to be upset about then. Life goes on."

Simon thought of what Hope said about faithfulness to God, and what she said about it being a heart issue.

"Look, you stayed in Bethel," Rich continued, "you met Hope, you've completed your little project here, and now everything can go back to how it was before. You can go back to doing all of the things you did before like umpiring, right?"

As soon as Rich said that everything can go back to how it was before, Simon's heart sank. He thought of everything that Hope said about knowing if God had truly been in the project like what it all meant and how they would know. And, of course, he thought of her question, 'Had anything really changed?'.

"No thanks, man," Simon said.

"*What?*" Rich pleaded.

"I've got more important things to do than umpire some little kids' baseball game," Simon objected.

"What are you talking about?" Rich asked, as if something blasphemous had just been uttered. "It's baseball. What's more important baseball?"

"Just about everything," Simon chirped.

"Like what?" Rich challenged, getting defensive. "Like this ridiculous project?"

"Ridiculous?" Simon shouted. "I'll tell you what's ridiculous, grown men dressing up in baseball uniforms to coach a baseball game for a bunch of 10-year-olds. What's that all about? Get over it! Grow up!"

Rich opened his arms with his palms out and looked himself up and down. "What's wrong with my uniform?" he asked. "This isn't some knockoff, this is the real deal. It's just like they wear in the bigs!"

"Life is not *all* about sports," Simon snapped.

"What are you talking about?" Rich said. "It's like I don't even know who you are anymore. Think of the fun we had playing ball. Think of all the things you learned about life while playing sports. It even got you an education."

Simon bit his lip and searched for a reply. He couldn't deny those things. "Yes," Simon answered, conceding the point, "look, I did love playing ball, and I did learn a lot from it. And it opened some doors for me. But, you guys have taken a good thing and made it your 'one thing'. It's like winning the 'Golden Cow' trophy validates your existence or something."

"Oh, so now you've got something against competition and winning?" Rich asked, astounded by what he was hearing.

"No, no, no, I like winning as much as the next guy, and I totally believe in the value of competition," Simon replied, trying to organize his thoughts. "But, that's not what life is all about. And it shouldn't be what youth sports is all about. As important as competition and winning is, it should not be the focal point. Not everything in life is a competition."

Rich starred at him in awestruck silence.

Simon sighed deeply and collected his thoughts for a moment. "Look," he said. "It's really a heart issue. It's not so much the winning as it is why you want to win. Who is it about? Is it about the boys? Or is it all about you? Because there's something seriously wrong with living vicariously through a bunch of 10-year-olds.

"Yes, sports are great, but at some point it ends. Then what? You guys make it the end all be all. Will these kids ever be able to move beyond the glory days of their youth? If these kids define themselves by playing sports, then what happens when they can no longer do that? If kids go through your program thinking that the best years of their lives are behind them at age eighteen, then you've done them a great disservice.

"Sports are what we do, it's not who we are. If it's only about winning, then you completely missed the boat. Kids should learn how to compete, how to play as a team. They should learn work ethic, self-sacrifice, and all that stuff. But, even then, it is ultimately meaningless if those things aren't learned in the context of what life is all about."

"Oh, so now you're going to tell me what life is all about," Rich scoffed.

Ignoring Rich's objection, Simon continued, "Hey, I'm not trying to demean what you do, you are a great coach. Your players look up to you. They admire you. God has given you ability that other people don't have…"

Suddenly, Simon's own words gave him pause. At once, he knew exactly what he needed to say. "…Wait a minute. I'm sorry. I may have spoken too flippantly about the importance of sports."

Rich rolled his eyes and gave a sigh of relief. "Thank you," he muttered. "Yes, you have."

"God has given you a specific talent, and he put in you a position of great influence at a crucial age for these kids," Simon said excitedly. "That could be *your* purpose, Rich. Think about it. That could be your 'one thing'. You could reach kids for Christ through baseball. You could teach those impressionable kids how to maximize their abilities to fulfill God's will for their lives! For His glory."

"You're nuts," Rich said flatly.

"No, I'm serious," Simon said. "I can totally see it now. Yes, competition is important because iron sharpens iron, and success is important because it builds confidence. Even losing can be good, if it builds character, but the key is keeping Jesus Christ and the Gospel at the heart of it all."

Rich was at a total loss for words. When faced with the truth, he was defenseless. Moreover, he was completely out of his comfort zone. Conditioned by Jack's rules at the tavern, he was unaccustomed and unprepared to participating in a political or religious discourse.

"Think about it," Simon continued, surprised by his own passion bubbling to the surface, "can you really say that you are satisfied with your life? You sit around and talk about the past, wishing you could go back and do it all over again. You spend all of your spare time trying to figure out how to win some trophy like it will fill the void you feel inside of you. Well, I have to tell you, it doesn't matter if you win four, eight, or a dozen titles, it never will be enough to fill that void. You will always want more.

"Because life is about more than a cause, or a goal, or a trophy. It's how we are wired. That void can only be filled by God. And baseball could be your mission field."

Simon's words had struck a cord, and now Rich was forced to confront his own demons.

"And let me tell you something about my little project here," Simon proclaimed, bringing it back around full circle to his own purpose. "This thing is *not* over. There's still more work to be done. A lot more to be done."

"Oh really?" Rich asked mockingly. "Like what?"

Simon had gotten ahead of himself in all of his zeal. Now unprepared to deal with the consequences of his bold statement, he haphazardly offered up a lame excuse to skirt the real issue.

"Like, like, like this basement for one thing," Simon said, flustered by the magnitude of making such a monumental decision about permanently staying in Bethel. "I've got to go through all of this stuff and sort out the valuables from the trash. Then I have to burn up the garbage and store up the treasure."

"Man, you have completely lost it, Freeman!" Rich said. "When you came back to town, I thought, 'Man, Simon is home. It'll be just like old times'. And it felt that way for a while, and then, I don't know, something happened to you. You've changed, man."

It was the unexpected confirmation that Simon needed to give him a boost of confidence. "Yes, I have changed," he said proudly, "and let me tell you why. I was saved. And I have recommitted my life to serving my Lord and Savior Jesus Christ." There it was. He had said it.

"Ohhh man, I don't want to hear that stuff," Rich complained, with a dismissive wave of his hand.

Upon hearing his friend's words, Simon was overcome with the reality of the depth of their meaning for his lost friend. He could see that Rich was confused and in turmoil after hearing the truth.

"But, you *do* need to hear that," Simon said, now gaining confidence. "Everyone needs to hear that. If you don't want to hear it because you are afraid of what you might have to give up and what you might have to change. You don't have to worry. I am telling you, you will get so much more than you ever have to give up. You need Christ, Rich. Without him there is no salvation and life has no meaning."

Rich started to backpedal towards the staircase with the wheels turning over in his mind. "I don't want to talk about it anymore," Rich said, cupping his mouth and shaking his head. "I-I don't even want to think about it…you just live your life, and I will live mine, and it'll all be fine."

"Jesus does not give us that option," Simon said almost pleading. "We can't just ignore it. He forces us to make a decision for ourselves about who He is. He loves you, and He is waiting with an open invitation for you to come to Him. All you have to do is confess your sins, ask for forgiveness, and acknowledge that He is your Lord and Savior. We can do it right now. I can help you do it. It just takes a little faith."

Rich's eyes glistened as he mulled over the offer. After a long pause, his face turned sour. "Look, I…I've got to go, man," he said softly. "I'm closing down the tavern tonight."

Then he turned and went away sad.

"Hey, Rich," Simon called out, taking a few steps towards the stairs.

Rich paused with one hand on the railing and turned to look back down at Simon. He had a downcast expression on his face.

"Just think about what I said, okay?" Simon asked. "Will you at least do that for me?"

"You just let me know if you can work the tournament," Rich said, flatly. "If you don't want to do it, I'll find somebody else."

Simon nodded as Rich ascended the steps and exited the building.

For a few minutes, Simon ruminated on Rich's abrupt change in demeanor upon hearing about Jesus Christ and His offer of salvation. It was just as profound and divisive as Hope had promised that it would be.

On the heels of his latest revelation, Simon was stricken by the dire condition of those who had never heard the Gospel. He not only thought about his close friend but also anyone else who may have never heard the Word. Suddenly, he had an overwhelming sense of urgency to reach the lost for Christ.

Simon closed his eyes and mouthed the words of a prayer. Hope's words reverberated in his ear, "…Do what you can, with what you have, where you are." Even though Rich had not immediately accepted his invitation, Simon had been obedient. There was no way to know when his offer would bear fruit, or if it would at all, but at least the seed had been planted. For the first time, he seriously contemplated the position of being a lowly teacher's aid. He could barely fathom reaching high by stooping low.

Unfolding his hands and opening his eyes again, he felt that he had his answer for Hope. It was now obvious to him that he still had a great deal of unfinished business left to do in Bethel. At peace with his decision, Simon excitedly reached for his cell phone before remembering what Hope had said about accidentally shattering hers into a million pieces at a truck stop.

Simon actually considered paying her a late night visit before reluctantly deciding that he had no other choice but to wait until morning before giving her the good news. With no one else to call or confide in at such a late hour, he did the only thing he could do; in an act of humble obedience, he set out to finish the work he had begun. Simon started separating the trash from treasure in the musty basement with great wisdom and discernment.

He surveyed the contents of the room, considering where to begin, before something on the floor caught his eye. It was the same New England Primer he had seen several weeks before it had gone curiously missing.

With Little Simon running around the building, it wasn't unusual for things to turn up missing from time to time. After all, it was one of the things that had perpetuated the ghost story and the legend of Jessie Joseph. If Little Simon had had any interest in it, it had since been lost. Now it lay, carelessly discarded on the sooty floor.

Simon thought of the Bible verses he had read from its stiff, yellow pages and bent down to retrieve the book from the floor. When he did, the picture that Jack had given him slipped out of his shirt pocket and fell onto the floor. With a furrowed brow, Simon reached down, picked it up, and held it up under the naked bulb. Mindlessly, he set the primer down on the large box and delicately unfolded the picture one more time.

Intently, his eyes surveyed the old piece of parchment paying particular attention to a handsome, rather unsuspecting figure who could have easily been arbitrarily placed into any other photo taken during the same time period. The figure was none other than Jessie Joseph. Simon studied infamous, young man's countenance and wondered what secrets it held.

He once again read the names singled out in the caption. Simon's index finger connected the names with each of the young, expressionless faces.

"What did it all mean?" Simon wondered. "What really happened on that dark day in 1935? And why on earth would Jack Lawless, of all people, give me that particular picture?"

No sooner had Simon entertained the question than something in the photograph caught his attention. It was something that he had not seen in any of the other photographs that he had previously collected. Simon grabbed the cord from which the bare bulb dangled and held the light up to the picture. In the far right corner of the photo, Simon recognized the edge of a second commemorative plaque hanging on the wall opposite of The Declaration of Independence. The hairs on the back of his neck stood on end as he made out the tiny words on the inscription.

The first line on the bronze plaque read, "You shall not st..." The next line down read, "You shall not give false t..." And the next line after that read, "You shall not covet your neig..." Just beneath that on the last row, it read "...or anything that belongs to your neigh..."

Simon dropped the picture to his side and stared blankly into the wall of the basement with his mouth wide open from shock.

"No way," Simon muttered in disbelief. There was no denying what the old photograph revealed. It was a plaque displaying the Ten Commandments. His mind raced, as he again considered what Hope had said about unfinished business. She made the observation that if God had truly compelled Simon to complete the project then it would ultimately further His Kingdom in some way. For the life of him, Simon had not been able to figure out how until that very moment.

The fact of the matter was that God did have a plan. Simon knew that if God had wanted him to return the entryway to its original condition, then that would mean *completely* returning it to its original condition. Now staring at the indisputable evidence, it was clear that that would involve reaffixing the bronze monument of the Ten Commandments to the wall in the entryway to the public institution.

Even as Simon to grapple with the problem of finding such a monument, his subconscious had already followed that line of reasoning to its logical conclusion.

As if magnetically drawn, he turned his head and looked into the deep recesses of what he had previously thought to have been an empty storage room. Thelma had been right. It wasn't completely cleared out after all. For there lying on the floor of the storage room was the bronze monument that had been taken down and long since forgotten.

Simon had been tripping over it this entire time without realizing it. Though the monument had been lying face down, he somehow instinctively knew that it was the very plaque pictured in the old, worn out photo. Solemnly, he stepped into the storage room, bent down, lifted the relic off of the dirty floor, and gently leaned it against the foundation of the basement.

To his delight, he found it to be much was less weighty than the Declaration of Independence. He realized that he would be able to hang it up without much difficulty. Over the course of the past month, through all of his hardships and failures, Simon had acquired all of the skills necessary to complete the work that God had begun in him.

* * *

After only a few short hours, the extension cord had been rolled up and the ladder had been put away. Simon swept up the last bits of sawdust into the dust pan, stood up, and backed away from the wall to gain a better perspective of his handiwork. He wiped the perspiration from his forehead with the back of his hand and let out a deep sigh of satisfaction.

Like an anxious child on Christmas morning, he dug out the black and white photograph from his pocket, unfolded it, and hurried down the steps to the base of the stairs just inside the front doors of the building. Expectantly, he turned, held the picture out as far out in front of him as his arm would reach, shut one eye, and did a side by side comparison between the past and the present. They were identical.

Overcome with an unexpected outburst of emotion, Simon dropped to his knees onto the mat by the front door and turned toward the Ten Commandments. He put his face to the ground, and began to pray to God, thanking Him for His great provision and faithfulness.

But his prayer was cut short as the front door flung open and hit him in the leg.

"Oh, I am terribly sorry, Simon," Dr. Al-Banna said, as he eased his way through the slight opening. "I didn't see you down there. I came back for my pager. I think I might have left it on the…"

"…That's quite all right," Simon said, quickly rising to his feet and brushing off his knees. Slightly embarrassed, he looked up and noticed the good doctor staring at the newly hung monument. His mouth was ajar and his brow was furrowed.

"What is this?" Dr. Al-Banna asked, wagging his index finger towards the wall above the stairwell.

"It's the Ten Commandments," Simon replied.

"Yes, I am aware of this," Dr. Al-Banna replied with a grave expression on his face, "but where did it come from?" His countenance revealed a sense of awe and wonder.

Encouraged by a hint of approval, Simon replied, "It had been laying face down on the floor of the storage room in the basement all of this time. I must have accidentally tripped over it a dozen times during the last few weeks without even knowing what it was."

"Really?" Dr. Al-Banna said, as he took a few steps closer to get a better look at it, "but why did you hang ?... I mean, how did you know where to...?"

"Someone left an envelope for me with this newspaper clipping that clearly shows the monument hanging from this wall above the stairwell in 1935," Simon said, as he presented the black and white photograph to Dr. Al-Banna. "Take a look for yourself."

Dr. Al-Banna took the picture from Simon's hands and held it out at arms length from his face. "I am afraid I don't have my bifocals with me," he said. Even with that being the case, there was no denying the incontrovertible evidence. "Who left the envelope?" Dr. Al-Banna asked, holding up the photo and squinting in an effort to gain greater clarity.

"It was Jack Lawless of all people," Simon said in a tone that belied his own skepticism.

"Jack Lawless?" Dr. Al-Banna asked, befuddled by the disclosure. "But, who is responsible for hanging the monument on the wall?"

"I guess... I am," Simon replied. "It really wasn't that heavy. And I must have picked up a few tricks of the trade from some of the guys over the course of the last forty days."

"*You* did this?" Dr. Al-Banna asked as he turned towards Simon.

"Yes," Simon replied. The tone in his voice revealed the pride he had taken in his work before considering that there was a possibility that Dr. Al-Banna might not approve.

Dr. Al-Banna slowly nodded. His eyes were intently locked on the monument. "Hmm," he muttered. "And it is your intention of keeping it here on the wall then?"

"Yes," Simon replied, anticipating a backlash.

"Under who's authority?" Dr. Al-Banna asked.

"W-well," Simon sputtered, "I think that I made it perfectly clear from the beginning that the goal was to restore the school to its original condition. I don't see how we can do that now without it...I mean...knowing what we know now of course... I mean, based on the picture there can be no denying it. That's just how it...*was*."

"Uh-huh," Dr. Al-Banna grunted.

"I guess you could say, then," Simon said, taking another run at it, "that whoever put it there in the first place gave me authority to hang it back up on the wall."

Simon stopped speaking and guardedly awaited a response.

"I think it is awesome!" Dr. Al-Banna said as a broad smile swept across his face.

"You do?" Simon uttered in disbelief.

"Of course," Dr. Al-Banna replied, as he stepped closer and ran his hand over the raised lettering.

"Whew," Simon said, letting out a gush of air. "You don't know what a relief that is to me. The last thing I wanted to do was offend you."

"Offend me? Why should it offend me?" Dr. Al-Banna asked, quizzically.

"Well, you are a Muslim…" Simon said, sheepishly.

"Ah, I see," Dr. Al-Banna said with a laugh. "It may come as a surprise to you then that on this particular matter that the Bible actually substantiates what was revealed to the prophet Mohammed in the Quran."

"No kidding? That's great news," Simon said, beginning to feel a little silly about having been so worried about bridging the subject with the doctor. "So, you *do* believe in the Ten Commandments then?" Simon asked just to be clear.

"Yes, yes," Dr. Al-Banna said, reassuringly.

"I thought maybe that was just a Judeo-Christian kinda thing," Simon replied.

"No," Dr. Al-Banna intimated. "The God of the Old Testament and the god of the Holy Quran are one-in-the-same. In all actuality, Christians and Muslims agree on many different points.

"For example, we both believe that God is sovereign. We both believe that He created the heavens and the earth in six days and rested on the seventh day. We believe that He made Adam and Eve and that the serpent deceived them, and that they were banished from paradise.

"We believe that man has free will. That man is easily led astray to sin. Both religions believe in things such as judgment and Heaven and Hades. We believe that god revealed himself through prophets in the days of old. Oh yes, there are many passages of the Quran that can be supported by the Old Testament."

"Really? I had no idea," Simon said, now completely disarmed.

"Muslims even believe in Jesus, the son of Mary and Joseph," Dr. Al-Banna said, proudly.

"Really?" Simon said excitedly.

"Yes-yes," Dr. Al-Banna said with a smile while admiring the stately, bronze monument. "It is true."

"Well, this is great news!" Simon said almost giddy. "I was so worried."

"Really? How do you mean?" Dr. Al-Banna asked.

"Well, I was afraid to say anything to you before, because I consider you to be a friend," Simon replied. "And I didn't want to offend you, but I truly believe in my heart that God intended for me- well, for all of us- to complete the renovation of the school. I know that may sound crazy to you."

"No, no, no, on the contrary, Muslims very much believe in seeking Allah's will to do good works," Dr. Al-Banna assured him. "What's more, the Quran tells us that in the day of judgment all of our meritorious works will be taken into consideration."

Simon frowned, and started to ask, "What are meritor…" Suddenly, he heard a strange buzzing sound being emitted from the front pocket of his shorts.

"That reminds me," Dr. Al-Banna said, snapping his fingers. "The reason I can back was to retrieve my pager," he said pointing at the front pocket of Simon's shorts.

"Ah, yes, your pager," Simon replied, as he dug his hand into his pocket and retrieved the source of the noise. "I found it on the podium and had meant to bring it over to you. Sorry, it must have slipped my mind after I got busy with all of this," he said apologetically as he handed over the device.

"Thank you," Dr. Al-Banna said. "Normally, it wouldn't be such an urgent matter to have it on me, but I need it just in case. The Cain's baby received her first round of treatment earlier today at St. Jude's." He extended his arm and squinted at the LCD screen before pressing a button to stop the incessant noise. "No. False alarm. Just my wife wondering where I have gone."

"I'm glad that it wasn't any bad news about the baby," Simon said. "I feel so bad for the Cain's. If dealing with a sick child weren't enough, I heard that the family was also having financial problems."

"It is for that reason that some people in town are throwing together a benefit to raise money for the family here tomorrow," Dr. Al-Banna said.

"I did hear something about that," Simon said.

"Yes," Dr. Al-Banna replied, "knowing that there would be a great deal of traffic coming in and out of the building as people voted on the referendum, they decided to host the event on the road in front of the school. They are going to have a band and some booths, games,…some food…"

"That makes sense," Simon said.

"By the way, that was a stroke of genius to have the voting booths moved from the town hall to the entryway of the school," Dr. Al-Banna said. "Am I to assume that you are responsible for that as well?"

"No, I can't take any credit for that," Simon admitted. "At the last minute, Tony came to me and said that the mayor wanted to do that or something. So, of course, I thought it was a great idea. I mean it tugging at people's heart strings and all couldn't hurt."

"Mayor Fields wanted to do that?" Dr. Al-Banna asked in disbelief.

"Who?" Simon asked.

"The new mayor, Kurt Fields," Dr. Al-Banna said. "You know, Rocky's father."

"No, I didn't know that," Simon said. "For some reason, I thought that Jack was the mayor."

"He was until very recently," Dr. Al-Banna said. "Jack stepped down due to other obligations. He said that he will soon be traveling a great deal."

"Huh," Simon grunted, "then I guess it was Kurt Fields who ordered that the voting booths be moved from town hall to the entryway of the school."

"That surprises me, actually," Dr. Al-Banna said, pensively. "He is a tenant farmer for Jack and stands to lose a substantial percentage of his profits in light of an increased property tax. After all, Jack is certainly not going to absorb the loss, you know?" Dr. Al-Banna said with a laugh. "Oh, anyway, it was also a good idea to do the benefit on the street in front of the school..."

Simon stood in silence contemplating all of the possible implications. Instinctively, he lifted his right hand and patted the tattered picture from the old newspaper in his shirt pocket and reflected on how it had come into his possession. Could it all merely be a coincidence? Why would Jack give him the photo that revealed the Ten Commandments at that time?

He thought about all of the people who would see the commemorative plaques for the first time hanging on the wall of a public school building as they walked up the stairs to the two voting booths on the landing. Not having thought about it before in all of his excitement, he now considered the potentially negative influence that it might have on the outcome of the vote.

Simon had sought God's will in completing this task, followed the conviction of his heart, and turned his faith into action. Now, just had Hope had done earlier, he had put himself out there, exposing the true motives of his heart and making himself completely vulnerable to scorn and ridicule. In the morning, his deep seeded convictions would be brought to light for everyone to see.

As the reality of it all sank in, Simon's expression momentarily turned to angst. Overwhelmed by the potential backlash and impact on the vote, he inadvertently let out a barely audible groan.

"...There's going to be bounce houses and concessions and face painting, and all that," Dr. Al-Banna said, referring to the benefit for the Cain family. "I heard that they are even going to put up barricades, close the road, and set up a makeshift stage for the band to play."

Suddenly, the good doctor noticed the expression on Simon's face. "What is the matter?" Dr. Al-Banna asked.

"What? Oh, nothing," Simon said, snapping out it, "it's just that I hadn't considered... What I mean is, I didn't think about..."

But, before he could elaborate any further, Dr. Al-Banna noticed the time on his watch and said, "Oh my, it is a quarter of twelve already," he said. "My wife will be wondering what has happened to me. I am sorry, but I must be going now."

In a gesture of respect and solidarity, he reached out to shake Simon's hand before turning to exit out the front doors.

"Sure, I understand," Simon said with a wave of the hand. "I really enjoyed our conversation. Have a good night. Oh, and I will say a prayer for the Cain family."

Dr. Al-Banna paused with his hand on the front door, smiled, and replied, "Yes, thank you. That is the best thing we can do for her at this point." Then he added in his native tongue, "God is great!"

When Simon heard the same words that the doctor had spoken earlier at the dedication ceremony, his countenance fell. He all of a sudden realized where he had heard the expression before. It was after the calamity on 9/11. The Arabic phrase for "God is great" that was uttered by the terrorists on that fateful day was "Allah-Akbar!"

Upon hearing the notorious expression, Simon recalled how Hope had challenged him to ask Dr. Al-Banna about his motivation and intentions for completing the project. Now he found himself staring face to face with the opportunity to do just that. In an instant, he had to decide if he would choose to take the path of least resistance or if he would dare to ask the fundamental question. As he teetered between courage and trepidation, the moment was slipping away.

His heart skipped a beat. The window of opportunity was quickly closing as Dr. Al-Banna opened the front door with a quizzical expression on his face. If Simon were going to ask him the ultimate question, the moment was now. He might not have another chance. With the door slowly closing behind him, Dr. Al-Banna gave an uncertain wave goodbye. It was now or never.

"Dr. Al-Banna!..." Simon said, letting out of gush of air.

The good doctor poked his head back into the doorway while holding it open with one hand. "Yes?" he asked

"May I ask you a question?" Simon inquired. His heart was up in his throat.

"Most certainly," Dr. Al-Banna answered, pushing the door ajar and holding it open with his hip.

"Why did *you* want to do the renovation?" Simon asked, nervously.

"'Why?' " Dr. Al-Banna asked.

"Yes," Simon repeated. "Why? For what reason?"

"Ah, 'for what reason'," Dr. Al-Banna replied.

"Yes, well, I guess what I mean is...," Simon replied, realizing the question came off a bit brash. "...Let me back up a step. For example, when I said that I felt like my ultimate goal was to fulfill God's will by completing the project, you mentioned something about meritoria...meritit.."

"Meritorious works," Dr. Al-Banna said.

"Yes, that's it... meritorious works," Simon said. "I have to admit that I don't know what that means."

"Oh, I see," Dr. Al-Banna said, as he leaned against the door. "Yes, you *did* the *work* that God called you to do. That pleases Allah. Therefore, he credits you. He gives you a merit for your good work. So, a meritorious work is one that is counted in your favor and added to the ledger of good deeds. It is how we ultimately gain entry into paradise. Therefore, you could say that my motivation for helping do the work as well. It was ultimately to please Allah."

Simon's heart raced, and he could feel his pulse pounding in his ears. "I am sorry," Simon heard himself say, but I don't totally understand what you mean."

"In the Quran, the prophet Mohammed tells us that we must pay for our sins by doing good works," Dr. Al-Banna said. "Let me see if I can explain. It is like a scale. When we break Allah's law and sin, it tips the scale against us. But, when we do a good, or meritorious work, it offsets the scale. Then, when we die, it is each Muslim's hope that we have earned enough good deeds to swing the balance in our favor."

"So, how does a Muslim know for certain if he has done enough works?" Simon asked in disbelief.

"He doesn't," Dr. Al-Banna said, flatly. "He won't know until the day of judgment comes. That is why it is so important for us to know Allah's will," he said, pointing to the Ten Commandments on the wall. "We need to know when we have transgressed, so we can make amends with god. There is no guarantee. Therefore, we must do our best to please Allah and pray for his great mercy continually because he is a gracious, forgiving god."

"But," Simon said, trying to process what he was hearing, "if that were the case, then no one would ever have enough good deeds to get into heaven!"

"What? How so?" Dr. Al-Banna asked, with a look of confusion on his face.

"Well, no one can keep the law," Simon said. "I mean, I know that I can't go five seconds without breaking a commandment. So, how could I ever possibly keep track of the number of sins I commit each day? Let alone pay for each one with a good deed?"

Looking at the laws written on the wall, Dr. Al-Banna quipped, "Do you steal? Do you murder? Do you commit adultery? Ha! You're not even married, yet."

The last one stung Simon. "It's-it's not just the act," Simon said, trying to articulate what he knew to be true. "It's like what Jesus taught us in the Beatitudes. It's about the desires of our heart and not just the act. If we covet, or hate, or lust, then we are in violation of the law.

"I can't even keep the most important commands, 'To love the Lord my God with all of my heart, soul, mind, and strength' and 'To love my neighbor as much as myself' much less any of the other commands."

"But, that's ridiculous," Dr. Al-Banna said, stepping fully back into the entryway and allowing the door to shut behind him. "Who can keep such a law? You said yourself that no one is perfect."

"Exactly! But, God is perfect," Simon responded, beginning to allow his passion to bubble to the surface. "Look at it this way. We agree that God is Holy, right? So, He cannot accept anything that is unholy or unrighteous to be in his presence.

"Therefore, if God is in heaven and if heaven is 'paradise', then there is no room for sin. Even one sin disqualifies us from entry into heaven because the standard is perfection.

"What you are telling me is that we can only sin with our bodies. But we don't take our bodies to heaven.

"We sin in our hearts more than anything. The act is only symptomatic of the desire. And when we do so, we are committing a crime, we incur a debt, and we separate ourselves from God."

"We break the law and are in debt, nothing more," Dr. Al-Banna said flatly.

"And, at the same time, we violate God's character," Simon said, with conviction. "Because the law also reveals to us who God is..."

"...No-no, the law is only his will," Dr. Al-Banna said, closing his eyes and waving his index finger. "It does not reveal his character, only his standard. For we cannot truly know god."

"I respectfully disagree," Simon objected. "The law not only reveals His will but also who God is. The Bible makes God's true nature known to us. Therefore, we are not able to go to heaven based on anything that we do. It is only because of what He did for us on the cross...because of His mercy. We are not saved by works, but by grace through faith alone."

"As I said, I will agree that we are only saved because of Allah's mercy, but, man is a morally autonomous agent," Dr. Al-Banna said, raising his voice slightly. "He is responsible for his own actions. He must earn his right to go to paradise."

"That's my point," Simon said, incredulously. "How could any man ever do enough good deeds, when he constantly sins from the time he is born to the time he dies?"

"But, man is not born into sin," Dr. Al-Banna argued. "The Quran tells us that man is weak. That he is foolish. That he is easily led astray. But, man is born without sin. He only learns sin from the world."

"No, no, the Bible tells us that when Adam sinned we all sinned," Simon said, empowered by all that he had learned in the past month. "We inherited it. It is in our family tree. It is a part of our DNA so to speak. No amount of good works could ever pay for that sin!"

"What you say if foolishness!" Dr. Al-Banna said, raising his voice another notch and stepping towards Simon. "If that were the case, how could god be just? No man would ever gain entry into paradise."

"That's precisely how God *is* just," Simon said almost pleading. "There can only be justice if sin is punished. And the punishment for sin is death. That is why we are in such great need of a Savior," Simon said. "We need someone to atone for our sins. We need someone to pay for the debt we owe, by standing in the gap between us and the judgment of a Holy and righteous God. We need someone who could take on our sins and receive our punishment in our place. Someone who could be a substitute for us. Someone else had to die as the punishment for man's sin."

"But, man is responsible for himself and himself alone," Dr. Al-Banna said, raising the inflection of his voice. "How can anyone else pay for our own sins? How can that be possible?"

"I am afraid that no one knows *how* God makes it possible," Simon had to admit. "But, I do know that it makes sense because the Bible tells us in Genesis that we are to make sacrifices, or atonement, for our sins. It goes back to the very beginning of creation. It goes back to Abraham and Isaac. In the Old Testament, a perfect bull or ram, or lamb without blemish, had to shed its blood in order to atone for the sin of man. That is why God provided a ram to serve as a sacrifice in place of Isaac."

"But, no one is perfect," Dr. Al-Banna retorted with his blood pressure beginning to rise.

"Yes, there was one man," Simon said loudly. "Jesus of Nazareth was perfect."

Dr. Al-Banna's face nearly boiled over in frustration. "This is why Muslims cannot understand Christianity," he stammered. "It is full of mumbo jumbo and contradictions. You say yourself that no man is perfect. And then you say that Jesus was a man. And then you say that Jesus was perfect. You say that he was the son of god and that he was god."

"How can you say that Christianity is full of contradictions?" Simon gasped. "You are the one who said Muslims believe in Jesus."

"We do," Dr. Al-Banna said proudly. "Jesus was a prophet, maybe only second to Mohammed himself. He was born to a virgin and performed many miracles."

"Yes, He was a prophet, but He was also more than a prophet," Simon stated. "He was no ordinary man," Simon said holding his arms out with his palms up. "The Bible tells us Jesus was God incarnate. He is God in the flesh. He had a human nature and divine nature. He was one hundred percent man and one hundred percent God. He was two in essence but one in person. As you say, he was born to the virgin Mary, who was found to be with child through the Holy Spirit. He did not inherit the 'DNA' of sin through Adam, because Jesus did not have a human father. Therefore, he was born sinless.

"While his human nature was exposed to the temptation of sin, he never gave in to that temptation. He did not sin, and that is how he became an acceptable substitute for our sins. He is the lamb without blemish. That is how He was able to die on the cross in our place. In that transaction, he paid for the wages of sin, which was death. He took on the sin of all mankind, and in exchange we were given His perfection. Jesus redeemed us, making us acceptable before God so that we may be adopted into the Kingdom of heaven. But, we are only given eternal life if we choose to accept the gift of grace through faith."

Dr. Al-Banna's anger boiled over, and he lashed out, "Jesus did not die on the cross! Allah have relations with a worry, and he would never allow one of his Holy prophets to die such a disgraceful death!"

"He did die on the cross," Simon snapped.

"He didn't!" Dr. Al-Banna snapped back.

"Then who did?" Simon asked pointedly.

"I don't know!" Dr. Al-Banna stammered, looking about the floor as though he had dropped something. "Judas or one of the other disciples, I don't know; but, it wasn't Jesus!"

"Not Jesus?" Simon said, almost exasperated. "We know that it was Jesus because only God incarnate could rise again from the dead three days later."

"But he didn't rise from the dead, no one rose from the dead," Dr. Al-Banna said almost writhing in agitation.

"He had to have risen from the dead because there was an empty tomb," Simon cried out.

"There was an empty tomb because the rest of the disciples stole whosever body it was!" Dr. Al-Banna said.

"No, you don't understand," Simon said, utterly amazed by Dr. Al-Banna's assertions. "Jesus died, was buried, and rose again on the third day so that we may have eternal life through Him. You said yourself that you believe Jesus performed miracles."

"I probably shouldn't even be talking about this," Dr. Al-Banna said.

"But, we *have* to talk about this!" Simon replied. "What kind of religion would discourage open debate about such an important matter as this?"

"Okay," Dr. Al-Banna replied. "Mohammad tells us plainly in Surah 9:1-17, that whoever believes in Jesus as the Messiah breaks the unforgivable sin of shirk, placing a man on the same level as god! Whoever does so is forever cursed!"

"'*Cursed*'?" Simon repeated in amazement.

"Yes, it says he will be cursed," Dr. Al-Banna repeated.

"Well," Simon said, leaning on all that he had learned from Jeremy's Bible over the course of the past month, "John 4:14-15, tells us that no one goes to the Father except through the Son!"

"Ha!" Dr. Al-Banna said, tilting his head back. "That is because the Bible has been tampered with. It has been corrupted!"

The two of them stood now only a short distance apart looking wildly into one another's eyes. They were at an impasse. The conversation had escalated quickly and reached an almost fever pitch. Now Simon and Dr. Al-Banna were both at a loss for words.

Out of the corner of Simon's eye, the monument to the Ten Commandments caught his attention. When it did, he was struck by a disturbing realization.

"Dr. Al-Banna," Simon said, maintaining his composure. "You said earlier that these laws from the Bible actually support what is written in the Quran even though other parts of the Bible have been corrupted."

"Yes," Dr. Al-Banna replied, doing his best to also keep his emotions in check. "Surah 15:9 clearly states that the Quran is the only authentic word of God that has been preserved."

"If that is the case, and you had your choice, what law would hang on this wall?" Simon asked, as he accidentally stepped on a 'Hope and Change' poster that someone had been left on the floor following the commencement ceremony.

In the midst of the tension filled room, an unsettling thought occurred to Dr. Al-Banna as well. He looked up at the monument to the Ten Commandments and wagged his finger in the direction of the virtually indestructible, bronze monument.

Instead of answering the question, Dr. Al-Banna asked his own question, "What is *your* motivation for doing the school renovation? What is *your* true intent here for hanging this plaque on the wall?"

Suddenly, Simon had the answer, and his response lit a fuse.

"My motivation is sanctification through obedience to the one true God; the Father, the Son, and the Holy Spirit," he replied unapologetically.

"That is the unforgivable sin!" Dr. Al-Banna adamantly replied. "I already told you that is the sin of Shirk which is to place man on the same level as God. Muslims believe only in monotheism, not polytheism. Praise be to Allah!"

"Christians would agree with you on that point," Simon replied. "I heard a great program on the radio by Dr. R.C. Sproul and Abdul Saleeb. They were talking about this very issue on a radio program that I heard one time.

"Dr. Sproul said that even he would not be comfortable saying that Jesus is God. Dr. Sproul said that Jesus was God incarnate. He said that there was a very important distinction between the two things. The formula for the Trinity is opposite of that for the formula for Jesus Christ. God is one in essence and three in person while Jesus is one in person, but two in essence.

"C.S. Lewis pointed out that even in praying to God we are participating in the Trinity. Jesus' death on the cross established a new covenant by which we can have an intimate relationship with God the Father through the intervention of the Holy Spirit in prayer.

"Dr. Al-Banna, you *can* know God. You can have that intimate relationship with Him. *You* can have assurance of one day joining God in heaven if you simply acknowledge Jesus Christ as your Lord and Savior. After all, He died on the cross as much for you as he did for me."

"Tell me, how can you follow a religion whose only assurance into heaven is through the disgraceful crucifixion of a Holy prophet?" Dr. Al-Banna challenged. "It is blasphemous!"

Upon hearing the good doctor's charge, Simon allowed his emotions to get the best of him. "How you can follow a religion whose only assurance for going to paradise is 'killing the infidel wherever you may find him'?" he asked. "Tell me, what is your take or opinion about Jihad?"

With that, Dr. Al-Banna seethed with anger. He turned about in circles jabbering in his native tongue while intermittently wringing his hands. He turned and approached Simon once again, wagging his finger in the young man's face. Through clenched teeth he said, "I can no longer be a part of this project. From this moment, I am renouncing my endorsement, and I am pulling all funding...I want back any and all donations that I have provided to date!"

Simon stared at the doctor, speechless.

Dr. Al-Banna made his way towards the door, as he angrily shouted, "This is an outrage! And tomorrow, the people of Bethel will see this, and they will know that your true intentions are proselytizing the students!" He reached back, grabbed the handle to the front door, and threw it open. "And then they *too* will be outraged!"

With that, the good doctor stepped out into the darkness. The door slammed shut behind him, leaving Simon once again standing in the glow of the giant chandelier. He was still in the throws of that awkward, uncomfortable feeling following an intense argument when something profound suddenly occurred to him. He turned and looked at the writing on the wall.

Hope had suggested that Simon might be able to gage whether or not he had been doing God's will by the degree of opposition that he faced. Naturally, Simon reasoned that if his argument with Dr. Al-Banna were any indication then he could be certain that he was in fact doing God's will. If that were the case, then he could also be pretty certain that persecution would soon follow.

Strangely encouraged by the proposition, Simon dug into his pocket to retrieve his cell phone. With still trembling hands, he began dialing Hope's number before remembering that she was currently without a phone. The thought crossed his mind to go over to her house, but then he thought wiser of it.

The Good News would have to wait until morning.

31

THE WISDOM OF THE WORLD

No sooner had Simon put his phone back into his pocket when he heard the sound of the front door being flung open.

Turning towards the entrance, Simon instinctively said, "Dr. Al-Banna, I…"

"'Dr. Al-Banna'?" Joey said with a laugh. "I don't know what you said to that guy but he was fuming mad."

"Yeah, I've never seen him that angry before," George said, walking through the doorway still wearing his dusty blue shirt, grey slacks, and black shoes from umpiring. "I…oh wow!" George cursed.

"That may have something to do with it," Joey said, holding his beer can up and extending his index finger towards the Ten Commandments.

"What do you guys want?" Simon asked, once again getting a sense of what kind of reaction the monument might bring about.

"We came to talk you into umpiring the tournament with us," George said. "Where did you get this thing anyway?" he asked, as he walked over to the monument and ran his fingers over the raised letters before taking a swig of his beer.

"Rich told us to come talk some sense into you," Joey said, unimpressed.

"Don't bother," Simon replied, "besides, you guys don't need me."

"But you know the rule book better than anybody," George said almost pleading.

Joey frowned at the notion, "I'm right here, dude."

"What?" George asked, innocently.

"Thanks, but no thanks," Simon said. "There's still too much to do around here."

"Too much to do?" George repeated. "Like what? Everything looks finished to me."

"It might look that way on the surface," Simon intimated while thinking of his conversation with Hope. "But, I still need to clear out the rest of the junk from the basement, and I still need to…"

"…What? You still need to offend everybody?" Joey said with a laugh before taking another drink of his beer. "Don't worry, that won't take very long." He said glancing at his watch. "What time do the voting booths open?"

"Yeah, dude," George said, looking back up at the Ten Commandments. "You realize that this isn't going to fly around here. Nobody's going to go for that."

"Listen, I made it perfectly clear from the very beginning that the goal was to restore the lobby to its original condition," Simon unapologetically replied.

"Yeah, but the Ten Commandments?" George quipped. "This is a public building. It's so inflammatory!"

"'Inflammatory'?" Simon repeated. "We have always been a Christian nation, founded by Christians."

"Whatever we once were, we are no longer a Christian nation," Joey said haughtily.

"What?" Simon sputtered. "That's ridiculous!"

"Is it?" Joey mocked. "What proof do you have?"

"What proof do I have?" Simon asked, as he turned to look at the plaque on the wall. "But, no one can dispute that this was here from the beginning. Take a look." He retrieved the tattered photo again from his pocket and handed it to George.

"You mean it was in 1935?" Joey mused. "That's not exactly from the beginning."

"Where did you get this?" George asked, as he carefully studied the photograph.

"Jack Lawless left it for me," Simon replied.

"Good ole Jacky boy," Joey said, sardonically.

"Was this up during the commencement ceremony earlier?" George asked.

"No," Simon sheepishly answered. "I just found the plaque lying on the floor of the basement a couple hours ago."

"So, no one has seen this? I mean besides Dr. Al-Banna, obviously," Joey said.

"No," Simon replied.

"Tsk, tsk, tsk," Joey said. "That's Jack for ya. I knew he wasn't just going to sit by and let this referendum pass."

"What do you mean?" Simon asked.

"Have you even thought about what affect this might have on the outcome of the referendum as people walk under this thing to cast their vote tomorrow?" Joey countered.

Simon's eyes danced over the bronze monument as he contemplated the question.

"Yeah, if Dr. Al-Banna's reaction is any indication you may have torpedoed your own cause," George said, handing the picture back to Simon.

"But, Dr. Al-Banna wasn't angry about displaying the Ten Commandments," Simon said.

"Then why was he so angry?" George asked.

"We simply had a disagreement about what they mean," Simon replied. "Dr. Al-Banna thinks the Commandments merely express God's will."

"And what do you think they mean?" George asked, genuinely interested.

"I think that they not only express God's will, but they also reveal to us His character," Simon said unabashed. Thinking about it further, Simon added, "We just have completely different beliefs about who God is and what He demands from us."

"Well, what do you believe?" George asked.

Acting disinterested, Joey strolled about the room studying the various tributes to American history.

"Well, I believe that God exists, that God is love, that He created the universe and everything in it," he said, nodding at the monument on the wall. " And that God is just..."

"Ha!" Joey laughed, staring at the intricate detail of the replica portrait of Abraham Lincoln."

"What?" Simon said with a frown as he turned towards Joey. "You don't believe that God is just?"

"If by God, you are referring to the same basic, unknown force that transcends all words and ideas then 'yes', I believe god is just," Joey said almost contemptuously as he turned to look Simon in the face. "But, if you are referring to the mythological God of orthodox Christianity then, 'no'."

"What's the difference?" George asked. "God is God, right? I thought you told me that they were all the same."

"Let's ask Simon," Joey said, walking towards the center of the platform at the top of the stairs. "Do you think that god is omnipresent?"

"Yes," Simon answered.

"Do you think he is omnipotent?" Joey asked smugly.

"Yes," Simon answered, suspiciously.

"And that he is omniscient?" Joey asked, taking another drink.

"Of course," Simon answered, trying to figure out where Joey was going with his line of questioning.

"Then I also assume that you would agree that god is the 'alpha and omega'?" Joey asked.

"What are you getting at?" Simon asked, cautiously.

"If you say that God is all of those things, then how is it just for the orthodox Christian God of love knowingly send the Magnus Opus of His creation to Hades?" Joey asked triumphantly.

George looked back at Simon with a grave expression.

"God doesn't 'send' people to Hades," Simon said. "At least, not the manner in which you are insinuating. We've already been over this."

"Well, you're telling me that God created man and that God is all-knowing," Joey said, lifting his chin. "Then at the very least you are saying that God makes some men, knowing full well that they will eventually go to Hades."

"That may be," Simon said. "I don't know, because I am not God...and don't pretend to be. But I think the most important component that you are missing is that either way, men do not know their own end. We do not know who goes to heaven and who goes to Hades in the end. So, for us, from our narrow and limited perspective it is still a choice. We hear the good news of the Gospel and make a choice to believe it or not believe it."

"I get what Joey is saying, though," George chimed in, engrossed in the theological exchange, "if God is love, then why make going to heaven a choice at all? Why not just send us all straight to heaven in the first place?"

"Again, I cannot fully know the mind of God," Simon said, realizing that he did not have exact Bible verses to draw from at his finger tips. "I can only read the Bible and draw conclusions from it. First of all, I would ask you a question. Didn't God already try the whole 'entitlement to paradise' route before creation? How did that turn out? I mean, all of the angels were given an eternal free pass to heaven, and it was still not enough to satisfy all of them. The second in command, Lucifer, rebelled and turned a third of the angels against God.

"So, I would hardly blame God, if He made us active participants in our own salvation through free will. But, at the same time, it would seem to me that God cannot deny himself. He cannot pretend to be what He is not, or pretend to not know what He knows. So, if he creates some men, knowing full well what the end result will be, it doesn't matter because to us it's still a decision that each of us has to make. That hardly makes it unjust, if we are all free to make our own decisions.

"Ultimately, my entire belief system hinges on the inerrancy of the word of God in the form of the Bible. That is how I *know* that God is right and just and fair. So, if God 'sends' men to Hades it is only because that was a just punishment for the path they chose."

"But *Hades*, come on, really?" Joey mocked. "Seems a bit dark for a God of love, doesn't it?"

"It is true that God is love," Simon replied. "So, I can only come to the conclusion that the punishment fits the crime.

"Why would God even give us the choice of Heaven or Hades in the first place?" George asked. "Why even put the Tree of Knowledge in the Garden of Eden to begin with?"

Joey shot George a sideways glance.

"I mean if it isn't just some mythological story contrived by man?" George sputtered.

"I don't know," Simon answered contemplatively. "Maybe love must somehow involve a component of free will. After all, is it really love if you don't have a choice? I don't think God wants a bunch of mindless robots. What kind of choice would it be if what you were choosing between something that wasn't equal but opposite? Isn't the opposite of God in heaven, Satan in Hades?"

"Jesus' free gift of eternal salvation is universal, but each person must choose whether or not to accept the gift of grace."

"How is *that* justice?" George asked, befuddled by the mystery. "How is it fair that through one man's bad decision to eat the forbidden fruit that every man is born into sin? That wasn't our choice."

"I don't think that anyone can honestly say that they would have been more obedient than Adam if faced with the same ultimate dilemma," Simon replied. "We constantly make bad decisions. Each bad or unrighteous decision that we make is a sin. And if God is just, he must punish sin. The punishment of even one sin is death. Each decision stands on its own merit. Therefore, no man can do extra works to pay for a previous sin, because each action, utterance, or thought is judged individually. So, once we commit even one sin there is no making up for it the next time around. What's done is done."

"So, we're all doomed," George replied.

"Yes!" Simon said excitedly.

"What?" George squawked.

"That's the bad news," Simon replied. "That's the dire circumstance that every man finds himself in. Perfection is the standard. Most people are never able to grasp how Holy God is. We are too busy comparing ourselves to each other, and we give ourselves a free pass by fooling ourselves that we really aren't that bad. Even our best actions are filthy rags compared to God's righteousness because we always have an ulterior motive for what we do. We are all filled with pride. That's the bad news, but people have to understand how bad the bad news is before they can understand how good the good news is."

"So, what's the good news?" George asked with a nervous laugh.

"God did not just leave us to our own devices," Simon replied. "He, himself, promised a Savior thought the prophets in the Old Testament. To fulfill the prophecies and the law, '...though He was rich, made himself poor...' by coming to earth in the form of a baby. And even though He was tempted in every way that we are tempted, He did not give into temptation. Jesus lived a perfect, sinless life. Then He voluntarily died on the cross as a sacrifice for our sins. On the third day, He rose again from the dead as predicted. Just as sin entered through the world through one man, God redeemed us through one man. In fact, the Son of Man was prophesied in Daniel 7:13. God's mercy is so great that all we have to do to receive eternal life in heaven is to accept the gift of grace through faith."

"Wow!" Joey said. "No wonder it is such a popular legend. It has all of the elements of a great story. But tell me, how is it just, and right, and fair for people who never get to hear it?"

"Again, you're asking me to be God in order to answer that question," Simon said, exasperated. "I have no idea. I guess I need to study the Bible more."

"Maybe, that's why He gave us a conscience, so that the law is written in our hearts, and we are without excuse."

"Ha! And that's justice?" Joey asked. "Do you know how many people have died never having heard your little legend?"

"But, that's why it's so important for us to share the Gospel with those who are lost," Simon replied.

"I bet," Joey mocked.

"One thing's for sure," Simon said defensively, "it's a more just system than having to perform an unknown number of good deeds to tilt the scales in our favor. That provides no assurance of going to heaven."

"Hold up!" George said, trying to make sense of it all. "There's nothing we *do* to receive eternal life? Therefore, there's nothing that we can *do* to keep us out of heaven."

"Yep, just believe and receive!" Joey answered sarcastically. "Pretty messed up system, huh?"

"Well, we have to make the choice, and it's not that we don't in turn do good works," Simon said. "Salvation is one thing, but using your talents to fulfill God's will for your life is another."

"Sad, isn't it," Joey said to George with an air of superiority. "Such a simpleminded religion."

"Come again?" Simon said, amazed.

"Don't get me wrong," Joey said. "All myths were contrived with the same purpose in mind- to explain the mysteries of the great transcendent common consciousness."

"'Contrived'?" Simon repeated.

"Contrived, created, concocted, however you want to put it," Joey said, leaning on the podium and looking down on George and Simon. "What were they teaching you at TCU anyway? All myths, like Christianity, are merely symbolic representations designed as a road map for finding one's way in a labyrinth of altruistic mysticism. The Bible is just one of many similar, ancient mythological tales of symbols, metaphors, and imagery intended to bridge the gap between what is seen and what is unseen, what is known and unknown.

"Naturally, they were heavily influenced by the culture and times in which they were written. These are the masks of God. But, if we sift through those superficial differences and look behind the mask, we can find the common threads, or the basic stuff, of what you call god."

"Religion was never meant to be taken in its literal form. And just think of how many wars have been started because of it. As we continue to evolve, peace will only come once we learn to do away with the differences of all of the world religions, and focus on their commonalities."

Suddenly, Simon felt his stomach turn as his mind raced to grasp the degree of danger that such a one world religion posed; it was far beyond even the threat posed by Islamic extremists.

"So, you're saying once that happens, we will truly know God?" George asked, mesmerized by the brilliance of Joey's words.

"No, I am saying something much more profound than that," Joey said, coming around the side of the podium. "I am saying that once we have the knowledge of god we will be our own gods!"

Once past the initial shock of such a grandiose assertion, Simon managed to regain his faculties. "So, you think that somehow by taking away the masks we will find what…?" Simon started to say.

"…Nothing, and as a result everything," Joey said, pleased with himself. "Quite a paradox isn't it?"

"Wow," George said in awe. "That's deep."

"No, there's nothing deep or profound about that," Simon replied. "It's not a paradox, it's a flat out contradiction. If that is the case, there's nothing *to know*."

"Right, and as a result we'll know everything that we need to know," Joey replied. "Once we remove the cultural rules that shackle our intellects, we will discover that the whole concept of right and wrong has been the greatest limiting factor of progress. Behind the masks of our cultures and legends, we will find that good and evil are one-in-the-same. If everything all came from the same source, then it must be inherently all good. Get it? Once we accept that, we will able to transcend right or wrong. Only then will we discover that it is human experience that is the primary purpose and objective to life. The more you experience and more knowledge you gain, the more you will come to know the great being of the universe, or what you call god, and the more that you are like god."

"Man," George said. "That is amazing."

"No, that's just stupid," Simon said, unapologetically.

"What? No, you don't get it," Joey said with a wave of the hand. "I didn't think you would. You're too narrow minded."

"What do you mean?" George asked Simon.

"Well, if that is the case, then all truth is relative," Simon said. "So, there is no truth. So, he can't claim to know the truth about anything if there is no truth."

"I'm lost," George admitted.

"It sounds to me like truth is determined by whoever is sifting through the myths and weeding out out fact from fantasy," Simon said. "It's like a buffet of ideas. I can choose to pick out what I like and leave the rest. And you can do the same, but arrive at a completely different set of truths which makes Joey's theory a gross contradiction. Because his only truth is that there is no truth; how is that just?"

"What can be more just than everyone being swept up into the Great Common Consciousness?" Joey said proudly. "There's no judgment or condemnation."

"What can be more just than having no consequences for anyone's actions?" Simon said miffed. "Sounds to me like total anarchy."

"You are so far out of your league," Joey said. "That's what I've been telling you George. Brilliance is limited by the intelligence of the listener. You can't explain things to people who can't understand."

"And you can't understand nonsense," Simon added.

"Dude, read a book!" Joey sarcastically snapped, dismissing Simon.

"Where did you get all of this dime store philosophy?" Simon asked.

"Dime-store philosophy, huh?" Joey said. "Oh, I don't know, from just a few dullards named Nietzsche, Freud, Jung, Mann, Joyce, Bastian...you may have heard of them. Or, then again, if you went to Texas *Christian*, so...."

"It's the result of being educated. You couldn't possibly understand this, but once you have that knowledge then you're able to see past all of these limitations and intolerances," Joey said, pointing at the Ten Commandments. "The saddest thing about it is that you don't even know that you have the most paralyzing limitations already built in. They were programmed in your brain when you were just a kid. I understand. Believe me. It took me a long time to get past Father Rite and my Catholic up-bringing."

Turning pale, Simon was beginning to understand the degree of danger such a philosophy posed on society.

"If all experience is truth, then there is no wrong," Simon said.

"Exactly!" Joey said. "That's what you have to get past. There is no right or wrong, that was written into myths in order to establish order in our primitive cultures."

"But, if there is no right and wrong, then who goes to heaven?" George asked.

"That's just it," Joey said. "When we die, we are simply absorbed into the supreme being of the universe. No one goes to Hades, because it doesn't exit. Now that, my friend, is justice.

"I'm telling you. Once you get it, that knowledge empowers you. At that point, you realize that you are capable of doing almost anything."

"Without a conscience?" Simon asked. "I bet! Anything and everything can be justified when you are your own god."

Dumbfounded, Simon looked back at Joey's highly impressionable protégé who was slowly nodding in agreement. At that moment, Simon became less concerned with any impact that he might have on Joey's hard line stance and more concerned with damage control on the malleable mind of George Lukas.

"George, take a step back and think about what Joey's really saying here," Simon said, desperate to reach him. "He is saying that the God that created this universe of precise structure and order, has a chaotic, indiscriminate nature." Looking at George's dusty umpiring uniform, an idea came to him. "Think about a baseball game for a minute. There are a set of rules, right?"

George nodded.

"Everybody has to play by the same rules in order for the game to be fair. What would happen if the foul line was only foul for one team and not for the other one? It would be bedlam. So, it would be like someone built a beautiful, pristine ballpark to very purposeful specifications and then tried to play a game without rules. Does it make sense to have players running around pegging each other in the back with baseballs, or smacking each other over the head with bats, or players declaring themselves safe after a close play at first; and, at the end of the game everyone's a winner?"

"Now, think again about the universe for a minute. When anyone hits a ball into the air, it's going to come back down. There's no denying that. There is an order to the universe. It is not complete chaos.

"Think about what we now know about the thousands of specialized components to a single cell organism that Darwin was not privy to. Think about the intricate complexities of the human eye. Think about the precise conditions of the earth's environment that makes life possible. It's not random! It is designed by a designer."

Joey yawned before taking another swig of beer.

"Now ask yourself," Simon continued passionately, "would the God who created such an ordered, systematic universe not have an equally ordered system of human laws like the law of human nature? There is ultimate truth. One plus one plus one plus is three in any language, in any place, and at any time. If I get on a spaceship and travel to the farthest star in the solar system the answer will still be three. It doesn't matter how many people say it's not three. That's still the only right answer.

"Everything that is living was born and one day will die. That's not chance; that's a fact.

"And when you do something wrong, aren't you aware of it? Something inside you knows it, whether it's your conscience, your soul, or the voice of God himself. There is a voice inside of you that tells you to do the right thing. And there is another voice that tells you to do the wrong thing, but there is a third, neutral voice, that implores you to do the right thing. You can't deny it. You were pre-wired to recognize it. Should someone who steals go unpunished? Should someone who murders go free? Should someone who…?"

"…Aborts a baby not be castigated or someone who is a homosexual not be vilified?" Joey mocked. "It's always the same thing with these Christians, George. They're so predictable in their arguments. See what I mean by narrow minded?"

"That's true! Order is predictable!" Simon nearly shouted.

"What?" Joey asked, confused.

"You said that Christians are predictable," Simon replied. "We should be predictable. That is my point. There has to be order in the universe. Without order there would be total chaos. How many possible answers are there to one plus one, and how many possible wrong answers are there?" One right answer sounds pretty narrow minded, doesn't it? Are we really being intellectually superior to claim equality to God or is that flat out arrogance?

"I don't have the authority to make the rules. It doesn't matter if I decide what is right and wrong. It only matters what God says is right or wrong. As a Christian, I defer to God's authority as it is written in the Bible about issues like abortion or homosexuality. Christians don't have the luxury of arbitrarily picking and choosing which rules to follow and which ones to ignore.

"Would you really want to live in a world where truth is relative? Would you really want to live in a society without prisons, judges, police officers, or laws? Does that sound like heaven on earth to you? No! Absolutely not! Relativism would be Hades on earth. Freedom cannot be achieved without rules and consequences for breaking those rules. It is not doing whatever you want to do whenever you want to do it. If that were the case, then the majority of people would constantly live in fear. Only the strong or elite or ultra rich would dominate the weak or the masses or the poor like in a feudal system. That's not a democracy. That's totalitarianism!

"Which would be fine with Joey because he sees himself superior to most people. In Joey's worldview, the masses are just sheep moving through this world, herded into the great, mystical unknown. To Joey, they're too stupid to figure life out for themselves, so they need someone as enlightened as him to tell them what to do. He thinks he's the man in Plato's allegory of the Cave, when really he's Napoleon in Orwell's *Animal Farm*. After all, ...'all animals are created equal, but some are created more equal than others...'

"Don't you see that Joey's worldview is justification for using whatever means necessary to fulfill the desires of his heart? This isn't some kind of New Age altruism or enlightenment. This ideology has been rolled out many times over the centuries in many different forms to subjugate the masses. If God doesn't make the rules, then men do. And men only make rules for their own power, position, and greed like Stalin, Hitler, Mao, Castro, or Chavez; ever heard of them, Joseph? God doesn't make rules to limit us. God gives us rules to protect us."

With haughty eyes, Joey dismissed Simon's claims saying, "Blah, blah, blah."

"You see!" Simon said to George. "The 'progressives' demand that we open up our minds and think, but only if we think the way that they thing. As soon as we formulate an independent, logical objection to a stated theory, they simply dismiss it, mock it, marginalize it, or ignore it completely."

"Dude, I feel sorry for you," Joey replied.

"...Or they attempt to disparage the messenger when they have no rebuttal for the message," Simon said to George.

"What you're saying is not even worthy of a rebuttal," Joey said, plainly.

"That's it?" Simon demanded. "If it's so easy to dismiss, then dismiss it."

Joey slowly shook his head with an air of superiority before taking another drink. After an awkward pause, he said, "Jack would have a field day with you."

"Jack Lawless?" Simon sputtered. "That's where you got all of this nonsense? How does a guy like that weasel his way into every aspect of society? I'll tell you how. He makes deals. Always making deals. He keeps prodding and probing to find the 'one thing' that makes a person feel completely dissatisfied. And once he finds it, he cuts a deal with you. He gives you your heart's desires in exchange for your soul. Either you are 'in' or you are 'out' with Jack, there's no in between. All he wants in return is your blind allegiance. Once you make that concession, he'll give you just enough to keep you temporarily satisfied, while your heart yearns for true happiness and meaning."

"You have no idea what you're talking about," Joey scoffed.

"Now who's close minded?" Simon asked. "Fine, George, I will ask you, 'who is the father of chaos?'," Simon continued. "You see, Joey is not the first person to oppose God's law by asking something like, 'Did God really say?'. Isn't it just like the followers of the father of deceit to stop just short of the complete truth in order to make what is right, wrong and what is wrong, right?

"Joey mentioned homosexuality earlier, but he only tells you some of the truth about it. You see, if you actually read the Bible, it's not just homosexuality that God abhors. A real, orthodox, Christian understands that God condemns any sexual act outside the bounds of marriage between one man and one woman. He finds all sexual immorality equally deplorable. So, the man who lusts in his heart after a women is equally guilty as the man who is in an adulterous relationship, or the man who participates in the act of homosexuality."

"Man, I didn't realize how bigoted you are," Joey chided.

"Bigoted?" Simon repeated. "Homosexuality is not a civil right."

"Oh yes it is," Joey argued. "It is just like the civil rights movement of the sixties."

"I have yet to see a black person decide not to be black," Simon replied. "And yet, I have heard of people who professed to be homosexuals who chose to turn away from that lifestyle. Being black is not a choice, but a person's choice to participate in a certain sexual act is. Those two things are nothing alike."

"Whoa, people's sexual orientation can't be helped," George said. "Some people are just born that way."

"I agree that people are born with certain inclinations just as any sinner might have an inclination or an urge to do something sinful," Simon replied. "But, don't you see that even people who choose to participate in homosexual acts would agree that there are limits to people's sexual urges? Wouldn't the vast majority of people agree that incest, or polygamy, or pedophilia is wrong?"

Joey looked away.

"Yeah, of course, anyone in their right mind would say those things are wrong," George admitted.

"Well, where does their sense of right and wrong come from?" Simon asked. "Where do their limitations come from, if not God? I'll tell you where. It is from their own preferences! It's completely arbitrary. For them, right and wrong simply drifts along with the secular trends of the day. They are only trying to justify their bad behavior."

"What you're saying is hate speech," Joey mocked. "That's the only quote unquote bad behavior here."

"Whoa," Simon quickly responded. "Since when is vocalizing my religious beliefs a hate crime? Ever heard of the 1st Amendment?"

"It does offend people," George sheepishly answered.

"Well, maybe I'm offended that certain people want to take away my inalienable rights," Simon replied. "How about that?"

"But, what you are saying is so intolerant," George said in disgust.

"Don't you see, George, being what Joey calls tolerant to the current cultural trends puts us at odds with an intolerant and righteous God," Simon insisted. "God is only just because he *does* punish evil behavior and perverse speech. God punishes those who deserve to be punished because of their poor choices. He is intolerant to sin. That is justice!

"God does not ignore evil behavior. And He certainly doesn't celebrate it. We don't throw parades for adulterers. They were also 'born with' sexual urges and inclinations. But, don't we expect people to exhibit self-control and fight those urges? Don't we expect people to be faithful to their spouses?

"There is nothing in the Bible either explicit or implicit that justifies adultery or homosexual behavior, but there are plenty of verses that object to those sinful acts."

"I think Pastor Algood might disagree with you," George said, having never heard justice explained in that way.

"That's because Pastor Algood is not boxed in by traditional, orthodox Christianity," Joey replied. "He is a contemporary Christian who has evolved in his understanding. He has taken the blinders off. At least Pastor Algood is on the right track. He fully grasps the concept of an energy or power that we can harness to achieve prosperity; to attain all of the richness and fullness that life has to offer."

Simon's face fell.

"What?" he asked. "He's actually preaching that nonsense from the pulpit?"

"It's only nonsense to those who are too limited in their capacity to understand," Joey said, condescendingly.

"Oh, no, I understand completely," Simon said. "We're back to the whole there is no truth except the truth that there is no truth. I'll tell you what it all of this sounds like to me. It's sounds like a re-packaged ancient religion called Hinduism. That religion only goes back thousands of centuries. How progressive of you! So, why don't we just follow the advice of one of your brilliant Harvard professors and all drop some LSD before the sermon so that we can fine tune our senses, transcend reality, and reach a higher understanding?"

"If that's what you want to do…," Joey coldly quipped.

"Oh, right, of course, because there is no right or wrong," Simon replied. Tell me, then, just what could possibly be the purpose of a life without accountability?"

"That's easy," Joey said, shaking his now empty beer can. "To follow our bliss."

"Well, there it is," Simon said, finally piecing it all together.

"What is?" George asked.

"The draw, the attraction, to subscribing to such an ideology," Simon said. "It is to destroy the conscience in order to justify your fleshly desires. Now I get it. It's a 'me' centered religion. You're worshiping yourself.

"But, what makes it so dangerous is that it is cloaked in a shred of truth. There is a power in the universe called the Holy Spirit. God does want us to be happy. We are all on a quest for truth, for knowledge and understanding. We do have very strong, deviant urges that feel so good that we can't even imagine that they could somehow be bad for us."

"So, what difference then does it make one way or the other if they are one-in-the-same?" George asked.

"It makes all the difference in the world!" Simon pleaded. "Because it's not all the same. His 'god' doesn't care about you one way or another. He is completely indifferent. To Joey's god, you have no meaning. Having a relationship with God is what differentiates Christianity from any other world religion. God is the only thing that can fill that void in our lives. He's the only thing that can make us complete or whole. He loves us, and we love Him because He first loved us. The purpose of life for Joey is to please himself because it's impossible to displease his god. The purpose of life for the believer is to use the talents that you have been given to please God. You, you,…"

Simon's brain locked up temporarily, searching for a way to make George understand. Then it divinely came to him.

"…Listen, George," Simon said. "You said that you are heading off in the fall to study cinematography at USC, right? Well, you may have all of the talent in the world to make incredible movies that will impact the entire world.

"What if you decide to use those talents to make a bunch of great movies that advocate Joey's worldview about the archetypal hero journey? And let's say millions and millions of people flock to the theaters to watch your movies, and you make a ton of money; maybe even become famous. It's all good, right?

"But, what if God was the One who gave you those talents for a specific purpose in order to ultimately glorify Him? Would it make a difference to God if you were leading people away from knowing Him by perpetuating all of this myth, this New Age nonsense? Do you think God would be pleased with you, when you could have just as easily have used your talents to not only entertain, but also to encourage the audience to seek a relationship with their Creator, ya know, like the Kendrick brothers did with *Flywheel* and *Facing the Giants*?

"Do you see the difference between Christianity and what Joey's suggesting? You weren't created just to follow your bliss and serve yourself. You were wonderfully, and uniquely created to follow God's will for your life, to serve and worship Him."

"Ha! Oh, yeah, right; now that's a contradiction," Joey croaked. "It's the old suffering servant motif. True fulfillment can only be reached by denying yourself and what gives you the greatest gratification."

"Yeah, it's called self-control," Simon snapped.

"Unbelievable," Joey lamented, "you can only be happy by making yourself miserable. Makes perfect sense to me.

"And I suppose the ultimate prize is having the distinct privilege of martyrdom, of dying some horrible death. Like being pelted with rocks, or getting your head chopped off, or being burnt at the stake. Yeah, right. No thanks."

"And according to you," Simon replied. "There is nothing wrong with any of that. After all, if it makes me blissful to set another human on fire or chop their head off, then go for it, right? There shouldn't be any punishment for a person who goes around killing or raping other people. I mean, if it's their bliss then why not?"

"Now you're starting to get it," Joey said, sarcastically, pointing to his brain.

"Then the only thing that would keep a person from doing something like that is a man-made law, designed to keep order," Simon said. "And if you can get enough people to agree, you can change or interpret the law to where setting someone else on fire is legal, right? That doesn't seem like justice to me."

"The truth will set you free, my friend," Joey said for effect, before leaning back to take one last swig of beer. "Just look at the evolution of laws in this country concerning gambling, pornography, drugs, abortion, and marriage. It's no different. The laws keep progressing."

"So, if *you*, believing what you just told me to be true, wanted to kill a person," Simon started to say while folding his arms and turning his head to one side, "the only thing to keep you from doing it would..."

"...The fear of being caught," Joey said calmly, squinting one eye while looking into his empty beer. Then he nonchalantly looked up at Simon and George who were speechless. "If I knew I wasn't going to get caught, it'd be kinda cool," he said, playing it up a bit. "Like I said, the more things that you can experience, the more you will know, the more you will be like god; empowered to control your own destiny."

Simon blinked several times, unsure of how to respond as he watched Joey be-bop back down the steps towards the front doors of the school.

"There can only be justice if God gives men rules, consequences, and accountability," Simon called out to him.

"There you go again with more of your contradictions," Joey said smugly. "First, you say God does all the work. He pays for all sin, and he offers it freely to all mankind which, by the way, reminds me of my Catholic up-bringing. Go to mass, ask for forgiveness, wipe the slate clean, go sin the rest of the week, and around and around we go. In the same breath you say, man is accountable for his own actions. Which is it? Can't have it both ways, you know."

"No, that's not it, that's not what I'm saying at all," Simon said, suddenly at a loss of words to articulate the relationship between salvation and sanctification.

"That's what I thought," Joey said, waving his arm for his friend to follow, "come on George, we're going to miss last call at the tavern."

George looked at Simon, glanced up at the monument on the wall, and then slowly slinked back down the steps towards the front door.

Even though Simon was unable to verbalize the distinction between faith and works, he was enlightened by a simple observation.

"There is one thing I do know," Simon called out. "You supposed intellectual elites have progressed so far that you have ended up back in the stone ages."

Joey stopped at the bottom of the steps and looked back over his shoulder. "How do you mean?" he asked.

"'You will not surely die'," Simon quoted. " '...when you eat of it your eyes will be opened, and you will be like God, knowing good and evil'. Yours has a prettier bow, but it's an old package."

"Ah, of course," Joey said, shaking his head. "Using a quote from the myth to substantiate the myth itself. To that I say:

> 'After Buddha was dead, his shadow was still shown for centuries
> in a cave- a tremendous gruesome shadow. *God is dead*, but given
> the way of men, there still may be caves for thousands of years
> in which his shadow will still be shown.- And we, we still have
> to vanquish his shadow, too.'

"Frederick Nietzsche," Joey quipped.

Without missing a beat, Simon replied, "You might as well have asked a blind man to describe the sunrise.

"You know there is another working theory on how all of those different civilizations could have common elements to their myths. According to your hypothesis, thousands of isolated, disconnected civilizations share common attributes in their stories that reveal the great common conscious. Your theory is almost like a pyramid with all of these separate stories as the foundation. By sifting through the stories to find related facts, the pyramid takes shape and reaches a pinnacle of common ideas that reveal singular truths about your mystical god."

"Yeah, so," Joey quipped.

"So, what if the pyramid were inverted?" Simon asked. "What if it were more like a family tree that began with Adam and Eve in the Garden of Eden? The real story is the base of the tree. As generations started to branch out and spread across the globe, they passed down the original story about God and Creation and Noah by word of mouth. As time and distance moved the various people groups further and further away from their place of origin, they simply added information to the stories in order to fill in the gaps. When they had finally written the stories down, the legends did share common facts, but now they also contained details based on each culture's environment and traditions.

"But, one people group, chosen by God, kept a very accurate account of the facts surrounding God and the origin of mankind.

"Your profound theory of anthropological mythology hinges on one tiny detail. You have to assume that every tribe and nation did not originate from one geographical location. It is predicated on the idea that all of those cultures independently came into being and independently discovered common truths about a 'Great Common Conscience' by observing the universe or by enlightenment.

"That's not profound. That's not even science."

Joey replied, "Okay, so tell me then, professor, seeing how you seem to be complete unimpressed by genuine scholarship? What do *you* consider the most profound idea that has ever been revealed to mankind then?"

Without hesitation, Simon said plainly, " 'Jesus loves me, this I know, for the Bible tells me so."

Joey stared blankly before blurting out, "Ha! That's what I thought. It's 'grade school' theology." Then he glanced back up at the monument displaying the Ten commandments. "You know," he said. "Things are looking up for you. You may get your chance at that martyrdom thing sooner rather than later."

"I am not afraid of that," Simon solemnly replied.

Joey turned and headed back down the steps. "Yeah, right, we'll see what your huddled masses have to say tomorrow morning," he called back over his shoulder. "Nice talk. Next time you might want to brush up on your comparative religion and ancient mythology. I suggest starting with the 'Bardo Thodal'. I think you might find it very interesting."

With a wave of his hand and a sardonic smile, Joey propped open the door and waited for his understudy who obediently followed him out the front door into the darkness.

Disgusted at his own ineptness, Simon vowed to be prepared for the next verbal exchange of that nature. At once, he ascended the stairs to the chorus room, sat down in the swivel chair, and set to the task of better arming himself for future debates.

Sometime in the wee hours of morning, Simon reluctantly surrendered to sheer exhaustion and drifted off to sleep, bringing to an end the longest day of his life.

32

THE ACCUSER OF OUR BROTHER

As the sun peaked over the grain elevator to the east of the school, Simon was dead to the world. He was still in the same position after drifting off to sleep the night before. Leaning back in the swivel chair, his mouth was wide open, his feet were propped up on the desk, and a Bible lay open in his lap. Scattered all about him were a sea of books and reference materials, most of which had been marked, highlighted, or underlined in some form or fashion. Frozen on the computer screen before him were the results of his last Google search. Scribbled on a scratch piece of paper in front of him were a variety of names, titles, and phrases such as, *Infinite Monkey Theorum*, Ravi Zacharias, *The Case for Christ*, G.K. Chesterton, *Common Sense*, C.S. Lewis' *Mere Christianity*, Norman Giesler, and Josh McDowell, and much, much more…

The shadows of the metalwork atop the grain elevator had slowly crept through the window across the hardwood floor and now lay criss cross over Simon's peaceful countenance. Suddenly, the murmurings of a clamor drifted up the stairs and nudged him gently from his stupor. His nose twitched a couple of times before he made a feeble attempt to reposition his slumbering body. With the noise growing in volume and intensity, Simon begrudgingly lifted his head and looked around the room through a squinted eye. Momentarily catching a glimpse of the grain elevator off in the distance through window of the chorus room, Simon nearly unlocked its riddle from the recesses of his subconscious that had plagued him ever since returning to Bethel only a few shorts months ago. But, just as he was about to put a finger on a distant memory, shouts of anger unmistakably rose above the clamor.

Simon shot up out of the chair, shook the cobwebs from his head, and set the Bible back down on the desk in front of him. Still groggy, he winded his way down the stairs towards the landing to see what the commotion was all about. Just as he turned the corner, he saw them. An angry mob of people standing on the stairwell at the base of the monument to the Ten Commandments passionately arguing and wildly gesticulating. As soon as they saw Simon coming down the steps, they accosted him. There were angry shouts and bitter words as the people demanded answers.

As it had turned out, the workers from the city who had delivered the voting booths early in the morning saw the controversial monument hanging on the wall. In no time, they had brought their discovery to the attention of the store owners that were just beginning to arrive at their places of work and to the attention of the farmers who were having their first cup of coffee at the tavern. With the help of Dr. Al-Banna and the miracle of social media, it wasn't long before the entire town was talking about the great controversy. Before long, a crowd of nearly five-hundred people had descended on the school, filled the lobby, and spilled out into the street. Conspicuously missing from the crowd was Jack Lawless who was only now returning from Clay Potter's property.

Having come to his senses, Simon looked down at his watch and saw that it was already half past seven. Somehow he had overslept. With the voting scheduled to begin in a half an hour, neither of the booths had been set up yet. Frantically, Simon surveyed the faces in the disgruntled crowd, looking for his trusted assistant. All the while, people were grabbing at Simon's shirt, tugging at his arms, and shouting in his face.

Finally, Simon spotted Tony who was trying to fight his way through the crowd at the front doors of the school. After catching his attention, Tony was able to understand Simon's hand gesturing amidst the commotion. The handyman turned and pointed outside. Simon rightfully took it to mean that the booths were sitting in front of the school building.

Still dazed by the surreal scene, Simon wrongly assumed that all of the outrage was over his negligence in getting the booths ready for the vote on the referendum. Consequently, he would quickly be able to restore order by setting them up.

"Where are they?" Simon shouted at Tony, as he made his way through the throng of people.

"Lyin' out front on the playground!" Tony yelled back. "But, I don't think…!"

"Well, let's grab them and get them in here!" Simon shouted, as he fought his way out the front door and onto the blacktop.

Just then, a group of men led by Dr. Al-Banna snaked their way through the crowd and made their way over to Simon who was about to bend down and pick up one end of a voting booth. The crowd quieted in order to hear what the good doctor had to say.

"There he is!" Dr. Al-Banna shouted.

Caught off guard, Simon set back down his end of the booth.

"What's all this?" Simon asked, just now getting a clear sense of the real source of the people's consternation. It had nothing to do with neglecting his duties and everything to do with fulfilling them.

Tony stepped away from his end of the voting booth and stealthily shrunk back into the shadows of the riotous crowd.

Dr. Al-Banna cleared a path for Pastor Algood, Lexus Helrigle, and Kurt Fields.

"Simon Freeman, are you the one responsible for this demonstration?" Kurt Fields sternly asked.

Sheepishly, Simon looked around as the crowd awaited his response.

"No, I am not *responsible* for any demons...," he began to say.

"...Simon, you know that it is unlawful to have any kind of religious symbol posted in a public setting," Pastor Algood scolded. "It is a breech of the Establishment Clause."

"Did you or did you not hang the plaque of the Ten Commandments on the wall in the entryway to the school?" Lexus Helrigle asked, in an accusatory tone.

"Well, yes, I..." Simon started to say.

He was quickly drowned out by the protestors who demanded to know by what authority he had done such a thing.

"Yes, Simon!" Dr. Al-Banna interjected. "Tell them by whose authority. Tell them what your true intentions are for doing such an offensive thing as this!"

"Yes, tell us! We demand to know! What's the meaning of all of this?" the crowd shouted in unison.

At that moment, Hope arrived. She tried to make her way through the crowd of people surrounding Simon. But, try as she might, she was unable to get by the angry mob. Straining to hear what was being said, Hope worked her way around to a flat bed trailer that had been parked in front of the school. The trailer was to be used as a makeshift stage for the benefit to raise money for the Cain family.

Hope stood on her tiptoes and careened her neck to see what was going on, but it was no use. Nonetheless, other observers were more than eager to share what they knew of the developments that were unfolding. She listened intently as many as four or five people filled her in on all that had taken place up to that point. As she did her best to decipher the deluge of bits and pieces of information, she was unable to contain the sparkle in her eyes or the brilliant smile that swept over her face.

Dr. Al-Banna waved both hands and quieted the crowd.

"Go on, tell them," the good doctor said to Simon. "What do you hope to accomplish by hanging this offensive monument on the wall?"

With nearly half the town of Bethel breathlessly awaiting an answer, Simon realized that the time had come to take a stand. Surprisingly, he didn't worry what to say or how to say it. At that time, in his moment of truth, he had somehow been given the words to say. Simon spoke eloquently of the series of events that had led him up to this moment which included his entire testimony and his calling to renovate the school. Simon boldly proclaimed his true intentions to end Bethel's curse through the complete restoration of the school.

About that time there arose a great disturbance about his testimony. The assembly of people broke into confusion. Some were shouting one thing, some another, while many others didn't even know why they were there. They just came to see what all the excitement was about.

Finally grasping the full magnitude of the moment, Hope seized the opportunity and climbed onto the flatbed trailer. Convicted by the Spirit, she nervously cleared her throat, cried out at the head of the noisy street, raised her voice in the public square, and made her speech. "How long will you simple ones love your simple ways?" she shouted, trying desperately to get the people's attention. How long will mockers delight in mockery and fools hate knowledge? Simon is right! We are living under a curse!

A hush came over the crowd of onlookers.

"But if we would just respond to God's warnings," she continued, "He would pour his heart out to us and make His thoughts known to us. Since we reject Him when he calls, and no one gives pays any attention when he stretches out his hand, since we ignore all of His advice and do accept His rebuke, He laughs at our disaster and mocks us when calamity overtakes us!

The large gathering of people listened in great awe and wonder at Hope's admonition.

"God *is* angry with us for the way we live!" she shouted to the now silent crowd. "I don't blame Him for not answering out prayers when we call out to Him.

"Since we refuse to accept His advice and spurn His rebuke," she said clearly referring to the Ten Commandments. "We hate knowledge and do not fear the Lord. We don't listen to His advice. We don't accept His rebuke. In the end, we all get what we deserve. And unless we change our ways, it will only lead to our destruction. Our waywardness will kill us and our complacency will destroy us!"

There was grumbling that rippled through the crowd, as Simon tried desperately to grasp the concept of the fear of the Lord.

"But, but…!" Hope yelled, "Whoever listens to God's word will live in safety and be at ease without fear of harm. So, Simon was right to put that monument *back* where it belongs," she said, beaming with pride as their eyes met for the first time through the crowd. It is *exactly* what this community needs at this moment in time!"

There was silence. Hope's breathing was labored She could hardly believe that she had somehow mustered up the courage to go through with her pledge. Just as a great sense of relief began to overwhelm her, a single, solitary clapping of hands could be heard from out of the shadows of the old school building.

All eyes turned to see Jack Lawless stepping up onto the flatbed trailer.

"Ha!" Jack said. "Well, that was quite a speech young lady. Yes, quite a speech. You'll have to pardon, me folks. Those of you who know me, and I would guess that that's just about everyone here from the looks of things, know my distaste for getting up in front of large groups of people. I ain't never liked being the center of attention.

"At any rate, as president of the school board, I thought it my duty to shed some light on a bit of information. Information that, uh, I myself have only been made recently aware of. There have been some developments that I think are relevant to the situation at hand. Even though the efforts of this young lad, Simon Freeman, seem to be commendable at first glance, I am afraid there are some very nefarious activities going on beneath the surface. I am afraid we have all been greatly, greatly deceived."

A murmur ripped through the crowd as all eyes volleyed back and forth between Jack, Simon, and Hope.

"It gives me no great pleasure to inform you," Jack said smugly, "that Mr. Freeman has in fact been embezzling money from private donors and misappropriating school funds. In turn, he has been using that money for, well…what could be described as reprehensible conduct."

Even though the vast majority of the crowd had been taken in, Hope remained unfazed by the wild allegations.

"That's a lie!" Simon said to his accuser.

Jack's face turned instantly violent and shouted, "*Is it?* Then he turned to his right and said, "Bring him up here, boys!"

Everyone in the crowd swayed from side to side in an effort to see whom Jack was referring to. Suddenly, there was more rumbling amongst the crowd as Little Simon Adamson appeared on the back of the flatbed trailer. Begrudgingly, the notorious outcast of the community made his way across the makeshift stage and stood next to Jack.

"Do you deny, Mr. Freeman, that you have a history with known prostitutes?" Jack asked pointedly. There was a collective gasp as all eyes turned to Simon.

Simon's face turned pale, as Hope's countenance fell. "Known history of…? What are you talking about? No!" Simon replied, flatly.

"So, are you going to stand there and tell me that you and Jez Bell never spent an evening together in the front of a pickup truck on Clay Potter's property?" Jack asked.

Hope was still undaunted by the hard line of questioning, having already heard all of the sorted details about that dreadful night.

"What?" Simon asked. His embarrassment belied his innocence. "Yes, but we didn't…"

"And did she receive money in exchange for her company?" Jack asked.

"…Well," Simon said, stuttering and stammering. "I didn't know she had been paid to be there. You see, Rich…"

"…I thought as much," Jack said, with an indignant expression. "And is it also true that you have been purchasing groceries and other items for Ms. Adamson on a regular basis for the past month in exchange for her services as well?" Jack asked, with a wicked grin.

Hope's heart was in her throat as she jerked her head around to look into Simon's eyes.

Simon's mind was reeling. He cried out, "No! *Absolutely not!*"

The crowd relinquished a collective groan.

"So, you deny, then, bringing her groceries?" Jack asked, pointedly.

Simon paused, trying to parcel his answer, "No, I don't deny that..."

He was unable to get the full answer out before the din of noise rose to a clamor.

Jack didn't wait for the crowd to quiet down before he spoke again. "Pastor Cross, did you or did you not see Mr. Freeman on multiple occasions go in and out of Ms. Adamson's home?" Jack asked, looking towards the very back of the crowd.

"But, I didn't go to their house to see her," Simon said, defensively. "And it wasn't for the reasons that you are accusing me of..."

"...Oh, I suppose you just went over there for conversation," Jack said, sarcastically. Then he knelt down next to the frightened little boy and said, "Go on, tell them, what you told me earlier. It's all right."

Simon's head was spinning. He looked towards Hope. Her face turned white as a sheet as the boy finished his damning testimony concerning the sordid details surrounding Simon, Jeremy, meth, and his mother.

After Little Simon finished speaking, Jack stood up and turned again towards Simon with an expression of great disdain. "And where do you suppose Simon got all of that money to feed his vile habit?" Jack asked.

Without thinking, Simon made his fatal mistake.

"But, I didn't go over there for Bambi Adamson, or for drugs, or anything like that!" he desperately blurted out. "I went there for him. I went there for the boy!"

As soon as the words come out of Simon's mouth, pandemonium broke out. A mob mentality swept through the crowd like a wild fire. Simon felt the first blow to his face, and he felt the cold trickle of blood run down his face. People grabbed him from all directions. They spat at him, cursed at him, and assaulted his person. Several severe blows were quickly delivered to his head and midriff. Dazed and confused, he suddenly felt a large, burly hand grab him by the scruff of the neck.

Simon squinted and braced himself for the blow as Rich clutched his collar with his left hand and pulled back his right. When the mountain of a man brought the giant fist down, he struck one of Simon's assailants square on the chin, dropping him to ground.

The brawny bartender picked Simon up, threw him over his shoulder, and pushed his way through the swarm of people like a fullback. With the crowd in hot pursuit, Rich raced his way down the back alley behind the tavern, circled back, and came around to the front of Thelma's Trophy Shop on Main Street. Rich figured that getting Simon into the custody of the local constable was his best chance for survival.

Still staggered by the blows to the head, Simon could not shake the deep sense of betrayal by the little boy whom he had been dutifully ministering to for the past month. He marveled at how Little Simon could have made-up such terrible things, after all that he had done for him. The inconceivable thought ran over and over in his mind as he lay slumped over Rich's shoulder, bounding down the back alley.

So many thoughts crowded his clouded conscious, as Rich ran away from the crowd. "Was he that horrible of a child?" Simon thought. "Was he that much of a monster? Why on earth would he do something like that to me? Where would he even get such an idea?"

All of these thoughts collided instantaneously in Simon's mind, as Rich turned the corner and headed back to Main Street. Just as Simon was about to write off the strange little boy as a lost cause, the burly bartender sprinted past the Cain's who were standing with the rear passenger door open to their SUV. The young parents were just about to get the sick little girl out of the car and place her in the stroller.

As he bounded past the young family, Simon's subconscious took a mental snapshot of the interior of the vehicle. That's when he saw it. It was the missing Baby Jesus from the manger in the basement of the school. It was lying in the car seat next to the sleeping child.

Instantaneously, Simon jerked his head up to verify what he had seen in a mere blink of an eye. Even though the car seat was already long out of sight, there was no question as to what Simon had seen.

"Baby Jesus?" Simon mused. There were only a handful of people who had unadulterated access to the basement.

Having only temporarily given their pursuers the slip, Rich reached the front door of Thelma's shop and wildly groped for the door handle, but the shop was locked. Frustrated, he set Simon down and banged on the door. Then he stepped forward, cupped his hand, and peered through the large glass window of the shop only to see Thelma sitting forward in her chair at her desk with her eyes closed, head bowed, and hands clasped.

Still groggy from the violent blows to his head, Simon tried to piece it all together, "...From the nativity scene?" Finally, it dawned on Simon. "Of course! Little Simon must have given it to her. He had to have. He was the only one who could have. He must have given Jesus wrapped in swaddling clothes to the Cain baby!"

Maybe, there was still hope for the wayward child after all.

Exasperated, Rich tapped on the glass and yelled, "*Thelma!*"

Suddenly awakened, Simon took off running. He doubled back in same direction from whence that they had just come. He was heading for the cellar doors that led to the tunnel beneath the school.

Rich frantically called out to Simon, urging his friend to come back. Winded and rubber legged, he started off after Simon before quickly realizing that there was no way that he was going to catch the fleet-footed centerfielder.

When Simon reached the back of the school building, he wrenched open the cellar doors and made his way down the long, narrow tunnel to Little Simon's hideout, but it was empty. There was no sign of the child. He knew that there could only be one other place to search for the lost child.

Hearing shouts echoing down the corridor from the angry mob, Simon raced out of the dark tunnel in the opposite direction. He emerged again in the basement behind the boiler. Quickly, he charged up the stairs, sprinted across the landing beneath the giant chandelier, and darted back out the front doors of the school building.

33

REFUSING TO ACKNOWLEDGE HIM

Dry, brown corn stalks waved in the breeze above Simon's head as he ran down the uneven row towards Clay Potter's abandoned farm. Dried blood from his lip smattered his button-down shirt, now drenched with sweat in the hot summer's sun as the stiff stalks mercilessly cut him. When he finally broke free from the row of corn, he stumbled out into a clearing on the opposite side of the field. Out of breath, he paused for only a moment leaning on his knees. He stared at the decaying home, the tattered barn, and the rusted windmill at the top of the bluff next to the threshing floor.

Determined, Simon ran up the hill, kicking up a cloud of dust behind him as he went. When he reached the dried up well, he fell to his belly, lifted the piece of plywood partially covering the hole, and looked down. At the bottom of the well sat Little Simon.

Startled, the dirty-faced boy yelled at him profanely, "Go away!"

His face was beet red, and he was still panting from the long run out to his hideaway.

"Simon, I need to talk to you, now!" Simon shouted. "Climb up here!"

"No!" Little Simon shouted, in a bratty tone.

"*Get up here, now!*" he growled through clenched teeth. "You get up here this instant or so help me…"

Realizing that his idle threat had no effect, Simon's eyes danced about as he searched for a lever. Suddenly, raising his eyebrows and lifting himself up onto his elbows, he calmly said, "Simon Adamson, if you don't get up here right now, I will go back into town, buy the strongest dead bolt money can buy, and lock up the cellar doors to the school.

"You wouldn't do that!" Little Simon said, looking up panicked.

"Oh, yes I would," Simon replied.

"No!" Little Simon, shouted while forcing his patented fake cry.

"You can count on it," Simon said, standing to his feet.

He looked down at the boy's greasy hair atop his head. It wasn't long before the little boy reluctantly rose to his feet and climbed up out of the well. When he reached the top, he paused for a moment with only the very top of his head sticking out as though he were having a change of heart. Before he could retreat back down into the hole, Simon yanked him out of the well by the boy's arm.

Holding him by both shoulders, Simon bent down on one knee and looked the child in the face. Still Little Simon refused to look him in the eye.

"Look at me," Simon demanded, as the boy refused to make eye contact.

"I said, look at me!" Simon yelled, taking him by the chin and forcing him to look into his eyes.

"No!" Little Simon screamed before punching, and biting, and cursing to pull himself free.

"Stop it, stop it…Stop it! I said," Simon growled.

Momentarily, the boy stopped fighting before spitting in Simon's face.

"You little…," Simon said, wiping his face. "You know what? I don't care. You are going to answer my questions either the easy way or the hard way."

"No!" Little Simon said, before violently kicking his captor in the shin.

"That does it!" Simon said. "You have been needing one of these for a long time." Then he wrestled the boy over his knee and gave him three hard swats on his behind."

Little Simon burst out with a real cry this time. He reached for his still stinging rear-end as Simon set him back down on his feet.

"Now," Simon said, kneeling down, holding both of the boy's shoulders and looking him in the eye. "You are going to answer my questions."

Little Simon, no longer struggling to free himself, stared at the ground in front of Simon, whimpering.

"Why did you say those things about me?" Simon asked sternly.

Stubborn and silent, Little Simon stood speechless still staring at the dirt.

"Answer me," Simon said, now in control.

Little Simon glanced back over his shoulder towards the well, contemplating an escape.

Simon, reading the boys thoughts, said, "Why do you go down there? You can't hide forever you know."

Still upset and heaving, Little Simon replied, "It's my cave."

"Your cave?" Simon asked.

"Yeah, 'member, I'm a vampire," Little Simon replied somberly.

Considering how messed up a kid had to be in order to make up such a delusion, Simon said, "Why do you want to be vampire?"

"Cause," Little Simon said, reaching up with the back of his hand and smearing his runny nose over a cheek muddied from tears.

"Cause why?" Simon asked, dropping one hand to his side and loosening his grip with the other.

Little Simon's answer was chilling. "Cause they won't come after me if I'm one of them'," he intimated, finally looking up at Simon.

"If you're 'one of them'?" Simon asked.

"Yeah, then I won't have to be afraid no more," Little Simon said.

"Afraid of what?" Simon asked.

"Ya know, vampires, zombies…or monsters," Little Simon replied, glancing at the abandoned house.

Simon dropped his other hand to the ground and steadied himself.

"What monsters?" he asked.

"Like the ones who come for my mommy, I hear them fighting in her room," Little Simon said.

Suddenly, Simon's stomach turned as he realized what the boy was saying.

"Have they ever come after you?" Simon dared to ask, temporarily distracted from his own plight.

Little Simon shook his head and replied, "No dummy! Cause I'm one of 'em. I'm a vampire, remember. That's when I climb out my window and go to my caves."

Simon understood the desire to run and hide. He looked down at the ground and bit his lip.

Little Simon muttered, "I don't ever want them to do that to me."

"What the monsters do to your mommy?" Simon asked, thinking he now understood.

The little boy nodded, sheepishly, before a look of terror came over his face, "And what the monsters done to Mr. Jeremy."

Simon jerked his head up and sat forward, "What *who* did to Mr. Jeremy?" Only now remembering that his body had been discovered only a few miles from Clay Potter's property.

"Jack," Little Simon said.

A shiver ran up Simon's spine, "*Jack?*"

"And them others," Little Simon said, staring blankly back down the hill to the abandoned farmhouse.

Simon glanced back in the direction of the stare before a cold realization set in. "Simon, this is important. Did you see what happened to Jeremy Warner?"

Again, the boy refused to make eye contact.

"Simon," he said again. "What did you see? Did you see Jack do something to Jeremy?"

Silence.

Simon's faced turned angry, before looking over at the well. "Listen, if you don't tell me what happened, not only will I put a lock on the cellar door to the school, I will come out here with a bag of concrete mix and fill that well. Now tell me what you saw."

Little Simon stared down the hill in the direction of the school and began to recount what he saw the night Jeremy was brutally murdered.

"They was out here that night, like they are sometimes," Little Simon said, almost in trance.

"Whose they?" Simon asked.

"Mr. Jack and some other guys," Little Simon said.

"And you were hiding in the well?" Simon asked.

Little Simon nodded. "I heard a car drive up, so I climbed up to see what was goin' on."

"Could you see the men?" Simon asked, his face white.

"Yeah," Little Simon said. "They burn stuff in a pot in the house. I seen it once. And lots of people come in and out all the time when Jack and them is out here."

Simon furrowed his brow and looked down in the dirt before imagining what a meth lab might look like. He looked back at the house with anarchy and satanic symbols spray painted on the exterior walls. He remembered the stories of burning sacrifices by the Satanic worshipers. "Who drove up in the car, Simon? Do you know?"

"It was Mr. Jeremy," Little Simon said.

Simon fell to both knees. "Jeremy Warner, the youth pastor?" Simon asked, his face now ashen.

"Uh-huh," Little Simon said.

"What happened, what did you see?" Simon asked, desperately.

"When he got out of the car, Jack and them come out of the house," Little Simon said, reliving that dreadful night. "Jeremy met them, he was holdin' somethin'; a book or somethin'."

"What did he say?" Simon asked, completely absorbed by the account.

"I don't know, somethin' bout how they shouldn't be doin' what they was doin'," Little Simon said. "He talked at them a long time."

"And what was Jack doing during all of this?" Simon asked with grave concern.

"Jack?" Little Simon repeated with fear and trembling. "Well, the other guys first grabbed Jeremy, like to shut him up and stuff."

"What happened next?" Simon asked, trying his best to decipher the story.

Little Simon turned his head as if trying to understand it himself. "Then, Jack just walked around whisper'n in everybody's ear while Jeremy's face turned white."

"Turned white?" Simon asked, confused. "What do you mean turned white? Like it turned pale or something?"

"No," Little Simon said. "It glowed...like a lamp."

"Glowed?" Simon repeated, trying to picture in his mind what the boy meant.

"Then Jack said somethin' and all em' guys laughed and stuff," Little Simon continued. Now he wasn't merely telling the story, but almost acting it out. "Then they grabbed Mr. Jeremy. He started fightin' and tell'n 'em to let him go."

Tears began welling up in Simon's eyes.

"What happened after that?" Simon asked.

Little Simon frowned like he was confused, "Mr. Jeremy was telling them all about Jesus and how they needed to 'pent. He kept sayin' 'pent for the dumb king snear, pent for the dumb king snear' or 'king dumb' or somethin' like that. But each time he said it, they just laughed harder and harder and harder. Then one of em' ran into the house and came back with some wood and laid it down around that post over there."

Simon looked down at two old laundry poles near the house. One rusted out and the other black with soot.

"Then Mr. Jeremy was shouting and his arms were goin' all over the place and stuff," Little Simon said, still pantomiming what he had seen. "One of the monsters punched him real hard in the face and Mr. Jeremy fell down. Then… and, uh, then a couple of em' dragged him over to a stump and held his fingers out like this." The boy said extending his hand out. "And they laid it on that stump over there and smashed them!"

Simon could feel a lump in his throat and his heart beat beginning to pound in his ears. He felt like he might vomit.

"…And Mr. Jeremy was yellin' an stuff. And- and another guy he-he come runnin' out of the house carryin' a chain. They dragged him over to the pile of wood and chained em' to the…to the…" he said pointing to the pole.

"…The clothes line?" Simon heard himself say.

Little Simon nodded, his eyes getting wider as he stared off in the distance towards the house.

"They chained Jeremy to the pole?" Simon asked, tears streaming down his face.

"Yeah," Little Simon said, getting excited as his body recoiled. "And the guy with the gold watch, lit a stick on fire with a lighter. And-and he walked over to the wood pile and set it down on it."

Simon was numb, overcome by the terrifying account. His mind raced as he considered for a moment how quickly the dry wood probably caught.

"What was Jeremy doing?" Simon demanded to know. "What was he saying to them?"

"He wasn't sayin' nothin' to them," Little Simon replied. "He was lookin' up to the sky and yellin' 'O' Father…O' God 'give them. And other stuff like that. And the whole time his face was still glowin'. And the fire was gettin' bigger and bigger. The other dudes was laughin' and like dancin' around drinkin' and thrown' their bottles into the fire. Jack just stood back in the distance, lean'n against the house, with his arms folded, smokin' a cigarette, just smilin'," Little Simon vividly recalled, gesturing with his hands.

Simon felt lightheaded and was sick at his stomach.

Little Simon was now in the moment, reliving it. "Then he just stopped," the little boy said, his arms falling to his sides. "Mr. Jeremy was lookin' up at the sky, like he was starin' at somethin'. And all them guys, they stopped and looked up. I looked too. But, I didn't see nothin'. And, and, and all of a sudden, Mr. Jeremy just…smiled," he said, the corners of his lips curling upward.

Simon expectantly waited for the boy to continue before frantically asking, "Then what?"

"He died," Little Simon said flatly as a look of terror came over his face.

"What is it Simon?" he asked the boy.

"He was lookin' right at *me*," Little Simon said.

"Who?...Mr. Jeremy?" Simon asked, confused.

"No," Little Simon said. "Mr. Jack."

Simon stood up. He was in complete shock. With the hot sun now beating down on him, he mechanically wiped the beads of sweat off of his forehead and stood to his feet. Almost paralyzed by the incredible story, Simon was at a loss of words. Suddenly, coming to his senses, he looked down at the forlorn child.

"We've got to *do* something," Simon said, excitedly. "We've got to tell someone what happened."

The little boy jerked his head up and stared at Simon with a look of horror on his face. Slowly taking a few steps backward, he shook his head decidedly.

At the same time the frightened boy took off running towards the well. Simon leaped after him. Catching him by the collar just before reaching the hole, Simon said, "No, no, no...Wait! I have to take you to the authorities. We have to tell the police!"

Little Simon was flailing his arms and yelling, "No! Let me go! He said he'd get me!"

"Calm down!" Simon said, securing the terrified little boy and kneeling down before him. "Calm down. Shhh! He won't get you. Nobody is going to *get* you."

"Yes, he will!" the boy yelled.

"They will protect us," Simon said, himself uncertain.

"No, they won't come after *you*!" the boy yelled, wrenching his body as he tried to pull away.

"What?" Simon asked, caught off guard by the comment. "Why you and not me? You're not making any sense."

The boy stopped struggling for a moment and looked at Simon, "Because you're one of them."

"What?" Simon said. "No, I'm not!"

"Yeah you are!" the boy said, angrily. "I seen you."

"You seen me?" Simon asked. "Seen me do what?"

"I seen you dig them bodies up in the graveyard," Little Simon said. "I heard what you said. Heard you yellin' at God. I saw your face." Furiously, he made another attempt to get away. "They won't come after one of their own. That's why I *have* to be a vampire!"

Defensively, Simon tried to justify what the boy had seen, "Simon, I...that was before...wait!" he said trying to secure the wild thrashing of the boy who was standing on the concrete slab next to the well. "Just wait a second. This is important. We have to tell someone about what you saw!"

"I did, I already did!" the now livid little boy yelled, "I told that man at the church. It didn't do no good. Now let me go!"

Simon was in shock, but managed to ask, "Pastor Pete? You told Pastor Pete?"

Then the Little boy dug his sharp teeth into Simon's forearm, causing him to loosen his grip.

"Ouch!' Simon said instinctively, clutching his arm as he watched the boy race past the well and into the cover of tall cornstalks in the nearby field.

Simon stood holding his arm with a look of shock on his face. His eyes wildly danced about as he tried to process everything that he had just learned.

* * *

Pastor Pete Cross stood precariously balancing himself on the tall ladder while assessing the water damage to the ceiling of the sanctuary due to the heavy spring rains. Not having the resources to actually repair the damaged roof, he concerned himself only with the minimal supplies that it would take in order to do a little patchwork.

Suddenly, the pounding of heavy footsteps on the creaky floorboards at the back of the sanctuary startled him. With his heart pounding, he deliberately turned his neck and strained to see out of the corner of his eyes to identify his unannounced visitor.

"Simon!" the pastor exclaimed, carefully steadying himself at the top of the ladder. "Where have you been, son?" Having achieved a less perilous position on the rungs of the ladder, the pastor could now fully turn to take a long hard look at the known fugitive. He was drenched in sweat and gasping for breath, having sprinted the mile back into town from Clay Potter's property. His shirt was torn and bloodied, his lip was swollen, and his hair disheveled. More than that there was an intensity about his countenance that belied his desperate condition.

"Pastor...Pete...," Simon gasped, trying to catch his breath as the Pastor Cross descended the ladder.

"Simon, what are you doing here?" the Pastor asked, as he stepped down from the ladder and approached Simon who was now leaning on his knees. "You are in some serious trouble. The authorities came by here earlier looking for you. They told me all about the wild allegations; the money, the extortion, drugs, soliciting prostitutes, human trafficking, and...even murder charges." With an expression of pity, the good Pastor took Simon by the arm and tried to ease him over into a pew, but Simon resisted. For the moment, the Pastor was still able to don the façade and spout the rhetoric that was expected of him.

"Murder?" Simon asked, blown away by the accusation.

"I'm afraid so," Pete replied in a somber town. "After you ran off, Jack started spreading the rumor that you were Jeremy's hook-up from Texas. And that maybe the two of you were in this thing together, or that somehow Jeremy was dealing for you. He even insinuated that maybe he double crossed you or something. So, you had to come here and take care of him yourself. Then he planted the seed that maybe the whole thing was about some torrid love triangle between you, Jeremy, and Candy Adamson."

"Jack, made those accusations against *me?*" Simon asked in disbelief.

"Well, not exactly," Pete replied. "He would say things like 'Is it possible that...?' and 'Is it a coincidence that...?' or 'You don't suppose that...?'"

"Well, we need to go to the police and straighten this whole thing out," Simon said between breaths, ignoring the pastor's words. "I was with Joey and George that night. They'll vouch for me.

"And you need to tell the cops who Simon really saw that night."

"Tell them what?" Pastor Pete asked, suddenly dropping the facade. "I-I'm afraid I already did. I told them all that I knew...about you going into the Adamson's house next door, just like..."

"What about Jeremy Warner?" Simon blurted out, tugging his arm away from the pastor. "I know about Jeremy. Simon Adamson told *me* everything! That's why we have to go tell the cops," he said passionately, backing towards the door and imploring the pastor.

Pete's whitewashed face fell. With his role as the caring, detached clergyman shattered, Pete stumbled backwards and collapsed into the pew. He was no longer just a detached observer.

"What are you doing?" Simon pleaded, as he took a few steps back towards the ashamed grey-haired man.

"We have to go," Simon said with a pained expression. "We have to *do* something about this, this injustice. They've got it all wrong about me and Jeremy. We have to tell someone..."

"...I already did," Pete said in a monotone voice, staring off into the distance.

"What?" Simon said now standing over the top of a broken man. "Who did you tell?"

"Jack," Pastor Pete said.

"*Jack?*" Simon gasped, spinning in a circle while wiping his face with the palms of his hands. "Why on earth would you tell, Jack?"

"You wouldn't understand," Pete said with his eyes welling up with tears.

"Wouldn't understand?" Simon yelled. "You bet I don't understand. Of all people, you go to the one responsible...you-you put an innocent kid's life in jeopardy? What could you possibly have been thinking?"

"I didn't tell Jack about Simon Adamson," the expressionless pastor said, choking out his words.

Simon rolled his eyes and let out a sigh of relief. "But, it doesn't make any sense," he lamented. "Why would you say anything to Jack?"

"Because..." the pastor snapped, glancing up at Simon. "It's not as easy of a decision as you make it out to be."

"What…to tell the truth?" Simon asked, accusingly.

"Who can believe everything a strange little kid like that says?" Pete said defensively, trying to convince himself. "It's just some 6-year-old kid's word versus Jack's. Besides, think of what a false accusation like that could do to a person's reputation. Think of all of the things such an accusation would set in motion…a trial, all the media attention…It would be like living in Hades."

"*So?*" Simon said, unable to comprehend the irresponsibility of the pastor.

"So, what if the boy was making it up?" Pete asked. "I needed to know the answer to that question. So, I went to Jack in private first, hoping that if he had committed a crime that I could get a confession or something."

"A confession?" Simon shrieked. "Are you out of your mind? You had to know Jack would just deny the whole thing."

Without even acknowledging Simon's assertion, Pete replied, "He had an alibi. I confirmed it myself. So, you can see there'd be no point in raising such wild allegations against a prominent business man and jeopardizing his reputation over some crazy conspiracy theory or the fantastic tale of a deranged child."

The word reputation rang in Simon's ears like a siren song. Bewildered by the bizarre reasoning of a man of the cloth, Simon raked his hand through his hair, trying to fathom Pete's motivation for the choices that he had made. As he searched the pastor's eyes, it suddenly dawned on him. It was all about *reputation*.

"You knew Jack would deny it," Simon said, pointing at the pastor. "You may have even guessed that he'd come up with some sort of phony alibi, but that didn't matter. Either way, once he denied it, you would be let off the hook. You did it, so that you wouldn't have to go public with the information because you knew you'd be in the middle of all of it. You did it to ease your own conscience!"

"Ha! Ease my conscience!" Pete said angrily. "There is no such thing. You have no idea the personal torture that I daily endure at the hands of my conscience. Besides, Jack and I have a deal. I won't pursue the matter any further, and he won't let everyone know that I'm just a big phony."

"Wow! How can a pastor make a deal with the devil?" Simon asked, dumbfounded. "It's all about you, isn't it? You're more concerned with preserving your precious reputation than truth. You put on this, this do-gooder front, piddling around, busying yourself with these little inconsequential distractions. But, it's just some kind of ploy to make yourself unavailable, so that no one can pin you down on the real hard issues. I've heard your sermons. You don't want to take a stand!"

The Pastor dropped his head into his hands as though he had finally been found out. To Simon it was a clear admission of guilt.

Simon stood straight up, turned his head, and blinked. "I'm right, aren't I," he said. "You're an imposter."

"That's right," Pete said, writhing in anguish. "I am an imposter, completely unworthy of my position."

"But, why?" Simon asked, still trying to comprehend.

"Because there is something that I did when I was a child that can never be undone," Pete said, his voice muffled through his fists and his face gripped with self-contempt.

Simon's mouth fell open as he intuitively reached into his pocket and withdrew the tattered piece of newspaper from his shirt pocket. Slowly, he unfolded the wrinkled photograph that Jack had given to him. Somehow Simon made the connection.

He looked at the picture and frowned, before offering it to the pastor. "Does it have something to do with this?" Simon heard himself ask.

The pastor lifted his eyes towards the photograph and took it from Simon's hands. His hand shaking, Pete now held the picture in his trembling hands and nodded affirmatively.

A chill ran down Simon's spine, and he spontaneously convulsed. Stunned by the turn of events, he slipped into the pew next to Pete. The pastor's face was sullen. His eyes were puffy and bloodshot as he scanned the young, innocent faces in the photograph that had haunted him for the better part of seventy-two years.

"You were there the day it happened, weren't you?" Simon asked, temporarily forgetting the immediate issues at hand.

"October 31, 1935," Pete said through a grave voice. "I will never forget that day. It was a cloudy, cold Monday morning, but us kids, we didn't care. Mr. Joseph had decided to let us have a Halloween party that day. Everybody was so excited. We had looked forward to that party for what seemed like an eternity. All of the students came to school dressed in costumes. My brother Andy and I were pirates. There were decorations all over the room and treats and games," Pete said allowing a glimmer of a smile to momentarily cross his face.

His voice now distant and detached. "I was in 2nd grade and Andy was in 1st at the time," he continued, "but in those days the classes were so small that each teacher taught two grades in the same room at the same time, you know?" He paused and blankly stared into space, as though he were traveling back in time.

"And Jessie Joseph was your teacher?" Simon asked, trying to prompt the Pastor.

Pete nodded.

"What was he like?" Simon asked, now completely captivated by the story.

"He was…," Pete started to say before turning his head and squinting. "…it's hard to say…most days, we all thought he was terrific. Everybody loved him. All of the kids fought for his attention and approval. But, then, other days…."

Simon leaned in, fully bracing himself for the worst.

"…He would change," Pete muttered. "His behavior was erratic. Some days he would be on cloud nine, laughing and joking with the class. Other days, he seemed as though he barely had the energy to drag himself to school. On those days, his hair would be disheveled and his face sullen. We didn't know which Mr. Joseph we were getting from day to day. As the days went on, the wild swings of emotion became more and more erratic. One day, we could do no wrong and the next we couldn't do anything right. One day you would be rewarded for a behavior, and do the exact same thing the very next day and get blasted for it. He enforced his rules based on how he was feeling, I guess. And when he handed down punishment, he did so with an iron fist. On the other hand, his rewards for doing something that he liked got more and more grand like letting us have the Halloween party for learning our math facts.

"But, his punishments got worse and worse as well. It didn't matter if it was something insignificant like not paying attention to the lesson or if it was something really bad like cheating. Any misbehavior was subject to the same severity, whether it was the switch, or missing lunch, or…being sent to the closet."

Simon remembered what Miss Harold said about the Adam and the closet, and the hairs on the back of his neck stood on end.

"Which Mr. Joseph showed up at Halloween party that day?" Simon wisely asked.

"He seemed really down, very distracted," Pete answered. "Like he was in no mood for a party."

"And what happened?" Simon dared to ask.

"Well, he just kind of let us get up from our seats and wonder around the room, while he sat slumped back in his chair, staring at the wall," Pete answered.

"What did you do?" Simon asked.

"We didn't know what to do," Pete said. "We just kind of started playing games. And the more we played, the louder we got. And the louder we got, the more agitated Mr. Joseph seemed to get. Then one of the decorations evidently fell from the ceiling onto Mr. Joseph's desk. We hadn't noticed at first. A group of us were standing around the metal wash tub, trying to bob for apples without much success I might ad."

"Who is 'we'?" Simon asked, trying to get a mental picture. "Your brother, Andy?"

"Yes, Andy, John Rash…."

Simon swallowed hard.

"….Evelyn Potter and Adam Potter," Pete continued. "None of us were exactly sure of the rules for bobbing for apples. So, we started to argue over whether or not you could use your hands because it seemed nearly impossible to do so otherwise.

"When it was Evelyn's turn to go, John, Andy, and myself were busy arguing over the rules. We didn't even notice that she was taking her turn until she came up out of the water holding an apple under her chin. She was so excited. She held it up in the air saying, 'I did it,' 'I got it!' 'I got it!' Mr. Joseph warned us sternly from the far side of the room to calm down, but no one bothered to acknowledge him because we were all jockeying for position to go next.

"Like I said, we hadn't noticed it at the time, but Mr. Joseph, at the imploring of some of the other students, begrudgingly set his chair on top of the desk and climbed up on top of it to hang the decoration back up that had previously fallen down from the ceiling.

"Well, Adam managed to get his face down into the water which made the rest of us really mad. But John was especially put off by the whole thing. So, when Adam used his hand to secure the apple under his chin and came up out of the water holding it, John went nuts. He was calling Mr. Joseph's name to tell on Adam, while he wrestled to get the apple away from Adam. They scuffled a bit until Mr. Joseph finally looked up to see Adam shoving John to the floor in anger.

"I think everyone gasped and immediately looked across the room at Mr. Joseph standing on the desk, holding the decoration high in the air. You could tell that he was completely annoyed with what Adam had just done.

"So, he scolded Adam and told him to go over and stand in the corner facing away from the classroom. But, Adam didn't go quietly. To him, the whole thing was a great injustice. He started to cry as he pleaded his case while slowly making his way towards the designated corner.

"Everyone else stood still in silence watching the whole thing unfold. Mr. Joseph got very stern with Adam, but he would not stop trying to justify his actions. He kept turning his head from the corner to plead his case. Finally, Mr. Joseph got tired of it and ordered Adam to go to the closet. It was a method that he had used many times before, but this was different, because the closet had been decorated to look like a tomb. A skeleton from the 6th grade science class was propped up in a little coffin that was covered in fake cobwebs.

"Well, once Adam realized that he was being sent to the closet, he went into hysterics, begging Mr. Joseph to change his mind. That only caused Mr. Joseph to dig his heels in all the more. It was just a battle of wills to him. But, to Adam... well, I think he was genuinely afraid.

"Reluctantly, Adam went over to the closet and stepped inside. Then Mr. Joseph told him to shut the door because he wasn't going to listen to any more of his whining. But, he didn't close it all of the way. He left a crack in the door. By this time, Adam was sobbing uncontrollably. Out of fear, he refused to let the whole thing go. He kept opening the door and stepping out into the room.

"Finally, Mr. Joseph had had enough. He was furious at what he perceived to be outright defiance. He started down from the desk but then suddenly stopped. Realizing that there was no lock on the door, he gave orders for me and Andy to hold it shut." Pete's voice gave way as a tear streamed down his face.

"We were just trying to do what our teacher told us to do, you know. We didn't know any better. So, we did. We held it shut. But that just sent Adam over the top. He banged on the door and yelled and screamed. By now, some of the other kids started to cry.

"And I don't know if John did it out of spite or because he thought he was helping out or what, but he ran over to help us hold the door shut. Mr. Joseph realized, I think, that he was about to lose control of the class, and he was determined not to give in to Adam's tantrum. I can still see him now slamming his fist on the desk before coming over to where we were holding the closet door shut.

"By that time, Adam was screaming and clawing at the door! Andy and I got out of the way as Mr. Joseph pushed against the door, demanding that Adam be quiet. John didn't budge. He just stood there under Mr. Joseph's arm, leaning on the door with this awkward smile on his face. The whole thing seemed like it went on for a long time, even though it was probably no more than four or five minutes. Finally, there was silence."

Tears were now streaming down Pete's face, and he was wringing his hands. "Mr. Joseph, you know, he was pretty pleased with himself, thinking that he had won the battle of wills. He cautiously stepped back away from the door and called out sternly to Adam who was still inside the closet. He told him that he could just stay in there for a while and think about his actions.

"What did you do?" Simon asked, his heart in his throat.

"No one knew what to do," Pete answered. "We were just kids. We just kind of stood around looking at each other. Everybody was stunned. Some of the kids were still sniffling, trying to keep from crying. It was terrible. Mr. Joseph told us all to go back to what we were doing, but how could we?

"Realizing that he may have gone too far, Mr. Joseph sighed deeply like he was exasperated by the whole thing. He went back over to the closet and talked through the door to Adam. He said, 'I hope you have learned your lesson. If you think that you can control your behavior, you can come out and join the rest of the class. But, there was no answer. Just an awful, awful silence.

"Mr. Joseph looked around the room at the other students, as though he were a little alarmed. When he opened the door...," Pete face turned to anguish. "When he opened the door, there was Adam on the floor. His face was blue and the ends of his fingers were bloodied from scratching at the door."

Simon could hardly move. The intensity of the story had nearly paralyzed him.

"Everything after that seems like one big blur," Pete managed to say. "There was a lot screaming and yelling and crying. Mr. Joseph scrambled to the floor and felt for a pulse. With this look of terror on his face, he got up from the floor, closed the door, and ordered John to go get the principal.

"Panicked, Mr. Joseph gathered us together away from the closet, got down on a knee, and tried to prepare us for what was going to happen next. He kept insisting that it was an accident. That no one meant to harm Adam and that everything would be all right. He said that. He said everything would be all right. Mr. Joseph kept saying over and over that we needed to support each other. That it would help the police if we all told them the same story about what had happened..

"Then,..." Pete's voice trailed off.

"Then, what?" Simon asked, gripped by the origin of the curse.

"It was pandemonium from there," Pete said. "Pretty soon the room was filled with teachers from the other classrooms, policemen, fire fighters, ambulance drivers, and even a large group of parents who had heard all of the sirens and raced up to the school. Then John who must have had some trouble getting the principal finally came back into the room.

"All twelve of us students were crowded around Mr. Joseph, huddled in the corner of the room," he continued. "I think we were all just in complete shock, wondering what was going on. I remember it like it was yesterday, standing next to Mr. Joseph. I stood there in my pirate costume still wearing my patch over my eye with my sword by my side, secure in its scabbard while the principal grilled him with questions. Then some guy, I think he was probably a detective or something, took Mr. Joseph by the arm. We thought they were going to take him to jail. But, we weren't going to allow it. We stood by holding on to him, begging them to leave him alone and pleading his innocence. I remember us saying that we all wanted to go with him.

"Mr. Joseph assured us that it would be okay, and that he was going to just step out in the hallway to tell the policeman what had happened. He promised that he would be right back, and that they would probably ask all of us what had happened, and he told us that we should all cooperate by telling them *exactly* what happened.

"But, when Mr. Joseph walked out of the room, I could still see him standing on the landing under the chandelier, talking to the officer who was taking notes. He had this very serious expression on his face, and every now and then he would glance back into the classroom.

"Well, evidently Mr. Joseph must have given them a slightly different version of all that had taken place, because the police came back into the room. They let Mr. Joseph go and quickly ushered John Rash out of the room. Even then, we clung to our beloved teacher because the cops were holding back our parents at the bottom of the stairs, so that we couldn't get to them.

"One by one, they took us aside and interviewed us. Being the good little boys and girls that we were, we told them everything just as Mr. Joseph had instructed us."

Simon, still trying to square the story with the legend, asked, "So, Jessie Joseph pinned it all on John? Wait. If that's the case, then how did Jessie end up going to prison?"

Reluctantly, Pete told Simon about his shame and the demons that have plagued him ever since that tragic day.

"We didn't know that John was being blamed," Pete said, trying to hold back the tears. "We were just a bunch of kids. We trusted Mr. Joseph when he said that everything would be okay. We were just so sad about Adam. We weren't thinking about blaming anyone. It was an accident. And that's what we told the police. But, evidently Mr. Joseph had given them a little more detail that implicated John.

"Little by little, as everyone tried to make sense of what had happened, we began to realize that John was being blamed for Adam's death, and that he was going to be put in jail or juvenile detention or whatever. Then somehow word got around about Adam pushing John to the floor and John getting angry and… I guess the whole thing just spiraled out of control from there.

"People were just in shock. Nothing like that ever happened in Bethel before. Not knowing the facts, people did what they do. They speculated and filled in the pieces that they didn't know. A lot of them began to make John out as some kind of little monster or something. It just wasn't true.

"So, I began to feel sorry for John. After all, John was my friend. Andy and I finally told our parents that it wasn't right. That they shouldn't blame John. And that he should not go to prison. But, my parents just wanted to stay out of it.

"After a week or so, as far I can remember it, a detective came to school. He pulled each of us out of class one by one and took us up to the chorus room. They started asking…well…more than asking. They were trying to get us to tell them what Mr. Joseph had *done* to us. They said that they knew already because John had told them all of the horrible things Mr. Joseph had done, but that they just needed to hear it from us too.

"I didn't know what to say at first. I was afraid they were going to put me in jail too. After all, Andy and I were the first ones to hold the door shut. But, then they said I could help my friend John. They said I could get him out of trouble if I would just tell them what they wanted to know about Mr. Joseph."

Pete started to sweat and shake as he recalled what happened next. "They wanted to know if Mr. Joseph had ever touched me. Of course, he had touched me. Had given me hugs and stuff. I was so scared. When I said things like, 'Mr. Joseph never hurt me' they would frown at me and talk angrily. I thought that maybe I might be in trouble too, if I didn't tell them what they wanted to hear. But, when I said things like, 'Mr. Joseph kissed me on the top of my head once' they got really happy.

"So, then they brought out a doll and had me show them all of the places that Mr. Joseph had touched me." Suddenly, Pete's face turned red. He slammed his fists into his knees and yelled. "I didn't know what they were doing! But, I was scared! So, I agreed with everything they said. All of the vile horrible things that they said. And when they were done with me, they did the same thing with Andy and the rest of the kids.

"And with each kid that came back to the room crying and afraid, it only made the other kids all the more on edge. We all told them what they wanted to know. We just agreed with them, so we could go. Simple as that. By the time they were done with us, they took Mr. Joseph away."

Pete paused trying to pull himself together, as Simon tried to comprehend the fallout. When he had reached the church only a short time ago, Simon's only purpose had been to seek justice for Jeremy. Now, enraptured by the intensity of a man's regret and the origination of town's haunted past, he temporarily put aside his original purpose for coming. Transfixed by the pastor's first hand account,

Simon waited breathlessly before asking, "Why did anybody have to be punished? I mean, it was an accident, right? Just a tragic accident."

"Yes, a horrible accident," Pete answered. "Too horrible. Maybe that's why. Maybe it was the blood. Maybe it would have been different had he just drifted off peacefully, but there was all of that blood from his fingertips. No, someone had to pay. Justice had to be served. Everyone thought as much, especially the Potters. They were devastated. When it was expected that John was at fault, they pressed hard to get their pound of flesh. So, by the time they realized that Jessie had been implicated, they had already cast their lot. It was just a sad twist of fate that all of their wrath would fall on Jessie's shoulders. It was especially difficult for Clay Potter."

Gripped by the irony of his own paralleled plight, Simon protested, "But, Jessie never did those any of the terrible things that they said. They were just false accusations coerced by overzealous investigators. Nobody was actually molested or abused the children!"

"No," Pete lamented. "None of the students were physically abused. Why is it that people crave all that's deplorable in this world? There has been a great deal that has been embellished to that story over the years. It's like everything else, what they don't know or can't explain they just make up. And for some reason, people tend to gravitate towards sensationalism.

"Even though none of those things actually happened, the full extent of damage brought about by the grim turn of events may never be fully realized."

"Why do you say that?" Simon asked intently.

"We are still in the throws of the shadows cast seventy-two years ago," Pete said through gritted teeth. "We're talking about very deep, unseen scars and the residual effects. Some of us who were alive at the time are still hemorrhaging on the inside.

"You see. I couldn't take the guilt anymore. I wasn't sleeping. I wasn't eating. The truth gnawed at my conscience until I finally gave in. About a year after the tragedy, I had my parents take me back to the investigators, and I told them everything."

"Everything?" Simon asked.

"How I made the whole thing up," Pete admitted. "How Mr. Joseph hadn't done any of the things that I said he did anyway."

"Well, what happened?" Simon asked. "Did they let him go?"

"They didn't know what to do," Pete replied. "Some of the other kids came clean too, but others didn't. Folks around here didn't know what or who to believe. So, they didn't *do* anything. They just let Mr. Joseph rot. People more or less made an unspoken pact to never discuss the matter. So, no one did- at least not in public; but behind closed doors, people greedily speculated and gossiped, and the legend grew."

"But, didn't you at least try to dispel the rumors and all of the inaccuracies?" Simon asked.

"I did, at first, even into my teens," Pete replied, "but what I discovered was this; when people have a conspiratorial spirit and a preconceived set of beliefs, dispelling myths and sharing truth only serves to push them farther away. The more I said anything, the more people clung to their own assumptions. It actually drove them away like they were somehow disappointed by the notion that it was just an accident. They actually wanted their little ghost story. They wanted to be scared...they wanted to be entertained.

"In the process, I think people didn't know who or what to trust anymore whether it be in authority or in rule of law. They lost their Faith. Their secure, insulated little world had crashed down around them. Cynicism grew. Nobody was above suspicion. Slowly and systematically all manner of law and discipline was compromised in this town. Even here," Pete said, lifting his chin to indicate that the very church they were sitting in was not above reproach. "Do you know what happens to a world without truth?" the pastor asked.

Simon shook his head.

"Everything becomes relative, and people become more concerned with being careful to not offend others than to actually seek the truth," he said, sardonically. "In Jessie's case, it was such a heated topic. People were very passionate about all of it because it hit them so close to home. It just had gotten to the point where there were two distinct camps splitting the community in half. One side who believed and those who didn't. So, in the name of peace, people did what they thought was prudent. They just agreed to disagree and leave it at that. People just wanted to move on with their lives. Out of respect no one brought up the subject for fear of its potential volatility."

"But, didn't Jessie appeal?" Simon asked.

"Yes, of course, several times," Pete replied. "Life was difficult for him in prison. You can imagine how prisoners accused of those crimes would be treated. Still, it was of no use. No one would hear his case. He died several years later of tuberculosis."

Pete sat forward in the pew, defeated.

In silence, Simon traced the current legend as he knew it back to the original event that started it all. He thought about the little coffin in the storage facility, the haunted chorus room, the scratches on the back door of the closet. Then he considered the footsteps and the mysterious lights. In turn, he thought of Little Simon whom he had perceived to be the ghost of Adam Potter. Next, he considered the graveyard.

"How is it Jessie came to be buried in Potter's field?" Simon asked.

"That's how folks around came to the conclusion that Jessie was definitely Clay's son," Pete said as though exhausted. "Clay demanded that he be buried in the family graveyard on his property."

"Hmmm," Simon muttered, nodding his head with a furtive brow. Then something else occurred to him. "How do you suppose the whole thing about the pattern of the tragedies materialized?"

"Well, like I said, this boy here," Pete said pointing to the photograph from the newspaper that Simon still clutched in his hands. "He died of pneumonia a couple of years later. I don't know. I guess people want answers for why terrible things have to happen. Did he deserve it? Did he or his parents do something that caused it? A senseless death leaves people asking the question, 'why?'.

"The tragedy was still fresh in people's minds, so I guess it was just a convenient explanation for some folks. From that time on, people couldn't help themselves. It was too enticing. Every time there was a tragedy someone would bring it up. Even though a lot of people thought it was complete nonsense, some still perpetuated the myth."

Simon felt foolish at being taken in by the fantastic story. He thought about all of the decisions that he had made based on that central belief. He thought of the school and the project and his purpose. Suddenly, he came to his senses and jumped to his feet. "But, we *know* what happened to Jeremy!" he pleaded, with a reinvigorated sense of urgency. "We have an obligation to tell the truth!"

"What do we *know*?" Pastor Pete snapped, looking up at Simon with an incredulous expression. "We only know what Simon Adamson said and what Jack said, nothing more."

"I don't think that you fully grasp the gravity of arbitrarily picking sides. You may not get that, but I do. Jessie died because of my false testimony, what I said."

"But, this is not a testimony without evidence," Simon said, challenging the pastor. "You don't seem to get it. People's lives are at stake here!"

"No," Pete said, dully. "You don't seem to get it. You have to *know* you are right, because people's souls are at stake here."

Simon then realized he had managed to get bogged down once again in the quagmire of the external, temporal world. He was focusing only on societal justice as it pertained to this life. Somehow he had missed the big picture and drifted away from the heart of the much deeper issue at hand.

For a moment, he assessed the situation, still unable to fully make the connection between the legend and his purpose. The ultimate question came to mind. How could returning a school to its original condition end a legend of a curse?

He had to stop and consider what they were really talking about here. How had he become convinced that God had orchestrated his return to Bethel or that God had wanted him to renovate the school? And what did it have to do with Adam, Jessie, or Jeremy and the real story behind the legend?

Coincidental circumstance explained most of the fallacies surrounding the legend. In retrospect, he could see how he had originally been duped into believing that he had been chosen to put an end to the cycle of tragedies. Now, after having all of the evidence at his disposal, Simon realized that he might not only be able to bring about justice for Jeremy, but also to Jessie after all of these years. In the process the rational explanation might put an end to the perpetuation of the legend. But, to what end? In so doing, would that actually be putting an end to a curse?

Maybe. But, it still didn't feel quite right. An element was missing. All of that evidence dealt with knowledge and the intellect and the senses. It still couldn't explain what he knew to be true in his heart and what had been confirmed by the message written on the marquee in front of the church. That he had communed with God Himself that night. That he had been called to complete a specific task on God's behalf. Ultimately, Simon felt led to complete the renovation for God. If that were the case, it was a purpose that surely dealt with something not temporary and tangible, but something eternal and ethereal. It was a calling that was grounded in faith and necessitated by his own free will. Something told him that Pete was unintentionally bridging the gap between earthly events and spiritual consequences. But, how?

"What did you mean by 'people's souls being at stake'?" Simon asked, making every effort to go beyond his cerebral limitations and understand how the two things might be interrelated.

"I mean," Pete said through gritted teeth as he rubbed his hands on the top of his thighs, "can you be so certain that you are right? How can you know for sure that Simon Adamson is telling you the truth? It is critical that you are absolutely certain, you know, because there are consequences to the conclusion you come to. Your beliefs become words. And our words, your words, my words, they affect other people. They are powerful. They not only have the ability to exonerate you, or Jessie, or Jack, but if we are wrong, they also have the power to condemn us before God.

"For example, who really knows if it was John or Jessie who was actually telling the truth? Maybe Jessie really did some of those horrible things to John and the other kids. I have no idea. I will probably never know for sure. After all, there were only a few us who retracted our accusations.

"Just think about it for a moment. At first, I supported Mr. Joseph because I thought that I was doing the right thing. Then I told the detectives what they wanted to hear because I thought that I was doing the right thing. Then I admitted that I lied about what I told the detective because I thought that I was doing the right thing. All of that was based on the evidence that I had at my disposal. In the end, my testimony played a role in determining other people's fate. Jessie and John both suffered greatly because of my words. As a result, there was ultimately no justice for either of them."

"You may have had some degree of impact on their lives," Simon said, "but, one person can't be held responsible for another person's ultimate fate." After critically analyzing his own words, Simon realized that he sounded more like

Dr. Al-Banna and the good doctor's explanation of the Islamic merit system for gaining entry into paradise. "Wait," he said, trying to sort it all out in his own mind. Suddenly, he realized that he was having trouble putting a finger on the line of demarcation between a person's own actions and the impact that they have on the lives of others. Simon followed the circuitous line of reasoning to its logical conclusion before stating, "Yeah, that's right! Each person will be judged individually according to his or her own choices. You can't be held responsible for what anybody else does."

"That might be a very comforting thing to believe," Pete said, with a gravelly voice, "but in reality that's just not how it all plays out. I learned the hard way that by impacting people's lives, you're impacting their souls as well. We don't live in a vacuum. What we think, say, and do affects other people. Suum Cuique is somnium for …'for those who judge themselves, by themselves are fools'…

"Listen, I went to seminary thinking I could *do* something to make up for this intense guilt. To make up for what I had done to Jessie and John. That if I devoted my life to serving God that somehow He could eventually forgive me."

Simon could hear the intensity in Pete's voice.

"I was so busy trying to free my own conscience that I didn't stop to consider how I might affect people by what I say from up there," Pete said, pointing to the pulpit.

"But that's a good thing, *right?*" Simon said, confused. "Your words can lead people to heaven…"

"…Or send them to Hades," Pete said, overcome with emotion.

"But, you can't just dig a hole and bury your talents!" Simon pleaded, referring to the parable in Matthew.

"But, don't you see?" Pete replied. "Where people spend eternity may hinge on something you say, or something you don't say, or say the wrong way. Or it could be that you misinterpreted the text or took it out of context. Or worse, you might not be able to live up to your own words and drive away nonbelievers. It is an enormous responsibility that I am not worthy of." Judging by the expression on Simon's face, Pete could see that he was starting to get through to the young man. "In that way, their personal responsibility is my responsibility, and I am afraid that I have miserably failed my flock."

Upon hearing the pastor's words, Simon thought of the negative impact that he had on Rocky, Mara, Andy, Shannon, and the Helrigles. "Yeah, I can see what you mean," he confessed. "Tell me something. How can you ever really *know* for sure that *you* have ultimately failed anyone?"

"Huh," Pete grunted as his face turned ashen, "believe me. I *know* that I failed John, not once but twice. Because of what I told the detectives John spent several weeks in juvenile detention. He was never the same after that, and no one treated him the same either. There was always an air of suspicion concerning him. And he knew it. He could sense it.

"The poor soul was either the victim of abuse or the cause of an innocent man going to jail. Either way, it took its toll on him. He never knew if he could really trust anybody or get close to them. After the tragedy, he just couldn't seem to cope with reality.

"He just couldn't get it together. As he got older, he chose to self-medicate with alcohol. Like me with the church or Andy with the school, we all needed a distraction, an escape. But instead of activity, John chose booze. I think deep down he blamed God for all of it. He wouldn't let me, or anyone else for that matter talk, to him about it until 9/11," Pete said, regretfully. "Until the Sunday following that fateful day, John Rash hadn't been to church since he was a boy."

"But, what's that have to do with…" Simon started to ask.

"…Don't you get it?" Pete asked. "That was my chance at redemption, to reach him, to get through to him and anyone else who was searching for answers that day. The events of 9/11 shook people out of their spiritual slumber. It was a harbinger from God. For a short period of time, people were talking about God, seeking counsel, opening their dusty Bibles, and praying. And for some of them, I knew that it might be their only shot at salvation.

"I prayed that week over the sermon. God, how I prayed. Each day, I would lay the papers out on the floor in my office before God, and I would fervently pray over the message that He wanted me to deliver. I wrote it and delivered it, fully convinced that I was merely acting as a mouthpiece for God."

"And?" Simon asked, suddenly thinking of himself and his own calling. "What happened?"

"I could feel the power of the Holy Spirit moving that day," Pete said. "It's impossible to describe, really. It didn't just seem like it was *me* speaking. It felt more like the Spirit of the Lord speaking *through* me."

"See, but that's what I'm saying," Simon offered. "That's a good thing!"

"Really?" Peter asked, sadly. "Then tell me, if it really was God speaking through me, then why would His message be rejected? That doesn't make any sense, does it?"

"No, I guess not," Simon replied. "But, how do you *know* that anyone rejected it? Maybe God was just planting seeds."

"At the end of the sermon, no one answered the alter call," Pete replied, distraught. "The following Sunday only about half of the sanctuary was full. And each following week there were fewer and fewer people who came to Sunday service. As for John, he sent me an email just before he committed suicide."

"What did the letter say?" Simon asked with a degree of skepticism. "Do you still have it? Can I see it?"

"You don't have to see it," Pete replied with tears now streaming down his face. "I've read it so many times that I can recite it, word for word. It said:

'Pete, my old friend,

I have never been able to come to grips with the past. It has taken so much out of me, and so much from me. I never understood why God could allow such a terrible things to happen. My entire life I have been consumed with such hate and bitterness. For years now, I have blamed the wrong person for my sorrows. After hearing your sermon today, I finally realized that I do not want to live that way any longer. I don't want to live in a world where God does not exist. So, I want you to be the first to know that today is the last day. I am going to rid Hannah Grace, my family, and entire world of this bitter, old man. I am going to die a death unto myself, and allow everyone to get a fresh, new start. Today will be a new day in Bethel. This is something that I must do. Thank you for freeing me of my torturous life!

Sincerely,
John Rash

Simon had to agree that on the surface it had the sound of a suicide note. But, it was cloaked in such ambiguity. "What did he mean by things like …'this old man,' or …'die a death unto myself'?" Simon asked. "Was he drunk when he died? Did they do an autopsy? Did they test his blood alcohol level?"

"What?" Pete asked, as if annoyed. "No. He was always drunk, so…?"

"Well, how do you know he jumped from the grain elevator?" Simon asked. "What if he was drunk? What he just slipped and fell or something?"

"Why on earth would he be climbing the grain elevator?" Pete asked, defeated.

Simon bit his bottom lip, furrowed his brow, and stared at the floor. "Yeah," he said softly. Then he looked back up and offered another possible, logical explanation. "Maybe he was just telling you that he was starting over. Maybe the letter is a paradox!"

"No," Pete replied, flatly.

"…'Today will be a new day in Bethel'," Simon continued. "I am just saying that the words aren't exactly clear cut."

"No," Pete replied, staring off in the distance through red, puffy eyes.

Simon thought for a moment more before it finally dawned on him. Trying to reconcile the difference between individual and collective responsibility, he finally came to a conclusion.

"Pete, even if it was a suicide letter," Simon said, "John was not rejecting *you*. He was rejecting God. You said it yourself. You prayed about the message. You sought God's will. Your conscience is clean!"

Now he was forced to consider his own situation. He thought of his calling to renovate the school and the people's rejection of the Ten Commandments.

"All you can do is what you can do where God has called you to do it," he said, remembering Hope's affirmation. "You did that! Peter, you may be the head of the church, but you are still just a man. You aren't infallible. You don't decide who is and who isn't forgiven. Only *Jesus Christ* can save us from our sins!"

Pete jerked his head up and scowled at Simon. Unexpectedly, Pete asked, "How do you *know that*? How can anyone really know if Jesus can really save us from the darkness in our hearts?"

"What?" Simon asked, startled by such a fundamental question coming from the lips of a preacher. "We know that because Jesus died on the cross."

"And?..." Pete asked flatly.

Simon suddenly thought of the moment that he had hit rock bottom. It was the night he had exhumed the bodies of Jessie and Adam in the graveyard.

"And...," Simon continued. "I know because of the empty tomb. Jesus rose from the dead three days later!"

"And how do you *know* that?" Pete objected.

"Because it's in the Bible!" Simon adamantly replied, sticking his hands out to his sides with his palms up. "The disciples did not find a body, just found the linen wrappings and the rolled up face cloth. Remember?

"I mean, come on! You are a preacher! Where is your backbone? Where is your faith? Where is your resolve?"

Pete looked back down at the floor, slowly shaking his head.

"It all goes back to what I was saying before," Pete muttered. "We make all of these claims, but how do we really know for sure? One person says one thing, and another person says something else. I mean, what if Dr. Al-Banna and Pastor Algood are right? What if the text was compromised or tampered with? What proof do we have that the record is authentic?

"How do we really know who or what to believe? Like, uh, like...Jesus says one thing and Mohammad says something else. You say the Bible is the inerrant word of God, while Dr. Al-Banna says it's the Quran! I'm asking you, how do you *know* who or what to believe?

"It's really no different from trying to decide if Jack or Adam is telling the truth. It's just one person's word against another's."

"But, you're a pastor for heaven's sake!" Simon spouted. "...'Blessed is he who does not see and still believes'..."

"Ha, I'm afraid it would take a miracle for me to believe at this point," Pete said, utterly defeated. "I would have to put own my finger in His side to know for sure."

Simon's eyes wildly danced about the room. "But, you have to believe because..." Simon stammered in a panic. He was suddenly at a loss for words as the seeds of doubt began to creep in. Then it hit him. It was a truth that was undeniable and unassailable. "I *know* in my heart because of what *I* personally experienced. I *know* beyond a shadow of a doubt that it was Jesus who spoke to me that night in front of the church."

All of a sudden, Pete looked up and raised his eyebrows.

"I know that He spoke to me that night when the lights came on the marquee out front, and I read the words 'Come, Follow Me'! That's how I know that the quiet, still voice in my head is God's and not my own."

With that, Pete's shoulders drooped, and a despondent expression came over his face as he turned away.

"What?" Simon asked, certain of himself. "What is it?"

The Pastor shook his head doubtfully. Then he looked back up and blankly stared into Simon's face and said, "That's it? That's what *led* you to stay in Bethel? That's why you worked so hard to complete the renovation? That's how you *know*?"

Simon nodded his head with a bewildered expression of his face.

"Simon, *I* turned on the light that night, *not* God," Pete said. "I couldn't sleep. I was in my study trying to put together my sermon and saw you leaning against the fire hydrant on the street in front of the church."

"...And the message?" Simon gasped in complete shock.

"It just happened to be the next one in the series, that's all," Pete replied, apologetically.

Simon turned away from the pastor and stared off in the distance. He was devastated. His whole world was spinning out of control. Slowly, he got up and wandered towards the exit.

"Simon," Pete called out to him. "Simon...!"

But, there was no reply. He left the church, completely demoralized and disillusioned.

* * *

Simon stepped out into the sweltering heat. He stood at the top of the stairs of the church in a complete haze. Looking down at the marquee, he was overwhelmed by the absurdity of it all. Was it all just one big coincidence?

He turned and lifted his eyes towards the steeple of the church. Even though he had walked in and out of these very same doors every Sunday for the past four weeks, he had never bothered to take a good, hard look at the church. Doing so now, all of the glaring imperfections from the withered siding to the tilted foundation came to light. A cursory glance was all he needed to realize that the dilapidated structure was in far worse condition than even the old school building. After all, it was far, far older.

An incessant, dull droning of a diesel engine finally caught Simon's attention. Turning away from the church, he looked across the street to see a brand new, black GMC Denali HD lurking in the shade of an overgrown Maple tree. A steady stream of smoke billowed out of the driver side tinted window that was cracked open a few inches.

Simon took a deep breath and dragged himself down the uneven, concrete steps. Expressionless, he made his way across the street, circled around to the front of the rumbling truck, opened the passenger door, and slid inside.

"Ha! Well, I'll be a monkey's uncle. Hello there!" Jack said, dangling a cigarette between his teeth. Sitting opposite Simon, he withdrew his hand from the steering wheel, pinched the cigarette between his thumb and index finger, and took one last deep drag before flicking it out the window. Excitedly, he rolled up the window, exhaled, and wafted the smoke with his opposite hand. "My boy, you are full of surprises! Just when I think I've got you pegged…" he said, rubbing his goatee as a broad grin swept across his face.

Simon didn't give him the satisfaction. Instead, he stared blankly straight ahead out the front windshield. Jack leaned to his right, reached out his hand, and turned down the radio just as John Lennon sang, "…imagine all the people, living for today…"

"Ah, don't you just love that song?" Jack dreamily mused, closing his eyes. He opened them again and said, "The Beatles…Ha! Ya know, they started off innocent as doves too…"Love, love me do", Jack sang off key. "But then eventually, they were singing …'Help, I need somebody, Help not just anybody'… Jack sang before bursting out into laughter. "Oh man, they had some God-given talent! No doubt. Then they started searching for the meaning of life, started doin' drugs, even visited my man, the Maharishi, and before long, the whole world was sing'n…'he's a real nowhere man, sitting in his nowhere land, making all of his nowhere plans for nobody'… Beautiful! Just beautiful! Really, confused everybody, ya know. They could just as easily have written lyrics that showed people the way, the truth, and the life. But, no. Ha!

"I just loved the sixties and everything about it. 'Free love' and all that nonsense. The women's libbers, Malcolm X, Marshall Davis, Bill Ayers, Loyd Jowers, Sirhan Sirhan…*Vietnam*! Are you kidding me? Ha! Business was good. Business was very good. One of my better campaigns, actually. I wish somebody would just bring it all back. Could happen, ya know?"

"Anyway, I digress," he said, taking a deep breath. "Simon, my boy! I thought for sure you would have run when you saw my truck. I would have put money on it. Ha! But, you didn't. Enlighten me."

"Run where? To what?" Simon asked, dryly. He was still looking out the windshield.

"Ha!" Jack said, raising his eyebrows. "That's what I like about you, boy. Sharp as a tack."

Slowly, Simon turned toward Jack with a disgusted look on his face. "The better question is," he said, " 'Why not just do away with me like you did Jeremy Warner? Simon Adamson told me all about it."

"Straight to the point," Jack said with a warm smile. "I like that. No beatin' around the bush. Doggone it, I wish you would have just accepted my offer to manage the new strip club off the interstate, or…,or the one at the bank. You could have just taken that job at the bank. Or politics! I could have introduced you to a good friend of mine named George Soros.

"But, I understand. I know that you would not have been happy in any of those positions. They were beneath you. I can see that now. I underestimated you. No, I have other plans for you."

"Potential?" Simon scoffed, turning away from Jack and looking out the passenger window of the truck. "You mean like Simon Adamson?" he asked accusingly.

"Ah yes, Little Simon Adamson," Jack said with a frown on his face. He forced another laugh once he processed the inference. Then he leaned forward, put the truck in gear, and began to drive. "I can't even keep a straight face. Unbelievable, boy! You understand more than I thought." Jack hung his wrist over the steering wheel as he slowly wound his way through the streets of Bethel. "Ah, yeah, Little Simon. Yes, he has some potential to be sure. He might just one day go berserk and take out a bunch of kids on the playground. Possible. But, then again, I can also see him deal'n meth for me one day. I mean, he ought to be able to make it himself by now, as many times as he's seen Rob and those guys do it out there at Potter's place.

"Who knows, maybe he'll be no better than a junky? At the very least, he can get himself a couple of girlfriends…then mess up his own kids before abandoning them altogether…" he said, before turning dark. "…like your daddy did."

Simon shot a cold, icy stare at Jack just as the wily, old man's pager went off. Jack leaned forward, dug around for the source of the obnoxious ringing. He held the device up in front of his face. Frowning, he clicked a few buttons before setting it back down on the console. "Sorry about that…my minions," the shrewd businessman muttered. "Thing rings off the hook, day and night. So many deals, so little time." He slung his wrist back over the steering wheel and leaned on the armrest.

"Now, where were we?" Jack asked. "Oh yeah, Adamson. But, nothing like the plans I have for you. Plans to…"

"…That's the reason you won't drag me down to Potter's place, dump some gasoline on me, and strike a match like you did to Jeremy?" Simon demanded to know.

Jack gritted his teeth and looked around at the scenery. "Tsk, tsk, tsk, poor Jeremiah," he muttered. "Now there's a guy who had so much promise in the beginning. He was insecure, confused, geeky, unpopular, but smart, real smart. I wish I could have gotten to that kid in Jr. high. That was my chance. 'Man', I said to myself, 'We got something here'. He was picked on, bullied, made fun of…you name it. He had this rage inside of him, ya know?

"I blame myself really. I think I handled him all wrong. I took him for the intellectual, introspective type. But, I pushed too hard. Tried to use his intelligence against him to channel his resentment into an air of superiority and contempt like I did all them Hollywood boys; Katzenburg, Spielberg, Geffen. Oh, how I love 'Tinsel Town'. But, boy, did I miss on that one. Ha! Jeremiah wasn't like those guys at all.

"We threw all kinds of propaganda at him. Ya know all of the usual suspects like Slick Willy, Jessie, Jimmy, FDR, Woodrow, Karl…you name it. Even tried to confuse him about his own sexuality just cause he was a little effeminate. And it was working at first," Jack shook his head as if he'd picked the wrong pony at the track. "Na! On second thought, he just didn't have it in him."

"Oh, but I do?" Simon asked with a scowl. "That's why you don't just put me out of my misery right now; because of my 'potential'?

"I've lost everything," Simon said as his anger began to boil over. "I've got nothing left. Now you're going to 'maximize' my potential in this forsaken little town. By making me bitter and angry? By-by putting me through some ridiculous trial? Maybe throw in a little public humiliation? A little jail time? That's your big plan for me?"

"Ha!" Jack said as he put the truck in park. Momentarily distracted, he reached for a dial on the AC unit, hit Max, and cranked up the fan.

"Hmmph," Simon scoffed.

"I like to keep it cool," Jack said.

Suddenly, Simon looked around and realized where they were sitting. Jack had brought him back to the school and parked his truck next to the clunker of a car that Simon had driven all the way from Texas.

A strange look came over Simon's face.

"No, no, my boy," Jack intimated, as he reached into his front pocket and pulled out a massive wad of singles that had been tied up neatly in a rubber band. "No sir. All you have to do, my good man, is nothing. I just want you to go." Then he tossed the roll over to Simon.

Catching it in his lap, Simon picked up the money before looking back at Jack with a disgusted, confused expression. "Go?" he asked. "Go where?"

"To the coast!" Jack replied. "To Jersey. To that big sales job. To the life you always wanted for yourself like the fancy car or big house. Go see the Big Apple, night life, the social scene. Think about the women! Eh?" he said with a wink. "Vacations in the Bahamas, time shares, a beach house, a cushy retirement; whatever your heart desires. You can even go to church and give a little to charity every now and then if it makes you feel good.

"You can leave this dump once and for all. Get on with your life. Forget any of this ever happened.

"So you got off track a little bit. Who doesn't from time to time? I get a little lackadaisical myself sometimes. It's human nature. Nothin' to be ashamed of.

"But, there's nothin' here for you anymore. You said it yourself. You've lost everything." Jack sat back, satisfied. He patiently waited for Simon's response, grinning from ear to ear.

"That's it?" Simon asked. "That's what you meant by reaching my potential?"

Jack held up his pinky and leaned toward Simon as if sharing a deep secret. "Remember?" he asked. "Life's all about that 'one thing'. Ha!" Then he slurred several obscenities. "I was tryin' to do it like Palance. But who can do that? Anyway. Go! Find that one thing that makes *you* happy and do it. Follow your bliss!"

Totally bewildered, Simon looked down at the large bank roll that he held in his hand.

"Consider it a charitable donation from the girls in Neoga," Jack said, jokingly. But, then he added. "Uh, I wouldn't touch my mouth after handlin' those singles by the way."

"But, the sales job hasn't even been....," Simon started to say, obviously distracted by the sudden, unexpected turn of events.

"...Yes, it has," Jack said, finishing Simon's thought. "A client of mine at the FDA told me this morning that the new drug has been approved. They're gonna announce it tomorrow."

Simon sat in silence for a moment before asking, "And just like that, you want me to leave Bethel? But, what about the cops and all of the charges?"

"Ha!" Jack said. "I wouldn't worry about the cops. It'll all just go away. Who do you think your dealin' with? Who do you think gets the Clintons out of their little jams? There are some amazing lawyers who work for me.

"Must have just been some sort of accounting error or somethin'. Miraculously, we will locate the short fall of school money, and a previously unknown alibi will step forward on your behalf."

"And the other thing?" Simon asked, wanting for his name to be cleared for Hope's sake.

"Just the wild imaginings of a strange, little boy," Jack smugly replied.

"What about the school, and the referendum, and the curse...?" Simon asked, looking over his shoulder at the grade school.

"Enough about the stupid curse. It's ancient history!" Jack said, momentarily losing his temper and slapping the steering wheel with the palm of his hand. Quickly, he collected himself again and calmly sold, "For the love of Pete, forget about it already. Why do you even care what happens? Where has it gotten you? All of the pain, and sweat, and tears, and time? Was any of it really appreciated? Wake up man! It caused nothin' but heartache and disappointment and...a warrant for your arrest. And you want to know, 'what about the school'? What about *you*? Think about yourself for once!"

Simon sighed deeply, chewed on his fat lip, and gazed forlornly at the old, defunct building. Contemplatively, he looked down at the bank roll that he was still holding in his hand. "And that'll be the end of it?" Simon asked, overcome by the thought of immediate clemency and liberation from his present condition.

"What? Oh yeah, absolutely the end of it," Jack said, rubbing his goatee. "Of course, *I'll* see you again. Don't you worry about that. I do a lot of business on the East coast. They know me well in New Hampshire, Vermont, Delaware, Connecticut, Massachusetts... Spend a whole lot of time in Manhattan and D.C. these days! Oh my, *a lot* of business in D.C. I have so many plans to roll out over the next eight years. Lord have mercy. Feels like I live there half the time.

"But, don't you worry. I will never be far away."

Furtively, Simon reached for the handle of the truck, opened the door, and slid out.

"It's been fun!" Jack said with a smile. "Drive careful, and oh, by the way, I wouldn't pull over for anybody on the side of the road. I've heard of people puttin' the hood up, actin' like they got car trouble, and then robbin' ya blind. Lot of wackos out there, ya know. Read about it in New York times only this morn'n."

Despondently, Simon shut the door to the truck. Through the tinted windows of his Denali, Jack watched Simon walk over to his car, unlock the door, climb into the driver's seat, and unceremoniously pull away.

The shrewd businessman reached into his shirt pocket, grabbed a cigarette, and clenched it between his teeth. He pushed off the floor board, leaned back, and dug into the pocket of his jeans in search of his lighter. Hungrily, he brought it up to his mouth, cupped his hands, and lit the cigarette. With an air of deep satisfaction, he sat back in the leather seat, cracked the window ever so slightly, and slowly exhaled.

V

EXCEPT THROUGH ME

"Then Jesus told him,
'Because you have seen me,
you have believed;.
Blessed are those who have not seen
And yet have believed."

-John 20:29

34

APOLOGY ACCEPTED

The scenery had not changed much in the five hours since Simon had left Bethel. The fields of withered, brown cornstalks and orange tangles of soybeans lined I-70 as far as the eye could see in either direction. Crunchy, baked grass grew in the median, and dry, droopy leaves hung limp from the trees. The very roots of vegetation sucked every ounce of water from the hard, cracked soil. It had now been forty days since the last rain, and the effect of the drought had begun to take its toll on the entire country.

Looking at the scenery, it was hard to believe that the same farmers who were complaining about the scorched earth were the same ones who had also griped about the torrential rains in the spring. Such wild swings of emotion in response to the delicate balance of nature were understandable for a profession whose livelihood depended as much on faith as it did raw determination. Still, the farmers weren't the only ones who were facing a terrible short fall come harvest time.

Steam seethed from under Simon's bloodied collar like the heat reflecting off the pavement on the horizon. For the better part of the morning, he had driven directly into the glaring sun. Even though it now mercifully hung high overhead, the hours of intense squinting had given him a splitting headache. To make matters worse, the air conditioning unit in his car was insufficient to overcome the sweltering heat outside. It wasn't long before the interior of the old, rusted out Impala began to feel more like a furnace. Beads of sweat dripped from Simon's forehead, only adding to his aggravation.

The distraught young man was unable to lose himself in thought. He was too busy replaying the unexpected turn of events over and over in his mind like a viral video. The hours of monotonous driving through the uninspiring countryside had done nothing to calm his restless spirit. In fact, somehow sitting idle had only served to add to his anxiety. Like a caged lion, he repositioned his body time and again in hopes of becoming comfortable, but it was of no use. He hadn't sat still that long in weeks. There was no way to deceive his tortured soul that had been rejuvenated by purpose only to be unceremoniously robbed of it.

His eyes wildly darted about, his fingers tapped uncontrollably, and his leg twitched with nervous energy. Desperate for distraction, Simon impulsively reached over to turn up the radio. As he randomly spun the dial, the speakers spit, crackled, and sputtered before finally landing on a station.

Out of the corner of his eye Simon caught a glimpse of the rolled up single dollar bills sitting in the passenger seat beside him. Keeping one eye on the road, he leaned over and snatched up the bank roll. Using his palms to steady the wheel, Simon took off the rubber band and began to unravel the wad of cash. Alternately, he glanced back and forth between the money and the road. Deftly holding the singles in one hand, he licked his fingers and counted out the bills.

"Sixty-six lousy bucks!" Simon shouted. "That's it! You've got to be kidding me. That'll barely fill up my next tank of gas."

He shook his head in disgust before thoughtlessly tossing the money back into the passenger seat.

"He'll see me in New Jersey, huh…whatever," Simon muttered under his breath. Angrily, he slapped the steering wheel with the palm of his hand, leaned his elbow on the door, and chewed on the knuckle of his index finger.

It was just one more slap in the face. The whole thing was a comedy of errors from the moment he had returned to Bethel. Thinking back on it now, he chastised himself for all of the stupid decisions that he had made since graduating from college. That was supposed to be the mark of a new beginning. It was supposed to be a fresh start.

Things were going to be different for him after earning his degree. Life was going to get much easier. He was finally going to have the things that he had always wanted. He was going to have a good job, some money, and a whole new life. He was finally going to be somebody.

"And I was on my way too," Simon thought as he berated himself for somehow getting off track. "Why did I ever go back to that forsaken, little town? I spent all of that time and money, and I have nothing to show for it!"

He shook his head in self-loathing and disfigured his face as if catching a whiff of something putrid. Only it wasn't a smell that was so reprehensible to him. It was a thought.

"How did I fall for all of that stupid curse garbage?" he asked, as he chastised himself. "I just need to forget that place ever even existed."

But, he couldn't help himself. Time and time again he went over the series of events that had led to his downfall. He thought of Rob and the guys retelling the legend, and the trip to the cemetery, and the little old lady who asked him if he was 'the one'.

"Oh, brother!" he said, rolling his eyes in total disgust. " 'The 'one'. Yeah, I'm 'the one' all right. I'm the one sucker who would fall for all of that nonsense."

Next, he thought of mistaking Little Simon Adamson for the ghost of Adam Potter. He thought of the small coffin, the night at the well, the footsteps in the hall, and the lights going on and off in the school. And chasing after the little freak as he ran down the stairs into the basement. Next, he thought ashamedly of digging up the graves of Adam and Jessie Joseph when he was at his breaking point. And then he remembered the light coming on the church marquee as well as the message. All coincidental. All explainable. And now totally immaterial.

As his car bounded down the highway, Simon beat himself up, recalling all of the stupid things that he had told people along the way. He remembered the things he said to Jeremy, and Pastor Pete, and Rocky, and Hannah Grace, and Miss Harold, and on and on and on. There had been no end to his self-righteousness, and subsequently, his total embarrassment.

Suddenly, he thought of Hope and the expression of disappointment on her face, and his heart sank. Spontaneously, he lifted his cell phone off of the seat beside him and checked it for any new messages. There were none.

As his emotions started to overwhelm him, he realized his pain and disappointment would have to be managed. He realized that now. It was as if a switch had to be flipped inside of him if you were going to survive. In order to disquiet the confluence of contradictory feelings raging inside of him, a loud, familiar voice audaciously rose above the noise and confusion in his brain. It was the kind of voice that covered up wounds, dug in foxholes, and built strong holds as the first line of defense in preserving some dignity and self-respect.

Unable to cope with his mounting deficiencies and obvious shortcomings, Simon allowed his ego to take charge and dominate his conscience. In no time at all, he was able to justify his actions. He soon took great comfort in convincing himself that it was understandable. He took great solace in the thought that anyone else would have done the same thing given the same set of circumstances. Before long, his ego was able to put a spin on the entire situation. He quickly dismissed any admission of wrongdoing and projected it onto the people of Bethel instead.

The longer the loud, defiant voice railed from within, the better Simon felt about himself. It was all well and good, he decided, to go back and see the town. To catch up with old friends. To hang out a while. To party. To play a little softball. To umpire a few little league games. There was no harm in any of that.

But, the voice insisted, Simon had crossed the line the moment he began to care again for those hicks. That was where he messed up. They were backwards, close-minded, ignorant, and utterly hopeless. If anyone was to blame for their hollowed out existence, it was them. They were the ones who chose their own miserable, insignificant lives. After all, he assured himself, it was the people of Bethel who were the ones who had all of their priorities out of whack. It was the people of Bethel who decided to place a higher premium on sports than education. They were the ones who were willing participants in their own little housing crisis. It involved everyone from the greedy realtors, to the unscrupulous loan officers, to the bank president, all the way down to the insatiable buyers. After all, they were the same ones who supported the strip clubs, the meth labs, the abortion clinics, and the Mosque or at the very least tolerated them. And they were the ones just going through the motions at church, or even worse, trying to tap into an undefined, all-powerful spirit as some sort of get rich quick scam. They were the ones who cut deals with the likes of Jack Lawless, trading their allegiance for handouts.

The more Simon listened to the loud, cynical voice, the more he realized that he was much better off getting out while he still had the chance. It was a blessing, really. All of a sudden, the dominant voice began to gain support by breathing new life back into Simon's self-esteem. After all, it was the same voice that had originally urged him to pursue the job in New Jersey in the first place. And it was the same one that implored him to leave Bethel from the very start.

After many miles of driving, his ego had somehow managed to quell his conscience's brief reign. Thankfully, it all but brought an end to the struggle for power inside of him. Simon liked the voice because it made him feel good about himself.

It was the people of Bethel who were to blame.

"That is one screwed-up little town," Simon thought. "If anyone had anything to be ashamed of, it was them. Look at all of the problems those people had brought on themselves. They had earned every bit of it, and they deserved everything that they had coming to them, including the likes of Jack Lawless."

A big part of Simon desperately yearned to buy into the propaganda. He would have to if he was going to turn his hurt and shame into anger and resentment, and anger and resentment into self-confidence and self-reliance. Just as Simon was about to accept his own contrived rationale regarding the error of his ways, he suddenly remembered what they did to Jeremy.

"Stupid sap," he muttered with his eyes glossing over. He scowled and chewed on his fat lip while blankly staring out the window. Finally, he bitterly said, "That's on them! That's not my problem anymore!"

After a minute of resigned silence, he burst out again. "I did everything that I was supposed to do," Simon snapped, trying his best to convince himself. "I did my part. I put my life on hold. I answered the call. I sacrificed my time, my money, my energy to do His little project for Him.

"But, not anymore. I learned my lesson. You can't help people who won't help themselves."

And yet, he was still unable to completely convince himself.

"You can't," Simon said in almost a whisper. "You just can't..."

A few more tortuous minutes passed by in total silence.

"If that's how they want things, then so be it," he thought. "It is what it is. It's not my concern anymore. Not my battle. Not my home. I'm not even a permanent resident. I was just a stranger passing through.

"From here on out, I'm going to control the controllables. I'm going to look out for number one!"

The boisterous voice inside of Simon had almost completely disquieted his nagging conscience. With a false bravado, he turned up the radio. The words of an old eighties song blasted through the speakers, "...I gotta do it my way or no way at all..." Disgusted, he quickly reached out and spun the dial. When he finally found a station that was coming in crystal clear, he withdrew his hand. The singer blared out the lyrics, "...they say that a hero can save us, I'm not going to just sit here and wait..."

Perturbed, Simon again spun the dial and landed on a sports talk radio station. Hoping to get absorbed in some trivial conversation about arbitration, he listened intently as the announcers disputed salary caps and bargaining agreements between multi-millionaires who *played a game* for a living. Discontented, he went to an old, tried and true method of distraction by conjuring up memories of scandalous movie scenes, but all that did was open old wounds.

"Ahh!" he blurted out, completely disgusted with himself.

Once more, he reached for the dial before landing on one of his favorite conservative talk radio programs. The host was categorically listing the problems with our country and warning of the radical voting record of the freshman Senator from Chicago. In the past, Simon would have gotten swept away by all of the incendiary rhetoric but not anymore. Now he realized that the host was only talking about the symptoms without getting down to the real heart of the issue. Frustrated and dissatisfied with FM radio, Simon flipped over to AM and landed on another station.

Immediately he recognized the familiar voice of Dr. James Dobson. It was a broadcast featuring the best of "Focus on the Family".

And Simon suddenly remembered his conversation with Jeremy while sitting in the bleachers at the ball field. Dr. Dobson's son, Ryan, was recounting the very same story that Jeremy had used to make a point about reaching the lost.

Simon listened intently to the replay of the radio broadcast as Ryan Dobson told the story of a towboat that accidentally pushed a barge into a concrete bridge support on the Arkansas River in Oklahoma. A portion of the bridge collapsed, but drivers on the interstate could not see the peril that lie ahead. Cars and semi-trucks shot off the edge of the bridge until a fisherman climbed up to the road and shot a flare into the windshield of a tractor-trailer. The semi stopped just short of falling off into the abyss. Then Ryan made a very poignant observation about the fisherman. The fisherman knew that the cars and trucks were driving to their eminent doom. He had to do something to save their lives.

Ryan then speculated about what that truck driver must have felt initially as a flare unexpectedly hit his windshield. Without knowing the danger that he was in, the driver was probably furious that somehow had the audacity to do something like that. The shock of the flare hitting his windshield could have scared him half to death. He could have even panicked and driven off the road. At the very least, he was probably enraged at whoever had shot the flare. Maybe he was even offended by it. It possible that he wanted revenge or justice.

But once the truck driver saw the damaged bridge, he quickly realized that the person who shot the flare had actually saved him from destruction!

Finally able to focus on something other than his own circumstances, Simon leaned back against the headrest and continued to listen. He was reflecting on the words of the talk show host as he drove over a bluff that provided a clear view of the long road ahead of him. Off in the distance, he could make out a small cluster of fire trucks, police cars, and ambulances with a long row of cars in single file line leading up to an accident. Even though it was several miles down the road, many cars and trucks had already began to obediently make their way over into the left lane. Simon slowed down and followed suit as he passed a roadside assistance vehicle with a large blinking arrow. It was followed by a long row of orange cones.

Suddenly a driver of a shiny, new Camaro took advantage of the slow moving traffic. Instead of falling in step with the other vehicles, the driver of the Camaro hit the accelerator and darted past as many of the other cars and trucks as possible before darting back in line and cutting off his fellow travelers.

Simon's heart skipped a beat as he anticipated the shrill sound of metal on metal. Somehow the cars had miraculously avoided a collision. Nonetheless, the narrow miss precipitated by the selfish act helped bring Simon back to his senses.

"Man," Simon said aloud, "that maniac could have killed someone just to move up one hundred yards and save thirty-seconds of driving. How selfish can a person be?"

All of a sudden, Simon was overcome with shame and embarrassment because he realized that he was just as guilty as the next guy. Consequently, he was in no position to cast dispersions at a person whose only crime was being completely ignorant. He was in no position to judge. After all, Simon had acted the exact same way until...

Purposefully ducking the rational explanation for the moment, Simon directed his attention towards the self-serving act. Yes, he was a hypocrite, but that didn't mean that he didn't now know the difference between right and wrong or that he couldn't recognize an injustice when he saw it. In fact, it was just the opposite. Now that his eyes had been opened, he had the obligation to do something about it.

Even as the long line of vehicles neared the scene of the accident, Simon could see even more cars in his rearview mirror begin to slide over onto the shoulder, ready to take advantage of the situation. Those inconsiderate drivers who were by-passing the long line of cars were not only trampling on the rights of the other drivers on the road, they were also jeopardizing everyone's safety and potentially blocking a path for the ambulances or other rescue vehicles.

Simon was beyond merely recognizing injustice and being indifferent to it. He was ready to take action. Calmly, he looked for a gap in the cars and trucks that were racing past him down the shoulder of the road. He waited for just the right moment and jumped out onto the shoulder, effectively filling the gap and stopping the deluge of vehicles. As a large Hummer filled his rearview mirror, Simon could hear the squeal of the tires. Clutching the steering wheel, he braced for a collision that never came. Even though he could feel the wrath of the driver voicelessly telling him off, Simon was overwhelmed with the satisfaction of righting a wrong.

Now moving down the road with the steady flow of traffic, Simon kept one half of his car on the shoulder and the other half in the right hand lane of the interstate. He decided that it was okay to be intolerant to the other drivers' untoward behavior because they were simply wrong. As deeply offended as the small of number of opportunists were, Simon knew that he was in the right. Little did he know that the vast majority of drivers who had been obeying the rules of the road were very appreciative for the courageous, selfless act.

Simon could no longer avoid the question, "Why?" His actions weren't born out of resentment or condemnation for the other drivers for he had been guilty of the same kind of selfish behavior in the past. It wasn't that anyone was committing a federal offense or anything like that. In fact, that kind of reckless driving took place all over America everyday.

So, if it wasn't for any of those reasons, then why did he do it? He first decided that it must be a mere matter of principle. A semblance of order had been restored. It was just the *right* thing to do.

Dissatisfied by his own answer, Simon had to ask himself what had changed.

"Why was it okay before, but now it wasn't?" Simon wondered.

As he considered the issue, he noticed that he was nearing the scene of the accident. His attention was momentarily diverted by the sheer number of emergency vehicles and first responders on the scene. Spontaneously, he mouthed a short prayer for those involved in the accident as well as for those tending to the injured. There was no self-pity over being slightly inconvenienced by the delay. There was no tantalizing desire to feed an insatiable hunger for sensationalism. No yearning to catch a glimpse of a mangled car, or a bloodstained road, or a body bag. There was only genuine sympathy and deep concern for his fellow man.

As he regained the speed limit, the real answer to his question dawned on him. He no longer saw the world in the same way. Pride, arrogance, perverse speech, and evil behavior were now reprehensible to him. Simon recognized that the loud, obnoxious voice he had heard stirring earlier was that of his own pride. His selfishness had become as detestable to him as the lies and false allegations that Jack had made against him. He could no more artificially inflate his own self-importance any more than he could make himself taller. It was impossible. The ridiculous voice that he had heard raging inside of him was nothing more than a tale told by an idiot, full of sound and fury, signifying nothing. In the end, he was certain that the voice that falsely inflated his own self-importance would only testify against him upon a hard cross examination on Judgement Day.

Simon had changed. Suddenly, he realized that it didn't matter if Pastor Pete had been the one who physically turned on the light to the marquee. The fact of the matter was that the Holy Spirit had been at work that night even if He had used a man to do it. Nor did it matter that the message was just the next one in the series. The invitation, "Come, Follow me" was both universal and yet profoundly specific to him in that moment. It was perfect, just like God is perfect!

At the time, Simon did not know the verse to which the words were referring. But, now, after studying Jeremy's Bible, he was aware of its full context. Matthew 4:19 read, "Come follow me, and I will make you fishers of men."

There was no denying it. Jesus had spoken to him that night. Simon had been saved at that moment and now he had an enormous responsibility to seek the will of God. If all of that were true, then it would be hard to argue that that particular moment wasn't part of a greater, highly orchestrated plan, and that his return to Bethel wasn't for a specific reason. And if that were the case, then there could be no doubt that God had also called him to complete the renovation after all.

Still, Simon had to square that revelation with everything else that had transpired over the last twenty-four hours. It was one thing to know what you know to be true. It was entirely another matter to be able to articulate it. Before he could get himself to turn his car around and head back to Bethel, he had to come to terms with Pete's fundamental question, "*How* did he *know?*".

Everything hinged on being able to reasonably answer that one pertinent question. Somehow Simon knew that the answer would also go a long way towards explaining another question that had been plaguing him. It might explain how the physical restoration of a building could ultimately further God's kingdom.

After all, truth was not relevant as Joey had ridiculously proposed. There is right and wrong, and there is good and evil in this world. It wasn't all just one-in-the-same. He had to look no farther than Jeremy Warner to know that. There was no doubt that he had been the victim of a horrific crime. And yet, if gone unchecked, his story would irreverently be folded up into the fabric of the overarching myth that had held Bethel hostage all of these years.

As Simon thought about the charred laundry pole, he remembered Joey's indignant indictment that the pinnacle of the Christian experience was martyrdom. If that were the case, then what good could possibly come from it?

* * *

After turning it over and over in his mind, Simon rightly concluded that there *can't be* any one piece of definitive evidence to prove what he knew to be true in his heart because that kind of tangible evidence would do away with faith altogether.

"No," Simon thought, "a single, solitary piece of irrefutable evidence would leave only one possible answer to the ultimate question. And only one possible answer leaves us without a choice to believe or not believe. Faith requires that we don't have just one possible answer and no alternative answers. On the contrary, faith requires a right answer with at least *one* alternative wrong answer if not many,

many more. Without a choice, we might as well be pre-programmed to worship and serve God like a bunch of robots.

"Wait a minute, what would be wrong with that?" Simon wondered, choosing not to accept the conclusion at face value, but instead challenging himself with a valid counterpoint. After all, things aren't what they always seem on the surface. "God is God. He makes the rules. If He wanted to make a bunch of mindless, worshiping robots, He could have done it. We, being His creation, wouldn't have been any the wiser because we wouldn't have ever known anything different. If that were the case, then ignorance truly would have been our bliss.

"So, why, then? Why give us a choice in the first place? No one would go to Hades. Everybody would be in heaven just like in Joey's little world. We would all love God. God would love us. There would have been no need for a Savior because there would have been nothing to save us from. Jesus wouldn't have had to die on the cross. Everyone would just do everything 'right' all of the time. There would be no tragedies or calamities. And we would have all lived happily ever after."

Momentarily, vexed by the conundrum, Simon went back over his line of reasoning a few more times before coming to a conclusion.

"Obviously, God *did* give us a choice about what to believe and what not to believe though," he continued, "otherwise we wouldn't have any disagreements about God or religion in the first place. And we all know that's not the case!"

Simon thought of Pastor Pete's advice and started again at the beginning.

"Okay, God is perfect, right?" Simon thought. "He doesn't make mistakes. And He only wants what is best for us. So, He must have given us a choice on purpose, not by accident. Therefore, He must have done it for a reason.

"If that's the case, then there must be something special about having the freedom to choose. There must be something vital about giving man free will. After all, at the beginning of the world, God gave Adam a choice in the Garden of Eden. Even before Adam, God must have even given the angels a choice. Otherwise, Satan would not have chosen to rebel.

"Hmmph," Simon mused. "God already tried the entitlement route for granting eternal life in heaven and look what happened. His second in command led a rebellion to overthrow His own Kingdom, taking a third of the angels with him. No, God doesn't want robots, but he doesn't want a bunch of ungrateful, malcontents either. God doesn't want minions; he wants humans.

"It goes to the heart of the fundamental question, 'why would a perfect and righteous God create angels or men in the first place?'. He certainly doesn't need us. He is already whole.

"Maybe, since God is love," Simon theorized, "it is reasonable to conclude that He created man in His own image out of love. He must have simply wanted to do it. It must have pleased Him. After all, He said as much in Genesis 1:31, 'God saw all that He had made, and it was very good'.

"And so," Simon concluded. "God must have also given us free will out of love for us. After all, He cannot deny Himself. He's not twisted or sadistic. That's not who God is. Like any good Father, He deeply cares for His children and wants the best for them. He creates us, sends us out into the world, sets us free, and waits for us to choose to come back to Him…to come and follow Him! But, why would He take such a risk, if not each and every one of his creation would choose to return to Him in the end?"

Simon frowned and readjusted his hand on the steering wheel. Without knowing, he alternately peeled the backs of his bare legs off of the vinyl seat. The pressure cooker conditions outside were slowly baking the interior of the old Impala.

"Maybe!" he said, excitedly, "it is because the highest form of love can only be reached when love is returned to the same degree. Maybe God is seeking a reciprocal relationship born out of choice like in a marriage! God wants us to choose to be with Him and only Him. Not simply to be forced to be with Him!"

"That would make sense!" Simon reasoned, thinking of his relationship with Hope. "It's obvious that the bond between us was strongest when our love for one another was reciprocated to the same degree. Hope said she was jealous because she wanted what was rightfully hers. She didn't want to share it. She wanted my complete devotion to her and only her!"

It was like being hit in the face with a two-by-four. Suddenly, Simon was faced with the realization that he might have not only irreparably damaged his relationship with Hope, but also with God. He was afraid that his own transgressions created a permanent imbalance that could never be swayed again in his favor. After all, infidelity destroys relationships.

Simon grimaced and let out a gush of air as though he had just been punched in the gut. He paused to reflect for a moment before continuing down the same line of reasoning. "When love is returned in kind, it creates a deeper, more intimate degree of caring. It binds people together, reaching far beneath the surface. It connects us at the very core of our being.

"And if I hadn't messed things up so badly with Hope, our love could have grown deeper, drawing us even closer together. Who knows? At some point, we may have even chosen to make the ultimate commitment to one another. To make a covenant. To become one. To choose to dedicate all of our affection and devotion to only one another even though there are millions of alternatives out there.

"It's no different with God! Love binds and unfaithfulness divides."

Simon's heart sank as he thought of the poor choices that had led to his own undoing.

"Deep down everyone longs for that kind of intimacy," Simon lamented. "That's what we're all seeking because it satisfies one our greatest needs. Everyone needs to love someone who chooses to love us in return. It is the most meaningful connection that we can have with another human being. And if we call that being in love, and if God is love, then God is the 'glue' that binds us together. So, God is at the heart of every successful marriage whether we are aware of it or not.

"Marriage is critical to our understanding of God because it symbolizes that relationship that He wants to have with us," he suddenly realized. "That's why it is sacred. It allows our puny little brains to get a tiny glimpse of an even more meaningful relationship that we are all desperately seeking. God ultimately fills the void in our lives that can never be filled by another human being.

"If the analogy is," Simon recalled, "that Jesus is the groom and the church is the bride, then no wonder Satan hates marriage between one man and one woman! No wonder the destruction of the family is at the heart of his campaign to separate us from God. It is the closest thing we have that allows us to understand the depth of love, commitment, and devotion that God wants out of our relationship with Him.

"He wants the same thing from us that we want from Him. He wants out heart, soul, mind, and strength. Just like a loving spouse, He doesn't want some of us some of the time. He wants all of us all of the time.

"But He even takes it a step further," Simon thought, recalling Jeremy's notes written in the margins. "He tells us that He is a jealous God just like a husband is jealous for his wife. A husband doesn't want to share his wife's body, and she doesn't want him to share his heart. God wants us to be completely faithful to Him all of the time. So, when there is infidelity in a marriage, when some of the 'glue' that should have been reserved for the spouse is applied to another relationship, there is betrayal, outrage, and suffering. Love is greatly diminished, trust is permanently damaged, and the bond, or covenant is considerably weakened, if not broken altogether...

"Oh man!" Simon said, shaking his head. Finally, he fully understood. "If that's the case, then Hope had every right to be angry when she found out I had lusted after another woman. The physical act was merely an outpouring of my unfaithful heart. It made no difference that I had not even met Hope before that night because I should have been saving myself for that one person with whom I would spend the rest of my life anyway. It was representative of my ability to keep a promise and fulfill a covenant.

"So, God didn't allow the existence of evil because He is sadistic!" Simon realized, having followed the line of reasoning to its logical conclusion. "The ultimate form of love is reciprocated love born out of choice. In order for there to be a choice, there had to be an equal and opposite option to choose from. For there to be free will, God had to allow evil.

"God doesn't just send people to Hades out of spite! It is only *after* we are unfaithful to Him by choosing to serve ourselves or other gods. That is when we invoke His justice and receive His wrath. When we reject God and choose to serve anything besides Him, we become adulterers. As a result, we get the opposite of Him. And what is the opposite of love? Hate. What is the opposite of life? Death.

What is the opposite of caring? Apathy. What is the opposite of perfection? Sin. What is the opposite of forgiveness? Vengeance. Instead of grace, we get justice. It is only a fair and just response to *us* rejecting *Him* first; not the other way around."

The scenery unceremoniously passed by as Simon cruised down the interstate in deep thought, only now starting to come to grips with what he was really doing by fleeing Bethel. He was not only making a choice to abandon Hope, he was also breaking the covenant that he had made with God.

"No," Simon thought, disgusted with himself. "There must be an infinite difference between choosing to return the love we are given and not even being given a choice in the first place. By simply giving us the choice, it necessitated the risk of God losing some of his children forever by their own volition.

"That would explain why a perfect, loving God would allow such evil in the world in the first place. He had to allow an alternative to Himself. Evil, Satan, sin, and Hades were merely the necessary byproducts of free will.

"But, God is perfect, and God is in heaven. So, heaven must also be perfect. That is the standard. Anything less than that cannot and will not be tolerated. So, both perfection and free will *must be essential* components for receiving eternal life and living in the presence of a Holy, righteous God.

"Wasn't that also the case in the Garden of Eden? God did not introduce sin and death from the beginning of creation. At first, there was only perfection. Adam and Even were living eternally in the presence of God. And yet, there was still free will. God only planted the Tree of Life and the Tree of Knowledge in the Garden. He gave Adam and Even a choice to be obedient or disobedient to Him. There was no sin until Adam chose to eat of the forbidden fruit. God didn't cause or allow bad things to happen to innocent people. He only gave Adam and Eve, and even Satan for that matter, the consequences they deserved because they were accountable for the choices they made. He handed down…*a curse!*

"Sin, suffering, and death only came about as the result of God's justice. He rightfully punished Adam and Eve for breaking their covenant and being disobedient to Him. Yes, love binds and unfaithfulness divides.

"Man's unfaithfulness separates us from God. There is nothing man can do to atone for the original sin that he inherited from Adam. Man is imperfect and unable to pay the debt he has incurred. So, he has to borrow someone else's perfection in order to pay for his sins.

"There was a curse in Bethel to be sure!" Simon decided. "And one man was called to put an end to it!- and it sure wasn't *me!* God sent His only begotten son. He came Himself to atone for man's sin. Only Jesus did not inherit Adam's sin because He was not born of an earthly father. He was born of the Holy Spirit through the virgin Mary. Jesus was God incarnate. He was both God and man. As God he was born perfect, as man he was exposed to the same temptations to sin as any other man. Given the gift of free will, Jesus chose to not sin. He chose to be obedient and keep His covenant with God the Father. As a result, He qualified himself as the perfect living sacrifice to pay for man's sins. Jesus is the unblemished lamb as was foretold in the story of Abraham and Isaac on Mt. Moriah.

"Jesus Christ paid the ultimate sacrifice by laying down his own life for man. He willfully and obediently died on the cross in our place to pay for our sins out of unconditional love for His creation. God shows us mercy and clemency. It only takes one simple choice to determine our fate. In order for us to receive eternal life, all we must do is choose to accept Jesus' free gift of salvation by grace through faith. Whether or not a person is allowed to enter Heaven is strictly predicated on whether or not a person chooses Jesus Christ as his or her Lord and Savior. That is all that is required of us. It is not out of works, so that no man can boast.

"God loved us enough to leave it up to us to decide. God didn't want us to settle for less than perfection. He didn't want to rob us of free will. He didn't want us to settle for the guarantee of mediocrity or merely eking out an eternal, robotic existence, because that would be less than perfect. He wanted to give us the opportunity to receive the greatest gift of all, to experience all of the richness and fullness of His love. He wanted us to be active participants in determining our own destiny.

"There is no doubt about it," Simon decided. "God is definitely pro-choice because He is pro-life. But He is also pro-accountability, and pro-justice, and pro-consequences!"

Except, unfortunately, Simon had made his decision. When given the choice, he had chosen to run from Bethel just like his father before him. Ashamed, he now considered the implications for making such a terrible decision.

* * *

God was waiting for Simon to return to Bethel like the prodigal son. Nevertheless, Simon spontaneously convulsed as he thought about Jack Lawless' accusations. If he did go back, Simon knew there would be a trial. He knew that there would be false testimony against him. And he knew that he would be persecuted just like Jeremy Warner had been persecuted.

All of a sudden, a Bible verse came to him. He remembered the words of John 15:18, "If the world hates you, remember that it hated me first."

"But why?" Simon asked himself. "Why would a loving God allow his followers to be persecuted? Why would He allow Jeremy Warner of all people to die such a horrible death at the hands of Jack Lawless? What would be the point? Don't all things work for the good of the believer?"

Simon pondered the veracity of God's promise that was written in Romans 8:28. Could he really accept Paul at his word? How could he know for sure that it wasn't all just another myth like the legend of Jessie Joseph?"

He took a moment to consider how the legend of Jessie had evolved. Some of the core details had remained unchanged from the original story while many details had either been altered or added over time. It didn't matter if they were born out of hyperbole or plain ignorance. Either way, it was now readily apparent that whenever there were gaps in the story or information that couldn't be easily explained, people were more than happy to fill in their own details.

He realized that the more active the imagination, the greater the deviation from the truth. Ironically, the more intelligent the listener, the easier it was for them to accept plausible, alternative explanations to the one true account. In fact, the closer the lies were to the truth, the more difficult they were to decipher. In that way, it was easy to see how someone as smart as Joey could allow his intellect to inhibit his ability to hear the truth. For people like Joey, the truth is limited to what they can understand. Therefore, anything mysterious or supernatural is beyond their comprehension.

Joey refused to accept the Biblical truth because he did not have the mental capacity to rationalize it or the supernatural insight to fully appreciate it. It was too hard for him to accept that the 'Great Common Consciousness' that imparted truth to people from distant, isolated cultures was actually the God of the Bible. It was a sad irony that Joey's superior intellect had all but stifled the internal compass God had pre-installed inside of him to recognize truth. All of Joey's acquired learning had actually poisoned the well from which a person draws wisdom, thereby sabotaging any chance he might have had at reaching an unadulterated conclusion to life's deepest questions.

Even though each one of us is born with it, the laws of Human Nature can be quieted or snuffed out altogether. That is why Satan is so intent on destroying, or at least, numbing the conscience. It is one of his most devious campaigns.

Not only does Joey and all of his *great* philosophers, writers, directors, and scientists ignore Biblical truth and discount the power of prayer, but they also see the conscience as the greatest impediment to fully experiencing the universe. To them, a person must overcome his conscience in order to acquire knowledge so that they can be like God or to be their own god. When in fact, the opposite is true.

The more they rely on human knowledge and their own experiences the less that they listen to the voice inside of them. They develop a tin ear. As a result, any number of different explanations pertaining to the origin of man or the creation of the universe sound good to them. To them each religion or culture's version of truth has equal validity.

Without wisdom and knowledge, they are no longer able to discern fact from fiction. The intellectuals have become so open-minded that the mere suggestion that there is an absolute truth has become completely absurd to them. In fact, they would argue that anyone who does believe in absolute truth is either simpleminded, or closed-minded, or both. Consequently, truth becomes relative.

That was Joey's fatal flaw as well. It explained his inability to sift through the thousands and thousands of ancient myths about creation and identify the one true account found in Genesis. Joey simply could not distinguish the hyperbole and inaccuracies of the heretical stories from the genuine article. They all sounded good to him. Any historical, empirical evidence that contradicted his foregone conclusions were conveniently ignored or dismissed altogether because they didn't fit the narrative.

Conversely, Simon had become convinced that the Bible was the inerrant word of God and the one true account of history. Ironically, he had arrived at that conclusion in large part due to his experience in trying to decipher a myth. Over the past month and a half, Simon was able to carefully examine all of the different accounts pertaining to the legend of Jessie Joseph. He used knowledge, wisdom, and discretion combined with research, historiography, and eyewitness accounts to sift through all of the hyperbole and inaccuracies to arrive at the truth. In the end, he was able to separate the wheat from the chaff.

In solving the mystery, he discovered that there was no single, solitary piece of evidence that had definitively proven what had actually taken place on that fateful day in 1935. By piecing together the evidence at his disposal, he was able to eventually solve the mystery.

"Joey, Pastor Pete, or anyone else for that matter, need to understand," Simon thought for moment, "it's not faith without evidence; it's faith in the evidence. Faith that God will provide the answer to our questions."

Individuals should be eager to sift through all of the different possibilities in order to flush out fallacies, while we train our ear to listen for the voice inside of us for the facts. People should welcome open debate and discussion, because ..."if we seek, we will find, and if we knock, the door will be opened to us."

Once Simon had done that with the legend of Jessie Joseph, it was like putting on a pair of glasses for the first time. Everything came into focus. After that, it was easy to see how the story had evolved over time. It was easy to see how people read into things. How people assumed Jessie was jaded and vengeful. How the residual tragedies were linked to the legend. How twelve gravestones on Potter's abandoned cemetery could be mistaken as that of the students from the 1st and 2nd grade classes. How the periods between tragedies were thought to be cyclical, even though their wasn't any kind of chronological pattern. Simon could even see how people could attribute such horrible accidents to a curse of some kind.

"Huh," Simon muttered aloud. "There was that word again, 'curse'!"

After his revelation about Jesus being the one chosen to put an end to the ultimate curse, Simon once again was forced to ask himself the ultimate question.

"Why then?" Simon thought. "If Jesus is the only one who can end the curse, then why have me put my life on hold to fix up a cruddy old building? What was the purpose? If it was somehow God's plan to bring about some kind of change, then why had it so miserably failed? What was the point? Why did it serve more to divide the town than bring it together? Wasn't it, after all, just a colossal waste of time, energy, and resources?"

He thought of the people's reaction to seeing the commemorative plaques. Was it merely a sad irony that only a few people opposed the hanging of the Declaration of Independence, but almost everyone opposed the source from which that document was given birth? The real persecution began when Simon hung the Ten Commandments back up on the wall. After all, he was only making the entryway look exactly like it did in the fall of 1935. Instinctively, Simon stuck out his tongue and felt his swollen lip.

People were upset about the taxes, but hanging the old, Judeo-Christian monument back up on the wall nearly incited a riot. Somehow that actually made him feel a little better considering Hope's assertion. The fierce opposition might be an indicator that he was in line with God's will. A smile slowly crept across his face, but soon vanished when he recalled the other way in which Hope said he would know if God had called him to complete the project. In the end, it would further God's Kingdom in some way, but that hadn't been the case. The renovation seemed to have had the exact opposite effect.

Simon furrowed his brow and thought for a moment. "Why?" he wondered, as he thought of Parker's eulogy at Jeremy's visitation. "If I put my life on hold and used my talents to follow God's will, then why would He allow so much pain, suffering, and persecution? Why put me through all of the trials and tribulations?"

The project hardly brought about the kind of positive impact on the community that he had hoped for. In one fell swoop, the community rejected the Ten Commandments, voted down the referendum, accused him of criminal activity, and nearly lynched him for all of his trouble.

"If someone were doing God's will," Simon thought, "then why would He allow them to be unjustly punished?"

It was the same question the people of Bethel had been asking themselves for decades. How could it be a part of God's plan for the innocent to suffer?

Suddenly, Simon thought about Little Simon Adamson, Jeremy Warner, Adam Potter, and even Sharon's never to be born baby. He tapped on top of the steering wheel with his index finger and leaned his elbow on the door, searching for a possible answer.

"It was one thing to punish the guilty," he mused. "That was justice. Anyone would agree with that, but why on earth would the God of love allow something tragic to happen to the innocent? Why would He allow a little boy to be neglected, a young man to be murdered, a small child to suffocate, and a baby's life to be snuffed out? That hardly seemed right, or just, or fair. Looking at it from that perspective, the people of Bethel truly did seem to be cursed.

There was a definite disconnect somewhere. It just didn't add up. Simon did not have a rational answer to explain God's seemingly indifference to injustice. Obviously, neither did each passing generation in Bethel since the day Adam Potter was laid to rest in the fall of 1935.

"So, that must be why they came up with the legend of Jessie Joseph in the first place," Simon rightly surmised. "It was a way to cope with the senseless tragedies that seemed to have no rhyme or reason. Being haunted by some vengeful ghost made more sense to them than it all being a part of a loving God's master plan.

"Still…," Simon observed, while driving down the interstate, "…if the legend of Jessie Joseph came into being as a way to explain the unexplainable, it was grossly insufficient because it failed to explain its genesis. As far as the average person knew, the legend was true. And if so, they might be inclined to ask themselves a question. What would make a young teacher do all of those unspeakable things to his students in the first place? In their minds, even if the legend were true, it didn't offer a compelling explanation for the motivation for Jessie's gross misconduct. If the whole point of a legend was to explain the unexplainable, then it had fallen short of achieving its ultimate objective."

"But, that was it, wasn't it?" Simon realized, slamming the palm of his hand on the steering wheel. "There was no sufficient explanation for it. That's what they couldn't wrap their heads around. They were unable to deal with something so sinister. That was the pivotal moment that changed Bethel forever. That would explain why they had begun to question their beliefs. And why they might turn their backs on God altogether. They simply couldn't process or understand why He would allow, much less cause, such inexplicable pain and suffering to their own children. And they definitely couldn't see how it could all work to the good of the believer.

Prior to that, life made more sense. Sure, there had been hardships from time to time. But for the most part, when good people did good things, good things happened to them. And the opposite was also true as well. When bad people did bad things, bad things happened to them.

But, after that tragic day, when so many of their innocent, young children seemed to have suffered at the hands of a man in whom they had placed so much trust, their whole world had been turned upside down. They didn't know who or what to believe anymore."

Simon continued to drive away from Bethel as he once again considered how making the school look exactly like it did prior to October 31, 1935 could put an end to their doubt and ultimately further God's Kingdom. There was some key element that was still eluding him. But, what was it?

He unconsciously bit his fat lip again as he ran back over the series of events from that fateful day according to Pete's eyewitness account.

"Okay, let me go over this again," he said aloud. "Adam Potter uses his hands while bobbing for apples. John Rash gets angry at Adam for cheating. They get into a scuffle. Jessie Joseph, who's not in the right frame of mind, turns to see Adam shove John to the floor. It's all typical boy stuff. The teacher overreacts and ultimately sends Adam to a time out in the closet as punishment. It sounds like that was common practice back in the day. Adam, who is completely freaked out by the skeleton laying in the coffin, refuses to stay there in the dark. Who could blame a kid for that? Jessie orders Pete and Andy to hold the door shut because there's no lock on it. Then, for whatever reason, John decides to jump in and help them like it was some kind of game. Sure, it would make no sense if it were an adult, but it makes perfect sense when describing the actions of a 7-year-old boy.

"Panic sets in for Adam who we now know had asthma. He keeps banging on the door, trying to force it open. Jessie takes it as some kind of act of defiance to his authority. Again, it all makes perfect sense. Determined to win the battle of wills, he goes over and holds the door shut himself. That's plausible. Pete and Andy step out of the way, but John stays put for some unknown reason. Adam totally wigs out. The poor kid starts screaming, banging, and scratching on the door. After all, he's only human. Evidently, Adam has a panic attack, hyperventilates, and dies. Jessie assumes that Adam's silence means that he has finally given in and accepted his punishment. It's not until they open the door and see Adam's blue face and bloodied fingers that the horribly reality of the situation sinks in."

Now Simon could clearly see how elements of the legend sprang from the one true account. It became obvious to him that without knowing the original story it would be difficult to sort out fact from fiction.

"Jessie shuts the door and sends John to go get the principal," Simon continued. "By now, all of the kids are very frightened. Of course, they were. Jessie, now realizing the seriousness of the situation, calls the rest of the students together, calms them down, and gets their story straight. After all, *he's* only human. Pretty soon, the police, firefighters, and some very worried parents all descend on the school."

He could see the natural chain of events unfolding in his mind. It all made sense.

"Not being the person everybody thinks that he is, Jessie decides to save himself. So, he pulls the detectives aside and incriminates John. The rest of the students rally around their beloved teacher at least when there's no threat of getting in trouble. And they corroborate Jessie's story. So, the cops take John away."

Simon shakes his head, as he tried to imagine what it must have been like that day.

"Understandably, the Potters are devastated and demand justice for their now deceased son, Adam. The pressure mounts on the police to take action. John suddenly becomes terrified of being punished for Adam's death. Who wouldn't? So what does he do? What any kid would do. He makes up a story.

"The detectives, being not overly excited about charging a child for such a horrible crime, become very willing to believe John's testimony. Still hungry for a motive, the cops unintentionally ask leading questions that cause John to describe how Jessie abused the students.

"One by one they pull the students out of the classroom, take them upstairs to the chorus room, and begin the intense interrogations. Now the little boys and girls are scared of getting in trouble. After all, they hear that John had been taken to jail, and they naturally assume that they might be next. So, what do they do? They tell the detectives exactly what they want to hear. The more gruesome the details they make up, the happier the detectives seem to be. And as a result, the stories get more and more outlandish and deplorable.

"They take Jessie away. John is released from prison. Some time passes before Pete's guilt gets the best of him. So, he confesses that he made the whole thing up about Jessie. A couple of other kids come forward and say the same thing. Now nobody knows who or what to believe. Nobody knows who is telling the truth. Pete still doesn't even know to this day. And he was there!

"So, nobody does anything. They let Jessie rot. He gets convicted, goes to jail, and dies years later of TB. Nobody, comes forward in his defense. The whole town just decides to bury the whole thing under the rug and move on as if nothing had ever happened. John spends the rest of his life self-medicating with alcohol while Andy and Pete spend the rest of their lives trying to make amends for the part they played in the death of their friend and the imprisonment of their beloved teacher.

"Except people are people, so even though they do their best to bury the past, in secret, behind closed doors, everyone talks about it and wallah, the legend of Jessie Joseph is born."

Simon repositioned himself and tightly wrenched the steering with both of his hands. It all made perfect sense now. If Jessie was as charismatic as everyone said, it was easy to see why the students wanted so desperately to please him. And it also made sense that they looked to him as the authority in the classroom. They naturally saw him as someone who would protect them. So, it is reasonable that they would obediently support his story about what had taken place, even after the cops took John away.

It also made sense why Pete felt so guilty about John going to juvenile detention. After all, his testimony had contributed to his incarceration. Furthermore, it was easy to see why Jessie had implicated John. He probably figured that it would not only clear his own name, but that the authorities would also be less likely to prosecute a child.

Consequently, it was easy to see why John then turned on Jessie and why the other students would change their testimony. It all had to do with fear and the threat of punishment. They were willing to say just about anything to avoid being taken to jail. And it also made sense that no one really came to Jessie's defense because no one ever knew for sure what had really happened.

"Even though the tragic accident wasn't nearly as gruesome as depicted in the legend, why *would* God even allow something like *that* to happen to an innocent child?" Simon unwillingly asked himself. He realized that he was no better equipped to answer that question than the people of Bethel. Now he understood how the people of Bethel must have labored over that question with each new passing tragedy.

What was the purpose? Was God punishing the children? Was God punishing the parents of Bethel for some hidden sin? And if so, why punish the next generation? Why not punish the parents? Simon was beginning to understand how maddening it was to not have clear-cut answers. He thought of Joey's original question the first time they met at the ball park. Is there any point discussing a question that has no definitive answer? It exhausts the mind and drains the soul.

The people of Bethel must have decided that there was no point, so they decided to bury it along with the bodies of Jessie and Adam. Outwardly, they had put on a facade for the rest of the world, but inwardly, they had become cynical and wary. As Simon drove down the interstate, he remembered Miss Harold's claim that Bethel changed after that tragic accident.

The parents felt as though they had failed in their duty to protect their children. They must have agonized over the wretched things that they imagined Jessie doing to their babies up in the chorus room. It must have challenged their most deeply seeded beliefs. Their doubt challenged their way of thinking. And eventually their new way of thinking must have ultimately culminated in observable changes in the community.

Tortured by the mistakes of their past, they secretly vowed to never let something like that happen again. They became hyper-vigilant of any potential threats to their children's physical or mental well-being. Before long, protecting the safety and self-esteem of the children became paramount. Parents did their level best to eliminate all potential dangers, hardships, or obstacles. The extreme measures all but vanquished their children's own trials or tribulations. Parents opted to fight their children's battles for them instead.

Shaken by the tragic events, the parents did not know what to believe anymore. Steeped in doubt, they were more reluctant to defend, much less advocate, the doctrines that their ancestors had regarded sacred. As a result, their society made small incremental shifts. Whenever their belief system was challenged, the people of Bethel acquiesced time and again to the philosophies, doctrines, and alternate religions that had crept in from other parts of the world. Before they knew it, truth had become relative. It was merely a matter of perspective.

The net result was the removal of anything deemed offensive or controversial from the public square. That was especially true of that referenced traditional, Christian teaching or symbols. After a while, the people of Bethel came to hold diversity and individuality in higher esteem than the doctrines espoused by their forefathers. Tolerance, acceptance, and political correctness came to rule the day. Everyone's beliefs began to enjoy equal merit in the market place of ideas.

Little by little, 'Do unto others as you would have them do unto you' gave way to 'To each, his own'. Residually, the egocentric dogma crept into the schools. The new way of thinking slowly began to erode the academic and disciplinary expectations of the children. Parents did their level best to keep their children from experiencing pain, turmoil, conflict, struggle, or disappointment in the classroom, even if it meant lowering expectations or nullifying consequences.

When that didn't work, parents sought legal counsel. Before long, an offended minority or a single dissenter could control the voiceless majority by using legal precedent as a lever. Slowly, but surely, anything even remotely offensive or controversial was eventually removed from the school as well. Consequently, a litigious culture was wrought in the name of understanding and tolerance. Any sense of accountability or responsibility had become completely compromised. Entitlement became pervasive. Students became convinced that the system owed them something, and they soon adopted a victim mentality.

Over time, the entire community unceremoniously divorced itself from God, thereby undermining the very source of all truth, wisdom, knowledge, and discretion. And in turn, they were unwittingly forfeiting all of their inalienable rights. All the while, they did an even greater disservice by self-identifying as a "Christian". They habitually continued to attend church and celebrate traditional holidays. As a result, the rest of the world viewed the hollowed out doctrine, blatant hypocrisy, and unbecoming conduct as evidence of a false religion. When, in fact, it was false Christians misrepresenting the one true God. The apostates wavering in their faith opened the door to new fangled ideas. Pretty soon any and all opinions, ideas, and beliefs were given equal credence. The supposed Christians had arrived at a place where they spent less and less time worrying about was right and wrong and more time worrying about how to deflect public ridicule or potential litigation.

Their great compromise was the removal of all Christian symbols or teachings. Little did they know that by eradicating God and His law, they had unwittingly vanquished any purpose and meaning from their empty lives. Naturally, the people of Bethel turned to other alternative sources to fill the void. An unfortunate, albeit predictable outcome, was that people gravitated to the things apart from God to keep themselves temporarily satisfied whether it was their careers, or status, or money, or drugs, or sex, or entertainment, or hobbies, or even sports. And good old Jack was more than happy to provide them with the means or at least offer a high interest, unsecured loan.

When the pursuit for personal pleasure took over as the quintessential hallmark of happiness in the community, it perpetuated the destruction of the family. Once God was removed from society, so was the glue that cemented long lasting relationships. As soon as people felt like they were not getting what they wanted out of a relationship, they often times just gave up on it. Spouses divorced, and parents abandoned their children.

Even if parents did manage to somehow stick it out, they often did so begrudgingly, because fixing a clogged drain, or changing a poopy diaper, or mowing the lawn, or doing the dishes, isn't much fun.

So people escaped into their own tawdry vices and guilty pleasures. By the time no fault divorce had become legalized, there was nothing to hold spouses accountable to one another other than a piece of paper at the courthouse. There was not enough glue to keep them together because there was not enough love. There was not enough love because God was not at the heart of the agreement anymore. Marriage was a contract to be sure, but it was no longer a covenant. It had become commonplace for children to grow up without a set of parents, or either *parent* for that matter, which had only further accelerated the cyclical, downward decline of the community. In the end, children like Simon Adamson were left to raise themselves on video games, cable TV, fast food, and Ritalin.

"So, that's what Thelma meant by Bethel never being the same since," Simon mused, as he considered everything that he had observed while living in Bethel. "That one tragic event caused all of that?"

He had come full circle back to that same nagging question. "If that is the case, then why would God cause or allow tragedies? There had to be a reason. There had to be a purpose. But, what? Can one act in one moment in time really be *that* pivotal?"

Then Simon thought of Jesus Christ.

His fleeting enthusiasm was stifled after realizing that the significance all hinged on whether or not the Bible really was the inerrant word of God. He immediately remembered the accusations made by Joey, Dr. Al-Banna, and even Pastor Pete. Was the Word reliable or had it been tampered with? Was it a historical document or just a myth?

Then Simon also remembered Wilson B's frustration over what he perceived as hypocrisy. He had admonished Simon for not applying the same rigor and scrutiny to both the legend and the Bible. In order to know if the Biblical account of Jesus was true, Simon would have to do the same thing that he had done in analyzing the legend of Jessie Joseph. He would have to carefully examine all of the circumstantial evidence and eyewitness accounts. He would have to use his deductive reasoning skills, apply wisdom, and decide for himself.

Consciously, he did his level best to approach the question without having a preconceived conclusion. Just as it was in the case of Jessie Joseph, Simon hoped that by retracing the series of events leading up to Jesus' ascension into heaven, he could determine the Gospel's validity. Daringly, he opened his mind and challenged his own beliefs.

Recalling mostly what he had learned while studying Jeremy's Bible, Simon went back over the events surrounding Jesus' death, burial, and resurrection.

"Jesus prays in the garden while the disciples sleep," Simon thought, seeing the events play out in his mind. "The authorities come to seize Jesus even though there was no real crime to charge Him with. They falsely accuse Him of blasphemy. Initially, Peter comes to the defense of his teacher. He violently lashes out with his sword, cutting off the ear of one of the Roman soldiers. But then, out of fear for their own potential punishment, Peter and the other disciples flee. Jesus is left alone. They arrest him. Jesus is tried in the court of public opinion. Pilate asks Jesus if He is the Christ. Jesus answers, "Yes, it is as you say'. He is then scorned, mocked, and brutally beaten. Fearing for his life, Peter denies any association with Jesus three times before the cock crows. No one comes to Jesus' defense. Jesus is crucified. He dies and is buried."

Simon took a deep breath as he considered the sheer magnitude of the series of events. As Simon reviewed the step-by-step account of the story, something occurred to him. It did not logically and neatly fall into place like the legend of Jessie Joseph. In fact, it made no sense whatsoever. First of all, there was no crime. Jesus was completely innocent. Secondly, false witnesses contrived stories to support the charge of blasphemy. But even then, Jesus did not deny the charges. Why not? Jesus showed no fear in light of the gravity of the situation. Jesus did not try to run, or displace blame, or incriminate one of his disciples. He did not fight back even while he was being brutally beaten. Jesus made no effort to save Himself. It was a very unnatural, inhuman thing to do.

At the very least, one would think that if Jesus was not the son of God, he would have admitted to being a fraud or phony when faced with the prospect of being crucified. When they laid Him down on the cross to hammer in the nails, one would think that if Jesus really was just a man He would have said just about anything to go free. One would think that in order to save his life, Jesus would have denied the allegations and admitted to being an imposter. None of the things Jesus did made sense, if He were just a man.

On the other hand what the disciples did made perfect sense because they were human. When they saw the soldiers coming for Jesus, they panicked. Peter lashed out in defense. It was a very logical and human reaction. Then, when they realized that they had come to arrest them, the disciples ran. Again, it made perfect sense. It made even more sense that the insistency of their denial would intensify as they saw what was happening to their teacher. What man wouldn't deny knowing Jesus at that point? Who wouldn't go into hiding after seeing their teacher crucified? Peter even called down curses on himself and swore that he didn't know Jesus. He flat out lied to save himself. Again, it was a very human thing to do. But, then again, who wouldn't? Would anybody dare to step forward and defend Jesus, let alone admit to being His disciple at that moment? Simon could honestly say that he would not have been able to do it.

Simon chewed on his bottom lip as he considered what happened next.

"Jesus' body is placed in a tomb," Simon thought. "It is sealed and guarded by Roman soldiers. The disciples wallow in remorse and self-pity, while hiding in the upper room. No one comes forward. They all think that their teacher is dead. No one dared to claim that Jesus is the Messiah not even to one another.

"But, that all makes perfect sense!" Simon exclaimed. "They were probably all sitting around wondering 'What just happened?'. They may have thought that Jesus was a liar, or that He was crazy, or something. At the very least, they probably thought they had been wrong in their assumptions about who He was."

Simon could sympathize with their doubt and what it meant for their lives.

For a moment, he thought about the similarities between the reaction of Jessie Joseph's students and the reaction of the disciples. In both situations, the fear of being punished caused them to lie. It quickly turned into every man for himself.

"When the heat and pressure were ratcheted up, they ran, and hid, and lied," Simon marveled. "They did what they thought they had to do to save themselves. And so did Jessie. But why didn't Jesus if he were in fact just a man?"

It defied logic. It was beyond explanation. In solving the mystery of the legend, Simon had discovered the body of Jessie Joseph still lying in the coffin, but Jesus' tomb was empty! Could the disciples have overtaken the guards, moved the stone, and removed the body themselves?

"That might make sense," Simon thought, "but why go to all of that trouble just to perpetuate a lie. Why risk being caught? How could it benefit them? Just so everyone would think that Jesus actually was the Christ? To what end? For power? For political control? For money?

"Were they simply trying to collect tithes and offerings," Simon doubtfully considered. "Were they trying avoid punishment for being a follower of Jesus by legitimizing His ministry? Maybe.

"Power and wealth. That would make the most sense. After all, a lot of people do stupid things for money.

"Either way, after three days," Simon continued, "the body of Jesus turns up missing whether they disposed of the body themselves or someone else did it for them. If the disciples were lying, they get together and concoct a story. After they get their story straight, they go out into the streets of Jerusalem and proclaim that Jesus was the Messiah.

"It's possible, I guess," Simon mused.

"So, unlike Pete Cross, or Andy Cross, or John Rash, or anyone else in Bethel who spent the rest of their lives trying to bury the terrible tragedy, the disciples inexplicably did the complete opposite. That made no sense whatsoever. They boldly spent the rest of their lives proclaiming the message of the Gospel and the resurrection of Jesus Christ as the Messiah prophesied in the Old Testament? To do what? To save *themselves*?"

Simon had to quickly reconsider his insufficient conclusion. "If the disciples lied for money, or power, or their own safety, how did it turn out for them in the end?" he asked himself. "Even if they lived off of the offerings or had held positions of power for a time, what happened to them? How did they die?"

As far as Simon knew, they all died horrible, violent deaths. They were all eventually scorned, mocked, and persecuted for claiming that Jesus was the Christ. Simon scowled again.

"If it were just one big hoax," he thought, "you would think that at least one of them would have confessed out of guilt and shame like Pastor Pete did. If not out of guilt and shame, then out of fear for their own lives like Jessie Joseph did.

When faced with the prospect of such a torturous ending like being burned alive, or stoned to death, or even crucified, surely *at least one of them* would have admitted to the conspiracy.

"The theory didn't even make sense, if someone else had stolen the body of Jesus. You would think just before their accusers flung the first stone, or lit the kindling, or hammered the first nail, that they would have admitted that they really didn't know for sure what had happened to Jesus' body. In fact, one would think in that moment the disciples would have said just about anything to avoid martyrdom like the way John Rash saved himself from retribution with the outlandish lies he had told the detectives about Jessie.

"It makes no sense that none of the eleven disciples did that," Simon realized. "Not a single one of them denied Christ's deity. You would think that at least *one* of them would have lied to save his own skin. But, that wasn't the case. On the contrary, they maintained their assertions about Jesus being the Messiah all the way to the grave.

Suddenly, the hairs stood on the back of Simon's neck.

"One event *can* change the course of history!" Simon thought. "God can use the tragic death of the innocent to further His Kingdom. After all, He caused, or allowed, the death of His own son in order to put an end to Adam's curse and bring about salvation for all mankind!"

It was just as Thelma Harold had said. There is no putting an end to the curse as far as we are concerned. One man was called to complete the task. God came to earth in the flesh.

"The crucifixion of Jesus was no accident!" Simon said as he banged his hand on the dashboard. "It was all part of a master plan. Jesus even predicted what was going to happen! He not only explained the law and prophets, He fulfilled them!"

Suddenly, Simon recalled Jesus' words while on the cross, "My God, My God, why have you forsaken me?" Then he remembered reading Jeremy's notes in the margin of his Bible. Jesus' paradoxical words were in reference to Psalm 22. In the Old Testament, David wrote, "My God, my God, why have you forsaken me? Why are you so far from saving me…Dogs have surrounded me; a band of evil encircled me, *they have pierced my hands and my feet:….*!"

Of course, God allows persecution for a purpose. After all, He allowed the disciples to be martyred to confirm the authenticity of their testimony. And how many people have been saved as a result of their testimony and persecution? Since that time, billions of Christians from every end of the globe have come to know Christ. They died for Jesus, just as He had died for them.

The words of John 15:13 suddenly came to mind, "There is no greater love than to lay down one's life for his friends."

Then it finally sank in. Simon realized that solving the veracity of the resurrection was very similar to solving the mystery surrounding the legend of

Jessie Joseph. There wasn't a single, solitary piece of irrefutable evidence that confirmed the one true account. Simon could arrive at a definitive conclusion simply through a thorough investigation of the facts at his disposal.

It wasn't faith without evidence. It was faith in the evidence. He could use his intellect to sift through all of the eyewitness accounts, historiography, and archeological records while applying wisdom, knowledge, and discretion to arrive at the truth. The quiet, still voice inside of him only served to confirm it.

There could be no doubt it now. The voice he heard inside of him was the same one that he heard that night while standing in front of the marquee. It was the same voice that called him to rebuild the entryway of the school to make it look exactly as it had in the fall of 1935. It was the same voice that was nudging him to turn his car around now.

Simon had his answer for Pastor Pete. Even so, his stomach tightened and his face went flush at the thought of going back to Bethel and facing the angry mob. He thought of the charges that had been brought against him and the certain persecution.

He was afraid, but now he was afraid of the right thing. If he was going to suffer, then it would ultimately be for his own good, for all things work for the good of the believer. God used the darkest of tragedies to bring about salvation. If that were the case, then He would use any means necessary to bring his children back to Him.

"If that is the case, then I need to reconsider what really is a *tragedy*," Simon thought. Jesus' death was tragic, but He still allowed it to happen. If Jesus did not die on the cross, then the entire human race would have been doomed. The real tragedy for us would have been if Jesus did not die on the cross. So, we really don't always know if something is a blessing or a curse while we are in the heat of the moment. Tragedies should not be limited to the things that only harm the flesh. Tragedies should be gauged by how they destroy the body *and* the body in Hades. We need to look beyond our own immediate, temporal circumstances and see the big picture.

"That was what Jesus did for us," Simon realized. "He took care of the big picture. He paid the ultimate price for us and put an end to the curse. So, we… What?…Turn around and blame Jesus for all of the problems in the world? Does that make any sense? We take Jesus out of public life because He might offend someone? Really? Is anything more offensive than eternal damnation?

"What if the fisherman in Ryan Dobson's story hadn't shot the flare into the semi truck's windshield. What would be more offensive? Shattering the windshield or allowing the trucker to drive off into the abyss?"

Simon came to the conclusion, "God will use any means necessary to bring us to Him because our circumstance is so dire. Even if it doesn't make any sense to us now, there is a greater purpose for the things that we go through in this life. There is an infinitely more wonderful plan that we can't see.

"So, we don't always know why things happen the way they happen. And we really don't even know if something if a blessing or a curse while we are in the middle of it. It is only our present circumstance. What seems so wonderful at the time might actually cause us to drift further and further away from God. And what seems so terrible might actually draw us closer to Him.

"Who, then, can really say what circumstance is and is not tragic for our *eternal* well-being? God is always in control, even though we might only truly see it for what it is in retrospect. Sometimes it is only later that we see how God was using a tragedy for a greater purpose. After all, the ultimate goal is for as many people to go to heaven as possible no matter the cost."

Simon expectantly sat forward in his seat looking for an exit. He now fully understood that salvation through Faith was one thing, while working out his own salvation, his sanctification, was another. Even if he kept driving, he would still be saved. Going back to Bethel was a matter of showing his love for God through obedience. Just as Simon made his momentous decision, he saw two flashing hazards lights emitted from an old Crown Victoria that was parked in the grass next to the interstate up the road.

"Oh man! Really? Now?" he said aloud as he listened to the still, quiet voice in his head.

* * *

If ever someone had a legitimate reason to not stop, it was Simon. Momentarily torn by the dilemma, he seriously considered driving on past the stranded vehicle that was sitting on the side of the road. Within a fraction of a second, the debate raged inside of him.

"Surely, they have a cell phone," Simon fleetingly thought. "Somebody will come along ...I mean, eventually...right?"

Then he remembered Jack's warning against helping strangers in distress.

"Huh, Jack...what a punk!" Simon muttered, shaking his head in disgust.

Obediently, Simon flipped on his turn signal, punched his hazard lights, and started to make his way over to the side of the road. A flurry of cars and trucks raced past him as he pulled off the interstate.

The wind turbulence coming off of a semi racing by made Simon's car sway on its springs. Slowly, Simon crept up behind the disabled vehicle. A jack lay beneath the rear axle of the white sedan, and there was a tire iron leaning up against the spare. With the bright sun reflecting off of the rear window, Simon could barely make out two dark figures sitting in the front seat of the Crown Vic.

Simon put his car in park, reached for the handle of the door, and looked back over his shoulder at the dense traffic. He was waiting for a break before daring to get out of his car. After a few minutes passed, he picked his moment. When the opportunity presented itself, he quickly jumped out of the driver's seat, slammed the door shut, and raced around the front of the car to safety. Immediately, the intense heat enveloped him like a heavy blanket.

In a matter of seconds, he was completely drenched in sweat as he approached the old, white sedan with the flat. Walking up to the passenger side door, he could clearly see the figures sitting in the front seat. They were careening their necks to get a glimpse of what they hoped would be their savior. Gleefully, an elderly woman rolled down her window.

"Oh, thank heavens!" she called out to Simon.

"Flat tire?" Simon asked, knowingly.

An old man sitting in the driver's seat leaned forward to look out the passenger side window. When he got a glimpse of Simon's shoddy appearance, he was a little taken aback. Nonetheless, he knew that they couldn't be too picky given their current circumstance.

"Yes," the man finally said, pushing his glasses back up onto his nose with his index finger. "I tried to change it myself, but I couldn't get one of those stubborn bolts loose. With my arthritis, I…"

"…You have no idea how glad we were that someone *actually* stopped," the old woman interrupted. "We have been sitting here for the better part of forty-five minutes. Howard has a 'condition', and I was afraid that he was going to have a stroke or something out there in that awful heat."

"Oh, Gladys," the old man muttered under his breath. "If it wasn't for that one rusted out lug nut…"

The woman, acting as though her husband hadn't said anything at all, continued speaking to Simon, …"We were starting to get worried. You see, our cell phone isn't picking up a signal, and we are about to run out of gas. And the *heat*…mercy me!"

"Hey, I have an idea. Why don't you turn off your engine and save some gas?" Simon asked in a loud voice to be heard over the rush of cars. "You can sit in the AC in my car while I change your tire."

"No, I don't think we could…do you mind…I mean it's just so hot…" the elderly woman said while reaching for the door handle.

Simon made eye contact with the older gentleman. He rolled his eyes as Simon gently helped the old man's wife out of the car. He herded the elderly couple back to the relative comfort of his car that sat idling on the side of the road.

"It'll only take me a couple of minutes," Simon promised as he ushered the woman into the passenger seat. Given his recent revelation, he was determined to get the job done and get them back on the road in record time.

It wasn't long before Simon had broken the bolt free and was able to change the tire. Drenched in sweat and caked in grease, he swiftly finished up with the tedious task. When he rose to his feet and hoisted the jack in the air, he could see the elderly couple giving him a silent ovation.

As Simon took the old woman by the elbow and guided her back to the car, she looked up at him and yelled in a gravely voice, "I am glad to see that there are still some Good Samaritans our there! You have no idea how much we appreciate your help. We could have been out here all night! I mean *nobody* was stopping. And Mildred will be wondering what happened to us."

"You're welcome, ma'am," Simon replied once again making eye contact with the older gentleman who gave the international sign for yapping with his thumb and index finger.

"Thanks again, son!" the old man called out before sliding into the driver's seat.

Simon assisted the brittle woman into the car and was about to shut the door before she stopped him. "Let us give you a little something for your trouble," she said, pulling out a folded up one dollar bill from her purse.

"That's okay. You keep it!" Simon said loudly, as a two more semi's roared past them. "Hey, the traffic's pretty thick. Let me guide you out. I'll walk back down the road a little ways and wave the cars over into the far lane so you'll have a little room."

The old man nodded affirmatively, and the elderly woman gave Simon a polite wave as she rolled the window back up.

Humbled by the opportunity to help a fellow traveler in need, Simon jogged back down the road and began motioning for the oncoming traffic to move over into the left lane. To his surprise, the traffic obediently made its way over, giving the old man time to get the Crown Vic back out onto the open road. Simon glanced back over his shoulder to see the big sedan heading off in the distance.

"Whew, they made it," he mumbled under his breath.

As Simon started to make his way back to his car, something lying in the tall grass on the side of the road caught his attention. Inexplicably, he found himself drawn to the unidentified object. Furrowing his brow and pursing his parched lips, he moved in closer to investigate.

With the flurry of traffic racing by, he reached down into the tall grass and picked up a white cross that was no more than three feet in length. He reverently held it in his hands and examined the weathered, splintery wood. Even though there were no words written on the cross, Simon knew exactly what it meant. It was a makeshift gravestone, marking the spot where some poor soul had crossed over from this life into the next.

The significance of the symbol was all the more striking given his recent epiphany. Determined to return the cross to its rightful spot, he set it on his shoulder and painstakingly searched the tall, prairie grass on the side of the road. A few drivers honked as they sped past him. He suddenly stood up straight and quizzically looked at the cars whizzing by before realizing what he must look like to them.

Now he understood. He never was just an innocent bystander or an objective observer. That was the real myth. It was a lie born of sin, conceived of the mind, and perpetuated by Satan. It wasn't Jesus' cross that He carried to Calvary. It was ours.

For the first time in his life, Simon came to the stark realization that he was just as responsible as the next man for the necessity of the crucifixion. In that moment, he was overwhelmed by shame and guilt before an all-encompassing feeling of gratitude overwhelmed him. All of a sudden, he had the urge to share the Good News of the Gospel with everyone.

The old man in Simon had died just as John Rash described in his letter to Pastor Pete. As a result, Simon would never be the same. He had been born again.

Just as Simon found the hole in the ground, he asked himself the ultimate question. What does a believer do, *after* he is saved? The answer was simple. He does whatever His Lord and Savior asks of him.

The restoration of the school wasn't just some assignment that God had asked Simon to complete on His behalf. It was a new way of life. Suddenly, he remembered the Bible verse in Matthew 16:24, "Whoever wants to be my disciple must deny themselves and take up their cross and follow me."

That was it! His head spun as he finally remembered what had been missing from the top of the giant grain elevator, and suddenly, he somehow knew why John Rash had climbed to the top of it on September 16ᵗ 2001. John did not commit suicide. Simon was sure of that now.

Using a large rock that he had found on the side of the road, Simon hammered the cross back into its rightful place. Then he sprinted back to the car, jumped into the front seat, and raced back to Bethel.

35

A TESTED STONE

With the lightning intensifying in the West, Simon reached for the last, rusted rung of the ladder that was still warm after baking all day in the scorching heat. The warm wind wildly whipped about him as he stepped out onto the top of the giant grain elevator, rising some 120 feet above the plains. Considering for a moment the perilous position that he had put himself in, Simon fearfully took in the breathtaking view. The harvest moon, yet to be overtaken by the impending cumulonimbus cloud, illuminated the corn, bean, and wheat fields that stretched out to the horizon in every direction.

Standing atop the massive elevator, Simon recalled what Rocky had told him about the threshing floor by the well on Clay Potter's farm, and his thoughts hung heavy in the sultry air.

"The harvest is plentiful," Simon said under his breath. "It was another one of Jack's half-truths. The harvest is plentiful, *but* the workers are few."

Remembering the ultimate purpose for his death-defying climb, Simon turned to face the elaborate metal works that rose another thirty feet above the roof of the three cylindrical, concrete grain bins. Cautiously, he eased his way around the iron beams of steel. Once on the other side, he found what he had been looking for. Three crosses stood no more than ten yards in front of the elevator's tangle of iron construction. For years, they had been hidden in plain sight.

Even though the center cross was over ten feet tall, it was dwarfed by all of the metal works rising up behind it. From the ground, it simply blended in with the background.

Simon reverently made his way over to the three crosses. The one in the center was covered in lights. However, he noticed that the bulbs were coated on the inside with a black film, indicating that they had burnt out a long time ago. Moving in closer to get a better look, he accidentally stepped on an extension cord that lay impotently on the ground.

Glancing from side to side, Simon noticed that neither of the other two crosses were adorned in lights. Instead, one was covered with a clear mirror while the other was coated with a dark, tinted glass.

With lightning flashing in the distance, Simon fell to his knees before the cross and began to pray. Just as he had suspected, Pete's sermon did not drive John to commit suicide by jumping off of the grain elevator.

For the past six years, Pete had unnecessarily carried that burden of guilt with him. John's vague email had controlled the pastor's life, weakened his faith, and diluted his sermons. As it turned out, it was just a grave misunderstanding. John had merely slipped off of the ladder. He was going to relight the cross atop the man-made mountain *because* he had been saved!

For a moment, Simon tried to fathom what his discovery would mean to Pastor Pete, Hannah Grace, and Mara Rash. As a result of John's supposed suicide letter, the good pastor had watered down his sermons and led the rest of his flock astray. Hannah Grace had been unnecessarily tormented because of her husband's uncertain, eternal fate. And Mara had been harboring such bitter hatred for God because of His apparent injustice.

Simon could not wait to share the good news with them, but before he could do any of that he felt strongly compelled to do something else first. Carefully assessing the condition of the center cross, he counted the number of bulbs, examined the fuses, and estimated the number of extension cords that would be needed to get the job done.

* * *

When Simon finally reached the bottom of the ladder, he let go of the last rung and dropped the remaining nine feet to the ground. He hit the pavement with a thud, stumbled, and fell over. After regaining his feet, Simon began to wipe the dirt off of his shorts.

From over his shoulder, a booming voice called out to him. *"Freeman!"*

Simon's heart skipped a beat as he spun around to see the giant figure lurking in the shadows.

"What on earth are you doing?" Rich asked with his massive hands on his hips. "I thought you'd be a thousand miles away from here by now."

There was an awkward pause as a bright light flashed all about them. It was followed by a roll of thunder that peeled off in the distance.

Not knowing what to expect, Simon hesitated. "I, well, uh, you see..." he stammered.

With a furrowed brow, Rich slowly moved towards him. "You lied to me," Rich said.

"*What?*" Simon replied.

"You promised me that you would never change," Rich said, lunging towards his old friend.

Simon's turned his head and winced just as Rich unexpectedly engulfed him with a massive bear hug.

"Whoa!" Simon said, involuntarily exhaling as he was being hoisted into the air.

After a few seconds, Simon tapped the big fella on the arm a few times with the palm of his hand. "Okay, okay," Simon grunted.

Rich finally set him back down on the ground. He let go and stepped away while wiping his eyes with the back of his hand.

"That was...I...I didn't know what to expect, I mean..." Simon started to say. "I guess I shouldn't be surprised. After all, you did pull me out of that angry mob. You saved my life, man."

"No, you saved mine," Rich said, trying to pull himself together. "You pulled me out of the empty life that I was leading."

"What?" Simon said in shock.

"I know," Rich said as a broad grin swept across his face.

"You 'know'?" Simon asked, confused. "You know what?"

"Everything!" Rich replied. Then he pulled a book out from under his arm and held it up under the glow of a nearby street light.

Simon leaned forward and peered through the darkness. It was Jeremy's Bible.

"After you ran off, I went to look for you in the chorus room of the school," Rich said. "I found this sitting on the desk, and I began flipping through the pages. I don't know, somehow it just all finally made sense to me. I finally got what you had been trying to tell me. Ya know?

"I-I cant' even describe it... It-it was like I was seeing things for the first time. My life. The mistakes that I have made. The time that I have wasted. And I thought of Jeremy and what they did to him." Rich paused for a moment looking down at the book he held in his giant hands.

"And I thought of you, Simon," he continued. "Suddenly I understood why you were doing what you were doing. And I understood what you have been trying to tell me this whole time. I knew why you had changed. Then I just started to bawl like a little baby or something. I got down on my knees right then and there and gave my life to Christ."

Simon was blown away by the testimony of his old friend.

"That's...awesome!" Simon finally blurted out. "I am so happy for you. You don't even know how relieved I am to hear that."

They both got teary-eyed before Simon spontaneously gave Rich another warm hug. After a second, they both remembered themselves. Simultaneously, they pushed each other away and tried to play it off. For good measure, Rich slugged Simon in the upper arm and smiled.

"Ouch!" Simon said, as he grabbed his tingling arm.

"Tell me something," Rich said.

"Yeah, what?" Simon asked, opening and closing his hand to make sure it was working properly.

"Do you really not like baseball anymore?" Rich asked in disbelief.

"America's pastime?" Simon asked. "Are you kidding me? I love baseball. I didn't want you to stop coaching. I just wanted you to get your priorities straight."

"Cause the way you were talking, it sounded like you were ready to take down the scoreboards or something," Rich said, expressing a sigh relief.

"No, no, becoming a Christian doesn't make you a communist or something," Simon replied. "I know that competition brings out the best in people. Iron sharpens iron, ya know?"

"Whew!" Rich said. "I'm just trying to figure out what all I have to give up now."

"I know it may seem that way at first," Simon said, "but it's really the opposite. I can assure you. It's not about what you are giving up. It's about what you are getting."

"Huh," Rich scoffed, "I don't know about that. After watching folks around here give you the Frankenstein treatment earlier today, it makes me wonder what I'm getting myself into."

"I know it seems counterintuitive," Simon replied. "I can tell you that living out your faith will give you a sense of inner peace and contentment like nothing you could have possibly imagined.

"Then you'll be looking for any way you can to serve God and share the Good News."

As Simon finished his assertion, he instinctively looked up to the top of the grain elevator. The wind was picking up, the storm clouds were quickly approaching, and the lightning began to close in on them. He knew that he was running out of time.

Suddenly, Simon looked back at Rich.

"Oh no," Rich said. "I've seen that look before."

"Do you happen to have the key to the concession stand with you?" Simon asked.

"Yeah...," Rich hesitantly replied.

"I'm going to need an extension ladder, a bunch of light bulbs, some fuses, and a few extension cords," Simon said.

Rich raised his eyebrows before looking up at the top of the elevator. "You know I'm terrified of heights," Rich said somberly. "Is there any kind of grace period before you start serving God?"

Simon shook his head and replied, "No. I'm afraid not."

* * *

It was nearly midnight when they finished. Simon leaned down and grabbed one cord off of the ground at the base of the cross. Then he picked up the end of a long line of extension cords leading down the base of the man-made mountain.

With lightning flashing all about him, Simon walked over to the edge of the elevator and yelled down to Rich who was waiting impatiently at the base of the silo.

"Okay, here we go!" Simon called out.

As soon as he plugged it in, the light from the center cross lit up the darkened sky. Simon dropped the cord to the ground and made his way around to the front of the cross. Passing by the tinted mirror of the first cross, he paused a moment to catch a glimpse of his darkened reflection. All of a sudden, a Bible verse came to him, "…If the light within you is darkness, how great is that darkness?"

Unable to look directly into the bright light of the center cross, Simon lowered his eyes and made his way over to the third cross. Shielding his eyes with his hand, he peered into his own perfect reflection and smiled.

From the base of the prodigious elevator, Rich could see the warm glow of light emitting from the heights of the tower. Even though he couldn't see the cross from his vantage point, he knew the source. He closed his eyes and dropped his chin to his chest. His expression was that of a man who had just discovered something deeply, deeply profound.

* * *

Huddled over her work bench, Thelma suddenly stopped, lifted her head, and peered out the window. She paused, dropped her chin to her chest, let out a deep breath, and set down the blue ribbon that she had been working on. The old public servant slid off of her chair and hobbled over to the large storefront window of her trophy shop.

In the reflection of the glass, she could see the stream of tears running down her cheeks as she stared at the brilliant cross proudly standing high atop the grain elevator. She lifted her glasses that had been hanging around her neck and put them on. Contemplatively, she took them off, sucked on one of the arms, and gazed at the floor.

Emboldened, Thelma lifted one eyebrow and allowed the glasses to once again dangle from around her neck. She gingerly waddled back over to her desk and snatched up the large stack of blue math contest participant ribbons. She took one from the stack and unceremoniously dumped the rest of them into the garbage can. Letting out a sigh of relief, she reached into the bottom drawer of her desk, took out several stacks of red, white, green, and yellow ribbons, and set them down on her work bench.

Then she made her way over to the shiny, golden calf trophy that had been sitting on a shelf behind her desk. Using a small pocket knife, she pried the 2007 Dairy League Champions label off of the massive trophy and set it down next to a smaller, more traditional looking trophy.

Cradling the gaudy Golden Calf trophy in both arms, Thelma made her way out the back door of the shop and headed down the back alley towards the incinerator.

* * *

Mesmerized by the warm glow of the cross, Simon failed to notice the billow of smoke rising above the tree line until the sound of a fire alarm rang out. He abruptly spun around to face the town that was sprawled out before him. His eyes followed the dark plume of smoke to the flickering flames that were shooting out of the window of the chorus room. Suddenly, out of the corner of his eye, he saw a shadowy figure dart out of the front doors of the school and dash off into the darkness.

Simon's jaw dropped. For a moment, he stood frozen from shock. Suddenly snapping out of it, he thought of Little Simon and the tunnel that ran beneath the school building. Quickly, he raced towards the ladder of the elevator and shouted down to Rich who had just made his way around the base of the tower to see what all of the commotion was about.

"*The school is on fire!*" Simon shouted, as he began the one hundred and twenty foot descent down the ladder.

Rich scrunched his face and lifted his hand to his ear. He was trying to make out what his friend was saying, but the words were swept away in the howling wind and booming thunder from the impending storm.

"*What?*" Rich yelled, cupping his hands around his mouth.

As Simon neared the bottom of the ladder, Rich finally understood what Simon had been yelling. Immediately, Rich took off in the direction of Main Street and raced towards the burning building.

At fifteen feet, Simon jumped from the ladder, hit the ground, and rolled. In an instant, he was back up on his feet and sprinting in the direction of the school.

By now, a few curious people had made their way out of the tavern to see if they could detect which direction the incessant alarm was coming from.

As Simon raced by them, he yelled, "The school's on fire! Call 911!"

By the time Simon caught up with Rich, he was standing on the sidewalk next to the school. Windows shattered as the hungry fire gasped for oxygen. Even from thirty yards away, they could feel the intense heat as the dense cloud of smoke agitated their eyes and the black soot choked out their lungs.

Covering his mouth with his fist, Rich blurted out, "It doesn't look good, man!"

"But, what if Simon Adamson's in there?" he replied, covering his mouth with his fist. "We can't just leave him down there in the tunnel! He'll never make it!"

"There's no way to even know if he's in there!" Rich replied, coughing.

Simon bit his lip and said, "I can't take that chance!" Then he unexpectedly bolted towards the cellar doors of the school.

"Wait!" Rich called out in a panic before taking off after him.

But before Rich could run him down, Simon had already pried open the cellar doors and headed down the steps that lead to the service tunnel. He was now navigating his way through the smoke down the long corridor that ran under the school.

* * *

From the other side of the building that had been set ablaze, Pastor Pete had also heard the fire alarm while painting Kilz over the water damaged, sanctuary ceiling. Carefully, he hurried down the ladder, trotted out of the front door, and stood at the top of the steps to the church. In utter disbelief, he blankly stared into the towering inferno across the street. From his vantage point, he could see two men open the cellar doors and descend down into the belly of the burning building.

"Please God, no!" Pete muttered under his breath. He quickly shuffled down the steps of the church as he fumbled for his cell phone in his pocket.

After hanging up with the 911 operator, the good pastor hastily made his way across the street. He tried to approach the building that was now completely engulfed in flames, but it was of no use. He was soon overwhelmed by the intense heat and suffocating smoke. Reluctantly, he withdrew to a safe distance and stood with a small crowd that had begun to gather on the sidewalk in front of the church.

The Pastor knew what he had seen. There could be no mistaking it. Two men had gone down into the cellar. His mind raced, "...But, who were they? And why were they risking their lives? Were they going after the little boy? Could it be Andy and Simon? Who else knew about the strange little boy's secret hideout?"

Overcome with emotion, the good pastor did the only thing that he could do. Pete fell to his knees on the sidewalk and prayed the most fervent, heartfelt prayer that he had dared to pray since the Sunday following 9/11.

While he was praying, Hannah Grace and Sharon made their way through the group of spectators and approached the pastor. Hearing Pete's audible, passionate plea, they were able to quickly ascertain what was happening. Two men had gone into the fire to save Adamson, and no one had come out of the blaze.

Obediently, the two women knelt down on the ground next to pastor, put their arms over his shoulders, bowed their heads, and began to pray along with him. Before long, a small cluster of believers had huddled together on the sidewalk in front of the church.

The wailing of sirens intensified as fire trucks, ambulances, and police cars descended on the burning building. Then something compelled Pastor Pete to open his eyes. He mechanically rose to his feet and instinctively walked towards the firestorm. As if in a trance, he somehow made his way past the first responders who were scrambling all around him.

Bewildered by Pete's bizarre behavior, the small cluster of people who had been praying also rose to their feet and cried out to their pastor, imploring him to turn around and come back. A couple of men started to go after him, but a police officer charged with securing the perimeter intervened. Despite the their adamant protests, the officer directed the men to return to the opposite side of the street. Reluctantly, they rejoined the growing group of believers who had gathered at the foot of the steps to the church.

Now standing no more than a stone's throw away, the good pastor peered into the blazing furnace. Through the red and orange flames, he could make out four figures walking around in the fire, unbound and unharmed, and the fourth looked like a son of the gods.

With great fear and trembling, Pete called out to them. "Come out!" he shouted. "Come here!"

Shielding their heads with their forearms, they turned and steadily made their way toward the pastor, but only two men ultimately emerged out of the billowing smoke and lapping flames. The larger of the two men appeared be carrying a small sack of potatoes over his shoulder.

As the pastor herded them to safety, he suddenly recognized Simon and Rich, and the small sack of potatoes was actually Simon Adamson. The little boy was draped over the burly bartender's shoulder as he bounded across the street. The frightened child was pounding on Rich's back, demanding to be put down. When they had finally reached the steps of the church, Pete could see that the fire had not harmed their bodies, nor was a single hair of their heads singed; their clothes were not scorched, and there was no smell of fire on them.

Rich carefully set the boy down on the sidewalk and collapsed onto the bottom step of the church as the sizable crowd gathered around them. The people bombarded the three survivors with questions as they carefully looked them over. But, they could find no signs of trauma on their persons. There were no third degree burns or broken bones. In fact, there wasn't so much as a scratch. The people were amazed and said nothing like it had ever been seen before in Bethel.

Pete stumbled backward away from the crowd with a dumbfounded expression on his face. Turning back again towards the fire, he suddenly realized that only three people had escaped.

"Where's the other one?" Pete hysterically cried out.

"'The other one?'!" someone in the crowd repeated. "What other one? There isn't anyone else."

"*No, no!*" the Pastor shouted. "There was a fourth man in the fire!"

"No, you're mistaken," another person replied. "There were only these two guys and the kid. Relax. We've got them pastor. They're safe and sound."

"What?" Pete said, raking his hand through his hair. "No, that can't be. There was another man in the fire. I saw him. I saw him with my own eyes. I mean, there was a *fourth* man in the fire. His hair was pulled back into a pony tail...and...and... He had a beard..."

The large crowd of people who had now gathered at the foot of the steps to the church turned towards the fierce fire.

Hannah Grace who had been tending to the small boy looked up at the pastor and said despondently, "Well, if there had been anyone else in there, he didn't make it out."

Gradually, the look of panic on Pastor Pete's face fell away, and a smile slowly crept across his face. Finally, he understood.

"'Praise be to God who sent his angel and rescued his servants!'," Pete muttered under his breath as he stared into the blazing furnace.

The raging fire was now burning out of control. High winds from the imminent storm whipped about the flames as firemen worked furiously to contain the blaze because the entire town was in danger.

Meanwhile, someone had already retrieved some cold bottles of water and emergency blankets for Rich, Simon, and Little Simon Adamson. The three survivors sat on the bottom steps of the church for a few minutes with the shimmery, silver blankets draped over their shoulders. Simon guzzled his bottle of water in between gasps of breath while Rich tilted his back and doused some of the water over his head.

Without warning, Little Simon forcefully wrenched himself free of Hannah Grace's embrace and fought his way through the crowd. "Get out my way! Let me go, I said! I want to go home!" the boy yelled as he ran away.

"Somebody grab that ungrateful, little twerp!" Rich shouted as he began to stand up.

"No, no, it's okay!" Simon said, grabbing Rich by the forearm and pulling him back down to the steps. "Let him go for now. We can't force him. It has to be his choice. I know where we can find him.

"We're going to have to be really careful how we pursue him. It's going to take time to gain his trust. We can't afford to scare him off. After all, we're going to need him as a witness."

Suddenly, some of the people in the crowd began to level a deluge of pointed questions. They wanted to know how the school had caught fire, and how they came to be in the building in the first place, and how they managed to escape virtually unscathed. It all seemed very peculiar.

"I saw the whole thing," Pastor Pete announced as he made his way back through the large crowd that had by now gathered at the steps to the church. "They went rushing in through the cellar doors to save the boy after the fire started."

Pete squatted down in front of Simon and Rich. His eyes darted back and fourth between the two young men as though he were sizing them up. "Did you see *Him*?" he asked.

"What?" Simon asked, confused.

"You know. Did you see the One who brought you out of the fire?" Pete asked, expectantly.

"You couldn't see anything in there," Rich chimed in. "It just felt like…"

"…Like we were *protected*," Simon marveled.

"Yeah, like there this shield around us," Rich agreed.

"So how did you know which way to go to get out?" Pete asked.

"We didn't," Simon replied. "I just kept my head down, closed my eyes, and prayed the whole time. And…wait a minute…did you say a pony tail and a beard?"

Lightning darted across the sky, and the fire raged out of control as a clamor rose from the enormous crowd about all that they had seen and heard. Some were calling it a miracle, while others were calling it a curse.

For the first time, Simon looked around at the faces in the crowd. Standing all around him were Pastor Pete, Hannah Grace and Sharon, Wilson B., Angie, and Ralph Livingood, George Lukas, Bill and Judy O'Neill, Father Rite, Pastor Algood, Parker Godsell, and even the Cain's with their sickly child. By the looks of things, more than half of the town from all walks of life had made their way to the steps of the church.

Then Simon turned and looked back at the school. He noticed a slightly smaller crowd had gathered on the other side of the burning building. Through the dense smoke and lapping flames, he could barely make out their faces.

The orange glow of the flames flickered and fluttered across their grotesquely distorted visages. There was Shannon Zeal, Lexus, Claire, and Jackson Helrigle, Ron Fields, Rob Ateitup, Andy Cross, Mara Rash, Rocky Fields, and Will Thornchuk. In all, the small crowd represented an equally diverse demographic of the community.

Before Simon could fully appreciate the significance of his observation, Hope forced her way through the throng of people. Simon stood up just as she unexpectedly threw her arms around his neck. She hugged him tightly as streams of tears ran down her cheeks.

Her embrace enveloped him like a tidal wave of grace and jarred him from his stupor.

"So, you're…you're not mad at me?" Simon asked, pulling back to look into Hope's radiant eyes.

"No!" she answered, her face beaming. "I told myself, 'If he comes back, then he's innocent'."

Suddenly, there was a horrible moan coming from the burning building as it succumbed to the fiery onslaught. A hush came over the crowd. They looked on in silence as the school tumbled to the ground.

Rich stood up next to Simon. "Oh man," he said, apologetically, putting his meaty hand on his friend's shoulder. "All of that work, for nothin'. Sorry, man."

Simon looked up at Rich and furrowed his brow. He bit his bottom lip and pensively thought for a moment. Then he turned and looked at the distraught people who had gathered around them. Simon could see the pain, anguish, fear, and uncertainty written on their faces.

In a matter of seconds, a murmur began to sweep through the crowd. Unfounded rumors were already beginning to circulate. Wild speculation passed over the lips of the bewildered witnesses who were simply trying to make sense of yet another catastrophic event in a long line of inexplicable tragedies that had befallen their beloved community.

That's when it hit him. The words from the pages of Jeremy's Bible flooded Simon's consciousness. Instinctively, he looked down at the callouses on his hands. Then he turned and looked up at the withered, old church with its chipped paint, busted out window panes, missing shingles, and sagging frame.

Simon spontaneously turned back towards the throng of people who had gathered at the foot of the steps to the church. Their dry, withered souls all of a sudden reminded him of the endless fields of crops that sprawled out in every direction from Bethel to the horizon.

Excitedly, Simon took Hope by the hand and raced up to the top of the steps to the church. He cupped his hands around his mouth and called out, "Listen to me!"

The crowd noise died down as the people turned toward Simon. Once he had everyone's attention, he began to speak.

"Listen to what I am about to tell you," Simon implored the onlookers. "I know that many of you are feeling very troubled about everything that has recently taken place in Bethel. Many of us are still trying to come to grips with the murder of my good friend, Jeremy Warner.

Since the time of Jeremy's tragic death and impending investigation, we have had the the long, hard drought, the heated debate over the school referendum, and the stunning allegations that Jack Lawless brought against me only this morning. And now we have the complete and utter destruction of our school.

"I know that seems like it has been one thing after another around here. And it's true. You could say that Bethel has had more than its fair share of tragedies over the years. But, I am afraid to tell you that, unfortunately, Bethel is no different from any other community across this great land of ours.

The people grumbled.

"I know, I know," Simon said, raising a hand to quiet the crowd, "it is hard to believe. It must seem like your whole world is falling apart right before your very eyes. It must feel like you are cursed!..."

The crowd fell silent. Only the crackling fire and the howling wind could be heard above the noise of the firefighters bustling about.

"...And you are!" Simon boldly stated.

"*What?*" Rich scoffed, walking up the steps towards him. "After all of this, you still think Bethel is under some stupid *curse?*"

"No," Simon replied.

Rich's shoulders slumped forward as he let out a sigh of relief.

"I think Bethel is under two curses!" Simon replied.

"What?" Rich asked.

"Listen to me!" Simon yelled above the noise of the crowd. "Neither of the curses that I am talking about are the result of a myth, or legend, or some kind of contrived ghost story. What happened in the school in October of 1935 was merely the accidental death of a 6-year-old boy. His death wasn't the cause of a curse. It was the result of one.

"God cursed Satan, Adam and Eve, and all of mankind because of original sin. Adam chose to disobey God and eat the forbidden fruit. Satan had convinced Adam that God's law was actually keeping him from having complete knowledge, so that he could be like God. So that he could be his own god. Adam sinned, and the price of sin was death.

"Don't you see? God didn't create sin out of spite or vengeance or something. No, God gave Adam a choice to be obedient or disobedient to His word. God gives us all free will because He loves us.

"In that way, we are all alike. We are all born into sin because we inherit it from Adam, and consequently, we all choose to sin on a regular basis. As a result, we all fall short of the law no matter what we *do*.

"That is why tragic accidents happen in the first place. And that's why each man is appointed once to die just like Adam Potter. Because that's the consequence of our choosing to sin. There's nothing that any of us can *do* about it. It is inevitable. That's the bad news.

"The Good News is that God chose one man to put an end to the curse nearly two thousand years ago. God came Himself. He came as God incarnate. He came as Jesus. Jesus was born sinless and chose not to sin, making Himself the perfect, unblemished sacrificial lamb. Jesus voluntarily took on the sin for all of mankind and died on the cross in our place. On the third day He rose again from the grave. He ascended into heaven and sits at the right hand of God the Father Almighty. All we have to do to receive salvation is choose to believe in Jesus Christ as the Messiah prophesied in the Old Testament.

"And so, we are all in the same boat. We are all equal. We are born into the same basic set of circumstances. We are given life. We inherit a debt that we cannot pay. We live. And we die. None of us can make up for our depravity. There is nothing we can do. We are all a bunch of charity cases. We are completely unable to provide for ourselves. We are completely at the mercy of our judge for leniency.

"None of us can can boast about our achievements. Whether we sin once or a million times, none of us is any better or worse than the other when it comes to salvation. We are all the same. We all fall short of the requirements to enter heaven. And we are all in need of a Savior. So, life is completely fair from that perspective. We all rely on God's mercy to receive eternal life by grace through faith. Jesus paid the price. All we have to do is accept His free gift. Yes, Jesus put an end to the first curse.

"Ultimately, each individual has to decide for him or herself whether or not to believe in the life, death, burial, and resurrection of Jesus Christ. If we choose to believe in Him, then we are no longer held responsible for our words, actions, and deeds as it pertains to salvation. We are off the hook! That's why we call it the Good News.

"But, there is a second curse born out of the first that cannot be overlooked. We are imperfect people living in an imperfect world. We continue to sin and suffer, even after we are saved," Simon said as a bolt of lightning flashed across the sky. "After the fall, God promised us that life would be hard, and He has been true to His word. Life is full of trials, tribulations, and yes, even tragedies. Thelma was right. There will always be tragedies. Bad things are always going to happen, even to *good people*, until Jesus returns.

"But, everything works for the good of the believer! Satan intends for tragedies to harm us, but God intends them for good in order to save our souls.

"Take me for example. God used my circumstances to prepare me. My muscles ached and my hands were ripped to shreds because of the difficult work of renovating the school, but God used my pain to shape and mold me. He gave me callouses, so that my hands would be able to withstand even greater wear and tear. He strengthened my muscles and improved my endurance. He taught me new skills and gave me knowledge so I could do even greater work for Him.

"Yes, we are all universally the same when it comes to our salvation, but we are all incredibly unique when it comes to working out our own salvation and our sanctification. God gave each one of us different attributes and different environments into which we are born. Not everyone was given the same abilities or the same deficiencies. In that way, life is completely 'unfair' because it is not the same for any two given people. The playing field is not level for everyone nor was it intend to be.

"There are some things that only *we* can do, even though there are many more things that we can't. There are many opportunities that await us, even though there are many more that don't. The unique talents and opportunities that each of us have been given make us individuals. And we are to use our individuality to fulfill a specific mission in the body of Christ.

"But, with great talent and opportunity comes great responsibility. Because we are each charged with performing a specific task, it is our duty to fulfill it. Each one of us is personally responsible, and each one of us will be held accountable for how well or how poorly we did our job. We are punished or rewarded based on our performance.

"And that's where we get completely confused at times. We have a hard time striking a balance between salvation and sanctification. Between charity and responsibility. Between universality and individuality.

"Being saved is not the end of the journey it is only the beginning. God wants an interactive relationship with us. He wants us to voluntarily return His love for us in the measure it was given. He wants us to invest in the relationship by taking personal responsibility for our own thoughts, words, and actions. Ultimately, God wants us to show our love to Him by our obedience to His law.

"We are not entitled to God's blessings. On the contrary, blessings and curses are God's just response to either our obedience or disobedience. In the end, we get what's coming to us.

"In that way, we have been no different from Adam in the Garden of Eden. When we choose to disobey the law, we are trying to make our own set of laws and standards. You could say that we have been trying to make ourselves our own gods. Satan has done a masterful job of convincing us that the only thing inhibiting us from having the knowledge of God is the law of God.

"But Satan has deceived us. He has made us believe that God's Ten Commandments are offensive because they are too narrow minded and prohibitive. He has tricked us into thinking that if there were no right and wrong then we could freely pursue the things that make us happy. But, that's a lie! The law *is* the standard. God revealed it to us for our own good. Good laws are created to protect, not limit or condemn.

"There has been a pattern of tragedies in Bethel. Every time something bad has happened in this town over the years, we have had a tendency to move farther and farther away from God. We have blamed Him instead of putting the blame on sin and Satan where it belongs. With each tragedy, we have taken more and more of God out of our society. As a result, we have broken our covenant with Him. In so doing, we have incited God's wrath and received His curses.

"By removing God from our society, we have created a vacuum. And we have an enemy who is more than happy to step in and temporarily fill that void, but Satan is a counterfeit. He is the opposite of God. He has no rules. Is goal is total anarchy. He is always trying to divide us by race, sex, religion, and socioeconomic status. He has only come to kill, steal, and destroy.

"And what has been the result? Like a well pouring out water, we have poured out wickedness, violence, and destruction. We have oppressed the alien, the fatherless, and the widow. We have shed innocent blood. We have lusted after our neighbor's wife. We have worshiped what our hands have made. Those who deal with the law do not know God, and our leaders have rebelled against Him. We have forsaken Him. No one is in awe of God anymore. As the bride of the church, we have committed adultery against God by seeking the company of prostitutes and pursuing our own desires. And we wonder why we are miserable, and we wonder why bad things keep happening to us."

Simon surveyed the crowd and the look of uncertainty on the faces of the people.

"God is a just God," Simon continued. "He will not withhold his judgment forever. That is what we should fear. If we continue to ignore God and His word and if we continue to disobey his commands, then He will discipline us like any loving Father disciplines his child.

The wind wildly whipped about as the impending lightning and booming thunder intensified.

"If we do not change from our wicked ways, God will punish us. The winnowing fork is in His hand. And He will clear His threshing floor. The unrighteous will blow away like chaff in the wind, and the righteous will fall back down to the floor to be gathered up by our Lord and Savior.

"If we continue on the path we have been on, then calamities and disease will continue to fall on our land. It will become a burning waste of salt and sulfur. Nothing planted will sprout. No vegetation will grow on it. It will be like the destruction of Sodom and Gomorrah. We have to turn from our wicked ways before it is too late. We have to repent! That is what Jeremiah was trying to warn us about.

Simon paused to allow what he was saying to sink in.

"He's calling for some kind of theocracy!" an unidentified voice called out through a puff of cigarette smoke.

"No! I'm calling for a Constitutional Republic," Simon objected as the wind howled and the thunder crackled. "And that is why Bethel is under a second curse. We *had* that society. But we lost our way. We lost our compass. Bethel was like every other town in America. The order of society and rule of law were built upon a divine document that was constructed by a group of brilliant men on the foundation of Biblical Judeo-Christian principles. No, Christians don't need a theocracy. All we have to do is tap into the system that is already in place. But, somewhere along the line, we stopped doing that. It's like the series of tragedies rendered us disillusioned and apathetic.

"But, since the fall of man, bad things have always happened. That's just how it is. There's nothing we can do about that. But, as I said, all things work for the good of the believer. God uses even the trials and tribulations in our lives to shape and mold us in his image. So, the incidents and accidents are no incidents and accidents at all. God uses tragedies as a catalyst for change. It is all part of a master plan to bring us closer to Him and to eventually bring us home. And it is all for His glory.

"No, we can't stop tragedies from happening, but we can change how we react to them. We can put an end to the second curse by restoring God to His rightful place in the heart of our community. Each time something good or bad happens, we can choose to draw closer to God.

"Look, we are the people! This is our community! We can decide for ourselves! Each one of us has to take up our own cross and follow Him.

"I know it feels like it may be too late for us. Like the end is near. However, no man knows the day or the hour of Jesus' return. I don't know if it is next week or a thousand years from now. All I know is that when He comes back He had better find us doing the work of His Father."

"It doesn't matter if you are a preacher, or a banker, or lawyer, or doctor, or a superintendent, or a principal, or a teacher, or baker, or a clerk…," Simon paused as he made eye contact with Rich, …"or a coach. God has called each of you to do what you can with what you have where you are at. It is not so much our circumstances as how we react to our circumstances."

The people were now riveted with Simon's words.

"It just takes Christians to start acting like Christians!" Simon replied. "You have a voice. Stand up for what you believe in and vote your conscience. Better yet, run for public office. Serve in your community.

"Stop backpedaling! Stop giving ground in the name of tolerance and political correctness. Stop looking the other way and ignoring the strip clubs, the Ponzi schemes, the abortion clinics, and any other abomination that is in our midst. Do everything in your power to remove from office and positions of authority and influence any community agitator, like Jack Lawless, who implements the rules for radicals to make deals, silence his opposition, and perpetuate lies for his own self-interest and financial gain.

"Get back into a right fellowship with God. Admit your sin. Ask for forgiveness. Repent. And begin your walk with Christ before it is too late.

"If we choose to do that, whether it be as an individual or a society, God will honor His covenant with us," Simon asserted. "By rebuilding the church, we can rebuild the family. Once we rebuild the family, we can rebuild the school. We will once again be a prosperous community, and our city will shine like a beacon for the rest of the world.

"So, I ask you," Simon said, raising his voice above a cannon of thunder. "What will our generation be known for? What will be our legacy? This is our time to decide! Will we waiver in our convictions and fall from grace, or will we stand up and be counted?

The people didn't know what to say because words couldn't express how they felt.

Simon pointed to the lit cross high atop the grain elevator. "Look, I didn't put that cross up there. I simply relit it. It was there long before me."

"But, that hasn't always been there," a familiar, skeptical voice challenged from the back of the crowd. "The town was here way before electricity. In fact, it was here way before that grain elevator was ever built for that matter. How do we really know what you are telling us is the truth? What other evidence do you have that this was once a *Christian* community?"

Simon was silent for a moment. He chewed on his bottom lip while the fierce wind swirled about and thunder reverberated through the night sky. Intuitively, Simon turned and looked up at the cross at the top of the steeple of the church.

"It's right here!" Simon said, gazing skyward. "Here's your evidence. At the center of every town and city across the United States, there is a cross atop a steeple proclaiming the truth of our proud history.

"No," Simon said with great confidence. "God did not simply call me to complete a renovation in order to end a curse. He called me to spark a revival!"

Inspired by Simon's revelation, Pastor Pete anxiously stepped out of from the crowd and asked, "So, where do we start?"

Simon turned and momentarily stared at the pastor. Then he glanced back at the church building before it suddenly dawned on him. With Hope by his side, Simon hurried down the steps. They made their way through the crowd and stood next to the foundation. Simon pointed at the capstone.

"We will start here!" he said with great enthusiasm. "Then we will pull the two plaques and the chandelier out of the ashes and go from there!"

Pastor Pete raced to the top of the steps, propped open the front doors, and invited the people into the church. With one cry, the remnant filtered their way into the sanctuary. The Holy Spirit moved, and on that day, many were saved day. Completely broken and contrite in spirit, they begged for forgiveness and repented of their sins.

But an even larger contingency who had previously only referred to themselves as Christians renewed their walk with Christ. Suddenly, the body was undaunted by the certainty of resistance and undeterred the promise of persecution.

As Pastor Pete began to preach the Gospel in its entirety, he started with 2 Chronicles 7:14. All at once, Hannah Grace realized that they were going to need more volunteers at the voter registration table.

* * *

Off in the distance, less than a mile outside of town, a single drop of rain smattered a speck of dirt on the threshing floor on Clay Potter's estate. Then another. And another. Not long after that rain mixed with hail filled the well and all but ruined the hiding place.

ABOUT THE AUTHOR

Colin Briscoe is a first time author. Colin originally conceived of the basic storyline while working as a maintenance man at Philo Grade School shortly after graduating with a degree in writing from Millikin University. Originally, it was intended to be a horror story written purely for entertainment. However, as God shaped and molded Colin over time, He also shaped and molded the purpose of the story. And what began as a story about death became one about eternal life. Colin has no impressive credentials or qualifications making him a prime candidate to be used by God for His glory